THE DWARVES

"You are mistaken, my friend. We are the älfar, and we have come to slay the elves," the voice said softly.

"The gates may be closed, but the power of the land will raise you from the dead and from that moment on, you will be one of us. You know the incantation; you will open the door."

"Never! My soul belongs to Vraccas!"

"Your soul belongs to the land, and you will belong to the land until the end of time," the velvety voice cut him short. "Die, so you can return and deliver Girdlegard to us."

The spear's sharp tip pierced the flesh of the helpless, dying dwarf. Pain stopped his tongue.

Sinthoras raised the weapon and pushed down gently on the battered body. The final blow was dealt tenderly, almost reverently. The creature waited for death to claim its prey, watching over Glandallin's pain-ravaged features and drinking in the memory.

Finally, when he was certain that the last custodian of the gateway had departed, Sinthoras left his vigil and rose to his feet.

BY MARKUS HEITZ

The Dwarves
The War of the Dwarves
The Revenge of the Dwarves
The Fate of the Dwarves

MARKUS HEITZ
THE DWARVES

Translated by Sally-Ann Spencer

www.orbitbooks.net

ORBIT

First English-language Edition 2009
Originally published in Germany as Die Zwerge by
Heyne Verlag, 2003
First published in Great Britain in 2009 by Orbit

19 20 18

A CIP catalogue record for this book
is available from the British Library.

ISBN 978-1-84149-572-9

Printed and bound by CPI Group (UK) Ltd, Croydon, CR0 4YY

Papers used by Orbit are from well-managed forests
and other responsible sources.

MIX
Paper from
responsible sources
FSC® C104740
www.fsc.org

Orbit
An imprint of
Little, Brown Book Group
Carmelite House
50 Victoria Embankment
London EC4Y 0DZ

An Hachette UK Company
www.hachette.co.uk

www.orbitbooks.net

"Appearances are there to be ignored, for the biggest hearts may reside in the smallest and unlikeliest creatures. Those who fail to look beyond the surface will never encounter true virtue—not in others and certainly not in themselves."

—From "Collected Wisdom of a Dead Stranger"
in *Philosophical Letters and Texts* from the
archive of the Hundred-Pillared Temple of
Palandiell in Zamina, Kingdom of Rân Ribastur.

"Dwarves and mountains have one thing in common: It takes an almighty hammer and a tremendous amount of persistence to overcome them."

—Traditional saying from the Murk
region, northeast Idoslane.

"Fleeing from an angry dwarf requires fleetness of foot. For consider this: The target of dwarven wrath must be capable of outstripping the irate warrior's flying ax. Those lucky enough to escape with their lives should take pains to alter their appearance. The dwarven memory is dangerously good. Even after twenty cycles the threat remains and no one can predict when the chamber might ring with vengeful dwarven laughter as a tankard smashes against the offender's head."

—From "Notes on the Races of Girdlegard:
Singularities and Oddities" from the archive of
Viransiénsis, Kingdom of Tabaîn, compiled
by the Master of Folklore M.A. Het
in the 4299th Solar Cycle.

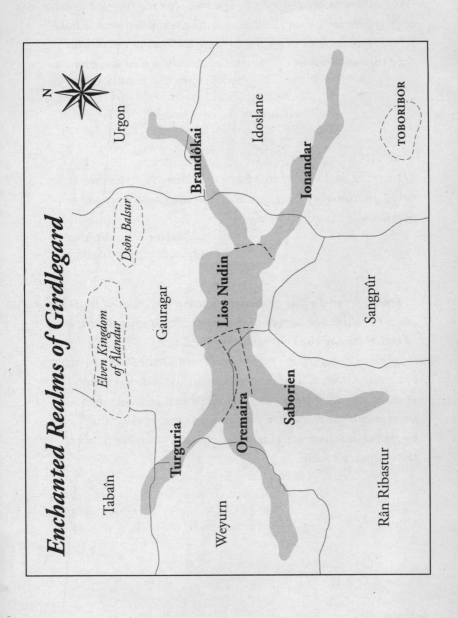

Enchanted Realms of Girdlegard

N

Urgon

Tabaîn

Elven Kingdom
of Alandur

Dsôn Balsur

Gauragar

Turguria

Weyurn

Oremaira

Brandôkai

Lios Nudin

Saborien

Idoslane

Ionandar

TOBORIBOR

Sangpûr

Rân Ribastur

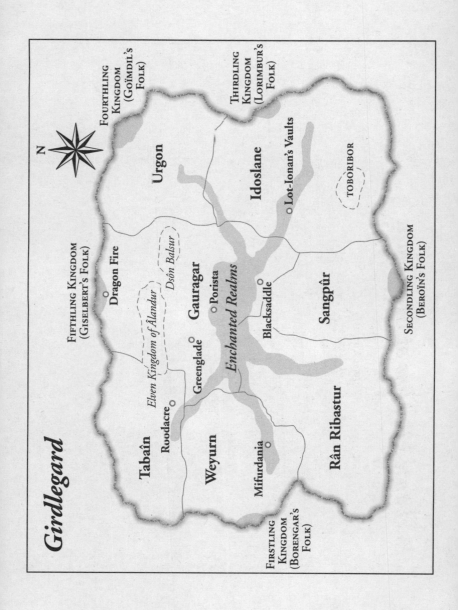

PART ONE

Prologue

Pale fog filled the canyons and valleys of the Gray Range. The Dragon's Tongue, Great Blade, and other peaks towered defiantly above the mist, tips raised toward the evening sun.

Slowly, as if afraid of the jagged peaks, the ball of fire sank in the sky, bathing the Northern Pass in waning red light.

Glandallin Hammerstrike of the clan of the Striking Hammers recovered his breath. Leaning back against the roughly hewn wall of the watchtower, he cupped his hand to his bushy brown eyebrows and shaded his eyes from the unaccustomed light. The ascent had been grueling and his close-woven chain mail, two axes, and shield weighed heavy on his aged legs.

There was no one younger to stand watch in his stead.

Only a few orbits previously, the nine clans of the fifthling kingdom had been attacked in their underground halls. Many had lost their lives in the battle, but the young and inexperienced were the first to fall.

Then came the sickness. No one knew where it had sprung from, but it preyed on the dwarves, sapping their strength, clouding their vision, and enfeebling their hands.

And so it was that Glandallin, despite his age, was guarding the gateway that night. Two vast slabs of solid rock erected by

Vraccas, god and creator of the dwarves, stemmed the tide of invading beasts. For some the sight of the imposing gateway was not enough of a deterrent; bleached bones and twisted scraps of armor were all that remained of them now.

The solitary sentry unhooked a leather pouch from his belt and poured cool water down his parched throat. A few drops spilled out of the corners of his mouth, flowing through his black beard. Elegant braids, the work of untold hours, hung from his chin and rested on his chest like delicate cords.

Glandallin replaced the pouch, took his weapons from his belt, and laid them on the parapet. The steel ax heads jangled melodiously against the sculpted rock, carved like the rest of the stronghold from the mountain's flesh.

A ray of sunlight glowed red on the polished inscriptions, illuminating the runes and symbols that promised their bearer protection, a sure aim, and long life.

Glandallin turned to the north, his brown eyes sweeping the mountain pass, thirty paces across, that led from the watchtower into the Outer Lands. No one knew what lay there. In times gone by, human kings had dispatched adventurers in all directions, but the expeditions were rarely successful and the few who returned to the gateway brought orcs in their wake.

He scanned the pass carefully. The beasts learned nothing from their defeats. Their vicious, choleric minds compelled them to throw themselves against the dwarves' defenses. They were bent on destroying anyone and anything in their path, for their creator, the dark lord Tion, had made them that way. The raids were conducted in blind fury. Raging and screaming, the beasts would scale the walls. From the first tinges of dawn light until the setting of the sun, armor would be cleaved from flesh, and flesh from bone. A tide of black, dark green, and yellowy-brown blood would lap against the impregnable gates, while battering rams and projectiles shattered as they hit the stone.

The children of Vraccas suffered casualties, deaths, and crippling injuries too, yet it never occurred to them to quarrel with their fate. They were dwarves, Girdlegard's staunchest defenders.

And yet we were almost defeated. Glandallin's thoughts turned again to the strange beings that had invaded the underground halls, killing many of his kinsfolk. No one had seen them approach. Outwardly they resembled elves: tall, slim, and graceful, but as warriors they were savage and ruthless.

Glandallin was almost certain that the creatures were not elves. There was no love lost between the dwarves and their pointy-eared neighbors. Vraccas and Sitalia, goddess and creator of the elves, had ordained the races with common loathing from the moment of their birth. Their differences had resulted in feuds, the occasional skirmish, and sometimes death, but never war.

Then again, he thought critically, *I might be wrong. Perhaps the elves hate us enough to draw arms against us — or maybe they're after our gold.*

A bitter northerly wind whistled round the mountaintops, gusting through Glandallin's braided beard. Suddenly, his brow furrowed angrily as his nostrils detected a stench that offended the core of his being: orcs.

Spilled blood, excrement, and filth — that was the perfume of orcs — mixed in with the rancid odor of their greasy apparel. They basted their armor with fat, believing that the dwarves' axes would slither over the metal and leave them unharmed.

No amount of fat will save them. Glandallin did not wait for the ragged banners and rusty spears to appear over the final incline of the path. Standing on tiptoe, he placed his callused hands on the coarse wooden handles of the bellows.

A low drone vibrated through the shafts and galleries of the fifthling kingdom.

The dwarf worked two bellows in rotation to produce a constant stream of air. Gathering in volume, the drone became a single piercing note, loud enough to rouse the soundest of sleepers. Now, as so often in their history, the fifthlings were being summoned to fulfill their noble duty as Girdlegard's protectors.

Sweating from the exertion, Glandallin glanced over his shoulder.

Tion's beasts had formed a wide front and were marching on the gateway, more numerous than ever before. Elves would have fled to the woods and a man's heart would have stopped at the sight of the monstrous hordes. The dwarf stood his ground.

The attack on the gateway came as no surprise to Glandallin, but the timing was unsettling. The coming battle would stretch the dwarves' resources more than usual. *More bloodshed and more death.*

The defending warriors lined up on the battlements on either side of the gateway, their movements slow, some lurching rather than walking, weak fingers wrapped loosely around the hafts of their axes. The band of dwarves stumbling to the defense of the gates numbered no more than a hundred brave souls. A thousand would have been too few.

Glandallin's watch was at an end; he was needed elsewhere.

"Don't forsake us, Vraccas. We're outnumbered," he whispered, unable to wrest his eyes from the stinking stream of orcs that poured along the path. Grunting, shouting, and jostling, they headed for the gates. The bare rock cast back their bestial cries, the echo mingling with their belligerent chants.

The strident noises jangled in his mind, and it seemed to

him that the beasts had somehow changed. There was a palpable air of confidence about the raging, shouting mob.

For the first time, he was afraid of the beasts.

What he saw next did nothing to ease his mind.

Scanning the ranks of the invading army, his gaze fell on a cluster of lofty fir trees. Since childhood he had watched them thrive and grow on the otherwise barren slopes.

Now they were sickly and dying.

The trees are faring no better than we. Glandallin's thoughts were with his wounded and ailing friends. "What strange forces are these? Your children need you, Vraccas," he prayed briefly, gathering his axes from the parapet.

With growing dread, he pressed his lips to the runes. "Don't abandon me now," he enjoined the blades softly, before turning and hurrying down the steps to join the small troop of defenders.

He reached them just as the first wave of beasts struck the wall. Quivering arrows rained down on the dwarves. Ladders were thrust against the walls, and orcs hastened to scale the wobbly rungs, while others set down their catapults and launched burning projectiles to reinforce the bombardment. Leather pouches, filled to the brim with paraffin, spluttered through the air and burst on impact, covering everything around them in an oily liquid and setting it ablaze.

The first salvo was aimed too low, but the dark hordes were undeterred by the sight of their front line burning in a storm of fire. Nothing, not the battery of stones nor the torrent of molten ore, could check their rapacious zeal. For every orc that was slain, five new aggressors scaled the walls. This time they were determined to breach the defenses. This time the gateway was destined to fall.

"Look out!" Glandallin ran to the aid of a dwarf whose shoulder had been pierced by an arrow. One of Tion's minions, a stunted creature with thick tusks and a broad nose, had seized his chance and squeezed through an embrasure, hauling himself over the parapet and onto the battlements.

Dwarf and orc stared at each other in silence. The clamor of voices, the hissing of arrows, the clatter of axes faded to an indistinct buzz.

Glandallin's ears were tuned to his opponent's heavy breath. The red-veined eyes, buried deep within the head, flicked nervously from side to side. The dwarf knew exactly what was going on inside the creature's mind. The orc was the first of its kind to have set foot on the battlement and could scarcely believe its good fortune.

A foul odor rose from the thick gray layer of tallow that coated its armor plating. The smell filled Glandallin's nostrils, drawing his attention back to the battle.

Shrieking, he threw himself against the beast. His shield jabbed smartly downward, shattering his opponent's foot, while he lunged with his ax from above. The blade smashed through the unarmored flesh around the armpit. The orc's arm, sliced cleanly at the joint, fell to the stony floor. Dark green blood sprayed upward from the open wound.

The orc let out a high-pitched scream, for which he was rewarded by a mighty stroke perpendicular to the neck.

"Tell your kinsfolk I am anxious to make their acquaintance!" Glandallin gave the dying brute a final shove and sent him tumbling against the parapet, where he took the next invader with him as he fell. They vanished over the side and plummeted to the ground. *With any luck, they'll crush half a dozen others,* thought Glandallin.

From then on the enemy gave him no respite. Running from one end of the parapet to the other, splitting helms, cleaving skulls, ducking arrows, and evading firebombs, he felled orc after orc.

Darkness was descending on the Stone Gateway, but Glandallin was untroubled by the fading light; even the thickest gloom could be penetrated by sharp dwarven eyes. But each blow and every movement took its toll on his weary arms, shoulders, and legs.

"Vraccas, grant us a moment to gather our forces," he coughed, rubbing his braids across his face to free his eyes of blood.

The dwarven deity took pity on his children.

A fanfare of horns and bugles bade the hordes cease their assault, and the orcs complied, pulling away from the walls.

Glandallin dispatched a lingering assailant and sank to the stone floor, fumbling for his drinking pouch. He tore off his helmet and poured water over his sweat-drenched hair. The cool fluid trickled over his skin, revitalizing his will.

How many of us remain? He stumbled to his feet and went in search of survivors. Of the hundred-strong army, seventy were left, among them the formidable figure of the fifthling monarch.

Nowhere were the enemy corpses stacked higher than at Giselbert Ironeye's feet. His shiny armor, made of the toughest steel forged in a dwarven smithy, gleamed brightly, and his diamond-studded belt caught the flames that licked from pools of burning oil. He climbed atop a stone ledge to speak to his folk.

"Stand firm!" Steady and true, his voice sounded across the battlements. "Be as unyielding as the rock from which we were hewn. Nothing—no orc, no ogre, no creature of Tion—will break us. We will cut them to pieces as dwarves have done for millennia. Vraccas is with us!"

The speech was met with low cheers and grunts of approval. The dwarves had been dealt a blow, but already their confidence was returning. They had grit and pride enough to stop the enemy in its tracks.

The warriors replenished their weary bodies with food and dark ale. With every sip and mouthful they felt stronger, more alive. The worst injuries were treated as time and circumstance permitted, gaping wounds sewn hurriedly together with fine twine.

Glandallin found himself a space on the floor beside Glamdolin Strongarm. The two friends ate in silence, watching the mass of orcs that had retreated a hundred paces from the gates. To Glandallin's eyes it seemed the enemy had formed a living battering ram, intent on smashing down the gateway with their flesh.

"Such persistence," he said softly. "I have never seen them as dogged as they are tonight. Something has changed." The thought of the dying trees sent a chill down his spine.

All of a sudden an ax clattered to the floor beside him. Turning just in time, he saw his companion slump forward. "Glamdolin!" He caught hold of the dwarf and was dismayed to see delicate beads of sweat glistening on his forehead, drenching his face and his beard. His reddened eyes were glazed and unseeing.

Glandallin knew at once that the mystery illness had claimed another victim, finishing what the enemy had left half-done.

"Get some rest. The fever will soon be over." Hauling Glamdolin's heaving body to one side, he settled him as comfortably as he could, knowing full well that the illness was probably fatal.

The long wait sapped the strength of dwarves and orcs alike. Fatigue, the warrior's enemy, set in. Glandallin dozed on his feet until his helmet hit the parapet with a thud. Awaking with a start, he looked around anxiously. Yet more of his kinsmen had fallen prey to the sickness. Fortune had turned her back upon the children of the Smith.

A bugle call rent the air, setting his heart racing.

In the cold light of the moon he watched the approaching rows of colossal silhouettes, four times as tall as the orcs. There were forty of them. Their hideous bodies were clad in poorly wrought armor and their monstrous hands clasped fir saplings, roughly fashioned into clubs.

Ogres.

The dwarves' defenses would crumble if the giants were to scale the walls. The cauldrons of molten slag were empty, the cache of stones depleted. For a moment Glandallin's doubts returned, but a glance at Giselbert's gleaming figure assured him that evil would be defeated in the time-honored way.

The mass of orcs stirred and a cheer went up as the ogres approached.

Marching to the head of the army, the enormous beasts, uglier and more oafish than even the orcs, deposited their grappling irons, the four prongs of which were the length of a fully grown man. They attached long chains to the stem of each hook.

The apparatus is ill suited to climbing, thought Glandallin. *The beasts intend to topple the walls.*

Whistling through the air, three dozen claws buried themselves in the stonework. A shouted order summoned the watching orcs to join the ogres in their tug-of-war. A crack of whips sounded and the jangling links pulled taut.

Glandallin heard the wall groan softly. The stronghold, built many cycles ago by his kinsmen, was no match for the beasts' raw power.

"Quick, bring the wounded to safety!" he bellowed.

The party of dwarves responsible for tending the cauldrons

left their stations and carried off Glamdolin and the other ailing warriors.

Masonry crumbled as a section of crenellated battlement ripped from the wall. The grappling hook went into free fall amid the showering stonework, killing two ogres and ten orcs. The enemy forces held their ground. Soon the hook was ripping through the air again, poised to sink its claws into the wall.

This time the dwarves retreated, abandoning the parapet just in time. They took up position in the barbican above the gates.

Glandallin listened as a large section of wall crashed and shattered on the ground below. The earth quaked and the invading army howled in triumph.

Good luck to them, thought Glandallin, endeavoring to stay calm. *I hope they dash their brains out on the doors.* The gateway was built to withstand more than a few paltry grappling irons.

He peered cautiously over the steel-plated wall. More reinforcements were on their way. Horsemen mounted on jet-black steeds galloped to the head of the army of ogres and orcs. Glandallin instantly recognized the pointed ears of the tall, slim creatures.

A red glow shone from the horses' eyes and their hooves struck the ground in a shower of white sparks. Two riders thundered to the gateway and gave orders to the troops. The orcs and ogres set about clearing the pathway of fallen masonry so the assault could start afresh.

Wheeling round on their horses, the riders found safe quarter from which to watch. One of the two creatures unshouldered a mighty bow and nocked an arrow against the woven bowstring. The marksman's gloved fingers held the weapon loosely as he bided his time.

Hastily, the fifthlings pushed boulders over the parapet and onto the beasts below. The enemy flinched, jostling to evade the projectiles, and three of the orcs turned to flee. The archer raised his bow. Before the deserters could take flight, the first arrow, too fast for Glandallin to follow, sang through the air and an orc fell to its knees.

Already a second missile, uncommonly long for an arrow, sped from the archer's bow. The second beast perished, shrieking, followed a moment later by the third. The remaining minions took heed of the warning and resumed their work on the pathway. The orcs did not venture a protest at the murder of their kinsmen.

By the coming of dawn, the path had been cleared.

The fifthlings marveled at the scene unfolding before their eyes. The sky had brightened in the east, heralding the rising of the sun, yet a thick bank of fog loomed in the north. Its luminous center, a maelstrom of black, red, and silver, flickered with coursing light.

In defiance of the wind, it rolled toward the gateway, sweeping over the beasts below. The raucous orcs fell silent, huddling nervously together and shrinking away from the fog. Stooping, the ogres allowed it to pass. As if hailing their leader, the riders bowed their heads and saluted the vaporous mass. The shimmering mist lowered itself gently to the ground and hovered in front of the horses.

Then the unthinkable happened. With a shudder, the first of five bolts on the doors shot from its cylinder. The gateway quaked. Someone had spoken the incantation, delivering Girdlegard into the clutches of the invading hordes.

"No!" bellowed Glandallin, turning his back to the enemy and leaning over the inner wall to seek the culprit below. "No dwarf would ever..."

Glamdolin Strongarm. Alone, the dwarf was standing by the doors, lips moving, hands raised in supplication.

"Silence!" Glandallin bellowed. "Can't you see what you're doing?"

His shouts fell on deaf ears. The second lock glowed brightly, illuminated by the runes. The bolt creaked back.

"He's been bewitched," muttered Glandallin. "The fog has infected his mind."

The third bolt left its ferrule and shot free.

At last the custodians of the gateway stirred. Springing to their feet, they darted down the staircase, racing to put a stop to the treacherous magic before it was too late. The fourth bolt drew back. With one bolt remaining, Glamdolin was still standing unchallenged on the pathway.

Time is against us, Glandallin thought grimly. "Forgive me, Vraccas, but I have no choice." He gripped his ax and hurled it with all his might and fury at his comrade-in-arms.

The blade sliced through the air, spinning, then plunged sharply toward the ground. Glandallin's aim was unerring and the ax drove home.

Glamdolin groaned as the weapon struck his shoulder. Blood spraying from the wound, he stumbled to the ground. Watching from above, Glandallin sent a quick thanks to Vraccas for guiding his blade.

His relief was short-lived. Death had come too late to prevent the traitor from achieving his terrible purpose. The final bolt shot back.

Slowly, the colossal gateway opened. The vast slabs scraped and dragged across the ground, as though reluctant to obey the treacherous command.

There was a grinding noise of stone on stone. The chink became a narrow channel, which widened to fill the breadth of the path. Time slowed to a crawl as the gates swung open.

One final creak and for the first time in creation the path into Girdlegard was clear.

No! Glandallin stirred from his paralysis and hurtled down the steps to join Giselbert and the remaining warriors defending the gates.

He was the last but one to take his place in the doorway. Already the others had closed ranks and were holding their shields in front of their bodies, their axes held aloft.

Shoulder to shoulder they formed a low wall of flesh against the tide of orcs, ogres, trolls, and riders. Forty against forty thousand.

The enemy hung back, fearing an ambush. Never before had the gates opened to allow their passage.

Glandallin's gaze swept the front line of monstrous beasts, shifting back to survey the second, third, fourth, fifth, and countless other grunting rows, all poised for the attack. He glowered from under his bushy eyebrows, forehead furrowing into a frown.

Giselbert lost no time in reversing the incantation. At the sound of his voice, the gates submitted to his authority, swinging back across the pathway but moving too slowly to stop the breach. Giselbert strode behind his troops, laying a hand on each shoulder. The gesture was a source of solace as well as strength, calming and rallying the last defenders of the gates.

Trumpets blaring, the riders ordered the attack. The orcs and ogres brandished their weapons, shouting to drown out their fear, and the army advanced with thundering steps.

"The path is narrow. Meet them line by line and give them a taste of our steel!" Glandallin called to his kinsfolk. "Vraccas is with us! We are the children of the Smith!"

"The children of the Smith!" the fifthlings echoed, feet planted firmly on the rocky ground beneath.

Four dwarves were chosen to form the final line of defense. Throwing down his shield, the king took an ax in each hand and led the surge toward the enemy. The dwarves, all that remained of Giselbert's folk, charged out to slay the invaders.

Ten paces beyond the gateway, the armies met. The fifthlings tunneled like moles through the vanguard of orcs.

With only one ax with which to defend himself, Glandallin struck out, slicing through the thicket of legs. He did not stop to kill his victims, knowing that the fallen bodies would hinder the advancing troops.

"No one gets past Glandallin!" he roared. Stinking blood streamed from his armor and helm, stinging his eyes. When his ax grew heavy, he clasped the weapon with both hands. "No one, do you hear!" His enemies' bones splintered, splattering him with hot blood. Twice he was grazed by a sword or a spear, but he battled on regardless.

The prize was not survival but the closing of the gates. Girdlegard would be safe if they could stave off the invasion until the passageway was sealed.

Until this hour his ax had defended him faithfully, but now the magic of its runes gave out. Glancing to his right, Glandallin saw a comrade topple to the ground, skull sliced in half by an orc's two-handed sword. Seething with hatred, and determined to fell the aggressor, Glandallin lunged once, twice, driving his ax into the creature's belly and cleaving it in two. A shadow loomed above him, but by then it was too late. He made a last-ditch attempt to dodge the ogre's sweeping cudgel, but its rounded head swooped down and struck his legs. Bellowing in pain he toppled against an orc, severing its thigh as he fell, before tumbling onward through the army of legs. He lashed out with his ax until there were no more orcs within his reach.

"Come here and fight, you cowards!" he snarled.

The enemy paid him no attention. Fired by an insatiable

hunger, they streamed past him toward the gateway. They had no need of stringy dwarf flesh when there were tastier morsels in Girdlegard.

Trembling with pain, Glandallin rose up on his elbows. The rest of his kinsfolk were dead, their mutilated bodies strewn on the ground, surrounded by scores of enemy corpses. The diamonds on Giselbert's belt sparkled in the sunlight, marking the place where the fifthling father had fallen, slain by a trio of ogres. At the sight of him, Glandallin's soul ached with sorrow and pride.

The sun rose above the mountains, flooding through the gateway and dazzling Glandallin with its light. He raised a hand to his sensitive eyes, straining to see the gateway. *Praise be to Vraccas! The gates were closed!*

A blow from behind sent pain searing through his chest. For the duration of a heartbeat the tip of a spear protruded through his tunic, then withdrew. He slumped, gasping, to the ground. "What in the name of...?"

The assassin stepped round his body and knelt beside him. The smooth elven face was framed by fine fair hair that shimmered in the sunlight like a veil of golden threads. But the vision bore a terrible deformity: two fathomless pits stared from almond-shaped holes.

The creature wore armor of black metal that reached to its knees. Its legs were clad in leather breeches and dark brown boots. Burgundy gloves protected its fingers from grime, and its right hand clasped a spear whose steel tip, sharp enough to penetrate the fine mesh of dwarven chain mail, was moist with blood.

The strange elf spoke to the dwarf.

At first the words meant nothing to Glandallin, but their morbid sound filled him with dread.

"My friend said: 'Look at me: Sinthoras is your death,'"

a second voice translated behind him. " 'I will take your life, and the land will take your soul.' "

Glandallin coughed, blood rushing from his mouth and coursing down his beard.

"Get out of my sight, you pointy-eared monster! I want to see the gates," he said gruffly, brandishing his ax to ward away the beast. The weapon almost flew from his grip; his strength was ebbing fast. "Out of my way or I'll cut you in two like a straw, you treacherous elf!" he thundered.

Sinthoras laughed coldly. Raising his spear, he inserted the tip slowly between the tight rings of mail.

"You are mistaken, my friend. We are the älfar, and we have come to slay the elves," the voice said softly. "The gates may be closed, but the power of the land will raise you from the dead and from that moment on, you will be one of us. You know the incantation; you will open the door."

"Never! My soul belongs to Vraccas!"

"Your soul belongs to the land, and you will belong to the land until the end of time," the velvety voice cut him short. "Die, so you can return and deliver Girdlegard to us."

The spear's sharp tip pierced the flesh of the helpless, dying dwarf. Pain stopped his tongue.

Sinthoras raised the weapon and pushed down gently on the battered body. The final blow was dealt tenderly, almost reverently. The creature waited for death to claim its prey, watching over Glandallin's pain-ravaged features and drinking in the memory.

Finally, when he was certain that the last custodian of the gateway had departed, Sinthoras left his vigil and rose to his feet.

I

A volley of raps rang out as the hammer danced on the glowing ore. With each blow the metal took shape, curving into a crescent as the iron submitted to the blacksmith's strength and skill.

Suddenly the jangling ceased and a pair of tongs swooped down and tossed the metal back into the furnace. The blacksmith gave a grunt of displeasure.

"What do you think you're doing, Tungdil?" the waiting man demanded impatiently. Eiden, a groom in the service of Lot-Ionan the magus, stroked the horse's nose. "The nag can't wait forever, you know. She's supposed to be pulling the plow."

Tungdil dipped his hands into a pail of water and used the brief hiatus to wash away the grime. The dwarf wore leather breeches and a brown beard clipped close to his chin. He was naked from the waist up, save for a leather apron. Running his brawny fingers through his long dark hair, he shook out the sweat and let the drops of cool water trickle across his scalp.

"The shoe would never have fit," came his brief response. He pumped the bellows, producing a tortured hiss like the breath of a wheezing giant. The air breathed red-hot life into the glowing coals. "Nearly there now."

He repeated the procedure, this time to his satisfaction, and fitted the shoe to the nag. A foul-smelling cloud of yellowish smoke enveloped Tungdil as the iron singed the horny sole. He dunked the shoe into the pail, allowing the metal to cool, then held it to the hoof again and drove nails through the holes. Setting the hind leg down gingerly, he retreated hastily. The animal, a strong, broad-backed gray, was too big for his liking.

Eiden sniggered and stroked the plow horse. "How do you like your new shoe?" he asked her. "The smith's a midget, granted, but at least he knows his stuff. Just watch you don't trip over him." He hurried from the forge and marched the horse toward the fields.

The dwarf stretched and gave his powerful arms a shake as he strolled to the furnace. The groom's jibes did not rile him; teasing, affectionate or otherwise, was something he was inured to, having grown up in Ionandar, the only dwarf in a human realm.

He stood more chance of finding gold by the wayside than encountering another of his kind.

All the same, I should like to meet one, he thought. His gaze swept the orderly forge, taking in the rows of tongs and hammers hanging neatly from the walls. *I'd ask about the five dwarven folks.*

The light in the forge was dim, but Tungdil liked it that way because it brought out the beauty of the fiery coals. He worked the bellows, chasing sparks into the chimney as he fanned the flames. For a moment his face lit up as he imagined the glowing red dots flitting through the sky and taking their place in the firmament to shine brightly as stars. It was the same satisfaction that he derived from letting his hammer bounce up and down on the red-hot metal. *Do real dwarven smiths do things differently?* he wondered.

"Why is it always so dark in here?" Without warning, Sunja, the eight-year-old daughter of Frala the kitchen maid, appeared at his side. A bright child, she was refreshingly untroubled by Tungdil's appearance.

The dwarf's kindly face creased from ear to ear. It was astonishing how quickly human children grew; the girl would soon be taller than he was. "You're as bad as cats, you children, sneaking up on me like that! I'll tell you all about it if you help me heat the iron." He tossed a lump of metal into the furnace.

Eagerly, the fair-haired girl joined him at the bellows. As ever, he pretended to let her take over, allowing her to believe that she was compressing the firm leather pouch with her strength alone. Soon the metal took on a reddish glow.

"Do you see now?" Reaching forward with the tongs, he gripped the nugget of iron and laid it on the anvil. "It's not for nothing that I work without light. A blacksmith needs to know when the metal has reached the right temperature. Left to slumber in its toasty bed of coals, the iron overheats, but raised too soon, the brittle metal can't be forged." Tungdil was rewarded with an earnest nod. The child looked exactly like Frala.

"My mother says you're a master blacksmith."

"I wouldn't go that far," he protested, laughing. "I'm just good at my job." He winked at her and she smiled.

What Tungdil didn't mention was that he had never received instruction in his trade. Watching his predecessor at work had been all the training he'd needed. Whenever the man set down his tools, Tungdil had seized his chance to practice, mastering the essentials in no time. Now, thirty solar cycles later, no job was too big or too difficult for him.

Lost in their thoughts, Tungdil and Sunja watched as the flames changed color: first orange, then yellow, red, white, and blue... The glowing coals sputtered and crackled.

Just as the dwarf was about to inquire what Cook would

be serving for luncheon, a man appeared in the doorway, black against the rectangle of light.

"You're needed in the kitchens, Tungdil," came the imperious voice of Jolosin, a famulus in the fourth tier of Lot-Ionan's apprentices.

"Well, since you asked so nicely..." Tungdil turned to Sunja: "Be sure not to touch anything." On his way out, he pocketed a small metal object and then followed the apprentice into the vaults of Lot-Ionan's school.

Two hundred or so students of all ages had been selected to learn the secrets of sorcery from the magus. To the dwarf's mind, magic was a slippery, unreliable occupation. He felt more at home in his forge, where he could hammer as loudly as he pleased.

Jolosin's dark blue robes billowed as he walked, his combed hair bobbing about his shoulders. Tungdil eyed the youth's fine garments and coiffure and grinned. *The vanity of the boy!* They entered a large room and an appetizing smell wafted toward them. Sure enough, cooking pots were simmering and bubbling above two hearths.

Tungdil saw at once why his services were required. The pots were suspended on chains from the ceilings, but one of them had slipped its pulley and was sitting in the flames.

Lifting the vessel required more strength than a woman could muster and none of the apprentices were willing to help. They considered themselves a cut above kitchen work, refusing to dirty their hands or burn their fingers when others, such as smiths, could do the work.

The cook, a stately woman of impressive girth, hurried over. "Hurry," she cried anxiously, reaching up to stay her escaping hairnet. "My goulash will be spoiled!"

"We can't have that. I'm starving," said Tungdil. Without wasting time, he marched over to the hearth, touched the chain lightly to gauge its temperature, then seized the rusty links. Cycle after cycle at the anvil had strengthened his muscles until even the heaviest hammer felt weightless in his arms. A pot of goulash on a pulley was nothing by comparison.

"Here," he said to Jolosin, proffering him the grimy chain, "hold this while I fix it."

The young man hesitated. "Are you sure it's not too heavy for me?" he asked nervously.

"You'll be fine," Tungdil reassured him. He grinned. "And if you're half as good at magic as you say you are, you can always make it lighter." He pressed the chain into the apprentice's hands and let go.

With a muttered curse, the famulus threw his weight against the dangling pot. "Ow!" he protested. "It's hot!"

"That's my goulash you're holding!" the cook reminded him darkly. Conceding defeat to her hairnet, she allowed her brown mop to fall across her pudgy face. "I don't care if you're a famulus. I'll take my rolling pin to you if you let go of that chain!" Her plump arms rippled as she balled her fists.

On discovering the source of the problem, Tungdil decided to punish Jolosin by delaying the repair.

"This won't be easy," he said in a voice of feigned dismay. Frala raised her pretty green eyes from the potatoes she was peeling, saw what he was up to, and giggled.

At last he made the necessary adjustments and checked the mechanism again. The pulley held and the goulash was safe. "You can let go now."

Jolosin did as instructed, then inspected his dirty hands. Some of the grime had transferred itself to his precious blue robes. He shot a suspicious look at Frala, who was laughing out loud. His color rose.

"That's exactly what you were hoping for, isn't it, you stunted wretch!" He took a step toward Tungdil and raised his fist, then stopped; the dwarf was considerably stronger than he was. Angrily, he stormed away.

Tungdil watched him go and smirked. "If he wants a fight, he shall have one. It's a pity he lost his nerve." He wiped his hands on his apron.

Frala fished an apple from the basket beside her and tossed it to him. "Poor Jolosin," she said with a chuckle. "His fine gown is all soiled."

"He should have been more careful." He shrugged and strolled over. Like him, Frala was responsible for the little things that contributed to the smooth running of the school. "But I'll excuse his clumsiness, just this once." His kind eyes looked at her brightly from among his laughter lines.

"You two deserve each other," Frala sighed. "If you're not careful, someone will come to a bad end because of your feuding." There was a splash as she dropped a peeled potato into the waiting tub of water.

"What did he expect when he dyed my beard? You know what they say: Make a noise in a mine shaft and you're bound to hear an echo." Tungdil ran a hand over his stubbly beard. "I had to shave my chin, thanks to his stupid spell. He must have known we'd be sworn enemies after that!"

"I thought orcs were your worst enemy?" she said archly.

"Well, I've made an exception for him. Beards are sacred and if I were a proper dwarf I'd kill him for his insolence. I'm too easygoing for my own good." He bit into the apple hungrily. With his left hand he took something from the pouch at his waist and pressed it into Frala's hand. "For you."

She looked down at her palm and saw three horseshoe nails painstakingly forged together to form a homemade talisman. She stroked the dwarf's cheek fondly.

"What a lovely gift. Thank you, Tungdil." She got up,

fetched a length of twine, threaded it through the pendant, and knotted it deftly round her neck. The talisman nestled against her bare skin. "Does it suit me?" she asked coyly.

"Anyone would think it had been made for you," he said, thrilled that Frala was wearing the iron trinket as proudly as if Girdlegard's finest jeweler had designed and forged the piece.

There was a special bond between the pair of them. The dwarf had known Frala since she was a baby and had watched her mature into an attractive young woman who turned the heads of Lot-Ionan's apprentices. These days she had two daughters of her own: Sunja and one-year-old Ikana.

Cycles ago, when Frala was still a girl, he had made tin figures for her to play with, showed her around the forge, and let her work the bellows. "Dragon's breath," she used to call it as the sparks flew up the chimney, accompanied by her laughter. Frala never forgot the pains he had taken to entertain her, nor how he cared for her daughter.

She shook the remaining potatoes into the tub and topped up the water. As she turned round, her green eyes looked at him keenly. "It's funny," she said with a smile. "I was just thinking how you haven't changed a bit in all the cycles I've known you."

Half of Tungdil's apple had already disappeared. Still munching, he made himself comfortable on a stool. "And I was just thinking how splendidly we get on together," he said simply.

"Frala!" the cook shouted. "I'm going for some herbs. You'll have to stir the goulash." The ladle, its stem scarcely shorter than Tungdil, changed hands. The cook hurried out. "You'd better not let it stick," she warned.

A delicious smell of goulash rose from the pot as Frala gave the stew a vigorous stir.

"All the others look older," she said, "even the magus. But you've stayed the same for twenty-three cycles. How do you think you'll look in another twenty-three?"

The topic was one that Tungdil was reluctant to consider. From what he had read about dwarves, it seemed he was destined to live for three hundred cycles or more. Even now it grieved him to think that he would see the death of Frala and her daughters, of whom he had grown so fond.

With these thoughts in mind, he popped the apple core into his mouth. "Who knows, Frala," he mumbled, hoping to dismiss the gloomy subject.

The maid had a particular knack for reading his mind that morning. "Can I ask you something, Tungdil?" He nodded. "Do you promise you'll look after my daughters when I'm gone?"

He choked on the sour apple pips, scratching his throat in the process. "I don't think we need to worry about that now. Why, you'll live to be" — he looked her up and down — "a hundred cycles at least. I'll ask the magus to give you eternal life — and Sunja and Ikana too, of course."

Frala laughed. "Oh, I'm not intending to meet Palandiell quite yet." She kept stirring dutifully, even though her forehead was dripping with perspiration. "But all the same, I'd...Well, I'd feel better if I knew you were there to take care of them." Her shoulders lifted in a helpless shrug. "Please, Tungdil, say you'll be their guardian."

"Frala, by the time you're summoned to your goddess, Sunja and Ikana will be old enough to look after themselves." Realizing that she was in earnest, he duly gave his word. "I'd be honored to be their guardian." He slid from the stool. "If the chain slips again, send Jolosin to find me!" He made his way out with a small bowl of goulash to sustain him until lunch.

On returning to the forge he found Sunja waiting for him with yet another commission from Eiden, two wooden barrels whose iron hoops had split. No sooner had he started work than the plow was brought in, needing urgent repair.

Tungdil relished the work. The fierce flames and physical effort made it a sweaty business, and soon perspiration was trickling down his arms and plopping into the fire with a hiss. Frala's daughter watched in fascination, passing him tools whenever she was strong enough to lift them and working the bellows with all her might.

The glowing metal yielded to his hammer, letting him shape it as he pleased. At times like this he almost felt like a proper dwarf and not just a foundling raised by humans.

His mind began to drift. He had reached the age of sixty-three solar cycles without seeing another of his kind, which was why he looked forward to being sent away on errands. The occasions when Lot-Ionan required his services as a messenger were regrettably few and far between. There was nothing Tungdil wanted more than to meet one of his own people and learn about his race, but the chances of encountering a traveling dwarf were infinitesimally small.

The realm of Ionandar belonged exclusively to humans. There were a few gnomes and kobolds, but their races were almost extinct. Those that remained lived in remote caves beneath the surface, emerging only when there was something worth stealing—or so Frala said. The last of the elven people lived in Âlandur amid the glades of the Eternal Forest, while the dwarves inhabited the five ranges bounding Girdlegard. Tungdil had almost given up hope of visiting a dwarven kingdom and finding out about his folk.

Everything he knew about dwarves stemmed from Lot-Ionan's library, but it was a dry kind of knowledge, empty and colorless. In some of the magus's books, the writers called the dwarves "groundlings" and poked fun at them, while others blamed his people for opening Girdlegard to the northern hordes. Tungdil refused to believe it.

But he could understand why so few of his kind ventured outside their kingdoms; his kinsfolk were almost certainly offended by such prejudice and preferred to turn their backs on humankind.

Tungdil was putting the finishing touches to the first of the iron hoops when Jolosin appeared at the door, wearing, as Tungdil noted with satisfaction, a clean set of robes.

"Hurry," he spluttered, panting for breath.

"Don't tell me it's the goulash again," said Tungdil, grinning. "Why don't you run along and hold the chain until I get there?"

"It's the laboratory..." Barely able to get the words out, Jolosin resorted to gestures. "The chimney...," he gasped, turning and hurrying away.

This time it sounded serious. The dwarf set down his hammer in consternation and wiped his hands on his apron. Once Sunja had been dispatched to join her mother in the kitchen, he chased after the famulus through the underground galleries hewn into the stone.

Border Territory,
Secondling Kingdom,
Girdlegard,
Winter, 6233rd Solar Cycle

Tens of hundreds of tiny grains of sand pelted their helms, shields, mail, and every inch of unprotected flesh.

Battered by the gusts, the brave band of dwarves struggled onward, mounted on ponies. Scarves muffled their faces but the cloth was no match for the fine desert sand, which worked its way through the fabric, clogging their beards and grinding between their teeth.

"Bedeviled wind," cursed Gandogar Silverbeard of the clan of the Silver Beards, king of the fourthlings' twelve clans. He tugged at his scarf, pulling it over his nose.

At 298 cycles of age, Gandogar was a respected leader and accomplished warrior. He stood a little over five feet tall and his arms were strong and powerful. His heavy tunic of finely forged mail was worn with pride, despite the trying circumstances. Beneath his diamond-studded helmet his hair and beard were brown and wiry. He led the party unflinchingly through the sand and scree.

"It's the sand that gets me. I've never seen a sandstorm below the surface," complained Bislipur Surestroke, the friend and mentor riding at his side. He was taller and brawnier than the monarch and his hands and arms were laden with almost as many golden rings and bangles. He looked every inch the warrior, his chain mail bearing the scars of countless battles. The freshest marks were just five orbits old, the result of a skirmish with orcs.

"Vraccas knew what he was doing when he sculpted us from rock. Dwarves and deserts don't mix." The verdict was shared by the rest of the troop.

The ponies that had borne them on their long journey to the secondling kingdom snorted and whinnied fractiously, trying to clear their nostrils but blocking them further with all-pervasive sand.

"There's no other way of getting there," Gandogar said apologetically. "You'll be pleased to know that the worst is behind us."

The band of thirty dwarves was in Sangpûr, a desolate human realm under Queen Umilante's rule. The landscape consisted of nothing but barren dunes and godforsaken wasteland, a vista so cheerless that the dwarves preferred to stare at the tangled manes of their ponies or the tips of their boots.

Their journey south from the Brown Range had taken them through the lush valleys and steep gorges of the mountainous state of Urgon where Lothaire reigned. From there they had ridden over the gentle plains of King Tilogorn's Idoslane, where the slightest hillock qualified as a mountain and shady forests gave way to fertile fields.

The passage through Sangpûr was the last and most grueling leg of the journey, a swathe of desert forty miles wide, lying at the foot of the mountains like a moat of fine sand. It was almost as though nature wanted to prevent the rest of Girdlegard, including the fourthlings, from reaching the range.

On occasions, the wind dropped and the veil of sand fell, allowing the mighty peaks to loom before them magically among the dunes. The dwarves felt the call of the snow-capped mountains and longed for cool air, fresh water, and the company of their kin.

Bislipur tightened the scarf around his cheeks and stroked his graying beard. "I'm no friend of magic, but if ever we needed a sorcerer it's now," he growled.

"Why?"

"He could command the wretched wind to stop."

A final gust swirled toward them; then the gales died unexpectedly. Only five miles separated the dwarves from the comb of rock that ran from east to west.

"You're not a bad sorcerer yourself," said Gandogar,

breathing a sigh of relief. He had never been especially fond of the world outside his kingdom and this latest foray had persuaded him that one epic journey in a lifetime was more than enough. "What did I tell you? We're almost there."

Rising out of the gloom of the mountain's shadows were the imposing walls of Ogre's Death. The stronghold grew out of the rock, the main keep hewn into the foothills, the battlements extending down the hillside in four separate terraces that were all but impregnable.

Cut into the walls of the uppermost terrace was the stronghold's entrance, eight paces wide and ten paces high. *Like an enormous mouth,* thought Gandogar. *It looks as though the mountain is yawning.*

As the company neared the stronghold, the doors opened welcomingly. Seventeen banners fluttered loftily from the turrets, bearing the insignia of the secondling clans.

"Here at last," Gandogar said thankfully. "To think we've ridden right across Girdlegard." The other dwarves joined in his grateful laughter. They were his retinue, a heavily armed band who had escorted him throughout the long journey to the secondling kingdom. Between them they were the cream of Goïmdil's folk, skilled in ax work and craftsmanship, the best warriors and artisans from each of the twelve fourthling clans. Many a legend told of the fighting prowess of the dwarves, which explained why the party had not been troubled by a single brigand or thief. They were carrying enough gold to make an ambush more than worth the risk.

Bislipur waved his hand imperiously and his summons was instantly obeyed. A little fellow measuring just three feet in height slid from his pony awkwardly and came running through the sand. He wore a wide belt around his baggy breeches and looked oddly sinewy in appearance, despite the considerable paunch that rounded his hessian shirt. The yellowed undergarment was paired with a red jacket and his blue cap was pulled low over his face, a pointed ear protruding on either side. A silver choker encircled his neck and his buckled shoes kicked up clouds of sand as he scampered through the dunes.

He bowed at Bislipur's feet. "Sverd at your service, but not of his own accord," he said peevishly.

"Silence!" thundered Bislipur, raising his powerful fist. The gnome ducked away. "Ride on and announce our arrival. Wait for us at the gates—and don't touch anything that doesn't belong to you."

"Since I don't have a choice in the matter, I shall do as you say." The gnome bowed again and hurried to his pony. Soon he was galloping away from the dwarves in the direction of the stronghold.

Even from a distance it was obvious that Sverd was no horseman. He bounced up and down in the saddle, clinging to his cap with clawlike fingers and relying on the pony to set their course.

"He'll unman himself if he goes any faster. When are you finally going to set him free?" asked Gandogar.

"Not until he's served his penance," Bislipur answered tersely. "Let's not delay." He pressed his heels into the pony's broad flanks and the animal set off at an obedient trot.

The fourthlings knew Ogre's Death from etchings and stories, but now they were seeing it for the first time for themselves.

Hundreds of cycles had passed since the last dwarf of Goïmdil journeyed through Girdlegard to visit his kinsfolk in the south. In ancient times the dwarven folks had come together every few cycles to celebrate festivals in honor of

Vraccas and thank the Smith for creating their race, but the fall of the Stone Gateway, the invasion of the orcs, ogres, and älfar, and the annihilation of the fifthlings had put a stop to that.

"Thank Vraccas we're here," sighed Gandogar, standing up in his stirrups to give his saddle-sore bottom a brief respite.

None of the company had any instinct for riding. As true dwarves, they would never consent to making a journey on horses; the beasts were untrustworthy and the saddles could be reached only by means of a stepladder, which was far too undignified. It was bad enough riding on ponies.

Their distrust of the animals ran so deep that two of the party refused to ride altogether and were traveling in small, easily maneuverable chariots at the back of the procession.

"We'll all be glad when the journey is over," said Bislipur, spitting sand from his mouth.

The woes of their travels were partly forgotten as Ogre's Death's magnificent masonry loomed into view. Gandogar's eyes traveled over the exquisitely ornamented turrets and walls — even the outermost rampart was a work of art, graced with plinths, statues, pillars, and other embellishments. *Our folk boasts the finest gem cutters and diamond polishers, but Beroïn's masons are second to none.*

The gates to the first of the four terraces swung open and Gandogar's company was admitted to a courtyard. Sverd had dismounted and was standing by his pony. Bislipur signaled for him to fall in at the rear of the group.

Dwarves seldom showed their age, but the figure who came toward them had seen three hundred cycles or more. "Greetings, King Gandogar Silverbeard of Goïmdil's folk. My name is Balendilín Onearm of the clan of the Firm Fingers and on behalf of our ruler, Gundrabur Whitecrown, high king of all dwarves, I welcome you and your company to the secondling kingdom of Beroïn's folk."

Clad in a tunic of chain mail, the stocky dwarf was carrying a battle-ax at his waist. His weapons belt was secured by a finely worked stone clasp. Marble trinkets had been braided into his graying beard and a long plait dangled behind him.

"Come, brothers, follow me."

He started on the path that rose toward the stronghold. As he turned, the fourthlings noticed that he was missing one arm.

Gandogar conjectured that the limb had been lost to one of Tion's minions. In all other respects, the secondling was powerfully built, perhaps because of the strength required for working with stone. His right hand was heavily callused, almost bearlike in size, the fingers exuding a power that lived up to the name of his clan.

The company followed Balendilín through several gateways until they reached the fourth and final terrace, where he signaled for them to stop. At last they could appreciate the full genius of the stronghold's design. Their host gestured to the doors that led into the mountain. "Dismount and leave your ponies here. We'll take good care of them, I assure you. The delegates are expecting you in the great hall."

He led the procession into a tunnel of such vast proportions that a dragon could have entered with ease. What truly took the visitors' breath away, though, was the masonry. Nine-sided stone columns, each measuring ten paces in circumference, rose like fossilized trees. The ceiling was so high as to be invisible, the columns soaring into space. *Perhaps the crown of the mountain is supported by pillars,* thought Gandogar, gazing at his surroundings in awe.

Stone arches, richly decorated with carvings, spanned the columns, inscribed with verses and citations from the creation story of the dwarves.

Ahead of them towered an enormous stone statue of Beroïn, father of the secondlings. The ancient monarch sat on a throne of white marble, his right hand raised in greeting and his left hand clasped about his ax. His foot alone was as long as five ponies and loomed to the height of a fully grown dwarf.

But that was just the start of it.

The walls, once coarse naked rock, had been polished to a sheen and the glinting surfaces engraved with runes and patterns. The stonework was so delicate, so precise, that Gandogar slowed to examine it.

There were underground galleries and chambers aplenty in his own kingdom, but nothing compared to the secondlings' skill.

He reached out and ran his hand reverently over the dark gray marble. It was hard to believe such splendor was possible.

"By Vraccas," he exclaimed admiringly, "I have never seen such artistry. The secondlings boast the best masons of any dwarven folk."

Gundrabur's counselor gave a little bow. "Thank you. They will value your praise."

The company walked between the statue's feet and through another door. There the passageway narrowed and the air felt suddenly cool. They had reached the entrance to the hall.

Balendilín turned to Gandogar and smiled. "Are you ready to stake your claim before the assembly?"

"Of course he is," snapped Bislipur before the king could speak.

Balendilín frowned but said nothing, stepping forward to

throw open the doors and announce the arrival of the long-awaited guests.

The great hall surpassed everything that had gone before it. Cylindrical columns towered to vertiginous heights and great battle scenes graced the walls, the sculpted marble surfaces commemorating past victories and heroic deeds. Lanterns and braziers of burning coal bathed the chamber in a warm reddish glow, but the air was cool, much to the delight of the travelers who had endured the heat of Sangpûr's deserts.

While Balendilín was introducing the new arrivals, Gandogar fixed his adviser with a stare. "You would have beaten Sverd for such insolence."

Bislipur clenched his jaw. "I'll apologize to the counselor later."

They turned toward the assembly. Five chairs, one for each of the dwarven folks, were arranged in a semicircle around a table. Elegantly carved pews were lined up in five blocks behind them so that the chieftains and elders could follow the proceedings and have their say.

One of the chairs, together with its corresponding benches, would remain forever empty, a painful reminder of the fifthlings' fate. There was no sign of the firstling monarch or chieftains, but the seventeen clans of the secondlings had taken their seats.

The table was covered in maps and charts of Girdlegard. Before the fourthlings' arrival, the delegates had been discussing the happenings in the north, but now their attention turned to Gandogar.

The king felt a rush of excitement. For the first time in over four hundred cycles the most influential and powerful dwarves of all the folks would be assembled in one room. Never before had he been in the presence of his fellow monarchs and distant kin and at last the names that he had heard so often attached themselves to beings of flesh and blood. It was a momentous occasion.

The other dwarves rose to greet the company with hearty handshakes. Gandogar noticed how the palms differed; some were callused or scarred, others tough and muscular, while a few seemed almost delicate. He was touched by the warmth of the welcome, despite the distrust and suspicion evident in some eyes.

Then it was time for him to greet Gundrabur Whitecrown, king of the secondlings and ruler of every dwarf, clan, and folk.

He stepped forward and struggled to hide his shock.

After five hundred cycles of life, the once stately high king was so weak that the mildest breeze was liable to extinguish his inner fires. His eyes, dull and yellowed, flicked back and forth, unable to settle. It seemed to Gandogar that the monarch stared straight through him.

Because of his great age, the high king did without cumbersome mail, his feeble body wrapped in embroidered robes of brown fabric. His silvery hair and beard swept the floor and in his lap was the crown that symbolized his office, too heavy for him to bear.

The ceremonial hammer lay beside his throne, its head etched with runes and its handle inlaid with gems and precious metals that sparkled in the light of the braziers and lanterns. It seemed doubtful that the monarch could summon the strength to lift the heavy relic.

Gandogar cleared his throat and swallowed his trepidation. "You summoned me as your successor, Your Majesty, and now I stand before you," he said, addressing the high king with the time-honored formula.

Gundrabur inclined his head as if to speak, but no sound came out.

"The high king thanks you for following his summons. He knows that the journey was arduous and long," Balendilín explained on the monarch's behalf. "If the assembly wills it thus, you shall soon wear the crown. I am Gundrabur's deputy and I will speak for the secondlings." He gestured for Gandogar to take his place at the table.

Gandogar sat down and Bislipur took up position behind him. The fourthling monarch leaned over to inspect the maps, only to realize that some of the delegates were staring at him expectantly. They seemed to be waiting for him to stake his claim more roundly, but Bislipur had warned him against showing his hand too soon. His priority was the situation in the north of Girdlegard and he was eager to see how his proposal would be received.

"Where are the nine clans of Borengar's folk?" he asked, nodding toward the empty seats belonging to the firstlings. "Not here?"

Balendilín shook his head. "No, and we don't know if they're coming. We've heard nothing from the firstlings for two hundred cycles." He reached for his ax and lowered the blade over the far west of Girdlegard. The dwarves of Borengar's folk were the keepers of the Silver Pass, the defenders of the Red Range against invading troops. The human realm of Queen Wey IV separated their kingdom from the rest of Girdlegard. "We know they're still there, though. According to the merchants of Weyurn, the Silver Pass has not been breached." He laid his ax on the table. "It's their business if they choose to stay away. We must vote without them."

The other members of the assembly murmured their assent.

"King Gandogar, you wish to ascend the throne, but first you must hear of the challenges that await you. The Perished Land is creeping through Girdlegard. Every pace of land conquered by Tion's minions is infected with a terrible force that turns nature against itself. Its power is such that even the trees become intent on attacking and killing anything that lives. People say that those who perish on this ground return to life without a soul or a will. The dead become enslaved to the dark power and join the orcs in slaying their kin."

"The Perished Land is advancing?" Gandogar took a deep breath. It was clear from the counselor's words that the magi had failed to stem the tide of evil. "I never trusted the long-uns' magic!" he said heatedly. "All those fancy fireworks and to what end? Nudin, Lot-Ionan, Andôkai, and the rest of them are too busy perfecting their magic with their too-clever-by-half apprentices. They scribble away in their laboratories and castles, studying the secret of elven immortality so they can scribble and study and scribble some more. And all the while the Perished Land is creeping forward like rust on metal that no one has remembered to treat."

His blunt words met with noisy approval.

"At least some good has come of it. The elves have been all but annihilated." Gandogar's heart leaped at the thought that the arrogant elves would soon meet their doom. It was his firm intention that he and his warriors would inflict the final blow. The elves had murdered his father and brother, but now the time of reckoning was near. *Soon the feuding and fighting will be over once and for all.* He was itching to tell the others of his plan.

"All but annihilated?" echoed Balendilín, frowning.

"Elders and chieftains, this is joyful news indeed!" Gandogar's cheeks were flushed and his brown eyes shone with enthusiasm. "Vraccas has given us the means to wipe out the children of Sitalia. The last of their race are gathered here." His index finger stabbed at the small dot on the map representing all that remained of the elven kingdom. "Listen to what I propose: Let us form a great army, march on Âlandur, and extract our vengeance for deeds that have gone unpunished for cycles!"

The delegates stared at him, dumbfounded. Bislipur's surprise tactics had worked.

"Gandogar, we gathered here today to elect a new high king," Balendilín said evenly, trying to deflate the excitement. It was clear from the murmured conversations that the fourthling king's proposal had struck a chord. "It is not for us to talk of war with the elves. Our duty is to protect the peoples of Girdlegard." He turned imploringly to the benches. "Friends, remember the commandment given to us by Vraccas!"

Gandogar scanned the faces of the delegates. He could see that they were torn. "First listen to what I have to say. Documents have come into my possession, ancient documents uncovered by Bislipur and handed to me. Hear what they speak of; then decide for yourselves what should be done." He took a deep breath, unfurled a roll of parchment, and read in a solemn voice:

And the elves were filled with envy.

Desirous of the dwarven treasure, they fell upon the fifthling kingdom and ambushed Giselbert's folk.

Fierce fighting broke out in the underground halls and at the Stone Gateway.

Some of the enemy were trapped by Giselbert in a gloomy labyrinth, never to be seen again.

But the treacherous elves used their magic to poison the children of the Smith. One by one the fifthlings succumbed.

The elves seized their chance and slaughtered the ailing dwarves. Only a handful of Giselbert's folk escaped the massacre.

Silence descended on the great hall. Gandogar's words echoed in the minds of his listeners, his commanding voice breathing new life into the ancient script.

Drawn by the smell of death and bloodshed, orcs and trolls marched on the Stone Gateway and gathered at the border.

The cowardly elves fled in terror, abandoning Girdlegard to its fate.

But before they fled, they used their cunning to open the portal. Giselbert and his remaining warriors defended the pass with the staunchness of true dwarves, but their depleted army could do nothing against the hordes.

It was then that evil entered Girdlegard.

He paused to measure the force of his speech. With a little more persuasion, he would have them on his side. Only Gundrabur's one-armed counselor was shaking his head.

"I do not trust these lines, King Gandogar. Why were they not discovered before now? It seems strange that a document incriminating the elves should emerge at this time. It suits your purpose rather well."

"The document was hidden, who knows for what purpose—perhaps by a doubting dwarf like yourself who lacked the conviction to go to war," came Gandogar's scornful reply. He raised his ax and buried the blade in the map, cleaving Âlandur. "You heard what the document says. They killed our kin and betrayed us! They must pay for their murderous deeds."

"And then what?" Balendilín asked harshly. "Tell me, King Gandogar, who would benefit from the destruction of the elves? Their deaths won't further our interests, nor those of mankind! No, destroying Âlandur will profit the Perished Land alone. We may as well join forces with the älfar and help them to victory. Is that what you want?" The counselor fixed his eyes on Gandogar, who suddenly felt dangerously exposed. "Our real enemies aren't the elves, Your Majesty. Vraccas didn't give us the authority to fight the peoples of Girdlegard. By my beard, none of us can stand the elves; it's in our nature not to like them. There have been skirmishes, even deaths, I know." He placed a hand on his left shoulder. "I lost a limb in a fight with four orcs, but I'd sooner sever my one good arm than raise it in a war against the elves. Our races have their differences, but Vraccas bade us protect the elves and we have never neglected our task. Do you propose to break his commandment?"

Gandogar fixed the one-armed counselor with a furious glare. Balendilín had sabotaged his plans for vengeance and nothing he could say would mend the damage. Through the silence he heard Bislipur grinding his teeth.

"The älfar are no friends of mine," he said at last. "No, this is about seizing our opportunity. Once the elves are defeated, I will lead our armies to victory against the Perished Land. Tion's minions have plagued Girdlegard for too long. The dwarves shall triumph where humans have failed!"

"You surprise me, King Gandogar," said Balendilín, an expression of open bewilderment spreading over his age-

and experience-lined face. "Surely you don't mean to defy the commands of our god? It seems to me your reason has been subdued by hatred." He paused and eyed Bislipur suspiciously. "Unless false counsel is to blame."

The delegates shuffled and muttered until a secondling from the clan of the Bear Hands rose to his feet.

"In my opinion, the matter is worthy of debate," he said firmly. "What if the document speaks the truth? Once a traitor always a traitor! The elves might leave their crumbling kingdom and found a new settlement by seizing human land."

"What if they betray another of our folks?" The speaker, a chieftain of the same clan, leaped up, burning with zeal. "The pointy-ears will stoop to any level. I can't say whether or not they murdered the fifthlings, but they should be punished all the same!" He left his place and stood alongside Gandogar in a public show of support. "You may be a fourthling, but I stand by your cause."

Shouts of approval sounded from the benches. The dwarves' low voices rumbled through the chamber until all that could be heard was a single word: *war*. Balendilín's calls for order were drowned out by the noise.

Gandogar sat back and exchanged satisfied looks with his adviser. *Girdlegard will soon be free of elves.*

At that moment an almighty bang rocked the hall. "Silence!" a voice thundered sternly through the din.

The delegates turned in astonishment.

Crown on his snowy head, Gundrabur stood perfectly erect before them, the ceremonial hammer in one hand. He had swung it against the throne so furiously that the marble revealed deep cracks.

His eyes showed no sign of age, only recrimination, as he looked down at the chieftains and elders. No dwarf was more majestic, more imposing than he. His former weakness and frailty had vanished, driven out by rage.

His white beard rippled as he raised his head. "Short-sighted fools! You should be worrying about Girdlegard, not settling old scores. Any race that pits itself against the Perished Land is our ally! The longer the elves can repel the powers of darkness, the better." His gaze fell on Gandogar. "You are young and impetuous, king of the fourthlings. Two of your kin were slain by elves and for that I am prepared to excuse your misguided call to arms. The rest of you should know better. Instead of indulging him in this lunacy, you should be voices of reason."

Gundrabur scanned the assembly. "The time has come to bury our grievances. An alliance is what we need, what I desire! The elves of Âlandur, the seven human sovereigns, the six magi, and the dwarven folks must stand united to repel the Perished Land. I . . ."

Just then the hammer fell from his grasp and crashed to the floor, chipping the flagstones. The high king swayed and sank backward into his throne, his breath coming in short gasps.

Balendilín instructed the delegates to retire to their chambers and await his summons. "We shall resume our meeting when the high king has recovered."

The representatives from the various clans filed out silently, Gundrabur's words still echoing in their minds.

Bislipur cast a scornful look at the wheezing figure on the throne. "He won't last much longer," he muttered to Gandogar as they made their way out. "When his voice dries up entirely, we'll have the chieftains on our side. They were ready to join us before the high king interrupted."

Gundrabur's chosen successor made no reply.

Enchanted Realm of Ionandar,
Girdlegard,
Spring, 6234th Solar Cycle

Jolosin sped through the underground vaults, followed by the panting Tungdil on his considerably shorter legs. They hurried down a gallery past oak-paneled doors leading to classrooms where young apprentices were taking lessons from more senior famuli. Only four students were taught by Lot-Ionan himself, one of whom would be chosen to inherit his academy, his underground vaults, and his realm.

On reaching the laboratory Jolosin stopped abruptly and flung open the door. Small clouds of white smoke wafted toward them, creating an artificial fog. "Get a move on," he barked at Tungdil, who was racing to catch up.

Breathing heavily, the dwarf stepped into the chamber and was instantly wreathed in mist. "Watch your manners, Jolosin, or you'll be fixing the problem yourself."

"Climb up the flue," the famulus ordered tersely, propelling Tungdil across the room. "Something's blocking the chimney." Suddenly the fireplace appeared out of nowhere and beside it a bucket, which seemed to contain the source of the smoke.

"I thought you were one of Lot-Ionan's best apprentices. Wouldn't a bit of magic do the trick?"

"I'm asking you to fix it," the famulus said firmly. "What would a dwarf know of sorcery? You're wasting everyone's time. My pupils can't see a thing in here." There was some low coughing and a clearing of throats.

"What's the magic word?"

"Pardon?"

"I should have thought a wizard would have a bit more charm."

Jolosin scowled. *"Please."*

Tungdil grinned, picked up the poker, and hooked it through his belt. "And as if by magic..." He stepped into the fireplace, where the embers had faded to a weak red glow. A quick upward glance confirmed that a thick layer of opaque smoke had sealed the chimney like a screen.

Climbing confidently, he set about scaling the flue. The soot was slippery, but his fingers found easy purchase on the uneven brickwork and he hauled himself up, rising slowly but steadily one, two, three paces until the hearth disappeared beneath him amid the smoke.

He reached up and nudged something with his fingers. "I think there's a nest up here. It must have fallen into the chimney," he called down.

"Then get rid of it!"

"I was hardly going to lay an egg in it." He braced himself against the wall of the chimney, took hold of the offending twigs with one hand, and gave them a vigorous shake.

The nest came free.

At that moment he received an unpleasant surprise. A torrent shot toward him, drenching him in a foul-smelling liquid that stung his eyes and his skin, followed soon after by a cloud of delicate feathers that tickled his face and his nose. Overcome with the urge to sneeze, he let go of the brickwork and fell.

Tungdil had the good fortune not to graze himself on any of the jutting bricks, sustaining nothing more serious than a few nasty knocks to the chest and landing in the remains of the nest, whose twigs had ignited among the embers. Clouds of ash fell around him and coated him in fine gray soot. He sprang up, fearful of burning his bottom, but the hot embers had already scorched through his breeches.

The raucous laughter left him in no doubt that he was the victim of a malicious joke.

At once the clouds cleared miraculously so the class of twenty young famuli could observe the humiliated and disheveled dwarf. Jolosin was leading the general merriment and slapping his thighs in glee.

"Help! The stunted sooz-man is here to get us!" he cried in mock horror.

"He stole the elixir from the skunkbird's nest!" one of his pupils jeered.

"You never know, it might be his natural smell," said Jolosin, dissolving into laughter all over again. He turned to Tungdil. "All right, midget, I've had my fun. You can go."

The dwarf wiped his face on his sleeve. His head was crowned with ash and feathers, but now it shrank menacingly into his shoulders and his eyes flashed with rage.

"You think this is funny, do you?" he growled grimly. "Let's see if you laugh at this!" He made a grab for the bucket, which felt cool to the touch, giving him all the encouragement he needed to hurl its contents. He raised his arm and took aim at the famulus, who had turned his back and was joking with his pupils.

A warning shout alerted Jolosin to the threat. Whirling round, the quick-thinking famulus saw the contents of the bucket flying toward him and raised his hands to ward off the water with a spell. In a flash the droplets turned to shards of ice and flew past him without drenching his freshly changed robes.

The tactic worked, but at a price, as the assembled famuli realized from the sound of tinkling glass. The hailstorm had passed over their heads, only to land among the neat rows of phials whose contents—elixirs, balms, extracts, and essences—were used in all manner of spells. The containers shattered.

Already the potions were seeping from the broken phials and mingling in pools on the shelves. The mixtures crackled and hissed ominously.

"You fool!" scolded Jolosin, pale with fear.

The dwarf bridled. "Don't look at me!" he retorted indignantly. "You're the one who turned the water into ice!"

Just then a shelf collapsed and a flurry of sparks shot to the ceiling, exploding in a flash of red light. Something was brewing in the laboratory, this time quite literally. Some of the pupils decided that enough was enough and ran for the door. Jolosin darted after them.

"This is all your fault! Lot-Ionan will be sorry he ever took you in. You won't be here for much longer, dwarf. Not if I can help it!" he shouted furiously, slamming the door as he left.

"If you don't let me out of here this instant, I'll strap you to my anvil and beat you with a red-hot hammer!" threatened Tungdil as he rattled the handle in vain. He suspected that Jolosin had placed a spell on the door and locked him inside to take the blame.

You won't get away with this! The dwarf ducked as something exploded behind him. Looking up, he scanned the room hurriedly for somewhere to shelter until he was released.

Beroïn's Folk,
Secondling Kingdom,
Girdlegard,
Winter, 6233rd Solar Cycle

Balendilín watched in concern as the last of the delegates filed out of the hall. The meeting of the assembly had taken an unexpected and unwelcome turn. It was a serious setback for the high king's hopes of uniting the peoples of Girdlegard in a grand alliance against the Perished Land.

Please, Vraccas, make that obdurate fourthling see sense, he prayed fretfully.

Once the hall had emptied, Gundrabur extended his hand shakily and reached for Balendilín's arm.

"Our planning will come to nothing," he said dully. "The young king of Goïmdil's folk lacks experience." With a weak smile he squeezed his counselor's fingers. "Or maybe he needs a wise adviser, my loyal friend."

He struggled upright and reached for his gleaming crown. His right hand, which moments earlier had wielded the heavy hammer, trembled as he lifted the finely wrought metal from his head.

"A war...," he muttered despondently, "a war against the elves! What can Gandogar be thinking?"

"Precisely nothing," his counselor replied bitterly. "That's the problem. There's no point reasoning with Gandogar or his adviser. I don't believe in their mysterious parchment for a moment. It's a forgery, I'm sure, written with the intention of winning support for a war that—"

"It served its purpose," the high king reminded him. "The damage has been done. You know how headstrong the chieftains can be. Some of them are itching to go to war with the elves, regardless of whether the document was faked."

"True, Your Majesty, but some of the fourthlings seemed rather more reticent. Gandogar's victory is by no means assured. The matter will be decided by a vote, with each chieftain following his conscience. We must convince the clans of both folks of the merit of our argument."

The two dwarves fell silent. A more lasting solution was needed to prevent Gandogar from reviving his plans for war at a later date. Once he was crowned high king, he would be able to implement his scheme with little or no resistance.

Neither Gundrabur nor Balendilín was worried about the military might of the elves. The dwarves' traditional enemy was considerably weakened, having suffered serious losses in the ongoing battle against the älfar, who profited from reinforcements streaming into Girdlegard via the Northern Pass. In the event of a war, the elven army would be easily defeated, but casualties would be inflicted on both sides and any loss of life among the children of the Smith would leave the gates of Girdlegard vulnerable to attack.

Gundrabur's gaze roved across the deserted chamber. "The great hall has seen happier times. Times of unity and cohesion." He bowed his head. "Those times are over. Our hopes of forging a great alliance have come to nothing."

A great alliance. Deep in thought, Balendilín stared at the five stelae at the foot of the throne. The stone slabs were engraved with the sacred laws of the dwarves, including the name of a folk with whom the others would have no truck: Lorimbur's dwarves in the thirdling kingdom to the east.

"For the sake of an alliance I would do the unthinkable and invite the thirdlings to join our assembly." The high king sighed. "In times such as these, old animosities must be forgotten. We're all dwarves, after all, and kinship is what counts."

The counselor was in no doubt that Girdlegard needed every ax that could cleave an orcish skull, but he also knew his fellow dwarves too well. "After Gandogar's rabble-rousing, the assembly will be in no mood for appeasement."

"Perhaps you're right, Balendilín. I know our vision of a united and unstoppable dwarven army is fading, but we cannot permit the assembly to sanction a war against the elves. We must convince the delegates that attacking Âlandur would be foolhardy." The high king's voice sounded weaker than ever. "We need more time."

"The timing depends on you," his counselor said gently. "Gandogar will not ascend the throne while you are strong enough to rule."

"No one should rely on the failing fires of a dying king." Gundrabur smoothed his beard. "We need something more decisive... We shall use the dwarven laws to silence the war-mongers and put a stop to the matter once and for all."

He descended the throne, negotiating the steps with utmost concentration. Every movement was small and considered, but at last he reached the stelae. Balendilín was at his side in an instant to offer him a steadying arm.

Golden sunlight poured through the slits carved into the rock, illuminating every flourish of the runes. Gundrabur's weak eyes scanned the symbols.

"Gandogar is certain to be elected," he muttered absently, "but if my memory serves me correctly, there is a way of delaying the succession. It will buy us some time so we can talk to the chieftains and strive for peace and an alliance with the elves."

His eyesight had dimmed with the cycles and was now so poor that he was forced to stand with his nose almost touching the stone. The law stated that the throne, currently occupied by a dwarf of Beroïn, should pass to one of Goïmdil's folk. On that basis, Gandogar's succession was secure. Tradition dictated that the heir should stake his claim and be elected by the assembly unless there was reason to contest the appointment.

"I'm sure it's here somewhere," he murmured to himself, fingertips gliding across the stone.

His efforts were rewarded. With a sigh of relief, he closed his eyes and pressed his brow against the cold tablet whose surface had been engraved long before he was born.

"After such a wretched beginning, the orbit has taken a

turn for the better. Listen to this." He straightened up and ran a crooked index finger over the all-important words. "Should the folk in question produce more than one possible heir, the clans of that folk must confer among themselves and decide on a candidate before presenting their preferred successor to the assembly," he finished in a satisfied tone.

His counselor read the passage again, fiddling excitedly with the trinkets in his graying beard. There was nothing to say that the chosen candidate would be the existing monarch: Any dwarf could stake a claim. *"Accordingly, a dwarf of any rank may be elected high king, provided he has the support of his kinsfolk."*

Balendilín saw what his sovereign had in mind. "But who would challenge Gandogar?" he asked. "The fourthling clans are in agreement. To be sure, there are those who doubt their king, but..." He stopped, baffled by the look of satisfaction on the high king's craggy face. "Or is there such a dwarf?"

"No," Gundrabur answered with a wily smile, thinking of the letter that had been sent to him several orbits ago. "Not yet, but there will be."

Enchanted Realm of Ionandar,
Girdlegard,
Spring, 6234th Solar Cycle

There was almost nothing left in the candleholders on Lot-Ionan's desk. The flickering light and short stumps of wax were sure signs that the magus had been in his study for hours, although it seemed to him that only minutes had elapsed.

He leaned awkwardly over the parchment, poring over the closely written runes. Inscribing the magic formula had consumed countless orbits, even cycles of his time. There was one last symbol to be added; then the charm would be complete.

He smiled. Most mortals had no experience of the mystic arts and were suspicious of magic in any form. For simple souls, the constellation of the elements was a mysterious business, but for Lot-Ionan, the sorcery that drove fear into the heart of peasants was nothing more than the logical outcome of elaborate sequences of gestures and words.

It was one such sequence that occupied him now. Everything had to be exactly right. One wrong syllable, a single character out of place, an imprecise gesture, a hurried movement of his staff, or even a sloppily drawn circle could ruin a spell or unleash a catastrophe.

The magus could name any number of occasions when his pupils had conjured fearsome beasts or caused themselves terrible harm because of their carelessness. It always ended the same way: with an embarrassed apology and a plea for help.

He never lost patience with his famuli. Once he had been an apprentice too. Now he was a magus, a master magician or wizard, as some folks called him.

Two hundred and eight-seven cycles. He stopped what he was doing, hand poised above the parchment. His gaze, alert as ever, took in his creased and blotchy skin, then roved over the jumble of cupboards, cabinets, and bookshelves in search of a mirror. At length his blue eyes came to rest on the shiny surface of a vase.

He appraised the reflection: wrinkled face, gray hair with white streaks, and a graying beard dotted with smudges of ink. *There's no denying I'm older, but am I wiser? That's the question...*

His beige robes had been darned and patched a thousand times, but he refused to be parted from them. Unlike some of his fellow magi, he took no interest in his appearance, caring only that his garments were comfortable to wear.

In one important respect the old scholar agreed with the common people: Magic was a dangerous thing. To minimize the fallout from failed experiments, he pursued his studies in the safety of the vaults.

Of course, the magus's motives for retreating below the surface were not entirely selfless. In the calm of the vaults he could forget about his fellow humans and their trivial concerns. He delegated the running of the realm and the settling of minor disputes to his magisters, functionaries picked expressly for the job.

The enchanted realm of Ionandar stretched across the southeastern corner of Girdlegard, covering parts of Gauragar and Idoslane, its borders defined by a magic force field, one of six in total. Certain regions of Girdlegard were invested with an energy that could be channeled into living beings, as the very first wizards had learned. Once transferred to a human, the energy became finite, but a person could renew his store of magic by returning to the field. No sooner had the magi made this discovery than they seized the land, divided it into six enchanted realms, and defended the territory against existing monarchs who had no weapons to match their magic powers. Generations of rulers had been forced to accept that swathes of their kingdoms were under foreign rule.

The force fields were the key to the magi's power. The six wizards' skills and knowledge had increased over time and now their formulae, runes, and spells were capable of working great beauty, terror, and good.

Keep your mind on the formula, he chided himself. Carefully wiping the tip of his goose quill against the inkwell, he lowered it to the parchment and traced a symbol slowly on the sheet: the element of fire. Every flourish of the quill was vitally important; a second of inattention would ruin all his work.

His diligence paid off. Satisfied, he rose to his feet.

"Well, old boy, you've done it," he murmured in relief. The formula was complete. If the sequence of runes worked as he intended, he would be able to detect the presence of magic in people, creatures, or objects. But before he put the theory into practice, it was time for a little reward.

Lot-Ionan shuffled to one of his cabinets, the oldest of a timeworn lot, and removed a bottle from the third shelf. He glanced at the skull on the label and took a long swig.

The liquid was not poisonous, in spite of the warning symbol. Experience had taught him that it was the most effective way of preventing his finest brandy from disappearing into thirsty students' throats. The precaution was by no means unwarranted: Some of his apprentices, especially the older ones, were only too partial to a drop of good liquor. Lot-Ionan was prepared to share his learning but not his precious drink. He had run out of barrels of this particular vintage, so the bottle was worth protecting.

Just then a powerful explosion rocked the walls of his underground chamber. Fragments of stone rained down from the ceiling and landed on his desk, while phials and jars jangled in the cabinets, bouncing so violently that their stoppers struck the shelves above. Everything in the higgledy-piggledy study rattled and shook.

The magus froze in horror. The open inkwell was dancing up and down on his desk, tilting farther and farther until . . . - Lot-Ionan's hastily uttered incantation came too late. Ink poured over the precious manuscript and his lovingly drawn runes were drowned in a viscous black tide.

For a second Lot-Ionan was rooted. "What in the name of Palandiell was that?" His kindly face hardened as he divined the origin of the bang. Gulping down the remains of his brandy, he turned sharply and strode from the room.

He raced through the shadowy galleries, practically flying past doorways and passageways, his fury at his wasted efforts increasing with every step.

By the time he reached the laboratory, he was seething with rage. Half a dozen famuli were talking in hushed voices outside the door, through which strange noises could be heard. They were evidently too afraid to go in.

"There you are, Estimable Magus," Jolosin began respectfully. "What a calamity! We got here too late. The dwarf slipped into the laboratory and before we could—"

"Out of my way!" Lot-Ionan barked angrily and unbolted the door.

The devastation could scarcely have been more complete if a mob of lunatic alchemists had rioted inside his precious laboratory. Equipment was floating through the air while small fires flared and spluttered at intervals throughout the room. The shelves dripped with valuable elixirs that had burst from the phials and formed foul-smelling pools on the floor.

Huddled in the corner behind an upturned cauldron was the culprit. His fingers were in his ears and his eyes were closed tightly. Despite his singed hair and scorched beard, there could be no mistaking who he was: Tungdil Bolofar.

There was another loud bang. Blue sparks shot through the air, missing the magus by a hairbreadth.

"Explain yourself, Tungdil!" Lot-Ionan thundered furiously. The dwarf, who evidently couldn't hear him, said nothing. "I'm talking to you, Tungdil Bolofar!" the magus bellowed as loudly as he could.

Looking up in surprise, the dwarf saw the lean wizard looming menacingly above him. He struggled out from behind the cauldron.

"This wasn't my doing, Estimable Magus," he said firmly. He shot an accusing glance at Jolosin, who was standing in the doorway with his pupils, doing his best to look surprised.

Lot-Ionan wheeled on him.

"Don't look at me!" protested Jolosin with exaggerated indignation. "I had nothing to do with it! You saw for yourself that the door was locked!"

"Silence, the pair of you!" For the first time in ten cycles, Lot-Ionan was in danger of losing his temper altogether. He surveyed the costly mess. "This feuding has to stop!" His ink-stained beard seemed to ripple with rage.

The dwarf had no intention of taking any of the blame. He planted his feet firmly on the ground. "It wasn't my fault," he said stubbornly.

The magus was visibly struggling to regain his equilibrium. He sat down on an iron-bound chest of wood and crossed his arms.

"Listen carefully, the pair of you. I'm not interested in hearing who was responsible for this disaster. *Nothing*, but nothing is more infuriating than being distracted from my work. Your explosion has cost me orbits, if not an entire cycle, of study, so forgive me for losing my patience. Enough is enough! I intend to restore peace to my school."

"Estimable Magus, you're not going to banish the dwarf, are you?" exclaimed Jolosin, trying to sound horrified.

"Enough! We'll discuss your part in this fiasco later, but first I need this nonsense to stop. The sooner we have peace in the vaults, the better!" He turned to Tungdil. "An old friend gave me the use of a few items and now he needs them back."

The dwarf braced himself. "You, my little helper, will run the errand for me. In one hour I shall expect you in my study, bag packed and ready to go. I'll give you the items then. Prepare yourself for a good long walk."

The dwarf bowed politely and hurried from the room. This was far better than he had expected. A journey on foot was scarcely a chore; the paths and lanes of Girdlegard were no challenge for his sturdy legs. *I might meet a dwarf,* he thought hopefully. *If this is supposed to be a punishment, he can punish me some more.*

The magus waited until the stocky figure was out of sight before turning to Jolosin. "You wanted to land him in trouble," he said bluntly. "I know what you were up to, famulus! There's never a moment's peace with the two of you around. Well, I've decided to put a stop to it. For the duration of Tungdil's journey I want you peeling potatoes in the kitchen. You'll have plenty of time to regret your bad behavior and pray to Palandiell for his speedy return."

Jolosin opened his mouth in protest.

"If I hear so much as a grumble from you or the slightest criticism from Frala or the cook, you can pack your bags and leave." The young man's jaws clamped shut. "Oh, and before you start your stint in the kitchen, you can clean up here." The magus waved at the mess that had once been his laboratory.

He shooed the remaining famuli from the room. On his way out, he picked up a broom from the corner and pressed it into Jolosin's hands.

"Don't get anyone to do your dirty work for you," he said, marching to the door. "Make sure it's tidy, and by tidy I mean *absolutely spick-and-span!*"

He slammed the door and the bolt rattled home.

II

Beroïn's Folk,
Secondling Kingdom,
Girdlegard,
Winter, 6233rd Solar Cycle

It was time for the high king to initiate his counselor into the plan. He handed him a letter. "It's from the magus of Ionandar. Lot-Ionan the Forbearing, they call him in his realm."

Balendilín knew the magus by reputation. His school lay in the east of Girdlegard and he was said to prize his solitude. Apparently, he spent most of his time studying in his underground vaults, inventing new charms and formulae, far from the worries of everyday life.

"He sends news of something most unusual: a dwarf," the high king explained. "The only dwarf in Ionandar, no less! He says he found him many cycles ago under peculiar circumstances and raised him in his realm. He wants to know whether any of our clans are missing a kinsman. He is eager to reunite him with his kind."

Balendilín skimmed the letter. "What do we know of the dwarf?"

"The matter is mysterious but intriguing. To my knowledge, no child has been lost in the past two hundred cycles."

"And it's your intention to present the sorcerer's ward as a long-lost heir to the throne?" The counselor laid the letter on the table. "But how?" he asked doubtfully. "A dwarf raised by long-uns won't know what it means to be a child of the

Smith. The fourthlings will never back him, especially not without proof of his lineage."

The high king shuffled to the conference table and lowered himself onto the secondling monarch's chair before his legs gave way beneath him.

"I expect you're right," he said in a strained voice. "Be that as it may, they can't do a thing until the candidate is here and the matter has been resolved. Even if I die, their hands will be tied." He looked squarely at his counselor. "If Vraccas should smite me with his hammer before the dwarf arrives, you must bear the burden of preventing war and preserving our kinsfolk."

Balendilín pursed his lips. "Your Majesty won't be leaving us yet. Not when your inner furnace still burns strong."

"You're a miserable liar, like all dwarves." Gundrabur laughed and laid a hand on his shoulder. "But from now on we must speak with false tongues in order to protect our kinsfolk from a war that could destroy them. You and I will fib like kobolds, Balendilín. For once we must make it our business to drive a wedge between the clans. Let us walk awhile and you can lend me your counsel. We shall weave a web of falsehoods around Gandogar and Bislipur and keep them from the throne until the last belligerent syllable has been squeezed from their lungs."

Balendilín helped the king to his feet. He had no faith in the plan succeeding, but he kept his misgivings to himself.

Gandogar was in good spirits when he woke the next morning and was summoned with the other delegates to the great hall. Proceedings were about to recommence and he felt confident that the high king would name him as his successor, after which the members of the assembly would endorse his choice with their votes. It was as good as decided already.

Gundrabur's plea for peace had rankled with him, but he no longer held a grudge. The aged dwarf's long reign had produced nothing worthy of posterity and he was destined to be forgotten before too long. It wasn't dignified to quarrel with a dying king.

Gandogar entered the hall and sat down, while Bislipur took up position behind him. The pews filled quickly as the chieftains and elders filed in.

A few of the delegates looked at him encouragingly and rapped their ax heads. Far from being threatening, the gesture was a sign of support.

Gandogar noticed an unusual trinket hanging from the neck of a secondling chieftain. He strained his eyes to take a closer look. The shriveled trophy was an elven ear worn with obvious pride by the chieftain, who nevertheless tucked it hurriedly under his mail as soon as the high king's arrival was announced. It was still too early for open displays of aggression toward a protected race.

Gundrabur appeared at the door, his sprightly appearance belying rumors of his impending death. Gandogar felt a wave of disappointment at seeing the high king in such excellent form, then immediately felt guilty for harboring such dreadful thoughts. He didn't actually want the old chap to die; it was just that Gundrabur's disapproving speech of the previous orbit had struck a raw nerve.

Tunics of mail creaked and rasped as the delegates went down on one knee to greet the high king. Axes on high, they signaled their unwavering devotion and their willingness to live—and die—as he decreed.

Gundrabur answered by lifting the ceremonial hammer and bringing it down smartly. The delegates were free to rise, which they did, amid much clunking of armor.

Balendilín stepped forward and turned his earnest brown gaze on Gandogar: "Gandogar Silverbeard of the clan of the Silver Beards, ruler of the fourthlings and head of Goïmdil's line, are you ready to assert your claim to the high king's throne?" he said ceremoniously.

Gandogar rose from his seat, pulled his ax from his belt, and laid it on the table. "Unyielding as the rock from which we were created and keen as this blade is my will to defend our race against its foes," came his solemn reply. Such was his inner turmoil that he failed to notice that Balendilín, not the high king, had taken charge of the proceedings. It occurred to him when the counselor cut in before he could continue.

"King Gandogar, the assembly has heard and noted your claim. A decision will be taken when we have heard the second candidate speak. You and he must decide which of the two of you will withdraw. Until then we must wait."

"Wait?" bellowed Gandogar, blood rushing to his head. He turned to search the faces of his chieftains, all of whom seemed genuinely surprised. "Who was it?" he thundered. "Which of you had the audacity to go behind my back? Step forward and make yourself known!" He reached for his ax, but was stayed by Balendilín.

"You do your kinsfolk an injustice," said the counselor. "Your rival is not here." He produced a letter and held it up for all to see. "The dwarf in question was separated many cycles ago from his folk. He is mindful of his heritage and has announced his return. He lives in Ionandar and is preparing to join us as we speak."

"Ionandar?" Gandogar exclaimed incredulously. "Vraccas forgive me, but what kind of dwarf lives with sorcerers?" He drew himself up. "Is this some kind of joke? A stranger writes a letter that you accept without question and now the ceremony must be delayed. What name does he go by?"

"His name is of no account. He was raised as a foundling and named by humans. But the items discovered with him show him to be a member of your folk."

"Hogwash!" Gandogar retorted angrily. "The letter is a fake!"

"And what of the document purporting to tell the truth about the elves?" Balendilín said sternly, one hand resting lightly on his belt.

"Silence, both of you!" The high king levered himself from his throne. "King Gandogar, do you presume to call my counselor a liar?" The old dwarf was powerful and majestic in his fury, his words thundering through the lofty hall. The fourthling monarch sounded shrill and petty as a fishwife by comparison. "You will abide by my decision. When the candidate arrives, the fourthling chieftains will decide which of you will make the better king."

Gandogar pointed to his retinue. "Why the delay? Ask the chieftains now and you shall hear whom they elect. Their minds are made up. How could a stranger—"

The high king raised a wizened hand. "No." He waved toward the engraved stelae. "We will follow the law as it was given to us by our forefathers. What they ordained will be fulfilled."

The silence that descended on the vast hall was by no means uniform in quality. For the most part it was born of astonishment, but in a number of cases it was prompted by helplessness and rage. There was no choice but to wait for the audacious stranger to appear.

Gandogar sat down heavily and pulled his ax across the table toward him. The blade left a deep white gouge in the polished stone, scarring the surface over which the masons had toiled so long.

"So be it," he said coolly. He dared not risk a longer speech for fear that he would say something he might regret. Turning, he cast an abject glance at Bislipur, who seemed a model of composure, but whose unruffled expression Gandogar could read. His adviser was already turning over the situation in his mind, searching for a solution. Bislipur could be relied on to be resourceful.

"The journey from Ionandar will take weeks. How are we supposed to occupy ourselves until the dwarf arrives?" asked Gandogar, eyes fixed on the sparkling diamonds on his armor. "What makes you think that our aspiring high king will find us?"

"Or that he'll make it here alive," added Bislipur.

"We'll have plenty to discuss in the meantime," said Balendilín. "The assembly will turn to matters of imminent importance for our clans." He smiled. "But your concern is touching. Rest assured that the dwarf will get here safely. We've sent an escort."

"In that case we should send one too," Bislipur insisted with forced benevolence. "The fourthlings are always happy to look after their own. Where should we send our warriors?"

"Your offer is most generous, but unnecessary. The dwarf will be a guest of the high king, so the high king has sent warriors of his own," Balendilín said diplomatically. "Given the stormy start to the proceedings, I suggest we take a break and cool our tempers with a keg of dark ale." He raised his ax and rapped the poll twice against the table. The clear ring of metal on stone sang through the air and echoed through the corridors.

At once barrels of dark roasted barley malt were rolled into the hall, and in no time the delegates were raising their drinking horns to the reigning high king and his successor, who most assumed would be Gandogar.

Bislipur laid his hand on his monarch's shoulder. "Patience, Your Majesty. Let us honor our forefathers by satisfying every requirement they name. It's important we don't give anyone the opportunity to question the legitimacy of your reign." They clinked tankards and he took a lengthy draft. The beer was thick and malty, almost sweet. "Ale like this can be brewed only by dwarves." He smiled, wiping the foam from his beard.

At length the atmosphere in the great hall became jollier and more boisterous and Bislipur could slip away unnoticed. Safely ensconced in a lonely passageway, he summoned Sverd and entrusted the gnome with a mission of great importance.

Enchanted Realm of Ionandar,
Girdlegard,
Spring, 6234th Solar Cycle

Whistling, Tungdil knelt by his cupboard and packed his large leather knapsack for the trip. He took a tinderbox, a flint, and a blanket, in case he had to spend a night in the open, as well as his fishing hook, a plate, and some cutlery. His cloak he rolled into a bundle and fastened to the outside of the knapsack with a leather strap. Lastly, he pulled on his chain mail and tweaked it with practiced movements until it lay flat against his skin.

He felt instantly better. There was something safe and incredibly homely about his shirt of steel rings. His attachment to his chain mail was a matter of instinct, not something he could explain.

He had the same feeling when he was working at the anvil. Routine jobs — forging horseshoes, nails, and iron brackets for doors, honing blades, or sharpening tools—came naturally to him. It was his dwarven blood, he supposed.

Hoisting his bulging knapsack to his shoulders, he picked up the ax that had been given to him by Lot-Ionan, hooked it through his belt, and set off for the magus's study. He knew the vaults like the back of his hand. The dim light posed no problem for his sharp dwarven eyes and his sense of direction never abandoned him underground. No two tunnels looked the same to him, owing to his ability to remember the slightest irregularity in the rock. It was a different story on the surface, where he was unable to find his way anywhere without a map.

He knocked briskly and opened the door. Lot-Ionan was sitting at his desk, dressed in the old beige robes to which he was so attached. He held up a sheet of parchment accusingly as the dwarf came into the room.

"Do you see this, Tungdil?" he said, throwing the paper disgustedly back onto the pile. "This is your doing! Orbits of study destroyed in the blink of an eye."

"I had no idea," the dwarf said with genuine contrition but determined not to concede any guilt. Stubbornness was another of his inherited characteristics.

"I know, Tungdil. I know." The magus's expression softened. "Go on, then. What really happened?"

"It was another of Jolosin's pranks. He played a trick on me, so I threw a bucket of water at him..." He bowed his head and his voice fell to an indistinct mumble. "He turned the droplets into ice and the shards hit some of the phials. He tried to lay the blame on me by locking me in the laboratory." He looked up and focused his brown eyes on his patron.

The magus sighed. "Six of one and half a dozen of the other, just as I thought. Still, I shouldn't have shouted at you like that." He motioned to the parchment. "Of course, it doesn't change the fact that I'll be spending the next few orbits reinscribing these runes. You had no business to be in the laboratory, Tungdil. No good comes of a dwarf meddling in magic or mixing potions. I thought you knew that by now."

"But it wasn't my—"

"What possessed you to take matters into your own hands? You had only to come to me and Jolosin would have been punished. I'm sending you on a journey, a long journey—which isn't to say I won't be pleased to have you back. On the contrary." He paused. "Rest assured that Jolosin has fared much worse; he'll be peeling potatoes until you're home. And should you decide to take a more circuitous route..." With a mischievous grin he left the rest up to Tungdil. "Well, are you ready?"

"Yes, Estimable Magus." Tungdil answered, relieved that his patron no longer held him solely to blame. "What would you have me do?"

After the frayed tempers of the laboratory, the atmosphere in the study, where they were surrounded by the clutter of Lot-Ionan's cabinets, gadgetry, and books, seemed all the more relaxed. Flames crackled softly in the fireplace and the magus's owl was napping in a corner.

"We'll discuss your errand later. All in good time." Lot-Ionan rose and retired with his steaming mug to the wing chair by the hearth. He stretched his slippered feet toward the flames. "There's no rush. Jolosin will be busy in the laboratory for a good while longer...Besides, there's something I'd like you to consider while you're away." His hand patted the chair beside him.

Tungdil set down his knapsack and took a seat. It sounded as though the magus had something important to say.

"I've been thinking." Lot-Ionan cleared his throat. "The two of us have known each other for sixty-two of your sixty-three cycles."

The dwarf knew what was coming. At times like this, when the mood was sentimental and the magus was feeling relaxed, he would pour himself a draft of beer, warm his feet by the fire, and journey into the distant past, recalling events that had happened over a human lifetime ago. Tungdil loved these conversations.

"It was winter and the winds were howling when there was a knock on the door and a band of kobolds deposited a bundle." He looked his ward in the eye and laughed softly. "It was you! Back then, without your beard, you could almost have been mistaken for a human bairn. They threatened to drown you in the nearest river if I didn't pay your bond. What could I do? I gave them their money and raised you myself."

"For which I shall be eternally grateful," Tungdil said softly.

"Yes, well, eternally . . ." The magus fell silent for a moment. "It seems to me that it might be time to let you go your own way." He laid a hand on the dwarf's thick shock of hair. "I've outlived my natural span and you've served me so loyally that your debt of gratitude, if ever there was one, has been repaid. Besides, if I don't come up with a more convincing charm against old age, my soul will be summoned to Palandiell."

Tungdil didn't like to be reminded that human existence was inescapably brief, even for the likes of the powerful magus. "I'm sure you'll find a way . . . ," he said hoarsely. "Er, didn't you want to tell me something?"

The dwarf's clumsy attempt to change the subject brought a wry smile to Lot-Ionan's face. "You were left here at your parents' behest because they wanted you to be the greatest wizard of the dwarven race, or at least that's what I told you. You saw through the story soon enough. Once I taught you to read, you learned enough about your kinsfolk to know it wasn't true."

"Dwarves aren't fond of magic and magic isn't fond of them." Tungdil couldn't help smiling. His hands were best suited to wielding a hammer and he could happily clutch a book from Lot-Ionan's vast library, but a sorcerer's staff was another matter. "Vraccas made us artisans through and through. There's no room in our hearts for magic."

"Indeed," the magus agreed in amusement, remembering the long line of minor disasters resulting from Tungdil's accidental encounters with the occult. "But you're too modest. You've crammed your head with knowledge like a scholar. You know more about the peoples of Girdlegard than some of my pupils."

"The credit is all yours, Lot-Ionan. You even schooled me in rhetoric."

"And that was no small feat. Adhering to the proper rules of disputation is a challenge for the obstinate tongue of a dwarf!" His face became serious. "I still curse myself for not asking the kobolds where they found you. At least then I'd be able to tell you which clan you belong to." He reached down to the floor and rummaged through a stack of papers to produce a map of Girdlegard, which he carefully unfurled. "I've sent word to Beroïn's folk," he said, pointing his index finger at the secondling kingdom. "Perhaps they'll know something of the circumstances surrounding your birth. Given the ripe old age you dwarves can get to, there's a reasonable chance your parents are still alive. Well, Tungdil, what do you say?"

The dwarf was visibly moved. His dream of meeting his clansfolk was on the cusp of being fulfilled. "That's...Oh, thank you, Lot-Ionan!" he said, overcome with excitement. "Have the secondlings replied?"

Lot-Ionan was delighted to see his enthusiasm. "Not yet. But I'm sure they'll be intrigued by the news of a lost dwarf. They'll be in touch; you can count on it. It's only a start, though. You shouldn't get your hopes up yet."

"I can't thank you enough," Tungdil said solemnly, still struggling to put his emotions into words.

"Now that we've got the map out, I may as well show you where you're going." Lot-Ionan traced a route from the underground vaults through Idoslane, across the border, and into the kingdom of Gauragar. His finger stopped just short of the enchanted realm of Lios Nudin, home of the powerful magus Nudin the Knowledge-Lusty, and came to rest over a peak named the Blacksaddle. "There you have it, three hundred miles on a northwesterly bearing. The paths are well marked and I'll give you the map to take with you, of course. Failing that, you can always stop for directions in one of the villages on the way." He rolled up the parchment. "As for your errand, I need you to convey a few items to my good friend Gorén. If you look in the ebony cabinet, you'll find a small leather bag with green drawstrings. I borrowed the contents for an experiment many years ago and their purpose has been served. The coins on the table are for you to take."

While Tungdil was scrabbling in the cupboard, Lot-Ionan leafed through a book, pretending to read. The dwarf pulled out a bag.

"Found it," he said finally.

"You should go, then, Tungdil, but remember to reflect on our earlier conversation. If we find your family, you'll be free to join them or remain with me, as you please," he said without looking up from his tome. Tungdil turned to the door.

"And one last thing: Be careful! Keep an eye on the bag and don't lose it: Its contents are valuable," he warned. At last he glanced up and smiled: "I strongly advise you not to open it. We don't want any mishaps while you're away. Palandiell be with you—and Vraccas too!"

"You can depend on me, Lot-Ionan."

"I know I can, Tungdil. Now, enjoy your trip and come back safely."

On leaving Lot-Ionan's study, Tungdil steered a course for the kitchens to stock up on victuals and tell Frala of the news.

He found her working at the large dough-trough. The stodgy mix of flour, water, and yeast took considerable effort to knead and her face glistened with sweat from the exertion.

"I need provisions," he announced with a grin.

"The magus is sending you on an errand, is he?" Frala smiled and gave the dough a final vigorous squeeze. "I'm sure we'll find something in the larder for Lot-Ionan's special envoy." She dusted her hands and led the way into a small room that Tungdil imagined was the closest thing to seventh heaven for a mouse.

Frala filled his knapsack with cured meat, cheese, sausage, and a loaf of rye bread. "There," she said, "that should keep you going."

"Not for three hundred miles, it won't."

"Three hundred?" she exclaimed in surprise. "Tungdil, that's not an errand; it's a serious journey! You'll need more food than that." She added two large sausages and some ham. "But don't let Cook see," she said, buckling the flap hastily.

They returned to the kitchen. "Aren't you going to tell me where you're going?" she asked impatiently.

"The Blacksaddle. The magus wants me to deliver a few items to one of his old apprentices."

"The Blacksaddle," Frala echoed thoughtfully. "I've never heard of it. But three hundred miles is an awfully long way. Which kingdoms will you pass through?"

Tungdil chuckled. "I'd take you with me and show you, but I don't think Lot-Ionan would approve—not to mention your husband and daughters." He showed her the map and traced his finger along the route.

"Through Idoslane and Gauragar! And Lios Nudin is barely a stone's throw away. Aren't you curious to visit?" she exclaimed in excitement.

"Not much happens in Lios Nudin," Tungdil said dismissively. "Nudin the Knowledge-Lusty does nothing but study. But Turguria would be worth a look."

"Why's that?"

"Turgur the Fair-Faced is on a quest for universal beauty. He wants to make everyone into paragons of elven grace—even bow-legged farmers and squinty-eyed maids. From what Lot-Ionan told me, he hasn't quite perfected his spells. Apparently, his experiments have led to such deformities that some of his subjects are too ashamed to leave their homes. It's probably a good thing I won't be going there. What if Turgur took it into his head to magic me to human size?"

"What a dreadful thought," said Frala with feeling. She stooped to embrace the dwarf. "May Palandiell and Vraccas bless you and keep you from harm." Before he knew it, she had unknotted her scarf and tied it round his waist. "Here, now you'll have a talisman too." Her eyes twinkled mischievously. "It'll remind you of me—and you'll have no excuse for forgetting my present!"

Tungdil looked into her lively green eyes and sighed. He

was so fond of Frala that it was hard to imagine life without her in a dwarven kingdom, especially now that he was guardian to Sunja and Ikana. His attachment to her was not in the least bit romantic; he felt bound to her like a brother, having known her since she was a child.

"Lot-Ionan wrote to the dwarves of Beroïn," he said, proceeding to recount his conversation with the magus. "He wants to find out where I came from. If the secondlings know my kin, I'd like to visit them in the mountains, maybe move there. The magus said I was free to choose."

The maid embraced him once more. "It looks as though your dream is coming true," she congratulated him. She smiled mischievously. "Jolosin will jump for joy if you decide to go."

"Maybe I should stay, then," threatened Tungdil.

A shadow came over her face. "You won't forget to come back and visit us, will you? I'd like to hear about the dwarves of the south," she said, her voice tinged with melancholy in spite of her genuine pleasure at the news.

"Frala, who knows if I even belong there? They might not know anything about me; I could have been hewn from the mountain without any kin. In any case, my first priority is Gorén. I'll see what happens after that."

A wail went up from the cot in the corner. Frala hurried to comfort Ikana, who had been sleeping snugly by the hearth.

"Say hello to your guardian, little one," she told her daughter. "He'll always be here for you, just as he's always been here for me."

The baby grabbed the dwarf's outstretched finger and pulled. Tungdil was almost certain that he heard a soft chuckle.

"She's laughing at me!"

"Nonsense! She's laughing *with* you! She likes you, see?"

"Don't worry," Tungdil promised the baby, "I'll buy presents for you and your sister too." He disengaged his calloused finger from her delicate pink hands. Now that Ikana no longer seemed so fragile, he would have liked to stay and play. She reached up and tugged a strand of his hair. He carefully loosened her grip. "So you want me to stay, do you?"

The trio made their way through the shadowy galleries to the northern exit. Sunlight seeped through the cracks in the doorway. Frala kissed him on the forehead. "Look after yourself, Tungdil," she said. "And come back safe and sound!"

A famulus pulled on a rope to open the door and the iron-bound oak panels parted with a groan.

Outside, the rolling grassy hills, bright flowers, and leafy trees were dappled with sunshine. The aroma of warm soil wafted in on the breeze and the tunnel filled with the spring warbling of birds.

"Do you hear that, Tungdil? Girdlegard is wishing you well," said Frala, filling her lungs with fresh air. "What glorious weather for a journey!"

The dwarf lingered for a moment in the safety of the shaded doorway. He was accustomed to having ceilings above him and walls that afforded protection on all sides. In the open, there was too much freedom for his liking and he had to acclimate himself all over again.

Not wanting Frala to think he was no braver than a gnome, he took a deep breath, stepped out into the sunshine above Ionandar, and marched purposefully away.

"Come back soon, Tungdil," she called. He turned and waved until the doors to the vaults were closed, then continued on his way. After a few paces he came to a halt. Screwing up his eyes, he winced in the dazzling light. His subterranean existence had made him so sensitive to the sun's powerful rays that he was obliged to shelter in the shade of a towering oak. He dropped onto the grass and laid the magus's bag and his pack of provisions beside him.

Hmm, not the most promising start, he thought to himself. He squinted at his surroundings, straining to see something of the landscape. The canopy of leaves afforded little protection from the glare.

It was the same at the beginning of every journey, but at least the terrain, a wide track winding gently over rolling countryside, would be easily mastered on foot.

He held the map above his head to block out the light and studied his route. Assuming the cartographer knew his business, the landscape would begin to change in the region of the Blacksaddle. A dense forest of pines surrounded the mountain, through which there was no obvious path.

So much the better. Tungdil ran his thumb over the blade of his ax. *Those trees will regret it if they get in my way.*

The sun followed its slow trajectory across the sky.

Little by little Tungdil's eyes adjusted to the sunshine as it weakened and mellowed to a soft orange glow. By dusk, his vision would be restored entirely, but time was running out if he wanted to cover a few miles and find a bed before nightfall.

Straightening up determinedly, he slung his packs on his back, returned his ax to his belt, and plodded on, all the while cursing the sunshine. Grumbling wouldn't get him there any faster, but it vastly improved his mood.

The sun was disappearing over the crest of a hill when Tungdil emerged from the forest on the fifth orbit of his uneventful journey and found himself confronted by palisades bounding a village of some considerable size.

Two soldiers patrolled the wooden watchtower above the gateway. At first neither noticed the diminutive figure outside, but at last one of the men motioned to his companion. Judging by their reaction, the dwarf was not regarded as a threat.

Tungdil was relieved. After four chilly nights in the open, camped among squirrels, foxes, and more greenery than he could tolerate, he was looking forward to finding a tavern with good beer, warm food, and a soft mattress. His stomach was grumbling already.

He reached the gateway, but the doors remained closed. The sentries leaned over the parapet and watched from above.

"Good evening to you both!" he bellowed up at them. "Be so kind as to open the gates! I should like a bed for the night and a roof overhead!" Even from a distance, he could tell that their armor was well made and well cared for. This led him to two conclusions: First, the suits had been crafted by a smith of considerable skill, and second, the metal was worn for protection and not effect. The sentries were no ordinary villagers.

These thoughts were followed by another revealing discovery. In the flickering torchlight he had taken the rounded objects on the palisades to be gargoyles, but on closer inspection they turned out to be skulls. The heads of three dozen dead orcs were impaled on the defenses.

Tungdil doubted the wisdom of baiting the enemy in this fashion. As a deterrent, an array of orcish skulls had about as much chance of warding off the orcs as a dead bird would protect a field from crows. In fact, the sight of the severed heads was more likely to incite the brutes to wholesale slaughter.

From this Tungdil deduced that he had crossed the border into Idoslane and that the men hired to defend the settlement were trained fighters but foolhardy with it. Only mercenaries paid by the skull would be reckless enough to provoke the beasts so gruesomely. The bloodied heads had been set out as bait to draw in nearby bands of orcs.

"What are you waiting for?" he called indignantly. "Let me in!"

"Greetings, groundling! This is Goodwater in the fair land of Idoslane. Have you sighted orcs on your travels?"

"No," he shouted, struggling to keep his temper. To be referred to as a "groundling" was more than he could bear. "And if you don't mind, I'm no more a groundling than you men are grasslings: I'm a dwarf."

The sentries laughed. At their signal, the right half of the double door creaked open and Tungdil was allowed to pass. Inside, another pair of heavily armed soldiers was waiting for him. They eyed him distrustfully.

"Well, blow me down," one of them muttered. "If it isn't a real-life dwarf! They're not as tiny as everyone says they are."

Tungdil was once again reminded that humans knew almost nothing about dwarves. He bristled under the sentries' stares. "If you've quite finished gawking, maybe one of you could inform me where I might find a bed."

The sentries directed him to the nearest tavern, which lay a short distance along the dusty street. Above the door, a shabby platter and a similarly dilapidated tankard indicated that the place sold food and beer, although, by the look of it, it wouldn't be anything fancy.

In spite of his best efforts to slip in unseen, the rusty hinges squealed excitedly as soon as he lifted the wooden crossbar and pushed open the door. It was hard to imagine a simpler yet more effective means of guarding against intruders: The shriek of neglected metal was impossible to ignore. The dwarf hesitated for a moment, then entered.

Seated at the tavern's roughly fashioned tables were ten villagers holding tankards of ale or mead. Tungdil's nose was assailed immediately by the smell of food combined with tobacco and sweat. The villagers wore simple garments: hessian or coarse woolen shirts to protect against the evening chill. Their feet were encased in thick stockings and laced shoes.

Two of the men nodded hesitantly in acknowledgment; the others were too busy staring. It was always the same.

The dwarf returned the greeting and took his place at an empty table. Naturally the furniture was far too big for him, but he made himself comfortable and ordered his supper and a large ale. In no time a steaming plate of cornmeal and mincemeat was laid in front of him, followed by a tankard of beer.

He tucked in ravenously. The meal tasted wholesome, a little burned, and somewhat bland, but at least it was warm. The pale watery beer disappointed his dwarven palate, but he drank it all the same. He had no desire to cause offense, especially when there was the matter of his lodgings still to settle.

One of the villagers was looking at him so intently that he could almost feel his piercing stare. Tungdil returned his gaze unflinchingly.

"What beats me," said the man, raising his voice so everyone in the tavern could hear, "is what a groundling would be doing in our village." A ring of smoke left his pipe and shot toward the sooty ceiling.

"Breaking his journey." Tungdil chewed his mouthful

deliberately, dropped his spoon into the gloop, and wiped his beard. A belligerent villager was the last thing he needed. It was obvious from his manner that the man was sparring for a fight. *Well, he's picked the wrong dwarf!* "I've no desire to argue with you, estimable sir," he said firmly. "I've spent the past few nights in the open, and Vraccas willing, I'd like to sleep on something other than twigs and leaves."

There was an eruption of mocking laughter. Some of the villagers prostrated themselves in front of the pipe smoker, calling him "sir" and "your honor"; one even went so far as to set an empty tankard like a crown on his head. They evidently found it amusing that Tungdil should address a humble villager in terms of respect.

"You think you're quite something, don't you, groundling?" The man hurled the tankard to the floor and faced his friends angrily. "Go ahead and laugh, you harebrained idiots! What if he was sent by orcs to spy on us? You won't find it so funny when he sneaks out of bed and opens the gates!"

The mirth stopped abruptly.

At once Tungdil realized he would have to tread carefully. On a practical level, that meant sticking to plain speech. It was bad enough that he was a dwarf, let alone a dwarf with fancy manners.

"Dwarves and orcs are sworn enemies," he said earnestly. "A dwarf would never throw in his lot with an orc." He extended his hand toward the man. "Here, have my word that I mean you no harm. I swear it by Vraccas, creator of all dwarves."

The villager stared at the sturdy fingers and weighed the matter in his mind. At last he gave the hand a brief shake and turned away.

The publican brought the relieved Tungdil another beer.

"Don't mind him," he said quickly. "We're all on edge at the moment. So many villages have been plundered these past few orbits. Orcs are rampaging through the northwest of Idoslane."

"Hence the mercenaries at the gates."

"They're here to protect us until King Tilogorn's soldiers rid us of the beasts." He turned to go.

"Wait!" Tungdil laid a hand on his grease-spotted sleeve. The man's words had given him faint grounds for hope. "Will there be dwarves among them? I heard King Tilogorn has dwarves in his pay."

The publican shrugged. "I couldn't tell you, little fellow, but it wouldn't surprise me."

"When do they get here?" he asked eagerly. The opportunity of setting eyes on a fellow dwarf was reason enough to delay his mission to the Blacksaddle. *All the more potatoes for Jolosin to peel.*

"By rights they should have been here three orbits ago," said the publican, signaling apologetically to the queue of thirsty customers at the bar. Tungdil let him go and returned to his supper, mulling over what he knew of Tilogorn and his kingdom.

The name Idoslane was derived from the land's bloody past. At the heart of the historical conflict was the throne. The Idos, the kingdom's great ruling dynasty, had plotted, conspired, and waged war on one another, bringing misery on themselves and their people, who bore the brunt of their feuds. Bit by bit the state was torn apart by their squabbling until every district was governed by a different member of the Ido clan. At last their subjects reached the limit of their endurance and felled every last sibling, cousin, and scion of the dynasty: Ido-slane.

A villager, rather the worse for wear, staggered to his feet and raised his tankard: "Long live Prince Mallen! May he drive King Tilogorn from the throne!" When no one joined in with his toast, he lowered himself to his stool, muttering darkly.

If Tungdil's memory served him correctly, Prince Mallen was the sole surviving member of the Ido clan. He lived in exile in Urgon, the kingdom to the north of Idoslane, and was forever conspiring to return to his country as its rightful king.

Tacked to the wall of the tavern was an ancient map of Idoslane, its yellowed parchment stained by smoke. The succession of rolling hills, forests, and plains made for a pleasantly varied landscape. It would have been idyllic, if it weren't for the orcs.

"Not a bad place, is it?" observed a fellow drinker, following Tungdil's gaze.

"Save for Toboribor." Tungdil pointed to the black enclave at the heart of the kingdom: The orcish stronghold was located on Idoslane's most fertile land. He picked up his tankard and joined the villager at his table. "Why are the brutes on the move?"

"They're bored, that's all. Orcs don't need a reason to plunder and pillage. They attacked a place a few miles from here and set fire to the fields and orchards. Their sort are just monsters. Robbing, fighting, killing... They don't know any better."

"And they're strong," said another, eyes widening theatrically. "There was a time when—"

"Not that old fable," groaned the publican, stopping at the table to refill their tankards.

"You don't have to listen. I was talking to the dwarf." In

spite of his injured tone, the storyteller had no intention of abandoning his tale. "I came up against a whole bedeviled mob of them. Great hulking beasts, they were. It was during my employ in Tilogorn's army. We—"

"Happier times, they were. The old prattler never had time to scare folks with his stories."

"What would a publican know about it? If you'd seen the accursed things, you'd have some respect." He turned back to Tungdil. "I'm telling you, dwarf, they were a terrible sight. A whole head taller than most men and ugly as sin: big flat noses, hideous eyes, and sticking-out teeth. It was worse for the young lads; they nearly died of fright."

"That's funny," murmured Tungdil. "I read a description just like that in—" He clamped his mouth shut, but no one had heard. To cover his embarrassment, he scratched his sunburned head. Any later in the season and his scalp would have burned to a crisp by now. The sun took a bit of getting used to.

"Half an orbit it took to kill those wretched brutes. My, they were tough! When I was young no one would hire mercenaries to keep the orcs from their gates. Orcs or no orcs, Idoslane was safe in our hands. Times have changed," he said regretfully, mourning the decline of Tilogorn's army and the passing of his youth. He glanced down and caught sight of Tungdil's ax. The blade had been put to good use in the woods and was looking somewhat neglected, with blobs of dried sap and splinters sticking to the bit. "Don't tell me you've been using a fine ax like that for hacking wood!" he exclaimed, aghast.

"I had to get through the undergrowth somehow." Tungdil reddened, hoping to goodness that no one would ask him to demonstrate his race's legendary axmanship. The truth was, he knew nothing of fighting.

Tungdil had learned everything he knew from Lot-Ionan, who took little interest in weaponry, sword fights, and close combat, leaving his ward without a military education. No one had ever shown him how to wield an ax in anger. The servants chopped wood or killed rats with their axes and that was as far as his handling of the feared dwarven weapon went. His race was supposed to be skilled in axmanship, but if faced with an aggressor, which well he might be, he was resigned to striking out haphazardly and praying that the beast would run away.

"The dwarves are great warriors, or so I've heard," said the veteran trooper. "Runs in the blood, does it? Is it true what they say about a single dwarf putting pay to a pack of ten orcs?"

Tungdil had long suspected that he wasn't a proper dwarf, but now his fears were confirmed. Listening to the men made him realize that his kinsfolk would laugh if they could see him, which put an end to his enthusiasm for meeting others of his race. Even the thought of the fairer sex seemed more alarming than appealing.

"Ten orcs," he said, hoping the trooper was right, "absolutely..." He yawned loudly, stretched, and rose. It was time to escape his own doubts, shake off his nosy questioners, and find a bed. "You'll have to excuse me: I need to get some sleep."

His fellow drinkers, their initial suspicions forgotten, were reluctant to let him go, but at length he was permitted to make his way to the second floor of the timber-frame house where the publican had quartered him for the night. The room was a dormitory, but a large one, and Tungdil had it to himself.

He used the washbowl to bathe his sweaty feet, which had been confined to his boots since the start of the journey.

Savoring the luxury of his third beer, he stood by the window and gazed out over the tiled roofs of Goodwater.

The settlement was a good size, numbering a thousand or so dwellings. The villagers seemed to make their living from the surrounding fields and orchards and what wealth they had was now threatened by orcs. Tilogorn's anxiously awaited army would have to hurry if there was going to be anything left to save.

Tungdil dried his weary feet, folded his clothes over a chair, and buried himself in the thick feather duvet.

Silvery light shone on the leather bag destined for Gorén, sorely testing his resolve.

Don't meddle with things that don't concern you, he told himself sternly.

Even as he fell asleep he thought of Lot-Ionan and Frala, whose talisman was looped through his belt. He missed the sound of her laughter. Tomorrow he would ask the publican for directions to the Blacksaddle and press on without delay.

Muffled sounds roused him from his sleep.

Two men were taking great pains to ready themselves for bed without making any noise. Outside a storm was howling and raging around the settlement.

A whispered exchange followed, during which Tungdil felt certain that he heard Lot-Ionan's name. He peered warily at the newcomers: a thin, well-dressed gentleman and a taller, broader fellow clad in leather mail with metal plating.

A merchant and his bodyguard? Their garments were clearly worth a gold piece or two. He caught sight of a simple yet striking trinket attached to the larger fellow's leather lapel. It was embossed with the seal of the magi.

They're envoys to the magi's council! "Are you headed for

Ionandar?" he asked, abandoning all pretense of sleep. Curiosity had triumphed over caution.

The broad man frowned. "What makes you think that?"

"The brooch." He pointed to the man's gown. "You must be envoys."

The pair exchanged looks of surprise. "Who are you?" the bearer of the trinket demanded. Tungdil introduced himself. "What news of Lot-Ionan?" the man said sharply. "Is he well?"

"Perhaps you could tell me a little about yourselves first," the dwarf requested with impeccable politeness. They supplied him with their names and occupations: Friedegard, a first-tier famulus apprenticed to Turgur the Fair-Faced, and Vrabor, a warrior in the service of the magi. "Lot-Ionan is in excellent health," Tungdil informed them. "You'll see for yourselves when you get there." He struggled to contain himself, then gave in. "Pray, what is the . . ." He reconsidered and began more plainly: "What do you want with the magus?"

"Our business is with Lot-Ionan, not his message boy," Vrabor said dismissively, loosening the buckles on his armor. "Why do you think the council sent an envoy and not a town crier?"

He had barely finished speaking when the storm outside whipped into a frenzy, gusting through chinks in the walls and emitting a strange, unnatural whine, which was followed almost immediately by a high-pitched whistle.

Tensing, the two men reached for their swords.

Not a night to be abroad, thought the dwarf as he watched the moonlit scraps of cloud chase across the gloomy sky.

Just then a slender face appeared at the window. Tungdil looked into the gray-green eyes and felt his mind go numb. The apparition was more bewitching than frightening: Long dark hair swept the beautiful visage, the occasional strand plastered against the rain-drenched skin. So pale, so perfect was the being that it resembled a marble sculpture of an elf, its bedraggled locks like fine fractures in the stone.

The dwarf stared helplessly, transfixed by the creature's gaze. The countenance was attractive—of that there was no question—but it inspired in him an almost physical revulsion. It was too beautiful, almost cruelly so.

"Over there..." His breathless warning was enough to alert the envoys, who looked up and dove for cover.

At that moment there was an explosion of glass as a long black-fletched arrow shattered the window and whined through the air, planting itself in the wall.

"You get rid of them; I'll deal with the window," shouted Vrabor to his companion. Seizing the heavy table, he upturned it and slammed it into the wall, then hurriedly jammed some furniture against the makeshift barricade. There were no other openings for arrows to enter.

Meanwhile Friedegard, eyes closed and head bowed, was chanting silently and tracing strange symbols in the air. In his right hand was a coin-sized crystal set in gold.

"Can someone tell me what's going on?" Tungdil scrambled out of bed and grabbed his ax because it made him feel safer.

The envoys listened in silence. Although the wind had abated, the rain was falling more heavily than before. They strained their ears, but there was no sound of the mysterious bowman. He seemed to have vanished with the tempest.

"Has the elf gone?"

"I can't be sure," said Vrabor. "Perhaps." He sheathed his sword and sat down on the bed, hands resting on the cross guard of his weapon. "They could be biding their time."

"They?"

"Älfar, two of them. They've been tailing us since Porista."

So it wasn't an elf after all... The älfar, a race crueler than any other, were sworn enemies of the elves. They hated their cousins for their purity, a purity that the älfar themselves had been denied. It was hatred and jealousy, according to the history books, that impelled them across the Northern Pass and into Girdlegard. "Is Lot-Ionan in danger?"

"Lot-Ionan will come to no harm," Vrabor assured him wearily. "The älfar are powerless against the magi and they know it. The arrow was meant for Friedegard and me; they want to know what we're carrying. We knew they were following us as soon as we left the capital of Lios Nudin, but they waited until they could be sure of our destination before they attacked. I'm sorry, groundling," he said, responding to the unspoken question in Tungdil's eyes. "I'm sure you're a loyal messenger and I know we're indebted to your vigilance, but our business is between the council and Lot-Ionan. You'll have to save your questions for your return."

"I'm a dwarf, not a groundling." Tungdil toyed with the idea of accompanying the envoys to Ionandar the next morning and telling the magus of what he had seen, but he decided against it. His mission to the Blacksaddle was more important. He sat down and laid his ax across his knees.

The rest of the night was spent in watchful silence, their fear of the älfar keeping tiredness at bay. None of them slept a wink, but Friedegard's spell seemed to have worked and there was no sign of their assailants. At last, with the coming of dawn, the tension finally fell away and Tungdil lay back and dozed.

III

Enchanted Realm of Ionandar,
Girdlegard,
Late Spring, 6234th Solar Cycle

Reclining in his wing chair with his feet on a stool, Lot-Ionan had made himself comfortable in a corner of his study and was leafing contentedly through a grimoire, one of the many that lined his walls. In addition to his slightly shabby beige robes he wore even shabbier slippers and his pipe lay beside him, tobacco at the ready. Steam rose from a glass of herbal tea on the table. The magus was savoring the peace and quiet.

"Do you hear that, Nula?" he asked the barn owl who was perched on the back of his chair and seemed to be studying his spells. "Not a sound. No noise, no explosions. I was loath to say goodbye to Tungdil, but I know it was the right decision."

Blinking approvingly, Nula replied with a gentle *twit-twoo*. Lot-Ionan knew full well that she couldn't understand him, but he enjoyed their conversations. It was an excellent way of collecting his thoughts.

"I suppose it was a bit mean of me, really," he confessed. "Gorén left the Blacksaddle goodness knows how many cycles ago. He abandoned the mountain after falling for the charms of a beautiful and intelligent elf." The owl blinked again. "You want to know how I heard about it? My former apprentice told me himself. It was all in a letter that he wrote from Greenglade. He seemed most contented with his new abode and gave a full account of the superior allure of elven women."

The thought of Gorén's mistress reminded Lot-Ionan of his age. He had long since lost interest in pleasures of the flesh; other matters took precedence in his mind.

"Tungdil will find out his new address, I shouldn't wonder. And when he does, he won't rest until he's tracked Gorén down and accomplished his errand." He took a sip from his steaming glass. The cold air of the vaults was conducive to study, but he found himself drinking countless cups of tea.

Nula blinked, this time almost reproachfully.

"What?" he said defensively. "Don't you remember how he and Jolosin ruined my work? You know how fond I am of Tungdil, but another incident of that kind while I'm rewriting the formula would be disastrous! I took the necessary measures to ensure a lengthy absence, that's all."

The owl seemed unconvinced.

"Come on, the journey will do him good! After everything he's read about Girdlegard, it's time he saw the country for himself. Besides, he'll be back before you know it, pleased as punch for finding Gorén on his own. And as for Jolosin, he'll never want to look at another potato, let alone eat one, and he'll be cured of playing tricks. We'll all be better off in the long run." His eyes fell on his solar calendar. "What's that I see? Nula, we're expecting an important guest!"

The circular slide rule indicated that Nudin the Knowledge-Lusty would be visiting that orbit. Needless to say, his fellow wizard would not be putting in a personal appearance. With five hundred or more miles separating their realms, they communicated via magic, availing themselves of an elaborate ritual that could be implemented only during certain phases of the moon.

Not that Lot-Ionan minded the distance. Nudin was fast developing into the most disagreeable character that Lot-Ionan had ever known. At the same time, he was becoming a formidable magus, his growing skill as a wizard correlating almost exactly with his objectionableness as a man.

Of course everyone developed his own personal approach to studying the mystic arts, but only Nudin seemed to think that being rude, bad-tempered, arrogant, and overweight would somehow serve his cause.

"I'll be honest with you, Nula: That man has spells and charms at his fingertips that others could barely decipher, let alone perform." He reached under the table and fished out a jug of water and a glass. After giving the latter a quick polish on his robes, he held it critically in the candlelight.

There were those who said that Nudin's rising power as a magus had not been gained through study and hard work. Rumor had it that he had cast a spell on his body and invested it with the ability to retain magic indefinitely. Lot-Ionan gave the gossip no credence, but even he was forced to concede that Nudin had changed in character and appearance.

At that moment the air cooled suddenly and a fierce gust of wind swept through the room, nearly extinguishing the candles. A faint bluish haze shimmered at the center of the study, gradually assuming the contours of a man. In the span of a few heartbeats, Lot-Ionan found himself staring at Nudin's imposing bulk.

The wizard of Ionandar appraised his dark-robed guest. Nudin seemed to have grown again—outward as well as upward. His paunch looked larger than before, which was possibly the reason for his especially voluminous malachite-green robes.

Chin-length mousy hair hung limply about his face and there were dark circles around his usually lively green eyes. The apparition was a perfect replica of the real magician, who at that moment was standing in the circle he had cast in his study in Porista, working the magic for his doppelgänger to appear.

The illusion was incredible. Lot-Ionan had never seen a more perfect demonstration of the phenomenon in all his 287 cycles. Apparitions usually shimmered slightly or were marred by minor imperfections, but this one was complete.

Nudin, holding a finely carved maple staff crowned with an impressive onyx in his left hand, languidly dusted his elegant robes with his right, dispatching the lingering blue sparks. Suddenly Lot-Ionan felt terribly underdressed.

"Do sit down," he said, gesturing to an armchair, and Nudin's doppelgänger lowered himself smoothly into the seat. Convention dictated that the same courtesies were extended to apparitions as to real guests; it was only polite. "Can I offer you a drop of tea or would you like something else?"

The question was not as absurd as it sounded. Even from a distance of five hundred miles, Nudin would be able to taste the flavor of anything consumed by his doppelgänger.

The visitor shook his head. "Thank you, my friend, but the news I bring will suffer no delay. You must come to Lios Nudin at once. The Perished Land is advancing."

Lot-Ionan stopped smiling; he had not prepared himself for tidings as dire as these. "How long has it been moving?"

"Some sixty orbits. I took a trip to the border and it came to my attention." Nudin looked anxious. "Our protective girdle is no longer as strong and reliable as it was. The damage is too great for me to repair; I need the council's help. The rest of us are in Lios Nudin already; we're waiting for you…" He trailed off.

"Go on," Lot-Ionan encouraged him, although he had a sinking feeling that there was worse to come.

"It's the älfar," explained Nudin. "They've been sighted in the south of Gauragar, many miles from Dsôn Balsur. Meanwhile, King Tilogorn is being plagued by marauding orcs. They're rampaging through Idoslane, burning down villages and laying waste to the land. He's sent his army to deal with them..." He looked grimly at his host. "It bodes ill, Lot-Ionan."

"The incursion of the Perished Land, the älfar, the orcs—they're all connected?"

"We certainly shouldn't rule it out," he said, refusing to commit himself. "You were summoned by the magi's council. Why didn't you respond?"

"Summoned?" Lot-Ionan made no attempt to disguise his surprise. "When?"

"I have it on good authority that two of the council's best envoys were dispatched with a message: Friedegard and Vrabor are their names. I believe you know them."

"Of course I know them! But where have they got to?" Lot-Ionan was instantly concerned for the pair's well-being, especially now the älfar were known to be abroad. "Thank goodness you decided to follow it up yourself. I'll set off as soon as I can. It shouldn't take more than a few orbits to get to Lios Nudin." Lot-Ionan expected Nudin to take his leave, but the apparition did not stir.

"Just one more thing," his guest cut in. "It's trivial compared to the other news, but all the same...Do you think you could bring my instruments with you? If you've finished with them, I'd very much like to have them back."

"Your instruments...Of course!" Many cycles ago Lot-Ionan had borrowed a number of items from Nudin on Gorén's behalf. The loan comprised a small handheld mirror, two arm-length remnants of sigurdaisy wood, and a pair of

silver-plated glass carafes with unusual etchings. After finding some reference to the items in a compendium, Gorén had
been eager to examine them more closely. Lot-Ionan could
no longer recall what conclusion he had reached, but he suspected it was nothing of particular interest. The more immediate problem was locating the things. He had a sudden vision
of the wrecked laboratory and hoped to goodness that Gorén
had not left the items there.

"I'll be sure to bring them," he promised.

Nudin seemed doubtful. "You do still have them, don't
you?" Lot-Ionan nodded in what he hoped was a convincing
fashion. "All right, well, make haste, old friend. Only the full
council can save Girdlegard from the terrors to come."

Nudin's double rose to his feet, positioned himself in the
middle of the room, and rapped his staff firmly against the
floor. The illusion shattered in a shower of sparks. Glittering
dust drizzled to the ground, disintegrating further and further until nothing was left. The interview ended as spectacu-
larly as it had begun.

Lot-Ionan leaned back in his chair. *If Toboribor's orcs
have joined forces with Dsôn Balsur's älfar, the peoples of
Girdlegard are in serious danger.*

He decided to combine his trip to Lios Nudin with a visit
to King Tilogorn in order to pledge his support. At least half
of Ionandar lay within the borders of Idoslane, so it seemed
only proper to loan the monarch his magical powers in the
battle against Tion's brutes. The magus rose. *Time is of the
essence; Nudin was right.*

He summoned his famuli and issued instructions regarding the luggage he required for the journey and the chain of
command among the students while he was away. Then he
removed his beloved robes and exchanged them reluctantly

for his little-worn traveling garb, comprising another set of robes, also in beige, but made of more durable cloth, and a mantle of dark blue leather.

His servants were busy grooming his bay stallion, Furo. The five-hundred-mile journey to Porista would take ten orbits at most, so everything he needed could be stowed in the saddlebags.

At length Lot-Ionan clambered somewhat stiffly onto his horse. Furo snorted excitedly as the magus leaned forward, stroked its mane, and whispered some enchantment in its ear.

With a loud whinny the stallion thundered out of the underground vaults and through the gates. Once out in the open, with the path ahead and fresh air all around, it picked up speed, accelerating from a canter to a gallop. The cobbles flashed beneath its hooves, covering multiple paces with each stride. Thanks to Lot-Ionan's art, the horse could outstrip any mount in Girdlegard and it relished its speed.

And thus Furo carried his master, who was clinging on for dear life, across Ionandar and beyond.

Kingdom of Gauragar,
Girdlegard,
Late Spring, 6234th Solar Cycle

The Blacksaddle? Never heard of it!" The morning could scarcely have got off to a less auspicious start. Tungdil pushed the map to one side as the publican placed his breakfast on the table.

Particles of dust danced in the wide rays of sunshine pouring through the plate-glass windows. It came as a relief to Tungdil that he could see without peering; his eyes had adjusted to the brightness already.

None of the good people of Idoslane could tell him anything about the Blacksaddle; it was not even marked on the tavern's ancient map.

"Is there anyone in Goodwater who could help me?" he persisted. "A clerk or a magistrate or someone?"

The publican shook his head regretfully, sorry to disappoint the outsider. Tungdil spooned his breakfast halfheartedly. The porridge was decent enough, but frustration had taken the edge off his hunger.

Privately he was still hoping that the villagers were too simpleminded to be relied on. The publican struck him as the sort who had never strayed more than ten or twenty miles from home.

Annoyingly, Goodwater was not marked either, but with a bit of luck one of the mercenaries would know the area sufficiently well to pinpoint its location and send him in the right direction.

No doubt Friedegard and Vrabor would have been of some assistance, but they had long since departed. Stopping only to give the publican a few gold coins to pay for the window, they had struck out for Ionandar and taken the arrow with them.

Tungdil was similarly anxious to leave. "Vraccas be with you," he called to the publican as he slung his pack and the leather bag over his shoulder and stepped out into the street.

The sentries from the previous night had been replaced with a new set of stubbly faces, but Tungdil lost no time in inquiring about the Blacksaddle. Thankfully, the mercenaries had heard of the wretched mountain and could point to

Goodwater on the map. It was getting on for midday when he left the settlement and set off down a narrow road, heading north as the sentries had advised.

"If you see any orcs, tell them where they can find their dead friends!" one of the men shouted after him, thrusting his spear at a festering skull and raising a cloud of flies.

He could still hear the soldier's laughter as he skirted the fields that he had seen in the distance from his window the night before.

Goodwater was an apt name for the place. Tungdil could picture what it would be like at harvest time: fields of corn blowing gently in the breeze, ripe apples hanging from the branches, and enough nuts for countless busy hands. Idoslane struck him as a beautiful place, with the obvious limitation that it wasn't underground. He never felt quite comfortable in the open.

At least there's a decent road. He dreaded the moment when he would have to strike out across the countryside. *It's beyond me how the pointy-ears manage to find their bearings when there's nothing but woods and fields.* From what he'd gathered from his reading, the elves had retreated to the glades of Âlandur as part of their quest to live in harmony with nature, art, and beauty. But the smug creatures' desire for perfection had failed to save them from their treacherous cousins, the älfar.

It's funny, thought Tungdil, remembering the face at the window, *the älf looked just the way I always imagined an elf.*

The northern elven kingdom of Lesinteïl had fallen long ago and now the kingdom of Âlandur was two-thirds under the dominion of the Perished Land. As for the elves of the Golden Plains, they were history: The älfar had seized their land, renamed it Dsôn Balsur, and made it their base, from which they sent out scouts to reconnoiter the surrounding land of Gauragar.

Gauragar's sovereign, King Bruron, was powerless to repel them. As warriors, men were no match for the älfar, and if it came to a battle, Bruron's soldiers would be lucky to draw their weapons before they were killed.

Tungdil thought of the envoys and tried to estimate the distance between the southeasterly tip of Dsôn Balsur in the north and Lot-Ionan's vaults in the south. Four hundred miles or more, he reckoned — a formidable distance, even for an älf.

Unless, of course, the Perished Land has edged southward and the älfar have extended their range. If that was the case, it would explain the envoys' business with Lot-Ionan: Any expansion southward of the Perished Land would pose a threat to the enchanted realm of Lios Nudin.

Tungdil kept a watchful eye on his surroundings as he walked: If there were orcs abroad, he had no desire to deliver himself into their clutches. He took particular care at blind corners, stopping to listen for clunking armor and weaponry or bestial snarls and shouts. To his considerable relief, he encountered no one and was spared the unenviable task of choosing to stand his ground or flee the orcs' superior might. By the time he reached the gaily painted pickets marking the border between Idoslane and Gauragar, it had been dark for about four hours.

His feet were weary, so he decided to journey no farther that night. Spotting a nearby oak, he walked over and scrambled into the branches, hauling his bags after him with a rope that he had purchased in Goodwater.

He valued his life sufficiently that sleeping like a bird in the treetops seemed a fair price to pay for the extra protection it afforded. The orcs were hardly likely to spot him and in the event of trouble, he would draw on his ingenuity to find a way out. Wrapping the rope twice around his body, he tied himself to the tree to stop himself from falling or being shaken from his perch, then closed his eyes—and dreamed.

He took a deep breath, filling his lungs with the fresh cold air that swept the majestic summits of the Great Blade and Dragon's Tongue. The Northern Pass appeared before him and his imagination took off, soaring high above the Gray Range like an eagle.

A sudden welter of monstrous shouts shattered the serenity of the mountains and echoed hideously against the age-old rock.

On looking down, Tungdil saw the mighty portals of the Stone Gateway and all around them Giselbert and the fifth-lings fighting to the death. Axes thudded into enemy armor, biting through sinew and bone, only to be torn out and planted in the next foe.

Still the hordes kept coming.

Tungdil stared in dismay when he saw the endless tide of assailants battering the stronghold. A foul stench of dead orc rose from the battlements where the stone was awash with green blood. He could practically taste the rancid fat on the creatures' greasy armor. The reek was so unbearable that he woke up, retching.

Tungdil opened his eyes and was surprised to discover that it was light. *What...?*

At the foot of the tree, a dozen fires were burning in a ring. Guttural laughter, low grunts, snarls, and angry curses sounded from below.

His blood ran cold. He was trapped: The bands of orcs so eagerly awaited by Goodwater's mercenaries had set up camp around his tree. No wonder he had dreamed of the fifthlings' battle against the hordes. His ears had heard the brutes, his nostrils had smelled them, and his sleeping mind had conjured the images to fit.

The dwarf pressed himself against the trunk, stiff as a statue, willing himself to become part of the tree. *What if they notice me?*

One thing was certain: A mob of this size would make short work of the handful of mercenaries in Goodwater.

Red flames blazed up from the fires, towering as high as several lances and alerting nighttime wanderers to the danger. For the dwarf amid the boughs, the warning came too late.

Tungdil totted up the heads in sight and came to the conclusion that over a hundred beasts were camped below — sturdy, powerful orcs for whom a wooden palisade would be no deterrent if there was prey on the other side.

He took another look and was seized with the urge to vomit. The meat being roasted over the fires and consumed with gusto was unmistakably human in form. Two human torsos were turning on specially constructed racks like chickens on a spit.

Tungdil had to fight back his nausea. It didn't take a genius to work out that the beasts' suspicions would be aroused by a porridge-spewing tree.

Judging by the color of the bandages, he deduced that the ragged strips of cloth covering the wounds of the handful of injured orcs had been torn from the uniforms of King Tilogorn's men. So much for Goodwater's eagerly awaited reinforcements. It seemed Idoslane's soldiers had underestimated the strength of the enemy and paid a high price, having been killed and eaten into the bargain.

Out of the frying pan and into the fire, thought Tungdil, remembering the previous night's brush with the älfar. *What have I done to deserve this?*

The poor villagers of Goodwater had no idea that the green-hided peril was heading their way. He was the only one who could warn them, but that was impossible with the beasts camped round his tree. His only hope was to bide his time, then climb down and creep past them while they slept.

Suddenly it occurred to him that he could use the situation to his advantage by sneaking a little closer to the fires. If he could eavesdrop on the orcs' conversation, he might learn something of their plans. He was familiar with their language in its written form, at least. It paid to have been raised by a magus with a very large library: Studying was his favorite occupation after working in the forge.

Unlikely as it might sound, there was a logic to the grunts, snarls, and shouts that passed for orcish communication. Scholars had studied the speech of orcs in captivity and discovered a language with an unusual emphasis on curses and threats.

His heart raced at the prospect of stealing closer to the stinking beasts. He would be finished if they caught him, but a dwarf was obliged to do everything in his power to protect the races of Girdlegard from Tion's ugly hordes. The Smith's commandments applied to every single one of his children, and that meant Tungdil too.

His mind was made up. He eyed the trunk, looking for the best way of reaching the ground without making any noise. Even as he was lashing his bags to the tree, a commotion sounded below. One by one the orcs rose to their feet amid a tumult of shouted exclamations. Guests were approaching.

The ring of orcs closed around the tree. The dwarf edged

away from the trunk, crawling as far along the tapering branch as he dared. At last he was close enough to hear what they were saying, provided he strained his ears. Thankfully the chieftains were forced to raise their voices above the din, which made things a little easier.

He reached out gingerly and pushed the leaves aside. The beasts were gathered in a large circle around three chieftains whose fearsome tusks had been sharpened and tattooed. At once the noise died down, the cheering fading into silence.

Tungdil heard the clatter of horseshoes. Two riders made their way through the ranks of waiting orcs, the hooves of their black steeds striking the ground in a shower of blue and white sparks. The crimson-eyed horses moved with feline fluidity and had nothing of the typical equestrian gait.

The tall, slender riders directed their steeds to the center of the circle and dismounted. Tungdil's instincts told him they were älfar.

The creatures were clad in finely tailored leather armor and from their shoulders hung long cloaks. Their black leather breeches were tucked into dark brown boots that reached above their knees and their hands were sheathed in burgundy gloves.

The first of the pair, an älf with long fair hair, held a spear tipped with a head as fine as an icicle. A sword dangled from his belt.

His companion's hair was pulled away from his face, his dark plait disappearing into the mantle of his cape. He carried a longbow in his hand and a quiver of arrows on his back. A pair of daggers was lashed to his thighs with leather straps.

Tungdil recognized the älf at once: It was the face he had seen at the window of the tavern. *Please, Vraccas*, he begged silently, *may Friedegard and Vrabor be alive.*

The fair-haired älf took charge of the proceedings, speaking in the common tongue. It was clearly below his race's dignity to communicate in the primitive grunts of the orcs.

"I am Sinthoras of Dsôn Balsur, here at the command of my master, Nôd'onn the Doublefold, commander of the Perished Land, to present the three princes of Toboribor with an offer of an alliance." His voice was cold, barely courteous. He was there to present a deal and his tone told them they could take it or leave it. "Prince Bashkugg, Prince Kragnarr, Prince Ushnotz, you have been chosen by Nôd'onn to conduct a campaign of subjugation and destruction the like of which has never been seen. You, the strong arm of the south, shall lead the orcs to victory and sunder the skull of mankind."

"And who shall be the commander?" demanded Kragnarr, who stood as tall as the älf but with twice his girth. The other princes were of smaller stature.

Bashkugg gave him an angry shove. "You think you're better than us, do you?" he shouted belligerently.

Kragnarr responded to the insult by lumbering round to face his challenger. He leaned across until their broad foreheads were touching. Neither moved as they stared at each other, clawed fingers clutching the pommels of their massive swords. Ushnotz proved altogether wilier and took a step backward, waiting to see how the squabble would unfold.

"My master intends to make you equal in rank," announced Sinthoras, straining to make himself heard above the snarling.

"No," growled Kragnarr quickly, promptly followed by Bashkugg.

The älf cast them a disgusted glance. Even from a distance Tungdil could tell that he would rather kill the princes than negotiate with them, but Nôd'onn had given his orders. It was the first time that Tungdil had heard mention of any name at the source of the evil.

"In that case, my master will grant the office of commander to whosoever conquers the most land." The älf held his spear loosely, but his taut stance betrayed his distrust of the beasts. His dark-haired companion seemed equally wary.

"Land?" grunted Ushnotz scornfully. "It should be corpses, not land! Whoever gets the most bodies will be commander!" He stroked his belly and the other two princes hastened to agree.

"No," the älf said firmly. "This is about territory, not corpses."

"Why?" thundered Bashkugg. "Why not corpses? My soldiers have to eat!"

"Content yourselves with killing the armies that are raised against you," the älf advised him coldly. "You know my master's will."

"Exactly," Ushnotz said slyly. "*Your* master. We've no obligation to obey him. He doesn't rule the south; *we do!*"

Sinthoras directed a pitying smile at him. "Not for much longer. My master is advancing from the north with an army of orcs who will seize the south faster than you can fashion cudgels from the trees." He looked each of the princes in the eye. "Give him your allegiance now and he will reward you with land of your own. Toboribor is nothing compared with what will follow. Each one of you will have your own kingdom with humans for slaves. But defy him, and you will cross swords with others of your race."

The threat of a green-hided army from the north with designs on their territory achieved its intended effect. A hush descended as the three princes digested the information, all memory of their quarrel forgotten.

From his post among the branches Tungdil listened and watched in disbelief. Nôd'onn, if that was the name of the Perished Land's lord, was forging all kinds of unholy alliances in order to subjugate the southern lands. The coming cycles would bring untold suffering for men and elves.

"Fine," Ushnotz said finally, although clearly unhappy with the solution. "I shall do as your master proposes — and he shall make me commander in chief."

Kragnarr glowered at him murderously. "Count me in as well," he snarled. "The tribe of the Kragnarr-Shorrs will conquer more land than the two of you put together." He jabbed a clawed finger derisively at the others. "*I'll* be commander, you'll see!"

"I wouldn't bet on it," Bashkugg retorted angrily. "My troopers will overrun the fleshlings' cities before you've even started!"

"You'll all have a chance to prove yourselves," said Sinthoras, reaching into his belt pouch and producing three plain amulets of blue crystal. He tossed them to the princes. "Leave here and go your separate ways. These are gifts from my master; they offer protection against the magic of our foes. You are to carry them always."

The meeting had almost reached its conclusion when a foolhardy orc sidled up to the älfar's steeds and sniffed the air hungrily.

Without warning, one of the horses whipped round, jaws opening as it pounced. Sharp teeth closed around the orc's shoulders and ripped out a sizable clump of flesh.

Green blood spurted from the wound as the orc retreated, shrieking. A second orcish trooper drew his sword and made to fell the rabid horse.

Before he could strike, the steed's hind leg lifted and sped into the orc's broad chest. There was a flash of blinding light and the orc was thrown backward, traveling several paces before crashing to the ground.

The trooper had no time to right himself before the second horse was upon him. Its forelegs stove in his chest, hollowing his breastplate. His stomach burst with a sickening bang. In an instant the creature's black jaws were at the orc's unprotected throat. There was a sound of crunching bone and the orc's anguished screaming broke off abruptly.

Tungdil watched in stunned horror as the steed swallowed the mouthful of flesh. The second creature let out a whinny of savage enjoyment.

The fair-haired älf issued an order in an unintelligible language and the steeds, horses in nothing save appearance, settled down at once, trotting obediently to their masters. The älfar swung themselves gracefully onto their backs.

"You know what my master expects of you. Make haste and keep to the terms of our agreement," Sinthoras said grimly, turning his steed to leave.

A wide corridor opened before him as the crowd parted hastily, drawing back from the animals' lethal jaws. At length the silence was broken.

The orc with the wounded shoulder shoved his way to the front. "Look what they did to me!" he shouted furiously, waving his gore-encrusted claws in Bashkugg's face. "The pointy-ears killed Rugnarr; the pointy-ears deserve to die!"

The powerfully built chieftain wiped the trooper's blood from his eyes. "Hold your tongue, you cretin!" he thundered, adding a string of foul-mouthed epithets. "They're with us."

"In us, I reckon! We'll eat 'em like we'll eat the fleshlings!" The threat brought grunts of approval from three of his tribe. Emboldened by their support, he nocked an arrow to his bow and took aim at the vanishing riders. "Mmm, what's tastier—älfar or horse?"

Tungdil knew better than to mistake the mounts for horses. He had read about shadow mares in Lot-Ionan's books. They were creatures of the night, unicorns who had been possessed by evil and stripped of their purity, their white coats, and their horns. They ate flesh and were ferocious hunters, driven by an all-consuming hatred of goodness in any form.

Bashkugg was tired of the trooper's posturing. Drawing his clumsily forged sword, he struck at the wounded orc's throat. The blade sliced halfway through the neck, withdrawing with a vicious jerk. The prince grabbed the second orc and hewed his head from its shoulders, holding it aloft for the others to see. With a terrible warning cry, he bared his fangs and dropped the dripping skull, grinding it into the ground until dark gray brains oozed through splintered bone. The other two orcs who had joined in the rebellion were put to the sword as well. The matter had been resolved in the traditional orcish way.

Cowed by the display of might, the troopers skulked back to their campfires, grunting and snarling, to resume their victory celebrations. The five bloodied corpses of their comrades, one trampled by the shadow mare and four slaughtered by the prince, were abandoned where they lay.

"What now?" Ushnotz wanted to know.

"I'll go south," decided Kragnarr. "You," he said, pointing to Bashkugg, "head west, while Ushnotz takes care of the east." The others nodded their assent. "What do we do about the fleshling settlement?"

"I say we attack together," Ushnotz said greedily. "It's not far and we can get a quick feed before we go our separate ways."

Bashkugg scratched his chin doubtfully. "Didn't the älf tell us not to—"

"The southern lands are our business, not theirs. Besides, this wasn't part of the ceal. The älf told us to conquer new territory; this is ours already." He smiled slyly.

"The fleshlings skewered my troopers' skulls on their palisades; I want revenge!" roared Kragnarr, his breastplate jangling as he thumped his brawny chest. "No älf can stop me from punishing them."

"At dawn, then?" proposed Bashkugg to a chorus of approving grunts.

Tungdil let the twigs spring back and retreated slowly along the branch. He had heard enough to know that Girdlegard was in serious danger, but before he could warn Lot-Ionan about Nôd'onn's designs he had to sound the alarm in Goodwater and deliver the bag to Gorén. The magus would know what to do about the threat; he would probably call a meeting of the council or, better still, summon the rulers of the human kingdoms as well.

It seemed to Tungdil that it was time for the magi and the human sovereigns to join forces against the Perished Land. They could even ask the dwarves to help them: A combined army, bolstered by his kinsfolk, would surely be victorious.

Tungdil waited until all but a handful of orcs were asleep, but even then there was no guarantee that his escape would be successful: Three dozen orcs had been posted around the camp's perimeter to keep watch for intruders.

The dwarf took a deep breath and decided on his route, picking a particularly bored and sleepy-looking sentry who had propped himself on his rusty spear and was fighting to stay awake.

After a good deal of deliberation he resolved to take his

packs with him. In view of his recent bad luck, it seemed too risky to leave them in the tree. The orcs would only discover them, and the last thing he needed was to lose the precious artifacts and admit his failure to Lot-Ionan and Gorén.

An eternity seemed to pass as Tungdil abandoned his hiding place as quietly as possible. Even the rustling of a branch would seal his fate.

He kept hold of the firm bark with both hands, sliding down gradually and taking care to avoid the light of the fire. Every now and then a twig would snag on his chain mail, but he succeeded in prizing himself free without a telltale snapping of wood.

At last he was back on solid ground, pressing his face into the grass and filling his nostrils with its fresh dewy scent. It was a welcome antidote to the pungent stench of orc.

Stealth had never been his strong point, so it seemed best to proceed on his belly like a caterpillar, pushing the bags in front of him while endeavoring to keep his posterior out of sight.

It turned out to be much harder than he'd hoped. The haft of his ax was forever jamming between his legs, his chain mail jangled with the slightest movement, and his boots struggled to find purchase on the slippery grass. His nerves were in tatters.

I knew I was a terrible climber, but trying to be quiet is worse, he thought, stopping to mop the sweat from his brow. Vraccas had intended the dwarves to fight in open combat. They took deliberate strides to get wherever they were going and built staircases when the gradient dictated. There was none of this sneaking around.

Barely ten paces separated the dozing sentry from Tungdil as he slithered past. Every feature of the trooper's hideous countenance was visible in the moonlight. Its face was criss-crossed with war paint and ceremonial scars and milky saliva dribbled out of its mouth and down its protruding tusks, dripping onto its fat-slavered armor. The nostrils in its flat nose flared from time to time.

The dwarf was tempted to bury his ax in the beast's oaf-ish head, but he doubted his proficiency and in any case, one dead orc would scarcely save Goodwater from attack.

Relieved to be out of the camp, he crawled through the grass until he reached an irrigation channel at the edge of the field and slipped inside, disappearing from view.

The ditch allowed him to reach the fringes of a wood without being seen and at last it was safe to stand up. *Now, that was an adventure by anyone's standards.* His clothes were coated in mud, but he had other, more pressing concerns. As far as he could recall, the wood was fairly small and the best course was to cut straight through it. He hoped to goodness that he wouldn't lose his way.

Having put a decent distance between himself and the orcs, Tungdil stopped worrying about trying to move quietly. Provided he could get to the village fast enough, there was still a chance that lives could be saved.

He settled into a steady trot and reached the edge of the wood in short order. With a sigh of relief he stepped out into the open.

Vraccas almighty! He froze at the sight.

Four hundred paces from the wood was another orc encampment, three times larger than the first. The field was carpeted with sleeping beasts. No fires were alight to alert him to the danger.

Tungdil retreated quickly before he was spotted. In spite of his best efforts, he failed to find an alternative route: If he wanted to reach the settlement, he would have to sneak past the sleeping bodies. Soon his misgivings were replaced by dwarven obstinacy. Determined to warn the villagers of the coming danger, he crept along the edge of the wood, trying to stay hidden while he picked out the best path through the camp.

Suddenly his boot met with resistance and he heard a faint click. Leaves swirled into the air and a metal jaw snapped shut, trapping his left calf just below the knee. The ground opened and Tungdil plummeted downward, landing headfirst. Everything went dark.

It was the pain that woke him.

When Tungdil came to, there was an excruciating throbbing in his left leg. Groaning, he struggled into a sitting position and gazed up at the dark earthen walls. Gleaming green fronds framed the opening of the pit; it was dawn already.

Clamped to his leg and strangling his blood supply was a contraption whose purpose he knew only too well. Villagers set traps like these to catch wolves. The metal teeth had pierced his leather breeches, leaving a crust of dark red blood around the wound. His calf throbbed dully.

Tungdil did not bother to prize the trap apart but took up his ax, gritted his teeth, and set about hammering the thin pins at the heart of the spring.

Every blow to the trap was a blow to his leg and he moaned softly in pain. Trying not to flinch, he worked on the metal determinedly until the jaws fell open and the pressure was released.

With cautious movements he removed the trap, then flung it away furiously. Using the loamy wall to support himself, he stood up and placed his injured leg gently on the ground.

Pain seared through his calf. Running was out of the question; hauling himself out of the pit was going to be difficult enough.

His concern for the people of Goodwater gave him the necessary strength. After tossing his knapsack out of the pit, he slung the leather pouch over his shoulder and wound his fingers around the roots protruding from the soil. Gasping, he hauled himself up and, with a final burst of energy, swung himself onto the grass, where he lay panting for air.

I'll be more careful where I put my feet in the future, he thought grimly. After a while he crawled to the edge of the wood. The fresh scent on the spring breeze was all the evidence he needed that the orcs had moved on. The field was deserted.

There could be little doubt where they had gone: Smoke was rising in the distance, gathering like a storm cloud in the sky. Tungdil scrambled up, shouldered his knapsack, and hurried off, shaking the dead leaves and mud from his hair.

Anger and loathing dulled the pain, driving him faster and faster until he realized that he was running after all. He wanted to be there with the people of Goodwater since his clumsiness had prevented him from warning them in time.

Such was his resolve that he paid no heed to the voice of reason that bade him take more care. Nothing could stop him from racing toward the settlement, spurred on by the ever-growing column of dark smoke.

That afternoon, sweat-drenched, he reached the top of the hill and looked down on the settlement.

Goodwater was ablaze. Breaches several paces across had opened in the palisades and there were two large gaps where the wooden defenses had been razed to the ground. Mutilated limbs and bodies littered the perimeter.

He soon spotted the remains of the mercenaries, heads

impaled on their spears. Their unseeing eyes stared down from the watchtower as the fire raged unchecked through the settlement, reducing the houses to charred shells.

There were no cries for help, no shouted orders to fetch water or quench the blaze. All Tungdil could hear was the crackling of flames, the roar of burning wood, and the crash of collapsing roofs and walls. There was no sign of life.

Clutching his ax, Tungdil marched toward the burned-out settlement. *Maybe I'll find a few survivors trapped among the ruins.* He gripped his weapon a little tighter as he passed through the gates and turned onto the high street, limping as he walked.

The warm wind smelled of scorched flesh, and flames were shooting out of the houses where panes of glass had shattered in the heat. The whole settlement was on fire.

Human corpses were strewn across the streets and pavements, bodies piled up like dead vermin. Some of the women were naked, the flesh of their breasts and buttocks gouged with bite marks and scratches. There was no mistaking their particular fate.

Shuddering, Tungdil stepped over the slaughtered villagers and listened intently for the slightest sign that anyone was still alive. It was deathly quiet.

All the while the heat was intensifying. The surviving walls acted like a furnace, trapping the fire and raising the temperature dangerously. The dwarf had no choice but to leave the dying settlement.

Back on the hilltop, Tungdil sat down and made himself watch Goodwater's final moments. *It's my fault.* He buried his bearded chin in his hands and wept in despair. Long moments passed before the tears of anger and helplessness began to slow.

Now he could see why his kinsfolk stood guard at Girdlegard's passes: Humans were powerless to defend themselves against the brutal beasts. Tungdil looked down through his tears at the burned-out settlement. Nowhere should ever be made to look like that.

He dried his salt-streaked cheeks and wiped his hands on his cloak. His calf was throbbing so painfully that he decided to delay his departure until the following orbit. Curling up on the hillside, he pulled his cloak over him and watched the flames flicker as evening drew in.

The fire raged long into the night until there was nothing left to burn. Red glimmers illuminated the ashes and Tungdil was reminded of the shadow mares' menacing eyes. *So much evil in such a short space of time,* he thought sadly.

Tomorrow he would press on with his errand and deliver the pouch. Then it would be time for him to persuade Lot-Ionan to take action before the orcs and älfar grew any more powerful.

When Tungdil woke the next morning, he was forced to concede that the sacking of Goodwater was not, as he had hoped, just a dream.

Gray clouds obscured the sun and the smell of rain hung in the air. There was nothing left of the settlement besides smoking embers, rubble, and burned-out houses whose scorched beams rose starkly into the sky like blackened skeletons.

The fields and orchards were covered with a white mist that advanced over the remains of Goodwater, hiding it from view. The land was mourning the villagers, laying a shroud over the settlement that only an orbit earlier had bustled with life.

The sight was too much for Tungdil to bear, so he gathered

his packs and set off. As he hobbled on his way, he tried to eat a little something from his provisions, but the bread he had bought in Goodwater stuck in his throat. There was a cloying taste of death and guilt. He stowed the loaf away.

The gashes in his calf were angry and painful. If he left the wound untreated, he ran the risk of infection or even gangrene, which could cost him his leg or, worse still, his life.

That aside, the journey passed without incident and he crossed back into Gauragar and camped that evening beneath the now-familiar oak. Its leafy canopy sheltered him from the downpour that started that night, only easing late the next morning.

By the fifth orbit the skin surrounding the crusty wound felt hot to the touch and thick yellow pus oozed from the scab. Gritting his teeth, Tungdil walked on.

There was no use waiting for help by the wayside. Instead he kept going, trailing his injured leg through the fine drizzle that was rapidly transforming the trail into a mud bath. At last he reached a small hamlet numbering six farmhouses. His forehead was burning.

A fair-haired woman in simple peasant dress, a milk pail in either hand, spotted the staggering figure. She stopped in her tracks.

Tungdil could barely make out her features; she was just a faint shadow. "Vraccas be with you," he murmured, then toppled over, landing face-first in the mud, his arms too weak to break his fall.

"Opatja!" the woman called urgently, setting down her pails. "Come quickly!"

There was the sound of hurrying footsteps; then Tungdil was rolled onto his back.

"He's feverish," said a blurry, misshapen figure, his voice

echoing oddly in the dwarf's ears. Someone was examining his leg. "He doesn't look good. It's gangrenous. We'll have to move him to the barn." Tungdil felt himself hovering in mid-air. "He'll need an herbal infusion."

"He looks funny," said a childish voice. "What is he?"

"He's a groundling," the woman answered.

"You told me they live in the ground! What's he doing up here?"

"Not now, Jemta. Take your brothers and sisters inside," the man said impatiently.

The air was warm and smelled of hay. Tungdil could hear mooing. The rain seemed to stop and the light dimmed. "Goodwater," he said weakly. "Goodwater has fallen to the orcs."

"What did he say?" The woman sounded worried.

"Pay no attention," the man said dismissively. "He's fever-ish, that's all. Look, he must have been caught in a wolf trap. Either that, or the orc had metal jaws." They both chuckled.

The dwarf clutched at the man's arm. "You're right; I'm feverish," he said, making a last attempt to warn them, "but the orcs are coming. They're heading in three directions: west, south, and east. Three tribes. At least three hundred troopers."

Footsteps approached rapidly. "Here's the infusion," said the girl. "So that's what a groundling looks like!"

"Ava, you go inside too," the man ordered. There was a brief pause; then Tungdil felt as though his leg were being dunked in boiling oil. Even as he screamed the world went dark around him.

...but he doesn't even have a proper beard!" Tungdil detected a note of disappointment in the girl's voice. "Grandpa said they always have long beards, but this one's shorter than Father's. It's like...scratchy wool.

"Do you think he's got gold and diamonds?" The speaker took a step closer. "Remember what Grandma told us? Groundlings are richer than anyone."

"Come back here!" hissed the girl. "You can't just search his pockets. It's rude!"

Tungdil's eyes flicked open. Squealing, the children jumped back in a flurry of straw. He sat up and looked around.

Nine children were gathered around him, staring with a mixture of curiosity and fear. Their ages ranged from four to fourteen cycles and they were clad in plain garments. Nothing they wore could have cost more than a single bronze coin.

His leg had been dressed and was throbbing a bit, but the pain was gone and his temperature was back to normal. They had taken good care of him.

"Vraccas be with you," he greeted them. "Could you tell me where I am and who was kind enough to tend to me?"

"He speaks just like us," said a redheaded boy with sticking-out ears.

The eldest girl, her brown hair in two plaits, grinned. "Of course he talks like us. Why wouldn't he?" She nodded at him. "I'm Ava. Mother found you five orbits ago. You fell over in the mud, but Father and the others picked you up and looked after you." She sent a fair-haired girl, Jemta, to fetch the grown-ups. "Are you better now? Do you want something to eat?"

"Five orbits ago?" To Tungdil it seemed more like a short doze. His stomach rumbled loudly. "Hmm, I suppose some food would be in order—and something to drink as well." He smiled; the children reminded him of Frala, Sunja, and baby Ikana. "Haven't you ever seen a dwarf before?" The harmless inquiry unleashed a deluge of questions.

"Which folk do you belong to?"

"Are you rich?"

"Where are your diamonds?"

"How many orcs have you slain?"

"Are all groundlings small like you?"

"Is it true you can smash rocks with your bare hands?"

"Why isn't your beard very long?"

"How many names have you got?"

"Stop, stop!" Tungdil pleaded, laughing. "I can't answer everyone at once. You can take it in turns, but first I have to tell your parents something." He wanted to save the news of the orcs for the grown-ups; there was no need to scare the children.

A fair-haired woman whom he vaguely remembered from his last lucid moment five orbits ago came in with a basket of victuals on her arm. The smell was enough to make his mouth water. "I'm Rémsa," she said.

"And I'm Tungdil. You saved my life and for that I'm eternally grateful." He lowered his voice. "But I'm going to have to ask you to send the children away."

"Why?" Jemta protested cheekily.

He grinned at her. "Because certain things aren't meant for young ears!" They left.

"You're not still on about Goodwater, are you?" said the woman. "You had all kinds of nightmares while you were ill."

"They weren't nightmares, Rémsa. It's the truth! The orcs, they...Never mind about that: You have to get out of here! They're coming. They're heading south, east, and west—three whole tribes of orcs, numbering a hundred troopers each. You'll be killed. They'll slaughter your animals and set light to your farms. You have to go!"

Rémsa placed a hand on his brow. "The temperature's

gone," she said thoughtfully. "You don't seem feverish…"
She unpacked some bread, milk, cheese, and cured meat and
laid them on the blanket to protect them from the straw. "So
it's true, is it? I'll tell Opatja and we'll send a messenger to
Steepleton. The privy council will know what to do."

"There's no time for that! They're on their way already!"
he said with as much urgency as the mouthful of sausage
allowed. Hunger had got the better of him and he was tucking in ravenously.

"You've been sick for five orbits, don't forget. They'd be
here by now if they wanted to attack. We'll send out a scout,
just in case."

"Is there any way of getting a message through from Steepleton?" A rider or even a carrier pigeon would reach the
major cities of Girdlegard faster than anyone else. Those
services were by no means cheap, but at least they could be
relied on to spread the news quickly.

"A message? I'll send someone who can note it down for
you."

"It's no trouble," Tungdil interrupted politely. "I can
write." He could hardly blame her for assuming he was illiter-
ate; most country people were unschooled. "I just need some
parchment and ink—and someone to take the letter as far as
Steepleton. It's for Lot-Ionan in Ionandar."

She nodded and checked the dressing on his calf. "You
were lucky not to lose your leg, you know. It's a good thing
we found you when we did; another orbit and you'd be wearing a wooden peg. That trap must have been a rusty old thing.
Make sure you eat and get some rest."

She gave strict instructions to the children to leave him in
peace, but they soon returned, giggling and bearing parchment and a quill.

From then on it was impossible to get rid of them. Knowing nothing of dwarves save for stories and legends, they were determined to satisfy their curiosity while they had the chance. They stared at him raptly, following every loop and flourish of the quill as he composed his message to the magus.

The letter contained a full account of all that had happened in Goodwater, the pact between the orcs and älfar, the designs of Nôd'onn, who was said to be the ruler of the Perished Land, and other salient facts. *I hope it gets there in time,* he worried silently. He made a second copy in case the first went missing en route, then lay back in exhaustion on his soft bed of straw.

As soon as the children saw that the letter was complete, they pestered him with yet more questions. This time Tungdil answered with one of his own: "Who can tell me about the Blacksaddle?"

"I can!" Jemta volunteered proudly. "It's almost three hundred miles from here. Father says it's near the highway. He knows all about Girdlegard from when he used to be a trader." She paused for a second. "I know — I'll go and get him for you. He'll describe it better than me." Jumping to her feet, she dashed out like a whirlwind and returned a few moments later with Opatja, a stocky gray-haired man. To Tungdil's delight, he came bearing a tankard of beer.

"The Blacksaddle, you say?" he asked. "An unnatural sort of place. There's a road, all right, but it doesn't lead straight to the mountain; you'll have to hack your way through the forest for the final mile or two." He picked up Tungdil's map and traced a rough route. "You can't miss it: a flat black mountain poking above the trees."

"Flat?" said the dwarf in surprise, taking a grateful sip of his beer. The children drew closer, listening intently.

Opatja nodded. "Think of it as a giant tablet of soap that slipped from Palandiell's hands. It's four hundred paces high, three hundred paces wide, and it runs for a full mile plus another two hundred or so paces." To show the dwarf exactly what he meant, he sliced a hunk of cheese and cut long vertical gouges into its sides. "That's from the wind and rain," he explained to the children.

"Ah, a table mountain! They call them that because the summit is flat like a tabletop. I read about them in my magus's library." He tried to imagine how the Blacksaddle would look in real life. Opatja's description had vaguely reminded him of a legend, but he couldn't for the life of him remember how it went. Oh well, the three-hundred-mile march would give him ample opportunity to search his memory.

"What do you want with the Blacksaddle?"

"I'm looking for a wizard, a former apprentice of my magus. He moved there some time ago and now Lot-Ionan is concerned for his well-being. He won't rest until I've seen him for myself."

Opatja contemplated Tungdil's injured leg. "Leave it a few more orbits before you set off. We'll give you some healing herbs so you can keep treating it while you're on the move." He picked up the letters to Lot-Ionan and rose to his feet.

"Thank you," Tungdil said warmly. "I'm most grateful to you."

"Don't mention it," replied the former merchant with a laugh. "I've never seen the little rascals so quiet!"

He left his guest with the children, who resumed their persistent questioning as soon as he was gone. They could hardly believe their ears when Tungdil told them he was sixty-three cycles old.

"Shouldn't your beard be much longer?" Jemta asked suspiciously. "I asked Grandpa and he said groundlings grow their beards to the floor."

"I'm a dwarf, not a groundling! And besides, I grew my beard for thirty cycles before I had to shave it off. It kept getting scorched by the sparks in the forge and then some scoundrel dyed it blue."

The boy with the protruding ears reached out to touch it. "It's much wirier and curlier than Father's!" he pronounced.

"You should try combing it! Imagine how long it takes to braid." The dwarf grinned and showed them one of his plaits. "It's willful and unruly, just like us. We dwarves hold competitions to see who can grow the longest, bushiest beards, and we decorate our braids with beads and metal trinkets. Most of my kinsfolk look like me. Very few of us have mustaches, sideboards, or chinstraps, and fewer still have no beard at all." He could tell them all about it, thanks to Lot-Ionan's books.

Giggling, the children fashioned their own beards by plaiting stalks of hay and sticking them to their chins with globules of sap scraped from the wooden beams.

"Do all groundlings...I mean, do all dwarves have beards?"

"Absolutely. If you see a clean-shaven dwarf, you can be sure that it's a punishment for something. An exiled dwarf won't be allowed home until his beard has reached the length of his ax haft. And since our beards grow so slowly, the banishment lasts for cycles." *Book-learning,* he thought sadly. *Book-learning passed on to me by humans.* He sighed.

Jemta seized her chance and snatched the straw from the chin of the jug-eared boy. "There, you're banished! Be off with you!"

In no time the battle of the beard was raging with all the

youngsters intent on banishing one another from the barn. In the end Rémsa reappeared and put an end to the fun. Amid loud protests, the children were made to say their good nights and go to bed.

The woman smiled at him warmly. "They've taken to you," she said. "They're not this friendly with everyone, you know. Good night to you, Tungdil. We'll ask Palandiell to mend your leg."

They actually like me. It came as a welcome surprise. Frala and her daughters would surely feel at home here. *So much has happened already; they won't believe the half of it!* He stroked the scarf that Frala had given him, then lay back and put his arms behind his head. If only he could have answered the children's questions about dwarven hoards and dwarven customs with proper authority instead of gleaning his knowledge from books. *It's about time I got to know my own people,* he thought.

IV

Kingdom of Gauragar,
Girdlegard,
Late Spring, 6234th Solar Cycle.

Tungdil soon had the chance to repay his hosts for their kindness in nursing him back to health. Two orbits later, when his leg was almost mended, he set to work in the hamlet's little forge, tackling all the jobs that the regular smith, the only one in the vicinity, was unable to do on account of a broken arm. From the man's point of view, the dwarf's assistance—unpaid, of course—was a godsend.

While the children worked the bellows and squabbled over taking turns, Tungdil placed the iron in the furnace and waited until it glowed red with heat.

The youngsters watched as he hammered the metal amid showers of sparks. With every thud of the hammer, there were squeals of delight.

The smith nodded at Tungdil admiringly. "It's not often you see such swift work," he complimented him. "And good quality too. Maybe it's true that metalwork was invented by groundlings."

"We're dwarves, not groundlings."

"Sorry," the man said with an apologetic smile. "I meant dwarves."

Tungdil grinned. "Well, no matter how fast I work, there's enough to keep me busy for a good long while. How about I stay another orbit? I can always leave for the Blacksaddle after that."

They were interrupted by Jemta. "Show me how to make nails!" she demanded.

"You want to be a smith, do you?" Tungdil patted the blond child on the head, then set about teaching her how to make a nail. While she ran off proudly to show her handiwork to her parents, he turned his attention to forging a new windlass for the well.

It was midafternoon when he left his perch to lie down in a tub of cool water. His clothes reeked of perspiration, so he climbed in fully dressed.

I'm surprised my skin doesn't hiss like hot iron, he thought. The cold water took his breath away, but then he sank luxuriously below the surface and came up, snorting and gasping for air. He was just wiping the water from his eyes when a shadow fell over the tub. There was a clunking of metal and the smell of oil.

Plate armor, thought Tungdil, blinking nervously.

A solid man of around thirty cycles was leaning against the outside wall of the forge, arms folded in front of his armored chest. Despite the various weapons about his person, he had no uniform or insignia to identify him as a soldier.

"Were you looking for me, sir?" asked Tungdil, stepping out of the tub. Water streamed from his clothes, drenching the sandy floor.

"Are you the smith?"

"I'm standing in for him at the moment. Is there something you'd like repaired?" The dwarf did his best to be polite even though he had taken an instant dislike to the man. The stranger's gray eyes bored into him as if to read his innermost thoughts.

"Two of our horses need shoeing. Are you up to it?"

That was enough to turn Tungdil against him forever. "I should hope so. What else would I be doing in a forge? I may as well ask you if you know how to ride!" The dwarf left the bath, trying to look as dignified as possible while leaving a trail of water behind him and making squelching noises as if he were tramping through a bog. His hair hung limply down his back.

Waiting outside on the narrow rutted road were six horses and four men in what looked like full battle dress. One of the horses was laden with kitchen utensils, leather packs, and two rolled-up nets.

The men were conversing in low tones but fell silent when Tungdil approached. They looked at him oddly but made no remark.

The dwarf instructed one of the men to work the bellows. Air hissed into the furnace, fanning the glowing coals until flames licked around them, quivering and flickering above the burning fuel. Tungdil was enveloped in heat, his hair and clothes drying in no time. He was in his element.

"Are you mercenaries?" he asked the fellow on the bellows. Unhurriedly, he chose a hammer and some nails while another man led in the lame horse. Tungdil held the shoe against the hoof; the fit was right.

"You could say that," came the curt reply. "We hunt orcs and criminals with a price on their head."

Tungdil placed the shoe among the burning embers and waited. "I suppose business is good at the moment," he probed. "What of the orcs who razed Goodwater?"

"Gauragar is a big place and Bruron's soldiers can't be everywhere at once. We've enough to keep us busy," the leader of the company said brusquely.

The conversation was over.

Working in silence, Tungdil hammered the horseshoe into shape and fitted it to the hoof. A cloud of yellowish smoke filled the forge. When the job was done, he demanded twice his usual price. The mercenaries paid without objecting and rode away. Tungdil watched them go and dismissed them from his mind.

The next orbit flew by and already it was time for him to leave. The children in particular were disappointed; they had grown fond of the stocky little fellow who showered them with metal trinkets.

Tungdil thanked his hosts profusely. "Without your healing powers a festering wound like that could have killed me." He dug out the extra money that he had taken from the mercenaries and handed it to Opatja.

"We can't accept this," the villager objected.

"That's your business, but I won't be taking it back. It's not often that a dwarf agrees to part with money." He was so insistent that the coins eventually found their way into Opatja's purse.

Rémsa gave him a pouch of herbs. "Lay them on your wounds before you go to sleep. Soon your leg will be as good as new." They all shook hands and he went on his way. The children followed him until the sky grew darker and rain clouds gathered overhead.

"Will you come and see us on your way home?" Jemta asked mournfully.

"Of course, little one. It's an honor to have made your acquaintance. Keep practicing, and you'll make a fine smith." He offered her his hand, but she darted forward and hugged him instead.

"Now we're friends," she said, waving and running back toward the hamlet. As she rounded the corner she shouted: "Don't forget to come back!"

Tungdil was so surprised that he stood there for a moment, hand outstretched, in the middle of the road. "Well, well, who would have thought I could win over a girl-child so easily?" He marched off in good spirits, thinking fondly of the people left behind.

The spring weather had taken a turn for the worse: Dark clouds covered every inch of sky and rain had settled for the duration. After a while, even his boots were soaked, his feet cold and swollen inside the sopping leather.

In spite of the unpleasant conditions, Tungdil was making good progress, but the thought of the orcs and the incursion of the Perished Land, as foretold by the älfar, preyed on his mind.

He remembered what Lot-Ionan had told him about the invasion of the northern pestilence. The Perished Land extended six hundred and fifty miles across Girdlegard, swallowing the whole of the former fifthling kingdom and much of the northern border besides and reaching another four hundred miles southward, where it tapered to approximately half that breadth.

Tungdil reached the shelter of a rocky overhang and examined his map. In his mind's eye he pictured the insidious evil as a wedge forcing itself into Girdlegard, its tip grinding against the magi's magic barrier and leveling off, unable to advance any farther.

Now it seemed that the Perished Land's ruler, the mysterious Nôd'onn, was intent on extending his dominion. And he was undoubtedly making progress, in spite of the magi's girdle. In the east, the älfar kingdom of Dsôn Balsur was eating its way into Gauragar like a festering sore, covering an area two hundred miles long by seventy miles wide. And while the Stone Gateway remained open, there was nothing to stop further armies of foul beasts from entering Girdlegard from the north.

The magi will have their work cut out now that Toboribor has allied itself with the northern blight. The wizards were powerful, but they could only be in one place at a time.

At least they'd be forewarned. According to his calculations, the message would have reached Lot-Ionan by now.

All around him, the varied landscape of Gauragar was

doing its best to recompense him for the dreadful events at the start of his trip. Even the rain could not dull the vibrant springtime colors, although Tungdil was too focused on his journey to pay much attention to the lush splendor of the knolls, woods, and meadows. At length he came to an abandoned temple, a small edifice dedicated to Palandiell. Light streamed through manifold windows, illuminating carvings that symbolized fertility and long life.

Palandiell commanded the loyalty of most humans, but she was too soft and indecisive for Tungdil's taste. He was a follower of Vraccas, to whom temples had been constructed in some of the larger cities—or so he had read in Lot-Ionan's books.

Some humans preferred Elria, the water deity, while others prayed to the wind god Samusin, who regarded men, elves, dwarves, and beasts as creatures of equal standing and strove for an equilibrium between evil and good. Tion, dark lord and creator of foul beasts, was more feared than admired in Girdlegard. *I don't know anyone who would worship him,* Tungdil thought in relief. Lot-Ionan's household, Frala included, prayed to Palandiell.

Tungdil had erected his own special altar and dedicated it to the god of the dwarves who had hewn the five founding fathers from unyielding granite and brought them to life. From time to time he smelted gold in his furnace as an offering: For all he knew, he was the only dwarf in Girdlegard to follow such a custom, but he wanted to give Vraccas a share of the best.

His brown eyes surveyed the ivy-covered walls of the derelict temple. *Perhaps men will have greater cause to pray to Palandiell in the future,* he mused.

Later he stood aside as a unit of well-armored cavalrymen rode by. Their mail, embellished with the crest of King Bruron, clunked noisily and mud sprayed from the horses' hooves, spattering his cloak. He counted two hundred riders in all. *Will that be enough to defeat a war band of orcs?*

From then on Tungdil regularly encountered patrol groups. By the look of things, news of the marauding hordes in Idoslane had traveled fast. Rather than relying on Tilogorn to put a stop to the destruction, King Bruron of Gauragar was taking steps of his own to hunt down the orcs.

It pleased Tungdil to see that the humans had heeded his warning. History would hardly remember the actions of Tungdil Bolofar, a dwarf without clan or folk who had alerted Gauragar to the danger by calling on a peasant family to send word to the authorities that Goodwater had been destroyed. What mattered was that *he* knew about it and it filled him with pride.

Most nights Tungdil slept beneath the stars, although occasionally he made his bed in a barn and once he allowed himself the luxury of a room at an inn. It seemed prudent to save the dwindling contents of his purse.

After nine orbits his leg was fully mended. The rigors of the journey had made a lasting impression on his girth and his belt sat two holes tighter than usual. Walking was good for his stamina and he no longer panted when he journeyed uphill. Even his feet had become accustomed to the daily toil. At night he sometimes dreamed of Goodwater, the horrors he had seen there still present in his mind.

It took another few orbits of marching before the Blacksaddle finally loomed into view. The mountain looked almost exactly like the model that Opatja had irreverently fashioned from cheese, except its sides were pitch-black.

Sunlight glistened on the deep gulleys running vertically down the mountain's sheer flanks. The forbidding rock jutted out of the landscape like an abandoned boulder and was surrounded by a murky forest of conifers. The trees looked small and fragile by comparison, although the smallest among them was fifty paces high.

In times gone by, it must have been a proper mountain with a summit towering miles above the ground. Perhaps the gods snapped it off as a punishment and left the base like a tree stump in the soil.

There was something vaguely sinister about the mountain. Tungdil couldn't define it exactly, but he knew he would never have gone there by choice. He could only assume that Gorén prized his solitude more than most.

Brushing aside these misgivings, Tungdil hefted his bags and continued along the gravel road that wound past the forest half a mile to the east. He kept looking for a path or a gap in the trees, but at sundown he was back where he had started and none the wiser for it all.

What a strange forest. Tomorrow I'll have to cut my way through the undergrowth if the trees won't let me pass. He could feel the tiredness in his limbs, so he set up camp by the roadside and lit a fire, keeping a watchful eye on the forest for predators.

Soon afterward he was joined by two peddlers who seemed thoroughly relieved not to be spending the night on their own. They stopped their covered wagons by his fire and unhitched their mules. Their consignment of pots and pans rattled and jangled louder than a battalion of armed men.

"Is there room at the fire?" asked the first, introducing himself and his companion. Hîl and Kerolus were everything Tungdil expected of the human male: tall and unshaven with long hair, plain apparel, and needlessly loud voices. They laughed, joked, and passed the bottle of brandy back and forth, but their jollity seemed forced.

"I don't mean to be nosy," said Tungdil, "but you seem a little on edge."

Hîl stopped laughing abruptly. "You're observant, ground-ling."

"Dwarf. I'm a dwarf."

"A dwarf. I see. I didn't know there was a difference."

"There isn't; but the proper term is dwarf. Just as you pre-fer to be called humans and not grasslings or beanpoles."

Hîl grinned. "My mistake."

"We're afraid of the mountain and of the creatures in the woods," said Kerolus. "That's the truth of the matter. We wouldn't normally stop here, but our poor old nags are beat." He broke four eggs into a frying pan and invited Hîl and the dwarf to share in his meal.

"So what's wrong with the mountain?" asked Tungdil, dipping a crust into the egg yolk.

Kerolus looked at him incredulously. "I thought every groundling, er, dwarf, knew about the Blacksaddle. Very well, I shall tell you the story of the mount that lost its peak..."

Hîl settled down by the fire and his companion began his tale.

Many cycles ago there was a mountain called Cloud-piercer, whose summit towered high into the sky. Taller and prouder than any other peak in Girdlegard, it was tipped with snow throughout the seasons and its loftiest pitches were made of pure gold.

Everyone could see the mountain's riches, but no one could reach them. The golden crown rested on impos-sibly sheer and unyielding slopes and the glare from the snow and the precious metal blinded any who looked at the summit for too long.

But the people's desire for the gold was overwhelming and they summoned the dwarves to their aid.

A delegation came to Gauragar to examine the golden

mountain and set about it with pickaxes, chisels, and spades.

Owing to the superior quality of their tools, they succeeded in burrowing their way into the mountain and digging a tunnel to the top. They hollowed out the mountain and carried away its treasures without being dazzled by the gold.

Of course, the people of Gauragar were furious and demanded to be given a portion of the trove. While the men and dwarves were quarreling, the mountain came to life, quaking with fury and bent on shaking the plunderers from its core. By then, of course, its flesh was riddled with shafts and tunnels, and the tip of the mountain fell in on itself, crushing the looters beneath its weight.

And now you know the story of how Cloudpiercer lost its summit and its glory.

Since then the denuded mountain has simmered with murderous hatred, its treacherous slopes darkening with malice as it plots its revenge against the races of men and dwarves.

The fire crackled loudly. Kerolus threw on another log to keep the flames going and drive out the darkness.

I knew there was something sinister about it, thought Tungdil. He wondered what it said about Gorén's character that he had chosen to make his home there: It seemed a strange place to live.

"Folk say that wayfarers who venture into the woods are set upon by monsters," the peddler added. "The mountain lures the creatures to it with the promise of easy prey. Sometimes hunger drives them out of the forest and into the towns. They eat anything, man or beast." He shuddered.

"Well, it's good to have company," Tungdil said sincerely,

steeling himself for the next morning's march among the trees. At least he had his ax for protection. "Wait till you hear my story."

He started to tell of his recent experiences, of his night in Goodwater and the meeting between the älfar and the orcs, but his account tailed off when he came to describing the destruction of the settlement. The memories were still too fresh.

Retreating into silence, he tried to get some sleep, but the trees had set themselves against him, creaking and groaning as soon as he closed his eyes. The forest seemed to take pleasure in keeping him awake.

Hîl and Kerolus were oblivious to the noise. Belatedly, it dawned on Tungdil why the men had partaken so freely of the brandy: Their senses had been dulled so completely that nothing could rouse them from their sleep. The task of watching over the camp and their lives was left to the unfortunate Tungdil.

With the coming of dawn, the rustling in the forest finally subsided and the peddlers packed their wagons, wished the dwarf a safe journey, and rode away, refreshed and alert. Tungdil hadn't slept a wink.

He gazed glumly at the forest, peering into the murk. Fretting wasn't going to get him anywhere and he had to press on. Gorén lived in the Blacksaddle, probably in the ruins of the dwarven tunnels, if Kerolus's story was to be believed.

Monsters or no monsters, I'm coming through. He gripped his ax with both hands and stepped among the trees. At once his whole being was assailed by malice and spite: There was no mistaking the mountain's displeasure at his approach.

Tungdil walked on regardless, intent on delivering the artifacts to Gorén so he could return to the comfort of Lot-Ionan's vaults. The sooner he accomplished his errand, the sooner he would be home. *Who knows, maybe the second-lings have replied to the letter already,* he thought brightly.

At length his obstinacy and determination paid off and he reached the foot of the mountain with the forest behind him and not a monster in sight. Maybe the beasts attacked only after nightfall; in any event, he had made it unscathed.

The sheer sides of the Blacksaddle towered above him, steep, dark, and unmistakably hostile. For a moment he was tempted to run away.

Even as he stood there, a volley of rocks sped toward him and he dove for cover just in time, the final boulder missing him by the span of a hand. Each one of the rocks had been big enough to kill him, but he refused to be daunted. He had to find Gorén.

Tungdil circled the base of the mountain without discovering any indication of a dwelling or path. He took to calling the wizard's name in the hope that he would hear him but was met with no response.

Muttering under his breath, he set out a second time around the mountain. This time as he scanned the dark fissured walls, he spotted a narrow flight of stairs hewn skillfully into the rock. The breadth of the steps suited him exactly, but a big-booted man would have struggled to keep his footing on the narrow stone slabs.

A hundred paces, two hundred paces, three hundred paces: Tungdil ascended the mountain, crawling on all fours and clinging to the sculpted steps; there was nothing else to hold on to.

From time to time the mountain cast stones at him or loosed an avalanche of scree. Pebbles grazed his hands and face, and a rock glanced off his forehead, tearing a gash in his skin. Feeling suddenly dizzy, Tungdil pressed himself against the flank of the mountain, letting go only when the world stopped spinning. He wiped the blood from his eyes, gritted his teeth, and climbed on.

"You can't shake me off that easily! Vraccas created the dwarves from rock so we would rule the mountains. I'll conquer you yet!" he bellowed.

He could tell from the angle of his shadow that the sun had passed its zenith and was sinking in the sky. A cold wind whistled around him, tugging at his bags. With every step his situation was becoming more perilous and he hardly dared consider the descent, but at last he mustered the courage to glance down at the fair land of Gauragar, four hundred paces below.

He had never seen such an incredible display of color and light. The sun and clouds were playing on the landscape, casting fleeting shadows over the meadows, fields, and forests. If he strained his eyes, he could make out settlements in the distance, the individual buildings resembling tiny blocks of stone. Rivers wound their way through the countryside like shimmering veins and the air smelled of spring.

The view was so spectacular that it almost stopped his breath. It gave him a sense of power and majesty, as if he himself were a mountain. He could see now why the dwarves had chosen to make their homes in Girdlegard's ranges.

He continued his ascent, climbing with new vigor and courage, until at last he reached a recess in the flank of the mountain some five hundred paces above the ground. It seemed as good a place as any to spend the night.

The alcove was large enough to shelter him from the fierce winds and protect him from further attempts on the part of the Blacksaddle to pelt him with rocks. He crawled inside cautiously. *Tomorrow will take care of itself.*

The sinking sun bathed the gloomy walls of his simple shelter in reddish light, playing on the textured rock. Tungdil stared at the fissured surface; there was something about the markings that reminded him of runes.

He blinked. *Surely not?* He ran his hand over the rock. *There's definitely something there.* Time and nature had worn away at the rock, but his searching fingertips found the shallow furrows of chiseled runes.

Tungdil had a sudden thought. Opening his tinderbox, he kindled a flame and scorched the haft of his ax. Taking the map from his pack, he laid it facedown against the wall and ran the charred wood across the parchment.

At first the improvised charcoal wouldn't stick to the paper, but at length he succeeded in shading over the runes. The symbols appeared on the parchment, pale remnants of an ancient script.

Long moments passed while Tungdil studied the markings, struggling to make sense of the strange, cumbersome formulations. At last, when he had translated the runes into modern dwarfish, he was able to divine the meaning of the lines.

Built with blood,
It was drenched in blood.
Erected against the fourthlings,
It fell against the fourthlings.
Cursed by the fourthlings,
Then abandoned by all five.
Roused by the thirdlings
Against the will of the thirdlings.
Drenched again
In blood,
The blood
Of all their
Line.

The mason had carved the verse in the shape of a tree, symbolizing renewal and the eternal cycle of life.

There was no way of gauging the age of the inscription, especially since the treatise on dwarven language in Lot-Ionan's library made no mention of such things, but Tungdil couldn't escape the impression that the runes were terribly old, a message from a long-forgotten era at least a thousand cycles past.

He breathed life into the words, reciting them aloud and listening raptly to the strange yet familiar syllables, so different from human speech. The language moved him, stirred him, churning his emotions.

He wasn't the only one roused by the sound. The ancient runes rolled through the folds and wrinkles of the mountain and woke the Blacksaddle too. Something shifted in its memory and its hatred of the dwarves returned with a vengeance, this time directed at Tungdil. The Blacksaddle quaked.

"I'm not going anywhere!" He pressed his back against the rock, determined not to be shaken out of the alcove by the shuddering mountain.

Just then the wall behind him stirred as well. Grinding and groaning it slid back to reveal a tunnel. The shaking stopped abruptly.

Tungdil decided it meant one of two things: Either the Blacksaddle was trying to lure him inside and hold him prisoner in its flesh, or Gorén was welcoming him to his den.

With that, the matter was settled. He collected his things, shouldered the bag of artifacts, and strode determinedly into the tunnel.

After barely three paces he felt an almighty shudder and the doorway closed on Girdlegard's night sky. The stars of

Girdlegard twinkled their farewell and the dwarf was trapped inside.

Enchanted Realm of Lios Nudin,
Girdlegard,
Late Spring, 6234th Solar Cycle

The lofty buildings of the majestic palace shone luminous white against the clear blue sky. Sable turrets rose among the domed roofs, sparkling in the sunshine. Like beacons, their shimmering brightness and imposing height lit the way to Lios Nudin from a distance of fifty miles. A traveler would have to be blind to miss Porista.

Lot-Ionan feasted his eyes on the view. The circumstances surrounding the council's meeting were worrying, but he was looking forward to seeing the others all the same. With a tug on the reins, he curbed his mount and rode through the city at a more sedate pace. Snorting, Furo made it known that he would rather gallop and feel the wind in his mane.

Tradition dictated that the meetings of the council took place in Porista's opulent palace, a custom upheld by Girdlegard's magi for two millennia. The reason for the venue was twofold: Firstly, the practical consideration of a central location, and secondly, and more crucially, Lios Nudin's heart-shaped form. Like a well of enchantment, Lios Nudin supplied the other five realms with magic, the energy flowing outward to Ionandar, Turguria, Saborien, Oremaira, and Brandôkai.

Lot-Ionan patted his indignant stallion on the neck and laughed. "There'll be plenty of time for galloping on the way home," he assured him, keeping an attentive eye on the crowds.

The walls of Porista offered shelter and protection to forty thousand men. Grassy plains extended for hundreds of miles in every direction and the population made a decent living from livestock and crops. Farming was profitable in these parts: Porista's produce was considered to be almost as good as that of Tabaîn, the northwestern kingdom nicknamed the Breadbasket because of its fertile fields.

Lot-Ionan steered his horse through the bustling streets, dodging carts and carriages and taking care not to trample pedestrians underfoot. He was already missing the tranquillity of his vaults.

At length he reached the gates of the palace, closed to ordinary mortals except by permission of the council. An invisible trap ensnared foolhardy individuals who tried to slip over the walls. Glued to the masonry like insects on flypaper, they were left to die of hunger and thirst, their magic bonds loosening only when nothing remained but bare bones. In matters of security the council was unbending: The palace belonged exclusively to the magi and their staff.

Lot-Ionan recited the incantation. The doors swung open as if propelled by an invisible hand and the magus rode on.

On reaching a sweeping staircase of buff-colored marble, he reined in Furo and slid from the saddle. His path took him up wide steps and through sunlit arcades on paving of elaborate mosaic. White pillars channeled the light from a vaulted glass roof to shine on the colored tiles and show off the intricate designs. The walkway led all the way to the conference chamber where his presence was awaited. He gave the password and the doors flew back.

The others were there already, seated at the circular table of malachite: Nudin the Knowledge-Lusty, Turgur the Fair-Faced, Sabora the Softly-Spoken, Maira the Life-Preserver, and Andôkai the Tempestuous.

With Lot-Ionan, they formed the council of six and dis-
posed of almost limitless power. Each used their magic to
pursue a goal of their choosing. Had the magi seen fit, they
could easily have toppled the seven human kingdoms of Girdlegard and annexed their land, but they were intent on perfecting their wizardry, not acquiring worldly might.

Lot-Ionan spoke first to Sabora, then greeted the others
in turn, before taking his place between her and Turgur. His
arrival was acknowledged with brief, stately nods.

Sabora clasped his hand and gave it a gentle squeeze. "I'm
glad you're here," she said, smiling warmly. Her high-buttoned
dress of yellow velvet, a straight and somewhat stern affair,
reached to the floor. Her short hair looked more silvery than
at their last meeting, but her gray-brown eyes were as lively as
ever. She sought his gaze. "Andôkai was beside herself with
impatience." She lowered her voice to a whisper so only he
could hear. "So was I, but for entirely selfish reasons."

Lot-Ionan returned her smile. Sabora made him feel like
an amorous young man. Their affection was mutual.

"We know why you didn't respond to our summons,"
Andôkai told him. Her harsh tone made it sound like a
reproach. She was attractive in an austere sort of way and her
physique was uncommonly muscular for a maga, lending credence to the rumor that she could fight as well as any warrior.
She wore her hair in a severe blond plait and her blue eyes
seemed to search for a quarrel.

"Friedegard and Vrabor are dead," Maira explained. She
was taller and slimmer than Andôkai, with red hair that fell
about her pale white shoulders. Her simple dress of light green
cloth was the perfect complement to her eyes and showed off
the gold trinkets hanging from her neck and ears. "The news
arrived just before you did." She looked over at Nudin. "It

seems to us that the evidence points to the älfar. We think the Perished Land sent them to thwart our meeting."

Lot-Ionan frowned. "The älfar are the Perished Land's deadliest servants, but they've never been known to venture so far south. Nudin tells me that our girdle is failing." He paused. "Enemy reinforcements are streaming into Girdlegard in greater numbers than before. Unless we seal the Northern Pass, we'll be meeting in Porista on a regular basis to renew our magic shield." He drummed his finger vigorously on the table. "Enough is enough! The Perished Land must be destroyed!"

"Oh, absolutely," Turgur said scornfully. The famously fair-faced magus had perfectly symmetrical features, a meticulously shaven chin, a thin mustache, and flowing black locks. Women of all ages swooned at the sight of him, for which he was hated and admired by others of his sex. He was far and away the most handsome man in Girdlegard. "Why didn't we think of it before? What a fabulous plan, Lot-Ionan."

"This is no time for sarcasm," Nudin rebuked him in a hoarse, rasping voice.

There was a brief silence as the magi reflected on their past attempts to defeat their invisible enemy.

"Our magic has done nothing to prevent the Perished Land from casting its shadow over Gauragar, Tabaîn, Âlandur, and the fallen kingdoms of Lesinteïl and the Golden Plains," Lot-Ionan said at last.

"And it's not for want of trying. We've used enough energy to topple mountains and drain oceans," added Andôkai, who knew all about destruction. Samusin, the god of winds, was her deity and she focused her magic on controlling even the slightest movement of air. Her mood was as changeable as the weather and her quick temper caused many a storm.

"It wasn't enough, though," said Turgur. "The Perished Land has dug its claws into our soil like a great dark beast and won't be shifted."

"No," Andôkai contradicted him. "It's lurking and ready to pounce. If we do nothing, it will attack."

Lot-Ionan cleared his throat. "I've been thinking. We know from experience that our combined power is enough to keep the threat in check. If we summon our apprentices to Porista and add their magic to the ritual, we may be able to defeat it." He looked expectantly at the others. This was no idle suggestion: They each had thirty or more famuli, all of whom could practice magic to some degree. "If we were to harness the magic of a hundred and eighty wizards, our strength would surely prevail."

"Failing that, we'll know for certain that neither might nor magic can defeat our foe," Nudin commented dryly.

The possibility was too dire for Lot-Ionan to contemplate. If nothing was capable of stopping the Perished Land's incursion, it was only a matter of time before Girdlegard fell. Every living thing, man, beast, or plant, would be forced to live out its existence as a revenant, dead and yet forever in the service of the northern pestilence. A shiver of fear ran through him. *No, we can't let that happen.*

Andôkai was the first to find her voice. She seemed anxious as she scanned the faces of the others. "I know some of you don't approve of my allegiance to Samusin, but I stand by my faith. We must act."

"I thought your faith would forbid you from driving out the Perished Land," Lot-Ionan said in surprise.

"Samusin strives for equilibrium, but in the blackest of nights, nothing survives, not even a shadow. If we stand by and do nothing, Girdlegard will be in thrall to the darkness," she explained. "Once the Perished Land is defeated, the balance will be restored. I'm in favor of the proposal."

The motion was put to the vote and received the council's unanimous support.

"Very well," Nudin said hoarsely, "but we should renew the existing girdle first. If our defenses crumble before the apprentices get here, we won't be in a position to undertake anything at all. I suggest we break for an hour and have some refreshments before proceeding."

The magi concurred with the suggestion and the council dispersed. Nudin beckoned Lot-Ionan to the north-facing window.

Seen from close range, the ruler of Lios Nudin looked bloated and swollen. The whites of his eyes were shot with red veins and his pupils glinted feverishly. It was clear to Lot-Ionan that he was seriously ill.

Just then Nudin was seized by a coughing fit and held a handkerchief to his mouth. With his free hand he steadied himself on his maple staff. He stuffed the handkerchief hastily away.

Lot-Ionan thought he glimpsed blood on the cloth. "You should ask Sabora to lay hands on you," he said anxiously. "You look...To be honest, you don't look well."

Nudin arranged his swollen features into a smile. "It's nothing, just a nasty cold. It's good for the body to have something to pit itself against." He gave Lot-Ionan an approving nod. "That was an excellent idea of yours, you know. Even Andôkai was convinced of the scheme, so the others are bound to fall into line." His face went a violent shade of purple as he struggled to suppress another cough. "We magi have pursued our own private interests for too long," he continued in a strangled voice. "I'm not talking about Sabora, of course;

she's always been different. But it's good to see that there are some things on which the council is prepared to take a stand. It's a pity it had to come to this first."

"Indeed," Lot-Ionan said uncertainly. For once Nudin seemed perfectly amenable and even his condescending tone was gone. If this was the effect of the illness, Andôkai and Turgur could do with catching it as well. "Are you sure we shouldn't be calling you Nudin the Solicitous?"

Nudin chuckled good-humoredly and ended up coughing instead. Lot-Ionan caught a clear glimpse of blood on his lips before he hurriedly dabbed it away.

"That does it. I'm sending you to Sabora," the white-bearded magus said firmly. This time it was an order. "The ritual will be draining and you look weak enough as it is."

Nudin raised his hands in surrender. "I give in," he rasped. "I'll go to Sabora. But one last question: Where are my arti-facts, old friend?"

Lot-Ionan had rather hoped that the matter had been forgotten. "I left them in Ionandar," he admitted. "I'll get my famuli to bring them when they come."

Nudin smiled. "Well, at least you know where they are now. Don't worry. There's no rush. The Perished Land is our primary concern."

"It slipped my mind entirely. I meant to go through the cabinet in my study and pack the things together, but after what you told me about the orcs and the girdle..."

Nudin gave him a pat on the back. "Don't worry about it." He swayed slightly. "Now, if you'll excuse me, I think I'll lie down." He turned and made for the door, his voluminous robes rustling softly and his staff tapping out a steady rhythm against the floor.

"Don't forget to see Sabora!" Lot-Ionan called after him.

Pensively, he gazed out of the window beyond the artful palace gardens and over the roofs of Porista to the horizon where the green plains fused with the bright blue sky. There was no sign of the Perished Land from this distance, but he knew it was there, only a few miles from the city.

After a while he felt a gentle hand on his shoulder and a delicate fragrance wafted through the air. It had been a long time since he had smelled that perfume and his old heart quickened. He placed his right hand over hers. "My favorite maga," he said, turning to face Sabora.

"My favorite magus," she replied with a smile.

He was always delighted to see Sabora. They shared the same attitude where aging was concerned: Neither attempted to disguise the passage of time. He found it reassuring that he wasn't the only one with wrinkles, especially when the others looked so young.

No one could accuse Lot-Ionan of being vain, but the meetings in Porista made him feel ancient. Andôkai, with her hundred and fifty cycles, looked no older than thirty, while Maira could be taken for fifty, despite being six times that age. Turgur, of course, was always refining his looks and maintained the appearance of a vigorous man of forty cycles.

Sabora guessed his thoughts. "Oh, Lot-Ionan," she commiserated, "they're getting older as well, you know." They embraced.

"So tell me about your work," she said when they finally drew apart.

"It was coming along nicely until one of my assistants ruined a vital part of the formula before I had a chance to try it out," he reported. "Still, it won't be long before I can render the presence of magic in people and objects visible to the eye. It should mean a breakthrough in our understanding of what magic energy really is. But let's hear about you. Can you cure all our illnesses and ailments?"

Sabora slipped her arm through his and they set off leisurely through the arcades. "I've mastered injuries and wounds and now I'm focusing my efforts on eliminating the plague. I've been quite successful, actually," she confided. "The trouble is, there's no shortage of people with new and mysterious diseases. The gods send us new ailments every day."

"You'll get there eventually," he said encouragingly. "Has Nudin been to see you? He looks dreadful."

Sabora shook her head. "I saw him hurry past earlier, but he didn't stop to talk." A mischievous smile spread across her face. "If it's his waistline that's bothering him, he'd better ask Turgur. He's the one who knows how to remodel his body and his face."

"He must be nearing his goal, don't you think? He seems to have lost more of his wrinkles since the last time I saw him. Everlasting beauty can't be much farther off."

They stopped in one of the palace's many gardens and sat down.

Sabora laid her head on Lot-Ionan's shoulder. "It's incredible, isn't it?" she said softly. "We all pursue such different goals, but for once we're in agreement."

"Maira's support was as good as guaranteed. I suppose you've heard that she's opened her forests to the purest animals of Girdlegard? She's determined to save them from the orcs. As the eldest among us, she knows better than anyone what the northern pestilence would do to Girdlegard."

"Yes, her realm is a sanctuary. The last of the unicorns have taken refuge in Oremaira." She paused. "If everything goes to plan, Girdlegard will be safer than it has been for eleven hundred cycles—and it won't be a moment too soon."

Lot-Ionan laid an arm around her shoulders, savoring her presence. Duty and geography made such moments all too rare. "I was pleasantly surprised by Turgur," he confessed. "He usually seems so self-obsessed. His life revolves around physical perfection, beauty, aesthetics, and yet…"

Sabora laughed. "I expect he's worried about his flawless blossoms and flower beds. He's lavished so much time on perfecting his gardens that it would be a pity to see them ruined by the Perished Land." She straightened up suddenly. "I heard Gorén was here. Wasn't he one of your apprentices?"

"Gorén? What would Gorén be doing in Porista? He lives in Greenglade."

"Turgur said something about a meeting he held with Gorén and one of Nudin's apprentices. It was here in Porista, the last time we met."

"Now, that sounds suspicious," the magus said jokingly. "Turgur the Fair-Faced meets two of his rivals' apprentices and steals their secrets. He'd know all about my work!"

"Much good it would do him: charmed beauty combined with the power of discerning magical presences, and…" She hesitated. "What *does* Nudin do?"

"He hasn't said." The magus shrugged. "Judging by the look of him, he doesn't have time for exercise, so it must be demanding." Now that he thought about it, he was intrigued; at the next opportunity he would ask Turgur what Gorén had wanted in Porista. "Let's forget about the others," he said tenderly, wrapping his arms around Sabora and hugging her gently. "We don't spend nearly enough time together."

"You're right," she said. "I'll ask Andôkai to swap kingdoms and then we'll be a little closer."

"I'm sure her subjects would welcome the change. The calm after the storm—isn't that what they say?"

"Still waters run deep," she informed him with a playful sparkle in her gray-brown eyes.

Kingdom of Gauragar,
Girdlegard,
Late Spring, 6234th Solar Cycle

Tungdil's sharp dwarven vision soon adapted to the darkness. The walls around him had been hewn cleanly from the dark flesh of the mountain and polished to a sheen. Smooth surfaces were the hallmark of dwarven masonry; he couldn't imagine a human laborer going to such lengths.

The chilling legend of Cloudpiercer had sounded convincing at the time, but he no longer gave it much credence. From the evidence around him, it seemed likely that the mountain had served as a dwelling, not a mine.

Tungdil clambered up a short flight of steps and came to an open portcullis. Beyond the raised grating, a heavy oak door reinforced with metal hasps and steel plating stood ajar. He knew there would be no way out if the door slammed behind him.

"Hello? Is that you, Master Gorén? Is there anyone there?"

For a while he listened to the dull echo of his shouts; then the deathly hush returned. He went in.

"Master Gorén, can you hear me?" he called. "My name is Tungdil. I'm here on an errand for Lot-Ionan." The last thing he needed was to be mistaken for an intruder. Hidden behind the door was a set of levers with which the portcullis could be raised or lowered. It made a dreadful racket, as he discovered by trying it out.

"Sorry," he shouted, hurrying on. It was time he found Gorén.

The tunnel delved deeper and deeper inside the mountain. After a while Tungdil could almost convince himself that he had stumbled on a dwarven stronghold. Staircases and passageways wound into the core of the enduring rock and for the first time he had a clear idea of what it would be like to live with his kinsfolk in one of Girdlegard's ranges. At length he came to the kitchen, a large chamber neatly hollowed from the rock, equipped with stoves and kitchenware that had not been used for some time.

"Master Gorén?" Tungdil sat down, lowered his packs, and waited awhile. A terrible thought occurred to him. *Who's to say that Gorén isn't dead?* Galvanized into action, he put aside his reticence and began to search the place for anything that might lead him to the wizard.

He flung open one of the doors and strode along a corridor. It took him to another chamber of vast dimensions, at least two hundred paces long by forty paces wide and full of plants. The allotment had been laid out in accordance with horticultural lore, but the plot had been sorely neglected and was overgrown with weeds. Despite the musty air, a system of mirrors provided the plants with adequate light, while slits in the ceiling took care of the watering, allowing rain to seep through and plop to the earth in a steady stream of drops.

Tungdil battled his way through the rampant vegetation, rejoined the corridor, and came to a study. The chaos inside was all too familiar. Every surface, including the floor, was littered with loose sheets of parchment, closely written manuscripts, and abandoned books.

"Surely he can't have written all this?" he marveled aloud. There was enough material to fill a good-sized library. Gingerly he riffled through the papers, looking for clues.

Most of the dusty tomes were written in a scholarly script known only to the magi and their senior famuli. He flicked through them, but their contents remained a mystery. *What was Gorén working on? Longevity? Perpetual health? Prosperity?* Reminding himself that it was none of his business, he focused on the task in hand: reuniting the artifacts with their rightful owner.

He continued the search, reaching behind a cabinet to pull out a bundle of letters. Two scholars had been in correspondence with Gorén about the nature, form, and guises of demonic possession, including known instances of men being inhabited by other beings and whether it was possible to be controlled by a spirit.

It seemed likely that one of the correspondents was a scholar of some distinction since his part in the discussion was written in scholarly script. The letters of the other, whom Tungdil judged to be a high-ranking famulus, were devoted to describing how an unnamed person had changed in character and appearance. Nothing in the correspondence gave him any indication as to Gorén's whereabouts.

The dwarf resumed his quest, searching the adjoining rooms and venturing farther and farther from the mountain's core as he rummaged through small laboratories, libraries whose contents had been partially cleared, and storerooms of potions and ingredients.

He turned the situation over in his mind. Although Gorén no longer seemed to be in residence, there was still the matter of the artifacts. Tungdil had promised Lot-Ionan that he would deliver them, so deliver them he would. A dwarf's word was binding. *And until I find him, Jolosin can keep peeling potatoes...*

Tungdil's eye was caught by a series of inscriptions that were unmistakably dwarven in nature. A cold shiver ran down his spine as he read. Carved into the rock were tirades of terrible loathing and murderous hatred. Whoever had wielded the chisel was bent on heaping dire accusations and dreadful curses on four of the dwarven folks and their clans.

Tungdil knew immediately what it meant: The mountain had once been home to Lorimbur's dwarves. Here in the human kingdom of Gauragar he had stumbled upon a chapter of dwarven history that was missing from most books.

He remembered the runes at the entrance to the tunnel. *Erected against the fourthlings, it fell against the fourthlings.* So Lorimbur's dwarves had built a stronghold in the heart of Girdlegard. But for what purpose? Had they intended to wage war on the other folks? Assuming he had interpreted the inscription correctly, the thirdlings had been defeated. In any event, a curse had been placed on the Blacksaddle to ensure that the stronghold was never used again: *Cursed by the fourthlings, then abandoned by all five.*

He could imagine the sequel. Gorén must have learned of the maze of tunnels in the mountain and decided to make his home there. As a wizard, he commanded the necessary expertise to lift the dwarven curse and turn the stronghold into a refuge where he could study in peace. *Built with blood, it was drenched in blood.* A famulus would never allow himself to be intimidated by such threats.

A sudden whisper caused the hairs on the back of his neck to stand on end. The walls were talking to him, muttering and whispering, animated by a ghostly presence that seemed to be closing in.

You're imagining things, he told himself.

There was a ringing and clattering of axes, chain mail jangled, and warriors shouted and wailed. The din grew louder and louder until a battle was raging around him, the shrieks of the maimed and wounded echoing intolerably through the rock.

"No!" bellowed Tungdil. He pressed his hands to his ears. "Get away from me!" But the clamor only intensified, becoming fiercer and more menacing. At last he could stand it no longer and took to his heels. Nothing could keep him in the mountain: His only desire was to escape from the Blacksaddle and its ghosts.

The whispers, screams, and crashing blades faded as he raced away.

Tungdil was not the sort to scare easily, but his courage had never been put to such a test. He would sooner endure scorching sun or pouring rain than spend a night in this place. Now that he knew the mountain's frightful secret he could already imagine the ghosts of his ancestors crowding round his bed.

He went back to scouring the tunnels and searched for hours without finding proof of Gorén's fate. The only clues to his whereabouts were love poems he had written to a certain elven beauty and the name of a forest that was circled on various crumbling maps. Tungdil surmised therefore that Gorén had moved to Greenglade.

For the dwarf to get there, his legs would have to carry him an extra three hundred and fifty miles on a northwesterly bearing. Greenglade lay at the edge of the Eternal Forest in the elven kingdom of Âlandur. According to legend, it was a uniquely tranquil place where the trees blossomed continually, irrespective of the seasons.

Tungdil mulled the matter over and smiled. *To think a wizard would leave his home for the sake of a pointy-eared mistress!* For his part, he had never been especially fond of elves, and this new development, which served to prolong his adventure, did nothing to improve his opinion of their race.

He was so wrapped up in his thoughts that he took a wrong

turn and failed to find his way back to the kitchen, where he had hoped to rejoin the passageway that led to the door. The diversion took him through yet more of the thirdlings' halls. It was obvious that the masons had intended the stronghold to make a stately impression, but the result was disappointing. Some of the galleries were lopsided, the steps were all shapes and sizes, and the intervals between them didn't match. The curse of Vraccas had robbed Lorimbur's folk of the most elementary of dwarven skills.

At length he came to a solid stone wall, carved with an arch of voussoirs. Tungdil read out the runes on the keystone, conjuring a chink in the otherwise featureless rock. A door took shape, grinding against the floor as it opened to let him pass. No sooner had he stepped out of the tunnel than the door rolled back behind him. Try as he might he failed to discover any cracks, fissures, or other signs of a hidden opening. In this at least the thirdlings had shown some skill.

The short walk through the dense pine forest helped his eyes to adjust to the light and by the time he was marching along the road to Greenglade the sun scarcely bothered him at all.

For once Tungdil appreciated the buzzing insects, sweet-smelling grasses, and sunshine: Anything was better than the Blacksaddle.

V

Enchanted Realm of Lios Nudin,
Girdlegard,
Late Spring, 6234th Solar Cycle

That evening the six magi assembled in the conference chamber to prepare for the ritual.

First they took away the chairs, leaving the malachite table at the center of the room. Then they traced a large white ring on the marble floor around it and filled the circle with colored chalk marks. The symbols and runes would serve to bind the magic energy conjured by their invocation and stop it from dispersing before it could be used. From there they would channel it into the malachite table.

It took hours to complete the preparations. Not a word was spoken, for the work demanded absolute concentration and an incorrectly drawn symbol would oblige them to begin the process all over again.

Lot-Ionan was the first to finish. Stepping back, he gazed at the malachite table, recalling its curious past. He had happened upon it fortuitously in a shop selling odds and ends. The dark green stone had intrigued him and on further investigation he discovered that the mine from which it was quarried was located on the fringes of a force field. His experiments had confirmed the stone's special properties: Magic could be stored in the malachite and set free upon command. In the following cycles, Lot-Ionan's discovery had saved Girdlegard several times over, for without the table to help them harness and channel energy, the magi would never have been able to hold back the Perished Land. Generations of wizards had turned the power of malachite to their advantage; now the council would draw on it again.

Turgur straightened up and looked at the circle in satisfaction. He shot a glance at Nudin. "He's up to something," he said in a low voice to Lot-Ionan. "Keep an eye on him."

"On Nudin?" Lot-Ionan asked, astonished. "Whatever for?"

Just then Nudin rose to his feet and glanced in their direction. A look of suspicion crossed his swollen features when he saw the whispering men.

"I can't explain now. I'll tell you later," Turgur promised. "You'll second me, won't you?"

"Second you?" The white-bearded magus had spent his life studying spells and conjurations and was baffled by Turgur's hush-hush tone.

Before he could probe any further, Maira summoned them to their places. The moon and the stars were shining brightly as the six magi stepped into the circle. It was time for the ceremony to begin. The copper dome parted, sliding back to unite the wizards with the firmament above.

Closing their eyes, they held their arms horizontally and began the incantation that would conjure the energy.

Each spoke according to his or her nature: Maira singing, Andôkai hissing and spitting, and Sabora whispering, while Turgur enunciated his words with a pride befitting his character. Their voices combined in a complex chant beseeching and commanding the magic to come forth.

Only Nudin and Lot-Ionan spoke as one person, reciting their formulae ceremoniously, as if respectfully addressing a king.

Lot-Ionan had not forgotten Turgur's strange whisperings. He stole a glance at Nudin through half-closed eyes and was relieved to see that there was nothing the least bit unusual about his behavior.

One by one the symbols surrounding Maira the Life-Preserver lit up, sheathing her in an iridescent column of light that reached high into the dark night sky. The maga of Oremaira was ready.

The glow surged around the circle, bathing each of the wizards in light. By now the citizens of Porista would be staring at the palace, transfixed by the extraordinary sight.

So intense was the flow of magic that the chamber crackled with energy, purple bolts of lightning scudding between the columns.

Maira laid her hands on the malachite table and the others followed suit. Lot-Ionan noticed that Turgur, eyes fixed on Nudin, seemed incredibly tense.

The energy coursed through the magi and flowed into the malachite, the dark green crystal pulsing with light. The six waited until the glow had intensified, then lifted their hands from the cool surface and stepped away.

"Go forth!" commanded Maira. "Go forth and strengthen the unseen girdle protecting our lands!" She recited the formula, and the magic in the malachite did her bidding, shooting from the center of the table in a dazzling blaze of white light.

As it streamed upward, Nudin seized his staff and thrust its tip into the flow. The onyx absorbed the light. A black bolt sped from the jewel, striking Nudin. As the energy discharged into his body, the wizard writhed and screamed in pain.

"The blackguard has betrayed us!" Turgur raised his arm, intending to dash the onyx from Nudin's staff, but an invisible shield protected the jewel.

As the last of the magic flowed into the onyx, the mala-

chite grew dull and the light of the circle was extinguished.
The ceremony was over. The energy had been harnessed and
released. Nudin staggered back in exhaustion and leaned
against a marble column for support.

Lot-Ionan turned to Turgur for guidance. The fair-faced
magus had obviously suspected that something was awry.
"He betrayed us!" Turgur raged furiously. "Nudin betrayed
us to the Perished Land. If only I'd seen it sooner."

"Explain yourself, Nudin!" stormed Andôkai, striding
purposefully toward him. She gripped him firmly by the
shoulders and for a moment it seemed as though she might
strike.

He beat her to it.

His fist raced toward her chin with such speed that she had
no opportunity to defend herself. Andôkai the Tempestuous
flew several paces through the air and slammed down on the
malachite table. She lay motionless.

"You'd better tell us what you've done," Lot-Ionan commanded sharply.

Nudin drew himself up and smoothed his dark robes. "Be
quiet, you old fool," he retorted, directing his onyx-tipped
staff at Lot-Ionan's chest.

The four magi reacted immediately, steeling themselves to
deflect a magic strike. Whatever was ailing Nudin had clearly
affected his brain. Madness was not uncommon among
wizards.

"Tell us what you've done," Sabora urged him. "This isn't
about power, is it, Nudin? Was this meeting a ploy to increase
your own strength? If Turgur's right, you're more foolish than
I thought." She looked to the others for support. "Lay down
your staff before it's too late."

"It's too late already," he informed her. "You made your

choice. For hundreds of cycles you've been fighting it, when all you had to do was listen. Much of what it says is true."

"'It'?" Maira queried, horrified. "You don't mean the Perished Land? Are you saying you talked to it?"

"I learned from it," he corrected her. "I can't protect Girdlegard without changing it first. It's up to you whether you decide to help me."

Lot-Ionan reached for his staff. As far as he was concerned, there was nothing to consider. "Your actions today have turned five friends against you," he said sadly. "Your thirst for knowledge and power has led you astray. You should never have listened to the voice of destruction."

"You are wrong to call it that." Even as Nudin began to speak, his left eye and his nostrils dribbled blood, leaving thin crimson streaks on his doughy face. He faltered.

"Can't you see what it's doing to you?" Maira said gently. "You still have the power to renounce it, Nudin."

"N-no," he stammered, agitated. "No, never! It knows more than all my books put together, more than all the magi and scholars combined." His voice took on a hysterical edge. "It's what I dreamed of. Don't you see? There's no choice."

"Only because you agreed to be a part of it. And what did the Perished Land demand in return for this wonderful knowledge? All Girdlegard and its inhabitants!" Turgur laughed scornfully. "You strike a poor bargain, my friend."

"None of us can help you," Sabora whispered. She shook her silvery head. "Nudin, how could you?"

"You've got it all wrong," he protested, disappointed. "It wants to help us; it wants to protect us from harm."

"Protect us?" Maira signaled to the others. "No, Nudin, there is nothing more harmful than the Perished Land. We must fight it." She took a deep breath. "And we must fight you too."

"You fools! Do you think you can hurt my friend?" Nudin dropped his voice to an unintelligible whisper and smote his staff against the floor. The marble cracked, a deep fracture ripping through the stone and channeling in the direction of the chalk circle. A heartbeat later it reached the table.

The malachite disintegrated like rock candy in hot tea, crumbling into a thousand pieces. Andôkai, whose motionless body was lying on the tabletop, landed heavily on the flagstones. Green shards rained around her, tinkling on the floor, but still she made no sound.

Lot-Ionan, the words of a counterspell frozen on his lips, gaped with the others in horror at the wreckage. The table, their precious focus object, had been destroyed.

He was still staring at the sparkling green fragments when a blue fireball whooshed overhead, on course for the treacherous magus. Before it could reach its target, Turgur's fiery projectile was torn apart by a counterspell.

"For Girdlegard," Maira shouted. "Stop the traitor!"

The sound of her voice startled Lot-Ionan into action. Pushing aside his fears for his realm and his disappointment at Nudin's betrayal, he focused on the challenge ahead. He knew the others were depending on his support, but in all his 287 cycles he had never once used his powers to kill or harm.

They assailed the traitor with fireballs and lightning bolts, then joined forces for a combined attack.

Flames and projectiles bombarded Nudin's shield and he disappeared amid the inferno. Sabora toppled the pillars on either side of him, bringing a section of ceiling crashing to the ground. Dust swirled around them, obscuring their view.

None of them dared to check on Andôkai; all energies were focused on Nudin.

"Let's take a look." Maira summoned a gust, propelling the dust through the open roof. As the clouds dispersed, they found themselves looking into thin air—Nudin the Knowledge-Lusty was gone, but there was nothing to suggest that he had been destroyed.

"He can't have survived," wheezed Turgur. "It's impossible. He must have—" His eyes widened in horror as he looked at his hand. The skin was wrinkling, its surface filling with age spots that blackened and turned into sores. A hastily invoked countercharm did nothing to stop the rot. The festering infection spread along his arm, eating into his chest, then his legs.

Sabora rushed to his aid. Without flinching she laid a hand on the putrefying skin. This time her healing powers failed her.

With nothing to hold his flesh together, Turgur slid to the floor. He tried to speak, but his rotten tongue twitched helplessly in his mouth. The fair-faced magus had been robbed of his beauty; a moment later, he forfeited his life. A deathly canker had eaten him alive.

Lot-Ionan struggled to contain his growing dread. Nudin commanded powers the like of which had never been seen. The Perished Land had taught him terrifying secrets.

Stepping out from behind a pillar, the false magus appeared at Maira's side. She shrank away.

"You had your chance," he rasped, drawing a few paces closer and stopping by the fallen Andôkai. "I asked you to help me and you refused. Much good will it do you. I'll show you what—"

At that moment, Andôkai, who had been lying seemingly

dead on the floor, shot up and drew her sword. The blade sang through the air and pierced Nudin's chest.

"Take that, you traitor!" she thundered, raking the sword upward. The metal tore through the left side of his rib cage and continued through his collarbone, hewing his shoulder. Nudin staggered and fell.

As he went down, he raised his staff and hurled it with all his might. The tip buried itself in Andôkai's chest. She gave a low moan and toppled backward, fingers clutching at the malachite splinters that littered the floor. Then she was still.

"Andôkai!" In an instant, Sabora was at her side, laying hands on the wound.

The sight of the traitor lying in a pool of blood allowed Lot-Ionan and Maira to draw breath. They knelt alongside the injured Andôkai, but their magic could do nothing to help her.

"We're not strong enough," said Sabora, scrambling to her feet. "Our powers have been depleted by the ritual and the battle. Try to stop the bleeding while I go for help. A rested famulus with a knowledge of healing might save her yet."

She took two paces toward the door and froze midstep. Her face took on a bluish tinge that spread rapidly through her body.

"Sabora?" Lot-Ionan reached out to touch her. A stab of cold rushed through his arm, freezing his fingertips to her skin. Sabora had turned to ice.

"Andôkai the Tempestuous lies still, Turgur the Fair-Faced has lost his looks, and Sabora the Softly-Spoken will forever keep her peace. What will become of Lot-Ionan the Forbearing, I wonder?" a voice rasped behind him.

Nudin? Lot-Ionan howled furiously, tugging his hand away from the maga's frozen arm and skinning his fingertips. His sorrow at the fate of his beloved Sabora turned to violent rage. "You'll pay for this, Nudin. You won't cheat death again!" A terrible curse on his lips, he whirled round to face the traitor. Nudin's staff was pointing straight at him. His robes were bloodied, but there was no sign of the grisly wound inflicted by Andôkai's sword; a rip in his cloak was the only evidence of the blade's gory passage.

Before Lot-Ionan could react, he was seized by an insidious paralysis. The heat seemed to vanish from his body, chilling him to the core, while his skin tightened so excruciatingly that tears rolled down his rigid cheeks. Only his eyes were free to move.

"Can't you see it's using you, Nudin?" Maira tried to rise from Andôkai's side, but slipped on the fragments of malachite and swayed. Nudin saw his chance. On his command, the splinters rose up like an uneven carpet of thorns. He hurled a curse at her.

Maira deflected the black bolt, but staggered and fell among the shards. The jagged crystals cut through her robes, slashing her skin and inflicting grievous wounds.

"Nudin, I'm begging you—" she whispered urgently.

"*No one* has the right to ask anything of me!" He stood over her and brought the staff down heavily with both hands. Maira let out a tortured scream as the onyx smashed into her face. There was a flash of black lightning. "From now on, I listen to no one."

Possessed of a crazed fury, he battered her head until the skull gave way with a sickening crack. Nothing was left of Maira's once-dignified countenance.

Panting for breath, Nudin drew himself up, triumph flashing wildly in his eyes. He looked at the bodies strewn around him.

"You've got only yourselves to blame," he shouted angrily, as if to justify his actions. "*You* wanted it to end this way, not me." He ran a hand over his face and found sticky smears of blood. Disgusted, he wiped them away with his gown. "It was your choice," he said more quietly, "not mine."

Unable to do anything but weep, Lot-Ionan cried tears of despair. The magi had been betrayed and destroyed by one of their own, a man whom they had counted as their friend.

The traitor dropped his guard. Lowering himself onto a chair, he tilted his head back and gazed up at the stars.

"My name is Nôd'onn the Doublefold," he told the glittering pinpricks of light. "Nudin the Knowledge-Lusty is no more. He departed with the council, never to return." He gripped his staff. "I am two and yet one," he murmured pensively, lumbering to his feet. Lot-Ionan followed him with his gaze as he strode toward the door.

"You too will die, my old, misguided friend," the treacherous magus prophesied. "Your whole being will soon be fossilized; you'll be nothing but stone." He fixed him with bloodshot eyes, a look of untold weariness and disappointment on his face. "You should have sided with me and not that backstabbing Turgur. Still, for old times' sake I won't deny you a proper view." His swollen fingers took hold of Lot-Ionan and he embraced him briefly, hauling him round to face Sabora. "Now you can watch her while you're dying. It won't be long before she follows. Farewell, Lot-Ionan. It's time I got on with saving Girdlegard — single-handedly, since the rest of you won't help."

He stepped out of Lot-Ionan's line of sight, and the doors slammed shut. Alone in the chamber and beside himself with grief, the magus of Ionandar surveyed his dead friends. The sight of Sabora, frozen and motionless, was enough to break his heart.

*Will the gods stand by and watch the ruin of Girdlegard?
Do something, I implore you!* Rage, helplessness, hatred, and
sorrow welled within him until despair took hold of his being
and nothing could check his tears.

At length the curse relieved him of his torment. The salty
rivulets petrified on his marble cheeks, forming a lasting
memorial to his anguish, while his breathing faltered and his
heart turned to stone. If death had not claimed the kindly
magus before daybreak, the sight of Sabora melting in the
merciless sunshine would surely have killed him.

When everything was still in the chamber, a colossal warrior forced himself through one of the windows, stepped over
the bodies, and knelt beside Andôkai. The palace echoed
with his bestial howls.

*Enchanted Realm of Lios Nudin,
Girdlegard,
Early Summer, 6234th Solar Cycle*

Tungdil was making swift progress. His boots devoured the
miles, carrying him on a northwesterly course ever closer to
Greenglade. The shortest route to his new destination took
him through the enchanted realm of Lios Nudin, home to
Nudin the Knowledge-Lusty.

It was unsettling to think that the distance separating
him from the Perished Land was dwindling with every step.
The southern frontier extended almost as far as Lios Nudin,
although Greenglade was a good hundred miles clear of the
danger. Nonetheless, if the girdle was to fall, Gorén would be
obliged to move elsewhere.

On the far side of the Blacksaddle he came across a mes-

senger post. Knowing that Lot-Ionan would be worried about
his whereabouts, he composed another short letter in which
he informed the magus of where he was going and what had
come to pass. He paid for the courier with the last of his precious gold coins.

The weather was treating him kindly. The sun shone
benevolently from the sky, a light wind kept him pleasantly
cool, and on the few occasions when the warmth threatened
to overwhelm him, he retreated to the shade of a tree and
waited for the midday heat to pass. His legs were much stronger now than at the start of his journey and he was barely
aware of the weight of his mail. The walk was doing him
good.

The landscape of Lios Nudin made little impression on the
dwarf. It was mainly flat with a few rolling hills, referred to
locally as "highlands." For the most part, fields and meadows stretched as far as the eye could see, dotted with grazing
cows and vast numbers of sheep, herded by attentive dogs.
Woodland was rare and tended to be sparse, although the
trees were of a venerable age. Having succeeded in taking
root, they had every intention of standing their ground.

With the exception of Porista, which lay a considerable
distance to the north of his route, there were few settlements
of note in Lios Nudin, Lamtasar and Seinach being the largest with thirty thousand inhabitants apiece.

However, the proliferation of smaller villages and hamlets made it easy for Tungdil to find work as a smith and he
offered his services in return for extra rations of cured meat,
bread, and cheese. It was no good asking ordinary country
folk to pay him in gold.

For four orbits he had been following the same road on
a westerly bearing toward the border, where he would cross

back into Gauragar and take a diagonal path northward to Greenglade.

With any luck Gorén won't have quarreled with his elven mistress and moved away. In his gloomiest moments Tungdil envisaged himself traipsing after Lot-Ionan's famulus forever, doomed to carry the blasted artifacts until he died. At least the journey was furnishing him with plenty of new experiences and even life on the surface no longer seemed quite such a trial.

Weeks had passed since the attack on Goodwater and the memory of the violence was fading, allowing him to take pleasure in his surroundings. He savored the different smells of the countryside and chatted to the peasants, reveling in their stories and their curious accents and dialects. Girdlegard dazzled him with her infinite variety.

At times he felt lonely and longed for the comfort of Lot-Ionan's vaults, where everything was reassuringly familiar. Nothing made him feel safer than narrow passageways and low ceilings and he missed his books and his chats with junior apprentices. Most of all, though, he missed Sunja and Frala, whose scarf was still tied to his belt.

Yet deep down he also nourished the hope that his kinsfolk, intrigued by the news of an abandoned dwarf, had sent word to Lot-Ionan and requested to see him. Every orbit he prayed to Vraccas that the magus's letter wouldn't be ignored.

It was afternoon when he noticed that the landscape was becoming more wooded. The gaps between the trunks diminished until at last he was in an airy sunlit wood. This was the beginning of the Eternal Forest and he had almost reached his goal.

On consulting his map, he found he was fifty miles west of Lios Nudin and a hundred miles southwest of the Perished

Land—safe enough, in other words. It would take a real stroke of bad luck to meet orcs in these parts.

A branch snapped loudly.

Tungdil's recent exposure to country noises persuaded him that the sound was more than just a cracking twig. A creature of sizable proportions was lurking in the wood. Reaching for the haft of his ax, he peered in the direction of the noise.

Another branch snapped.

"Who goes there?"

The shouted question startled the stag that had been nosing among the trees for the lushest grass. Its white rump bobbed up and down, then vanished from view.

Tungdil shook his head at himself. *What did you expect it to be?* he chuckled. As he wandered through the forest, a sense of calm and serenity settled over him. There was something incredibly peaceful about the trees and it rubbed off on his mood. Even the birdsong was fresher and more joyful, the forest-dwellers greeting him like an old friend whose visit was long overdue.

The dusty road gave way to a grass track that meandered through the woods like a green ribbon unfurled by nature. Every step felt luxuriously soft and springy and even the hot sun, which had reached an oppressive intensity in recent orbits, seemed pleasant beneath the dappled leaves. A light breeze chased away the muggy summer air and Tungdil felt he could walk forever.

Soon he became accustomed to the sounds of the glade and the rustling and crackling became more frequent. Deer and wild boar tore through the undergrowth at his approach. There were animals everywhere, and like him, they seemed to sense the peacefulness of the forest and feel at home there.

I won't get too friendly with the elf maiden until I've

learned more about her, he decided. His race and hers were sworn enemies, but Tungdil saw no sense in hating someone who had done him no harm. *I'll see how she treats me first.*

A branch snapped again. Judging by the racket, the culprit was a fair-sized animal, most probably a stag. Tungdil peered ahead, hoping to glimpse its magnificent antlers.

Another branch broke, twigs snapped, and a voice cursed—in orcish.

The harmony of the forest shattered like a bauble beneath a blacksmith's hammer. Orcs spilled out of the bushes and Tungdil, who moments earlier had been basking in a sense of security, was confronted with the prospect of being eaten alive. A penetrating odor of sweat and rancid fat filled the air.

The first beast, a particularly hideous specimen, stepped onto the path. He was armed to the teeth and nearly twice the height of Tungdil.

"Bloody greenery. We'd move faster if we burned the blasted forest down." The orc snatched furiously at a twig that had wedged itself in his armor. He still hadn't seen the dwarf.

The troopers who followed him out of the bushes were more observant. "Hey, Frushgnarr, take a look at that!"

The square-jawed head whipped round. Two small deep-set eyes glared at Tungdil as the orc opened his wide mouth in a blood-curdling shout: "A groundling!" He drew his toothed sword. "I love groundlings!"

"If only the sentiment was mutual." The dwarf strained to see past him and paled. The orcs were still coming, pouring out of the woods. At thirty he stopped counting. There was no hope of evading them this time. Like a true child of the Smith, he would go down fighting and take an orc with him. He would have liked to prove his credentials before he met his Maker, but at least Vraccas would know that his intentions were sound. "Now you're here, I'll have to kill you."

"You and whose army?" the orc jeered.

Tungdil lowered his bags. It was maddening to know that he had come so close to completing his mission, but he drew unexpected courage from his frustration.

"Army? I don't need an army when I've got my ax!" His inborn hatred of the beasts, common to all dwarves, was awakened by the foul creatures' odor. An image of Goodwater, houses burning and villagers slaughtered, flashed before his eyes. The bookish part of his brain shut down and he threw himself, shrieking, upon the nearest orc.

The beast parried his blow with a shield. "Are you sure you don't need an army?" he grunted scornfully. Snarling, he took a step forward and lunged.

The dwarf retreated hastily and backed into a tree. At the last second he ducked, the sword whistling past him, almost grazing his head. It buried itself in the bark.

On seeing the orc's sturdy thigh in front of him, Tungdil swung his ax toward the unprotected flesh. "Take that!" Dark green blood gushed from the wound, streaming down the beast's shin.

Abandoning his sword in the tree, the orc reached for his dagger to stab the dwarf instead. Tungdil's mail stopped the blade from penetrating, but the impact sent him reeling. Fighting to stay upright, he tripped over his bags and fell.

"So much for your ax, groundling! Prepare to die!" The orc hurled the dagger at him but missed.

Tungdil, who had succeeded in tangling himself in the straps of his bags, was still trying to free himself when his opponent decided to retrieve his sword, wrenching it out of the tree.

The beast limped toward him, snorting with rage and brandishing his blade. It hurtled through the air.

As the dwarf dove to one side, the bag of artifacts jerked after him, landing on his back just as the blade made contact.

The famulus's precious possessions absorbed the blow, but the splintering and jangling left Tungdil in no doubt that the artifacts had paid dearly for saving his life. *Who knows if they'll ever get to Greenglade?* His fury redoubled.

"I'm not done yet!" Rolling onto his front, he used his momentum to plant his ax in the orc's right thigh, almost severing his leg.

The beast yelped and fell to the ground beside the dwarf. Tungdil rolled away from him, sprang to his feet, and drove his ax into the creature's throat. He heard the bone crack. "Who says I need an army?" he panted. For the first time in his life he had slain a beast of Tion. He hoped to goodness that Vraccas would be satisfied since it was likely to be his last.

The band of thirty or so orcs stormed toward him. He knew there was no chance of him surviving the attack.

If I'm going down, one of you is coming with me. Tungdil squared his shoulders and tightened his grip on the ax. He could imagine how the fifthlings had felt when the northern hordes had assailed the Stone Gateway. There was nothing for it but to follow their example and die an honorable death.

The lead orc was only ten paces away when a bright, defiant bugle sounded close by. He heard clattering armor and a peal of colliding blades; then shouts went up as dying orcs tumbled to the ground. To Tungdil's astonishment, reinforcements had arrived. He was too grateful to worry about who they were.

"The groundling has friends," roared the chief of the band.

"Bring me their flesh!" The green-hided beasts turned away from Tungdil to confront the enemy that had attacked them from behind.

The elf maiden must have sent her warriors. I can't stand by while they risk their lives on my behalf. He ran after the orcs, darting forward to drive his ax into the back of a dark green knee. The beast toppled like a tree.

That makes two, Tungdil thought grimly.

One of the orcs engaged his blade while the rest piled in on the new arrivals, hiding them from Tungdil's view.

Tungdil soon realized that his unexpected victories had given him more confidence than was merited by his skill. His third opponent saw through his feints and swiped at him relentlessly.

The dwarf checked five savage blows before his luck ran out. A fierce strike dashed the ax from his hand and it landed in the grass. For want of another weapon, he drew his bread knife. "Come here, you brute!"

"Gladly, groundling!" The orc gave a grunt of delight as he eyed Tungdil's knife. "What's that, a toothpick? Just what I need to clean your flesh from my jaws!" He raised his sword.

Kingdom of Urgon,
Girdlegard,
Early Summer, 6234th Solar Cycle

A joint army?" Lothaire laughed out loud. Urgon's sovereign was a youth of twenty-one cycles. He flicked his long blond hair and gestured for more water. "You want us to fight together against the Perished Land?"

King Tilogorn nodded. At forty cycles, he had a thin, earnest face and shoulder-length brown hair. He had journeyed to Urgon with the sole purpose of forging an alliance, but after four hours of discussion in the gloomy chamber there was no indication that the message had got through. In the meantime, the sun had passed over the mountains of Urgon and was sinking behind their peaks.

"It is rumored that the girdle is weak. If the magic fails, the orcs will attack our lands with a strength and ferocity more devastating than anything that has gone before." Tilogorn pointed to the map. "The seven human kingdoms of Girdlegard must unite. Your help is vital if I am to persuade Umilante, Wey, Isika, Bruron, and Nate of our cause."

Lothaire sipped his water and stared at Tilogorn over the rim of the glass. "You're serious about this, aren't you?"

"Absolutely. Our survival depends on it."

"Shouldn't we leave it to the magi to repair the girdle before we—"

"The magi will take care of the magic, but we must be prepared to fight. I've dispatched a messenger to Lios Nudin to request a meeting with the council. I'm expecting word any orbit."

"Why would the magi deign to meet with mere mortals? Andôkai has never honored me with a visit, despite claiming swathes of my kingdom as her own."

"Consider yourself fortunate; it's not for nothing that she's called the Tempestuous." He laughed, then became serious. "The magi rarely show themselves, and they tend to keep out of our affairs, but this is different, I assure you. They know their duty."

Lothaire studied the map, pondering the Perished Land, whose frontier posed no immediate threat to Urgon. "I don't know, Tilogorn. My kingdom is as tranquil as ever."

"But will it stay that way?" Tilogorn replied patiently, doing his best to talk Lothaire round. "I know your lands are easier to defend than the plains of Gauragar or Idoslane, but the Perished Land commands orcs, älfar, and other foul creatures. Nowhere is safe."

"The beasts shall be thrown from my mountains and drowned in my lakes. Their heavy armor will be the death of them," announced Lothaire with customary haughtiness. "My men are hardened warriors. Every day they seek out trolls in our ranges and put them to the sword. I ride with a single bodyguard, knowing that he will defend me single-handedly against a hundred foes."

"Do not confuse the älfar with simple-minded trolls. All it takes is a well-aimed arrow and your bodyguard will be dead. The hordes in the north are more numerous than you can imagine; their power is infinite, yours is not." With a sweep of his hand, Tilogorn gestured to the former elven kingdoms. "They insisted on fighting alone and were conquered. Isn't it our duty to learn from their mistake? We must fight like with like: Only a vast army can protect us from the beasts."

"But what of the Perished Land's curse? Those who die on its territory are said to join its ranks."

"I've heard the stories too. We must burn the corpses so none can return as soulless warriors. We shall create a battalion to follow our army and set fire to the dead." Tilogorn sensed that Lothaire was almost persuaded. "Then you'll fight with me, King of Urgon?"

"Our armies shall follow my lead."

"The command will be shared. Our strengths will complement each other." Tilogorn paused. "Besides, my men will never take orders from a ruler younger than themselves." He held out his hand. "Are you with me?"

Lothaire smiled. "Very well. Our army will be the mightiest in the history of Girdlegard, powerful enough to lay waste to Dsôn Balsur and hound the älfar across the Northern Pass. Although maybe we should kill them and be done with it... Yes," he said excitedly, "we'll destroy them altogether and then we can deal with the orcs. Peace will return to our kingdoms. It's a worthy plan." He shook Tilogorn's outstretched hand; then an anxious look crossed his face. "Er, there's one more thing. You remember Prince Mallen of Ido?"

Tilogorn snorted. "How could I forget the last of the great Idos? He lives in your kingdom, does he not?"

"He heads my army," Lothaire corrected him. "Rest assured, when the time comes to rid your lands of orcs, he will forfeit his command. No one shall accuse Lothaire of Urgon of scheming to plant the last of the Idos on Idoslane's throne."

Tilogorn took little comfort from the speech. "What if he incites rebellion in our troops? He is sure to have supporters among your men."

Lothaire sipped his water. "He's a reasonable man at heart. Perhaps your powers of persuasion will work on him as effectively as they worked on me." Before Tilogorn had a chance to reply, the young king rose and walked to the door. "I'll summon him to you. If you can convince him of our cause, the kings and queens of the other five kingdoms will be no trouble at all." He disappeared into the corridor.

His guest leaned over the table to study the map.

"Greetings, King of Idoslane," a voice said sardonically. "Who would have thought that we would ride to battle side by side? Fate plays games with the best of us, irrespective of rank."

Turning, Tilogorn saw Lothaire reentering the room with the speaker, a man of some thirty cycles, his features nondescript. His finely crafted armor bore the insignia of the Ido and testified to his wealth, although fashions had changed in the meantime.

"Prince Mallen of Ido?" It was less a greeting than an expression of surprise. "I remembered you differently."

"Yet you recognize the coat of arms to which Idoslane rightfully belongs...Are you comfortable on my throne?"

"You need not worry about my comfort, Prince Mallen. You and your coconspirators have not unseated me yet. The people are clearly fonder of my family than they were of yours. You serve Urgon's army, I hear?" Tilogorn asked brusquely.

"I am an exile. I have to do something to earn my keep."

"The Idos have a reputation for fighting—especially among themselves. Your bloodthirsty feuds brought suffering on the people and cost you your throne." He bit his lip. Barbed comments were hardly going to help his cause. "Forgive me, I didn't mean to—"

"Oh please, King Tilogorn, spare me the history lesson," Mallen said dismissively. "Tell me something interesting, such as what I can do to aid my country and return a free man."

"If you wish to help your country, bury our quarrel until Girdlegard is safe," Tilogorn entreated. "I'm sorry I spoke so harshly."

"You're sorry." Mallen was as distrustful as ever. "Well, we agree on one thing: An invasion of orcs or älfar would only harm Idoslane." He glanced at the map. "It may surprise you to learn that I'm in favor of a truce between us. I agree to your proposal, on the condition that I can enter Idoslane at will."

Tilogorn hesitated.

"I miss my country and the few friends loyal to my line," Mallen said evenly. "There'll be no more conspiracies, I swear. May Palandiell be my witness."

This time the king held out his hand. "I can see in your eyes that your concern for Idoslane is genuine. I shall take you at your word."

"Make no mistake," Mallen warned him. "There is no friendship between us. Only the gods know what will become of us once the hordes have been defeated, but let us focus on saving our kingdom for now."

Lothaire, who had been hanging back, stepped in. "Excellent. Good sense has prevailed, it seems. I propose that we inform the other monarchs and make haste to raise our troops." He escorted them through the corridors of his palace.

Tilogorn stole sideways glances at the other two, trying to read their expressions.

Lothaire was visibly excited at the prospect of battle, but Mallen's face was inscrutable, revealing only that he shared Tilogorn's profound anxiety about the future.

Just then, they fell into step, their boots ringing out in unison against the marble floor.

"Hark," said Tilogorn, drawing their attention to the harmony of their stride. "Past cycles have driven a wedge between our dynasties, but now we move as one. If only it didn't take a common enemy to bridge the gulf between neighbors."

"It's no use dwelling on the past," replied the sovereign of Urgon. "Blaze a trail for others to follow, and follow they will. It's the only reasonable thing to do."

"Well spoken, King Lothaire," Tilogorn said approvingly. "I think the two of us" — he nodded at Mallen — "have shown that we are reasonable men."

VI

O ver here, you runt," a voice cried lustily in dwarfish. "Come here so I can slaughter you!" A squat figure pushed its way between the orc's legs, whipped out two short-hafted axes, and planted them in the orc's vulnerable nether regions.

Oinking derisively, the diminutive warrior jerked the weapons out of his opponent's crotch and launched himself into the air like an acrobat, seemingly unhampered by his heavy mail. On his way down he struck again, hewing the neck of the orc who was doubled up in pain. The axes sliced from both sides, almost meeting in the middle. The beast crumpled to the ground.

"By Beroïn's beard," the warrior scolded Tungdil, "what were you doing dropping your ax?"

"You're a...dwarf!" Tungdil gasped in surprise, scrambling to his feet.

"Of course I'm a dwarf! What did you think I was? An elf?" He bent down, picked up the ax, and tossed it to Tungdil. "Don't let go of it this time. We'll save the talking for later." With a grim laugh he threw himself back into the frenzied scrum.

Tungdil spotted a second dwarf, identical to the first in every detail except his beard. He was slashing vigorously at his opponents with a crow's beak, a kind of spiked war hammer equipped with a curved spur as long as his lower arm.

"I thought you said you wanted our flesh? Too bad you didn't bring more of your friends!" shouted Tungdil's rescuer, taunting the orcs. "Your pig-ugly mothers must have slept with a hideous elf to make monsters like you," he boomed. "With a one-legged, mangy, no-eared elf. She probably enjoyed it!" When one of the orcs lunged forward, snarling with rage, the dwarf dispatched him with a flash of his axes. "Come on, don't be shy," he harried them. "You can all take a turn."

His fellow warrior preferred to work silently, wreaking his own brand of deadly havoc, slicing through limbs and hewing torsos with well-aimed swipes.

By now the orcs numbered just four, their slain comrades littering the ground around them and drenching the soil with their blood. Closing ranks, the last of the beasts prepared for a joint attack. The dwarves immediately drew together, standing back-to-back.

"Huzzah! That's more like it!" shouted Tungdil's savior, his eyes gleaming maniacally.

Rather than wait for the orcs to engage them, they whirled their way forward into the mob, spinning on their axis like a dancer in a music box, each warning the other in dwarfish of any threats from behind.

This unconventional strategy secured the dwarves a speedy victory against their more numerous foes. The last orc went to his death to the sound of their laughter and cries of "oink, oink!"

Tungdil was profoundly impressed. The dwarven warriors had dispatched an entire band of orcs without incurring so much as a scratch. He gazed at them in dumb admiration, then realized he had done nothing to help.

"May the fire of Vraccas's furnace burn in you forever," the second dwarf greeted him. "My name is Boëndal Hookhand of the clan of the Swinging Axes and this is my twin brother,

Boïndil Doubleblade or Ireheart, if you prefer. Secondlings, the pair of us." His friendly brown eyes studied Tungdil shrewdly.

"You can see straightaway that he wouldn't stand a chance against a band of orcs," his brother said, guffawing. "He had enough trouble with just one of those runts. What kind of idiot drops his only ax?" He checked himself and looked at Tungdil. "I'm assuming you weren't planning to strangle them with your bare hands?"

"Oh no, sir," said Tungdil. "I'd be dead by now if you hadn't come along." He blinked. There was something peculiar about Boïndil's eyes, a strange flicker that gave him a rather frenzied look. He was probably still fired up from the battle.

"There are no sirs here," said Boëndal with a smile. "We dwarves were all hewn from the same rock."

"Absolutely, I'm sorry. All the same, you saved my l-life," stuttered Tungdil, his relief at being rescued already eclipsed by the excitement of meeting others of his race: For the first time since Ionandar—for the first time *ever*—he was face-to-face with real dwarves. A thousand questions jostled for attention in his head.

Boëndal's plait rippled down his back like a long black snake as he shook his head good-naturedly. "You don't have to be grateful. We'd do the same for any dwarf."

"Even a thirdling," chortled Boïndil, "although we'd give him a good hiding as well." He bent down to wipe his gore-encrusted axes in the long grass.

"It took us a while to find you." Boëndal paused. "You *are* Tungdil Bolofar, aren't you?"

"What a name!" his brother grumbled. "Bolofar! It's not some magical piffle paffle, is it?"

Tungdil's astonishment was stamped on his face. "Yes, that's me," he said slowly. "But how did you—"

"What's the name of your magus and the purpose of your journey?" the twins demanded.

"Lot-Ionan the Forbearing is my magus, and as for my journey…" He paused, then continued firmly. "You have my undying gratitude and deepest respect, but the purpose of my journey is my own private business and I'm not ready to share it with you yet."

Boïndil roared with laughter. "Pompous as a scholar, but I like his spirit." He clapped Tungdil on the back. "Don't worry. Lot-Ionan told us that he'd sent you to look for Gorén. We wanted to be sure that we had the right dwarf."

"The right dwarf?" For a moment Tungdil was mystified; then he remembered Lot-Ionan's letter to the secondlings. "My clansfolk want to meet me!" He could barely keep the excitement from his voice. "But why the escort? Is it because of the orcs?"

"That too, but it's more a matter of getting you safely to the high king. Gundrabur is expecting you as a matter of urgency," explained Boëndal, tearing a scrap of cloth from an orcish jerkin and carefully wiping his crow's beak.

His brother produced an oily rag and polished his gleaming axes. "Someone should get the orcs an escort," he chuckled. "Vraccas knows they need all the help they can get."

"The high king," Tungdil whispered, awestruck. "What an honor! But why would he want to see me?"

"We're supposed to get you back to Ogre's Death so you and the other contender can stake your claims to the throne." He made it sound like the most natural thing in the world.

"My claim?" Tungdil echoed incredulously. He looked at the twins' craggy faces. "What claim? Which throne? What's this got to do with me?"

"He should change his name to Baffledbrain!" wheezed Boïndil. "Well, fry me an elf if the poor fellow isn't quite ignorant! Let's get away from these snout-features before the stench makes me vomit. I say we walk another mile or so, set up camp, and tell him everything, agreed?" He looked to his twin for confirmation.

Tungdil wasn't consulted on the matter, but luckily for the others, he was dying of curiosity and followed without a fuss. They marched for a while, then left the path and camped in the woods.

"There's nothing better than a decent meal after a hard-fought victory." Boïndil kindled the fire, skewered some cheese, and held it above the flames.

"And after a defeat?"

"If you're dead, your belly won't bother you. In any event, Vraccas will give you some victuals from his smithy."

The smell of molten cheese was overpowering. Tungdil choked. "I think I know that aroma. I smelled it when I pulled off my boots after twenty-one orbits of walking."

"Oh, our food isn't good enough for you, is it?" said Boïndil, trying to copy Tungdil's look of disdain. "This is the best cheese in the kingdom, I'll have you know. Come on, give him a piece, Boëndal. It's time he got used to the taste. Living with humans has spoiled his palate."

His brother cut a slice of bread and handed it to Tungdil with some cured ham and cheese. "Right, I suppose you want an explanation. I'll make it brief: The high king is dying and a fourthling must claim his throne. Gundrabur found out about your secret because of the magus's letter."

"My secret?" groaned Tungdil. "I didn't know I had one." He still hadn't convinced himself to eat the cheese. It was all a bit too much.

"It's time you learned the truth, then. You weren't stolen by kobolds. The long-uns made that up so you—"

"Long-uns?"

"It's dwarfish for *men*—just a little joke. In any event, the magus didn't want to burden you with the story until it was time." Boëndal handed him the water canteen. "So there you have it: You're a fourthling."

Tungdil thought about Girdlegard's geography. "I can't be. The fourthling kingdom is miles away."

"There was a good reason for the distance," Boëndal said soberly. "You're the son of the fourthling king—illegitimate, mind. The birth was kept a secret and you were entrusted to the care of friends. When the queen found out, she was furious. No bastard child of her husband's was going to lay claim to the throne while she was around to stop it. She wanted you dead."

"Are you going to eat that cheese?" Boïndil interrupted. "It'll fall into the fire if you don't get on with it soon." Tungdil handed him the skewer wordlessly and the warrior wolfed it down. "Much appreciated."

Boëndal resumed his account. "Your adopted family took pity on you and carried you off. They took you to Lot-Ionan for one simple reason: No one would ever think of looking in a magus's household for a dwarf."

"You do realize that dwarves have no truck with the long-uns' wizardry, don't you?" Boïndil said suspiciously.

"Quiet!" his brother shushed him. "Just let me finish." He turned back to Tungdil. "So now you know why you grew up in Ionandar, miles from your kinsfolk. When the assembly of dwarves heard of your existence, it was obliged to summon you in accordance with our laws and consider your claim to the throne."

Tungdil held the canteen to his lips and took a long draft. "I don't mean to be rude," he murmured weakly, "but it can't be true. Lot-Ionan would have told me."

"He intended to tell you on your return." Boëndal produced a letter from his pack. It was written in the magus's hand. "He gave me this, in case you didn't believe us."

Tungdil unfurled the parchment, fingers trembling, and scanned the lines. The story was true, down to the last detail.

All I wanted was to meet a few of my kinsfolk, not be crowned king of all dwarves. "I'm sorry," he said, "but I can't do it. I'll gladly accompany you to Ogre's Death, but the other contender should be crowned." He laughed wryly. "How could I rule over anyone? No one will ever accept me as a dwarf. They'll think I'm a—"

Suddenly a morsel of stinking cheese was thrust under his nose. "Stop grousing," snapped Boïndil. "It's a long way to Ogre's Death. We'll make a dwarf of you yet." The molten cheese wobbled threateningly. "You may as well start now." He still had a faintly crazed look in his eyes. "Go on, taste it!"

Tungdil pulled the warm cheese from the stick and popped it in his mouth. It tasted revolting. His fingers would reek for orbits, not to mention his breath. "I can't do it," he said firmly. "I promised to deliver the pouch to Gorén."

"You don't have to come right away," Boïndil said magnanimously. "It's not far from here to Greenglade village. We'll go with you."

His brother nodded. "And you don't have to worry about the magus; he's given us his blessing already."

"What if you were to return without me?"

The brothers exchanged a look.

"Well," Boëndal said thoughtfully, "I expect they'd crown Gandogar, but no one would ever accept him as the rightful king." He fixed his brother with a meaningful stare.

"Exactly," Boïndil put in quickly. "There'd be all kinds of arguments and whatnot. Some of the chieftains might even...well, they wouldn't take orders from him, so before you know it, there'd be terrible feuds and..." He gazed into the flames for inspiration, then rushed on. "It could all end in war! The clans and the folks would fight each other, and you'd be to blame!" He sat back with a satisfied expression on his face.

Tungdil didn't know what to make of it all. Too much had happened since that morning. Having never raised his ax in anger, he had slain two orcs in succession and now his kinsfolk were trying to bundle him onto the throne. He needed time to reflect. "I'll think it over," he promised them, curling up beside the fire and closing his eyes wearily.

Boïndil cleared his throat and began to sing. It was a dwarven ballad with deep mysterious syllables that charmed the ear, telling of the time before time began...

Desirous of life, the deities fashioned themselves.
Vraccas the Smith was forged from fire, rock, and steel.
Palandiell the Bountiful rose from the earth.
The winds gave birth to Samusin the Rash.
Elria the Helpful, creator and destroyer, emerged from
    the water.
And darkness fused with light in Tion the Two-Faced.
Such are the five deities, the...

For Tungdil, the song ended there. It was the first time in his life that he had heard a dwarven ballad sung by his kin and the sound was so soothing that it lulled him to sleep.

Tungdil awoke with the smell of cheese in his nostrils and his mind made up: He would go with the twins to the secondling kingdom. His doubts had been conquered by a desire to meet more of his kin.

"Just so you know, I haven't changed my mind about being

high king," he told them. "I'm doing this only because I want to see my kinsfolk."

"It's all the same to us," Boëndal said equably. "The main thing is you've decided to come." He and his brother packed their bags and they set off briskly. "The sooner we get to Greenglade, the sooner we'll be home. Eight hundred miles are a good long way."

"We'll accompany you to the edge of the village and no farther," snapped Boïndil. "We want nothing to do with that elf maiden. It's bad enough having to walk through an elfish forest, let alone visit an elf house or whatever they build for themselves." He made a show of spitting into the bushes.

"What did the elf maiden ever do to you?" Tungdil ran his hand over Gorén's bag; there was no avoiding the fact that some of the artifacts were no longer in their original state. The encounter with the orc's sword had done them no favors, which made him doubly certain that the beast had deserved its fate. "Six hundred miles!" he muttered crossly. "Six hundred miles through Gauragar, through Lios Nudin, past beasts and other dangers without the artifacts coming to any harm, only for a confounded orc to ruin everything. Another three or four hours and I could have handed them over, safe and sound!" He hoped the wizard would be understanding.

Boïndil's mind was still on the elves. "Oh, *she* didn't have to do anything! Her race has caused enough trouble as it is," he blurted out angrily. "Those self-satisfied, arrogant pointy-ears are enough to—"

Overcome with fury, he whipped out his axes and fell upon a sapling, swinging at it with unbridled rage.

Boëndal, an impassive expression on his face, lowered his packs, pushed his long plait over his shoulder, and waited for the outburst to end.

"He does this sometimes," he explained to the dumbfounded Tungdil. "His inner furnace burns stronger than most. Sometimes it flares up and he can't contain his anger. It's why we call him Ireheart."

"His inner furnace?"

"Vraccas alone can explain it. Anyway, take my advice and keep out of his way. It's fatal to challenge him when he gets like this." Boëndal sighed. "He'll be all right again once his furnace has cooled."

Boïndil finished hacking the sapling to pieces. "Bloody pointy-ears! I feel better now." Without a word of apology, he wiped the sap and splinters from his blades and carried on. "We need to find a proper name for you," he grumbled. "Bolofar is no better than Bellyfluff, Sillystuff, or Starchyruff; it's plain daft! We'll come up with something on the way." He glanced at Tungdil. "What are your talents?"

"Er, reading…"

"Book-learning!" Boëndal burst out laughing. "I should have guessed you were a scholar! But we can't call you Pagemuncher or Bookeater. Dwarves should be proud of their names!"

"Reading's important. It—"

"Oh, books are very useful when it comes to fighting orcs. You could have killed the whole band of them with the right bit of poetry!"

Boïndil looked at Tungdil and frowned. "No one could call you a warrior, but you've certainly got the build for it. Your hands are nice and strong—with a bit of practice, it might come right."

Tungdil sighed. "I like metalwork."

"That's not exactly unusual for a dwarf. How about—" Boëndal trailed off and sniffed the air attentively. His brother did the same. "Something's burning," he told them, alarmed. "Wood and…scorched flesh! It must be a raid." Boïndil pulled out both axes and broke into a jog. The other two followed.

The trees grew farther apart as the path rounded a corner and emerged into a clearing. Until recently, the spot had been home to a settlement, but the elf maiden's haven at the heart of the forest had been ravaged by flames. Charred ruins hinted at the former elegance of the many-platformed dwellings that were set about the boles of the tallest trees. The carved arches, smooth wooden beams, and panels embellished with elven runes and gold leaf were so perfectly at one with the forest that they seemed to have grown with the wood.

But most of the gold was missing and the beauty of the glade had been savagely destroyed. For the second time on Tungdil's journey, the orcs had got there first. He tried in vain to recapture something of the leafy harmony, but the desecration was complete. "By Vraccas," he gulped. "We'd better see whether—"

"Absolutely," Boïndil said cheerily. "With any luck, we'll find a few runts. You've got to hand it to them: We couldn't have done a better job ourselves!"

"It's what you'd call rigorous," his brother said admiringly, gripping the haft of his hammer. As true children of the Smith, the twins were unruffled by the wreckage around them; it wasn't in their nature to feel pity for elves.

Tungdil felt differently. Wandering through the smoldering ruins, he lifted up planks and peered under girders in the hope of finding Gorén alive. Instead he found corpse after corpse, some of them horribly mutilated. At the sight of the carnage, memories of Goodwater came flooding back and he stepped away from the bodies, closing his eyes to the horror. The images stayed with him, more gruesome than ever in his mind.

Pull yourself together, he told himself firmly. *How are you going to recognize Gorén if you find him? Where would a wizard hide if he survived?* Tungdil's gaze settled on the largest dwelling, which had come off slightly better than the rest.

"Keep an eye out for any trouble," he called to the others. "I need to find out what's happened to Gorén."

"I've changed my mind," Boïndil shouted jauntily to his brother. "Forget what I said earlier about not going in. We might find some orcs."

While the twins began patrolling the ruins, Tungdil climbed the sagging staircase toward the front door. The charred steps groaned beneath his feet, but at last he reached the first platform and walked across the blackened planks.

The house was pentagonal in form, with the bole of the tree at its center. Linking the rooms was a corridor that encircled the trunk, its inner wall comprised of bark. Rope bridges led out to the sturdier branches where colored lanterns swung mournfully in the breeze.

Leaves were already floating to the ground, as if the tree were mourning the elves who had lived among its branches for so many cycles.

Tungdil gazed at the fluttering foliage, then tore himself away and searched the rooms. There was no sign of Gorén or any survivors, but the library had been spared the worst of the damage and he came upon a sealed envelope addressed to Lot-Ionan and some objects wrapped in a shawl.

He picked up the envelope and hesitated. *Surely these are exceptional circumstances by any standard?* He broke the seal, scanned the contents, and sighed. *Yet another errand for me to run!* In the letter, Gorén thanked Lot-Ionan for the loan of some books. The wizard had evidently intended to return them by courier, which meant Tungdil had landed himself another job.

There was a second letter, written in scholarly script and therefore indecipherable to anyone but a high-ranking wizard. He packed it away with the other items and continued his search.

A shudder ran through the platform. It started as a slight tremor, but in no time the planks were shaking violently. The wooden dwelling groaned and creaked furiously; then the commotion stopped as suddenly as it had begun. The dwarf took it as a sign that it was time for him to leave.

He hurried into the corridor and stopped in surprise. The tree was moving, its leafless branches squeezing and crushing the groaning timber of the house. The trunk gave a ligneous grunt and swayed to the left. A gnarled bough swung toward him.

"Hey! You've got the wrong dwarf! I'm not the one who killed the sapling!"

The tree took no heed of his protests and swiped at him again. Tungdil ducked, the cudgel-like branch smashing into the paneled wall behind him. He darted to the steps, but found himself engulfed in a sea of white. In his confusion he thought for a moment that it was snowing; then he saw that the haze was made up of petals that were swirling around the tree. The flowers and trees of the forest were hurling their blossoms at him, the glade's shattered harmony turning to violent hatred.

The house shook again, this time cracking some of the joists and sending debris crashing to the ground. Tungdil clattered down the steps to safety.

The twins were no less surprised than he was. Weapons at the ready, they were eyeing the glade suspiciously.

"It's nasty elfish magic!" shouted Boïndil above the din of rustling leaves. "They've turned the trees against us."

"We'd better get out of here," Tungdil called to them. "The trees mean to punish anyone who—" He broke off as a Palandiell beech loosed a shower of withered leaves, exposing the gruesome secret hidden among its naked boughs.

They had found the elf maiden. Her delicate white visage, previously obscured by a thick screen of leaves, stood out against the murky bark. From the neck down she was a skeleton, stripped entirely of flesh but glistening wetly with crimson blood. Long metal nails pinned her slender limbs to the trunk.

The sight was too much, even for the otherwise imperturbable twins. "Vraccas almighty," exclaimed Boëndal, "what kind of mischief is this?"

"That settles it," his brother decided. "We're leaving before the same thing happens to us."

"Not yet," Tungdil told them. "I need to keep looking for Gorén." The horror exercised a strange attraction on him and he walked on, obliging his companions to follow. "The wizard's body might be somewhere round here too."

On closer inspection, it looked as though the elf maiden's bones had been gnawed. Her murderers had finished the job by driving a nail through her mouth, pinning the back of her skull to the bole of the tree. In place of her beautiful elven eyes were two empty sockets.

"They pinned her to the tree and ate her alive," said Boïndil. "It's a bit too fancy for runts. They eat their victims on the spot and suck out their marrow."

Tungdil swallowed and took another look. Even in death, the elf's face had retained its beauty. For all his inborn antipathy toward her and her race, he was sorry she had ended so gruesomely.

Boëndal rounded the tree and discovered further corpses as well as a trail of curved black prints. "They're hoof marks, but they've been burned into the soil. What do you make of that, scholar?"

Tungdil remembered the two riders who had parleyed with the orcish war bands on the night before Goodwater was destroyed. "Shadow mares," he murmured. "They strike sparks as they walk. The älfar ride them." It explained why the elf maiden had suffered so cruelly before she died: The älfar took pleasure in torturing their cousins.

"Älfar?" Boïndil's eyes flashed with enthusiasm. "It's about time we came up against something more challenging than those dim-witted orcs! How about it, brother? I say we blunt our axes on Tion's dark elves!"

Tungdil, his gaze still riveted on the skeleton, was beset by awful visions of the mistress of Greenglade writhing and screaming on the tree while shadow mares ripped the flesh from her bones. The urge to vomit became uncontrollable and he covered his mouth with his hand, unwilling to forfeit the last shreds of credibility in front of the twins.

One corpse, a male body crumpled not far from the tree, excited their particular attention. A circle of scorched earth bounded the patch of grass where the dead man was lying, pierced by arrows. By the dwarves' reckoning, seven orcs had perished in the towering ring of flames.

Tungdil was as good as certain that magic had been involved. "I think we've found Gorén. He probably conjured the ring of fire to defend himself."

Hands trembling, he searched the dead man's pockets and brought out a small metal tin engraved with Gorén's name.

"He would have done better with a shield," Boïndil said dryly. "I always said that magic can't be trusted."

His brother's gaze was fixed on the rustling trees that were shedding their leaves furiously in spite of the season. "There's something wrong with this place," he decided. "If we hang around much longer, those trees will tear up their roots and attack us. We're leaving."

"What about Gorén and the others?" objected Tungdil. "Don't you think we should—"

"What about them? They're dead," Boïndil said breezily.

"Elves, elf lovers, and orcs." Boëndal set off at a march. "They needn't concern us."

As far as the twins were concerned, the matter was settled, so Tungdil fell in behind them, hurrying through the ruined village in the direction from which they had come.

Before they reached the path, he glanced round to bid the wizard and his mistress a silent farewell and apologize for leaving them without a proper burial. It was then that he saw something strange.

An easel, he thought to himself in surprise. In spite of the surrounding wreckage, it was standing upright, as though the painter would be back at any moment. Tungdil felt sadder than ever at the thought of the elf maiden or one of her companions abandoning their work in terror. The unfinished painting was a silent testimony to the moment in which the invaders had arrived.

I wonder what she was painting. "Back in a minute!" he told the others as he clambered over the charred timber, curious to see the elven artwork.

Boëndal sighed resignedly, setting his beard aquiver. "We've got our work cut out with this one."

"You can say that again," Boïndil said testily, wiping his sweaty brow with the end of his plait. Muttering under their breath, the secondlings hurried after their charge.

They caught up with him in front of the easel. There was something very obviously wrong with the picture: It showed the settlement in the aftermath of the attack.

There was no denying that the artist was incredibly gifted. The scene had been painted entirely in shades of red, every detail of the destruction reproduced with chilling precision on the smooth white canvas: corpses, the burned-out shells of buildings, scorched trees.

Tungdil peered at the work more closely. *There's something funny about that canvas*. He walked to the back of the easel and paled. The reverse of the painting was a damp, shiny red. He reached out gingerly to touch it, then whipped his hand away. *Skin!* The scene had been painted on skin so flawless that it could only belong to the mistress of the glade. Tungdil had a nasty feeling that the paint was far from conventional too. He showed his grisly discovery to the twins.

Two smaller pictures had been propped up nearby. The first showed the tortured face of the elf, her eyes dull with pain and fear. The second depicted her crucified body in all its gory detail. Tungdil knocked them over in disgust.

"It's still wet," said Boëndal, peering at the easel. "The freak who painted these pictures could be back at any time."

"So much the better," growled Boïndil. "We'll see how he likes to be flayed alive."

"I've never seen anything so monstrous," said Tungdil. Any admiration he still felt for the artist's talent was overshadowed by his revulsion at the foulness of the work. He shouldered the easel and hurled it into the burning embers of the fire. The two smaller pictures met the same fate.

Silently they turned to leave the village, but were halted by an aggressive snort. It was followed by angry neighing and a furious whinny.

A black steed left the forest and stepped into the clearing twenty paces to their right. Its eyes gleamed red, and white sparks danced around its fetlocks as its hooves clipped the ground.

Mounted on the shadow mare was a female älf, tall and slim with long brown hair. She was clad in mail of stiff black leather with polished tionium trimmings.

"What do we have here?" The hilt of her sword was visible

above her head and in her right hand she held a curved bow. A clutch of unusually long arrows of the kind favored by älfar protruded from a saddlebag. Tungdil needed no reminder of their murderous force.

"The stinking groundlings have ruined my pictures, have they? In that case, I'll need some fresh paint." She sat up in the saddle to get a better look at the dwarves. With her delicate features and fine countenance she could have passed for a creature of Palandiell, save for the gaping eye sockets that proved she was no elf.

"I hope your blood doesn't clot too fast," she said, reaching with her free hand for an arrow. "I won't be able to paint the finer details unless it's nice and fluid."

"I was beginning to think we'd been cheated of our battle." Boïndil grinned. "Quick," he instructed in dwarfish, "make for the ruins or she'll shoot us down like rabbits."

The first arrow came singing toward them just as they were ducking behind a timber wall. It passed through the wood as if it were parchment and struck Boëndal's mail with a *ping*. The black tionium cut a gouge in the metal, causing the dwarf to curse.

Keeping low, they scurried deeper into the smoldering village, hoping to throw off the älf, then attack her from behind.

Tungdil peered around the next corner and spotted the slender nose of the mare. There was something feline about the way it slunk through the ruins, branding the ground with its hooves. The earth gave a low hiss as the false unicorn passed over it, nostrils flaring as it tracked its prey.

Suddenly the dwarf had a terrifying thought. The mare's saddle was empty. *Where's the rider?* The älf was at large in the village. He closed his eyes, trying to forget everything he knew about her race.

When he opened them again, Boëndal and Boïndil were gone. He wasn't afraid anymore; he was panicked.

"Psst," he hissed, "where are you?" He tightened his grip on his ax, cursing the twins for abandoning him in the ruins. *First they tell me I'm no warrior; then they leave me at the mercy of a shadow mare and an älf!*

Someone touched his arm. Tungdil started and lashed out with his ax. The blade buried itself just below the man's rib cage. The dwarf stared at him in horror. "Gorén? I thought you were dead."

The wizard looked at the wound distractedly and ran his fingers across the gaping flesh. He fixed his gaze on Tungdil. "Nothing," he moaned softly. "I feel nothing." He plucked an orcish arrow from his body. "Nothing," he said again, this time more desperately. He reached for a wooden beam, locking the dwarf in his empty stare. "All I can feel is hate..."

"Hang on, Gorén, I..." Tungdil leaped aside as the wizard brought the beam crashing toward him. It smashed into a wall.

The din was enough to alert everyone to their presence. There was a clatter of hooves and the shadow mare whinnied.

Tungdil made his escape by crawling under a sunken ceiling. Anything would be better than being discovered by the mare.

"Nothing..." Gorén straightened up and swayed drunkenly out of the ruined building, dragging the beam behind him.

The shadow mare leaped toward him, trampling him to the ground. Tungdil watched as its forelegs crushed the wizard's abdomen in an explosion of sparks. To the dwarf's horror, Gorén rolled over and picked himself up.

The truth hit him in a flash: Greenglade had fallen to the Perished Land. *Any who die here will rise again as revenants!* The forest wasn't grieving for the elf maiden; the canker had spread into the soil, poisoning the tree roots and filling the trunks and branches with malice.

But that's impossible! Unless... Tungdil realized with horrible certainty that the girdle had failed. *I can't go to Ogre's Death without warning Lot-Ionan that the shield has been breached. If the Perished Land has encroached this far, it might be advancing on other fronts as well.*

But first he faced the immediate problem of leaving the glade alive, and the odds were stacked against him.

The shadow mare had picked up his scent and was heading his way. Its hooves struck Tungdil's hiding place and the timber erupted, crackling with light. The steed was intent on driving the dwarf into the open.

Tungdil had no choice. He rolled out, hoping to throw himself under the nearest piece of debris, but the shadow mare was faster.

In a single powerful leap, it soared over the wreckage and landed beside him, its head shooting forward to seize Tungdil's right shoulder in its jaws. The dwarf's chain mail saved him from its sharp teeth, but the pressure was excruciating.

"Get your filthy teeth off me!" Tungdil's fighting spirit came to the fore, and he forgot his terror, swinging his ax at the steed.

But the shadow mare had no intention of relinquishing its quarry. Jerking its head, it shook Tungdil back and forth like a doll. Without warning, its jaws flew open and he sailed through the air, landing on the ashen grass with a thud. The shadow mare whinnied, carving deep furrows as it pawed the ground. Tungdil was still coming to his senses when it thundered toward him.

The twins sprang into action. As the mare drew level with them, they burst out of their hiding places on either side of its path.

"Here, horsey, horsey," shouted Boïndil, driving an ax with both hands into the steed's right knee. Boëndal's crow's beak carved into its left foreleg.

The black beast staggered and fell, tumbling along the ground in a pother of ash. In spite of its obvious agony, it tried to drag itself up again, but the dwarves rushed in.

"You're not a horse anymore, you're a pony," Boïndil yelled at it. "How do you fancy fighting eye to eye?" The shadow mare lunged at him and was rewarded with an ax blow to the jaw. "Try sinking your teeth into that!" The mare jerked away, thereby sealing its fate.

Boëndal embedded his beaked war hammer into its long bony nose and hauled the beast in. Not for nothing was Hookhand his second name. Triceps bulging and heels digging into the ground, he dragged the mare closer so that his brother could sink an ax into its neck.

"So you want to bite me, you worthless bunch of bones," cried Boïndil, hefting his ax to strike again. The blade severed the shadow mare's spinal cord and it slumped to the ground.

Boëndal put one foot on the steed's nose and levered the crow's beak out of the corpse.

His brother grinned at him. "Now for the pointy-eared rider!" He signaled to Tungdil to stay hidden. "Make yourself scarce, scholar, and watch how it's done!"

They crouched next to the mare's fallen body and waited. Tungdil started to tell them about his encounter with the revenant, but they waved him away. All that mattered for the moment was dispatching the älf.

Before long an unnatural scream, more drawn out and high-pitched than the voice of any human female, rent the air.

Waggling his eyebrows in gleeful anticipation, Boïndil straightened his plait and steeled himself for combat. "Music to my ears."

Boëndal listened intently, then leaped to his feet. His brother followed.

I should be out there helping, not watching like a coward. Tungdil felt compelled to do something, even if only to act as a decoy. Sighing, he was about to emerge from his hiding place when two skeletal hands grabbed him from behind and thrust him to the ground.

"Who are you?" a musical voice demanded. Damp, foul-smelling bones fingered his face. "A small man or maybe a groundling..."

The dwarf was rolled onto his back and found himself looking into the tortured face of the once-beautiful elf. She too had become a revenant. Robbed of her eyes by the älfar, she had torn herself from the trunk of the beech and was groping blindly through the ruins.

"Let go of me!" shrieked Tungdil, reaching for his ax. His arms were clamped so tightly that he went for his dagger instead. The blade clunked harmlessly against her rib cage.

"Who gave a dwarf permission to enter my glade?" she demanded imperiously. A bony hand tightened around his throat. "Are you in league with the älfar? Do you hate us enough to ally yourselves with these monsters?"

Tungdil fought back his fear and realized that there was something different about her tone of voice. Unlike the wizard, she seemed to be in possession of her will. "Listen to me, my lady," he pleaded. "Lot-Ionan sent me here to return some items belonging to Gorén."

She turned her fathomless gaze on him. "I'm changing," she whispered fearfully. "Something's happening to me. They killed me, but my soul...my soul..." She trailed off. "You say Lot-Ionan sent you? My beloved Gorén thought highly of his magus." She released her murderous grip. "You'll find a book in the house; it's in the library. Gorén was going to send it to your master, but then the älfar attacked and—"

"I've got it already," he broke in excitedly.

"Don't let them have it!" she instructed. "Take it to Ionandar and give it to the magus; he'll know what to do as soon as he reads the letter." Her skeletal fingers clutched at him again. "Swear you'll do it!"

Tungdil stammered out a solemn oath, swearing first by Vraccas and then by the magus. The elf seemed satisfied and backed away.

"Now behead me," she said softly. "I can't allow the Perished Land to steal the little I have left." She stretched out her bony arms. "Do you see what they've done to me? Without your help, I'll be yoked to their evil forever, a blind servant of destruction."

There was something almost mesmerizing about the two dark pits in her face. Tungdil hesitated. "But I—"

"Everything I loved has been taken from me: Gorén, my beauty, my home, my glade." She raised her left hand and poked a finger gingerly into her empty eye sockets. "Look, even tears are denied me. Have pity on me."

Her face and voice spoke so eloquently of her sorrow that Tungdil had no option but to comply. He rose to his feet, took a few shaky steps toward her, and swung his ax. As the elf's head rolled through the debris, her skeletal body slumped to the ground. The lady of the glade was dead.

The trees around them gave a piteous groan, the crackling and rustling mingling with the sounds of a raging battle. Tungdil remembered with a start that the twins were locked in combat with the älf.

They still don't realize! he thought in alarm, quickly pulling himself together. *If we don't decapitate the corpses, they'll rise up and attack us.*

Meanwhile, Boëndal and Boïndil had discovered that their opponent had no intention of playing by their rules. The älf was nimble as a cat, ducking, skipping, and leaping to evade their blows. But for all her agility she had yet to penetrate the dwarves' heavy mail.

"Over here!" Tungdil lunged forward and hurled his ax. The älf spotted the missile just in time and stepped aside briskly.

Suddenly Gorén loomed up behind her, swinging a plank. She heard the wood whistling toward her, but it was too late to move.

The plank connected with her back, catapulting her forward. With a cackle of frenzied laughter, Boïndil rushed up and took aim at her thinly armored thighs. "Fight on my level, no-eyes!"

The axes sliced deep into her flesh and the älf shrieked in agony, only to be winded by Boëndal, who rammed the butt of his crow's beak into her belly. Before she could make another sound, Boïndil raised his blades and hewed her neck.

"What did you do that for?" he asked the wizard indignantly. "Couldn't you see we almost had her?" Puzzled, he stared as Gorén staggered toward him. "Hang on, shouldn't he be dead?"

"He won't die unless you behead him!" Tungdil called out to him. "This is the Perished Land. You've got to chop his head off!"

"Well, if you insist..." Boïndil dodged the wizard's clumsy attempts to fell him and sliced off his head with a single strike of his ax. Gorén was no more.

"Seeing as we're here, we should probably take care of the rest," said Boëndal, nodding in the direction of the ruins.

Brought back to life by the dark power, the charred corpses of the orcs and the elves were beginning to stir. The Perished Land made no distinction between its own soldiers and those who had died at their hands, so the twins were obliged to execute their task with utmost rigor, fighting and beheading every single revenant in order to deliver them from their fate. Tungdil chose to watch.

"They could have tried a bit harder," complained Boïndil when the gory business was over at last. "At least it's out of my system, though." Sure enough, the glint in his eyes was slowly fading. "Shall we go?"

They set off on a southerly bearing, quickly leaving the ravaged village behind them.

Perhaps the trees wanted to do a last favor to those who had slain one of the despoilers of the peaceful glade, but in any event they made no attempt to block their path. Creaking and groaning, the leafless boles and boughs swayed menacingly, stooping low and swinging above their heads, but allowing them to pass.

The only other sound was the crackling of dry leaves beneath their boots. They saw no sign of the forest's many animals; even the birds were too afraid to sing.

"There's been a change of plan," Tungdil informed the twins, recounting his promise to the elf. "Ionandar is far enough west to be safe from the Perished Land and Toboribor's orcs. We need to tell Lot-Ionan about Greenglade and give him the books. The elf maiden seemed to think at least one was important."

"But we won't get back to Ogre's Death for ages!" objected Boëndal. "We're late enough as it is, without walking an extra six hundred miles."

"I'm afraid there's no choice," Tungdil said firmly. "It's either that or ask to see the council in Lios Nudin."

"That's the spirit," chuckled Boïndil. "Cussed as a dwarf!"

Boëndal relented. "All right, we'll go to Lios Nudin. The high king has seen so many cycles that he won't begrudge us the odd orbit here or there. Vraccas will keep his fires burning." He took a sip from his water pouch.

His brother turned the conversation to Tungdil's fighting prowess. "You didn't do too badly, considering you haven't been taught," he commended him. "But there's one thing you need to remember: Never throw your ax unless you've got another one in reserve. Of course your technique needs a bit of working on, but I'll soon have you fighting like a proper dwarf. Mark my words, Tungdil: The runts will be as scared of you as they are of me."

Tungdil could see the sense in being tutored by Boïndil. "The sooner we get started, the better." He nodded.

They walked until the light faded and they were obliged to stop and rest. After a while Boëndal launched into a dwarven ballad about the age-old feud between their kinsfolk and the elves. When he saw the look of dismay on Tungdil's face, he trailed off into silence: The last thing they needed was a song about destruction and death.

"What do you know about my folk?" Tungdil asked.

"The fourthlings?" Boëndal scratched his beard and unpacked a wedge of cheese to melt above the fire. "Goïmdil's folk are made up of twelve clans and they tend to be shorter, scrawnier, and weaker than the rest of us—typical gem cutters and diamond polishers, I suppose." He looked Tungdil up and down and nodded. "I've never heard of any fourthling scholars, but in terms of your build...Actually, you're a bit too big. Your shoulders are too broad." He thought for a moment. "I'm not trying to offend you, you know," he said simply. "Vraccas made us just the way we are."

"What else do you know?" persisted Tungdil, who found the answer too vague to be revealing.

The brothers looked at each other and shrugged.

"You'd best see for yourself once we get there. It's been

hundreds of cycles since the folks had anything to do with each other," Boëndal explained. "I'll tell you what, though: We may not know much about Goïmdil's dwarves, but you can ask us anything about the secondlings. Our seventeen clans boast the finest masons in all the dwarven kingdoms, and the mightiest human stronghold isn't a patch on Ogre's Death. It'll take your breath away, you'll see."

Boëndal talked and talked, waxing lyrical about the fortifications and ornaments that were the envy of the other folks, while Tungdil listened contentedly, eagerly anticipating the moment when he would see his kinsfolk's architecture for himself.

Enchanted Realm of Lios Nudin,
Girdlegard,
Summer, 6234th Solar Cycle

The orbits wore on as the three dwarves journeyed to Porista to request an audience with the council.

At Boïndil's insistence, they had taken the precaution of walking through the undergrowth parallel to the road, but by the fourth orbit they were tired of scratching themselves on branches, finding thorns in their chain mail, and avoiding twigs that seemed determined to poke Tungdil in the nose or eye. They rejoined the dusty road, keeping an eye out for other travelers.

Tungdil still bore the scars of his recent ordeals. His sleep was haunted by nightmares and on stopping to fill his pouch from a stream, he noticed that the reflection looking back at him was older, more weathered, and more serious than before. The horrors he had witnessed were inscribed on his face.

Determined not to fall victim to the orcs, Tungdil applied himself to his daily training sessions with Boïndil. He was a fast learner—uncannily fast, his tutor said. While the two of them practiced fighting, parrying, and feinting, Boëndal sat and watched them, smoking his pipe and keeping his thoughts to himself.

From time to time they came upon wayfarers or a settlement and Tungdil was always sure to mention Greenglade and warn anyone from venturing too close to the Perished Land.

The long line of carts rolling into Lios Nudin reinforced his advice. With war bands of orcs terrorizing Gauragar, people preferred to trust Nudin the Knowledge-Lusty rather than rely on King Bruron to protect them.

It was midafternoon when Tungdil fell back a few paces. Guessing that he wanted to answer a call of nature, the twins walked ahead.

When Tungdil set off again, feeling much relieved, he came to a junction, only to find that Boëndal and Boïndil were nowhere to be seen. A signpost pointed east to Porista, so he set off at a jog.

A short distance along the road was a wooden caravan, its sides painted gaily with pictures of scissors, knives, axes, and other implements. The horses had been unhitched and the driver had abandoned his vehicle in a hurry.

"Hello?" The rear door was ajar, allowing Tungdil to peer into the darkness within. There was something odd about the situation. "Is everything all right in there?"

He drew his ax, just in case. If runts had ambushed the caravan, they might be hiding nearby. *Where are Boëndal and Boïndil when I need them?*

"Hello?" he called again, climbing the two narrow wooden rungs that led up to the door. He pushed it open with the poll of his ax and glanced around the little workshop. Drawers had been turned out, cupboards pulled open, and in the far corner a pair of shoes poked out from under a cabinet.

He stepped inside. "Hello in there! Is something the matter?" The smell of metal was mixed with a sweeter, almost sickly, odor. *Blood*. Tungdil had seen enough to suspect that the wearer of the shoes was no longer among the living. *I knew it!* There could be only one explanation for the string of calamities unfurling around him: His journey was cursed.

Hooking his ax on his belt, he bent down and gave the feet a shake. "Are you injured?" On receiving no response, he lifted the cabinet to free whoever was trapped underneath. It was a dwarf, or rather, the body of a dwarf. His throat had been cut and his head was missing. A ring of crimson gore encircled his neck, indicating that he hadn't been dead for long.

"What in the name of Vraccas is going on?" Tungdil was so perturbed by the sight of the dead dwarf that he let go of the cabinet, dropping it onto the corpse. As he stepped away, he tried to think logically. The poor victim was obviously an itinerant dwarf whose smithy had been ransacked by highwaymen. His death was an unfortunate consequence of the dreadful human greed for precious metals and coin.

No one deserves to be left like that. Tungdil grabbed the feet again and was dragging the corpse from beneath the cabinet when something clattered to the floor.

On closer inspection, the object turned out to be a blood-encrusted dagger, and although there wasn't much light inside the caravan, he was sure he had seen it before: It belonged to the brigand whose horse he had shod several weeks earlier.

Just then he heard the *clip-clop* of hooves. Peering warily out of the narrow window, he uttered a strong dwarven oath. Five armed bandits had come to a halt beside the caravan. He flattened himself against the wall and hid behind the door: Concealment was his only hope of survival against a band of seasoned warriors. Unlike Boëndal and Boïndil, he wasn't ready to fight five against one.

Heavy footsteps approached, the ladder groaned, the caravan wobbled, and a shadow blotted out the sunlight falling through the door.

Tungdil gripped his ax with both hands.

A man entered, mumbling indistinctly, and knelt beside the corpse. "Someone's been in," he called to the others. "He wasn't lying like this before." He scrabbled around for his knife. "Don't let anyone near the caravan, and hide the darned honey pot," he ordered. "The last thing we need is for people to ask what we're doing with the head of an ugly groundling."

"Stands to reason what we're doing. Earning our money like everyone else," said one of the company, laughing coarsely.

"No need to shout about it," snapped the murderer. "The little fellows are hard enough to get hold of, without every last Tom, Dick, or Harry competing for the loot. Ah, here it is!" He picked up the dagger, wiped the blade on the corpse's jerkin, and returned it to its sheath.

Straightening up, he stood for a moment in the light of the window, his mail reflecting the sun. A beam hit Tungdil's blade and rebounded. "What in the..." The murderer whirled round.

Tungdil had to act while the element of surprise was with him. Rushing forward, he drove his ax into the man's boots, cutting through the leather and cleaving the bone. In his panic he struck with such force that the blade embedded itself in the wooden floor. It took all his strength to pull it out.

The brigand bellowed in pain. If his companions hadn't noticed the commotion, they were certainly aware of it now.

"It's no worse than you deserve!" Tungdil grabbed his ax and fled. Whooping and yelling to spook the horses, he leaped out onto the road.

The panicked animals shied away, unseating their riders, who had dropped their stirrups and were preparing to dismount.

Tungdil didn't wait for them to recover, heading instead for the dense forest to the right of the highway. He knew there was no room between the trunks for the men to pursue him on horseback and the undergrowth would slow their progress if they chased him on foot. For once his diminutive stature was an advantage. Besides, daylight faded quickly beneath the thick canopy of leaves and his eyes were accustomed to seeing in the dark.

"Catch the dwarfish bastard," the company's leader commanded. "We'll get a fortune for his head."

Tungdil tore through the forest, stopping occasionally to listen. Loud curses and snapping branches informed him of the brigands' dogged pursuit, but the gap between them was growing. After a time, their heavy footsteps faded entirely, and he knew that he had given them the slip.

Leaning back against a tree trunk, he stopped to recover his breath. No amount of marching could have prepared him for sprinting through a forest, laden with bags. He made a quick check of his things; the pouch with Gorén's artifacts was still slung from his shoulder, rattling and jangling as soon as he moved. The bag had been making strange noises ever since his misadventure with the orc.

Still listening attentively for his pursuers, he took a sip of water. *The brigands are hunting dwarves for a reward*. He could scarcely believe it. Of all the terrible things that had happened, this new revelation shocked him to the core. Putting gold on dwarven lives ran counter to the laws of Girdlegard and it was hard to see the sense of it: What would anyone want with a disembodied head?

As soon as he had recovered sufficiently he made a beeline

through the forest toward the nearest path. To his astonishment, Boëndal and Boïndil were coming the other way.

"About time too!" Boïndil called out to him. "You went the wrong way!"

"I went the *right* way," Tungdil corrected him. "You missed the turn to Porista!"

Boëndal took a closer look at him. "What happened, scholar? Did you run into trouble?"

"Just my luck to miss all the excitement," his brother grumbled moodily. Then he laughed. "I know, I bet a squirrel was after his n—"

"Headhunters," Tungdil cut him off. "They're decapitating dwarves in return for a reward."

"What?" screeched Boïndil, eyes rolling wildly. His voluminous beard billowed. "Where are they?"

"I don't know," Tungdil told him, "and to be perfectly honest, I'm just glad they've stopped chasing me."

They stopped in a clearing to decide what to do.

"Did they say who was paying them?" Boëndal asked.

"No, but I've seen them once before. They didn't lay a finger on me at the time—too many other people nearby, I suppose." *Given half a chance, they would have killed me*, he realized with a shudder.

"Sounds like the thirdlings are up to their tricks again. They're probably paying the bounty hunters to wipe out the rest of the dwarven race, or it could be a ploy to turn us against the long-uns so we end up feuding with them as well as the elves." Boëndal looked at his companions. "There'll be plenty to talk about when we get back to Ogre's Death."

They unpacked their blankets and spent the night under a dense roof of leaves. It seemed prudent to do without a fire: It was dark enough for the flames to be seen for miles around and the mere snapping of a twig seemed alarmingly noisy in the stillness. Tungdil snuggled down and put his hands behind his head, only to sit up abruptly and pluck a beetle from his thick shock of hair. "It's strange," he mused out loud, "but the two of you must have left Ogre's Death at roughly the same time as the headhunting began."

Boïndil, who had coiled his long plait into a pillow, frowned. "You mean it's nothing to do with the thirdlings? You think they were after us?"

His brother shook his head. "That hardly seems likely, Boïndil. No, our scholar thinks they were after him. Am I right?"

Tungdil sighed. "I'm probably making too much of it, but didn't you say I had a rival for the throne?"

Boëndal saw what he was getting at. "Gandogar Silverbeard would never do a thing like that," he said firmly. "He's an upstanding dwarf!"

"I don't know what you're getting so offended about," his brother said reproachfully. "He isn't even a secondling."

"No, but he's a dwarf, an honorable dwarf with some funny ideas." He thought for a moment. "Besides, Gundrabur didn't tell anyone about Tungdil until after we'd left. No," he insisted, "the headhunting is another nasty thirdling ploy. It's bad enough that one of our folks has turned against us, but we can't start suspecting Gandogar. Our race will be doomed if we can't trust one another; it mustn't be true, it can't be."

They lay in silence, pondering the matter uneasily until they fell asleep.

Tungdil's dreams were filled with all kinds of unsettling nonsense. Hordes of orcs and älfar were pursuing him with shaving soap and razors, determined to cut off his burgeoning beard. In the end they caught him, held him down, and shaved his face; it was humiliating and infuriating to be lying on the ground with cheeks as naked as a baby.

The thought of it jolted him from his restless sleep and he got up, ate some of his provisions, and offered a fervent prayer to Vraccas, asking for protection from bounty hunters and safe completion of his mission.

You're not making it easy for me, Vraccas. Tungdil longed to be back in Ionandar's vaults with Frala, Sunja, and Ikana; even the prospect of seeing Jolosin no longer seemed so bad.

The long journey made friends of the trio and Boïndil devoted every spare moment to instructing Tungdil in the art of combat.

"So tell me, scholar," Boëndal said softly one evening when his brother was snoozing by the fire, "what do you make of the first dwarves you've ever been acquainted with?"

Tungdil grinned. "Do you want my honest opinion?"

"Of course."

"Boïndil has the fierier temper. His fists move faster than his thoughts and he generally acts on impulse, although once he decides himself on something, no one will convince him otherwise."

"I didn't need a scholar to tell me that. Go on!"

"He hates orcs and elves with a vengeance and his life is devoted to warfare. He fights with uncommon zeal."

"You know my brother well." His twin laughed. "Just don't let him hear you say so! And what of me?" he inquired eagerly, passing him a pipe.

"You have a gentler temperament. Your mind is sharper and you're willing to listen to other people's ideas." Tungdil drew on the pipe. "Your brown eyes are friendly, whereas your brother's...I can't describe the look in his eyes."

Boëndal clapped his hands softly. "True, all true."

"Why did the two of you become warriors?"

"Neither of us has any talent for masonry, so we decided

to join the guard. The secondlings are custodians of the High Pass, the steep-sided gorge through the Blue Range. At ground level, the pass is fifty paces wide, but its walls are over a thousand paces high, and the sides slope inward after eight hundred paces, leaving the path in shadow except for a short span of time when the sun is directly above."

"Sounds pretty gloomy to me."

"Throughout our history a handful of custodians have defended our kingdom against invaders, no matter how powerful their ranks."

"Don't you have a portal like the fifthlings' Stone Gateway?"

"No, our forefathers cut a trench in the path, forty paces long and a hundred paces deep. On our side of the trench they built a rampart with a mechanical bridge. The engineers worked on the design for almost as long as it took for the masons to hew the trench." Boëndal paused, recalling the genius of the engineering. "They made a collapsible walkway from thin slabs of stone. It's incredibly light but can bear any load. At full extension, it rests on columns that rise up at the pull of a lever from the base of the trench, but the bridge can be retracted instantly by means of chains, cogs, and ropes."

Tungdil was lost for words. "That's...I've never heard anything like it! But what happens when orcs or ogres force their way onto the bridge?"

"We send them crashing into the trench. Tion's creatures are forever littering the fosse with their bones." He laughed softly. "One lot were so determined that they catapulted each other to the opposite side. Most died on impact; the others felt the fury of our axes."

Tungdil joined in his mirth. "If I were trying to cross over," he said thoughtfully, "I'd fill in the fosse or climb down and up the other side."

"They thought of that too, but they didn't stand a chance.

There was only one occasion when our folk came close to going the same way as poor Giselbert's dwarves." Like every second-ling, Boëndal knew this episode of his kingdom's history by heart. "An army of ogres had the same idea as you. On reaching the trench, they didn't even try to find a way of bridging it; they just climbed down carefully, waded through the bones of their ancestors, and appeared before us in their hundreds."

"But the secondlings managed to stop them?"

"Why do you think it's called Ogre's Death?" Boïndil chimed in chippily. "Can't you keep the noise down when I'm trying to get some sleep?" He rolled closer and gazed into the fire. "I'm wide-awake now, thanks to you!"

He fetched some cheese from his pack and melted it over the flames. This time Tungdil accepted a morsel. It didn't taste nearly as bad as he'd thought.

Boëndal resumed his story. "The ogres had got as far as storming the ramparts when their chieftain was killed. That was our salvation. Without their leader, the ogres didn't know what to do and our warriors succeeded in pushing them back to the edge of the trench. They fell to their deaths. But that was a long time ago, when Boïndil and I were still in nappies. There hasn't been a single attack on the High Pass for at least thirty cycles."

"No wonder." His twin guffawed. "The beasts are too scared of us. Actually, the High Pass has been so quiet lately that Gundrabur decided to send us in search of you." He looked across the fire at Tungdil and his brown eyes glinted. "You were right, of course. I was born to fight. Combat is my calling; it's who I am."

"And I go where he goes. Twins belong together; find one and you'll find both. It's just the way it is."

"Does every dwarf have a calling, then?" asked Tungdil, wondering what his might be. "Do you think I'll be a stone hauler or a trench digger, or will I be an artisan with a proper talent?"

"Most fourthlings are gem cutters and diamond polishers. Maybe trinkets are your thing?"

Tungdil had never taken much of an interest in precious stones. Lot-Ionan possessed a few items of jewelry and Tungdil had enjoyed looking at the sapphires, rubies, diamonds, and amethysts because of the way in which they caught the light. He had never felt the slightest urge to craft a sparkling jewel from uncut stone, though.

"I don't think so." There was a hint of disappointment in Tungdil's voice. "For as long as I can remember, I've been drawn to the forge. The smell of molten iron, tongues of fire that writhe like living things, the ring of the hammer, the hiss of hot metal as it enters the water—ever since I saw my first anvil, that's what being a dwarf has meant for me."

"You'll be a smith, then," Boïndil said approvingly. "A scholarly smith. Very dwarflike."

Tungdil shuffled closer to the fire and tried to divine the secrets of his inner self. He pictured mountains of diamonds and then a column of dancing orange sparks rising from a furnace. He felt more affinity with the furnace. Gold appealed to him too, though; he loved its soft warm shimmer.

"I like gold as well, you know," he confessed in a whisper. "I pick up any lost gold I can find—gold pieces, gold jewelry, gold dust dropped by prospectors. I collect it all."

The brothers roared with laughter. "He's got himself his own private hoard! If that isn't properly dwarven, I don't know what is. You'll be a warrior soon," Boïndil promised him, reaching for the pipe.

"I don't know," Tungdil said doubtfully. "The way you and Boëndal can fight and win against the odds. I'll never—"

"There's no such thing as having the odds against you," Boïndil broke in. "Some challenges are bigger than others; that's all there is to it."

"All the same, I feel safer at the anvil; a forge is where I belong." Tungdil decided not to dwell on the matter, so he opened his knapsack and pulled out Gorén's books. The brothers watched as he slid the volumes out of their wax covering and examined them carefully.

"Well, what do they say, scholar?" Boïndil demanded impatiently. "Maybe that's your calling, to be a learned scribe or an engineer. The dwarves are renowned for being prodigious inventors."

"I can't make head or tail of them." To his immense disappointment, even the wording on the spine was written in scholarly script. "They were written for magi." In some ways it was surprising that Gorén, an ordinary wizard, had been able to read them at all.

Tungdil tapped his forehead and scolded himself for being so slow. He had forgotten that the elf maiden would have been familiar with the workings of high magic. *She must have helped Gorén unlock the secrets of the books.*

He stroked the leather binding of the books. *Why are their contents so important to the älfar? Since when have the elves' dark relatives been afraid of parchment and ink?*

"We'll find out soon enough from Lot-Ionan," he said, trying to rally their spirits. He was just returning the books to their wrapping when his gaze fell on the bag of artifacts. It had suffered visibly from the journey. In spite of the hardwearing leather, the pouch was bleached from the sun and scuffed in several places, and there were sweat marks and grease stains where it had come into contact with his food. A faint line stretched across its surface like a scar, an eternal reminder of its run-in with the orcish sword.

The longer Tungdil looked at the pouch, the more he desired to look inside. He had been fighting the urge to undo the colored drawstrings for some time.

What harm is there in looking? Surely I've got the right to know what I've been lugging about all this time. Besides, Gorén is dead. Tungdil's self-control failed him.

Trying to look nonchalant, he reached for the pouch. He didn't want the others to know that the magus had forbidden him to look inside. He untied the knot and the drawstrings came open.

At that moment an ear-splitting, bone-shattering bang rent the air. A volley of sparks shot upward and exploded in a blast of color.

"By the hammer of Vraccas and his fiery furnace!" Leaping to their feet, the twins stood back-to-back, weapons at the ready.

Tungdil swore and tugged at the drawstrings, but the fireworks continued until he tied the knot exactly as it had been before. Lot-Ionan had booby-trapped the bag. He must have reckoned with his inquisitive nature and decided to teach him a lesson.

"What in all the peaks of Girdlegard was that?" Boëndal asked peevishly. "Not some magical nonsense, I hope."

"I just wanted to see...Well, I wanted to see if the booby trap worked," fibbed Tungdil, trying to breathe evenly. He was every bit as startled as the twins. "The magus put it there to, er, he put it there to stop the bag from being stolen!"

"All that noise from a little leather pouch?" Boïndil stared incredulously at the bag. "I still don't see what the fireworks are in aid of, unless the magus wanted whoever stole it to earn a fortune as a street magician."

"It's so I'll know where it is and be able to get it back," Tungdil told him, inventing an explanation that was rather more flattering than the truth. He didn't want them to know that his nosiness was to blame.

"If he didn't want it stolen, why didn't he put a proper spell on it?" growled Boïndil. He spat contemptuously in the bushes. "I always said that the long-uns' magic was no good."

His brother joined in. "He could have conjured a hammer to whack the villain on the head!" he suggested.

"Or a drawstring that crushes his wrists! That would teach the blackguard to keep his hands off other people's belongings."

Boëndal sat back down. "The magi work in mysterious ways. All that power and no common sense."

Tungdil swallowed, thankful that his punishment had been mild by comparison. "I'll pass on your ideas," he promised.

"We'll tell him ourselves!"

"No," he said quickly. "It would be best if you didn't. He doesn't take kindly to anyone interfering in his business, especially if they're strangers." He could feel his cheeks burning as he spoke, but luckily for him, the twins were busy poking about in the fire, trying to retrieve a portion of cheese that had been dropped in the confusion.

"A stunt like that could have been the death of us in Greenglade," muttered Boïndil. He looked at Tungdil sternly. "Leave the bag alone in the future!" Sighing, he impaled the morsel on a stick, dunked it briefly in some water to wash away the ash, and popped it into his mouth. "No harm done," he said.

But Tungdil had taken the lesson to heart. *From now on I won't touch the bag except to sling it over my shoulder and take it off at night.* For all he cared, it could be stuffed full of gold; nothing could persuade him to open the drawstrings.

VII

Rantja scanned the crowd. Assembled in the atrium were 180 trainee wizards, the best famuli in Girdlegard, all waiting to be welcomed by Nudin the Knowledge-Lusty. At the behest of their respective magi, they had journeyed to Porista to lend their magical power to the crusade against the Perished Land. The high-ceilinged room echoed with their expectant chatter.

"The girdle must be in trouble if lowly apprentices like us are being summoned to keep out Tion's hordes," said a voice in her ear. "You look prettier than ever, Rantja."

"Jolosin!" she exclaimed in delight, shaking his out-stretched hand. It was then that she noticed his navy blue robe. "Oh my, you're a fourth-tier famulus already. How long did you have to pester Lot-Ionan before he caved in?"

"Only thirty-two cycles old and already in Nudin's fifth tier! I'm impressed," teased the dark-haired famulus admiringly. "How are you?"

"Fine." She smiled, then said soberly, "At least I *was* fine until I heard about the threat to Girdlegard." She pointed to the cuts on his fingers. "What happened there?"

"Don't ask," he muttered gloomily. "But between you and me, I'm working on a spell to make potatoes peel themselves. It's a relief to be out of the kitchen and doing something useful." He glanced around. "Have you seen the council?"

"No. Even my magus has disappeared," Rantja said anxiously. "What do you make of it?"

"All I know is that the rituals require their full attention, so they might not be able to brief us until later," he said uneasily. He took a leather pouch from his shoulder and tightened the green drawstrings. "Has it ever been this bad before?"

Rantja shook her head.

The doors swung open, and Nudin the Knowledge-Lusty stepped into the room. He was swaying slightly and his face looked drawn and tired.

"Welcome to Porista," he greeted them, his voice cracking as he spoke. To some of the famuli it sounded as if two people, a man and a woman, were talking at once. "These are dark times for our realms. Come this way and see for yourselves what the Perished Land has done." The magus turned toward the conference chamber, motioning the apprentices to follow.

"Are you sure he's not wearing heels?" Jolosin whispered, surprised. "He's bigger than when I last saw him—and fifty pounds heavier at least."

"I know. Everyone keeps saying he looks taller."

"*Much* taller, not to mention fatter. But men of his age aren't supposed to grow. A botched experiment, perhaps?"

They were less than a pace behind him now, and a sweet, almost putrid odor filled their noses. Jolosin put it down to moldering aftershave, but the magus seemed oblivious to the smell.

Just then Rantja skidded across the flagstones and would have fallen, if Jolosin hadn't reached out and caught her in time. "Thanks," she said, straightening up and hurrying on, propelled by the famuli behind them. The incident was over too quickly for anyone to notice the long crimson streak on the floor. The magus was leaking blood.

Nudin walked briskly, striking his staff against the marble at regular intervals and leading them through a maze of arcades and corridors until they reached a double door. His onyx-tipped staff glistened darkly as he raised his left hand.

"Steel yourselves," he warned them, and recited the incantation to open the doors.

Even before the doors were fully open, a fetid smell wafted out of the room, causing the famuli at the front of the queue to cover their faces. Rantja swayed and clutched at Jolosin, who steadied her bravely while he tried not to retch.

The magus was apparently unaffected by the stench. "See for yourselves why Girdlegard needs your help!" Hesitantly, the famuli entered the chamber.

There were cries of distress as the shocked apprentices surveyed the remains of their tutors: a statue, a heap of clothing, a rotting corpse, and in the case of Andôkal, a body so mutilated that its features were no longer recognizable.

"Palandiell have mercy on us," gasped Jolosin, staring in horror at Lot-Ionan's marble face. He would never have wished such a dreadful fate on his magus, no matter how many potatoes the wizard had forced him to peel. "Girdlegard is finished," he muttered despairingly, depositing the leather bag at the foot of the statue. Lot-Ionan had specifically asked him to bring it, and now he was dead. "If the council could do nothing, what hope is there for—"

He was silenced by the sound of a staff striking the floor. A hush descended on the chamber as everyone turned to face Nudin.

"We underestimated the power of the Perished Land," he said shakily. "It waited for us to channel the magic into the malachite, and then it attacked. The table was destroyed and I myself was almost killed. My good friends here"—he waved his staff in the direction of the fallen magi, whose rotting remains and frozen corpses reflected nothing of their former power— "were unlucky. As their most senior famuli, you are the highest-ranking wizards in Girdlegard." He stopped to cough up a mouthful of blood and staggered backward, leaning against the fossilized Lot-Ionan for support. "The attack has taken its toll on me, as you can see. It is our duty to repair the table as quickly as we can, for only then will we be able to repel the Perished Land. The survival of humankind depends on our success; ordinary armies will be helpless against the pestilence."

The famuli looked at one another bleakly, shaken to the core by Nudin's sobering words and the sight of their dead mentors.

"They were so powerful, but the Perished Land subdued them," whispered Jolosin despondently. "How are we supposed to—"

"We should give them a proper burial," Rantja said distractedly. "We can't just leave them here." She was trembling.

"Girdlegard is relying on you to be strong," Nudin exhorted them. "If you don't act now, we'll lose our only hope of repelling the Perished Land. You can mourn the dead when it's over." He traced a circle on the floor with his staff. "Gather round, join hands, and repeat the incantation after me."

The famuli did as instructed, Rantja and Jolosin standing side by side and drawing strength and comfort from each other.

Nudin took his place in the circle and laid his staff on the floor. His fat, clammy fingers reached for Jolosin's free hand and the unfortunate famulus clasped them with revulsion. "If you please, Estimable Magus, I've brought the artifacts you loaned to Lot-Ionan." He turned in the direction of the bag, and Nudin nodded curtly.

Then they began the incantation, calling on the magic to come forth and enter the splinters of the table.

The hours wore away.

Enchanted Realm of Lios Nudin,
Girdlegard,
Summer, 6234th Solar Cycle

It was raining at daybreak, or pouring, to be precise.

Summer in all its glory reigned over Girdlegard, but for the duration of a few hours the sun had retreated, allowing the sky to cloud over and quench the parched soil.

No doubt the vegetation was grateful for the downpour, but the dwarves were unimpressed. Huddled under a tree, they waited grumpily for the rain to stop.

"Now you see why we live in the mountains," scowled Boïndil, who was taking the opportunity to shave his cheeks. Over the past few orbits he had become increasingly restless. His warrior's heart longed for action so that he could swing his ax and shriek and spit at some orcs, but the chances of that in Lios Nudin were depressingly slim.

"What if he goes into a frenzy?" Tungdil asked Boëndal in a whisper. "Should I hide in a tree?"

The dwarf wrung the rainwater out of his plait and grinned from ear to ear. "You'll be safe so long as I'm around to direct his fury onto something else. I try to steer him clear of anything that breathes, and it works quite well, for the most part."

They kept their eyes fixed on the nearby thoroughfare, watching the carts and carriages roll past. One young couple seemed more interested in each other than in driving their oxen. The dutiful animals kept up a steady trot.

The sight of the lovers reminded Tungdil of a subject that had been bothering him for a while. He wondered whether to ask the twins' advice, although he was beginning to feel embarrassed about his ignorance of dwarven life. For someone who had spent his formative years surrounded by books, he asked incredibly foolish questions. *So much for being a scholar!*

Curiosity got the better of him eventually. "What do girl dwarves look like?" he asked, avoiding their gaze.

There was silence.

The patter of rain on the leaves seemed deafeningly loud. The brothers let him stew for a while; then Boïndil said: "Pretty."

"Very pretty," added Boëndal, amplifying his brother's terse reply.

"Right."

There was silence again.

Overhead, the shower was easing, the drumming raindrops fading to a steady drip-drip of water trickling from the twigs and branches.

He tried again. "Do they have beards?"

Silence.

Tungdil became acutely aware of the rich variety of noises made by falling rain.

"Not beards, exactly," said Boïndil.

"More like wispy down," explained Boëndal. "It looks lovely."

No one spoke.

The sun burned a path through the dark gray cloud, and summer triumphed over Girdlegard. Tungdil decided to broach an even more delicate topic. "When men dwarves and girl dwarves—"

He broke off under the secondlings' withering stares. Boëndal took pity on him. "It's high time our scholar got to know his kin," he said dryly. He glanced up at the tree. "The downpour's over; let's go." He stood up, followed by his brother.

"You didn't answer my question!"

"You didn't *ask* a question, and anyway, you're the one with all the learning, not me."

"Do girl dwarves fight too?"

"Some do, but in our clan they mostly stay at home," said Boëndal as they moved off along the road. "Our womenfolk devote themselves to domestic duties: herding animals in the valleys, stocking our pantries, brewing beer, and making clothes."

"No good ever came of the sexes fighting side by side," Boïndil added darkly. He seemed to be speaking from experience, but there was something in his voice that warned Tungdil not to probe.

"Don't make the mistake of belittling their talents, though. They're just as proud as we are. Some of the best masons and smiths in the kingdom are women. When it comes to artisan contests, they use their chisels and hammers so proficiently that other competitors stop and marvel at their work."

"Anomalies and exceptions," growled Boïndil, who was obviously of the opinion that certain tasks were the preserve of male dwarves. "For the most part they belong by the hearth. The kitchen is their calling."

Tungdil had been listening attentively. "It's like that in human kingdoms too," he told them. The idea of female dwarves seemed more appealing than ever and he was eager to become acquainted with their kind.

At last they reached Porista. Tungdil gazed in wonderment

at the turrets and domes of the palace, but his companions exchanged bored smiles, needing no further evidence that human architecture was inferior to their own.

Tungdil had been hoping to find Lot-Ionan and unburden himself of Gorén's books and artifacts, but he was sorely disappointed. At the palace they were told that the council had dispersed some orbits earlier and that Nudin the Knowledge-Lusty was not receiving guests. There was nothing for it but to follow Lot-Ionan to Ionandar.

They were on their way out of the city when Tungdil spotted a stable in one of the side streets. The horse inside it looked strangely familiar.

"Wait here," he instructed, striding toward the chestnut steed. He felt sure he had shod her not so long ago. He lifted her right foreleg and examined the shoe. The nails were unmistakably his own. "It's them," he hissed.

"Friends of yours?" asked Boëndal, whose crow's beak was resting casually on his shoulder. His brother was absent-mindedly stroking his freshly shaven cheeks in search of stray whiskers.

"Not exactly." Noting the bulging saddlebags, Tungdil fetched a bucket, turned it over, climbed on top of it, and fumbled with the buckles. The bag came open and the dwarf rummaged inside until his fingers came into contact with a jar. He pulled it out quickly.

"Remember the dead dwarf in the caravan?" His instincts had been right; the jar unscrewed to reveal a head. The bounty hunters had shaved the poor fellow's hair and beard so that the grisly trophy would fit inside the container, which was filled with honey to stop the air from getting in, thus preventing decay. Streaks of blood trailed through the golden fluid, staining it red. "We've found the villains who killed him."

There was a clatter of chain mail and the brothers were beside him like a shot. Neither spoke as they stared in horror at what had been done to their kinsman for the sake of a reward.

"By the blade of Vraccas, I'll cut them to pieces," roared Ireheart. Fury ignited within him, flushing him red and prompting his axes to fly into his hands. "Just wait until I—"

The door swung open and one of the headhunters walked into the stable from the house. Tungdil knew him immediately, and the recognition was mutual as the man stopped abruptly and swore. After considering the three dwarves for a moment, he decided that the odds were against him and fled.

"Cowardly as a runt," scoffed Ireheart. "Come back here and fight!" He chased him into the house, and there were sounds of a brief but energetic skirmish that climaxed in the man's dying screams.

"Don't—" Tungdil's shouted warning came too late. "He would have been more use to us alive," he finished mildly. He could hardly blame Boïndil: The fiery warrior was at the mercy of his temper and came to his senses only when his opponent lay bleeding on the floor.

"We'll wait for the others to return," Boëndal said phlegmatically. "Didn't you say there were five of them in total?" Tungdil nodded, and they took up position in the stable.

It was early evening when the men returned. Judging by their sullen faces, their honey pots were empty and their efforts had been in vain.

Waiting for them behind the door was the vengeful Ireheart, an ax in each hand and seconded by his brother, who had concealed himself among the straw. The twins were so accustomed to fighting together that any intervention on

Tungdil's part was likely to be a hindrance, so he lurked in the background and kept out of the way.

Once the men had entered the stable and dismounted, Boëndal and Boïndil nodded to each other and launched their assault.

"Leave one of the villains alive!" shouted Tungdil, joining the tail end of the charge.

Alerted by the commotion, one of the headhunters turned and reached for his sword.

The blade was only halfway out of its scabbard when Boïndil's ax thudded into his left hip. The force of the blow sent him tumbling against the wall. Before he could recover, the dwarf's second ax hit his right calf, hewing skin and sinew and shattering his knee. The man collapsed in screams of pain.

Satisfied with the crippling effect of his blows, Ireheart moved on. Cackling terribly, he hurled himself on the next of his foes.

His brother was left to deal with the remaining men. Shoulders squared, he charged toward the first of the two, leveling his crow's beak as he ran.

His opponent had enough time to snatch his shield from the horse and thrust it in front of his body, but he underestimated the weapon's force. The spike at the tip of the crow's beak pierced the metal, ripping through the shield and stabbing the man in the arm. Wood and metal had done nothing to repel the weapon; now flesh and bones yielded too. The soldier screamed.

Boëndal jerked the spike out of the shield and rammed the poll against the man's unprotected knee. The force was enough to smash the joint and buckle the leg. The second headhunter was down.

"I'll show you what happens to spineless dwarf killers!" Boiling with rage, Ireheart slashed at his opponent with fast, powerful strokes.

Tungdil could see that the men were doing their best to parry the frenzied blows of their attackers, but their expressions revealed the hopelessness of their plight; where there was fear, defeat often followed, and so it was this time.

Boïndil whirled his axes above his head. Unable to guess the direction of the attack, the panicked headhunter turned to his horse.

His legs outpaced the dwarven warrior, but his speed was no match for Boëndal's weapon. The crow's beak soared through the air, hitting the man's back just as he was swinging himself into the saddle. The impact cracked his ribs, stopping him momentarily. It gave Ireheart enough time to catch up.

"You're too tall for my liking, long-un," he snorted, slashing at the man's legs and severing his tendons. His victim toppled, and Ireheart dealt him a double blow to the collarbone that finished him off.

The dwarf went in search of the fourth headhunter, who was cowering behind the mound of straw. "Now it's your turn!" Ireheart's chain mail was spattered with his opponents' blood and his eyes glinted crazily. "Who do you pray to? Palandiell? Samusin?"

The man cast down his sword and raised his hands. "I surrender," he said hastily.

Ireheart bared his teeth. "Too bad," he growled, thrusting his axes into his enemy's unprotected midriff. The man collapsed amid agonized groans. He died quickly but painfully, as Tungdil could tell from his muted whimpers.

Tungdil surveyed the stable. The chief headhunter, whom

Ireheart had put out of action at the beginning of the fight, was lying in a pool of blood. He seemed to be fading rapidly. The dwarves hurried over.

"Who pays for your handiwork?" demanded Tungdil. "Tell us, and you'll be spared."

"We'll leave you to drown in your blood if you don't," Ireheart said threateningly.

"Bind my wounds," the man implored them, pressing his hand to the flowing gash in his hip. "In the name of Palandiell, have mercy on me." The blood was flowing so fast that Tungdil doubted anything could save him; the magic of a magus, perhaps, but certainly not a bandage.

Ireheart turned on him furiously. "Tell us, or I'll let my axes do the talking!" Before he could make good on the threat, the headhunter expired.

The dwarves left his side and hurried to the remaining survivor, whose shield and arm had been pierced by Boëndal's crow's beak.

The man was gritting his teeth. Pride prevented him from screaming aloud, but the pain from his shattered knee was almost too much to bear.

"Be m-merciful," he stammered. "I don't know much, but I'll tell you. We heard about the reward in Gauragar—they were offering gold in return for groundlings' heads." He pointed to Tungdil. "It was just after we met him."

"Who's *they?*" bellowed Ireheart. He laid the bloodied blade of one of his axes against the man's throat.

"The guild! The master of the guild!" he choked fearfully. "He sent us here. We harvest the heads and every thirtieth orbit he sends a man to fetch the jars. We get our share of the reward—thirty coins apiece for each head."

"The guild? What guild?" demanded Tungdil.

"The guild of the bounty hunters." The man groaned as the pain threatened to overwhelm him. "Let me go now. I've told you everything I know."

Tungdil believed him, but he knew the twins would never let him live. His murderous deeds would have to be punished.

"You're not going anywhere." Ireheart's axes settled the matter before Tungdil could object. The headhunter had breathed his last.

"Come on," Boëndal said evenly. "We need to get out of here before the watchmen arrive."

Hefting their bags, they hurried out of the city in the direction of Ionandar. At first they were worried that someone would find the bodies and chase after them, but no one did.

Tungdil felt a pang of conscience. "It wasn't right to kill them," he said, as they were sloshing their way through puddles and mud. "We should have handed them over to the watchmen along with the jar."

Boïndil's eyes narrowed. "Are you telling me I should have let the villains live?" He shook the raindrops from his beard. "They would have been tried and hung anyway. What difference does it make?"

"They deserved to die, I know. But if we'd..." Tungdil couldn't think of how to describe his nagging guilt in a way that Ireheart would understand.

Boëndal leaped to his brother's defense. "No, scholar, there are no two ways about it. They murdered for money and died because of it. What does it matter that we killed them? Boïndil's right: The long-uns would have hung them, but we saved them the trouble—*and* we avenged the dead dwarf." He tossed his plait over his shoulder to signal that his mind was made up. "It was the right thing to do."

Tungdil could find no argument that might persuade him

otherwise. He was still too much the scholar to understand his companions' dwarven way of thought.

"We need to press on," Boïndil reminded them in a more conciliatory tone. "The high king is waiting." The battle in the stable had cooled his raging temper and he was calmer again.

Enchanted Realm of Lios Nudin,
Girdlegard,
Summer, 6234th Solar Cycle

I can't keep this up for much longer," Rantja muttered despairingly.

"You mustn't stop now," whispered Jolosin. "If any of us leaves the circle, the ritual will be broken. I owe it to my magus; we all owe it to Girdlegard to keep going."

Just then he heard a change in Nudin's voice. The croaky rasp became a high-pitched purring that didn't seem to belong to him at all. After a while it lowered to a bass tone so deep that it vibrated through the apprentices' bodies. None of them, not even the highest-ranking famuli, had heard anything like it.

And yet it worked.

Pulsing with light, the dark green fragments of malachite rose into the air and came to rest three paces above the floor. Even the splinters in the decaying flesh of Maira the Life-Preserver left her body, exiting with a gentle pop as they bored through her skin.

"What did I tell you?" said Jolosin, giving Rantja's hand an encouraging squeeze. "We're nearly there now."

Nudin the Knowledge-Lusty began a new incantation and

the famuli resumed their chanting, only to break off shortly afterward, unable to follow the words. Babbling and gibbering incoherently, the magus had lost his thread. With the rest of the circle reduced to silence, the ritual was doomed.

Meanwhile, the fragments of malachite clustered together in a flat disc, ten paces in diameter. The glowing circle began to spin.

"Is this part of the ritual? I've never done this before," hissed Jolosin. Rantja made no reply.

The disc spun faster and faster, the splinters drawing closer as the speed increased. Soon the individual fragments joined together in a circular sheet of flawless crystal.

"My magus knows what he's doing," Rantja whispered proudly, breathing a sigh of relief.

A hush descended on the room as the ring of apprentices watched in awed silence while the glowing malachite morphed under Nudin's command. At last the impressive spectacle drew gasps of admiration and relief from some of the famuli.

"We did it!" Jolosin was about to throw his arms around Rantja but was stopped by the magus, who tightened his grip on his hand.

Nudin spoke, uttering a single, unintelligible word.

A splinter flew out of the disk and pierced Jolosin in the chest. No one noticed.

"What..." Groaning, the young man tried to free his hand and touch the spot where the jagged splinter had entered his flesh and buried itself deep inside his chest. He could feel the blood seeping from the wound and trickling down his abdomen, but Nudin was gripping him firmly in his cold, clammy clasp.

"Estimable Magus," Jolosin said, his voice strained with pain, "I'm...I'm hurt. I've been hit by a shard."

Nudin turned his pale bloated face toward him. His pupils were dilated, almost obscuring his irises. Then the black dots turned the color of tarnished silver. His misty eyes glinted.

"I know, my boy. I needed your magic. There was no other way." He squeezed his hand reassuringly. "It won't hurt for long." The magus closed his eyes.

Another tiny splinter of malachite flew across the room and hit Rantja. From then on, the splinters followed in quick succession, striking the apprentices so rapidly that half of their number had been wounded before the others noticed. They called to the magus for help.

"Stay where you are or everything will be ruined," he commanded, eyes still closed.

The remaining famuli were unpersuaded by his words. Rather than stay and be killed by the lethal crystal, they decided to run for cover, but by then it was too late. As they tried to pull away, they realized with horror that their hands were stuck together, tying them to one another until they too were struck by shards.

The malachite disc sent dark bolts in the direction of each famulus, green light caressing their bodies eagerly in search of the splinters and slipping inside the wounds.

Nudin looked up, an insane glimmer in his eyes. Throwing open his cloak, he uttered another incomprehensible command.

At once a finger-length shard of malachite flew toward him on a bolt of green lightning and planted itself in his chest. The beam intensified, pulsing and rippling with light, while the tendrils of energy binding the famuli to the crystal faded and dimmed. Soon they were gone altogether.

"Victory!" The magus's shriek of triumph was too shrill and powerful to be human. He laughed exultantly. "The time for dissembling is over; Nôd'onn the Doublefold is once more!"

The famuli slid to the floor. Jolosin, Rantja, and the others were incapable of speech; the malachite had wrested the magic from their bodies and plundered their strength.

The more fragile among them were the first to succumb. Their hearts stopped, their breathing failed.

A small band of famuli, Jolosin and Rantja included, summoned the energy to drag themselves across the floor in a desperate effort to reach the doors.

The magus plunged his fingers into his chest and was feeling around for the splinter. He withdrew the bloodied fragment, gazed at it dreamily, then replaced it in the wound. He took a step toward the malachite disc.

"You served your purpose, now be gone!" No sooner had his onyx-tipped staff made contact with the hovering crystal than it fell to the ground, littering the floor with myriad splinters.

Don't just stand there, he told himself sternly. *Let the next phase begin!* Gathering the leather bag brought by Jolosin, he hurried to the door, skewering three crawling famuli as he passed. A tidemark of blood stained the white maple of his staff.

On reaching the doorway, he stopped and looked back, scanning the foul-smelling room. The stench of decay would soon be overwhelming, but it was all the same to him. His work was almost done and he was leaving the conference chamber for the final time.

It was then that he noticed Rantja and Jolosin. With a brutal swipe of his staff, he crushed the famulus's skull. His own apprentice had nearly reached the door, but he nudged her back into the chamber with his boot.

Rantja rolled onto her back, tears streaming over her face, and uttered a healing charm. Her magic failed her.

The magus stooped to stroke her long brown hair. He knew the famula well and she was talented, one of his most gifted pupils, in fact. She would probably have made it into his discipleship in Lios Nudin, but he knew that she couldn't be relied on to cooperate with his plans.

"The malachite splinter inside you has left you weak and helpless," he told her. "The magic is gone. You'll die like the others, Rantja."

The young woman stared up at him accusingly. Her dark eyes were full of contempt for the magus whom she had trusted implicitly and who had forfeited her respect.

Nôd'onn looked away, surprised at how much he was affected by his dying apprentice. "I didn't want to kill them," he said defensively. "There was no other way of obtaining their magic. What was I supposed to do? Andôkai, Lot-Ionan, Maira, Sabora, and Turgur refused to help me, and you and the other famuli would have turned against me too. I knew it was going to be difficult, but I did it because I had to. This is my destiny. Girdlegard must be protected from evil."

"There is no greater evil than the Perished Land," she said, breathing in rapid gasps. "The gods will punish you for betraying our circle."

Nôd'onn thought for a moment. "Perhaps you're right. But the vengeance of the gods is a small price to pay for saving mankind." He got to his feet and stepped out of the chamber. "And mankind can be saved only by the Perished Land and the chosen few."

"You're mistaken," whispered Rantja. Her gaze faltered. "You're..." A sigh ran through her body and her head slumped back, falling to the side.

"No," Nôd'onn contradicted her sadly. "I'm right, but no one understands. My dear friend told me this would happen."

Closing the doors with a wave of his hand, he turned away quickly and hurried through the palace to the vaults. There was a dull thud as the doors of the chamber slammed behind him, sealing Girdlegard's most powerful wizards in their tomb.

Clumping down the stairs, Nôd'onn reached the room where the energy was at its strongest. From Lios Nudin, the force field extended outward in five directions, supplying the other realms. He was about to change all that.

The magi and their highest-ranking famuli had been taken care of, but there was still the matter of the lowlier apprentices. Nôd'onn was incapable of stopping the flow of energy, but he intended to reclaim the young wizards' meager powers by other means.

First there's something I need to attend to. He loosened the green drawstrings, opened the bag, and turned it upside down.

An hourglass hit the floor, shattering on impact, followed closely by two amulets, which tinkled against the marble. A roll of parchment landed on top.

Nôd'onn stared at the motley collection. *These aren't my things!* he thought furiously, scattering the pool of sand in all directions with his staff. *Confound Lot-Ionan!*

He reminded himself of the need for calm. Besides, he could always ask the orcs to retrieve the items from Ionandar.

Focusing his mind, he used his powers to search for the force field and, on finding a connection, uttered the charm provided by the Perished Land, thereby releasing the magic he had plundered.

VIII

To speed their progress, the three dwarves bought ponies and rode without stopping, dismounting only to spare their aching backsides. Even then they kept moving, continuing on foot.

Over the course of the journey the twins taught Tungdil a number of ballads that were known to all dwarves, irrespective of folk or clan. Little else remained of the common heritage linking all the children of the Smith.

The melodies were simple and easy to remember, embellishments and ornaments playing no part in dwarven songs. To Tungdil's ear, they sounded rather melancholy, a tendency he attributed to the gloominess of the underground halls. The mood was noticeably lighter in songs such as "Glinting Diamond, Cold and Bright" or "There Is a Golden Shimmer in a Faraway Range," where the lyrics told of great treasures and gold, and he enjoyed the drinking song "A Thousand Thirsty Gullets, A Thousand Flagons of Beer," taught to him by Boïndil, who had procured a keg of beer.

Tungdil awoke the next morning and cursed his pounding head. According to Boëndal, it was all the fault of the long-uns' ale, which was vastly inferior to the dwarves' own beer.

Farther along the way they encountered Sami, a peddler with stubbly cheeks and peasant's clothing, who had strange stories to tell. "Some people say that the cleverest famuli in the other five realms have left for Lios Nudin," he informed Tungdil, who was examining the array of trinkets on offer while the twins waited patiently. He wanted to buy something for Frala before he forgot.

"Any tidings from Greenglade?"

"The elf maiden is dead. The northern pestilence laid waste to the forest, and King Bruron is worried that wayfarers might get themselves killed. He wants to set fire to it." Sami made a show of unpacking his herbal soaps. "Perhaps you groundlings could do with some of these."

"Just because we're dwarves doesn't mean we stink!" growled Ireheart. "I'll put you in a lather, you lanky-legged rascal!"

"My mistake," Sami said hurriedly. "I thought he wanted something for a lady friend."

"Actually, Boïndil, the peddler's probably got a point," Tungdil said slyly, throwing him a bar of plain soap. He also bought a jasmine-scented soap, a patterned comb, and a doll each for Ikana and Sunja.

Boïndil sniffed the soap, scratched at it, and put a shaving in his mouth. "Ugh, it tastes disgusting! I'm not washing with that!" He tossed it disdainfully into his bag.

"So the Perished Land is still advancing?" probed Boëndal.

"It looks that way. Most of Âlandur has fallen already and the elves are under constant attack. Some have fled to the plains of Tabaîn, or so I've heard." The peddler packed the gifts in coarsely woven cloth. "Everyone says the älfar are getting the better of them. They've taken the other elven kingdoms, and if you ask me, Âlandur will be next. It's only a matter of time before the älfar conquer the last of their land." He handed the parcel to Tungdil. "A silver coin, please, master groundling."

"Dwarf," Tungdil corrected him.

"Pardon me?"

"We're dwarves, not groundlings."

"Of course," Sami said, again hurriedly. "Absolutely." He cast a distrustful glance at Boïndil, who was admiring his shaven cheeks in a mirror.

Tungdil was still digesting the news about Âlandur. "What do you think the assembly will have to say about it all?" he asked the twins.

"Serves the elvish tricksters right," said Boïndil with a shrug. "Most of them are dead already and the others will follow if they set foot in our range. The pointy-ears aren't welcome near Ogre's Death; I don't care whether they call themselves elves or älfar, they won't be moving in with us."

Tungdil scratched his beard. "What of the orcs?" he asked Sami.

"Oh, they're in three places at once, if you believe the rumors." The peddler looked at them dolefully. "It's not safe on the roads anymore. Tion's creatures are on the rampage and King Bruron can't do anything to stop them. Innocent folks like us have to fear for our lives and our wares."

Boïndil scanned the horizon longingly and licked his lips. Tungdil heard him making "oink" noises under his breath.

A while later they took their leave of the peddler and rode on.

To keep their purse stocked with coins, Tungdil jobbed as a smith, helped by the brothers, who also ornamented window frames and doorways with wonderful carvings. That way they kept themselves in ham and cheese while making good progress toward Lot-Ionan's vaults.

"You've got bits of cheese in your beard," Tungdil said to Boïndil at the end of a meal.

"What of it?"

"Well, it's not nice to look at," he answered, trying to be diplomatic.

Boïndil ran a hand over his chin and dislodged the largest morsels.

"There's still…"

"Look here," Boïndil told him brusquely, "the rest can stay where it is. It keeps the whiskers sleek and smooth." As if to emphasize the point, a bread crumb fell from his lips and landed in his beard.

Tungdil had an image of the hairs coming to life and feeding on the scraps. It would explain why nits weren't a problem; the whiskers would gobble them up before they had a chance to settle. "Surely the girl dwarves must have something to say about your—"

"There you go again!" Boïndil clapped Tungdil on the back and grinned lewdly. There was cheese between his teeth. "Always on about girl dwarves."

"Patience, scholar," Boëndal advised him. "Play your cards right, and you'll find out firsthand. You're not bad-looking; I'm sure we'll find you a suitable lass."

"And then what do I do?"

"You make eyes at her, of course." Boëndal gave him a playful dig in the ribs. "You sing her a song. You give her a hand-forged ring. Then you kiss her feet, cover her in a nice thick coating of her favorite cheese, swing her four times in a circle, and the gates to her Girdlegard will open."

"That's…It doesn't say that in the books," said Tungdil, bewildered. He looked at Boëndal, whose eyes sparkled roguishly. Boïndil couldn't contain himself any longer and let out a side-splitting guffaw.

"Idiots," huffed Tungdil. "It's not funny, you know. I can't help it if I've never met a female dwarf."

"We didn't mean to offend you," apologized Boïndil, wiping away tears of merriment. "But maybe you should try it; it seems to work for Boëndal!"

That was it; his brother dissolved into laughter too, the gentle hills of Ionandar echoing with their mirth.

"Just be yourself," said Boëndal, endeavoring to be serious. "I can't speak for everyone, but it's no good pretending to be something you're not."

"He used to say he was a poet," his brother chuckled. "His lady friends never believed it, but with you it might work."

"What sort of presents do they like best?"

"Ah, very cunning," exclaimed Boëndal. "Sorry, scholar, but you can't bribe your way into a lady's heart. There's no secret formula. Either she likes you, and she'll tell you as much; or she doesn't."

"And she'll tell you about that too," Boïndil added merrily.

"I wouldn't wish *that* on anyone," said his brother, "but if she likes you, well…anything is possible. But enough about womenfolk."

Their journey continued, and after several orbits Tungdil began to recognize his surroundings, which meant they were getting closer to Lot-Ionan's vaults.

He was looking forward to seeing the famuli and being reunited with Frala and her daughters. *They'll never believe that I'm an heir to the throne!* To prove that he hadn't forgotten her, he knotted Frala's scarf around his belt.

After a while they came to a river. A ferry was moored on the opposite bank near the ferry master's house and smoke was rising from the chimney.

Tungdil reached up to ring the bell that was suspended from a tree beside the berth. That way the ferry master would know to come and fetch them.

Boïndil grabbed his hand. "What are you doing?"

"I'm calling the ferry, unless you'd prefer to swim," said Tungdil. "It's either that or get the boat."

Boïndil eyed the swirling water. The river was lapping

against the banks. "We'll go a different way," he decided.
"It's too deep here. We could fall in and drown."

"You could fall off your pony and break your neck," Tungdil countered sharply. "Come on, Boïndil, it's too far to the
next crossing—two orbits, at least." When he saw the twins'
stony faces, he knew it was useless to protest. "It's this way,"
he sighed, pointing upriver. "But I don't see what's wrong
with the boat."

It was all the encouragement that Boëndal needed to launch
into the story of why dwarves and water didn't get along.

"Long ago, Elria put a curse on us. Elria was born of water
and water was her element. From the beginning, she took
a dislike to the dwarves—Vraccas's fire-loving, furnace-
tending children couldn't have been more different from her
water-dwelling creatures. To protect her children, she put a
curse on the dwarves, and now any dwarf who ventures into
water outside his kingdom is doomed to drown."

Lakes, rivers, ponds, or streams—according to the twins,
even puddles could pose a mortal danger, and they avoided
water at all costs.

"It's an excellent excuse for not washing," Tungdil told
them.

They rode until nightfall and arrived the following orbit at
the ford. When the time came to cross, the brothers waded nervously through the fast-flowing water, the river swirling ferociously about their thighs as if it intended to carry them off.

It was evening when they finally neared the entrance to the
tunnel leading into Lot-Ionan's vaults. Boëndal and Boïndil
grew uneasy at the thought of wizardry and spells.

"I didn't like coming here the first time," grumbled Boïndil.
"Lot-Ionan is a nice enough fellow, I'll grant you, but he's a
magus. At least we dwarves have the good sense to know that
hocus-pocus never did anyone any good. We stay away from

it. If Vraccas had wanted us to dabble in magic, he would have given us wands." He stared at Tungdil suspiciously. "You understand that, don't you? I hope he hasn't given you any daft ideas..."

"I can't weave magic," Tungdil said soothingly. "I've never even tried." He stopped for a second and looked at the brothers imploringly. "Promise me you'll treat him respectfully. Without his charitable intervention, there wouldn't be another claimant to the throne. In fact, it's only because of his salutary—"

"Listen to him!" Boëndal said sarcastically, mimicking his voice. "Do you hear the scholar speaking? Quite the gentleman, isn't he? He must be refining himself for highfaluffing conversations with a more h-h-educated race."

"*Highfalutin,*" Tungdil corrected him with a smile. "All right, point taken. Either way, be nice to him or say nothing at all. You can wait at the gates if you'd rather. I'll be fine on my own."

It was already dark by the time they got there. Even from a distance Tungdil could see that the door to the tunnel was ajar. It was usually bolted and protected with a magic incantation, but one of the famuli must have forgotten to do his job.

Tungdil grinned mischievously, his tanned face creasing around his eyes. Whoever was guilty of such negligence would soon regret it. He intended to give the vault's inhabitants the shock of their lives.

"Tut-tut," Boïndil said disapprovingly when they reached the open door. "The confounded thing better not close behind us. What if it's a trap to catch innocent travelers?"

"Why would the magus want to trap travelers?" his brother inquired.

"To try out new gobbledygook on them, of course! You don't think he'd experiment on his own apprentices, do you? He needs to be sure that his wizardry works." He looked to Lot-Ionan's protégé for confirmation, but Tungdil chose not to get involved. Boïndil unhooked an ax from his belt and mumbled threateningly into his beard. "If any of those wand-wielders so much as looks at me oddly, I'll show them what for."

Boëndal burst out laughing. "Don't worry, I'll be sure to punish them if they turn you into a mouse or a bar of soap." He gave the butt of his crow's beak an affectionate pat, but his brother was frowning grimly.

Tungdil noted their squared shoulders; it was clear from their posture that they were ready to fight. He decided to head off any possible misunderstandings by leading the way.

"Keep the noise down," he told them. "I want to take them by surprise."

Boïndil looked skeptical. "Seems to me that's just asking for trouble. What if they put a spell on us by accident? They might not recognize you in time."

Tungdil waved dismissively and stepped into the vaults. At once he was surrounded by the familiar aroma of paper, papyrus, parchment, and a hundred dusty books, mixed in with the smell of stone and a hearty whiff of supper. "Boiled potatoes and meat," he declared.

He looked over his shoulder at the twins, who were more interested in studying the tunnel and speculating in low tones about who had built the vaults and why.

"You can tell it's the work of long-uns," Boïndil was saying. "Do you see this? I noticed it last time as well. To think they didn't bother to work with the rock! They've cut through the strata with no concern for the veins." He pointed at something. "If they'd troubled themselves to look properly, they wouldn't have got themselves into such a mess. Even I could do better, and I'm a warrior!"

"A precarious design." Boëndal was gazing at the ceiling that was propped up every few paces by pillars and struts. "There's too much sand in the soil. An engineer or a miner would never have taken such a risk." He prodded the ceiling gently with his crow's beak, loosing a shower of mud and stone. "I'm no expert, but they should have dug the whole thing out. See how the warmth has dried the sand strata and made them all crumbly? Your magus needs a lesson or two in how to dig tunnels. It's a good thing we're here."

"Shush," Tungdil reminded them firmly. "You'll spoil the surprise."

"No sentries, no alarm system, nothing!" Boïndil rolled his eyes. "No wonder Vraccas told us to take care of the long-uns! The whole place would be easier to conquer than a dead dragon's den. Dwarves are more careful," he continued in a whisper still loud enough for Tungdil to hear.

Tungdil tiptoed on. His eyes had adjusted to the dim light, but the vaults were too quiet for his liking. There was no chattering of voices or banging of doors. If it hadn't been for the tantalizing smell of supper, he would have suspected the magus of moving his school elsewhere.

"Maybe they've abandoned the vaults and left the cook behind," mused Boïndil out loud. "Hardly surprising, given the state of the place."

The comment earned him a reproving look from Boëndal. "Surely they'd take the cook with them?" he couldn't help asking.

"Not necessarily." Boïndil grinned. "He might be so bad at his job that they've made him stay and practice until the ceiling caves in. Either that, or he's stewing in his soup."

Tungdil was too intent on reaching the magus's study to listen to their chatter. He knocked on the door. No one answered, so he walked straight in.

"I'll wait out here with Boïndil," Boëndal called after him. "We don't want to spoil the reunion."

On entering the room, Tungdil could scarcely believe his eyes. One half of the study was in a state of chaos with books, sheets of paper, and scribblings strewn over the floor; the other half was impeccably neat.

Tungdil had never seen such orderliness in Lot-Ionan's study. The books were stacked on the shelves in alphabetical order, the paper had been left in tidy piles, and the quill and inkwell were in their proper places.

He must have dreamed up a new charm that makes the mess tidy itself, he thought, impressed. He could see the logic in trying it out on one half of the study, but there was still no sign of the magus. *I hope the spell didn't tidy him away.*

He wandered round the chamber, looking for anything that might explain the silence in the vaults.

Boïndil sighed loudly. "Waiting is a hungry business," he declared. "I'm off to find the kitchens. If we ask nicely, they might spare us a bite."

"We should take Tungdil with us," his brother said anxiously. "The long-uns won't know who we are, don't forget."

"All the more reason for introducing ourselves." Boïndil was too hungry to worry about being cautious. "You can wait if you like, but there's a hole in my belly stretching down to my knees." He strode off.

Boëndal was reluctant to let him go anywhere unsupervised. They were guests at the school, and guests were expected to behave with a modicum of decorum, which didn't come naturally to his twin.

"Tungdil, we're off to the kitchens," he shouted. "I'll keep an eye on Boïndil, don't worry!" He hurried to catch up with his brother, who was disappearing around the corner.

The twins had no trouble finding their bearings in the vaults. Vraccas had given his children an infallible sense of direction when it came to orienting themselves underground. They knew instinctively whether a passageway would slope upward, downward, or curve gradually to one side, and they had no need of the stars to plot their course. In this instance, they were guided by the tantalizing smell.

All the rooms they passed were empty: There wasn't a soul in sight.

"Maybe it's dinnertime," Boëndal suggested hopefully, trying to ignore his growing unease.

They made for the passageway, where the smell of meat was strongest. Their tunics and armor clanked softly while their heavy boots clumped rhythmically on the floor. At last they reached a door that led into the kitchen, judging by the splashes and smears.

Boëndal tried to surge ahead to make a more orderly entrance, but his brother beat him to it. He gave the door an almighty shove.

Four great hearths burned in the high-ceilinged room, but otherwise the kitchens were as deserted as everywhere else. Curiously, there was evidence of recent activity: The stoves were roaring and supper simmered and hissed in covered pans. Large round cooking pots hung above two of the hearths, chunks of meat rising to the surface and sinking into the bubbling brown broth.

By now Boëndal had a definite feeling that something was wrong. Abandoned rooms and brimming cauldrons: It simply didn't add up. *What's going on?* He scanned the kitchen carefully.

"This is more like it," Boïndil said cheerfully. He let go of his ax, tore off a piece of bread, and headed purposefully for the nearest stove. Balancing on a stool, he lifted the lid of a pan and peered inside—juicy slabs of simmering meat and gravy. His mouth began to water. "It would be rude not to taste it."

He dunked a sizable hunk of bread into the sauce and prepared to swallow the morsel in one bite.

"Stop!"

His brother's warning brought him to a sudden halt. "What now?" he snapped, his stomach growling in protest at being neglected for so long. "Can't you see I'm eating?"

Boëndal had positioned himself next to the door, crow's beak at the ready. Judging by his stance, he was anticipating trouble. "I don't mean to spoil your appetite, but take a look over there."

Boïndil followed his gaze. The butcher's block, used ordinarily for chopping and filleting meat, was piled high with bones that had no place in a kitchen. Four skulls in particular held their attention: They were human in form.

It took a while for Boïndil to link the bones to the broth, but then he hurled away the dripping bread in disgust and jumped to the ground, drawing his axes.

"When I get hold of that magus, there won't be a spell in the world that can save him," he muttered darkly.

"Humans and wizards aren't usually cannibals," Boëndal told him. "If you ask me, there's been a change of guard. The magus didn't forget to lock the door; someone attacked." He peered into the corridor. "It's time we found our scholar."

Walking back-to-back, they retraced their steps through the eerily empty passageways, Boïndil leading and Boëndal following and watching his back.

Tungdil sat down on the footstool next to Lot-Ionan's armchair and waited impatiently for the magus to return. For want of anything better to do, he dusted off his garments. All he could think about was what the magus would say when he made his report. He had already decided to start with the most important business—Gorén's books. There was no reason to believe that Lot-Ionan would divulge their mysterious contents, but Tungdil hoped he would.

Just then he heard someone approaching from the corridor. He knew at once that it couldn't be Boëndal or Boïndil; the soft footsteps belonged to a light, unarmored man.

Tungdil was too bored to pass up an opportunity to amuse himself and, leaving the knapsack and bag of artifacts beside Lot-Ionan's chair, he leaped to his feet and hid behind the door, intending to jump out and scare the unsuspecting famulus. Chuckling silently in anticipation, he peered around the door.

The young man who came into the room had short black hair and was dressed in the malachite robes of Nudin's school. He made straight for Lot-Ionan's papers and set about sorting through his documents with shocking disrespect.

What in the name of Vraccas is he doing? Tungdil watched from his hiding place as the famulus sifted through a stack of notes, thereby solving the mystery of the unusually tidy room. Next he made himself comfortable at the magus's desk and set to work on the higgledy-piggledy documents and books, sorting them into piles and jotting the details on a list.

Tungdil looked on in amazement. *Who allowed one of Nudin's pupils to forage through Lot-Ionan's things? What's he doing here anyway?* If Lot-Ionan wanted someone to tidy his study for him, he had plenty of likely candidates in his own school, but Tungdil knew that the magus was very particular about his work. The documents that the young man was handling were strictly private and no one was permitted to look at them, least of all an apprentice from another enchanted realm.

Dragging footsteps sounded in the corridor and a second figure appeared at the door. The famulus looked up crossly, not bothering to hide his annoyance. "What is it?"

Tungdil pressed his face to the crack in the door and peered at the newcomer. All he could see was a broad back and a coarsely woven shirt.

"I've finished in the kitchens," said a deep, sluggish voice. The dwarf placed it immediately: It was Eiden, the magus's groom.

"Good. Then find yourself a quiet corner and stay out of my way," came the famulus's sharp reply.

Eiden stayed where he was, filling the doorway like a fleshy statue. "I'm hungry," he said dully.

"Why don't you gnaw on some bones in the kitchens?" the famulus said impatiently. "But remember not to touch the meat—it's for our sentries. Now, leave me in peace."

"I want meat," the man insisted.

"Go!" The famulus picked up a letter opener and hurled it at him. Whether he intended to wound the groom or whether it was a poorly judged throw, he succeeding in striking Eiden in the chest. The man groaned and staggered from the room.

At last the dwarf could see his face, which was ashen and horribly mangled. A club had crushed the right side of his head and his visage looked barely human.

At the sight of his torso Tungdil took a sharp intake of breath. The pale fabric of Eiden's shirt was caked with blood from two deep gashes to his collarbone and chest. The afflicted flesh was decaying, the skin around it yellow.

Tungdil was instantly reminded of Greenglade and its gory revenants. *No,* he thought, *the Perished Land can't have breached the magic girdle.* Lot-Ionan had gone to Porista to renew the barrier and preempt an attack, and in any event, the Perished Land's dominion ended 450 miles north of Ion-andar's vaults. *Then why is Eiden still alive?*

A gust swept through the room and a blue shimmer appeared in the air, gradually assuming the contours of a man. It was Nudin the Knowledge-Lusty.

The famulus rose and bowed before the apparition. "I've been searching the school as you requested, Estimable Magus," he reported, straightening up to face the bloated wizard. "There's no sign of the items you mentioned. Good-ness knows why the old man needed so many laboratories and libraries." He decided to get his excuses in quickly. "The vaults go on and on. It's a lot for me to manage on my own."

"Which is why I shall be joining you in person."

Tungdil hardly dared to breathe, lest he give himself away. Vraccas seemed intent on making him eavesdrop on all kinds of awkward conversations. He had seen Nudin once before, but he remembered him as being slimmer, healthier, and decidedly less cruel. The Nudin before him was like a carica-ture, an uncharitable likeness drawn by a detractor.

"Lot-Ionan told me that the items were in a cupboard," the magus continued, swiveling to survey the room. There was something oddly high-pitched about his gravelly voice. "Have you searched the place properly?"

"Not yet," the famulus admitted. "I thought the books were more important, so I decided to hunt for them first."

Nudin shuffled toward the large cabinet from which Tungdil had retrieved the artifacts at the start of his errand. "There's no proof that the books even made it to Ionandar. According to the älfar, a war band stole the books from Greenglade after the orcs had razed the place. Dwarven bandits, apparently."

"But didn't you tell them to...I mean, how—"

"The älfar are good allies." Nudin's doppelgänger stopped in front of the cabinet and propped his staff against the wall.

It took some effort for his swollen, spectral fingers to depress the handle, but he got there in the end. "Their only weakness is their love of art. For this particular älf, it proved fatal." Bending down, he reached into the cabinet and came up with a leather bag identical to the one that Tungdil had been carrying. "It looks as though our search has been rewarded."

He loosened the drawstrings and tipped out the contents. Five rolls of parchment tumbled to the floor. His grunts of displeasure seemed to indicate that he had been hoping to find something else.

Tungdil peered out a little farther. His packs were hidden by Lot-Ionan's chair, but he had an uncomfortable feeling that Nudin would be delighted to discover them.

It was then that it dawned on him: The ties on his bag were blue, but the magus had said something about green drawstrings. *I took the wrong bag! I marched for miles across Girdlegard, and Gorén's artifacts were here all the time!*

From the point of view of his errand, it wouldn't have made any difference if he had got to Greenglade and found Gorén alive—he would still have been carrying the wrong set of things. But something told him that his mistake had worked out well.

Tungdil couldn't quite make sense of it all. He had no idea why Nudin and his apprentice were behaving as if the school belonged to them, much less why Eiden was acting so oddly when really he should have been dead, but the fact that the magus had allied himself with the älfar was clearly bad news. Nudin the Knowledge-Lusty seemed to have changed sides.

He had to find out what had happened to Lot-Ionan and his famuli without alerting the intruders to his presence.

"One more thing," said the apprentice, riffling through the papers on the desk. He pulled out two pieces of parchment that Tungdil recognized as the letters that he had sent. "Lot-

Ionan received a couple of letters from someone called Tungdil who was looking for Gorén on his behalf."

He passed the correspondence to his master, who scanned the lines with bloodshot eyes. "Tungdil..." he said musingly. "Of course! The old man kept a dwarf of that name. It's perfectly possible that he's the one who took the artifacts and the books." He tossed the letters onto the desk. "Traveling dwarves are a rarity in Girdlegard, so it shouldn't be hard to find him. I'll ask the älfar to deal with it, and they'll deliver him, dead or alive." He nodded to the famulus. "It's a pity you didn't mention it earlier, but at least we're getting somewhere. You shall have your reward when I join you. Until then, keep searching. You never know what might turn up." The apparition flickered and faded, then vanished altogether.

After his many ordeals, Tungdil was beginning to think that nothing could shock him, but he hadn't reckoned with listening in silence while someone plotted against his life. His mettle was being thoroughly tested.

The famulus smiled smugly and sat down at the desk. He had pleased his master and secured a measure of the approval that he so craved. He buried himself once more in the documents.

He was just dunking his quill into the inkwell, ready to add another entry to the list, when he happened to glance toward the armchair. The straps of Tungdil's knapsack were protruding from one side.

"What...?" He got up slowly and crossed the room to examine the object that had materialized without his knowledge. He stooped to pick up the leather bag.

Tungdil drew his ax. Speed and surprise were of the essence: He had to strike before the famulus saw him and cursed him. He tensed his muscles.

Even as he prepared to charge, a commotion sounded in the corridor, stopping them both in their tracks.

For once the twins were making a genuine effort to be quiet. They didn't know who had invaded the vaults, but it seemed safest to hack them to pieces without giving them any warning. Whoever had butchered the long-uns would surely jump at the chance to eat a dwarf—but a crow's beak in the belly or an ax through the gullet was bound to cure their greed.

They heard lumbering footsteps.

Boïndil signaled for his brother to freeze, and they waited for the creature to stagger around the corner. There was a whiff of rotten flesh; then a man stumbled toward them, groaning.

His injuries were so horrific that it was a wonder he was alive. No ordinary mortal would have survived such wounds, but on seeing the dwarves, he yelped in excitement and lunged toward them with surprising speed, spurred on by the prospect of fresh meat. His eagerness was no match for the warriors' experience.

Boëndal saw the blow coming, skipped sideways, and jabbed him in the knee. The revenant swayed.

In falling, he hurled himself on Ireheart, who greeted him with a war cry and a pair of flashing blades. The secondling avoided the toppling body and reached out to cleave the man's left arm. Teeth grinding in anger, Eiden dragged himself across the floor, baring his teeth at the twins.

"Would you believe it? He's coming back for more!" observed Boïndil in astonishment. "I know revenants are supposed to hate the living, but this is ridiculous." He decapitated the man, thereby putting an end to his undead life.

The brothers set off at a run to find Tungdil. It seemed

likely that other bloodthirsty revenants would be roaming the vaults, in which case the heir to the throne could be in danger.

On reaching the door to the study, they saw a young man in malachite robes standing by an armchair, holding Tungdil's leather bag.

Their noisy skirmish in the corridor must have prepared him for their arrival. "Burn, you scoundrels!" His right arm flew up, fingers pointing at the dwarves, and he opened his mouth as if to speak. The door slammed shut.

The brothers blinked in surprise. "Surely he didn't need a spell for that?" said Boïndil.

"Why didn't he just close it before we got here? I told you wizards are weird."

"Magical mumbo jumbo. Leave it to me!" Launching himself at the door, Boïndil stormed inside, shrieking.

The young man had fallen backward and was lying motionless inside a cabinet. The doors were open and the shelves had slipped their brackets, scattering their contents on top of him. His forehead had been gouged in the process, and he was bleeding from the wound.

Tungdil straightened up and rubbed his head. "I should have put on my helmet before I head-butted him in the belly," he declared.

"Didn't I tell you those lessons would pay off?" Boïndil patted him on the back. "You've got the makings of a first-class dwarf!"

"It's about time someone explained what's going on," his brother said impatiently. "There's human broth on the stove and revenants roaming through the corridors. What kind of character is your magus, anyway?"

"None of this would be happening if Lot-Ionan were here." Tungdil gave a brief account of the eavesdropped conversation between Nudin and his famulus, then listened while the twins described the scene that had greeted them in the kitchen. In combination, the stories proved beyond a doubt that Nudin had seized the vaults and emptied them of their inhabitants.

Surely he can't have killed them all? Tungdil sat down, overcome with horror and dismay. *What of the apprentices, the servants, Frala, Sunja, and Ikana?* He refused to believe that the lunatic magus could have murdered a wizard as powerful as Lot-Ionan. *He's alive. I just know it!* He clung to the hope that Lot-Ionan had escaped with his senior famuli and was preparing to do battle with Nudin. *I have to find him!*

"The dwarven assembly needs to hear about this," ruled Boëndal. "Let's get out of here."

"No," Tungdil said firmly. "Not until I know where Lot-Ionan has got to." He looked at the unconscious apprentice. "I bet he could tell us." He knelt down and boxed his ears. It had the desired effect: The famulus's eyelids fluttered open.

Boïndil stood guard at the door while his brother placed the spiked tip of his crow's beak in the gap between the young man's eyes. "If you so much as think of cursing me, I'll ram my weapon through your brains." He obviously had every intention of carrying out his threat. "I crack skulls as if they were eggshells."

Tungdil bent down toward him. "Tell us where Lot-Ionan is," he demanded, torn between wanting an answer and fearing the truth.

"Are you the dwarves from Greenglade?" The famulus seemed perplexed. "But aren't you supposed to be—"

"Answer the question!" Tungdil told him roughly. Boëndal leaned on his crow's beak, applying just enough pressure to pierce the famulus's skin. Blood welled up around the metal spike as it bore into his brow. "Tell us where he is, or we'll kill you."

"Don't hurt me," the apprentice whimpered. "I'll tell you anything you want! He's dead. Nôd'onn killed him."

"Nôd'onn, commander of the Perished Land?"

"It was in Porista. He killed them all!" The terrible truth was out: With the other magi dead, there was no one in Girdlegard who could rival the traitor's power. "Nôd'onn cursed the force fields so no one else can use them."

An icy dread took hold of Tungdil when he realized what the famulus was saying. "So Nudin is Nôd'onn? Nudin commands the Perished Land?" The evidence had been staring him in the face, but either he hadn't realized or he hadn't wanted to. He felt like shrieking at the famulus or cutting him to pieces on the spot, but he forced himself to ask another question. "What does Nôd'onn want with the books and the artifacts?"

"I don't know. Nôd'onn told me to look for them, but he didn't say why. I swear I don't—"

Tungdil whacked him with the poll of his ax, returning him to his faint. Once he was safely tied up and locked in the cupboard, they debated what to do with him. It was obvious that they couldn't release him. A wizard with hostile intentions posed a serious threat and there could be no justification for not killing him while they still had the chance.

The tension over, Tungdil lowered his guard and gave in to his grief, mourning the loss of his adopted family and friends. Tears rolled down his cheeks, coursing through his beard, and he wiped them away with Frala's scarf. She had given him the talisman for luck, but now it was all he had left to remember her by. *I won't let your deaths go unpunished,* he promised his oldest friend.

Just then a familiar stench rose to his nostrils. Tungdil looked up and exchanged glances with the twins. They too had smelled the rancid butter, which could only mean one thing: orcs. He picked up his ax and rose to his feet. "Let's see if I can remember those lessons." They strode grimly to the door.

Beroïn's Folk,
Secondling Kingdom,
Girdlegard,
Late Summer, 6234th Solar Cycle

Rumor had it that the high king was on his deathbed. In fact, according to some reports, Vraccas had smitten him already and he had taken his place in the eternal smithy.

There was no need to look far to find the source of the gossip. So eager were the fourthlings to see their own king on the marble throne that they were only too happy to spread tidings of Gundrabur's demise. Come what may, they were determined to have their war against Âlandur, whether the elves were guilty of treachery or not.

At every discussion, no matter how big or small, Bislipur was there, tirelessly kindling the rumors, his every waking moment devoted to fanning the fires of his destructive campaign. No one seemed to need less sleep than Gandogar's devious adviser, except perhaps Balendilín, whom he regarded as a personal enemy.

"If only Vraccas would hurry up and smite the high king with his hammer," muttered Bislipur on returning to the chamber where he was staying as the secondlings' guest. He lowered himself crossly onto his bed. *I'm not making any progress.* Some of the fourthling delegates were starting to doubt the wisdom of going to war. *That blasted Balendilín is ruining everything. The sooner I take care of him, the...*

"Master, I bring news for you," a reedy voice announced from under his bed. "Not that I'd *choose* to tell you anything. In fact, I didn't want to come at all."

Bislipur stood up and kicked the bedpost. "Come out from there, you wretched gnome!" Sverd had barely emerged from his hiding place when Bislipur's calloused hand closed round his neck and lifted him into the air. He shook the gnome vigorously, like a cat would stun its prey, then tossed him roughly into the corner. "You're not to sneak into my chamber without my permission, do you understand?"

Sverd rose groggily and straightened his red jacket. "I wasn't sneaking, master. You weren't here, so I hid in a place where no one would find me, like you said." He tugged his hemp shirt over his rounded belly, covering his hairy green skin. His pointed ears stuck upward, as if pinning his cap to his head. There were few of his kind left in Girdlegard.

"Shall I tell you the news, master?" asked Sverd, his large round eyes filled with mock innocence. Streaks of mud and dirt covered his saggy breeches and his buckled shoes. He had tramped for many miles. "And if I do, will you let me go?"

"You'll go when I've finished with you." Bislipur rested his hand threateningly on the magical silver wire that allowed him to tighten Sverd's collar from any distance. "Talk or I'll strangle you."

"I wish I'd never tried to steal your hoard," the gnome whined piteously. "I regret it, really, I do." He looked at the dwarf expectantly, hoping to see a flicker of pity in the stony face.

"No wonder your kind is dying out if they're all as weak and pathetic as you." Gandogar's adviser stayed as cold and unbending as the many valuable trinkets that he wore. He tugged on the wire, tightening the leather band around the neck of his slave.

Sverd struggled to loosen the magic collar, but with no more success than at any other time during his forty-three cycles of bondage. The choker contracted and he sank to his knees, wheezing and panting. Bislipur waited until he was almost unconscious before slackening the leash.

"Thank you, master. Thank you." The gnome coughed. "Another joyous orbit at your side. How can I repay you?" He sank onto a stool. "Your pernicious plan failed. By all reports, the heir to the throne is still alive. Sadly, the same can't be said for our bounty hunters. There were no other takers for your cowardly mission and I didn't have time to start a proper search. Girdlegard is changing."

Bislipur took no notice of his reluctant henchman's sneers. From the beginning of his enslavement, Sverd had been trying to provoke him into killing him, but Bislipur chose to ignore him. The gnome deserved to suffer. "What happened?"

"I trailed the dwarf and the secondlings to Lot-Ionan's vaults. They were attacked by orcs…"

Enchanted Realm of Ionandar,
Girdlegard,
Late Summer, 6234th Solar Cycle

The beasts' approach could be heard from a hundred paces. Suddenly the clunking of their armor was interrupted by a clamor of snarls and grunts: The orcs had discovered the lifeless revenant.

On rounding a bend in the passageway, the three dwarves found themselves face-to-face with their foes. The exit to the vaults lay fewer than three hundred paces ahead, but it seemed to Tungdil that every inch of that distance was filled with orcs. A bristling thicket of weaponry blocked their escape.

"What fun!" enthused Ireheart, squaring his shoulders. "See how narrow the tunnel is? We'll have the pleasure of killing every last runt!" His whirled his axes energetically.

"Oink, oink! By the hammer of Vraccas, this is excellent sport!"

"The three of us will fight in formation," his brother told Tungdil soberly. "I know you've never done this before, but stand back-to-back with us and make sure you can feel us behind you. That way we'll all be safe." His brown eyes sought Tungdil's. "Trust us to watch your back, and we'll trust you. You're a child of the Smith, remember."

Tungdil took up position, wedging his back against the twins'. *Trust in the others,* he reminded himself, his heart thumping wildly. *Stand by me, Vraccas.* He swallowed and forgot about his fear. *For Lot-Ionan, Frala, and Girdlegard!*

"No more talking now!" Ireheart snapped at them, his eyes flashing wildly. "We've got skulls to cleave and shins to splinter!"

As the twins commenced their dance of death, Tungdil did his best to keep pace with them, nearly tripping over himself in his eagerness not to ruin their guard.

During the first few rotations, Tungdil could still see most of his surroundings. He glimpsed leering orc faces, saw green-hided flesh encased in various types of armor, spotted pillars among the jumble of legs, and occasionally sighted a whirling black plait.

But soon they were moving so fast that it all became a blur. Swords, daggers, and cudgels swooped toward him and he focused on dodging or parrying the blows. From time to time his ax met with resistance and after a while his blade was coated in glistening green, leading him to suppose that some of his blows had struck true.

It was the same basic strategy that the twins had used in the Eternal Forest. Back-to-back, the dwarves spun onward, boring their way through the enemy ranks, striking out furiously and never stopping for an instant, making it impossible for the beasts to land a proper blow.

Tungdil was glad of his chain mail. He lacked the secondlings' experience and was unable to field every strike, but his metal tunic protected him from the worst of it. He was willing to endure bruises, grazes, and even broken bones if it meant staying alive and saving the artifacts from Nôd'onn's fleshy hands.

He could hear Boïndil laughing behind him, his frenzied cackles competing with the orcs' dying shrieks. Boëndal was far less vocal, preferring to conserve his breath.

After a while the strain was beginning to tell on Tungdil's arms, but the battle was far from over. In addition to the orcs in front of them, there was also the problem of the survivors who were attacking from behind. In his despair, Tungdil came up with an alternative solution.

"The struts!" he yelled, straining to lift his voice above the jangling steel. "Cut down the struts!"

"Good thinking, scholar." Boëndal checked a blow, then rammed the offender with the butt of his crow's beak. A few moments later his weapon powered into a wooden pillar.

The force of the blow sent a strut crashing to the floor, followed by a shower of stone and dirt. The three dwarves repeated the maneuver until the unsupported ceiling collapsed behind them. Tion's minions disappeared under an avalanche of debris as ton after ton of rock blocked the tunnel, securing their rear.

The surviving orcs ran for the exit, afraid of being buried alive. Ireheart chased after them, swinging his axes furiously and felling all in his path. He stopped just short of the exit and waited for his companions.

"Come on," he urged them breathlessly. "There's another

twenty of these runts waiting outside. It would be a shame not to kill them."

They closed ranks again. For all his hatred of orcs, Tungdil secretly hoped that the surviving beasts had seized their chance and fled. His weary arms were reluctant to lift much higher than his belt.

Spinning in formation, they whirled out of the tunnel and into the darkness outside. The stars cast a silvery shimmer over the waiting orcs. A hundred pairs of green eyes glinted menacingly in the moonlight. The beasts were growling and snarling under their breath.

"I thought you said twenty?" Tungdil muttered accusingly, his heart quailing at the sight.

"Like I told you, some challenges are bigger than others," Boïndil assured him, glossing over his mistake. "This is one of the bigger ones."

"Should we go right or left?" asked Tungdil, who was keen to establish their strategy.

"Straight through the middle. If they start slaying one another by accident, we'll have a better chance of making it unscathed. I'll deal with their chieftain, and when we're out the other side, we'll attack the flanks and hew down the rest."

"Tungdil is new to this, remember," his brother put in. "The high king told us to bring him back to Ogre's Death, not to purge the countryside of runts."

Tungdil was profoundly relieved. He hadn't wanted to say anything for fear of disappointing the twins, but Boëndal was less reckless than his brother and his sharp eyes had noted his exhaustion.

"Oh, all right, then," conceded Boïndil a little indignantly. "We'll go straight through the middle and forget about the flanks."

The plan established, they decided to act, not wanting to

give the orcish archers an opportunity to use their bows. At first their tactic worked perfectly and they were mowing their way toward freedom at a tremendous rate when the enemy received unexpected support.

The ranks thinned around them as the orcs backed away, clearing a path.

"Hey! Come back here, you pug-faced monsters!" bellowed Ireheart, venting his frustration at the retreating beasts. "I'm not finished with you yet!"

The orcs continued to back away from them, and a lone man stepped forward instead. Tungdil knew the bloated figure from the apparition that had conversed with the famulus. The dark green robes cloaking the swollen body belonged to Lot-Ionan's killer.

The wizard looked doubly repulsive in the flesh. Blood trickled down his cheeks and his skin hung in flabby folds, occluding his features. He smelled as if he had been rolling in a pile of rotting rubbish.

"You've done well to get this far, but enough is enough," he purred. Fixing his gaze on Tungdil, he extended a bloated hand. "Give me the artifacts and the books you stole from Greenglade. After that, you can go."

Tungdil gripped his ax stubbornly. "These items belong to my master and I'll be damned if I'm giving them to you."

Nôd'onn chuckled. "How terribly valiant of you." He took a step toward them. "The artifacts belong to me. I'm in no mood for a discussion." The end of his staff struck the ground and he leveled the onyx-encrusted tip at Tungdil.

No sooner had he done so than the knapsack and the leather bag jerked away from Tungdil, struggling against him and trying to wrest themselves from his grip. He hung on to the straps as best he could, but his efforts were no match for the wizard's sorcery. The leather ripped and slipped from his fingers. He brought his foot down on one of the drawstrings just in time.

"I'll destroy the pouch and everything in it," he threatened, raising his ax.

"Be my guest. It would save me some work." Nôd'onn held his right arm on high, splayed his fingers, then clenched them into a fist.

The bags left the ground with such force that Tungdil could do nothing to stop them. Their flight ended when they dropped into the arms of an enormous orc, who clutched them to his chest with a grunt.

The magus was seized by a coughing fit. Blood leaked from his nostrils and he wiped it hastily away. "Go back to your kingdom, dwarves, and tell your ruler that I require his land. He can give it to me willingly, or my allies will take it by force. The choice is his." He gestured in Tungdil's direction. "Take him with you. I don't need him."

The two brothers said nothing. Gripping their weapons with steely determination, they were biding their time for an opportunity to attack. When the requisite diversion presented itself, they would hurl themselves on Nôd'onn and cut him to ribbons, but it was no good attacking while they were under the surveillance of the wizard and his hordes.

Suddenly there was confusion in the ranks. Beasts were pushing and shoving, and angry words were exchanged; then a particularly strapping specimen drew his sword against his neighbor and, snarling furiously, buried it up to the hilt in his gut. Within the space of a few heartbeats, the orcs were slaughtering one another.

Ireheart squared his shoulders, a sure sign that he was preparing to attack. His brown eyes were fixed on Nôd'onn's knees.

"Tungdil, you chop up his staff," he ordered in dwarfish. "The fatso won't stand a chance against the three of us." As always, he showed not a flicker of self-doubt.

"Ordinary weapons won't harm him." Tungdil glanced out of the corner of his eye at the iron-clad beast who was guarding the knapsack and the artifacts. "Our priority is to get the bags. Nôd'onn seems determined to destroy them, so they're obviously important."

Ireheart nodded. "You know what to do, Tungdil. On my signal..." The dwarves were preparing to leap into action when someone got there first.

From the crest of a nearby hill, a bolt of lightning flashed toward the magus and struck him in the side. Gasping, he dropped his staff and crumpled to the right.

The next bolt sped toward the orcs, reducing ten of their number to charred metal and flesh. The remaining beasts snarled in confusion, looking for the source of the attack. Spotting the figure at the top of the hill, they closed ranks and charged.

Nôd'onn raised his head and stretched out his right palm; the staff sprang into the air and flew into his hand.

This was the opportunity that the dwarves had been waiting for. Shrieking, Ireheart bore down on him, planting his axes into his legs, while Boëndal swung his crow's beak above his head and rammed it into Nôd'onn's broad back. He raked the blade upward, and the magus slumped to the ground.

The wizard's orcish protectors were too distracted by the arrival of the powerful new adversary to notice his plight. As they raced up the hill, black clouds formed above them, and a roll of thunder announced the coming storm.

The first orcs were paces away from their target when the

tempest was unleashed. Lightning crackled to earth, striking the front line of orcs and splitting their skins like sausages in boiling water. The dazzling flashes blinded those farther back, and the assault on the summit faltered and stopped altogether.

A wind whipped up, raging among the beasts and knocking them over like skittles. Pitching into one another, the orcs were hurled against trees or dragged to their deaths by the gusts.

Meanwhile, Boëndal had skewered the magus on his crow's beak and was pinning him to the ground. Ireheart leaped to his brother's aid, raining four fearsome blows on the magus's neck and cleaving his vertebrae. Nôd'onn's head rolled across the grass, and foul-smelling black blood spilled from the gushing stump.

Ireheart opened his breeches and was about to sprinkle the corpse with dwarven water, but was stopped by his brother. "The artifacts!" Boëndal reminded him sternly, pulling him away.

A moment earlier, Tungdil had summoned his remaining strength for an all-out assault on the orc who was guarding his bags. He let his instinct, combined with his recently acquired knowledge, guide his ax. The beast fell sooner than he expected, the speed of his victory taking him by surprise. *I can hold my own without the twins,* he thought, gratified, quickly grabbing the bags.

Boëndal ran up, his plait swinging vigorously as if it were alive. "We did it! Girdlegard is free of the traitor."

They hurried off, with Tungdil and Boëndal in the lead and Ireheart covering their backs. "It was child's play," he boasted, taking the opportunity to slay another couple of orcs. "We showed the traitor who's..." Ireheart's eyes shifted sideways and he let out a terrible howl of rage. "By the beard of Beroïn, I thought we'd..."

Nôd'onn was rising to his feet. His headless body straightened, and he stretched out a hand, beckoning to his skull, which flew toward him and settled on his severed neck. Not a scar remained to show where Ireheart's axes had raged. The magus seemed as strong and alert as ever. He ordered the remaining orcs to deal with Tungdil and his companions, then turned to the hill to destroy his magical foe.

"Seize the artifacts and the books," he boomed through the darkness. "And kill the dwarves!"

The onyx on the end of his staff throbbed with light as he raised his hand toward the knoll. The ground quaked, a deep furrow opening in the earth and burrowing toward the figure on the hill. Bolts of lightning shot from the dark clouds, only to melt harmlessly into the protective shield that cocooned Nôd'onn's body.

I knew it! Ordinary weapons can't harm him. Tungdil grabbed his companions. "This way," he panted. "The path leads south."

The trio raced off, slipping into a ditch to throw off their pursuers. They listened to the heavy trample of boots as the orcs charged past without seeing them.

"We should have stood our ground," Boïndil whispered crossly.

"And been killed!" Tungdil pushed himself deeper into the warm soil of the trench. "Didn't you see what he did back there? He got up, even though you'd beheaded him! It proves he's more powerful than the Perished Land." He pointed to the leather pouch that they'd managed to salvage. "The key to his destruction is in that bag."

"You're the scholar," Boëndal told him. "Find a way of

killing him and leave the rest to us. It's time we got back to Ogre's Death. Our kingdoms are in danger and we need to warn the assembly of Nôd'onn's plans. You might be the only one who can stop him."

"I don't know about that." Tungdil's hopes were centered on their mysterious rescuer, who had fought magic with magic, thereby saving their lives. *Please, Vraccas, let it be Lot-Ionan,* he prayed, unable to fight his tiredness any longer as he drifted off to sleep.

Beroïn's Folk,
Secondling Kingdom,
Girdlegard,
Late Summer, 6234th Solar Cycle

...and I was following them into the woods when they suddenly disappeared," said the gnome in conclusion. He tugged at the leather collar that had left him with a weal around his throat. "I had to get out of there quickly because the orcs were on my tail."

Bislipur was already deep in thought. Sverd's news obliged him to rethink his plans. "They're on their way here, then," he muttered to himself.

"Who? The orcs or the dwarves?" When Bislipur didn't answer, Sverd tried another tack. "You're not going to keep the news to yourself, are you? Didn't you hear what I said? The magus wants to *attack* the dwarven kingdoms! Only a real scoundrel would—"

Bislipur limped to the door. "Wait here," he ordered. "Don't show yourself unless I tell you."

"Yes, cruel master." With a sigh, the gnome settled on a stool, his short legs dangling above the floor.

*   *   *

Bislipur rapped on Gandogar's door. "It's me," he shouted. "Put your cloak on. We've got business to attend to."

Gandogar stepped out into the corridor and gave his adviser a bewildered look. "Wouldn't you rather come inside?"

"The exercise will do us good. Besides, there's enough gossip about me already. Apparently, I spend my time behind closed doors, plotting against the high king." He snorted derisively. "They're welcome to see us talking, if that's what they want."

Gandogar threw a light cloak over his mail and followed Bislipur through the stone labyrinth that was Ogre's Death.

All around them were carvings and ornaments. The secondlings had sculpted great artworks out of the humble stone, but the masonry was all the more striking because of its lack of pretension. Gandogar marveled at its simple beauty, but his reverie was cut short.

"I was just saying," Bislipur repeated softly, "that everything will be ruined if they keep us waiting any longer. The high king is an obstinate fool."

"Then what do you suggest?"

"I've consulted with the other chieftains. They think we should defeat the elves before the Perished Land gets there first."

At last he had Gandogar's attention. "Then let the Perished Land defeat them. It would solve the problem for us."

"Actually, Your Majesty, it would make our task harder. Remember what the Perished Land does to the fallen? They rise again! Our warriors would never prevail against an army of undead elves. The Perished Land is immensely powerful, remember." Bislipur's mail clunked slightly as he limped beside his king. "And what if the elves were to flee the threat and ensconce themselves somewhere quite unreachable?

Their crimes against the dwarves would go unpunished and your father and brother would never be avenged."

Despite the urgency in his voice, Bislipur was careful to speak softly. Anyone who saw them talking would assume they were preparing for the coming assembly—which was exactly what he intended.

"It's time you were made high king and led the folks against Âlandur. The Perished Land has lain dormant for some time. If it stirs, we must be back in our stronghold so we can wait in safety until the trouble has passed."

"You heard what Gundrabur said," the fourthling sovereign reminded him. "The laws were written by our forefathers, and I can't and won't defy them."

Their path led them to a beautiful sunlit valley whose verdant slopes were dotted with sheep and goats. Rocky peaks towered on either side with clouds stacked above them. To Gandogar, it seemed as if the mountains had impaled the bad weather on their summits to clear the skies for the pastures below.

"How peaceful it is here," he sighed, lowering himself onto a boulder. "I wish our assemblies were as harmonious as this."

Bislipur's cold eyes scanned the grassy slopes. "If you ask me, the other dwarves are exactly like sheep. They flock together, bleat until they get their food and beer, then fall into a self-satisfied slumber." He laid a hand on the monarch's shoulder. "You're a true king, Your Majesty, and you shouldn't be made to wait while some guttersnipe of a dwarf strolls across Girdlegard to challenge what's yours. Force a decision and the delegates will support you; I'll make sure of it."

"You're asking a great deal, Bislipur." The king rose, and they strolled back to the tunnel that led into the mountain and deep inside the Blue Range.

At length they came to a series of stone bridges whose backbones arched over dark, fathomless chasms. These were the ancient mine shafts, now empty and abandoned. The secondlings had plundered the mountain's riches and left deep gashes in its flesh.

Bislipur walked in silence, allowing the king to reflect.

"But what of the laws?" muttered Gandogar, turning the matter over in his mind. "I can't force another vote without challenging the laws of our forefathers and defying the high king's decision."

"It would take courage, the courage to do what's best for our race. You need to act now, Your Majesty. You've never been afraid to take a stand."

The passageway led over one of the kingdom's many quarries, where sheets of smooth marble were being hewn from the rock. A river meandered peacefully to the right of the stoneworks. The king and his adviser stopped on a bridge 180 paces above the laborers and gazed at the bustle below.

"Gundrabur might die at any moment," said Bislipur, still pressing for a decision. "Surely you don't mean to make us wait until the stranger arrives and the hustings have been held? What if the Perished Land attacks while the throne is vacant? Without a high king, there'd be no one to organize our defenses and lead us to victory. The folks would squabble among themselves and our race would be destroyed."

Gandogar pretended to ignore him, but the speech resonated with his own deliberations. He had been pondering the same questions, although he was still no closer to deciding what to do. *The laws come from Vraccas, but should we stick to them slavishly? What if it means forfeiting opportunities and exposing ourselves to danger?* He gave up and focused on the laborers below. They were working with incredible care and precision, handling the stone with as much consideration as if it were alive. Each sheet of marble was measured painstakingly before being prized from the mountain with pick axes, crowbars, hammers, and chisels. Water mills powered the blades of the enormous saws.

Dust hung in the air like gray mist and the laborers wore cloths to protect their mouths and noses. A thick layer of powdered stone covered any piece of equipment not in regular use.

It made Gandogar proud to think that he would soon be king of the dwarven folks. The children of Vraccas had their differences, but they were dwarves—united by ancestry, heritage, and a common foe.

Should we suffer because of our laws? He pictured the faces of his father and brother who had been felled by elvish arrows. *They were killed in cold blood.* His fists clenched and his face darkened.

He had made up his mind. "Very well, Bislipur, we shall act. I am the one who is destined to unite the children of Vraccas and what better way of strengthening the bonds between our kingdoms than a joint campaign against the elves? Victory over our enemies will pave the way for a new united future and put an end to this feuding and quarreling."

"And your name will be linked forever with the start of a glorious era," Bislipur added approvingly, relieved that his constant sermonizing had eventually paid off.

"We've wasted enough time already. I shall tell Gundrabur that he has thirty orbits to hold a vote in which my succession will be confirmed."

"And if he dies before then? He's old and infirm..."

"Then I'll be crowned, whether the mountebank has got here or not. Let's go back. I'm tired and hungry."

Privately, Bislipur was already working on his next assignment, unwittingly conferred on him by the king.

A great deal can happen in thirty orbits, he thought grimly. Murder was not the worst of his crimes, and a little more skulduggery would be neither here nor there. But this time he needed to do everything right.

"Coming, Your Majesty," he replied. Leaning over the parapet, he peered into the open quarry. *Anyone who had the misfortune to plummet from such a height would never be seen again.* He had just the assignment for Sverd.

Enchanted Realm of Ionandar,
Girdlegard,
Late Summer, 6234th Solar Cycle

Come on, scholar, time to get up," a voice whispered in his ear. A wiry beard scratched his throat and he was roused from his carefree dreams.

Boëndal and Boïndil were peering out of the ditch, scanning the woods for roaming orcs, but the beasts had continued their search elsewhere. Tungdil and the others were free to head south toward the secondling kingdom.

What a mess, he thought glumly. Things had turned out worse than he could have imagined. His errand had seemed simple enough, but now he was caught up in a succession crisis and everyone he had known and loved was dead, leaving him and his two companions to flee for their lives across Girdlegard while a crazed magus waged war on their kingdoms and tried to steal his bags. *And I don't even know what's inside them.*

Tungdil pulled the twigs and foliage out of his hair and beard. He was still fretting over Nudin's threat: The magus had declared war on all Girdlegard, men and elves included, and was planning to do battle with the dwarves.

"You look as though something's bothering you," said Boïndil, handing him some bread and cheese. He pointed to the woods. "Come on, you can eat on the way."

Tungdil fell in behind them. "Warning the dwarven kingdoms is a big risk. Nudin wouldn't mention the invasion unless he thought he could win."

Boïndil snorted. "Ha, that was before we chopped off his head!"

"Not that it had much effect," his brother reminded him gravely. "What did you make of it, scholar? Is it normal for magi to survive a mortal wound?"

Tungdil shook his head. "Wizards are just ordinary humans. They live a little longer than most, but they're susceptible to injury like everyone else. Lot-Ionan once cut himself on a knife and wove a spell to heal the skin. I asked whether his magic could counteract death, but…" He pictured Lot-Ionan and Frala and was too choked to continue. His companions didn't press him.

"Magi don't have the power to thwart death," he said finally.

"Nôd'onn was definitely dead," Boëndal told him. "He had my crow's beak buried in his back and his ugly mug was rolling on the ground. Maybe it's something that only dark wizards can do."

"If you ask me," said Boïndil, "it's a special kind of jiggery-pokery taught to him by the Perished Land."

Tungdil didn't know what to make of it all. Seeing the magus recover from his beheading had put pay to any theories about him being a revenant, leaving the dire possibility that Nudin had discovered the secret of eternal life—in which case, Girdlegard was doomed.

"We should have chopped him into tiny pieces and burned the lot," growled Boïndil.

"It wouldn't have worked," said a voice from the trees. The clear tones rang through the forest. "No known weapon can harm him. Swords, axes, magic—nothing will kill him. I tried and failed."

The trio whipped out their axes, and Ireheart wheeled round to cover their rear. "It can't be an orc," Boëndal whispered to Tungdil.

"Maybe, maybe not," said his brother. "I'm game for any kind of challenge, big or small."

The man who stepped out from among the pines drew a gasp of amazement from Tungdil. He had never imagined that a human could attain such dimensions; this one had a chest like a barrel and was as tall as two dwarves.

Although Tungdil had seen pictures of suits of armor in Lot-Ionan's books, nothing had prepared him for the sight of a real plated warrior. The man's breastplate, gorget, spaulders, and greaves were made of fine tionium and forged in such a way that the metal mimicked the curve of bulging muscle. The rings of a mail tunic, worn to give extra protection, were visible between the plates. A thin layer of cloth separated the segments of metal and dampened the clunking.

Sabatons protected the warrior's huge feet, and his head was encased in a helmet. A demon's face stared out from the elaborately engraved visor and a ring of finger-length spikes encircled his helm like a crown.

In his left hand he held a shield, while in his right he gripped a double-bladed ax, the mighty weapon raised effortlessly as though it were made of mere wood. A cudgel and a scabbard hung from his belt, the long blade resembling a dagger because of his great size. And as if this arsenal were not weighty and powerful enough, a two-handed sword was slung across his back.

Boïndil glanced over his shoulder to see what was going on and was instantly transfixed by the colossus.

"Swap places with me," he begged his brother. "You cover our backs and I'll bring down this mountain of metal." His eyes flashed eagerly. "That's what I call a *big* challenge. Better than a pack of runts!"

"Shush," Boëndal silenced him sharply. "Wait and see what he wants."

"His voice seems very high for a man of his size," said Tungdil, bewildered.

A blond woman with a severe face and a long plait stepped out from behind the warrior. "The voice wasn't his." Her blue eyes pierced the trio. "It was mine."

Tungdil appraised her commanding features and striking garb and wondered whether they had met before. She was athletic in appearance and wore black leather boots, gloves, and a tunic of dark brown leather, slit at the sides to give maximum movement. Her right hand rested on the pommel of her sword. There was something about her that reminded Tungdil of a woman that Lot-Ionan had once described.

"Are you Andôkai the Tempestuous?" he ventured at last.

The maga nodded. "And you need no introduction: Tungdil and his two friends who cheated Nôd'onn's wrath." She pointed to the warrior who was standing motionless beside her like a sculpted god of war. He was five heads taller than her. "This is Djerûn, a loyal ally."

Boëndal eyed her suspiciously. "What do you want?"

Tungdil took over quickly. "What's happened to Lot-Ionan? Is he alive?"

Andôkai looked at him with angry, tortured eyes. "Lot-Ionan is dead—and so are Maira, Turgur, and Sabora.

They're all dead. Nôd'onn didn't want them to interfere with his plans, so he killed them."

Tungdil bowed his head. It hurt to have the truth confirmed. The pain of losing his foster father gnawed away at him, leaving a void inside.

"Our senior famuli met a similar fate. Nôd'onn was careful to ensure that none survived who could challenge his power," she continued grimly.

"Then it was you who cast lightning at him!" Boïndil said excitedly. "I hope you caused more damage than we did."

"He survived. I did everything in my power to kill him, but it was useless. As soon as I saw him recover from your attack, I feared the worst, and I was right; we can't do anything to stop him."

"Wretched long-uns," Boëndal muttered crankily. "We dwarves tear our beards out patrolling the ranges and fighting Tion's hordes, and what do the humans do? Plot their own downfall! Vraccas should have made us into nannies, not warriors. Humans can't be trusted on their own."

"I'm afraid you're probably right." Andôkai took a step toward them. "I came here because I wanted to ask what Nôd'onn was after." She crouched in front of Tungdil. "We were watching from the hillside. You must have something that he covets. What is it?"

"Er, nothing really," he fibbed. "Just a few things that belonged to Lot-Ionan. I kept them to remember him by, but Nôd'onn wanted to destroy them. He and my magus can't have been good friends."

"There was a time when they liked each other well enough." She smiled wryly. "Lot-Ionan wasn't terribly fond of me."

That triggered Tungdil's memory. As far as he could recall, Lot-Ionan had disapproved of her values and her worship of Samusin. *If the twins find out that she keeps orcs in her realm, things could turn nasty, and we're bound to come off worse.* Not only would the maga attack them with her wizardry, but her companion looked capable of snapping trees with his hands.

"To be honest," said Boïndil, who had decided not to beat around the bush, "I don't much like you either. You go your way, and we'll go ours. We've problems enough of our own."

"Problems?" Andôkai said scornfully. She straightened up. "Your problems won't seem important when Nôd'onn invades. The dwarven kingdoms will fare no better than the realms of men and elves. The magus has allied himself with the Perished Land and together they seek absolute, unlimited power." Her chin jutted out and she eyed Boïndil with a look of contempt. "Run along and hide in your mountains. Tion's creatures will storm your strongholds from both sides."

"What do you propose to do?" asked Tungdil.

"We're leaving," she said frankly. "I'm not foolish enough to think that I could stop the Perished Land. No army will be mighty enough to challenge Nôd'onn, regardless of what the kings of men may think. What good would it do to stay? I'd only be condemned to become a revenant—a fate which, Samusin willing, I'm anxious to escape." She searched the dwarves' faces. "And you? If you're headed for Ogre's Death, we'd like to join you. Rest assured, we'll leave by way of the High Pass and never see you again, but we could journey as friends until then."

The dwarves discussed the matter in private and decided to accept the proposal. Boïndil's objections were overruled: The other two had learned from their encounter with Nôd'onn and could see that the maga would be a useful ally when facing the dangers ahead.

Boïndil made a show of complaining, but fighting with words was not his strong point and Tungdil argued him into a corner with his scholarly speech. "Fine," sulked the secondling, "but don't say I didn't warn you."

Tungdil informed the pair of their decision.

"But remember, we're the ones in charge!" Boïndil glared at the maga's companion contemptuously. He was obviously longing to pit his strength against the colossal warrior. "Hey! What's wrong with your tongue? Maybe if you took that bucket off your head, you'd be able to speak!"

"Djerûn is mute," the maga rebuked him sharply. "Remember your manners or I might have a thing or two to say about your height…"

"My manners are my concern," huffed Boïndil, smarting. He tossed his plait over his shoulder and turned back to the warrior. "Take my advice and keep out of my way," he warned, quickening his pace to lead the procession. "I deal with the orcs, all right? No doubt you'll learn soon enough."

Tungdil fell into line behind Andôkai, and they set off. *I'll wait until this evening to find out more,* he decided. It would be easier to ask his questions without the twins listening in.

Estimable Maga, how did Lot-Ionan die?" Andôkai had withdrawn a few paces from the fire and was sitting on her cloak, gazing into the flames. Instead of addressing her in dwarfish, Tungdil deliberately chose the language spoken by junior wizards. He wanted to demonstrate that he was educated and not a simple working dwarf.

It had taken a while for him to summon the courage to sit down beside her and engage her in conversation.

Back propped against a tree, Djerûn was positioned nearby.

The giant's weapons were arranged neatly on the grass in order of length, easily reachable with either hand. Owing to his visor, it was impossible to tell whether he was dozing.

"Lot-Ionan schooled you well, it seems," she said slowly, eyes still fixed on the flames. "An educated dwarf is a rarity in Girdlegard. Well, dwarves are rare enough." She paused. "I could tell you how your magus died, but the story of Nudin's treachery would only grieve us both."

"I want to know why Nudin changed."

"So do I, Tungdil." Andôkai turned and looked at him bitterly. "I don't suppose we'll ever find out." She recounted what had happened in Porista that night. "Nudin struck out at me without warning. He drew on his magic to deal me a blow that knocked me senseless. I didn't regain consciousness until later." She paused, resting her chin on her hands. "I cut him down with my sword, but he plunged his staff into my chest. After that I was too dazed to register anything but the sounds of the struggle." The maga took a deep breath, stretched out her legs, and looked up at the stars. "They must have fought him all the way. The sound of their screams will be with me forever. As for me, I could feel the blood seeping from my body and there was nothing I could do."

"But you survived."

"Thanks to my bodyguard." She glanced tenderly at the unmoving giant. "Nôd'onn must have forgotten that Djerûn had accompanied me to the palace. As soon as the lunatic magus had gone, he broke into the room and treated my wounds. I was too weak to confront the traitor, so Djerûn stole a corpse from the morgue, dressed it in my clothes, and left it with the other bodies. We wanted Nôd'onn to think he was safe." She reached for a branch and tossed it into the fire, sending sparks crackling into the night sky. "He is safe," she said dismally.

"And Lot-Ionan? What…"

"By the time Djerûn found me, your magus had been turned to stone. Nôd'onn turned him into a statue." A tear of helpless rage trickled down her cheek.

"A statue," whispered the dwarf, drawing closer to the fire. "Isn't there any way to…"

The maga shook her head but said nothing. They sat in silence, their thoughts with the dead. Stars twinkled in the firmament, and long moments passed.

"So you're leaving Girdlegard," Tungdil said wearily. "Where will you go? Aren't you worried about your realm?" He wiped the back of his hand across his face. He had been staring unblinkingly at the flickering flames, and the heat had dried his tears, leaving a salty residue in his eyes. "Will things be better elsewhere?"

"I'd be a fool to throw myself in front of a rolling stone when there's nothing else to stop it," she said softly. "It's not in my nature to prolong suffering without good cause. I shall give up my realm without a fight. What good would come of resisting? I may as well take my chances across the border now that Girdlegard's defenses have fallen." It was clear from her tone that the matter was closed. "I need to sleep."

After thanking the maga for her confidences, Tungdil withdrew and joined the twins to tell them what had happened in Lios Nudin.

"The wizards are really dead?" Boïndil skewered another piece of cheese from his seemingly endless supply. "So much for their miraculous powers."

"The strongest shield is useless when the sword is wielded by a traitor," his brother said wisely, munching on a hunk of toasted bread. "The long-uns are a wretched lot. I can't imagine what the gods were thinking when they created them."

He chewed his mouthful vigorously. "It's bad enough that they kill each other without dragging the rest of us into it."

Tungdil reached for a helping of molten cheese and popped it into his mouth. He had developed a taste for the pungent delicacy, which he regarded as a sign of progress as far as his dwarven credentials were concerned.

Boïndil gave him a nudge and pointed his cheese skewer at the mismatched pair on the opposite side of the fire. "Would you believe it? He's still wearing that bucket. I bet it's stuck on his head!"

Boëndal was more respectful. "It's his height that gets me. Granted, I don't know much about humans, but he's by far the biggest long-un I've ever seen. He makes orcs look like children."

"What if he's not really a long-un?" his brother said suspiciously. "He could be a baby ogre or Tion knows what." Already he was on his feet, preparing to march over and confront the giant. "I'm telling you, if there's a green-hided runt hiding in that armor, I'll kill it on the spot." He grinned dangerously. "The same goes for the lady. So what if she's a maga? She's not much use to Girdlegard now."

Tungdil's face flushed with panic. He wouldn't put it past Andôkai to have one of Tion's monsters at her side. *I can't let Boïndil pick a fight with Djerûn. If he starts on the giant, Andôkai will join the fray and we'll all be in trouble.*

"No, he's a man, all right," he said firmly. "Haven't you heard about the human giants? I read somewhere that they join together in formidable armies. The orcs are scared stiff of them!"

It was a nerve-racking business lying to his kinsfolk, but he knew it was for the best.

"How do they get that big?" persisted Boïndil, reluctant to

let the matter drop. He jiggled his axes, hoping to find some reason that would allow him to test his strength against the giant.

"Um, it's their mothers... You see, they..." Tungdil tried feverishly to dream up an explanation; almost anything would do. "Straight after birth, the mothers tie ropes to their arms and legs and stretch them as much as they can. They keep doing it, every morning and every night," he blustered, "and it works, as you can see. They've got a fearsome reputation on the battlefield. They actually grow into their armor; they can't take it off."

The brothers looked at him incredulously. "Their mothers really do that to them?" Boïndil was shocked. "It's pretty gruesome, don't you think?"

"That's what it says in the books."

Boëndal looked the warrior up and down. "I'd like to know what he weighs and how much he can lift."

The three dwarves stared at the giant, trying to work out whether or not he was asleep. His demonic visor shone in the flames, grinning at them mockingly.

Boëndal shrugged. "Sooner or later he'll show his face. He'll have to lift his visor when he eats."

IX

It had been a long time, perhaps thousands of cycles, since Girdlegard had last seen a band of travelers as strange as the company that had been toiling through Ionandar and Gauragar for several orbits.

First to appear over the hilltop was Djerûn, his formidable armored body provoking horrified panic among any peasants who happened to be tending the land.

The dwarves led the way, but their stocky figures took longer to loom into view. Boëndal and Boïndil walked ahead, with Tungdil in the middle and Andôkai and the giant a few paces behind. Djerûn was forced to take miniature strides in order not to outpace his mistress and the dwarves. The maga had offered a farmer a ridiculous number of gold coins to part with his horse, which now bore the weight of her bags and the giant's spare weaponry.

Tungdil was still trying to work out whether to tell Andôkai about the books. He had no idea what was written in the scholarly tomes, but it was encouraging to know that Nôd'onn feared their contents as much as the artifacts. *Who knows if I can stop him, but Andôkai surely can. She's the last of Girdlegard's magi.* He was determined to do whatever it took to make her stay. Slowing his pace a little, he fell in beside her. "I've been thinking about your magic and I can't figure out why it still works. Didn't Nôd'onn corrupt the force fields?"

"Why do you ask?"

"It's important?"

"For you or for me?"

"For Girdlegard."

"For Girdlegard! Very well, Tungdil, how could I refuse?" She smiled balefully. "I was never as kind-spirited as my fellow magi. My god is Samusin, god of equilibrium, who cherishes darkness as well as light. Thanks to him I have the ability to use both. It's harder for me to store and use dark magic, but the corruption of the force fields hasn't really affected my powers. Nôd'onn knows that, but he wasn't expecting me to survive. Not that he's got anything to worry about—my art is nothing compared to his." Shielding her eyes with her hand, she squinted into the distance. "There should be a forest ahead. I can't stand this sun much longer."

You've got to ask her now, Tungdil told himself. He summoned all his courage. "Maga, suppose there was a way of stopping the traitor. Would you try it?" he asked.

There was silence. Just as the tension was becoming unbearable, Andôkai spoke. "Would this have something to do with the contents of your bags, little man?"

"We found something in Greenglade," he told her, giving a brief account of what had happened in the woods. "Nôd'onn sent in the älfar, but we got there first."

"Are you going to show me?"

Tungdil thought for a moment and decided that there was no point leaving the matter half-solved. He slid the package out of his knapsack, removed the wrapping, and handed over the books.

Andôkai opened each of the tomes in turn and leafed through the pages, her face remaining an inscrutable mask.

Tungdil couldn't help feeling disappointed: He had reckoned with her amazement. Seeing her dispassionate expression made him fear the worst.

At length she returned the volumes. "Was there anything with them?"

"What are they about?" he asked, deciding not to give away anything until he'd found out more.

"They're anthologies: descriptions of legendary beings and mythical weapons, and an obscure tale about an expedition across the Stone Gateway into the Outer Lands. It says in the preface that a single survivor returned, mortally wounded but bearing manuscripts that are reproduced in the book. Why Nôd'onn should take an interest in the volumes is a mystery. I suppose he's just as knowledge-lusty as before."

"What else do they say?"

"Nothing."

"Nothing? Nôd'onn wouldn't have sacked Greenglade for nothing! He had us chased by a war band of orcs just to get his hands on the books!" He glared at the maga defiantly. "With respect, maga, I think you're wrong. There's something important in those volumes, even if you can't see it."

"Are you daring to....?" The mistress of Brandôkai stopped and erupted into laughter. "Did you hear that, Djerûn? Here I am, traipsing along a dusty road, being corrected by a dwarf who thinks he knows best!"

The giant kept walking, impassive as ever.

"I didn't mean to cause offense," said Tungdil, "but at least I'm not as arrogant and sure of myself as you are. I shouldn't wonder if there's elfish blood in your veins!"

"Fighting talk, little dwarf!" she said in amusement. She nodded in the direction of the twins. "The other two would have drawn their weapons and settled the matter another way, but you learned from Lot-Ionan, I can tell." Suddenly she was serious again. "I'll take a proper look at the volumes tonight. Maybe you're right and there's more to them than I thought."

"Thank you, Estimable Maga." The dwarf inclined his head respectfully and quickened his pace to catch up with the twins. "We'll soon find out what the magus wanted with our books," he announced proudly.

"What? You didn't tell the wizard-woman about them, did you?" gasped a horrified Boïndil.

"Not only that; I showed them to her."

The secondling shook his head reprovingly. "You're too trusting, scholar. It's time you became a proper dwarf and stopped acting like a human."

"I see. So you'd like me to splice her skull if she disagrees with me, would you?" said Tungdil, his temper beginning to fray.

"I'd like to see you dare," Boïndil retorted with venom.

Boëndal quickly squeezed between them. "Stop it!" he said firmly. "Spare your fury for the orcs; I doubt we've seen the last of them. For what it's worth, I think Tungdil was right to tell the maga. I don't like being hounded because of a couple of books I know nothing about."

His brother just grunted and surged on.

"I never said traveling with us would be easy," Boëndal said with a grin.

Tungdil sighed, then burst out laughing.

Dusk was falling when they set up camp. The air had cooled and there was a smell of earth and grass. A band of crickets was chirping its evening concert.

The dwarves divided up their dwindling provisions—the sight of the Blue Range's summits in the distance reassured them that they would soon be feasting on fresh dwarven treats. Meanwhile, Andôkai kept her word and studied the books.

Not wanting to distract her, Tungdil allowed the maga to read in peace, approaching only to bring Djerûn his supper. Like every other evening, he placed a loaf of bread, a chunk of cheese, and a large slab of meat beside the warrior.

This time he was determined to keep an eye on the giant while he ate; so far neither Tungdil nor the twins had seen behind the metal visor.

"Djerûn will sit the first watch," said Andôkai without looking up from her reading. "The rest of you can get some sleep."

"Suits me fine," said Boïndil, then burped. He shook the worst of the crumbs from his beard, coiled his plait into a pillow, and settled down next to the fire. "Listen, long-un," he told the giant, who was sitting motionless as usual, "don't forget to wake me if you see any orcs. It's about time they had a taste of my axes."

The twins seized the chance to get some sleep, and in no time loud snores were reverberating through the woods, setting the leaves aquiver.

Andôkai slammed down her book. "Now I know why they always take the first watch," she said irritably. "It's a wonder their snores never woke me. How am I supposed to concentrate when they're making such a din?"

Tungdil chuckled. "Imagine what it sounds like in Ogre's Death."

"I don't intend staying long enough to find out."

Tungdil looked at her rippling muscles as she stretched. She was impressively strong for a woman—stronger even than the scullery maids who were used to hard labor.

"Have you found anything new in the…" Tungdil checked himself. He had resolved not to ask her about the books.

Hugging her knees to her chest, she rested her chin on her hands and turned her blue eyes on him. "You think I'll change my mind if the books tell us how Nôd'onn can be defeated."

"Samusin is the god of equilibrium; surely it's your duty to strive for a balance between darkness and light," he said, appealing to her faith since honor alone was not enough to persuade her. Her decision to abandon her realm was proof enough of that.

Andôkai laid a hand on one of the leather-bound volumes. "If I could find a spell or a charm that would cause Nôd'onn's downfall, I would take the traitor on," she said earnestly, "but the books contain nothing of the kind—just far-fetched stories and myths."

"So you're turning your back on Girdlegard?"

"My art is useless against Nôd'onn's power. I was lucky to escape." She flicked through the book, opening it at random. "Maybe there *is* some kind of hidden meaning. All I know is that I don't have the key."

Tungdil decided to come clean. He produced the letter that Gorén had written in scholarly script. "This was with the books. I suppose it might help."

"Is there anything else you're not telling me, or is this the last of your secrets?"

"It's the last, I swear."

Andôkai accepted the sheet of parchment, folded it, and placed it between the pages of one of the books. She rubbed her eyes. "The darkness is hardly conducive to study. I'll read it tomorrow." She returned the volumes to their wax paper wrapping, arranged the parcel as a pillow, and nestled her head on top.

"Tomorrow?" Tungdil had been expecting her to read the letter at once. He sighed; the maga was a troublesome person to deal with. He settled down next to the fire and glanced at Djerûn.

The giant was still wearing his helmet, but the food was gone. Tungdil cursed: Talking to Andôkai had distracted him from looking at Djerůn's visor, although, now that he thought about it, he hadn't been alerted by a telling clunk of metal. There was something unnerving about the maga's companion.

Beroïn's Folk,
Secondling Kingdom,
Girdlegard,
Late Summer, 6234th Solar Cycle

Balendilín barely had a moment to himself. On reaching his chamber, he discovered that two dwarves from the fourthling delegation had requested to see him.

Not a moment too soon. It's about time Gandogar put a stop to this foolishness. He turned round and hurried to the meadows, where the delegates were expecting him.

The high king's counselor was feeling remarkably upbeat. For weeks he had poured most of his energy into rebutting the rumors about Gundrabur's failing health, and rightly so: The high king had a strong heart and an even stronger will, which he employed in persuading the assembly to await the arrival of the other pretender to the throne. Such was his success that there was talk of strengthening the bonds among the folks in more permanent ways.

It's going almost too well, thought Balendilín, gripped by a sudden apprehension. He stepped out of the passageway and onto a bridge across a chasm fifty paces wide. Deep in thought, he made his way over the disused copper mines two hundred paces below.

It bothered him that Bislipur never seemed to tire of rekindling the passions of those who favored a war against the elves. He and Gundrabur would have achieved much more if it hadn't been for the fourthling's inflammatory speeches. *He's a rabble-rouser. You can guarantee his influence is at the heart of Gandogar's misplaced zeal.*

Just then he noticed a movement in the mouth of the tunnel ahead. Bislipur was on the bridge in front of him, his left hand resting lightly on his ax. For a moment Balendilín wondered whether the fourthling could have heard his thoughts through the thick stone walls. There was something threatening about his demeanor. Balendilín stopped and waited. "Were you looking for me?"

"Do you know what they're calling it?" Bislipur shouted, his voice echoing against the rock. "The *quarrel of the cripples:* one-armed Balendilín against Bislipur the lame. Is that how you see it?"

Balendilín paused, hoping to hear sounds of other dwarves, but the tunnels were deserted. He and Bislipur were alone. "*Quarrel* is too strong a word," he answered. "You have your convictions, I have mine, and we're both trying to persuade the assembly of our views." He took a step forward, then another one. Bislipur did the same. "What is it that you want?"

"To serve the dwarves." Bislipur said, grim-faced.

"What is it you want from *me?*"

"A change of heart. How can I persuade you that the future of the folks and clans lies with Gandogar and me?"

"If you persist in campaigning for a war against the elves, I will never be able to support your king," Balendilín said frankly. He stood his ground and Bislipur stopped too. Fifteen paces remained between them.

"Then a quarrel it is," Bislipur told him harshly. "Until Gandogar has been elected, I shall regard you as an enemy and a danger to the prosperity and safety of our race. The others will come round to my view." He walked toward Balendilín, who was advancing along the bridge. Only an arm's length separated the two dwarves. "It's about time the high king was spared your counsel so he can come to his senses at last."

By now they were so close that their noses were almost touching.

"To his senses? That's rich, from you." Balendilín stared at Bislipur and saw implacable hatred and enmity in his eyes. "Let me tell you this," he said, trying not to betray his fear, even though Bislipur undoubtedly intended to harm him. "Your war against Âlandur will never happen. Even the fourthling chieftains are having second thoughts."

"The throne is ours. You're no match for Gandogar and me." The words were spat violently, Bislipur's pent-up fury ready to erupt at any moment.

"I didn't realize you were bidding for a joint succession."

Neither flinched as they glared at each other, eyes locked in combat. All of a sudden Bislipur's air of menace fell away.

"Well, good luck with your lost cause," he said breezily. "May Vraccas be with you." He stepped past Balendilín and continued along the bridge.

The high king's counselor closed his eyes and swallowed. Having resigned himself to a duel, he could scarcely believe that he was going to make it across the chasm without a fight. Bislipur's whistling reverberated through the tunnel, the simple melody repeating itself and overlapping as he strode away.

It was a relief to leave the bridge and feel solid ground beneath his feet. *At least I know he means business,* thought Balendilín philosophically. He pressed on, anxious not to keep the fourthling delegates waiting.

He was just approaching a bend in the passageway when the floor seemed to shake. The movement was so slight that a human would never have detected it, but the dwarves had learned to take notice of the faintest vibrations in the rock. Something heavy was heading his way.

The next instant, he heard agitated mooing and thundering hooves. From what he could gather, a herd had been startled on its return from the meadows.

Balendilín scanned his surroundings, searching in vain for a niche that would save him from the cattle's charge. There was no choice but to regain the bridge, climb over the parapet, and balance on the narrow ledge.

He turned and sped back along the passageway, spurred on by the sound of horns scraping against the polished walls. Panting heavily, he reached the end of the tunnel and the bridge came into view; the animals were right behind him.

Without hesitating, he swung himself over the side and steadied himself on the ledge. The momentum nearly carried him into the abyss, but the daring maneuver paid off and the cows streamed past behind him.

Vraccas be praised!

There was a jolt and the bridge cracked audibly. He could see the first fissures running through the rock.

It was only then that it occurred to him that the bridge was not designed to bear the weight of stampeding cows. It had been built for dwarves, not cattle. The herd exceeded its strength by a matter of tons and the rhythmic pounding of their hooves had a devastating effect.

The first crack opened at the midpoint of the bridge where the stone was at its thinnest. The struts beneath it snapped, heralding the next stage in the disaster.

A section of stone measuring four paces in length gave way, sending a number of cows plummeting into the abyss. From there the destruction spread along the bridge. Slab by slab the stone fell away, cows tumbling to their deaths, their moos becoming fainter and fainter. At the back of his mind Balendilín was aware that there was still no sign that they had hit the bottom.

His position was precarious in the extreme. With the bridge crumbling before his eyes, he was faced with a choice of dying among the cows or casting himself voluntarily into the abyss.

At last the herd stopped surging and the dwarf summoned the courage to leap into their midst. Barely had his feet touched the ground when the stone gave way beneath him. Grabbing wildly at the edge, he managed to catch hold of a jagged overhang and clung on for dear life.

An able-bodied dwarf would have hauled himself to safety easily, but Balendilín, dangling by his only arm, had no means of saving himself and no prospect of being rescued. He knew it was merely a matter of time before his muscles gave out.

"Is anyone there? Help!" he shouted, straining his voice to alert his kinsmen to his plight. With any luck, someone would be on their way to retrieve the wayward herd. "Over here!"

The cows were calmer now and answered his cries with gentle, mindless moos. Two of the animals ventured to the edge and, sniffing at his hand, licked it heartily. Their saliva collected in a pool, making his position more dangerous than before.

It seemed to Balendilín that three grown orcs could not weigh more than he did. His arm was getting longer, while his voice grew hoarse.

Suddenly the herd parted as someone barged through their midst.

"Over here," he called, relieved that help had arrived before he lost his grip. "I'm falling!"

Dust showered over him, coating his hair and his beard, and he found himself looking into the green face of a gnome whose sizable nose was tipped with a wart of impressive dimensions. The creature's round eyes stared at him greedily and its clawlike fingers slithered down his arm.

"Nearly done." Sverd leaned over the edge and fumbled with Balendilín's belt. "Just one moment," he told the unfortunate dwarf.

A clasp clicked open and Sverd straightened up, a look of satisfaction on his face. He brandished Balendilín's purse and the jewel-encrusted belt. "Much indebted to you, I'm sure! You can let go now." Chuckling maliciously, he beat his retreat.

"You can't just leave me!" Balendilín shouted, aghast. "Come back!" It was too late: His fingers slipped and in spite of his frantic efforts, he failed to get a purchase on the saliva-covered overhang. He steeled himself for the long slide into darkness.

At that moment, an ax sped toward him, the short metal spur catching in the rings of his mail shirt. Balendilín was reeled in like an anchor on a chain.

Breathing heavily, he lay on the floor beside his rescuer, who was panting from the strain.

"Gandogar!" Balendilín could not conceal his astonishment at being saved from his fate by the fourthling king.

"You and I may not always agree with each other, but we're hardly enemies," said the monarch, smiling wryly. "First and foremost, we're dwarves, children of the Smith. Our enemies are Tion's minions, not the other clans or folks. That's how I see it, in spite of our differences." He straightened up and helped the royal counselor to his feet. "What happened?"

Balendilín seized his hand thankfully. Gandogar had spoken from the heart and his heroic intervention was evidence enough of his sincerity. "Something must have startled the cattle," he said.

He didn't elaborate further. He wasn't prepared to blame Bislipur and Sverd for engineering the "accident" until he had firm proof. The gnome's appearance on the scene had convinced him that Bislipur was behind his attempted murder; Sverd always acted on his master's command.

"I owe you my life," he said earnestly. "It doesn't mean I think you're right about the elves, but I'm deeply indebted to you all the same."

"Spoken like a true dwarf," the king said warmly. "Besides, I didn't do anything that you wouldn't have done for me."

"Oh really?" Balendilín paused and smiled. "I'm not sure I would have helped."

Gandogar looked at him, shocked. "I..."

"How could I have rescued you with only one hand?" Balendilín burst out laughing and, after a short silence, Gandogar joined in. It saddened the counselor that the fourthling monarch was so determined to go to war; he had a feeling that Gandogar would make an excellent king.

Later, when Balendilín regained his chamber, he knew without a shadow of a doubt that the whole episode had been a trap. The delegates who supposedly wanted to see him were an invention.

At least his purse and his buckle had been deposited by his door. The gnome must have thought better of harboring evidence of his despicable crime. Balendilín replaced the purse, fastened his belt, and vowed not to give his would-be murderers another chance.

Kingdom of Sangpûr,
Girdlegard,
Early Autumn, 6234th Solar Cycle

Autumn left the travelers in no doubt that it was a force to be reckoned with, particularly at night. Even though they were deep in the south of Girdlegard, having crossed the border into Queen Umilante's realm, there was little warmth to be found in the desert, only a constant barrage of tiny grains of sand.

No sooner had darkness drawn in and the sun sunk below the horizon than the air took on a nasty chill. Andôkai wasted no time in lighting a blazing fire, in spite of the twins' disapproval. To Boëndal's mind, the comfort it provided was outweighed by the risk of attracting orcs and other riffraff; it seemed foolish to court danger when they had come so far and were almost at their goal. Somewhat begrudgingly, Boïndil agreed with him. But the maga ignored them anyway and persisted in tossing logs into the flames.

They were only eight or so orbits from Ogre's Death when they came to a village among the dunes. The settlement was situated next to a tranquil lake, which made it a popular and flourishing trading post. Tungdil and the others decided to grant themselves the luxury of a night's shelter.

For merchants returning home from the secondling kingdom, the village was a last oasis before the long journey through Sangpûr, where nothing awaited them but desolate wasteland and the occasional brigand.

"It's safe here," Boëndal assured them. "The traders like dwarves because they know we offer decent, solid wares that fetch good prices when they sell them in other towns."

The party still attracted considerable attention, but only, as Tungdil realized, because they were accompanied by a walking tionium tower. Children crowded round them, marveling at Djerûn, who bore the fuss with equanimity. The giant was accustomed to causing a stir.

Visitors to the settlement were accommodated in tents by the lake. Depending on the needs of each party, the canvas and wood constructions could be expanded or reduced in size, with the option of adding an extra floor to create a two-story dwelling not dissimilar to a house.

Djerûn was too tall for a standard model, so they opted for a two-story tent and removed the upper floorboards. The

wind was freshening, so they retreated under the canvas, lit a
fire in the corner, and got the kettle boiling.

"Just think," Tungdil said excitedly, sipping his steaming
mug of tea, "I'm about to meet my folk. I can hardly wait!"

"I'm not surprised," Boëndal agreed, smiling at him
warmly. "And the others will be pleased to meet you too. The
delegates will be dying of impatience."

"Ugh!" his brother interrupted. "Why would anyone drink
this stuff? I'm off to find some beer. There aren't any sensible
buildings in this village, but they're bound to sell something
that tastes better than tea!" He got up and left.

"So tell me, Tungdil," said Andôkai, who had been poring
over the books, "what makes you special enough to merit a
royal escort?" Gorén's letter rested on her knee. It was the
first time she had taken any interest in why the twins had
been sent to find Tungdil.

He hesitated. "What does it matter?" he said disdainfully.
"The Estimable Maga is abandoning Girdlegard. I don't see
why she needs to know."

Andôkai broke off her study, taken aback by Tungdil's harsh
tone. "Dear me, I've incurred your eternal displeasure, have I?
I'm sorry to disappoint you, but you're wasting your breath if
you think you can stop me by appealing to my conscience."

Boëndal glanced at Tungdil, eyebrows raised.

As far as Tungdil was concerned, the maga had no right
to give up on her homeland so easily. She wasn't the only
one who stood to lose by staying in Girdlegard. In spite of
his excitement at being reunited with his folk, he knew that
his chances of survival were slim, unless of course there
was something in the books that could help them vanquish
Nôd'onn. But unlike the maga, he was determined to fight
beside his kinsmen to the end.

Rain pattered against the canvas. Fat droplets left mean-
dering tracks on the outside of the tent and pitted the dusty
ground. Autumn showers were nothing unusual in Sangpûr's
deserts. In most other places, the wet and dry weather would
have been ideal for agriculture, but the soil was impossibly
barren in these parts. Trees and plants rarely took root and
were tended jealously by their owners.

Just then the tent flap swung open and a cloaked intruder
appeared in their midst.

Like a statue conjured to life, Djerûn leaped into action.
His left gauntlet closed around his two-hander; then he raised
the sword with both hands, dropped into a half crouch,
lunged forward, and brought the blade whistling toward the
stranger's throat.

"Stop!" the maga commanded. Djerûn froze.

"Forgive me," stammered the man. "I didn't mean to
startle you. I was told to deliver this." Hands trembling, he
deposited the keg of beer and fled, worried that the giant
would change his mind and cut him down regardless.

"Good work," Boëndal said admiringly. "I wouldn't have
thought it possible that a man could move so fast wearing all
that armor."

Djerûn returned to his former position, cross-legged on the
floor. Boëndal's comment failed to elicit a response from the
giant or his mistress.

The secondling persevered. "The warrior is your business,"
he told Andôkai, "but our sentries won't let him cross the
High Pass unless he's prepared to show his face and declare
his lineage."

"What kind of foolishness is this?" the maga said irritably,
weary of the constant interruptions. "We'll be leaving Girdlegard! What does it matter what he looks like or where he

comes from? You'd be well advised to focus on your defenses, instead of interfering in the business of travelers who can't wait to leave your land."

"Whether you're coming or going is of no concern to us," Boëndal said emphatically. "No beast of Tion will set foot on our pass."

"Hang on," Tungdil told him, "he's just an elongated—"

Boëndal didn't let him finish. "I played along to keep the peace, but we're almost home now." He looked at Andôkai grimly. "When we reach the Blue Range, the giant will be bound by the same laws as everyone else. You're welcome to seek your own route through the mountains, but you won't be crossing our kingdom if you're hiding something danger-ous behind that mask."

"I'll take my chances," said the maga, returning to her book.

"*Your chances!*" exploded Boëndal. "Do you mean we've been traveling all this way with a creature of darkness?"

"That's not what I said. Besides, I don't recall there being anything in the creed of Samusin to forbid it."

"Samusin? I won't have any truck with *him*." The dwarf's face hardened and he rose to his feet, the long shaft of his crow's beak clasped in one hand. "Tell me what's behind the visor."

"That does it!" Andôkai closed her book with a snap. "Nôd'onn himself could be hiding inside that armor and I wouldn't tell you! Djerûn is with me." If anyone had been wondering how Andôkai the Tempestuous had earned her name, the matter was now resolved. "Who cares if he's an ogre or a dark spirit or Tion knows what? He's the perfect traveling companion and he doesn't stink like a pig—which is more than can be said for you and your brother!" Her blue eyes glinted menacingly as she swept the long blond hair from her face. "He'll raise his visor when he's good and ready, and if you don't like it, too bad!" She pointed toward the main village. "Did you notice the bathhouse on your way in? I recommend you pay it a visit. It's a wonder the birds don't die of asphyxiation when you're around."

She fixed him with an icy stare and opened the second volume with a thud.

The silence that followed was broken by the sound of someone running toward the tent. The next moment, Boïndil burst through the door.

"Pointy-ears!" he spluttered. "Pointy-ears from Âlandur! The trader said they—" He noticed the keg of beer abandoned forlornly on the floor. "I thought you'd be thirsty!" he said, shaking his head in surprise. He pierced the lid with his ax, filled his tankard, emptied it in a single draft, and burped. "Not bad," he pronounced, helping himself to more.

"You were saying?" Andôkai reminded him sharply, diverting his attention away from the beer.

"Er, elves!" Boïndil sat down on a leather stool. "I bought the keg from a trader who told me what's been happening in Âlandur. He thought we'd be drinking to the ruin of the elves. From what he said, their kingdom is all but done for. He reckoned they were scouting Girdlegard for new places to live."

"In Sangpûr?" the maga said incredulously. "Why come this far south when there's nothing but sand, dust, and stone? It doesn't make sense. What would an elf want with a treeless desert?"

Tungdil glanced at Boëndal, who was clearly thinking on similar lines.

It took another sip of beer before his brother caught on.

"Are you saying they're älfar?" he ventured finally. Ideas invariably took longer to penetrate Boïndil's mind.

"Nôd'onn wants the books," Tungdil explained patiently. "A motley company like us doesn't go unnoticed. They must have followed us here and waited until nightfall to enter the settlement. As soon as it's dark, you can't see their eyes and there's no way of telling they're not elves."

"In which case, they could be either," Boëndal pointed out. "I say we post a watch. If they're älfar, they'll be after us. Why else would they be staying in the village, if not to steal the books? From now on, none of us leaves the tent, no matter what. We'll let them come to us."

"Nonsense, we'll go after them!" Boïndil said fiercely. "If they're älfar, we'll kill them, and if they're elves...we'll kill them too! The pointy-ears deserve to die." It had been a while since he'd last used his axes.

Andôkai listened, then signaled to Djerûn and settled down to sleep.

"No, brother," ruled Boëndal, "we'll leave them in peace. The whole village could turn against us if we start a fight. We're not in our own kingdom yet, remember. Cool your temper. I'll take the first watch."

Tungdil yawned and finished his tankard of beer before lying down on a pile of rugs. His fingers clutched the haft of his ax, making him feel a little less exposed. He wasn't sure what to think, but in some ways he was hoping that the älfar would attack. At least that would persuade Andôkai of the importance of the books.

Tungdil was just dozing off when a shouted warning woke the desert oasis. The dwarves were on their feet in a flash, weapons at the ready. Andôkai had drawn her sword and was monitoring the tent flap and the walls.

Ax raised and shield held in front of him, Djerûn knelt by the entrance, blocking it like a wall. His helmet glinted, the demonic visor coming alive in the dying firelight. For a fraction of a heartbeat, Tungdil thought he glimpsed a purple glow behind the eyeholes.

Boëndal damped the flames lest their shadows be seen through the canvas. The three dwarves stood back-to-back, the maga beside them.

For a few moments it was quiet; then agonized screams rent the air. Now sounds could be heard from the other tents as people emerged from their flimsy shelters, their voices mingling in a clamor of questions as each tried to establish the cause of the noise. Willowy silhouettes and strange shadows flitted across the canvas walls, while all around there was a clunking of metal as shields knocked against tent poles, armor was donned, and weapons were unsheathed. Roused abruptly from its slumber, the village among the dunes was preparing to fight.

"What's going on?" asked Tungdil in a whisper. "Do you think it's a trap?"

Just then a human voice cried out in terror, "Orcs!" Swords met in a ringing din. The battle had commenced.

The beasts stopped skulking through the settlement and abandoned all pretense at stealth. Listening to their grunts and snarls, Tungdil was reminded of Goodwater, of Ionandar, of those who had died…

He was torn between staying in the tent and running to the aid of the people outside. His instinct was to help, but for all he knew, the älfar were out there, waiting for him and his companions to emerge.

"What do we do?" he asked the battle-hardened twins.

"We wait," came Boëndal's strained reply. He tightened his grip on his crow's beak.

The clash of swords was getting louder and more violent, mingled with the screams of dying men. Sounds of fighting echoed from every corner of the village. The orcs had evidently surrounded the settlement and were attacking from all sides simultaneously, making it impossible for anyone to escape.

As the fighting raged around them, Tungdil and the others followed the progress of the battle on the walls of their tent, men and orcs locked in combat like figures in a shadow theater.

Boïndil held a whispered conference with his brother. At last a decision was reached. "We need to get out of here," he announced. "The runts will sack the settlement and we can't risk Tungdil getting—"

An orc burst through the tent flap, grunting and waving his sword. He ran full tilt into the expanse of unforgiving metal that was Djerûn's shield.

Nose gushing with blood, he staggered groggily to the side, only for the giant to hew his collarbone with a downward swipe of his ax. The force of the blow cleaved armor and bones, slicing the orc diagonally in two. Blood and guts spilled from the body in a horrible, reeking mess.

"Hey! I thought I told you to leave the runts to me," protested Boïndil. "The next one's mine, all right?"

A second orc stormed into the tent, and Andôkai called out to Djerûn, who swung his shield obediently to the side. The beast ran on unhindered, failing to notice his fallen comrade or the colossal warrior.

"That's more like it!" Boïndil rushed forward and stopped the beast without ado. Felled by his axes, the orc died with a final grunt.

"No more tomfoolery, Boïndil," his brother said sternly. He cut a slit in the rear of the tent and peered through the gap. "All clear." The sharp blade of his crow's beak tore neatly through the canvas and he slipped outside. When he was sure it was safe, he signaled for the others to follow.

They had taken no more than a few paces when a long, slender shadow appeared in front of Boëndal and attacked.

Only the dwarf's helmet prevented the sword from cleaving his skull. Even so, the force of the blow brought him to his knees.

"Elf or älf, prepare to die!" His brother hurled himself at the figure with a blood-curdling shriek.

As their assailant stepped back, his cloak fell open to reveal a black metal breastplate that reached to his thighs. His beautiful face and pointed ears removed any doubts about the identity of their attacker.

Another älf appeared out of nowhere and challenged Djerûn, while a third bore down on Andôkai. Stretching out her hand, the maga conjured a glimmering black sphere and cast a bolt of lightning in his direction.

Tungdil expected the creature to burst into flames, but his hopes were disappointed. The älf produced an amulet, which intercepted the spluttering charm, absorbing the magic and leaving the target unharmed. Cursing, the maga drew her sword.

Tungdil glanced round, looking for a possible fourth attacker. To his horror an älf leaped from a nearby cart and landed in front of him. His eyes took in the crimson gloves, long spear, and golden hair... It was one of the two älfar who had parleyed with the orcs near Goodwater. *Sinthoras!* His lips appeared to be moving.

"Speak up!" commanded Tungdil, dwarven bloody-mindedness conquering his fear. He had no intention of surrendering.

"Look at me: Sinthoras is your death," the fair-haired älf

whispered softly. *"I will take your life as I have taken the life of every groundling before you."*

"We'll see about that. Vraccas helped us to kill one of your kind in Greenglade and he'll help us again." Tungdil decided not to wait for the älf to attack. "For Lot-Ionan and Frala!" Raising his ax, he charged.

Sinthoras laughed, easily evading the energetic but poorly planned attack. Realizing at once that he was dealing with a novice, he decided to have some fun with his victim before dealing the fatal blow.

His spear flashed forward, its long, tapered point boring through Tungdil's mail shirt and passing through his undergarments. The tip pierced his left shoulder, deep enough to hurt him but too shallow for serious harm. The wound enraged the dwarf further and he redoubled his efforts, little realizing that the älf was toying with him.

Slowly but surely Sinthoras drew his victim away from his companions, leading him into the jumble of tents. While the älf skipped and danced ahead, Tungdil blundered among the guy ropes and tent pegs, grimly focused on staying on his feet.

The älf's weapon approached with such speed that Tungdil gave up trying to block its attack. One moment the creature would be in front of him; the next his spear would be buried in his back. He was losing blood from myriad perforations that smarted abominably.

At last Tungdil looked round and realized his mistake. Amid the confusion of ropes and tents he had lost sight of the others and even the giant was gone. A moment later, Sinthoras vanished as well. The älf was enjoying his murderous little game.

Wherever Tungdil looked, men were fighting with a courage born of despair, knowing with grim certainty that the orcs would show no mercy. Meanwhile, the beasts kept coming at them, more determined than ever to sink their teeth into the traders and their wares.

A number of tents had been pulled to the ground and the canvas caught fire. Flames and glinting swords reflected in the surface of the lake, the watery image of destruction warped by rippling waves.

"Where are you hiding?" Tungdil was learning to his cost that älfar were harder to deal with than orcs. He decided to rejoin his friends while he still had the chance.

But Sinthoras wasn't finished with him.

"Over here!" The älf loomed up behind him, thrusting his spear violently into the dwarf's right shoulder.

Something seemed to tear inside Tungdil's arm, the pain surging through him like liquid fire. His hand opened and the ax fell from his grasp.

The dwarf's tormentor pulled his legs from under him, tipping him face-first to the ground. Crouching over him, Sinthoras threaded the spear through his mail shirt on a level with his heart. The metal spike ground against the rings.

"What did I tell you?" said a whisper in Tungdil's ear. "*Sinthoras is your death.* It would have been wiser to leave the books in Greenglade, but it's too late for that now."

"Go ahead and kill me, but answer me one thing: What do you want with the books?"

Sinthoras laughed. "Only a groundling could be so simple-minded! To think that you've been lugging around the volumes, and you don't even know what they are!" He thought for a moment. "They're precious, more precious than anything you can imagine. A single syllable is worth a sack of gold. They could make you the wealthiest being in Girdlegard—or the most powerful, if you kept the secret to yourself. Acting on their contents would make you a hero beyond compare." He leaned on his spear and lowered his voice to a malicious whisper. "All this you had—but you lost it. I'll take even more pleasure in killing you now."

Tungdil shuddered as the älf muttered unintelligibly in his own dark tongue. At any moment the spear would reach his heart and put an end to his life.

Before the weapon could penetrate farther, a shadow fell over them and something whirred through the air. The älf dove to safety, only this time the maneuver was anything but elegant. He hit a tent, the canvas collapsing around him.

Djerûn strode past the stricken dwarf and went after the älf. Using the lower edge of his shield as a knife, he beat down on the muffled body, first with his shield, then his ax, until the bloodied canvas lay still. Three orcs tried to stop him but were slain on the spot.

Tungdil wondered whether he was hallucinating when he saw what happened next.

The giant, whose back was turned to Tungdil, opened his visor—or so the dwarf concluded from the movement of his arm—and tore a chunk of flesh from an orcish corpse. He raised the dripping meat toward his face.

What is he doing? Grunting with pain, Tungdil lifted himself onto his knees, leaned on his ax for support, and called to the giant.

Djerûn whirled round in surprise and pushed down his visor.

In the light of the burning tents, Tungdil caught a brief glimpse of a skull with wide jaws, long fangs, and slits for eyes. The helmet clicked into place and violet light glimmered through the demon's eyes. The chunk of flesh had vanished, but it was obvious from the mutilated corpse and the green blood dripping from Djerûn's gauntlet that something extraordinary had occurred.

He's not an orc or an ogre, so what kind of creature is he?

Djerûn gestured with his ax in the direction from which he had come. Tungdil followed his lead, relying on the giant to slay the orcs who barred their path. He was finding it difficult enough to walk with his injuries.

Before they were out of the maze of tents, Boïndil rushed toward them, a panicked look on his face. His lips twitched and his jaw tightened when he saw the blood on Tungdil's shirt; he didn't need to be told that the giant had saved his charge's life.

The trio hurried on, arriving in time to see Andôkai drive her sword through the neck of a dying älf who was flailing at her feet. She snatched up the amulet that had warded off her magic power. Her leather armor seemed to strain at the seams as she gasped for breath, her physical strength exhausted.

She greeted Tungdil with a brief nod, then led the company out of the village on a southerly bearing. Between them, Djerûn, the twins, and the maga had put pay to three älfar.

Boëndal stoically ignored the blood trickling down his neck. It took more than a blow to the head to make a dwarf complain.

Tungdil gritted his teeth and followed at the rear. His wounds could be bandaged just as soon as they had got the books to safety, which meant throwing off Nôd'onn's henchmen and making their way to Ogre's Death as quickly as they could.

Three orcish sentries were waiting for them at the top of a dune. Djerûn drew his sword.

"That's enough from you, long-un!" In no time Ireheart was at his side, hacking savagely at the beasts. The rage he felt at neglecting his duty to Tungdil was channeled into his blows and he cut down two of the beasts in the time it took Djerûn to slay one.

"At least I'm faster than you," he told the giant.

Down in the village, the noise of the battle was fading. From the jeering and grunting it was obvious that the orcs had prevailed against the inhabitants of the desert's lone oasis. Flames were spreading from tent to tent and the orcs were loading chopped-up corpses onto carts. A band of runts spotted the travelers on the crest of the dune and set off in pursuit. Two dozen beasts scrambled up the sandy slope behind them.

"You'd think they'd have the sense to give up." Andôkai waited until they were almost upon them, then raised her arms and uttered an incantation.

A tearing wind swept out of nowhere, gusting and circling until it formed a tornado four paces in diameter, becoming stronger and fiercer with the maga's every word. Sand, scree, and boulders were sucked into its midst; then, on Andôkai's command, the gale unleashed its force on the orcs, who were hanging back in confusion.

The wind and debris peeled the skin from their bones. Grunting and yelping, the orcs fled the lethal gust.

"Carry on without me," Andôkai told the dwarves. "I'll keep the orcs busy for a while."

The trio resumed their march and soon the maga was back in their midst, with Djerûn behind them, on the lookout for any attacks from the rear.

This time, though, the orcs let them go. Unlike the älfar, they weren't equipped to deal with magic, and the night of looting and destruction had been profitable enough.

X

I call on the assembly to decide the matter without further
delay," said Gandogar loudly, his voice ringing out across
the great hall. With the intention of cutting a regal figure, he
had put on full mail and was wearing his diamond-encrusted
helmet. "Thirty orbits have passed, thirty orbits in which..."

He continued his address, the chieftains and elders listening in silence.

Gundrabur's eyes were closed and the ceremonial hammer
was resting on the arms of his marble throne. His counselor
was following the speech without visible emotion. He had not
succeeded in uncovering any evidence to incriminate Bislipur
or Sverd, and worse still, the mood among the delegates was
tipping in favor of war.

"You saw the smoke! It came from a village across the border with Sangpûr." Turning slowly, Gandogar scanned the
semicircle of dwarves; he knew he had to make eye contact
if he wanted to win their trust. "The settlement was razed to
the ground by orcs. Tion's runts are marauding through the
countryside, brazenly attacking the races of Girdlegard. We
can't *afford* not to know who our next leader will be. Every
orbit brings new dangers. According to the traders, strange
things are happening in the enchanted realms and Âlandur
is in turmoil. Some say that the elves have abandoned their
kingdom and are scouting for land elsewhere. We must act!"

"Here or in Âlandur?" said a bewildered voice from the benches.

"Here *and* in Âlandur!" bellowed Bislipur, before Gandogar had a chance to reply. His dwarven blood was boiling over with impatience and he couldn't endure the prospect of another interminable speech. "Âlandur must be invaded before the pointy-ears give us the slip and vanish Vraccas knows where!" He raised a clenched fist. "Destroy the elves and avenge our murdered kin!"

The call was taken up by most of the delegates, although a few of their number abstained from the general excitement, some signaling their disagreement by frowning or shaking their heads.

Gandogar's gaze settled on a chieftain who was wearing his withered elf's ear with pride. The call to arms had been resoundingly successful, but there was still the matter of the succession, and the elderly monarch showed no sign of preparing to vacate the throne.

At that moment, Gundrabur's eyes opened wearily. "Silence!" he commanded. "Baying for blood like beasts... You should be ashamed of yourselves!" He raised a gnarled hand and pointed to the dwarf who was sporting the grisly trinket. "Get rid of it!"

The chieftain looked to Gandogar for support.

Seizing the hammer, the high king rose from the throne and made his way from the dais to confront the disobedient dwarf. His wrinkled fingers gripped the chain and snapped it from the delegate's neck. The shriveled ear dropped to the floor.

"I'm not dead yet, and while I'm your high king, I shall set our course," he thundered. "The assembly will wait!"

"No," Gandogar contradicted him, "we have waited long enough. Beyond these walls, orcs are laying waste to Girdlegard and the elvish villains are getting away. I will sit and wait no longer!"

Balendilín stepped down from the platform and strode over to the fourthling monarch. "You forget yourself," he said, hand resting lightly on his belt. "The high king deserves your respect." The reprimand was delivered without any of the usual formalities behooving Gandogar's rank.

"The high king has been wearing the crown for too many cycles to know what's best for our folks!" Gandogar snapped back. "I won't put up with this nonsense any longer. Why should I sit back and do nothing when we should be seizing our opportunity and getting vengeance on the elves? Âlandur is as good as defeated! We need to attack while we can, not sit here, wasting our energy on pointless discussions. Orbit after orbit, all we ever do is talk and drink!"

Balendilín squared his shoulders. "Think carefully before you continue, King Gandogar. Our laws were not made to be broken by you." He pointed to the stone stelae engraved with the sacred commandments of the dwarves. "They're the very basis of our existence. Defy them, and you'll be endangering the fragile unity of the folks. Why not take a hammer to the tablets if that's your intention? By all means, write your own laws, but remember: History will be your judge."

Hand on his ax, Bislipur stepped forward, positioning himself at Gandogar's side. The atmosphere in the great hall was unbearably tense; for the first time it seemed that the difference of opinion was going to end in blows.

Suddenly, the doors swung open.

"Get out!" Gandogar shouted furiously. "We don't need more confounded beer!"

But this time the interruption wasn't the fault of attendants bearing tankards. A herald walked in. "The second candidate has arrived!" he announced.

The delegates whirled round and stared excitedly at three squat figures silhouetted in the doorway. Behind them stood a human female and an armored giant. A buzz of whispers filled the room.

"Let me speak with him," said a visibly relieved Gundrabur. "The assembly is dismissed." Balendilín helped him back to the throne and they waited for the delegates to leave the hall.

The departing dwarves cast curious glances at the stranger standing between the twins, but no one dared to address him. Then Bislipur drew level.

He stopped and took a menacing step toward Tungdil. "You're not one of us," he said scornfully. "Go back to Lot-Ionan and leave us to settle our own affairs. You needn't have bothered coming; we've decided on a successor already."

"Oh really? Let's hope he's as good as this one," Boëndal said coolly. He stepped in front of his charge. "Didn't you hear what Gundrabur said? The assembly is dismissed."

Boïndil joined him and flashed the fourthling adviser an insolent smile. "Looking for trouble, are you? I'll shave your miserable chin with my axes, you see if I don't." Bislipur merely snorted and left. The doors closed behind him, shutting Andôkai and Djerûn outside.

The high king motioned for the trio to approach. He and his counselor looked at Tungdil warmly. "The lost dwarf has returned to his kinsfolk," he said, rising to clap a hand on his shoulder. "Thanks be to Vraccas for bringing you here."

Tungdil bowed his head, overcome with emotion. He wanted to say something, but his throat was dry with excitement. He felt sweaty and grubby, and his body ached all over in spite of Boïndil's efforts to treat his wounds. In fact, the shoulder that the high king was gripping was particularly sore. All in all, he was too tired and disheveled to appear before Gundrabur, but the king of all dwarves generously refrained from commenting on his state.

The monarch turned to the twins. "You've done yourselves and the secondlings proud. Ogre's Death boasts no finer warriors than you," he lauded them. "You can be sure of my gratitude. Retire to your chambers and get some rest."

Boïndil stared at the floor, uncomfortable at being praised. He hadn't forgiven himself for what had happened in the desert oasis when Tungdil had nearly been killed. It was mortifying to think that his charge would have died without Djerûn. Gloomily, he left the hall with his twin.

"You'll hear our side of the story in a moment," promised Balendilín, "but why don't you tell us about your journey first?"

This was the moment that Tungdil had been waiting for. He tried to swallow his nerves, but it was hard not to be distracted by the great hall's monumental galleries, pillars, and statues. It was all so very *dwarven*.

"Gladly," he said, "but what of Andôkai and Djerûn? They were loyal protectors during our travels. I trust they will be provided for?" Without really meaning to, he had adopted a more flowery way of speech, perhaps because of his magnificent surroundings.

Balendilín gave his word that the maga and her companion would be taken care of, so Tungdil launched into his account, beginning with Lot-Ionan, the vaults, and his errand, then proceeding by means of the Blacksaddle, Greenglade, the fate of the magi, the treachery of Nudin (or Nôd'onn, as he called himself), his run-in with the bounty hunters, Gorén's mysterious books, and the älfar's attempts to track them down, then concluding with the magus's threat to the dwarven kingdoms and his plans to bend Girdlegard to his will.

Soon his cheeks were flushed with talking, but he tried to state the facts plainly, without glossing over the horror or embellishing his report.

He spoke without faltering, save for one occasion when he was understandably thrown. It happened when three serving girls opened the doors and walked into the hall. Tungdil, who yearned to become acquainted with the fairer sex, was transfixed by the mysterious creatures who had colonized his imagination for as long as he could remember. They were a little shorter than he was and not as broadly built, but their ample robes betrayed an unmistakable fullness of figure. Fine, almost imperceptible fluff covered their plump faces from the cheekbones to the lower jaw. The wispy down matched the color of their hair and, unlike his own bristly whiskers, their furry skin seemed soft and smooth. This then was the origin of the myth about bearded women. Tungdil found them utterly beguiling.

His remaining composure crumbled when they turned to him with shy, friendly smiles. His heart started beating so wildly that he had to abandon his story until they were gone. Gundrabur and Balendilín made no comment, although the one-armed counselor could barely suppress a grin.

At last Tungdil concluded his report, ending with a brief account of the attack on the desert oasis. He reached for his tankard, which smelled enticingly of beer. The dark liquid washed over his thirsty lips, coating his tongue with its powerful malty flavor. A single sip was enough to convince him that humans knew nothing of beer. It tasted so good that he could have kissed the dwarf who had invented the recipe, but instead he took another swig.

"These are ill tidings," Gundrabur said sadly. "We intend to be honest with you, Tungdil, so you shall hear of our problems too." His counselor described the dwarves' predicament, including the proposed war, the question of the succession, and the rift among the delegates, as succinctly as he could. "It seems from what you've told us that an alliance is imperative. The races of Girdlegard must unite and fight together against the Perished Land."

Tungdil sighed. "An alliance won't save us if we can't make sense of the books or the artifacts. There *must* be a way of getting to Nôd'onn or he wouldn't be so afraid. The trouble is, we can't do anything without Andôkai and she's determined to wash her hands of Girdlegard. Without her power and knowledge, our chances of defeating the evil are no better than any of the other realms'."

"And we must watch powerlessly while the northern blight advances," Gundrabur murmured somberly, closing his eyes. "Then it is settled: I shall appeal to the maga for help."

Tungdil said nothing, although he doubted the efficacy of the scheme. No amount of dwarven reasoning could influence the workings of the maga's mind. The thought of Andôkai reminded him that Djerûn had been permitted to enter the stronghold without raising his visor. At the time it hadn't occurred to him, and it clearly hadn't registered with the sentries or the twins, who had blithely waved the armored warrior through their gates. *She must have put a spell on us.* He decided not to say anything, least of all to Boïndil, whose hot temper would explode in incandescent fury. The last thing they needed was for Djerûn to be challenged to a duel.

He took the opportunity to broach the subject of the succession. "I don't mean to sound ungrateful," he said, determined to nip the matter in the bud. "You've done me a great service in reuniting me with my folk, but I can't be made king. I was raised by long-uns and learned the dwarven ways from books—extremely *inaccurate* books, I might tell you.

My rival is a much more suitable candidate, so I intend to renounce my claim and vote in favor of him. We need a high king whom everyone will respect."

"Your speech and sentiments do you credit," Gundrabur praised him, "but the fact is, we made up the story about your birth. Lot-Ionan played along because we swore him to secrecy. I'm afraid you have no claim to the throne; there's no proof that you're even a fourthling."

Tungdil's mind was reeling. "But why...I mean, I don't see why you made me come all this way just to tell me it isn't true..."

"Think of all the good that has come of it already," Balendilín said soothingly. "It's put us in a better position to do something about Nôd'onn. And if we hadn't sent the twins to look for you, the orcs would have killed you in Greenglade."

"True, but..." He fumbled for the right words. "What of the delegates? All this time, the assembly has been waiting for me, and I'm not even a genuine heir!"

He felt as if the ground had been tunneled from under his feet. After the ordeals of his journey he had just been getting comfortable, and now he had nowhere to call home.

"Please don't be angry with us," Gundrabur entreated him. "If Gandogar is crowned, our race will be locked in combat with the elves, and we can't let that happen. Our idea was to postpone Gandogar's appointment until the assembly had been persuaded of the folly of waging war. When your magus wrote to us with news of a foundling dwarf, we took the liberty of inventing a story about your lineage to buy some extra time."

"We were hoping to find a solution—an ancient law or suchlike that would force the assembly to vote against a war," Balendilín explained. "Fighting the elves would be ruinous for both our races, but Gandogar just won't see it. I expect you think we're as dishonest as kobolds, but our intentions are honorable: We want the best for our race."

Tungdil kept his mouth shut for fear of saying something he might regret. He helped himself to more beer and emptied the tankard in a single draft. "And did you find anything?"

"Not exactly," the high king confessed. "That's why we're asking you to join our conspiracy and challenge Gandogar for the throne."

"What good would it do?" Tungdil shrugged. "They'd never elect me."

"No," agreed Gundrabur, "but if I'm not happy with the assembly's choice of heir, I can veto the succession."

"And what then? Would you rather our folks fought each other than waged war on the elves?"

"It won't come to that," Balendilín reassured him. "Our laws state that the heir must challenge his rival to a duel. Of course, the rival candidate would have to be backed by some of the chieftains and elders, but roughly a third of the delegates have been won over to our cause. That should suffice."

"And then Gandogar will have the privilege of slicing me in two." Tungdil scowled. "I still don't see how it changes anything."

The high king and his counselor exchanged glances.

"Swear that you won't breathe a word of this to anyone," Balendilín demanded, eyeing Tungdil solemnly until he complied. "We need to banish Bislipur and Sverd from Gandogar's circle. Bislipur is obsessed with the idea of wiping out the elves and his zeal has rubbed off on Gandogar. Thanks to Bislipur's constant whispering, the fourthling king rarely has time to think for himself." He frowned. "The villain tried to kill me. I can't prove it yet, but I will."

"But assuming you succeed," Tungdil said doubtfully, "won't Gandogar still go ahead with his plan?"

"We'll open his eyes to the perfidy of his mentor and the folly of an elven war. Gandogar is a good dwarf at heart; his adviser is to blame." Balendilín paused and looked at Tungdil intently. "But I need more time; and for that we're depending on your help."

"You'll be doing your kinsmen a great service," Gundrabur assured him. "They'll realize it eventually. History will record how a foundling dwarf named Tungdil was hewn by Vraccas to save his children from destruction."

"I'll do it," agreed Tungdil, "but I'll need your full support."

"We'll do everything we can for you," promised Balendilín. "You're an honorable dwarf, Tungdil. Forgive us for burdening you with our troubles before you've even had a chance to rest. Now that we've settled the important business, you should get some proper sleep. You'll have one orbit in which to recover and prepare yourself for the hustings." The one-armed counselor smiled at him encouragingly.

"Buy us some time, and we'll forge a better future without the likes of Bislipur," the high king exhorted him. He picked up the ceremonial hammer and held it out to the dwarf. "Swear on the hammer that brought us into being that you won't tell a soul."

Tungdil gave his word and left the great hall. Outside, Andôkai and Djerûn were still waiting in the corridor.

"They said we could stay for a while," she said evenly. "As it happens, I could do with a break. These past few orbits together have been horribly stressful."

"My sentiments exactly," said Tungdil, leaving the maga to decide whether it was the journey or her company that he found such a trial.

An attendant arrived to take them to their rooms. As they followed, Tungdil marveled at the splendor of their surroundings. The masons had worked the walls with incredible finesse and the smooth surfaces were decorated with sculpted reliefs and chiseled inscriptions. Dwarven runes inlaid with precious metals shimmered in a kaleidoscope of silver, gold, and red.

But what really caught his attention was the staircase. He had always thought of steps as being rectangular, smooth, and plain.

These were a revelation. Each slab of stone was different from the next, the flat treads decorated with elaborate patterns and the uprights engraved with runes.

It was only when he read the runes in sequence that he realized the purpose of the design: The staircases spelled out stories that served to distract the weary secondlings from the grueling ascent. Tungdil could tell from Andôkai's expression that she too had noticed the runes and was reading with interest.

The stories told of glorious days of old, evoking heroic adventures, each more impressive than the last. Tungdil climbed eagerly, relishing every step until at length they reached their chambers.

Andôkai disappeared inside her room before he could inquire about the books. He was sure that her change of heart was connected to something she had seen or read.

Maybe Gundrabur will be lucky, he thought hopefully as he shuffled to bed.

That's the beauty of being among friends," said a deep voice. "You don't even have to lock the door."

Tungdil woke with a start and sat up drowsily, only to discover Bislipur in his room.

"Good morning, Tungdil." Somehow the greeting sounded suspiciously insincere. "We'll talk properly at the hustings, but I'm sure you're as impatient as I am to have a little chat."

"I wasn't really expecting visitors," Tungdil said hesitantly.

The sudden appearance of Gandogar's adviser had thrown him slightly. In fact, now that he thought about it properly, walking in without an invitation was downright rude. His friendly feelings toward Bislipur as a kinsman had withstood their bristly encounter in the great hall, but this was something else.

Bislipur sat down on the bed and gave him a long stare. "You think you're one of us, do you?" he mocked. "A poor little foundling, raised by a wizard, but of genuine royal blood—it sounds like a fairy tale, doesn't it?" He leaned forward. "Because *it is!* I'm not going to beat about the bush: You're an impostor. What proof do you have of your lineage?"

"You'll see soon enough," Tungdil said firmly. If it hadn't been for his conversation with Gundrabur and Balendilín, he would have stepped aside for his rival. Only last night he had been assailed by doubts about the wisdom of maintaining the deception, but now, thanks to Bislipur's obnoxious behavior, his mind was made up.

"None of the fourthlings can remember a case of a missing child."

"And I suppose you know them all in person and every detail of their lives. That's really quite a claim." Tungdil stood up. He had a feeling that the long hours spent reading in Lot-Ionan's library and studying the art of disputation would stand him in good stead. All of a sudden he felt naked without his chain mail and his weapon. He threw on his tunic and belted his ax to his waist. His confidence flooded back. "Wait until tomorrow and you'll hear the full story."

"I've got a better idea," said Bislipur. "Cancel the hustings, and we'll adopt you as one of our folk. All we ask is that you agree to back Gandogar. Retract your claim and you'll never want for anything."

"Supposing I refuse?"

"Supposing you refuse?" Bislipur laid a muscular hand on his ax. "If you refuse, you'll see what happens when a fourthling—or a fake fourthling, in your case—turns against the leader of his folk. None of us will submit to your rule. Even if you're elected, you'll never really be king."

Tungdil could tell from the muffled fury in his voice that Bislipur meant business. "That's for the assembly to decide, not you," he informed him, doing his best to sound like a prospective monarch. "Now go," he commanded.

"Supposing I refuse?" the thick-set dwarf said mockingly.

"Supposing you refuse?" thundered Tungdil, placing a hand on his ax. "If you refuse, I'll throw you out myself! I've dealt with enough orcs and älfar to know what to do with a dwarf who sneaks his way into my chamber while I'm asleep." His brotherly tolerance of Bislipur had given way to undisguised dislike. "Get out!"

Bislipur wavered for a moment, unsure whether he should commit to a trial of strength. To Tungdil's relief, he decided to see himself out. "You'll regret this," he threatened by way of a farewell.

"That's a risk I'm prepared to take," Tungdil retorted. Alone in his chamber, he stood in front of the mirror, put his hands on his hips, and squared his shoulders. Rather than get dressed, he practiced looking steely until he was confident of his ability to assume a determined expression whenever he pleased. It took considerable willpower not to crawl back into bed.

He was in the process of removing his nightshirt when someone knocked on the door. Without waiting for an answer, a female dwarf in a skirt and leather blouse strode in and placed some fresh linen on the marble dresser. She giggled when she saw him rooted to the spot. *I should say something*, he thought, racking his brains desperately, but already she was gone.

"I guess it takes practice," he muttered, pulling on his clothes absentmindedly. His mind was whirring with a thousand different thoughts.

It was dispiriting to know that he was still a foundling dwarf. For the first time in his life he was surrounded by others of his race, but deep down he was the loneliest soul in all Girdlegard. In fact, he'd been better off when he'd lived among humans; at least then he'd belonged to Lot-Ionan and the school.

It didn't help that he was obliged to pose as a fourthling and put on a show of happiness at being reunited with his folk. For all his honest intentions, it made him feel like a terrible fraud.

Keen to distract his thoughts, he reread Lot-Ionan's letter about his provenance, memorizing every fabricated detail until he was sure that none of the delegates could pick a hole in his story. There was nothing else to do in his chamber, so he wandered into the corridor and roamed the majestic stone passageways while his stomach growled hungrily.

Dwarves streamed past him, clad in leather aprons and covered in a dusting of rock. Tungdil guessed from their appearance that they were heading for the quarry. They smiled and called out to him and he returned their greetings with a nod.

Soon afterward he was intercepted by an attendant who marched him off to breakfast. Tungdil understood the real purpose of the summons when he was welcomed to the table by Balendilín, who wanted to prepare him for the hustings.

"It's all under control," the counselor assured him. The trinkets on his braided beard swung back and forth as he spoke, which earned him fascinated glances from Tungdil. "Three dwarves from Gandogar's delegation have agreed to say they remember hearing a rumor about a missing child. Their testimony, together with the letter from your magus, should give us the credibility we need. After that, you'll make your speech and then—"

"My speech?" said Tungdil, looking up sharply from the array of pungent cheeses, salamis, pickled mushrooms, and roasted lichen. All of a sudden he stopped caring about the absence of ham, porridge, and bread: The prospect of addressing the assembly had banished any thought of food.

"It needn't be terribly long. You can talk a bit about your journey and your encounters with Nôd'onn and the Perished Land. You'll lose the vote, of course, but that's no great inconvenience; we'll proceed to the next stage of our plan." Balendilín's eyes twinkled. "It's all under control," he said again.

"I'm glad you think so." Tungdil sighed and piled his wooden plate with a small helping of everything. He told the counselor of Bislipur's visit.

"That's just the kind of underhanded behavior I'd expect from him." Balendilín seemed to take the news in stride. "You know what it means, don't you? We're on the right track. The scoundrel wouldn't bother with you unless he thought you were a threat."

Tungdil didn't share his optimism. He hadn't forgotten that Bislipur had tried to murder Balendilín, and he saw no reason to suppose that the fourthling wouldn't do the same to him.

"There's one more thing," said the counselor. "The maga and her bodyguard have gone."

"Gone?" Tungdil echoed, aghast. *So she's really left us? How could she give up like that and leave Girdlegard to its fate?* "When did she leave?"

"This morning, just after dawn. We had to let her cross the pass. There wasn't any justification for detaining her, and besides...how do you stop a maga?"

"You don't." Tungdil put his head in his hands. It was hopeless; no one apart from Andôkai had anything like Nôd'onn's power and now she was searching for force fields beyond the Blue Range. She must have given up on Gorén's books. *Why couldn't one of the other magi have survived instead?* He felt certain that Maira or Lot-Ionan would have stayed and led the fight against the traitor.

"We'll have to rely on you to decipher the tomes," said Balendilín. "You can always consult our archives, if you think they'll be of use."

"You should ask your historians. I'm sure they'd do a better job than me," muttered Tungdil.

Balendilín shook his head. "They don't know the magi's writings as well as you do. No one understands the long-uns better than you." He looked encouragingly at the dejected dwarf. "I know it's a heavy burden, but a great deal is at stake. We'll never forget it."

"I'll do my best," he promised, forcing down his mouthful. He hiccuped discreetly. His palate had adjusted to the cheese, but his stomach was proving less adaptable — not unreasonably, considering the quantities involved. To round off the meal he poured a mug of sour milk and stirred it through with a spoonful of honey. Dwarven cuisine was a lot better than he had thought.

Excusing himself from the table, he made his way back to his chamber, this time looking fixedly at the floor so as not to be distracted by the magnificent marble carvings. The speech that was taking shape in his mind was going to cover all the events of the previous weeks and more.

Tungdil drained the strong malt beer from his tankard, wiped his beard, and looked up at the assembly. The delegates had listened patiently while he'd read out Lot-Ionan's letter and tried to establish his lineage as the illegitimate offspring of the dead fourthling king.

True to their word, three of Gandogar's chieftains claimed to recall a rumor about a missing heir. Bislipur instantly accused them of lying.

"I expect you're wondering why I think I would make a good king," said Tungdil, raising his voice above the tumult. The beer had settled his nerves and quashed his inhibitions about appearing before an assembly of dignitaries and chieftains. "The fact is, I know better than anyone the dangers that lie ahead. I know the power of the Perished Land; and I know we need to stand united. It would be fatal to squander our strength on a campaign against the elves. Their numbers may have dwindled, but their army is not to be mocked."

"We're not afraid of the pointy-ears!" Bislipur shouted, incensed.

"Maybe not, but dead heroes are no use to us at all," Tungdil retaliated. "The elves have been fighting the älfar for hundreds of cycles. What chance would we have of defeating them? Their bowmen are the best in Girdlegard. Before we get within three hundred paces, they'll bombard us with arrows!"

"Not if we sneak up on them," Bislipur objected.

"You can't honestly believe they won't notice an army of a thousand dwarves! Friends, this war will end in our defeat." He looked at them beseechingly. "Darkness has eaten its way into the heart of our lands. Vraccas entrusted the safety of Girdlegard to our race; it's our duty to defeat Nôd'onn and expel Tion's minions—and if the elves and humans are able to help us, we must ally ourselves with them!"

"The high king's puppet has learned his part well," sneered Gandogar.

"Our minds think alike because we both see reason. If there was anything between your ears but sheer bloody-mindedness, you might see sense as well." A ripple of laughter swept the room.

"The elves must be punished," shouted Bislipur, drawing himself up to full height. "You heard how they betrayed our kinsfolk and allowed Tion's beasts to storm the Stone Gateway. Their crimes cannot go unavenged!"

"And what of Nôd'onn? A war against the elves would weaken us dangerously." Tungdil thumped his hand against the marble. "Of course, if we really want to make things easy for the magus, we could always open our strongholds to the orcish invaders! Is that what you want? Maybe you should ask the runts if they'd like to join us in a campaign against the elves!" He waited for the commotion to settle. "In my possession are two tomes belonging to Lot-Ionan in whose household I was raised. Once I have unlocked their meaning, we will hold the key to defeating Nôd'onn and the Perished Land." He neglected to mention that even Andôkai had failed to make sense of the books. "Just think of the glory if the dwarves were to save Girdlegard! Our heroism would humiliate the pointy-ears far more than military defeat."

There was a hum of excitement from the benches. Books that could defeat the Perished Land; that was news indeed!

"He's lying!" roared Bislipur. "Since when did magic ever help the dwarves? It brings us nothing but trouble! Magic is to blame for the dark wizard's power!"

"I say we fight the elves, then retreat to our ranges until the humans have settled the matter for themselves," added Gandogar, springing to his feet. He hurried to the middle of the assembly to be sure of the delegates' attention. "Don't listen to the foundling who learned our lore from books. He'll never understand our ways." He laughed. "A high king who knows nothing of his race? It's downright ridiculous!"

"It can't be that ridiculous or you wouldn't be so het up,"

Tungdil said pointedly. There was another low rumble of laughter. He was doing Lot-Ionan proud with his witticisms, although the beer could take some of the credit. *I mustn't get carried away,* he told himself.

Gundrabur had heard enough. He raised the hammer and pounded it against the marble table. "Both candidates have made their cases and the assembly must decide. Delegates, remember you are voting for your future high king. Those in favor of Gandogar Silverbeard of the clan of the Silver Beards, raise your axes!"

Tungdil counted the glistening blades. To his great surprise, Gandogar's share of the vote had dwindled to less than two-thirds among the fourthling chieftains. When his own name was called, the number of axes was far greater than expected. Balendilín gave him an approving nod.

Tungdil's personal victory did nothing to change the end result: The majority had voted in favor of Gandogar, which amounted to a mandate for war. Bislipur held his head high. It was clear from his triumphant expression that he thought his work was done.

"At this stage in the proceedings, it falls to me, the reigning high king, to approve the assembly's choice," declared Gundrabur. "Regrettably, in view of King Gandogar's foolish determination to steer our race toward destruction, I see no option but to declare him unfit for office. For that reason, I nominate Tungdil in his place. Who will back me?"

Gandogar and Bislipur watched in stunned silence as a third of the delegates raised their axes, thereby investing Gundrabur with the authority to proceed.

The hammer crashed noisily against the marble. "Then the succession shall be decided on merit. Our candidates will prove their ability in a contest: Gandogar and Tungdil will each nominate a task, two further tasks will be set by the assembly, and the fifth task will be drawn at random. You have seven orbits to prepare." With that, he called the hustings to a close.

Dazed, Tungdil made his way along the line of supporters who were queuing to pat him on the back, wish him well, and intercede with Vraccas on his behalf. Faces, beards, and chain mail loomed on either side of him, disappearing in a blur. His mind was reeling from the uncommonly strong beer and the exhilaration of success. It was incredible to think that dozens of dwarves had been won over by his arguments, but there was no escaping the knowledge that his triumph was founded on a lie.

Although the chances of discovering anything about his provenance were slim, Balendilín had promised to do what he could to investigate without arousing suspicion. The counselor was too tactful to mention the possibility that the foundling was descended from Lorimbur's folk, and the notion of it seemed ludicrous to Tungdil, who felt comfortable living in Ogre's Death and shared nothing of the thirdlings' murderous dislike of other dwarves. In any case, there were more urgent matters than establishing his origins. First and foremost, he needed to practice his axmanship in case Gandogar opted to challenge him to a duel. And he still had to settle on a task of his own.

No one knew what to expect from the fifth and final task. Each candidate could nominate four challenges and one would be drawn from a pouch. Only Vraccas could predict the outcome.

Tungdil returned to his chamber to find Gorén's books and the contents of the leather bag strewn across his bed. *Andôkai must have broken the spell and examined the artifacts!*

He turned over the fragments of two silver-plated decanters

and studied the runes. *What a pity!* If the inscriptions were to be believed, it took a single drop of liquid for the vessels to fill themselves over and over again. Mixed in with the shattered decanters was a broken hand mirror. The fractured glass cast back a cracked reflection of his bearded face. *Seven years of bad luck.* He chuckled grimly as he picked up a shard. To be cursed by a mirror was the least of his problems.

He turned his attention to a couple of lengths of wood. They were as long as his arm and had a gray, almost metallic shimmer to them. The grain was wayward and irregular. *What are they?* He supposed they could be cudgels. *But what would they be doing in the bag?* He tossed them carelessly onto the bed.

The maga had written him a note. Furious with her for leaving Girdlegard and for rummaging through his things, he left it unread. Then curiosity got the better of him.

The mystery is solved, or as good as.

You were right: There *is* a way to defeat Nôd'onn and the books explain how. However, the means are beyond us, which is why I'm leaving Girdlegard for good.

The first book is an account of the Outer Lands that tells of a place called Barrenground, where demonic beings have the power to enter human souls, take possession of them, and invest them with extraordinary power. Men possessed of such demons are driven by an urge to destroy goodness wherever they find it and bend everything to their will.

The second book tells of a race called the undergroundlings who invented a mighty ax to destroy the demonic power.

The blade of this ax must be made of the purest,

hardest steel, with diamonds encrusting the bit and an alloy of every known precious metal filling the inlay and the runes. The spurs should be hewn from stone and the haft sculpted from wood of the sigurdaisy tree.

The ax must be forged in a furnace lit with the fiercest of all flames and its name shall be Keenfire.

This is the weapon with the power to slay the demonic spirits. Keenfire can slice through flesh and bone, cutting through the human body to destroy the evil presence within. Any harm that has been done reverts to good.

Regrettably, I was unable to make sense of one passage, which means I cannot vouch for the method's success. The task is as good as hopeless.

All the same, it explains why Nôd'onn is interested in the artifacts. The bag contains two fragments of sigurdaisy wood.

The sigurdaisy is extinct in Girdlegard, but its wood is exceptionally hard, so hard that it can't be worked with ordinary tools. Humans used to believe that the trees were sacred and they burned the wood for its powerful aroma and deep crimson flames. They stopped conducting the rituals when all the trees were gone. I once witnessed a sigurdaisy fire in honor of Palandiell, but that was over a hundred cycles ago.

Even if were possible to make such a miraculous weapon, no one would get close enough to Nôd'onn to slay him. The whole business is ridiculous.

If the dwarves have any sense, they will cross the ranges and settle in the Outer Lands. Maybe the undergroundlings will give them shelter.

My work here is done.

Tungdil read and reread the letter until there was no further doubt: Lot-Ionan's murderer was not completely invincible. They had everything they needed to kill him—even the wood.

He hurried to find Balendilín. The counselor had lit a number of oil lamps, which bathed his chamber in light. Like the rest of Ogre's Death, the room was hewn from rock and the masons had even thought to sculpt a bed and cabinets. It looked as if the mountain had created a furnished chamber especially for his use.

Tungdil handed him the letter.

"There is mention in our records of distant kin on the far side of the mountain," he said when he saw the reference to the mysterious undergroundlings. "The inhabitants of the Outer Lands seem to have more experience of fighting the Perished Land."

Tungdil brandished the piece of parchment. "It explains why Nôd'onn was desperate to get his hands on the books and the bag! Well, it's too late now: His secret is out. Balendilín, you've got to tell the human sovereigns of our discovery before they lose all hope. They need to keep the magus fighting while we work on the weapon. If only they can keep him busy until then!"

Balendilín studied the passages relating to the making of the ax. "We'll have to enlist the help of the fourthlings: Their skill in diamond cutting is unsurpassed. Our people can take care of the stone, but as for the best smiths…"

"Borengar's folk!"

"Yes, but none of their nine clans are here. The firstlings ignored our summons. Giselbert's fifthlings were exceptional blacksmiths, but their line was snuffed out." Balendilín scowled. "And that's not the only hitch. The fieriest furnace in Girdlegard belonged to the fifthlings. Its name was Dragon

Fire and the hardest metal would melt in its flames. But the Gray Range has been in the hands of the Perished Land for over a thousand cycles." He rested his head in his hands. "The maga was right. It's not possible."

"We can't give up now. Call a meeting and let the delegates decide. We need to send word to the firstlings and ask for their assistance. Then we'll..." He trailed off. "Well, I'll take a look in the archives. Maybe I'll find something that will help."

"Good luck to you, Tungdil."

The dwarf left the chamber and headed for the vaults, where the written record of the secondlings' history was preserved. Now that the initial excitement was over, he was left with the sobering realization that they were barely any closer to saving Girdlegard from Nôd'onn's grasp.

I'm not giving up! The very hopelessness of the situation made Tungdil more determined than ever to succeed.

He settled down to his task with all the stubbornness and persistence typical of his race. It was his solemn intention not to leave the secondlings' archives until he found something of use.

Tungdil hurried back and forth, fetching ancient tomes, rolls of parchment, and stone tablets from their places in the vaults. He piled everything on a table to examine it at length.

Lot-Ionan must have known that my schooling would come in handy. Some of the parchment was so fragile that it tore or crumbled at his touch. It made Tungdil appreciate the durability of the marble tablets that lasted an eternity, provided they weren't dropped.

After a good deal of reading, he found evidence to back up Balendilín's vague assertions about the undergroundlings. According to the archives, a race of dwarves on the other side of the ranges went by that name. Whether or not Vraccas had created them was anyone's guess, but they seemed to have

much in common with the children of the Smith. They were accomplished metal workers and shared the dwarven passion for the forge.

On the fourth orbit he learned the secret of Dragon Fire, and his optimism, which had survived in spite of everything, was dealt a grievous blow.

The flames of the fifthlings' fiery furnace had been lit by the white tongue of Branbausíl, a dragon who had roamed the Gray Range until Giselbert's dwarves stole its fire, killed it, and seized its hoard. Argamas, its mate, had taken refuge in Flamemere, a small lake of molten lava at the heart of the fifthling kingdom. The creature had never been seen again.

The stolen fire enabled the dwarves to heat their furnace to phenomenal temperatures and create alloys from metals that had never been melded. Dragon Fire was powerful enough to melt tionium, the black element created by Tion, and combine it with palandium, the deity's pure white metal.

Later records indicated that the furnace had fallen with the fifthlings. Neither the älfar nor any other creature of Tion could find a use for the strange white flames, and Dragon Fire had been extinguished.

Tungdil's only hope lay in finding the dragon's mate who had escaped the dwarves' axes. If the firstlings could provide a smith and Argamas could furnish the fire, Keenfire could be forged and Nôd'onn defeated.

"More traveling." He sighed. *We'll have to go west to the firstlings, then north through the heart of the Perished Land to the lost fifthling kingdom. But how are we supposed to cross Girdlegard without Nôd'onn finding out?*

He put the question to Gundrabur and Balendilín when he met them in the great hall to report on his findings and share a keg of beer. The king and his counselor looked at each other knowingly.

"There is a way," the high king told him, "a secret way that has faded from memory over the cycles. My predecessor told me of it." He lit his pipe and sucked on it vigorously. "It dates back to the glorious orbits of old. In those happy times traveling was easy. We used underground tunnels that criss-crossed the whole of Girdlegard, linking our kingdoms."

"Tunnels...So we could travel unseen. With ponies we could—"

"You won't need ponies. You'll get there soon enough." Gundrabur pulled his cloak tighter and sent for another blanket. His inner furnace was burning worryingly low.

Tungdil frowned. "I don't follow."

"You've seen the wagons carrying iron ore through the mines?"

"Sure, but..." Then he grasped what the high king was saying. "We can go by wagon?"

Gundrabur smiled. "Indeed. Our forefathers used wagons to travel by the shortest route from the firstling kingdom to the secondling kingdom and the secondling kingdom to the fourthling kingdom and so forth, unimpeded by marshland, wilderness, rain, or snow. They could convey troops wherever they wanted in no time at all. Within a matter of orbits an entire army could cross from north to south undetected by men, elves, or magi."

"That's the answer!" Tungdil cried excitedly. "If the tunnels are still intact, we'll be able to forge the ax before the dark magus has time to defeat the human armies and conquer their kingdoms."

"I can't guarantee what kind of state they're in," warned Gundrabur. "According to the ancient records, some sections of the tunnels have collapsed. Balendilín, fetch the maps."

"Why hasn't anyone come across them since?"

"The entrance lies in an area of the Blue Range that

became polluted with sulfurous gas. Our kinsfolk abandoned that side of the mountain and the tunnels were forgotten."

At length Balendilín returned with two ancient maps showing the path of the tunnels through the secondling kingdom. The tunnels cut straight through the heart of the Blue Range and were well hidden, with numerous mechanisms and traps securing them against intruders. Even if Tion's creatures had known about the tunnels, there was no way of breaking into them, so the forces of darkness were obliged to conduct their invasion overland.

"Well, that's settled," Tungdil told the others. "I'll do it."

"Good," said Balendilín with a smile. He refilled their tankards. "In that case, you should be the one who tells the assembly of the tunnels' existence. The delegates will be impressed." They clunked tankards and drank.

Vraccas made me party to this knowledge so that the dwarves could liberate Girdlegard from evil," said Tungdil, coming to the end of his impassioned speech. "Why else would he have given me the artifacts and books?"

"Forgotten relics from a glorious era!" Gandogar said scornfully. "Nothing you've stumbled upon is of any practical use. A miracle ax to be forged secretly in a furnace fired by dragon's breath at the heart of the Perished Land—it can't be done! If you ask me, the whole thing's a fiction, a legend that found its way into our archives by mistake!"

"You may not believe it," Tungdil cut in, "but Nôd'onn clearly does. He wiped out a whole settlement to get his hands on the books. He tried to kill me too! Why would he be so worried if it were just an old story? Clansmen," he begged the assembly, "we need to send an expedition. Vraccas will see us through this."

"Of course he will," jeered Bislipur. "If you don't mind my

asking, how exactly were you intending to slay the dragon? They're tough old beasts, but tell it one of your stories and the poor thing will probably die of laughter on the spot."

The roars of merriment were enough to convince Tungdil not to put the matter to the vote. The motion would only fail. Common sense had yet to bludgeon its way into the delegates' thick skulls.

"To business," Gandogar said impatiently. He threw off his cloak, revealing a shimmering mail shirt. His adviser handed him his shield and his ax, while another fastened his helmet. "The purpose of this meeting is to decide the succession. Let the contest begin! For the first task I challenge my rival to a duel. Victory will go to whoever draws first blood or forces his opponent to his knees."

In an instant Boïndil and Boëndal were at Tungdil's side, helping him on with his armor. His metal tunic looked cheap and dull compared to Gandogar's glittering mail. "Beware of his shield. He's bound to try to ram you with it," whispered Boïndil. He clenched his fists. "If only I could take your place," he growled. "I'd hammer him into the marble."

"You've been wonderful teachers," Tungdil reassured the twins as he buckled his chinstrap. "And I'm not just talking about the past few orbits; you taught me a great deal during our journey as well. If I lose, it won't be because of you."

The two candidates stepped into the semicircle between the throne and the benches. Balendilín acted as referee. His eyes smiled reassuringly at Tungdil. "Fight valiantly and honorably," he told them as he backed away. The rivals were alone in the arena.

The fourthling king lost no time in launching his attack. Tungdil parried blow after blow, all the while trying not to be distracted by the twinkling diamonds on Gandogar's ax. He watched the swooping trajectory of the blade from behind his shield, retreating farther and farther until his back came up against a column.

As the next blow swung toward him, Tungdil ducked and struck back. There was a shrill metallic shriek as his blunted ax scraped over Gandogar's hastily raised shield and struck the lower edge of his helmet. Head spinning, the king staggered back.

"Now attack!" yelled Boïndil, caught up in the excitement. Fired on by his success and the encouragement of his tutor, Tungdil rushed forward.

Not if I can help it. Bislipur had no intention of allowing Gandogar to be defeated. Sverd was standing beside him, so he gave him a little shove. The gnome pitched forward and struck his head on a tankard. Beer slopped to the floor.

The incident was Tungdil's undoing. In his haste he didn't notice that the slippery marble floor was as treacherous as an ice rink. His right foot skidded to the side; he struggled to keep his balance and flailed out vainly with his ax.

"Foolish gnome!" Bislipur unleashed a volley of curses, threatening to thrash the hapless Sverd and tighten his collar until it cut off his breath.

"The scoundrel did it on purpose!" protested Boëndal.

"He's just clumsy, that's all. He'll pay for this, believe me!" said Bislipur, still pretending to be furious with the gnome.

None of that was any comfort to Tungdil, who skidded past Gandogar just as the latter straightened up and took aim. The king's ax thwacked his back with enough force to send him spinning out of control. Cursing, he lost his footing and forfeited the task.

A cheer went up from the fourthling corner where Gandogar's supporters were gathered. The jubilation turned to mocking laughter when Tungdil struggled to his feet. The contest wasn't unfolding quite as he'd hoped.

"Now for my task," he shouted above the din. The great hall fell silent.

"What is the nature of the challenge?"

"We shall both transcribe a text. The first to finish wins."

"What?" Gandogar protested. "I'm a king, not a poet!"

"You don't have to be a poet; all you have to do is write. A good monarch must have a steady hand and a smart mind to guide it; how else would he make the laws? But maybe fighting is your only virtue..." Without further ado he sat down at a desk and waited for Gandogar to follow suit.

"What if I refuse?"

"If you refuse," said Balendilín, "you'll lose the challenge and the tally will be one task each, leaving the succession to be decided by the final three challenges."

"Besides," Boëndal added snidely, "it would be cowardly not to accept. The scholar wasn't afraid to face your ax. I hope the fourthling leader isn't frightened of a quill!"

The gibe and resulting hilarity prompted Gandogar to lay down his shield and helmet and take a seat at the desk.

The referee called for the rolls of parchment and chose one at random. "You may begin."

In no time the scholar, as Boëndal jokingly called him, was scribbling furiously, while his opponent glared at the runes and scratched awkwardly at the parchment with his quill. The dwarves devoted themselves to the task in industrious silence.

"Finished," declared Tungdil at length. His work was scrutinized and found to be faultless. Gandogar took longer and made several errors along the way. Balendilín awarded the task to Tungdil.

The twins whooped in delight, pleased that their charge had used his cunning to secure a draw. "Too bad you lost that one, eh, Bislipur?" Boïndil shouted cheerfully.

At Balendilín's request, the delegates noted down their

challenges and the slips of paper were collected. Gandogar would draw first, then Tungdil.

"For the next challenge," announced the referee, "you will forge an ax from the poorest quality iron and strike it ten times against a shield without fracturing the blade."

Tungdil had spent so much time at Lot-Ionan's anvil that he was sure he would prove the superior smith. Balendilín declared a break in the proceedings while the necessary equipment was set up in the hall and soon the high-ceilinged chamber was echoing with the sound of ringing hammers.

Tungdil hit his stride, working in time with a dwarven ballad that had been taught to him by the twins. Not to be outdone, Gandogar belted out a song of his own and hammered all the more furiously.

"You'd think it was a singing competition." Boëndal grinned and hoisted his belt. "If that doesn't please Vraccas, I don't know what will."

"Tungdil is the better singer, so Vraccas will favor his cause," said his brother.

The singing continued until both candidates had finished their blades. Balendilín instructed them to attach the ax heads to iron hafts; then each took up the other's weapon, ensuring the blade's exposure to maximum force. They positioned themselves in front of their shields and at the referee's signal, the contest began.

"Let's see how His Majesty fared in the forge," said a sweat-drenched Tungdil, preparing to strike. The blade, still glowing with heat, traced an orange semicircle through the gloom of the hall, hitting its target in a shower of sparks. The ax withstood the blow.

"Better than you thought," retorted Gandogar. He struck the shield with equal force and the blade held true.

They dealt six further blows apiece, but on the eighth

strike Tungdil heard a faint crack when Gandogar's ax hit the shield. He knew the next blow would be its last. "Take a look at this," he called to the king. The blade fractured, shattering into countless shards. Panting, Tungdil threw the haft to the floor and fumbled for his water pouch.

A murmur went through the watching crowd. The fourthling king tensed his muscles, summoning all his strength for the final blow. The shield groaned and shuddered, but the blade survived the strike.

"Hurrah for the smith!" boomed Boïndil. "Two-one to Tungdil. It was the singing that did it. Even the poorest metal can't resist a good tune."

Gandogar laid down his ax in order to shake his opponent's hand. "I didn't think anyone could forge such a fine blade from such woefully inadequate metal. You are the undisputed master of the forge—but I shall be king of the dwarves. The next victory will be mine."

"We'll see about that."

Already Balendilín was unfolding the next piece of paper. There was no time for the dwarves to catch their breath. "The fourth challenge will be a race. Each candidate will be given a tankard of molten gold and must carry it to the end of the first meadow and back before proceeding to the gates. In addition to your chain mail, you will be given a pack weighing precisely forty pounds. The first to return with a full tankard wins the task."

To ensure that both competitors ran the full distance with their tankards, Balendilín dispatched a pair of dwarves to the meadow and another to the gates.

This is my kind of task, thought Tungdil, hefting the knapsack to his shoulders. He was accustomed to the heat of the forge and as for carrying gold, it was more a privilege than a burden. Even the thought of racing with a forty-pound knapsack didn't deter him: He had walked hundreds of miles across Girdlegard with two heavy packs.

They were handed their tankards, thick-rimmed glass vessels with a thin layer of pewter plating. The contents had been heated to several hundred degrees and would sear through the flesh on contact with the skin. There was an obvious risk of serious injury; even the steam rising from the molten metal was treacherously hot.

"Go!" shouted Balendilín. With that, the race was underway.

Gandogar surged forward, barely glancing at his tankard as he focused on his course. Tungdil took the opposite approach, feasting his eyes on the pool of liquid sunshine. He had marched for enough miles to have faith in his footing.

Soon the king was in the lead and had vanished from the hall. Tungdil followed leisurely. Balendilín had said that the task would be won by the first to return with a *full* tankard. He would rather take his time and bring back his quota than waste any of the precious gold. He even stopped and set down his tankard occasionally to give his calloused smith's hands a chance to recover from the heat.

He had almost reached the valley when Gandogar raced past in the opposite direction.

"You'd better hurry if you want to beat me, Tungdil," he shouted. There was an unmistakable whiff of scorched skin, but the king kept going regardless, content to let his fingers suffer. As far as Tungdil could tell, not a drop of gold had been spilled.

He stopped in the meadow, gave his hand a quick rest, and set off in hot pursuit. *I shouldn't have counted on Gandogar making a mistake,* he admonished himself.

It wasn't long before his hand began to shake. He was feeling the effects of the duel and the metalworking contest, but no amount of self-pity was going to help him win the task. He was just approaching the gates when Gandogar ran past, sweating and cursing, on his homeward leg. The fourthling smiled cockily at Tungdil, his tankard still full.

"We're even now! One last challenge and victory will be mine," he vowed.

That was enough to revive Tungdil's competitive spirit, and he hurried after Gandogar, determined to pass him as quickly as he could.

Just then a small creature darted into the passageway and collided with his legs. Tungdil stumbled and caught himself. "What in the name of Vraccas..."

The molten gold was swirling dangerously, ready to spill over the edge, but Tungdil had no intention of releasing his grip. A golden wave slopped over the side and splashed onto his skin. The pain was excruciating, but he gritted his teeth and continued without so much as a curse. His eyes scanned the passageway furiously, but the offending creature was gone.

Owing to the mishap, he reached the hall in second place and without his full quota of gold. He had lost by either reckoning. But Gandogar's victory had not been won without sacrifice and his poor scalded hands were being treated with ice and water by a nurse.

This time it fell to Tungdil to congratulate his rival. He refrained from shaking his hand out of consideration for his burns. "Well, you kept your promise this time," he said, immersing his own tender skin in the ice-cold water.

"Don't worry, I intend to keep *all* my promises," Gandogar informed him, turning quickly away.

Tungdil held up his hand to inspect the damage. The gold

had solidified, leaving a permanent coin-sized patch on his skin.

The golden stain made his right hand glisten in the light of the coal lamps, catching Boïndil's eye. "Take a look at that, brother."

"Tungdil Goldhand! That's what we'll call him," said Boëndal. "I hope he likes it. I reckon it suits him well."

"It's a darned sight better than Bolofar," his twin agreed.

"Attention, delegates," called Balendilín. "The score stands at two all, so we must progress to the fifth and final challenge, on which the choice of successor and the future of the dwarven folks shall rest." He instructed the rivals to note down a maximum of four tasks.

It has to be something I can definitely win… Tungdil thought for a moment, then grinned. *Of course!* The perfect task had occurred to him in the nick of time.

Each slip of paper was folded in the same fashion and placed in a leather pouch held open by Balendilín. The counselor pulled the drawstrings, gave the bag a good shake, and paced along the row of dwarves, stopping in front of Bislipur.

"Once the task has been drawn, there can be no complaints about the fairness of the choice. Bislipur, my friend, I should like you to pick the challenge." He held the pouch toward him.

The thick-set dwarf seized the bag without any pretense at politeness. He fixed the counselor with a stony glare.

Without looking down, he reached inside the bag, swept the bottom, and came up with a slip of paper. He was about to unfold it when the parchment slipped out of his fingers and fell back into the pouch. His hand plunged after it and he thrust the note wordlessly toward Balendilín.

"No," said the referee. "You picked the task; you read it."

Bislipur shifted his gaze from the counselor's face to the note. He unfolded the paper and scanned its contents. "Oh," he said breezily, "that's not the one I drew first." He reached inside the bag again.

"Rules are rules." Balendilín snatched the pouch away. "You made your choice; now read out the challenge."

Bislipur's jaw was clenched as if to hold back the challenge and prevent it from reaching the delegates' ears. He took a deep breath, hesitating for so long that Tungdil began to hope.

"The fifth and final task is an expedition," he announced, his voice trembling with rage. "The candidates are challenged to journey to the Gray Range and return with Keenfire. The winner will wield the ax against Nôd'onn."

There was a faint sigh as Gundrabur released his pent-up breath in relief. Balendilín closed his eyes and permitted himself the briefest of smiles.

No one could have anticipated that the greatest challenge to Gandogar's succession would come from a task chosen and read by Bislipur himself. It was obvious that Tungdil was far cleverer than his fellow dwarves had thought. Silence descended on the hall as the delegates digested the unexpected twist.

Tungdil stepped forward quickly to forestall any protests about the nature of the task. "I issued the challenge, and I accept." He turned to Gandogar.

The fourthling king was visibly seething. "Ditto," he growled.

"Stop! We must draw again," insisted Bislipur, knowing that an expedition to the Gray Range would sabotage his plan for a war against the elves. "You saw me drop the first note. This isn't the right one!"

Balendilín stood his ground. "What do you propose I do?

We'll never know which note was drawn first. No, the decision must stand. Both candidates have accepted the challenge, and the outcome will decide the succession."

"But what of the delay?" protested Bislipur. "An expedition will saddle us with orbits of uncertainty."

"Please don't worry unduly," Tungdil said politely. "I'll endeavor to return as quickly as I can." The delegates laughed. "If you'll excuse me, I need to get going and choose my traveling companions. There's no time to waste." He signaled to Boëndal and Boïndil to follow. "I would never have got this far if it hadn't been for you. With your agreement, I should like you to accompany me on my expedition to the Gray Range. Can I count on your assistance in escorting me there and back again?"

Boïndil guffawed. "Did you hear that, brother? He's the same old scholar!" He turned to Tungdil. "We'd be honored to join you, but only if you promise to drop your fancy speech. Besides," he added with a tinge of sadness, "there's the matter of restoring my good reputation after I failed you in the desert."

Tungdil placed his hands on the brothers' shoulders. "Don't worry, Boïndil, I'm sure you'll have more than enough opportunities to save me from certain death."

The dwarf grinned and his brother nodded. "You earned yourself a new name today, scholar." Boëndal pointed to the shimmering metal grafted to his skin. "Tungdil Goldhand. What do you think of that?"

"Goldhand..." Tungdil held up his right hand. "Yes, I rather like the sound of it." His hand hurt devilishly, but he managed a smile. *Goldhand — a proper dwarven name.*

The delegates dispersed and Bislipur and Gandogar stormed out of the great hall, leaving the high king and his counselor alone.

"Was that your idea?" inquired Gundrabur, reaching for his pipe.

Balendilín laughed softly. "Not at all. I would never have come up with such a preposterous suggestion. If you ask me, Tungdil was sent here by Vraccas himself." He ascended the dais and stood by the throne. "He'd make an excellent high king, you know. His ideas are pure gold."

"Tungdil chose wisely," agreed the monarch. "Whichever of the candidates comes back first, Girdlegard will be the real winner — and of course the dwarves. Our task is to make sure nothing untoward happens while the two of them are away."

"It means keeping your inner furnace alight a little longer," Balendilín reminded him anxiously.

Gundrabur levered himself out of his throne and stuck his pipe between his teeth. "Vraccas knows our need and will stay his hammer until the time has come," he said, undaunted.

His counselor watched him go, then sat down on the footstool to examine the contents of the leather pouch. His efforts were focused on finding the slip of paper that Bislipur had originally drawn. He knew it as soon as he saw it because of the nick in one corner. Bislipur's expression on reading the challenge had discouraged him from intervening and correcting the mistake.

And rightly so, as he discovered when he opened the note. If Bislipur had kept hold of the paper, Tungdil would be cutting diamonds instead of preparing for his quest. *He would have lost the challenge and Gandogar would be high king.*

He unfolded the other slips of paper and laughed out loud: four times diamond-cutting and four times an expedition.

Thank Vraccas for Bislipur's clumsiness! he thought, chuckling in relief.

XI

Knowing that he would require the services of a mason, Tungdil had asked the high king's counselor to recruit a suitable artisan from the secondling clans. Balendilín felt strongly that the final decision should rest with Tungdil, and so it was agreed that a group of candidates would be selected for him to take his pick. Not long afterward a one-eyed dwarf knocked on Tungdil's door.

Tungdil looked him over in surprise. "Are you the only one? Balendilín promised to narrow it down, but I didn't expect him to be quite so ruthless. Who are you?"

"Bavragor Hammerfist of the clan of the Hammer Fists, mason and stoneworker of two hundred cycles." His bearlike hands reminded Tungdil of Balendilín. His black hair hung loose about his shoulders, and his beard was artfully shaped around his cheeks and chin. "My masonry is second to none and my right eye sees twice as keenly as two. Nothing escapes me, not the tiniest fault in the stone nor the slightest flaw in the working of it."

Tungdil explained that the expedition required a mason to fashion the spurs for an ax. Since the blade was to be forged in the Gray Range, the other components of the weapon would be made and assembled there. "Which means journeying through the Perished Land. It's bound to be hazardous — only

Vraccas knows what will befall us." Tungdil left the briefing at that and looked the mason in the eye. A dark red ring encircled the brown iris. *How peculiar.*

"Count me in," said Bavragor. He held out his hand. "Let's shake on it. Do you promise that I, Bavragor Hammerfist, will be your one and only mason?" Tungdil obliged by clasping his hand and giving his word. The mason grinned and seemed almost relieved. "When are we leaving?"

"In two orbits' time. I need to recruit a diamond cutter from the fourthling delegation."

"Then I'll start packing. A weapon like Keenfire deserves my finest tools." He hurried from the room.

Tungdil had expected the interview to last a little longer, but he soon forgot about the mason and turned his attention to finding a diamond cutter.

None of the fourthlings could be expected to join his company of their own accord, so he was obliged to ask Gandogar to spare him a suitable dwarf. The strategy was safer than it sounded: The fourthling delegation was composed of first-rate artisans and warriors, as tradition dictated.

The more Tungdil thought about it, the less inclined he was to ask his rival for a favor, but in the end he swallowed his pride, reminding himself that vanity was a luxury when Girdlegard's future was at stake.

He was just leaving his chamber when he saw four dwarves hurrying down the passageway toward him. One by one they introduced themselves. "Balendilín sent us. He says you're to choose."

Bewildered, Tungdil stared at the bearded countenances looking at him expectantly. "I've made my choice," he said. It hadn't occurred to him that there might be other candidates. Now he was regretting his haste. "I chose Bavragor."

"Bavragor Hammerfist? Not Bavragor who polishes the stone with the beer on his breath?" said one of the dwarves incredulously. "Not the merry minstrel?"

"He got here first."

"He didn't make the final cut! You can't take him!" The masons looked at him, aghast. "He's been trying to drown himself in beer for as long as anyone can remember. Four full tankards are barely enough to steady his hands!"

"I gave him my word. I can't go back on it now." Tungdil's cheeks flushed with fury when he realized that he'd walked straight into the one-eyed mason's trap. *I shall ask him to release me from our agreement.*

The secondlings directed him to Bavragor's favorite tavern, and Tungdil marched off to give the trickster a piece of his mind.

He soon found the place. A line of lamp-lit columns ran down the center of the barrel-vaulted chamber, and lanterns dangled from the ceiling, casting golden halos through panes of tinted glass. At the far end was a stone-hewn counter where four barmaids were filling tankards from huge dark barrels and carrying them to the waiting clientele. The band was made up of two krummhorns, a stone flute, and a drum, whose task consisted mainly of accompanying the rowdy choir.

ravragor was sitting at a table with a group of laborers
me straight from the quarry and were covered in
brating his selection for the expedition in
ion, waving his tankard and singing
rough the room. Beer slopped
n leather breeches with

"Ah, the high king to be!" The mason raised his vessel. "Three cheers for Tungdil Goldhand!" His drinking companions joined in, raising their tankards and scrambling to their feet in a fog of gray dust.

Tungdil seethed. In a few determined strides he crossed the tavern, tore the tankard from Bavragor's hand, and slammed it onto the table. "Balendilín didn't send you to me. You tricked me into giving you my word and now I want you to release me."

"Oops, careful there. That's good beer you're spilling." The mason gave him an innocent smile. "I didn't actually say that Balendilín sent me, did I?"

Tungdil was lost for words. "Well, no, you didn't, but..."

Bavragor picked up his tankard. "Was it part of the deal?"

"Yes...I mean, no..."

"Look, here's what happened: I came in, asked for the job, and you agreed. We shook hands, you gave me your word of honor, and that was that." He took a long gulp. "In any case, you made the right choice: There's no better mason than me. I expect you saw my work when you got here: inscriptions, statues, the lot. Pretty impressive, I'd say." He raised his right hand. "This is the hand you shook, and your grip was true. The sooner you find a diamond cutter, the better; we can't hang around forever." He turned back to his fellow drinkers and launched into song.

Tricked by a drunkard! Speechless with ra stomped off to find Gandogar. He tried to and think about it logically. Perhaps best mason in the secondling up for his barefaced che

He was halfwa out laughi

onstrate that a little bravado could go a long way. The Smith had shown a fine sense of irony in saddling him, the false heir to the throne, with an impudent drunkard who had bluffed his way into the mason's role. *I'll have to remember to pack enough brandy and beer to steady his hands when we reach the Gray Range. At least Balendilín will be able to tell me whether he's really as good as he claims…*

Tungdil fetched one of the two lengths of sigurdaisy wood and entered the assembly room where Gandogar was waiting.

The fourthling monarch was sitting at the table with five of his entourage. Tungdil was struck by their glittering jewels and diamonds; compared to the secondlings, their tunics and mail were unashamedly ostentatious.

"It is not in my nature to make others beg. You don't need to explain yourself, Tungdil. I know what you want." He pointed to the delegates, who rose to their feet. "Take your pick. They're all expert craftsmen, masters in the art of cutting and polishing gems."

Tungdil paced along the line of dwarves, studying their faces and allowing his instincts to guide him.

The artisans were a little on the small side, but for some reason he was drawn to the puniest of the lot. Something told him that this was the one. The dwarf's beard glittered with diamond dust that had caught in his curly whiskers. It looked as though thousands of tiny stars were shimmering under his chin. Tungdil's mind was made up.

"Goïmgar Shimmerbeard," said Gandogar, introducing him. "A fine choice," he added.

The artisan's nervousness turned into full-blown panic. He turned to his monarch. "But, Gandogar, Your H¹ ness…Surely you won't make me…You knov can't…"

"I gave Tungdil a free choice," Gandogar said sharply. "Do you want me to break my promise? You're going with Tungdil, and that's that."

"B-but, Your Majesty…" the artisan stuttered desperately.

"Think of the reputation of our folk. Do exactly as Tungdil tells you, and if you get to the Gray Range before us, be sure to cut the diamonds as conscientiously as you would for me. Farewell—and, Goïmgar, come back in one piece."

The king rose and signaled for the remaining four dwarves to follow. When he reached the door, he stopped and turned.

"I don't want you to come to any harm, Tungdil Goldhand, but as the rightful heir, I can't honestly wish you well. Vraccas will lead me to victory and expose you as a sham. I will be Gundrabur's successor."

"You can have the title, King Gandogar," Tungdil said graciously, handing him the sigurdaisy wood. "Just remember to slay Nôd'onn and protect Girdlegard and our kingdoms from harm."

He hurried away without waiting for a reply. The scrawny artisan followed him, eyes cast gloomily to the floor.

Tungdil, Bavragor, Goïmgar, and the twins were sitting in the central hall of the library, a ribbed vault lined with lamps and mirrors that afforded sufficient light for reading and study. All around them were tablets and rolls of parchment, the collected knowledge of hundreds of cycles. The archive, the secondlings' repository of the past, seemed the ideal place to hold a meeting about the future.

Tungdil unrolled a map showing the territory between the ranges. "We'll go down and take a look at the entrance to underground network," he told them. "With a bit of luck ing of Vraccas we'll be able to travel west—"

"You mean north," interrupted Bavragor. The strapping dwarf leaned forward and pointed at the Gray Range. "We need to go north."

"Sure, but first we'll go west to Borengar's folk. The first-lings have always been the best smiths. They're the only ones capable of forging the blade."

"That's as may be," objected Bavragor, giving Tungdil a searching look with his right eye. "But who's to say they're still there? For all we know, they may have been wiped out by orcs." He reached for his beer. "We should take a smith with us and head north right away."

"Ah," said Boëndal, "so we've got a new leader, have we? Don't tell me you want to be high king as well?"

"I wouldn't mind being high king if it meant I could lock up maniacs like your brother," the mason retorted harshly.

Boïndil frowned, his hand moving automatically to his ax. "Careful, one-eye, or you'll end up blind."

"They never liked each other," Boëndal explained in a whisper. "The incident with Bavragor's sister only made things worse."

Tungdil sighed. He had a nasty feeling that the journey was going to be harder than he'd thought. "His sister?"

"I'll tell you later," hissed Boëndal. "They'll only end up fighting—or worse."

"What are we going to do with the dragon if we actually find it?" asked Goïmgar. The skinny artisan was barely half the width of Bavragor or the twins. "If you ask me, the whole thing sounds dangerous. Orcs, the Perished Land, älfar, a dragon..." He swallowed nervously. "I must say, I am a bit...concerned."

"Concerned? It's going to be *fabulous!*" bellowed Boïndil, clapping him on the back. Goïmgar winced in pain.

"We all like a good bit of orc-baiting, don't we? It's good dwarven fun."

True to his name, Goïmgar's beard shimmered in the candlelight. "Speak for yourself. I'd rather be in my workshop."

Boïndil eyed him suspiciously. "You do know how to use an ax, don't you? You sound more like a whining long-un than a child of the Smith." He jumped up and threw him an ax. "Come on, then, show us how you fight!"

The ax clattered across the floor and slid to a halt in front of Goïmgar, who left it where it lay. He patted his sword. "I'd rather use this and my shield," he said peevishly, offended by the secondling's mocking tone.

"Call that a sword? It looks more like a bread knife. A gnome would be too embarrassed to use a pathetic blade like that." Boïndil whinnied with laughter. "By the beard of Vraccas, you must have been hewn from soapstone!" He sat down, shaking his head in despair. Bavragor chuckled into his beer, emptied his tankard, and burped. On the subject of Goïmgar, the two archenemies were united in scorn.

Boëndal turned his attention to the map. "We'll be able to get to the firstling kingdom without coming up against the Perished Land. Let's hope we can use the tunnels. I wonder what kind of state they're in."

"I expect we'll find out when our wagon hits a broken sleeper and we plunge to our deaths," Goïmgar said despondently. "No one's been in the tunnels for cycles and cycles. It'll be a miracle if—"

"Now I know why Gandogar said we could take you with us. What a pumice-hearted weakling you are! I've never heard so much wailing and sighing," Boïndil said scornfully.

Bavragor eyed him coldly. "If you'd been at my sister's funeral—"

"Enough!" Tungdil silenced them. He was starting to have serious doubts about his ability to hold the group together. *Vraccas give me strength.* "Is this an expedition for dwarves or for children? No one would ever guess that you're older than me! We're not visiting a gold mine or a salt works. We're supposed to be saving Girdlegard."

"Oh, I thought we were risking our lives so you could steal the throne," Goïmgar said spitefully. Bavragor turned his tankard upside down and caught the last drops in his hand. He licked them up regretfully.

Tungdil smiled at the artisan. "No, Goïmgar, that's not true. Our priority is to forge a weapon that will slay Nôd'onn and give us the means to fight the Perished Land. Without Keenfire we don't stand a chance." He hadn't let on that he was missing a section of the instructions for Keenfire that Andôkai hadn't managed to translate.

"Is that how you're planning to persuade the firstlings to lend us their best smith?" the mason asked derisively. "They've probably never heard of the magus or the Perished Land."

Tungdil looked from Bavragor to Goïmgar and back again. "Why are the two of you so keen to make problems before we've even started?" he asked frankly.

Bavragor scratched his beard. "I'm not the one who's sitting here chatting," he retorted. "But if you want my opinion, we'll need more than Vraccas's blessing if we're to forge the blade and make it back across Girdlegard."

"Then take it from me that he'll give us his blessing and more. If you'd experienced half the adventures that I went through on my journey, you wouldn't be so skeptical. And remember, Bavragor, we're not doing this for me, we're doing it for Girdlegard and the dwarves." *And for Lot-Ionan,*

Frala, Sunja, and Ikana, he added silently. He smiled. "Just think: If we're lucky, we'll find some gold."

"Well, I'd drink to that, but I need some more beer," said the mason. He lumbered out of the room.

Tungdil turned to Goïmgar. "What about you? Do you see why we're doing this?"

"Absolutely. For Girdlegard, like you said." The flippant response did little to satisfy Tungdil, who tried to look him in the eye. Goïmgar stared fixedly at the bookshelves that lined the walls from floor to ceiling.

It wasn't long before Bavragor returned with an even larger tankard, having drunk at least half of its contents on the way. "To the next high king!" he said loudly, omitting to stipulate which of the candidates he had in mind. "I hope he achieves all his goals." He downed the rest of his drink.

"He hasn't even stopped for breath," Boïndil said in astonishment. "There must be a lake of the stuff inside him."

Bavragor wiped the froth from his beard. "Back in a minute," he said, rising to leave.

"Stop!" commanded Tungdil in a firm but friendly voice. "You can drink all you like as soon as we've finished." Bavragor sat down sullenly, dropping the empty tankard to the floor. The hallowed library echoed with the noise. "Our first stop is the Red Range. If the firstlings haven't heard about Nôd'onn, we'll tell them of the danger and ask for the loan of a smith. Then we'll continue through the tunnels to our next stop, the Gray Range."

He picked up another map and laid it out in front of the dwarves. "This is an ancient map from the 5329th solar cycle, showing the main paths through the fifthling kingdom."

Boëndal peered at the yellowing parchment. "Look, there's Flamemere. That's where we'll find our dragon."

"And then what?" Goïmgar inquired weakly.

Tungdil leaned back on his chair. "The way I see it, there's no need to actually fight the beast when all we need is a bit of its fire. Boïndil, if you dance around on its tail for a while, the rest of us can wait until it spews flames, at which point we'll jump out, light our torches, and hurry to the furnace."

"Can I slay it, or am I only allowed to dance on its tail?" asked Boïndil, practically bursting with excitement. Goïmgar gave him a sideways look.

"If it makes you happy, you can slay it—but only *after* we've got the fire," his brother instructed him firmly. "Dead dragons don't breathe flames."

"The furnace is near the entrance to the stronghold." Tungdil gave Boïndil a stern look. "I know you're looking forward to killing some orcs, but the fifthling kingdom will be crawling with them. If you take them on, neither you nor the rest of us will come out of there alive. You're going to have to be reasonable."

"Fine," Boïndil said obstreperously. He crossed his arms in front of his chest. "I won't kill the stinking orcs—yet. I'll slaughter the lot of them when it comes to the showdown with Nôd'onn." He glared at the others. "And let's get this straight: If we run into orcs on the journey, the first ten are mine. You can fight among yourselves for the others."

"Not on your life," muttered Goïmgar, just loud enough for Tungdil to hear.

He changed the subject. "Goïmgar and Bavragor, have either of you had much experience of humans?" They shook their heads. "I'll give you some tips on dealing with them in case we end up traveling overland for part of the way. But first you should get some sleep. We'll be leaving in the morning."

Bavragor and Goïmgar set off in the direction of their chambers.

"What about us?" asked Boëndal.

"We've got some exploring to do." Tungdil and the twins followed a stairway that wound deeper and deeper inside the mountain, taking them toward the ancient tunnels that had carried their forefathers through Girdlegard at incredible speed.

Tungdil walked in front with the map, while Boïndil and Boëndal trailed behind, staring wide-eyed at galleries and passageways whose existence they had never suspected. None of their folk had entered this part of the kingdom since it had been contaminated by sulfur hundreds of cycles before.

The air smelled dank and a little staler than usual, but there was no hint of gas. From time to time they came across a skeleton of a sheep or a goat that had lost its way and died a slow and painful death of thirst.

They followed the stairway for what seemed like hours. Broad-backed bridges of stone carried them over plunging chasms whose depths shone with a mysterious yellow glow. They passed mighty waterfalls and many-columned chambers as splendid as their own great hall. Overcome with wonderment, they walked in silence, hearing only the tread of their boots and the sound of rushing water. Soon the path sloped upward again.

"To think these shafts have been here all the time," said Boïndil, unable to keep quiet any longer.

"It's what happens when things aren't used. They get forgotten. I bet it's been free of poisonous gases for ages," his brother remarked.

"Aha!" Tungdil pointed to a door measuring four paces wide and three paces high and inlaid with golden runes. "This must be it."

They held up their oil lamps and scraped away at centuries of accumulated grime until they could read the runes. The inscription was written in an ancient dwarven dialect, and it took a bit of concentration for Tungdil to work it out. At last he recited the lines to the twins:

Whether finding friends
Or fighting foes,
May Vraccas be with you
And bring you safely home.

As he uttered the last syllable, the door creaked back, allowing the three dwarves to enter. Inside was a vast chamber filled with all manner of cogs, their teeth meshing vertically and horizontally in a confusion of rust and verdigris. Various rods connected them to a series of cauldronlike vessels and the apparatus was topped with chimneys of all shapes and sizes. There were hatches below.

Boëndal studied the machinery with interest. "To think the three of us have restored to life a forgotten miracle of science," he said reverently.

"Not yet we haven't." Tungdil took a closer look at the cauldrons and discovered slim tubes of glass, each with a single leaden ball. The tubes were calibrated and the cauldrons marked with the dwarven symbol for water. He knelt down to look inside the hatches and came across traces of ash. He laughed and thumped the sheet of metal. "Bavragor would say it's a distillery, but I reckon it's some kind of engine."

"How does it work, scholar?" asked Boëndal, while his brother disappeared behind the array of cauldrons and crankshafts.

Tungdil had seen diagrams of similar devices in Lot-Ionan's

books. "Think of it as a kind of mill," he explained. "The gears turn and drive the equipment."

"Look at this!" called Boïndil from the far side of the machinery. "There's more stuff over here!" They followed.

At the center of the chamber was a starting ramp with eight metal rails sloping gently toward eight closed doors. The uppermost end of four of the rails terminated in a wooden barrier, slung over with decaying sacks of straw.

"Those must be tracks for the wagons," said Boëndal.

Tungdil nodded. "We'll be gliding along a monorail. It's a hundred percent safe."

"Try telling that to Goïmgar," joked Boëndal.

Tungdil glanced across at Boïndil, who had discovered a depot of a hundred or so wagons in a corner of the hall. "Let's take a look."

There were various different designs of wagon. Some boasted ten narrow benches, while others had a single seat and were obviously meant for freight.

Near the front of each vehicle was a lever. Tungdil took hold of one and jiggled it gently. There was a squeaking sound from below. He peered beneath the carriage. "Brakes," he announced. "If you pull on the lever, the wagon slows down. We'll have to scrape off the rust, though."

"Hang on, scholar," said Boëndal. "How do you propose to lift the wagons onto the rails?" He glanced at the starting ramp, which was two paces high at its uppermost end. "They're too heavy for us to carry."

"True." Tungdil pointed to the ceiling. "But look up there."

"Hoists! We can use the hooks to raise the wagons and place them on the rails. I say we give it a go and see what happens."

They collected some leftover charcoal and set light to it with their oil lamps. Next they set out to fill at least one cauldron, which they did by drawing water from a pool at the bottom of a nearby waterfall.

"What now?" Boïndil asked eagerly.

"We wait," said Tungdil.

They dozed for a while, worn out from their exertions, until Boïndil woke up and grabbed Tungdil's arm. "Look!" he shouted. "The lead ball just moved!"

Tungdil sat up. The ball had risen and was dancing excitedly halfway up the glass tube. Hot steam shot from two of the vents.

"Well, well," exclaimed Boëndal, watching attentively to see what happened next.

The crankshaft turned on its axis and the first of many gears screeched into action, achieving half a rotation before grinding to a halt. A third valve opened and a hiss of air escaped.

"It's powered by steam," explained Tungdil, full of admiration for the engineers who had designed the contraption millennia ago. "It's like a water wheel, except it's turned by steam instead of water." The twins looked at him blankly. "Surely you must have tried holding a lid on a boiling pan?"

"What do you think I am?" Boïndil said testily. "A cook?"

His brother understood what Tungdil was getting at. "The steam turns the gears and the gears power the hoist, so the wagons can be lifted onto the rails without us breaking our backs!" He looked at the thicket of rods and wheels. "It'll take more than just one cauldron of water to get that going."

"It shouldn't be a problem," said Tungdil. "We're leaving tomorrow morning and by then we'll—"

Boïndil spun round and glared at the door. "Did you hear that?" he growled, already keyed up for a fight.

"An orc by the sounds of it," teased Tungdil. "You'd better go and look."

"Too right!" He set off at a jog, stopping to peer both ways at the door. Picking up a stone, he weighed it in his hands and turned to the right, only to whirl round and cast his missile into the shadows.

There was a loud squeal, then the rapid patter of footsteps in the darkness. Tungdil saw a small yet somehow familiar silhouette dart past the entrance where Ireheart was waiting, ax in hand. The creature was too quick for him.

"What was it?" Tungdil asked Boëndal. "Did you see anything?"

"No, but from the way it took off, I shouldn't think it was a threat." He watched his brother traipse back dejectedly.

"Shame it wasn't an orc," he grumbled. "I would have killed the little critter if it hadn't been so fast."

"We're nearly done here anyway," said Tungdil. He pointed to the row of eight doors. "We can head back once we've had a look at these."

"Even I know what's behind them," protested Boïndil, who had been longing to whet his ax on a worthy opponent. "Rails, that's what."

There were eight levers at the top of the starting ramp. Tungdil pulled the one next to the first rail and the corresponding door swung open. The rail continued through the opening, into utter darkness.

"It's going to be quite some journey," said Boïndil. "We'll be as good as blind in there. It's darker than a troll's backside."

His brother laughed. "Stop exaggerating. You know per-

fectly well that we don't have any trouble seeing in the dark."
Even so, he had to concede that the tunnel would pose a considerable challenge. Visibility was limited to about ten paces.
"The long-uns would need torches," he said.

"We should use torches as well," Tungdil told them. "If we get too accustomed to the darkness, we'll be dazzled by the least bit of light. What happens if there's a cleft in the rock? Even the tiniest chink of sunshine would blind us."

Boïndil, always the intrepid explorer, disappeared through the opening and took a few paces along the rail. Tungdil read the inscription chiseled into the wall.

"It leads to the firstling kingdom," he announced for the benefit of the twins. He was beginning to understand how the underground network had worked.

Four of the rails carried outgoing passengers away from Ogre's Death, and the other four were for wagons returning home. The wooden barriers and straw sacking served to absorb the impact in case the brakes failed.

He turned the matter over in his mind and paced along the row of doors. "Look at this," he exclaimed, stopping suddenly. "There's even a tunnel to the thirdling kingdom!" *Maybe the folks were more united back then. Why else would they build a tunnel to Lorimbur's dwarves?*

"It's probably so we could attack them," boomed a hollow voice inside the tunnel. "By the beard of Vraccas, it's pretty tight in here," cursed Boïndil. "No more than a dwarf's breadth either side of the wagon, I reckon."

Tungdil ignored Boïndil's typically warlike explanation of the tunnel's purpose and chivvied him along. "It's time to get going!"

"Hang on, I'm nearly at the end and...Whoa, the tunnel goes straight down! We'd better not tell Goïmgar or he'll die of fright." Boïndil's muffled laughter grew louder as he finished his reconnoiter and returned. "Look at the state of me!" He was covered from head to toe in spiderwebs, the desiccated corpses of countless insects sticking to his beard. He fished the cobwebs from between the rings of his tunic and dusted his whiskers.

"There's obviously plenty of wildlife in the tunnels," observed Tungdil, reaching for the lever to close the first door.

Boïndil sighed. "And all of it totally harmless. Still, any spider more than so big," he said, measuring out a space the size of his head, "belongs to me!" They all laughed.

Before they made their way home, they put out the fire beneath the cauldron and locked the door by reciting the verse. Without the sun to guide him, Tungdil wasn't sure how long it had taken to climb the hundreds of steps from the bustling heart of the kingdom to the forgotten hall, but it seemed from his rumbling stomach that they had been walking for some time.

They were sweaty and tired when they finally joined the other delegates in the dining hall. Ignoring the curious glances cast in their direction, they sat down wearily at the table.

"We won't show them the tunnels until tomorrow," Tungdil told the twins. "The last thing we need is for Gandogar to rush off and get ahead. We'll have our work cut out racing him to the Gray Range as it is."

"What are you complaining about?" grinned Boïndil, cutting a slice of fungi about the size of his plate and sprinkling it with pungent cheese. "You've got the best warriors, haven't you? Nôd'onn's days are numbered, just you wait and see."

"Boïndil's right," said his twin, "although there *is* one thing that bothers me. Remember the description of Keenfire?"

"Which part?"

"The purest, hardest steel for the blade, stone for the spurs, precious metals for the inlay, not to mention diamonds for the bit," Boëndal reeled off.

"We'll take everything with us," said Tungdil, guessing the nature of his concern. "I asked Balendilín to supply us with ingots and gems. He said that our task was important enough to merit a donation from the secondlings' hoard. He's giving us everything we need."

"Gold, silver, palandium, vraccasium, tionium, and a handful of diamonds...Vraccas almighty! Every bandit in Girdlegard will be after us'"

"Don't forget the steel, granite, victuals, and other provisions," Boïndil reminded them. "I know we've got sturdy legs, but not even an ogre could carry that much."

"If everything goes to plan, we'll be traveling by wagon so we won't need to worry about transporting the materials. And if we're forced to leave the tunnels, we'll buy a pony to carry our valuables. It'll be fine; you'll see."

The twins said nothing and focused on their supper, but Tungdil knew from their silence that they were unconvinced.

"Fine! What do you propose we do? Quarry the ancient mines of the fifthling kingdom for precious metals and steel?" He sighed and reached for a morsel of cheese.

"We could take some extra diamonds and buy the precious metals on the way. In fact, we could buy the metals once we get there," suggested Boëndal.

"Too risky," ruled Tungdil. "What if we end up with no tionium? We'd be missing a vital component of the ax."

He raised his fourth tankard to his lips and emptied it in a single draft.

"The decision stands: We're taking everything with us." He stood up briskly, cursing himself for drinking too quickly as the beer rushed to his head. "We'll manage," he said encouragingly and left the hall in the direction of his chamber, swaying slightly as he walked. Feeling rather too full and somewhat light-headed, he stretched out on top of his bed and fell to thinking about the small silhouette that had darted past the door. He was sure he recognized it from somewhere.

Suddenly he was assailed by doubts. *I hope we'll really manage. What have I let myself in for?* Tired from hours of walking, he fell asleep in his clothes.

Tungdil was roused from his dreams by a vigorous shake of his arm. He sat up blearily and groaned. *I thought dwarven beer wasn't supposed to give you headaches?*

"They've gone!" he heard Balendilín saying. "Tungdil, are you listening to me? They've gone!"

He opened his eyes. The high king's counselor was standing at his bedside, with Bavragor, Goïmgar, and the twins in the background. They were clad in their mail and looked ready to leave. "What are you talking about? They're behind you," murmured Tungdil, struggling to move his tongue.

"Not them! I'm talking about Gandogar. His party has left." This time Balendilín's voice was louder and sharper. "You'll never catch them if you don't leave now."

Tungdil slid out of bed. His body and mind were in no fit state to embark on a high-speed journey in the dark. "Don't worry," he said soothingly. "They'll take forever to reach the Gray Range. Ask Goïmgar how long they needed to get here!"

"They're not traveling on foot," Boëndal broke in. "They've all vanished except Bislipur, and no one knows where they've gone."

"They didn't go through the gates," added Boïndil.

Suddenly it dawned on Tungdil: "Sverd!" In an instant he was wide-awake. Bislipur's gnome had followed them and eavesdropped on their conversation until Boïndil had scared him away. *Which means Gandogar knows exactly how to operate the rails.* Sverd was every bit as devious as his master.

Tungdil wriggled into his leather jerkin and pulled on his mail, leather breeches, and boots. At last he was ready for the adventure to begin. He told Bavragor and Goïmgar to follow the twins through the disused passageways and light the fires beneath the cauldrons.

"I want the wagons to be on the rails by the time I get there. I've got a thing or two to say to Bislipur first."

He asked Balendilín to accompany him. "I see you've chosen your mason," the counselor remarked.

"Not exactly." Tungdil sighed. "Bavragor volunteered himself and I fell for it. It's too late to go back on my word, but I wouldn't mind knowing why everyone is so against him. Is his drinking really that bad?"

Balendilín drew breath. "Either he's sober, in which case he's bitter and rancorous; or he's tipsy, which means he won't stop singing and playing the clown—the merry minstrel, they call him. As far as his masonry is concerned, he's past his peak."

"You mean he's not the best mason?"

"Oh, he's the best, all right. You only need look at the parapets, halls, and passageways to convince yourself of that. But Bavragor hasn't used his chisel for ten cycles or more. Thanks to his perpetual drinking, his hands can't be trusted to do what his mind commands. No other mason has ever come close to rivaling his art, so yes, he's the best." He pursed his lips. "I didn't want to recommend him because his mood is unpredictable and he may not be as skilled as he was. Either way, it's not worth dwelling on now."

They found Bislipur breakfasting in the dining hall with a group of fourthling delegates. His companions broke off their whispered conversation to warn him of Tungdil and Balendilín's approach.

"Still here?" said Bislipur, feigning surprise. "I expected more of you, Tungdil. Strike while the iron is hot — isn't that the smith's motto?"

"I was waiting for Gandogar," retorted Tungdil, struggling to contain his rage. "Why isn't he here? And who told him how to get to the tunnels?"

Bislipur eyed him dismissively. "We did some exploring of our own," he said casually. "Besides, there was no agreement about departing together. Gandogar and his company were ready, so they left. They'll be back with Keenfire before too long." He wrinkled his nose. "You're the one who spent last night in his cups and frittered away the morning in bed. You should be setting Bavragor an example, not the other way round."

"Then let the race begin. We'll soon see who gets to the firstling kingdom and recruits the best smith. Your monarch will be wishing he'd had more of a lead."

Bislipur picked up his mug of hot milk. "Well, don't let me delay you. You're free to go whenever you please." There was a rumble of laughter from his companions.

"Where's that gnome of yours?" Balendilín asked sharply. "I hope he isn't snooping on your behalf. He wouldn't be plotting anything untoward against Tungdil, would he?"

Bislipur jumped to his feet and drew himself up threateningly. "How dare you insult my honor, Balendilín Onearm. If you had enough limbs to defend yourself, I'd challenge you to a duel."

"You can guarantee it will come to that if you continue to provoke me," the counselor said evenly. "All I want is your assurance that the expedition will be conducted without interference from you."

Bislipur put his hands on his hips. "Vraccas forfend that I should interfere! That's precisely why I stayed behind—so no one would wrongfully accuse me."

"And what of your little helper?" demanded Balendilín.

"The same applies," Bislipur said haughtily. "Of course, I don't always know what he's up to. Sometimes he gives me the slip."

Tungdil didn't believe a word of it. *We'll have to keep our eyes open*. He excused himself brusquely and hurried out of the hall.

"So, Bislipur," Balendilín said softly, "why don't you tell me why you really stayed behind?"

The dwarf laughed balefully. "I've given you one good reason already, but since you insist: I'm here because I don't want *you* deciding our future if the high king was to die. I owe it to my folk to ensure that the secondlings don't seize the crown while the legitimate heir is away." He leaned forward. "When I say *legitimate heir,* I don't mean your puppet. He isn't one of us."

"Nonsense," Balendilín said flatly. "Tungdil is a fourthling. You heard the evidence just like everyone else."

Bislipur took a step toward him. "I'll tell you where Sverd is," he whispered. "He's on his way to our kingdom to study our archives and speak with those who would know of a bastard child." His eyes narrowed. "The story of Tungdil's origins is an outrageous lie, an insult to the honor of a king who was faithful to his queen until his dying orbit. Sverd will bring back proof that your puppet is a liar, a slanderer, and a fraud, and I shall take pleasure in exposing the deceit. I'll smash the charlatan's ambitions as thoroughly as this ax has splintered hundreds of orcish skulls. Make no mistake, my friend, everyone involved in this trickery will meet the same fate. I swear it on Vraccas's hammer."

Balendilín considered the threat and decided that Bislipur stood a good chance of uncovering the deceit. If Tungdil was to return victorious, he would have to be protected from the allegations until Nôd'onn was defeated. The crusade against the magus was more important than anything else.

"That's good to know," he said equably. "Like you, I'm an honest dwarf with nothing to fear from the truth. I look forward to seeing which of our candidates is the first to return. In the meantime, I'm sure you won't mind if I examine the authenticity of your document about the elves. I think it's important to establish who was really responsible for the fifthlings' fall. Of course, if the text you provided turns out to be a forgery, I'll know who to blame." He nodded curtly and left the hall.

Bislipur sat down and watched the one-armed counselor disappear into the corridor. "Much good may it do you! Just wait and see who'll soon be sitting on the throne," he muttered darkly.

His ambitious plans had been foiled by the appearance of the impostor, but he had no intention of giving up. *I'm not letting cycles of preparation go to waste. We're going to war, no matter what.*

In the event that the delegates changed their minds about a military offensive, he had another trick up his sleeve.

Bislipur turned back to the breakfast table to refill his plate. He cut himself a slice of ham and stared at the streaks of white fat amid the soft pink flesh. Suddenly it came to him: *My enemies' enemies are my friends.*

* * *

Tungdil threw his most important belongings into a knapsack and hurried down the passageways at a jog. As an afterthought, he had briefed Balendilín and Gundrabur about the eight rails leading out through the mountain: Gandogar was gone already, but the other delegates deserved to be told of the forgotten depot of wagons and machines.

On reaching the hall, he found his companions awaiting him with faces as long as elves'. The air was damp and sticky and he was perspiring from every pore.

"Someone has gone to great lengths to delay us," Boëndal explained grimly. "Take a look at this."

The rail that sloped toward the firstling kingdom was lying warped and twisted on the floor. The oppressive warmth came from steam that was escaping from countless perforations in the sides of the cauldrons. Even if it was possible to repair the rail, they had no means of moving the heavy wagons.

"So much for letting the best dwarf win," Boëndal said testily. "Although it's flattering that Gandogar feels threatened enough to cheat."

"I'd rather do without that sort of flattery. Besides, I don't suppose Gandogar had anything to do with it." Tungdil bent down and examined the rail more closely. Someone had used the pulley system to prize it from the ground. "If you ask me, Bislipur decided to give his monarch a helping hand." *What are we supposed to do now?*

Goïmgar had stationed himself a few paces away and was cultivating a detached expression. Meanwhile, Bavragor was leaning against one of the perforated cauldrons and drinking from his pouch. He licked his lips contentedly, sealed the pouch, and walked over to inspect the damage.

"It's simple, really," he breezed. "All we have to do is swap the rails." He pointed to the neighboring rail that served as the disembarking point for passengers arriving from the firstling kingdom.

"You've been drinking," Boëndal said reproachfully.

The mason didn't bother to look at him. "So what? I don't complain when you've been eating. Beer just happens to be my sustenance." His huge calloused hands thumped the metal track. "We'll send for one of our smiths and let him take care of it." His right eye settled on the punctured cauldrons. "As for these, we should fetch a tinker from the trading post. I expect our artisans could handle it, but it's more a job for a tinker. And while we're at it, we may as well ask the womenfolk in the brewery. They know a good deal about vats."

Tungdil stared at him in surprise. All of a sudden the one-eyed dwarf was bubbling with enthusiasm and confidence. Balendilín had been right: The mason's mood was unpredictable. "Good work, Bavragor; those are excellent suggestions," he said approvingly.

"I know." Grinning, the mason rewarded himself with another draft of beer.

The combined efforts of the tinker and his apprentices, assisted by the women from the brewery, resulted in the cauldrons being repaired to the point where they could withstand the build-up of steam for long enough to get the machinery going.

It took a further two orbits to undo the rest of the damage. At last the cauldrons were filled with water and fired from below, the gears moved smoothly, and the hoists did as instructed. By the afternoon of the third orbit their wagon was stationed on its new rail, ready to begin its journey into the unknown.

Tungdil and Boïndil sat at the front, with Bavragor and Goïmgar on the next bench and Boëndal at the rear. Their luggage, including comestibles, equipment, and the materials for Keenfire, was shared among them and stowed at their feet.

Tungdil turned round and scanned the faces of his companions. There was no telling what awaited them at the bottom of the first steep drop or how much of an advantage Gandogar had gained. Everyone looked understandably grave.

"Trust in Vraccas," he said, shifting his gaze to focus on the door ahead. His left hand grasped the lever beside the rail. He pulled it back and the door swung open, clearing their passage into the darkness ahead.

"And now to save Girdlegard..." He let up on the brakes and the wagon rolled gently down the ramp toward the tunnel.

"What if Gandogar sabotaged the rail?" Goïmgar asked anxiously. "Or what if we're too heavy and fly off the side?"

"Let's hope we don't find out!" There was a crazed glint in Boïndil's eyes as they rushed toward the final pitch. "Here we come!"

Gathering speed, the wagon reached the point where the tunnel took a sudden plunge. Its passengers held on tightly as the vehicle tipped over the edge and careered into the abyss.

Ireheart whooped in excitement, Boëndal held on for dear life, Bavragor burst into song, and Goïmgar petitioned Vraccas, while Tungdil wondered whether any of his companions were sane.

XII

The windswept dwarves sped through the tunnel, hair and beards streaming behind them as the wagon thundered along the rail, swooping and juddering at an incredible rate. The speed of the descent pinned them to their seats, and Tungdil felt himself being pushed and pulled in ways he had never thought possible.

Bavragor had stopped singing after choking on something that had flown into his mouth, leaving Boïndil to whoop and bellow with untrammeled enthusiasm, exhilarated by the stomach-turning ride.

Goïmgar was praying with his eyes closed and beseeching Vraccas to protect him from harm. His mortal terror betrayed a lack of confidence in Gandogar's sense of fair play.

The carefully hewn walls flashed past so rapidly that all they could see was a blur of polished stone. After a while the tunnel opened out, becoming at least as wide as the wagon was long.

"You'll burst my eardrums if you keep yelling like that," Boëndal told his twin. "It's even noisier at the back because of the wind."

Boïndil roared with laughter. "Isn't this *fun*? It's a million times faster than boring old ponies. I'd like to shake our forefathers by the hand!"

"I don't know," grumbled Bavragor, wiping brandy from

his eyes. "They could have made it a bit easier for me to drink."

Tungdil smiled quietly. Being with other dwarves almost made up for the ordeals he had suffered since leaving Ionandar, and he had no regrets about visiting Ogre's Death, even though it meant embarking on another trip. At least this time he wouldn't be traveling alone. "If only it weren't for their blasted feuding...," he said, not realizing that he was speaking aloud.

"Blasted what?" Boïndil bellowed. "Speak up! I can't hear you!" Tungdil gave a helpless shrug.

Their steep slide into darkness ended as abruptly as it had begun and they continued at a more agreeable pace, with a few gradual climbs and the occasional gentle downhill.

They clattered over two junctions without being thrown off the rail.

"I hope we're on the right track," called Boëndal from the rear. "Has anyone seen any signposts?"

"I saw some levers before both sets of points," Tungdil shouted back. "There was dust and lichen all over them. I don't think anyone's used them for some time." He hoped to goodness he was right.

The tunnel stopped widening, and the view, now that they had slowed enough to see it, was disappointingly monotonous. Save for the odd patch of lichen or moss, the walls were smooth and unchanging. Twice they spotted stalagmites on the rail; then the wagon ran over them, snapping them in two.

"There's your proof that Gandogar didn't come this way," said Bavragor, uncorking his leather drinking pouch and using the leisurely tempo to drink a few sips before the next descent. "Do you think they might have switched the points?"

"No," Tungdil said firmly. "The levers definitely hadn't been touched." *Where else could they have gone, though?*

"Maybe they lifted the wagon across the rails so we wouldn't be able to tell," surmised Boïndil.

Tungdil didn't argue, but privately he was wondering whether Gandogar's company had taken an entirely different route. *What if they've found another tunnel that will get them there more quickly?* It was conceivable that Gandogar had come into possession of a proper map that showed more than just entrances and exits. Then again, maybe Bavragor was right and the points had been changed so that he and the others had been tricked into traveling in the wrong direction while Gandogar and his companions raced west. He decided not to mention his concerns.

Meanwhile, the wagon was purring along the rail as if it had been making the journey every orbit for a hundred cycles. In time the tunnel widened again and they reached a vast hall that served as an interchange with three other rails. They rolled to a halt.

Tungdil jumped down stiffly. "Come on, you lot, let's see where we go from here." He was glad of the chance to stretch his legs after hours of sitting down.

Between them, they explored the hall and discovered an array of hoists and cauldrons similar to the setup in the secondling kingdom.

"It's a kind of junction," murmured Boëndal, shouldering his crow's beak. He scanned the hall to make sure nothing had taken up residence in the underground network without the dwarves' knowledge.

"Hey, Shimmerbeard! What are you doing?" boomed Boïndil.

The fourthling sprang away from the wall, revealing a tablet of light gray granite. It was roughly the height and width of a gnome and held in place with long rusty nails. "I was…." He cleared his throat. "I was wiping the dust away," he said defiantly. "I wanted to see what it said."

"It looks like a map," said Tungdil, hurrying over. "Well done, Goïmgar. You've got sharp eyes."

He knew the fourthling didn't deserve his praise: Goïmgar had been scratching out the lines with his dagger to disadvantage the expedition and allow the fourthling king to get ahead. Tungdil had no means of actually proving it, so he kept the observation to himself and made a quick sketch of the map. *I'll have to keep an eye on him.*

"Look, Tungdil," Bavragor said cheerfully. "We're on the right track; it's this way."

"That's all we need: directions from a one-eyed dwarf," muttered Goïmgar just loud enough for Bavragor to hear.

The mason turned on him, snarling with rage. His right hand shot out, his fingers winding their way into the artisan's wavy beard and pulling him close.

"Come here, you pathetic excuse for a dwarf," he growled, raising his free hand and peeling back his left eyelid to expose the shriveled remains of an eye. A shard of rock was impaled at its center. "You think I'm blind, do you? Ha! Let me tell you about my eye. One orbit the mountain tired of my masonry and exacted its revenge. A splinter of rock as sharp and fine as a needle flew up and robbed me of my sight, but Vraccas took pity on me and made the other eye ten times as strong. That's *ten times,* Shimmerbeard. My one eye sees more clearly than ten!" He pushed the delicate artisan away and laughed grimly. "It sees the slightest flaw in the rock, the pores of your skin, and the fear in your eyes; what do you have to say about that?"

Goïmgar backed away from the mason's mighty hands and rubbed his chin. He had endured the humiliation silently, but now that Bavragor had released him, he felt brave enough to vent his fury in a threat. "You'll regret this, Hammerfist. Just wait until Gandogar is high king: The mountain won't be the only one to exact revenge!"

"That's right, run to Gandogar! You're a coward as well as a weakling."

"Let's call it quits now," Tungdil said sharply. "You've both said more than enough." In fact, Goïmgar's threat about Gandogar being high king was proof that he intended the expedition to fail. "I don't want to hear another insult from either of you. In any case, it's time to go."

He strode back to the wagon, the other four following in silence. The strained atmosphere was a worrying portent for the company's future.

What happens when I can't stop them from quarreling? His spirits sank lower when he remembered that Bavragor and Goïmgar weren't the only ones at loggerheads: Boïndil and Bavragor couldn't stand each other either. Only the calm and practical Boëndal hadn't made any enemies. *Who knows how long that will last? It's not easy being a leader,* he thought gloomily. *Vraccas give me strength.*

Boïndil, ever hopeful of finding someone or something to fight, wandered over to the mouth of the tunnel. He opened the door and peered inside. "It goes straight down. The wagon will need a bit of a push; then the slope will take care of the rest."

The next leg of the journey awaited them. They hauled their vehicle to the top of the ramp and jumped aboard, save for Boëndal, who waited a moment longer to give them a final shove. Soon they were hurtling westward, squeaking and rattling through the tunnel to the kingdom of Borengar's folk.

Enchanted Realm of Lios Nudin,
Girdlegard,
Late Autumn, 6234th Solar Cycle

The scouts returned on horseback with news that Porista was going about its usual business, untroubled by the twin-flanked advance of forty thousand soldiers under the command of Girdlegard's finest human warriors.

Gentle sunshine bathed the lush green countryside, bringing out the rich autumn hues of the trees. Everywhere the foliage was putting on a last show of splendor before the winter frosts.

All the same, the air was decidedly chilly, so Tilogorn and Lothaire had erected an assembly tent to guard against the winds. They stood outside and listened to the scouts' report.

The first envoy sent to Porista to negotiate on their behalf had returned with a list of preposterous demands, not to mention tidings of the magi's deaths. Many orbits had passed since then, but the brief exchange had taught them that Nôd'onn was the real enemy and would have to be destroyed.

Clasping flasks of hot tea, the kings of Idoslane and Urgon studied the sketched map of fortifications and marveled at Porista's meager defenses. A single wall protected the city from attack.

Tilogorn was wearing plain but solid armor. He was heartened to see Porista's vulnerability: There were villages in his kingdom that were better defended than the capital of Nôd'onn's realm. "Victory will be swift, provided the magus doesn't jinx us. We made the right decision in not waiting for reinforcements."

"Between us we'll bring the villain to his knees. He can't be in two places at once: One of the gates will fall and Porista will be ours," Lothaire said confidently, checking the buckles on his lightweight leather mail.

Each was wearing armor in keeping with the style of combat in his kingdom. In Idoslane, Tilogorn was accustomed to fighting heavily armed and powerful orcs, which called for heavy-duty protection against axes and swords, whereas a solid suit would be impractical in Urgon because of the lakes and hills. Agility and speed were of the essence when death was the likely consequence of stumbling on a narrow mountain pass.

The mismatched sovereigns were in command of an army that was similarly diverse. Each of the seven human kingdoms had sent units to Porista, but the other monarchs were content to let Tilogorn and Lothaire direct the motley troops. Another forty thousand soldiers were already on their way, ready for the next stage in the campaign: the assault on Dsôn Balsur.

Queen Umilante had sent her lightly armored and sparely clad warriors to line up with Queen Wey IV's waterguards and Queen Isika's guerrillas, whose favored territory was the forest. Not a soldier among them had ever stormed a city, and so it fell to Lothaire's and Tilogorn's units, who, along with King Nate's cavalry, formed the mainstay of the army, to show them what to do.

It's a good thing we're attacking Porista first. The men could use the experience before they cross blades with the älfar. Lothaire pointed to the city gates. "Tilogorn, you attack the northern gate; I'll approach from the south. The catapults and ladders are ready and waiting." He held his head high. "I'll go in first. Take up position with your twenty thousand men, but don't advance straightaway. As soon as you see my signal, charge through the other gate and attack the palace from the north."

"Agreed." Tilogorn reached for his helmet. "Then let's rid Girdlegard of Nôd'onn. After that we can focus on routing the älfar and the orcs. May Palandiell be with us."

"She's with us already, there's no doubt of that." They shook hands, mounted their horses, and rode to join their units three miles from Porista's walls.

Lothaire ordered the fanfare to be sounded and the men raised their standards in a billowing sea of cloth. The divisions attacked from the south as agreed, the first wave of soldiers pushing wheeled screens of wood in front of them to shield their advance.

Porista waited until they were within firing distance before waking from its doze. A dark shadow whooshed toward them, arrows and missiles raining on the troops.

The men huddled behind their wooden defenses and all but a handful escaped the storm unscathed. Lothaire's archers returned fire and the advance continued behind the moving screens. The men reached the wall, flipped the panels over, and held them aloft while others banged posts into the soil on which to balance the wooden shields. With the makeshift roofs overhead, there was no risk of injury from bombardment from above. Soon ladders were clattering against the walls.

It was then that Nôd'onn gave them a taste of his might.

Tilogorn was watching on horseback while his foot soldiers stole toward the northern gates. There was no opposition worth speaking of: Porista's guardians had been tricked into thinking that the opposite side of the city was the focus of the attack. By the time news of a second invasion reached the troops in the south, Tilogorn and his men would be through the northern gates and advancing on the palace.

We'll soon decide the matter in our favor, he told himself firmly. There was something unsettling about fighting magic with manpower, but he couldn't think of any other way.

Tilogorn had opted to ride at the head of the five-thousand-strong cavalry and he planned to bear down on the palace and take the magus by storm. In a battle against the wizard's magic, he needed every advantage of speed and shock to survive.

Two lone riders looped toward him, raising their flags as a signal for the king and his units to advance.

"Palandiell protect us." Tilogorn checked each of his weapons, making sure his sword and dagger were at hand. On his orders, the bugles were sounded, heralding the attack. The first eight thousand men swarmed toward the gates like ants. Lothaire had used the same tactic on the other side of the city, only two miles farther south.

The attacking force met with almost no resistance. A few arrows were loosed from the parapets but the damage was minimal.

In no time ladders had been laid against the walls and the first of Tilogorn's warriors were scaling the defenses to grapple with the handful of plucky soldiers left in charge of the northern gates.

Tilogorn watched as Idoslane's flag was raised on the ramparts. He buckled his helmet and pushed down the visor. "For Girdlegard!" He and his five thousand cavalrymen pounded toward the open gates.

The first block detached itself from the parapet and shot toward them like a missile from a catapult. The slab of stone, as long as a forearm in its shortest dimension, struck a soldier in the chest, his body compressing like honeycomb beneath the mass of granite.

It was the start of a bombardment more gruesome than anything the men had ever witnessed. Most of them weren't destined to survive it.

Block by block, the city wall was coming undone. Starting from the top, the stone slabs hurled themselves from the parapet, hitting the attacking army with such force that neither shields nor armor could save them. The massive projectiles crashed straight through the wooden barricades, flipping them over or smashing them to pieces and showering the nearby troops with a lethal hail of wood and stone.

Each of the blocks met its target. Everywhere armor was shattering, bones splintering and granite embedding itself in the ground. Shouts of terror gave way to screams for help and the anguished howls of the dying. Soon there was nothing left to support the ladders and they toppled back among the troops.

"Pull back!" commanded Lothaire, wheeling his horse about. A block struck his stallion's head and it fell to the ground, twitching.

The king tumbled from the saddle and was trapped beneath the fallen mount. When at last he dragged himself free, he realized that his leg was wounded, perhaps broken. Barely able to stand, let alone walk, he was rescued by two of his guards, who carried him to a ditch, the only place that offered any protection against the flying granite.

"Curse the magus and his wizardry," muttered Lothaire, gritting his teeth as pain shot through his injured leg. The situation was worse than anything he had imagined: Nôd'onn was using his terrible powers to bring death and destruction to the allied troops. He tried not to think about the quantity of blocks in the wall; it was a formidable arsenal by anyone's standards.

At last, when the thudding and pounding had ceased, the king raised his head and looked out of the ditch.

The flat ground at the foot of the gates was littered with stone slabs of varying sizes: Even the base blocks, each the length of a fully grown man, had lifted from the foundations and hurled themselves at the troops. Limbs, broken lances, warped shields, and snapped spears protruded from beneath the masonry, the hunks of stone providing grisly markers for every corpse.

Lothaire's gaze traveled over the debris and settled on the unprotected streets and houses beyond. Bereft of its wall, the capital of Lios Nudin lay defenseless before him. Only the watchtowers on either side of the gates were still in place.

"This is our chance," he said, straining to speak through the pain. "We've got to attack." With the help of his guards he left the trench to spur on his army.

Barely three thousand of his twenty thousand men had survived the bombardment, and over half of those had taken flight, their courage defeated by the invisible malice at work. *Who can blame them?* he thought bitterly.

The sight of their leader strengthened the soldiers' resolve and Lothaire was soon surrounded by a loyal cohort of fifteen hundred men, all determined to invade the city and storm the palace.

Just then the masonry came back to life. The biggest blocks were the first to move, rising one by one and lowering themselves into position. Next came the smaller slabs, piling one on top of the other until the wall loomed once again above the horrified troops, only this time it glistened red with the blood of their comrades.

That was the moment when Lothaire stopped believing that Nôd'onn could be defeated. Lowering himself onto the blood-drenched grass, he stared at the insurmountable obstacle in their path. Fragments of armor, broken weaponry, and mutilated body parts stuck to the wall like trophies, daring the army to launch another doomed assault. *Ye gods, what can I do?*

Weapons at the ready, his soldiers hesitated. Lothaire was still praying for inspiration when the voice of the magus sounded from above.

"How thoughtful of you to bring me an army, King Lothaire."

"Enjoy your monstrous work while you can," Urgon's ruler shouted furiously. "Your cruel dominion will soon be over."

There was a flash of dark green cloth and the magus came into view through an embrasure. Lothaire looked up at the great white oval of his bloated face.

"You thought you were invading a defenseless city. It wasn't your only mistake. The human eye is easily misled." He raised his arms and gestured with an elegance belying his bulk. "All the best with your final battle, King Lothaire. Don't worry: This time you'll be fighting humans, not stones." He withdrew and disappeared behind a merlon.

On looking round, Lothaire was rooted with horror. The grass beneath him was turning gray before his eyes. All around him the trees were drooping, the branches shedding their richly colored leaves, whose pigment faded as they fell. This was the true face of Lios Nudin, disguised by the magus to trick them into setting foot in the Perished Land.

Lothaire knew what it meant for him and his fifteen hundred men.

The Perished Land knows no such thing as death. Lothaire

had heard stories about the northern pestilence and the thought of it made him shudder with horror. Closing his eyes, he prayed to Palandiell and other benevolent deities to deliver them from their fate.

His desperate prayers were cut short by the sound of low groans from all over the battlefield. The dead soldiers were rising, clambering clumsily out of block-shaped craters and pushing their way through shattered blockades. Depending on the extent of their injuries, they crawled, limped, or staggered toward the surviving troops. A few walked without impediment, but their open wounds and terrible deformities gave them away. Already there were a hundred of them, each clutching a sword, lance, or other weapon, and their ranks were swelling all the time.

"But they're ... It's impossible! What are we to do?" cried a terrified officer.

"We fight our way out," ruled Lothaire. "If we stay, our courage will be of no greater use to anyone than it was to these men; the Perished Land will enslave us. We'll head south." His loyal guards had been waiting for his signal and offered him their shoulders to lean on. A dozen warriors surrounded the trio and shielded the wounded king. "Make haste! And may Palandiell be with us!"

With that, Lothaire and his men surged forward to break through the ring of undead soldiers who had once been their allies.

The cavalry thundered through the deserted streets of Porista with no regard for their own limbs or the safety of their mounts. Tearing round the corners, many of the horses skidded on the treacherous cobblestones and careened into houses. Those behind leaped over the bodies and galloped on.

Their goal was already in sight. Towering above the rest of the city, Nôd'onn's palace, once the seat of the council of the magi, pointed them on their way.

To Tilogorn's relief, the citizens of Porista did nothing to halt the charge. The assault on the gates had gone according to plan and now the invaders could focus on the purpose of their mission — subduing the magus himself.

The king trusted entirely to the power of numbers, believing his army to be stronger and more powerful than any wizard's spell. To think otherwise would be irresponsible — the men would sense his hesitation and an anxious army was easy to defeat.

The riders streamed through Porista like a torrent of shimmering water, channeled by the streets into three separate tributaries, which flowed toward the palace walls and collected in the marketplace outside the palace gates.

Ahead of them a crowd of people had gathered in front of the entrance. Judging by their dress, they were ordinary citizens, mainly women and children, who barred the way without weaponry or aggression.

From the throng of three hundred souls an unarmed youth stepped forward with his hands in the air. "Leave the magus in peace, men of the east," he called. "He has done nothing to hurt you and wishes you no harm."

Prince Mallen, clad in the armor of the Ido dynasty, pushed his mount through the rows of horses and drew alongside Tilogorn. "Nôd'onn has bewitched them," he whispered urgently. "Break them up or we'll lose our advantage." He glanced nervously at the turrets. "We're a sitting target out here."

"Prince Mallen? Didn't Lothaire..."

"The attack failed. Girdlegard is depending on you and your men."

I was right to fear the wizard's magic. He sat up tall in the saddle. "Move aside, good people. Our quarrel is with Nôd'onn, not you."

"You can trample us into the ground if you like," their spokesman retorted. "You'll have to kill us if you want to get past." He turned his back to them and returned to the others, who closed ranks, leaving no room for a horse to pass.

Tilogorn ordered three hundred riders to advance in a line and push the crowd through the gates. The row of armored horses bore down on the townspeople like a wall of steel, pushing them aside, while a second line of cavalrymen prevented them from rushing back to the entrance.

Suddenly one of the riders tumbled from his horse, clutching his leg and howling in pain. A moment later, a citizen of Porista took his place in the saddle and whipped out a cudgel spiked with nails. The unsuspecting rider to the left was struck in the face before the right-hand neighbor could reach across and run the intruder through. As the young man fell, his simple garments disintegrated, revealing an armor-plated orc. The snarling beast hit the ground and died.

With that, the spell was broken and the unarmed crowd became a war band of orcs. It was conclusive proof, if any were needed, that Nôd'onn was in league with Tion and his minions.

"Cut them down!" shouted Tilogorn. "Kill every last one of them! It's an illusion!"

The formerly peaceful crowd hurled themselves on the cavalry, attacking the horses and riders with cudgels, axes, and notched swords. Thrown off guard by the transformation, dozens of soldiers were killed.

On recovering from the initial shock, the riders discovered that it was impossible to land an accurate blow amid the jostling bodies. They endeavored to leave the scrum.

The green-hided beasts chased after them, hacking at the horses' legs, slashing their flanks, and hanging off their manes like rabid dogs until the poor animals bolted in agony and terror.

Wild with panic, the horses charged the waiting units, and the chaos was complete.

Meanwhile, the orcs were everywhere, snarling, striking, and ducking out of sight. The horses kicked out, making no distinction between friend and foe, whinnying, snorting, and pawing until they were seized by an overwhelming urge to flee. Even the best riders were unable to stop the stampede: The instincts of the herd were stronger than any bridle or spurs.

Mallen and Tilogorn lost valuable time as they struggled to round up their men and regroup in the marketplace. By then the foot soldiers had arrived and were readying themselves to join the charge through the gates.

In the blink of an eye, the orcs disappeared, leaving only the dead and wounded as evidence that a savage confrontation had occurred. The two commanders didn't stop to worry about the whereabouts of the enemy, but gave the order for the gates to be breached.

Three thousand riders tore into the palace forecourt. Tilogorn dispatched the units in different directions and the search for Nôd'onn began. Racing up the broad, flat steps, the horses sped through the corridors and halls, unimpeded by defenders or orcs.

"Stay down here and continue the search," Tilogorn instructed the bulk of his men. He eyed the highest turret, where his instincts told him that Nôd'onn would be waiting. "I'm going up there." He dismounted and wound his way up the flight of stairs with Mallen and three hundred men. As the staircase narrowed and steepened, he lifted his visor so he could breathe.

On entering the first chamber, he glanced at the large window through which the southern streets of the city could be seen. An armed unit was heading for the palace, the flags of Urgon and their other allies fluttering in the breeze.

"Look, Mallen," he said, relieved to see the reinforcements. "King Lothaire has taken the gates. The wizard is at our mercy."

The fair-haired prince of Ido stared in astonishment. "But Lothaire was...I mean, I thought I saw him..." He trailed off, puzzled, and followed the king. Buoyed by new courage and energy, they strode down the corridor until they came to an imposing door, which they opened by force.

Their persistence was rewarded. Twenty paces away a colossal figure in dark green robes was standing with his back to them. The magus was studying the commotion at the base of the turret and didn't turn round.

Without waiting for Tilogorn's order, the men spread out and silently leveled their bows. The target was so broad that it seemed the arrows couldn't fail to hit their mark, but on nearing the magus's back, the tips rusted, the shafts disintegrated, and wood dust trailed through the air. Soon nothing remained but fragments of metal, which tinkled against the marble floor.

"Welcome, King Tilogorn," the magus greeted them, his back still turned. "You have entered the enchanted realm of Lios Nôd'onn. What brings you here?"

"The plight of our kingdoms," Tilogorn replied steadily, drawing his weapon in readiness for a duel. "You are a danger to Girdlegard."

"And you, King Tilogorn, have invaded my realm, stormed

my palace, and threatened my life. Should I consider you a danger?"

"You're a traitor, Nôd'onn — a murderer and a traitor."

"A murderer, yes, that much is true. But I killed only because I had to, because I wanted to save Girdlegard — like you. Humankind is facing a much greater danger, a danger that only my friend and I are powerful enough to combat, and for that we need mastery over Girdlegard. The races of men, elves, and dwarves must cede their lands for the greater good — or die." Turning at last, he looked at them sadly with watery green eyes. "It pains me greatly that some have chosen death already. You'll join me, won't you?" He took a step toward Tilogorn and held out his hand.

"Never!" The king signaled for his men to attack and a dozen soldiers stormed forward.

They were still charging when their weaponry, mail, clothes, flesh, and bones perished like the arrows. The unseen power worked so swiftly that there was no opportunity for them to retreat. A semicircle of dust surrounded the magus, four paces from his feet; then an autumn gust dispersed the disintegrating men. The remaining soldiers drew back in fear.

"You underestimated my power, King Tilogorn," the magus said slowly. "You refused a hand extended in friendship. Your men are paying for your arrogance."

The fresh wind carried the sound of fighting to Tilogorn's ears. He listened intently.

"You thought the battle was over, did you?" Nôd'onn gestured to the window. "Why don't you see for yourself what has become of King Lothaire and his men?"

Tilogorn kept the magus in his sights and sent a soldier to the window to report on the skirmish below.

"They're fighting our men," he said in consternation. "The

soldiers are waving Urgon's banners, but they're...They're joining forces with the orcs!" He gasped. "Palandiell have mercy on us! The dead soldiers are rising! They're still alive, and they're killing our troops!"

Nôd'onn chuckled. "You have been treading the Perished Land for some time, King Tilogorn. I created the illusion to draw you to me and sure enough, you brought me the army I desired—"

He broke off midspeech, racked by violent coughing. Blood dribbled from his lips and two dark streams formed beneath his nostrils. He sank to his knees, still spluttering, and more blood gushed from his mouth, forming a crimson pool on the immaculate marble floor.

"This is our chance," shouted Tilogorn, rushing toward him. "For Girdlegard!" His soldiers joined the charge.

Most of the valiant warriors were turned to dust, but the magus's weakness had damaged his magic shield. Thirty men, among them King Tilogorn, penetrated his guard and were able to attack. Three, then four arrows embedded themselves in the bloated body, and the soldiers rushed in, hacking at Nôd'onn's prostrate form. Seconds later, Prince Mallen joined the fray.

Terrified that they too would fall prey to some wizardry, the men attacked with preternatural force. Their arms rose and fell in a savage frenzy, the blows raining harder and faster all the time. Blood seeped from every inch of the mutilated body, washing over the floor and poisoning the air.

Tilogorn saw a flicker of movement in the open wounds. *There's something alive in there,* he realized with a shudder. He threw all his strength behind his blade. "Die, why don't you!"

"No!" screeched Nôd'onn. Even as he spoke a gust of wind swept his assailants off their feet, knocking them backward. "Girdlegard will be ruined without me!" Black lightning shot from the onyx on his staff, zigzagging in all directions and incinerating the flesh and armor of all in its path.

"Don't listen to him!" Tilogorn sprang forward and raised his sword. "Keep fighting," he gasped. His right arm swooped toward the magus. "Keep—"

A bolt raced toward him and seared through his armor, piercing his heart. With a groan he sank down and let go of his sword, which clattered to the ground and disappeared among the muddle of legs and feet. He was filled with a sense of crushing failure.

"Congratulations, Prince Mallen," Nôd'onn said mockingly. "I suppose this makes you Idoslane's new king." He stepped forward and made to shake his hand. "The question is: Will you join me, or lose your kingdom as quickly as you gained it?"

The last of the Idos didn't stop to consider. Picking up Tilogorn's sword, he helped the wounded king to his feet. "Let's go," he said to Tilogorn. "We'll deal with Nôd'onn another time." He dragged the monarch to the door, protected by a guard of men.

The magus watched incredulously. "Not you as well?"

"How could I ally myself with Idoslane's enemy?" Mallen lifted Tilogorn's arm over his shoulder and half carried, half propelled him down the stairs. Nôd'onn strode after them.

"Then you shall die together!" he shouted hysterically. "You're no use to me!"

A volley of bolts crackled toward them, searing through the last remaining guards. Mallen slung Tilogorn over his shoulder and raced down the stairway. "I'm not leaving you with that monster. I'll get us out of here if it's the last thing I do," he said, gasping under the strain.

"Rule our kingdom more wisely than your forebears." Tilogorn was fading, his voice little more than a whisper. A trickle of blood leaked out of his mouth and onto the prince's armor. "Listen carefully: Wait for the other units at a safe distance from Porista. Rescue the wounded and be sure to burn the dead. If you don't, you'll face an army of revenants that nothing and no one can defeat. Whatever happens, Nôd'onn mustn't be granted his invincible undead."

"You can't die on me, Tilogorn. I need you to help me exact our revenge." The prince had to fight for breath as he struggled beneath the extra weight. "Don't tell me you're prepared to leave your kingdom to an Ido!" he said harshly, hoping to stir the king's anger and galvanize his will to live. "What's the matter with you, Tilogorn?"

"Promise me you'll make a better king than your grandfather. Promise that you won't tear Idoslane apart!"

"You have my word."

"Burn the dead," the king whispered. "You must save Idoslane. Palandiell be..." The tension left his body.

I shall honor my promise, Tilogorn of Idoslane. Mallen laid the body gently at the foot of the turret. *To regain the throne at such a price...* He took the dead king's sword, clasp, and signet ring and ran on.

It was only through sheer determination and good fortune that he and his remaining men escaped the violent fury of the revenants.

As they left the city, they set fire to the buildings, creating a sea of flames that no amount of wizardry could contain. Even the rain invoked by Nôd'onn could not prevent Porista from being razed to the ground, leaving nothing save the palace and the foundations. King Lothaire and King Tilogorn were never to rise from the blaze.

XIII

B y now the five dwarves had a rough sense of how far they were from their destination. At first they hadn't noticed the numerals on the tunnel walls, marking the completion of each twenty-five-mile stretch. In no time they covered an incredible two hundred miles.

After a while they rolled to a halt in another large hall and decided to rest for a few hours before embarking on the next descent. Traveling by wagon was less tiring than walking, but their muscles were sore after hours of sitting uncomfortably and being thrown from side to side. Even the constant rattling was wearying after a while.

Boïndil told the others to stay seated while he stood on top of the wagon and scanned the dusty floor for prints. "Either they've been pulverized or no one's been this way in ages," he said. He jumped down and vanished in a thick gray cloud.

Boëndal thought for a moment. "The rail doesn't look especially clean. Gandogar must have taken a different route."

Tungdil unfolded the map he had sketched in the previous hall. "It's possible, I suppose."

"I hope the ceiling collapses on top of him," scowled Boïndil, searching the hall for firewood. He found a stash of abandoned timber, but it turned to dust in his hands. There would be no melted cheese on toasted mushrooms after all.

They ate their meal in silence, each absorbed in his thoughts. Bavragor took long drafts from his drinking pouch and eventually burst into song, ignoring his companions' objections. His powerful voice reverberated through the hall, echoing down the tunnels.

"For pity's sake, be quiet! We don't want every creature below the surface knowing that we're here," snapped Goïmgar.

Boëndal grinned. "I don't think it's much of a secret. He hasn't stopped warbling since we left."

"Poor little Shimmerbeard," teased Boïndil, laying his axes in his lap and setting to work with his grindstone. "You're not scared, are you? Don't worry: My brother and I are here to protect you." He tested each blade with his thumb. "It's a long time since they tasted orc flesh. They're almost as impatient as me."

"Orc flesh? Down here?" Goïmgar asked anxiously.

"Who can tell?" the secondling replied. Boëndal and Tungdil saw the strange glint in his eyes and knew at once that he meant to have some fun: The poor artisan was about to be scared witless. "The tunnels have been abandoned for hundreds of cycles. All kinds of creatures could have moved in without us knowing." He tapped out a noisy rhythm with the butts of his axes. "It won't be safe until we get rid of them. From now on, it's war!"

"That's enough, mighty warrior," Tungdil warned him.

Boïndil laughed, spurred on by his fiery spirit. "Show yourselves, you ogres, trolls, orcs, and beasts of Tion! Come out and be hacked to pieces by the children of the Smith!" He had to shout at the top of his voice to drown out the mason's singing. "Come out, so I can kill you!"

"Don't provoke them," Goïmgar pleaded, edging away until he was sitting with his back against the wall. "You shouldn't bait them like that."

"Someone once told me about hideous beasts that live down here and plague the dwarves," said Bavragor, joining

in the fun. He oiled his throat with another helping of whatever he kept in his mysterious pouch. "Tion created them as
our natural enemies, like he created the älfar to wipe out the
elves."

"Someone once told *me* about innocent creatures dying in
agony because of your singing," quipped Boëndal.

"More than likely," said his brother. "You'd better keep
your mouth shut, Bavragor. I won't have you chasing away
my orcs."

The mason gesticulated rudely and launched into another
rousing song, only to be silenced by Tungdil. "We need to
know if anything's sneaking up on us," he explained. Goïmgar
and the twins hastened to agree.

"All right, you win." Bavragor lowered his voice to a hum
and curled up in his blankets. Soon he was snoring at a volume to rival his singing. The twins settled down for the night,
but Goïmgar stayed exactly where he was. At last Tungdil
handed him a blanket since he clearly intended to sleep with
his back against the wall.

"I saw what you were up to," he said softly when he was
sure that the others were asleep.

"I don't know what you mean."

"You know, when we stopped in the other hall. You were
trying to ruin the map so we wouldn't be able to read it.
Why?"

The diminutive fourthling glared at him defiantly. "I was
dusting it."

"Not with the tip of your dagger, you weren't." Tungdil
looked at him intently and tried to meet his eye. "I wish you'd
stop seeing me as the enemy."

"Don't flatter yourself," the artisan said coldly. "You're not
the enemy. You're nobody, not even a fourthling. You can say
what you like about your lineage; all I know is you're not one

of us. If you want my opinion, you're a common thief who's trying to steal the throne, and I won't let you get away with it. I know what King Gandogar said about obeying your orders, but I'll see to it personally that the rightful heir is crowned."

"Is that why you didn't want to join the expedition?"

"Maybe—or maybe I don't like traveling, fighting, and enduring all kinds of unpleasantness when I'd rather be at home. The journey to Ogre's Death was bad enough, but now I'm risking my life for a liar."

"This isn't about being made high king," Tungdil said earnestly. "Frankly, the whole business is rather a bore."

Goïmgar looked at him in astonishment. "Then why are you here?"

"All I care about is forging Keenfire so we can fight Nôd'onn and put a stop to the evil. Girdlegard is in danger and we dwarves are the only ones who can save her inhabitants from the magus's deadly scheme. That's what I'm interested in—not the throne."

"How do I know you're not lying? In your position, I'd swear blind that my beard was blue and the mountain was made of cheese. And besides, what if we get to Ogre's Death first? According to the rules of the contest, you'd have to be king. I don't see why we're hurrying if you're not interested in the throne."

Tungdil could tell that the discussion was going nowhere. It would take more than a single night to convince Goïmgar that he was mistaken about his intentions. The fourthling didn't trust him one bit.

In any case, Tungdil didn't like to be reminded about the uncertainty of his ancestry. All his efforts were focused on playing the part of the long-lost heir, but deep down he felt lonely and confused. It was only the thought of Lot-Ionan and Frala that gave him the strength to keep pretending. He would do anything to lead the company to the fifthling kingdom so that Keenfire could rob Nôd'onn of his power and his life.

"There's no point arguing," he said glumly. "You should get some sleep. I'll keep watch." He wrapped himself in a blanket to ward off the underground cold. At that moment he heard something. It sounded like a single strike of a hammer on rock.

Goïmgar stopped fussing with his bedding and froze. "An ogre," he whispered tremulously. "Or the ghost of a dwarf who died here when the tunnels were being built..."

Tungdil made no reply. *It could be anything,* he thought. Reaching for his ax, he listened to the darkness. There was silence. "It was probably just a stone," he said slowly, relaxing his vigil. "A bit of stone falling from the ceiling and hitting the floor. It's nothing to worry about."

"Shouldn't we wake the twins? I bet they'd know what to do."

"It was nothing," Tungdil said firmly. "Forget it and go to sleep."

Goïmgar pulled up his blanket until his beard was completely hidden, then balanced his shield across his chest. Tungdil heard him draw his sword. At last, the artisan decided that it was safe to close his eyes.

Tungdil rose quietly and paced up and down, listening at the mouths of the tunnels for footsteps or any sound of movement. *I wonder what it could have been...*

Silence. The underground network was at peace.

Even so, his uneasiness remained. *There's no reason why other creatures shouldn't have occupied the tunnels.* He hoped to goodness that Boïndil's bluster hadn't elicited an unfavorable response.

Tungdil waited until they were back in the wagon before telling the others what he and Goïmgar had heard. Boïndil was torn between excitement and pique, thrilled at the thought of possible antagonists, but angry with Tungdil for letting him sleep. He made a show of sulking and refused to say a word.

The wagon tore through the tunnels like the wind, accelerating, slowing, rolling uphill, and swooping back down. Twice they ran out of momentum and had to push the vehicle to the next downward slope.

For Bavragor, the interludes were an excuse to belt out a stirring melody, presumably to lift their spirits while they toiled. To make matters worse, he switched to a mournful love song and succeeded in antagonizing Boïndil so much that he could barely contain his rage.

Anyone would think he was baiting him on purpose. In fact, Tungdil was under the impression that the brawny mason was throwing just a fraction of his weight behind the wagon in order to make Boïndil take the strain. He took Bavragor aside and confronted him with his suspicions.

"Of course I'm doing it on purpose," the mason said without batting an eyelid. "I want him to suffer every mile of the way."

Tungdil looked at him reproachfully. "You know that's not fair."

Bavragor just shrugged.

"Is it because of your sister?"

The mason glanced back at the twins. Boëndal was handing his heavily perspiring and thoroughly exhausted brother some water. "Yes," he said slowly, taking out his own drinking pouch and removing the bung. There was an instant smell of brandy. He took a sip and wiped a few stray drops from his jet-black beard. "Yes," he whispered a second time, staring absently into the distance. He lowered his head.

"What happened between your sister and Boïndil?" Tungdil asked gently.

Bavragor raised his head slowly. His jaw was clenched and a single teardrop leaked from his patch and rolled down his cheek. He couldn't speak, so he took another draft.

"Is it because of her that you're drinking yourself to death?"

He put the pouch away. "No, I drink to forget how good I used to be," he said sadly. "Not that it helps, of course. Every corner of Ogre's Death is filled with my masonry. My sculptures and engravings look down at me and mock my useless hands." He leaned back against the wall and let his gaze sweep the room. "Do you know why I came on this mission?" he asked abruptly. Tungdil shook his head. "To get out of Ogre's Death and never go back." His hoarse voice was full of drunken earnestness. "I'm tired of being pitied. I want to be remembered as Bavragor Hammerfist, mason extraordinaire who sculpted the spurs for Keenfire and gave his life for the dwarves — not as drunken old Bavragor whose chisel danced over the rock of its own accord." He smiled wanly. "I promise to do my bit for the dwarves and for Girdlegard, but I won't return from the fifthling kingdom." He took another long draft to show that his mind was made up.

Tungdil's heart went out to the mason. Bavragor wasn't the noisy, occasionally rude but fundamentally cheerful and resilient character he had taken him for. "We can't leave you in the fifthling kingdom," he protested, realizing at once how feeble he sounded. "We'll need your fists in the fight against Nôd'onn."

Bavragor reached for his arm and squeezed it tightly. "No, Tungdil, you need warriors like the twins, true fighters whose confidence never falters." He released his grip. "Don't worry, my hands are steady enough to sculpt the strongest, most beautiful spurs ever fashioned by a dwarven chisel. I'll tell you about my sister another time. For now, I'd like a moment with my pouch."

Tungdil got up and strolled over to the twins, who were snacking on ham and cheese. *Poor Bavragor.*

Boëndal had observed the conversation from a distance, but refrained from asking questions because he didn't want Boïndil to get wind of the mason's distress. He offered Tungdil a morsel of goat cheese. "Well, scholar, only two more orbits and we'll be in the firstling kingdom — assuming we don't have any problems with the wagon."

"Gandogar will be there already," Tungdil said gloomily.

"For all we know, he might have gone the wrong way." Boïndil laughed and wiped his glistening brow. "I hope his blasted shortcut leads him straight into a fathomless chasm." Goïmgar glared at him. "You can stare all you like," Boïndil told him, rising to the silent reproach. "The king of the dwarves is sitting right here. Your king is a warmonger, a cowardly — "

"That's enough, Boïndil!" Tungdil interrupted. "I know you'd rather be fighting than trundling along in a wagon, but you're going to have to keep your temper under control." He waited until Boïndil had finished growling. "Right, let's get going. The sooner the first leg of the journey is over, the better." He stood up and the other four followed him to the wagon. *Will they ever stop squabbling?*

"I wonder what it's like in their kingdom," mused Boëndal, preparing to get the wagon rolling. "The firstlings are supposed to be consummate smiths. Do you think they'll forge me a weapon to beat my trusty crow's beak?"

"Good thinking, brother," his brother applauded him. "Not many axes are as good as mine, but I'll lay them aside if the firstlings can do better."

The wagon crept along the rail. Boëndal waited until they were inches from the downward slope, then jumped in and they thundered into the tunnel.

Beroïn's Folk,
Secondling Kingdom,
Girdlegard,
Late Autumn, 6234th Solar Cycle

Bislipur knelt before the high king. "I came because you summoned me," he said, rising. "Not because you can change my mind."

His obdurate tone left Gundrabur and his counselor in no doubt that the private meeting in the great hall would come to nothing. They could only hope and pray that Vraccas would knock some sense into Bislipur's intransigent skull. Gundrabur motioned for the burly dwarf to be seated.

Bislipur appraised him intently. *He looks weaker. His fingers are shaking and he can barely lift his arms. Nature is on my side.*

"We should have been straight with each other from the beginning," said Balendilín, taking his place beside the king. "We're tired of game playing. I know we don't share the same opinions, but it's no excuse for scheming like kobolds."

"Our folks have been offered a unique opportunity, and I'm trying to persuade the assembly to take it. Is that what you mean by scheming?" Gandogar's adviser retorted.

"His Majesty and I have been wondering what could possibly motivate you to agitate for war," Balendilín said forthrightly. "It baffles us that you should wish to lead the children of the Smith against the elves when a battle of far greater magnitude awaits us."

Bislipur seemed to find the topic too tedious to be worthy of anger. "Your Majesty, there's nothing to be gained by talking. Your concerns are as unintelligible to me as mine to you. I've got better things to do than —"

"Better things?" Balendilín cut in. "Such as what?"

"Private cogitation," Bislipur answered dourly. Without waiting for the high king to dismiss him, he got up and limped to the door.

"You're going to cogitate, are you?" Gundrabur called after him. "Well, here's something for you to consider: None of the fourthlings knows anything about your family."

The dwarf stopped short, but didn't turn. "What are you insinuating?"

"I'm not insinuating anything. I thought you should be warned."

The elderly monarch paused and Balendilín took over. "You questioned Tungdil's lineage, and you're entitled to do so. But I'm sure you've heard the maxim about scorched dwarves not playing with fire..."

Bislipur strode toward him, his huge hands clenched into fists. "And you dare to accuse *me* of scheming like a kobold," he snarled. "What do you want?"

"Nothing—although, of course, we may find ourselves obliged to share our suspicion that your ancestry is no clearer than that of the high king's nominated successor," the counselor said gravely. "Incidentally, the document accusing the elves of treachery was a fake."

"You're lying!" Bislipur struck the marble table with a resounding thwack.

"You don't look like a child of Goïmdil. No other fourthling comes close to rivaling your stature. You've never been seen polishing diamonds or fashioning trinkets, but your reputation as a strong and talented fighter is known even to the orcs. I learned this from my inquiries," Balendilín told him coldly. "Anyone with a less charitable mind would be inclined to think you're one of Lorimbur's dwarves."

"I have never heard such scandalous bile in all my life! By

my beard, if you weren't a helpless cripple I'd fight you for insulting my honor with your lies!"

Balendilín listened in satisfaction. He had no evidence for his allegations, but he seemed to have touched a nerve. "This is what we propose: First, that you cease your scheming until one or the other of the companies returns from the expedition; and second, that you make it known that the elves' involvement in the fall of the fifthling kingdom can't be proven, since the document was forged. For our part, we'll say nothing of the doubts surrounding your lineage."

"The outcome of the expedition must decide the succession," Gundrabur added. "Are we agreed?"

Jaw clenched, Bislipur nodded curtly.

"How about a beer to seal the truce?" proposed Balendilín.

Bislipur turned away. "Drink all you like. I have matters to attend to." He smiled balefully. "You needn't worry: I'll keep my word and say nothing about the succession. As for the business about the elves, I assume you'll permit me to convene an assembly so I can explain to the delegates." He took leave of the high king without bowing. *I'll show you yet,* he thought grimly. *You're both mistaken if you think I care about your truce. From now on, I'll be more discreet about my scheming.*

An attendant appeared at the far end of the corridor. He was carrying a pitcher in one hand and three tankards in the other.

Perfect timing, thought Bislipur. *The high king's refreshments. This is my chance.* He waited until the dwarf was level with him, then stumbled and clutched at him, knocking him over. Like a shot, Bislipur reached out and caught the pitcher and two of the tankards, allowing the third to shatter on the marble flagstones.

"I'm really sorry," he said apologetically. "My lame leg is a curse on these slippery floors. Still, I managed to save everything except one of the tankards."

It took a moment for the attendant to recover. He got up shakily and looked at the debris. "Er, actually, the tankard was for you. I'll go and fetch a—"

"Don't trouble yourself," Bislipur interrupted. "I wasn't thirsty anyway. You may as well clear up the mess."

The attendant stooped and gathered the pieces into his apron. "All done," he said, straightening up again. "Now, if you pass me the other tankards and the beer..."

Bislipur hesitated and gave the pitcher a little shake, watching the layer of white foam slop back and forth without mingling with the beer. "Light on top and dark below," he said thoughtfully. He returned the vessels to the waiter. "Let's hope light will triumph over darkness in Girdlegard as well. You'd better hurry; the high king is thirsty."

Humming contentedly, he set off to find the fourthling delegation, while the attendant continued down the corridor toward the great hall.

Underground Network,
Girdlegard,
Late Autumn, 6234th Solar Cycle

The next downward pitch gave the wagon a burst of speed that sent them careering through the tunnel. For the first time Tungdil was obliged to pull sharply on the brake. *Any faster, and we'll come flying off the rail.* There was a flurry of sparks and a terrible squealing and screeching.

"It's worse than Bavragor's singing," Boïndil objected, shouting above the noise. Obligingly, the mason burst into song, thereby adding to the din. Boïndil rolled his eyes despairingly.

The tunnel opened out and they found themselves inside a natural grotto, shooting along an enormous bridge hewn from stone. A river raged beneath them, drowning out the squealing of brakes. Tendrils of spray splashed against the sides of the wagon; then they were back in the tunnel and racing on.

"Did you see that?" marveled Tungdil.

"How could we miss it?" Goïmgar said unhappily. "We could have fallen in and died."

Tungdil was bubbling with enthusiasm. "What a spectacular bridge! Our forefathers must have been incredible masons."

If Bavragor had been in the driver's seat, he would have turned back to take another look. "I bet it was sculpted by secondlings," he said proudly. "We're the only folk who could build a bridge like that." He paused, waiting for someone to contradict him. "In that case, I propose a toast..." Suddenly the wagon started to judder and rattle. "Steady on, Tungdil! You're spilling my drink and we don't want Goïmgar spewing all over the place."

Tungdil was less inclined to joke. "There's gravel on the track. I'm worried we'll—"

They felt a terrible jolt and the wagon tilted dangerously to the right. Orange sparks shot to the ceiling.

Before the dwarves could react, the wagon lurched, turned over, bounced, turned over, and crashed to a halt. The tunnel ahead was blocked with fallen stone.

Tungdil was catapulted into the air and had to curl into a ball to preserve his limbs. He hit the ground with a thud, grazed his face on the rock, and whacked his helmet against something unyielding. *I suppose it was bound to end this way.* He sat up groggily, looking for the others.

The twins were already on their feet. Like Tungdil, they had scuffed and torn their breeches, but seemed otherwise unharmed.

Bavragor picked himself up with a groan, clutching his hip. Only Goïmgar was lying still beside the battered wagon. His breath was coming in faint gasps.

"Vraccas have mercy!" Tungdil made his way unsteadily toward the stricken dwarf. Much to everyone's relief, Boëndal and Boïndil took charge of the examination and declared the artisan to be intact.

"We'll have you up in no time," said Bavragor, administering a sip from his pouch. "I hope you appreciate the sacrifice I'm making."

The fragile fourthling wasn't much of a brandy drinker and came to with a splutter. Sitting up sharply, he yelped and clutched his right shoulder. He grimaced in pain. "It's broken, I know it is!" Boëndal bent down to take a closer look, but Goïmgar waved him away. "No! You'll only make it worse!"

"Keep acting like that and *I'll* make it worse," Boïndil growled menacingly.

"Come on, Goïmgar," Tungdil pleaded. "Boëndal and Boïndil are warriors. They know about injuries."

"Cuts and bruises, maybe, but not broken bones," said Goïmgar, shrinking away. Groaning loudly, he struggled to his feet, his right arm dangling limply. "I've broken my collarbone," he whined. "I can't move my arm."

"Here, have a sip of this to ease the pain," said Bavragor, tossing him the pouch. Goïmgar reached out and caught it with both hands. The others turned on him accusingly.

"You lava-livered liar!" barked Boïndil. "Stringing us along, were you?"

"I thought it was broken," Goïmgar protested hastily. "But I guess it was, er…dislocated! What a stroke of luck! I put it into joint when I moved. Did you hear it click?" He lifted his arm gingerly and feigned discomfort. "Hmm, it's still quite sore, but I should be able to put up with it." He returned the pouch to Bavragor. "You can keep your rotgut. It tastes like poison."

"Next time I'd advise you to try a bit harder," fumed Boïndil. "Hoodwink us again, and I'll wallop your backside until it's redder than a forge."

If only I hadn't chosen him in the first place, Tungdil thought ruefully. *I didn't realize I was hanging a millstone around my neck.* He could see now why the fourthling monarch had let him pick Goïmgar: The artisan was a pest. *From now on I won't believe a single word he says.*

Tungdil decided to focus on their immediate plight: The tunnel leading west to the firstlings was completely blocked by an avalanche of rock, and the ingots and gems for Keenfire were scattered across the floor. He beckoned to Bavragor. "When do you think the roof collapsed?"

The one-eyed mason inspected the rockfall, clambered all over it, and ran his fingers over the fractured stone. At length he returned. "Quite recently. There's a fair bit of dust about, but it must have come down with the ceiling. See how shiny these edges are?" He patted the warped chassis of the wagon. "We were lucky the wagon derailed itself when it did. If we'd hit this lot at full tilt..."

"Do you think it was sabotage?"

Bavragor rubbed the dust from his one good eye. "I can't say for sure, but it wouldn't surprise me." He stroked the wall lovingly. "It seems strange that the tunnel would collapse of its own accord after all these cycles."

"It was probably your singing that did it," Goïmgar said witheringly. "Your singing and the idiot's lunatic yells."

"You're the one who keeps whining. If I were the mountain, I'd cave in on myself rather than listen to your voice," the mason retorted.

"You're both wrong," said Boïndil, not wanting to be outdone. "The tunnel split its sides laughing because of Goïmgar's size."

The artisan opened his mouth to protest, but Tungdil ordered them to pile up the ingots and cover the treasure with rocks. "We're going up to the surface," he decided. "The next hatch isn't far from here. We'll leave the underground network, find a settlement, and buy a pony." He unfurled the map. "We can reenter the tunnel here. It's only eighty miles overland."

"That's all very well, but what are we going to do without a wagon?" asked Boëndal.

"If we don't find a wagon when we get to the tunnel, we'll buy a couple of extra ponies and ride the last two hundred miles." Tungdil rolled up the map and helped the others to stack the heavy ingots. He put the wood in his pack.

He sneaked a sideways glance at his four companions. *All this squabbling is bad for the mission. I need to make them work together or I won't have a company to lead at all. Help me, Vraccas.*

They bowed their heads and delivered a quick vote of thanks to their creator for saving their lives, then marched back through the tunnel. At last they came to a narrow flight of steps that zigzagged steeply to the surface.

Bavragor led the way, but Goïmgar refused to follow. "Where are we?" he demanded suspiciously.

"According to the map, we'll be entering Oremaira," said Tungdil. "It used to be ruled by Maira the Life-Preserver, but there's no telling what's happened since Nôd'onn took charge."

"Not another enchanted realm," moaned Boïndil. He laid

his hands on the hafts of his axes. "Still, it might be a chance to slay a few runts. I just hope the magus doesn't plague us with any of his tricks."

The rest of the company nodded in mute agreement.

After a long and arduous ascent the five dwarves reached a door inscribed with runes. Weapons at the ready, they prepared themselves for the outside world.

The stairway led out into a cave some four paces high and seven paces wide. The noise of a waterfall roared in their ears. Water was streaming past the mouth of the cavern and tumbling down the mountainside, sending showers of spray that spattered their dusty mail, helms, and cloaks. Faint rays of sunshine sloped through the watery curtain, forming pools of light on the dank rock floor.

"Bloody typical," shouted Boïndil, straining to drown out the noise. "I'll wash when I'm good and ready, not because of some blasted waterfall."

His brother laughed. "And when might that be?"

They found a narrow path that led past the waterfall toward a rocky plateau. *With a bit of luck, we'll be able to see for miles*, thought Tungdil.

"Come on," he chivvied the others, "let's see where we are."

One by one they edged past the cascading water, treading carefully because of the slippery stone. None of them escaped without a good soaking and Goïmgar was nearly knocked off his feet.

It was around about noon when they emerged into the autumn sunshine. A rainbow was shimmering in the waterfall and the air smelled fresh and moist. They reached the edge of the plateau and peered down at the fifty-pace drop. The firs, pines, and spruces formed a dark green mass of bristling spears. Judging by the gathering clouds, they were about to be rained on.

To the west, a vast lake shimmered on the horizon, but in the north they could see a collection of houses ringed by a wall. The settlement lay on the other side of the forest, and beyond that were fields.

Tungdil was heartened by its proximity. *It shouldn't take more than an orbit to get there.* "Vraccas has been merciful," he told the others. "We'll have our pony in no time."

"A town full of long-uns," Goïmgar said glumly. "What if they don't like us?"

"Stop whining! We don't need the hillside caving in on us as well," snapped Boïndil. "I don't know why you're worried about long-uns. They might be tall, but I'm strong."

"Let me do the talking," said Tungdil, alarmed. "I've dealt with humans all my life."

The others saw no reason to argue, so they set off to find a way down from the plateau, taking a narrow path that led through the forest below.

There wasn't much light beneath the canopy of conifers. The mist, fine and wispy in the upper branches, thickened toward the ground, forming a dense milky layer around the dwarves' waists. Their eyes needed time to adjust to the sunlight and they were grateful for the gloom.

"Maira turned these woods into a sanctuary for unicorns," Tungdil told them. He felt a rush of excitement at seeing the forest that he had read so much about. "If we're lucky, we'll see one."

Boïndil looked at him blankly. "What's the good of that? We can't ride them, can we?"

"No, but they're beautiful creatures and they're rare. The älfar hunted them almost to extinction."

"Quiet, isn't it?" said Bavragor. "You'd think no one else

lived here. Maybe I should sing something. The unicorns might show themselves if they know we're here."

"Unicorns are timid animals. Singing—"

"Isn't *caterwauling* the word you're looking for?" Boëndal chimed in softly.

"Either way, making a noise won't help. Legend has it that they only approach young virgins," explained Tungdil.

"Young virgins, eh?" said Bavragor. "That's me out, then. I don't suppose any of you…?" He look slyly at Tungdil, who tried desperately not to blush.

Just then Boïndil stumbled into something and came to a halt in the fog.

"What do we have here?" he said in surprise, feeling his way through the mist with one of his axes. The blade met something soft and came up tinged with blood. "Here, give me that," he said, grabbing Goïmgar's shield and waving it back and forth until the bloodied body appeared through the mist.

"It's a horse," exclaimed Bavragor, staring at the white-coated mount. "At least…Hang on a minute, it's not a unicorn, is it?"

Tungdil knelt beside the dead animal. Its throat hung in shreds, chunks were missing from its flesh, and its beautiful horn had been wrenched from its skull.

"It *was* a unicorn," he said sadly, stroking the animal's white flank. Lot-Ionan's books described the unicorns as pure creatures, incapable of malice or evil, but their gentle nature had done nothing to save them from their fate. "Nôd'onn's hordes must have got here first."

"Do you think they're still around?" Boïndil asked hopefully. "They might be lurking in the bushes."

Goïmgar retreated hastily, only to fall over backward in the mist.

For a moment he was lost; then he reappeared, shrieking. His hands were stained with blood. "There's another one," he shouted, sheltering behind the others. "I need my shield! Give it back to me this instant!"

Boïndil strode off and fanned away the mist where Goïmgar had fallen. A light wind gusted through the milky swathes and helped to clear their view.

They stared in silence at the gruesome sight. Strewn across the ground were twelve dead unicorns and three times as many orcs. The fabled mounts had been brought down by arrows and slashed to pieces, but not before they had gored their attackers with their fearsome horns and hooves.

As the mist continued to clear, the outlines of a corral made of tree trunks loomed into view. The unicorns had been rounded up and slaughtered.

"They hunted them down," Bavragor said, aghast. "Aren't unicorns almost extinct?" he asked Tungdil.

"There used to be just over a dozen of them," Tungdil answered shakily. Even in death, the unicorns looked dignified, peaceful, and pure; they must have been exceptionally beautiful before their mauling by the vilest of beasts. "There can't be more than a couple of them left."

"Girdlegard is in a bad way," Boëndal said sadly. "It's time we got a move on and bought a pony. Nothing except Keenfire can stop Nôd'onn from taking innocent lives." Setting aside their sorrow, they scrambled over the stockade and set off through the forest.

How many more deaths? The sight of the murdered unicorns reminded Tungdil of how much he wished Lot-Ionan, Frala, and her daughters were still alive.

Boïndil was still brandishing his axes, hoping to encounter an orcish war band and work off his pent-up rage. Suddenly a strange look came over him and he smiled. His brother reached silently for his crow's beak.

"Smell that?" Ireheart whispered excitedly. "Oink, oink!"

The next moment, the rancid odor of fat-smeared armor reached Tungdil's nostrils too. It smelled doubly repugnant among the fresh moss, damp earth, and fragrant pines. "We can't stop now, Boïndil. We're going straight to the settlement."

"Not until I've split their ugly skulls," Boïndil growled defiantly. His fiery spirit had been trapped for so long that his inner furnace had overheated, driving him to open mutiny. "Come out, you runts! Come here and be slaughtered!" He threw back his head and let out a long, drawn-out grunt.

His call was answered by grunting and snarling amid the dense trees.

Goïmgar shrank back, disappearing behind his shield. "Shut up, you lunatic!" he hissed fearfully. "They're..."

The clunking and jangling of armor was getting closer all the time. Eyes closed, Ireheart listened in rapt concentration. "They've climbed the stockade," he told them. "There must be"—he listened intently—"oh, twenty of them at least!" He swung his axes impatiently. "They've found us. They're picking up speed!"

His eyes flew open and he was off, grunting and oinking as he ran. With an apologetic glance at the others, Boëndal chased after him. There was a short pause, then the sound of steel impacting steel. The woods echoed with the din.

It was all too much for Tungdil. *If he's not careful, his inner furnace will melt his mind.*

"Well," Bavragor asked quizzically, "aren't we going to help them?" He raised his war hammer.

"I should think not!" snapped Goïmgar. "It's their fault for starting it. Let them finish it themselves."

"No, we'll fight together," ruled Tungdil. "And after that, we're heading for the settlement as fast as we can."

They hurried off. Charging ahead, Bavragor hurled himself on the nearest orc with a bloodcurdling howl. The beasts were too busy surrounding the twins to spot the new arrivals and were taken off guard. Their response was predictably poor.

Moments later, two dozen orcish corpses littered the forest floor—no thanks to Goïmgar, who had avoided all contact with the enemy by hiding behind the mason's back.

Ireheart was responsible for most of the carnage, but Boëndal and Bavragor had fought with such ferocity that Tungdil had barely had a chance to land a blow.

"Serves them right, the stupid runts," laughed Boïndil, mopping his sweaty brow. "They won't be killing any more unicorns now!" He kicked out at one of the corpses. "That's for Tion," he told the dead orc. "Be sure to give it to him with my regards."

"Shush," Goïmgar hushed him. "Did you hear that? There's more!" He raised his shield and sneaked fearful glances over the top.

Boïndil nudged his brother boisterously. "Look, a two-legged shield!" He turned in the direction of their new adversaries and grinned. "This is my lucky orbit!" Listening attentively, he tried to calculate the number of approaching orcs. "One, two, three..." His voice became more measured and less exuberant. "...four, five." His carefree expression was gone. "One, two, three..." His eyes widened and he squared his shoulders defiantly. "This is a challenge worthy of a dwarf."

By now they could hear the clunking of armor.

"Exactly how many are there?" Tungdil demanded. He had a bad feeling about Boïndil's idea of a challenge.

"Five plus two," Ireheart said laconically. "Most of them are advancing head-on, but a smaller party is closing in from the right."

"Only seven?" Goïmgar breathed a sigh of relief and emerged a little from behind his shield.

"Five dozen infantry, plus two on horseback," Boëndal explained.

Tungdil grabbed Ireheart by the shoulders. "That's not a challenge; it's lunacy. We need to get ourselves safely behind those walls." Goïmgar didn't hang around for the discussion; he fled toward the town.

Ireheart refused to budge.

"This time you'll do as I say," Tungdil ordered him. "You've had your fun. You need to put our mission first."

The warrior fidgeted moodily. "All right, all right. Those runts don't know how lucky they are—but they'd better not catch up with us, or I'll show them what for!" He turned on Bavragor. "As for you, keep your confounded hammer away from my orcs. If I wanted your help, I'd ask for it."

"My help?" scoffed the mason. "I was helping your brother, not you. Nothing would give me greater pleasure than seeing you sliced down the middle by an orcish sword!"

"Not now," Tungdil scolded them, setting off at a jog.

They raced through the forest, crashing through branches, snapping twigs, and doing everything they could to throw off their pursuers. There was no sign of Goïmgar, who had disappeared ahead.

From the sound of the bugles, it was obvious that the orcs were fanning out to hunt them down, but the dwarves' smaller stature worked to their advantage, allowing them to slip through the undergrowth while the beasts blundered and stumbled behind them.

Soon they reached the fringes of the forest where the trees grew farther apart.

Panting and wheezing, Tungdil risked a glance over his shoulder and realized that the dark silhouettes of their pursuers looked bigger than before. *It's going to be close,* he thought.

Once out of the forest, they settled into a steady trot. Salvation lay half a mile away in the shape of the settlement's walls: Goïmgar was almost halfway there already.

What in the name of... Tungdil blinked, not trusting his eyes. The dark forest seemed to be keeping pace with them, advancing on either side. Then he heard the jangle of chain mail and the clatter of armor and realized the truth: *We're in the middle of a raid.*

A division of orcs left the shelter of the trees. There were a thousand of them or more, all advancing toward the settlement in a living line of weaponry. The line became a circle as orcs closed in from every direction. The town was surrounded—and so were the dwarves.

"Run!" Tungdil urged the others. "Run for your lives!"

Enchanted Realm of Oremaira,
Girdlegard,
Late Autumn, 6234th Solar Cycle

Goïmgar reached the protective walls of the settlement and hammered on the locked gates. Faces peered down at him from the battlements. "Let me in!" he shrieked. "In the name of Vraccas the Eternal Smith, save me from these beasts!"

"You'd think he'd put in a good word for the rest of us," snorted Bavragor, as he and the others struggled to catch up.

A panel opened in the gates and Goïmgar pushed his way through. The door slammed behind him. It remained closed, even when his companions arrived.

"Hey! What about us?" Bavragor bellowed.

Not again, cursed Tungdil. *Surely he won't abandon us out here?*

The orcs were dangerously close. Arrows whined toward them and landed just short.

Raising his axes, Boïndil turned to face the oncoming hordes. "Looks like I'll get my battle after all," he said, bringing the polls of his axes together in a loud, ringing beat. "Oink, oink!"

"Open the door!" shouted Tungdil. "We're dwarves! Dwarves like the other fellow. We're on the same side!"

There was no response.

The first beasts were already upon them. Ireheart dealt with them swiftly and bloodily, but their agonized howls brought orcish reinforcements to the scene.

The twins got down to business, fighting so savagely that the floor was awash with green blood. None of the orcs came within striking distance of Bavragor and Tungdil, who were standing at the back. After a while, Ireheart took an arrow to the leg, but he stood his ground, laughing manically and sending orcs to their deaths.

At least a dozen of the beasts had been massacred before the door finally opened to let them in.

Ireheart, still intent on slaying his opponents, had to be dragged inside. Boëndal talked to him in a low, soothing voice until the crazed glimmer left his eyes.

Bavragor gave Tungdil a satisfied look. "What did I tell you? He's a nutcase! A dangerous, unpredictable lunatic."

Tungdil made no reply.

Their reception committee was made up of thirty heavily armed and armored men. The soldiers eyed them suspiciously, not sure what to make of the dwarves. Goïmgar was waiting by the door, his face a deathly shade of pale.

The captain stepped forward. "Who are you and what do you want?" he asked gruffly.

Tungdil introduced them by name. "We're dwarves on a mission to track and kill orcs," he explained. "It's our Vraccas-given duty. We heard Girdlegard was in terrible danger, and we're trying to help the humans as best we can."

"Killing orcs is our specialty, as you probably noticed," added Ireheart. "I wanted to stay and flay the beasts alive, but the others were worried about being outnumbered."

Boëndal knelt down to inspect the damage to his brother's leg. The arrow had passed through the flesh without hitting the bone, so he snapped off the arrowhead and extracted the shaft from the opposite side. His brother endured his ministrations uncomplainingly, wincing only slightly when an herbal dressing and bandage were applied.

The captain was impressed by his stoicism. "In that case, Mifurdania welcomes you," he said. "The present moment augers well for orc hunters, but less favorably for our town. You'll have plenty to do here. Report to me when you're ready to join our ranks."

He hurried away. Ten of his soldiers stayed behind to barricade the door, placing a steel panel across the gates and securing it with sturdy bolts. There was a clattering and banging as the orcs laid siege to the gates, but after a time they retreated, defeated by the steel.

"That was close," Bavragor said to one of the guards. "Why didn't you open up earlier?"

The man glanced at the pale-faced Goïmgar, who was

cowering in a corner. "He said to bolt it behind him," he told them. "You'd better ask him."

With that, the soldier turned away and returned to his comrades who were reinforcing the steel cladding with all available means. The gates were required to withstand the impact of a battering ram, hence the need for supporting struts and bars.

"That's not what I s-said," stammered Goïmgar. "I told him to bolt it after *you*." Bavragor took a menacing step toward him, and the artisan sidled out of the gate tower, ready to flee through Mifurdania's streets.

"You've been nothing but trouble since we set out," the mason accused him, waving his mighty fists in Goïmgar's face. "I'll beat you to a pulp, you miserable liar."

"And I'll shave off your shimmering whiskers with my axes," added Boïndil.

That did it. Picturing himself bruised and beardless, Goïmgar fled, vanishing into the bustling town.

"Stop!" Tungdil shouted after him, but the artisan didn't look back. *I should have known this would happen.* Tungdil fixed Bavragor and Boïndil with a stony glare. "Congratulations," he said with heavy sarcasm. "How extraordinarily helpful of you both! We're on an urgent mission and thanks to your childish taunting, a vital member of our company has taken to his heels. Perhaps a nice game of hide-and-seek will take our minds off the fact that *we're surrounded by orcs*." This time Tungdil didn't bother to conceal his rage; he wanted them to know how furious he was.

Bavragor and Boïndil stared sheepishly at the floor.

"He nearly got us killed," ventured Bavragor.

"Says who?" snapped Tungdil. "You didn't let him finish. You had only the guard's word for what happened and you threatened to beat him up."

"Why else would he take off like that?" protested Boïndil. "If that's not the sign of a guilty conscience, I don't know what is!"

"Unbelievable: The one time you're in agreement, and it has to be this. Once we've tracked down Goïmgar, we'll get to the bottom of the matter—by discussing it *calmly*." He scanned the streets and spotted a tavern. "I want the two of you"—he nodded at Bavragor and Boïndil—"to take yourselves over there and wait at a table for Boëndal and me to return. Don't get into any arguments—and remember what I told you about dealing with humans."

Bavragor scratched his beard. "But where are you going?"

"To find Goïmgar, of course! Do you think he'd show himself in front of you? You scared the living daylights out of him." Tungdil hurried off, signaling to Boëndal to follow.

Bavragor and Boïndil did as instructed and found themselves a table in the tavern. They ordered a hot meal to fill their bellies and a tankard of beer to while away the time.

The other drinkers stared in open amazement at the two dwarves whose mail was covered in orcs' blood. Stone-faced, the pair returned their glances and focused grimly on their meal.

At last Boïndil emptied his tankard and took the first step toward ending their feud. "Listen, about what happened between me and—"

Bavragor held up a hand to silence him. "I don't want to hear it," he said, spurning the attempt at a truce. "I wish she'd never had anything to do with you. I told her so from the beginning, but she was too stubborn to listen. Don't expect me to forgive you, because I won't; I want you to be tortured by your conscience for the rest of your life." He poured the contents of his tankard down his gullet and burped. "After what you did, I don't even want to share a table with you."

He got up and strode to the door. "Tell Tungdil that I've gone to buy a pony."

Boïndil watched him go and bit his lip. The publican brought him another tankard of beer.

Meanwhile, Boëndal and Tungdil had split up and were scouring the streets of Mifurdania in search of Goïmgar. Tungdil had made straight for the battlements and was reeling from his first bird's-eye view of the town.

The sheer number of houses was incredible. Mifurdania consisted of nothing but roofs, the solid expanse of thatching and tiles interrupted only by marketplaces or temples. A dwarf on the run from a beating and an unwanted shave would find no shortage of places to hide.

Tungdil permitted himself a final sigh, then put his mind to finding Goïmgar. Before he made his way down into the jumble of houses and streets, he crossed over to the other side of the battlements and looked out at the forest. For the time being, the orcs had retreated and were setting up camp among the trees. There could be no further doubt that Mifurdania was under siege. *We're trapped,* he thought glumly.

Tungdil started down the street that the fourthling had taken. At first he called out Goïmgar's name, but after a while he fell silent, discouraged by the townspeople's stares.

It seemed to him that Goïmgar's disappearance was the predictable outcome of the quarreling among the group. *Please, Vraccas, help me find him.* He peered down every alleyway and searched every courtyard, but the missing fourthling was nowhere to be found.

At length he came to a marketplace where a man in bright garments was standing on a platform, ringing a bell and shouting at the top of his voice.

"Roll up, Mifurdanians, roll up for Theater Curiosum and learn the truth about Nudin the Knowledge-Lusty. Witness the grisly circumstances leading to his reincarnation as Nôd'onn the Doublefold and resulting in Girdlegard's demise," he called stirringly. "Marvel at our celebrated actor, the fabulous Rodario; be transported by Furgas, the best prop master in Girdlegard; allow yourselves to be spirited away to a world where the sun always shines!"

The man took a sip from his hip flask, seized his torch, and sent a tongue of fire crackling over the townspeople's heads.

"Mifurdanians, for one orbit only this rare entertainment can be viewed in our magnificent theater for the bargain price of three small coins. Don't delay a moment longer—we won't be performing tomorrow if the orcs have their way!" There was scattered laughter from the crowd as he mimed his own beheading. "What are you waiting for, Mifurdanians? Roll up and join the queue!" He motioned to the building behind him. "The players are ready and the spectacle awaits! Leave your worries at the door!"

The townspeople were already streaming through the double doors, glad of the chance to forget their woes.

Tungdil clambered onto the platform. "Excuse me," he asked the man, "have you seen a fellow who looks a bit like me?"

"Like you?" The man grinned. "You're not exactly the ordinary type." He made a show of rolling his eyes and squinting; then his features fell back into place. "Hang on a minute; he wouldn't be a bit scrawnier, would he? Scrawnier, but with a bushier beard?" Tungdil nodded. "In that case, he's in the Curiosum already." Tungdil leaped down from the platform and joined the back of the queue.

He paid for a seat in one of the boxes in order to get a better view. It seemed a strange time for Goïmgar to be cultivating a passion for the arts. *Maybe he thinks Bavragor and Boïndil won't find him if he hides among the crowd.*

The auditorium was shaped like a circle with a raised platform at the center, allowing the stage to be seen from every side.

Tungdil noticed that the building was made entirely of wood. The stalls and galleries groaned with the weight of the audience, but the theater bore the strain valiantly.

Perfume and perspiration battled for mastery of Tungdil's nose. He caught a whiff of petroleum from the lamps in the rafters, the lone source of light in the windowless room. The noise of the chattering spectators made him think of a gaggle of geese.

Tungdil found his seat in a narrow booth with flimsy walls. The hard wooden bench was so low that he had to perch on the backrest and place his feet on the cushions in order to see the stage. *Come on, Goïmgar, where are you?* he thought impatiently.

His brown eyes searched the audience without discovering the familiar features of the dwarf.

He must be somewhere, he thought. He could only hope that Goïmgar was seated on the other side of the theater, hidden from view by the crimson curtains that were draped around the stage. He waited patiently for the performance to begin.

Suddenly the lights went out and the voices dropped to a whisper. A tense silence descended on the room.

The first soft notes sounded from the orchestra, inviting the spectators to enter the actors' world. The musicians, seated in a separate gallery, continued the melody, while a winch squealed into action and the curtain went up on the stage. Tungdil found himself looking at a grassy plateau.

The scenery was so convincing that he almost had to pinch himself. He could practically feel the wind and smell the soil.

Overhead, daylight flooded into the theater as prop hands unveiled the windows in the roof. The glass panels were arranged in such a way that only the stage was illuminated, leaving the wings and the rest of the auditorium shrouded in gloom.

It didn't matter to Tungdil that the spectators were seated in the shadows: His eyes were accustomed to seeing in the dark. At last he could survey the whole auditorium and continue his hunt for the missing dwarf.

He barely noticed that the performance was underway, having more important things to think about than humans in fancy dress. He scanned the audience attentively, but could see no sign of Goïmgar.

I may as well keep looking outside. He stood up with the intention of leaving and was amazed to see a beige-clad figure on the stage. He froze.

Surely it can't be... Resting on a rock, delivering a monologue, was an elderly man with a white beard. *Lot-Ionan!* The fair-haired woman clad in armor, hand resting encouragingly on his shoulder, looked exactly like Andôkai. Tungdil listened to see whether the voices were as he remembered them.

In no time the purpose of his visit was forgotten and he was focused on the plot. The actors were so convincing that he felt as if the real Lot-Ionan and Andôkai were before him, even though he knew that the magus was dead and the mistress of Brandôkai had left Girdlegard forever.

"Come, Lot-Ionan," said Andôkai, "the time for forbearance is over."

ENTR'ACTE

W̶e must fight the Perished Land!"

Lot-Ionan sighed. "We can halt its advance, but that is all." He ran a hand over the lush grass. Barely half a mile away the meadows gave way to a bleak expanse of withered vegetation and gray earth: No living plant could survive within the Perished Land. "It is not in our power to defeat it."

Andôkai chose not to reply, turning instead to ascend the slope where the other magi were waiting. Lot-Ionan followed, leaning heavily on his staff. At last the six members of the council were assembled on the grassy knoll, looking down on their foes.

A few paces away, the promontory fell away in a sheer cliff. The wind gusted toward them, whipping at their clothing and carrying the foul cries of the invaders to their ears.

Held back by the magic girdle, the beasts were pushing, shoving, snarling, and jostling in their eagerness to breach the unseen barrier and invade the lands beyond.

Seen from above, their massed ranks were a rippling sea of darkness. Orcs toting all kinds of lethal weaponry mingled with hideous trolls, ogres, and other vile beasts, forming a ragged and disorganized force. All had left their homeland north of Girdlegard and swarmed over the Stone Gateway like a plague of locusts, laying waste to towns and villages in an orgy of destruction.

The rulers of men had sent an army to stop them, but the

beasts had cut them down. Now only the magi could check the invasion and hold back the Perished Land.

"Let them come to us," said Andôkai. "Stay your magic until they're in reach of the village, then attack."

Maira looked at the buildings below. Nestled at the foot of the mountain, the little wooden huts seemed to be clinging to the hillside for support. "They must be terrified," she said softly, her voice full of compassion. "How desperate they must feel."

"Utterly desperate," agreed Turgur, whose splendid robes were more suited to a banquet than a war. "Which means, of course, they'll be doubly grateful when we come to their rescue."

Nudin the Knowledge-Lusty was too busy scanning the enemy ranks to respond. It was exciting to see so many new and unfamiliar creatures, and he was looking forward to learning more about their kind. *I'll spare a few of them and question them later, but I won't tell the others. They'll only accuse me of being too lenient with the beasts.*

Maira seemed to read his mind. "Every last beast must die, Nudin. We can't let the Perished Land encroach any farther."

Nudin nodded, already focused on the battle ahead. Everything hinged on the magi intervening at the critical time. Without his efforts, they would never have discovered the flaw in the girdle: He had used the malachite table to pinpoint the problem and identify a place where they could wait for the beasts and take them unawares.

Just then a loud crackling filled the air. The Perished Land was launching an attack on the girdle and at length it gave way. Snarling and shouting, Tion's minions charged toward the village, the ogres and trolls outpacing the orcs and the diminutive bögnilim squawking in frustration at the rear.

At once Andôkai summoned a storm, and the sky darkened above the promontory, bright lightning flickering between the roiling clouds. The first volley of bolts shot toward the charging hordes.

That was the signal for the others to join in. Together they unleashed their magic against the forces of the Perished Land.

Orbs of fire soared through the air, wreaking havoc among the troops. The earth gave birth to strange creatures of rock and dust who hurled themselves on the orcs, while the ground opened up, swallowing ogres and trolls.

The assault on the village faltered, then failed. The first to retreat were the short-legged bögnilim, who sought shelter in the Perished Land, little realizing that the destruction of the girdle had laid them open to attack. The magi's missiles scorched through the ranks of the fleeing creatures, setting them ablaze.

Every effort was made to destroy the beasts entirely, so that nothing could be salvaged by the Perished Land's dark power. Corpses were consumed by tongues of fire, cremated by lightning, turned to dust, or dashed to pieces against the ground.

Andôkai whipped up a fearsome gust that tore into the last dogged attackers, sweeping them back into the Perished Land. Meanwhile, the other magi were preparing to restore the girdle and make it stronger than before.

With a sweep of his robed arm, Lot-Ionan summoned the waiting apprentices, who hurried over with the malachite table. The six magi joined together for the complex ritual, channeling their energies and harnessing the magic to restore the barrier, thus securing Girdlegard against future attacks. At last it was safe for the villagers to leave their houses and thank their deliverers with waves and cheers.

As for the magi, their relief was tempered by the knowledge that the northern pestilence had spread. The Perished Land had extended south, claiming every inch of territory trodden by Tion's beasts and advancing as far as the gates of the village, where the new girdle was in place.

Turgur waved back at the devoted crowds. "We should let them thank us in person," he said. "The simple souls would be delighted to have us in their midst."

Nudin managed a weary smile. "Do the simple souls need Turgur or does Turgur need the simple souls? Be careful about casting yourself into their adoring arms, fair-faced magus. It's an awfully long way down." The others chuckled gently.

"I vote we retire to our tents, recover our strength, and enjoy a glass of wine," proposed Maira.

"Someone needs to tell the villagers to leave their homes without delay. Next time the Perished Land attacks, they might not be so lucky," said Nudin. "I'll take care of it while the rest of you relax."

Andôkai gave him a hard look, but said nothing.

A narrow path led down from the promontory to the settlement below. On nearing the village, Nudin was showered with gifts of bread, fruit, and wine as the villagers offered him simple tokens of gratitude.

Nudin acknowledged their generosity by stopping and accepting a sip of wine. He lost no time in warning them of the continued threat. "I'll send some men to help you with the move," he promised. "We'll find a safer place for you to make your homes."

He helped himself to an apple, then made his way back, skirting the edge of the battlefield without venturing into the Perished Land.

Here and there the ground was still smoldering, the energies unleashed by the magi vaporizing the soil and turning grains of sand to glass. The earth was pocked with craters and furrows and everywhere reeked of death.

The shallow sound of breathing brought him to a sudden halt. He listened, heart pounding, trying to locate the wounded beast. The death rattle sounded again and this time he was able to trace its source.

Gingerly, he stepped over the corpses and poked about in the jumble of body parts until his staff uncovered the injured beast. Lying beneath the vast torso of a troll was a bögnil, unable to free itself from the colossal weight. It looked rather like a stunted orc.

"Don't be afraid," Nudin reassured it in the language of Tion's beasts. "I'm not going to hurt you."

The bögnil stuck out its tongue and fumbled for its sword.

"I'll make a deal with you," said the magus. "I'll get you out of your predicament, but only if you answer my questions. I want to know about your species: where you come from, what kind of society you live in, and how you employ your time when you're not invading Girdlegard." He produced a roll of parchment and an inkpot from his satchel. "Remember: I have the power to ensure that you speak nothing but the truth." The creature stared back at him with soulless eyes and blinked in confusion. It didn't know what to make of the crazy stranger who was proposing something more complicated than rescue or death. It still hadn't responded when a long black arrow bored through its throat and pinned it to the troll.

"Andôkai?" Nudin wheeled round and blanched. Even a confrontation with the tempestuous maga would be preferable to this. He watched in horror as four älfar slipped through the magic girdle, effortlessly breaching the unseen barrier. The lead älf set another arrow to his string and leveled the bow at Nudin.

Just you try it! Nudin's hastily conjured charm stopped the quivering arrow in midflight and sent it speeding back toward the archer. A look of panic crossed the creature's dark eyes in the instant before he died.

Nudin raised his left hand and killed two of the älfar with searing bolts of light. He restricted himself to stunning the fourth älf with the intention of interrogating him.

Stooping down, he examined their faces. Their elegant features reminded him of their cousins, the elves of Âlandur and the Golden Plains, whom Turgur admired for their flawless beauty. His gaze settled on the amulets fastened around their necks.

Protective charms, he muttered in astonishment, taking one of the crystals in his hands. The mystery of how the älfar had crossed the girdle was solved. *The Perished Land has found a way of sending its most lethal emissaries through the magic barrier. I must tell the council of this.*

He disarmed the stunned älf with a curse, then roused him from his faint. The creature's eyes opened, revealing fathomless pits. In the bright sunlight, Nudin could see that he possessed neither pupils nor irises. The magus held up the amulet. "Who gave you this?"

The älf returned his stare.

Nudin invoked a truth spell to coax out his secrets, but the creature spoke in an unintelligible tongue. Like elvish, the language was melodious and elegant, but with a sinister, darker tone.

The learned magus was none the wiser. He stood up, took a few steps back, and incinerated the creature in a towering blaze. Its three companions and the bögnil met a similar fate.

"It won't be long before the Perished Land renews its attack," he muttered fretfully.

Still, he thought to himself, *there's no need to spoil the celebrations. The news of the amulets can wait until breakfast.* After exhorting the sentries to be doubly vigilant, he retired to his tent.

* * *

That night Nudin was visited by the strangest of dreams.

Fog settled around his tent, pushing through the canvas and swirling around his bed. Tiny streaks of black, silver, and red rippled through the gloomy mist as it snaked through the bedposts, encircled the mattress, and contracted warily around the sleeping man. At last it was so close that Nudin appeared to be hovering on the glimmering cloud.

A wisp of vapor, long and spindly as a finger, slid toward him and touched his hand. The magus awoke at the soft, velvety touch.

"Don't be afraid," a voice whispered. "I'm not going to hurt you."

Nudin sat up slowly and examined the flickering mist. "Afraid? My name is Nudin the Knowledge-Lusty, not Nudin the Timorous," he informed it calmly. "Who are you?"

"The soul of the Perished Land," came the whispered reply. "It is time for you to make your choice."

"What choice? The Perished Land kills its enemies. Is that what you mean by choice?"

The mist rose a few inches and wrapped itself around Nudin's feet, stealing slowly along his legs. It felt warm and soft. "You can choose to rescue Girdlegard—or join the other magi in hastening its doom. That is your choice."

"The magi are committed to rescuing Girdlegard. You are its doom," the magus said firmly.

"My power can protect these lands and the races that inhabit them—men, elves, and dwarves," the mist replied. "I want to secure Girdlegard against the coming threat, but your magic won't let me." The mist arranged itself into a human face, opening and closing its mouth in time with the voice. "The tide of evil will soon be upon us, streaming through the Stone Gateway or surging over the western ranges to swamp

Girdlegard and wash me away. The belt of mountains will stay standing, but everything within them will be destroyed."

"Why should I believe you? What kind of soul nourishes itself on the souls of the dead?"

"The greatest of souls," the voice purred. "I do not feed on them; I gather them to me for their protection. When the threat has passed, I shall release them to their gods. For now, while Girdlegard is in danger, I need their power."

"Be gone," Nudin commanded. "I have heard enough of your lies."

The mist began to dissolve away. "Listen to my proposal," it whispered. "I need your body. Lend it to me for a while and acquire my knowledge while I borrow your form. You will learn things beyond your wildest dreams, things whose existence exceeds the power of your imagination. I know charms devised by illustrious magi in faraway lands; I know nature, life, and the stars; I know mankind in ways that you will never glean from books. With my knowledge, you will be the wisest, most powerful magus in the history of Girdlegard and your name will be Nudin the All-Knowing." The particles melted into nothingness. "The All-Knowing..."

The All-Knowing... Nudin woke with a start, sitting upright in bed and glancing frantically round the tent. Unable to discover anything unusual, he told himself off for being foolish and settled back to sleep.

At breakfast the next morning he sat in silence, his mind on other matters, while his colleagues discussed their projects and plans.

He said nothing of his peculiar dream and omitted to mention his encounter with the älfar, keeping the news of the amulets to himself.

*   *   *

The messenger arrived just as Nudin was preparing for bed. He read the letter and froze.

Lesinteïl, the elven kingdom of the north, was in the hands of the älfar. They had breached the magic girdle and overwhelmed the unsuspecting elves.

According to the letter, the first settlements had been taken in a matter of orbits. The älfar had overrun the kingdom before the elves had had time to raise a proper army, and the outcome of the battle had never been in doubt.

Now the northern pestilence was creeping through the exalted lands of Lesinteïl, destroying the blossoming beauty that centuries of nurture had elevated to its highest form.

Nudin hurled the roll of parchment to the floor and clambered into bed. In less than forty-eight hours, the council would meet to erect a girdle around the fallen kingdom. Already the älfar were using their newly conquered land to send war bands into Gauragar, Idoslane, and Urgon to extend the boundaries of the Perished Land.

Nudin felt a stab of conscience. Unlike the other magi, he had a good idea of how the älfar had breached the girdle. He tried telling himself that nothing could have stopped them, even if the council had known.

That's not quite true, his conscience contradicted him. *If you'd shown them the amulet, they would have studied the inscription and erected a barrier impervious to its power. By saying nothing, you allowed the älfar to advance.*

"But I..."

Lesinteïl fell because of you. You broke faith with the council and betrayed the elves.

Pulling the covers over his head, Nudin tried to silence his troublesome conscience by falling asleep.

But sleep brought no delivery. That night the soul of the

Perished Land cajoled its way into his dreams and the whispering mist paid another visit to his bed.

"Have you made up your mind? Has Nudin the All-Knowing resolved to rescue Girdlegard?"

"You breached the barrier and took Lesinteïl. How did you do it?"

"Nudin the All-Knowing wouldn't need to ask." The mist slipped beneath the covers, where it soon became pleasantly warm. "The first elven kingdom is mine. Âlandur will be next, and the magi can do nothing to stop me. My protective power will extend deep into the south of Girdlegard, but I'm running out of time."

"Protective power? You're seizing the lands by force!"

"Only for a heartbeat in the continuum of time. Remember, Nudin, no one relinquishes freedom gladly. Rulers and races are like children and I am their mother. I protect them from harm." The swirling mist became a human face. "Imagine a small boy whose mother won't let him play with a dog. She picks him up because she knows that the dog is dangerous, but he resents her intervention. He kicks, screams, and struggles against her, not realizing that the dog would bite him as soon as it had the chance." The voice paused for a moment. "The mother chases the dog away, then sets her son down and lets him play as he pleases. The boy is too young to understand, but in time he'll see that she did the right thing. His resentment will turn to gratitude because she helped him *in spite* of his protests."

The analogy made perfect sense. Nudin's conscience warned him against the silver-tongued whisperer, but he shut out his inner voice. "You've explained it to me, so why can't you explain it to the rulers of the other realms and kingdoms? And why ally yourself with beasts? Orcs and älfar are feared by men and loathed by elves and dwarves: Why choose them to carry out your will?"

The mist swathed the bed, covering every inch of his body and shrouding his eyes. It felt like the caress of a thousand soothing hands. "Girdlegard is in danger. I didn't have time to choose my allies; I had to take what I could find. My creatures can be counted on to bring me rapid victories. It's the best way of protecting Girdlegard from the threat."

"And this threat, have you fought it before?" Nudin asked sleepily. He was struggling to focus.

"More times than I can remember, but the enemy is powerful, swift, and wily. Victory has always eluded me. We need time to prepare ourselves properly if we are to win." The caressing intensified, the whispers multiplying and echoing through Nudin's mind. "I need your body, Nudin. Lend me your form and I will give you my knowledge, a knowledge greater than any possessed by mortal man. Remember, when our enemy has been vanquished, your body will be your own. You will always have the power to drive me out. You must make your decision, Nudin."

"What if your knowledge isn't as spectacular as you claim?"

"Watch. I will show you." The mist contracted around his temples, pulsing furiously with streaks of black, silver, and red.

The soul of the Perished Land gave Nudin's dreaming consciousness a glimpse of the marvels that would soon be his.

Strange runes danced before the awestruck magus and unintelligible languages filled his ears. Images flashed through his mind—snatches of spells and curses, strange and formidable landscapes in the Outer Lands, and faraway cities and palaces more splendid than anything known to men, elves, or dwarves.

He drank in the wonderful sights and sounds, thirsted for more, and was rewarded. Plunged into an endless stream of images, he bathed in knowledge and imbibed its wisdom until the vision was brought to a halt.

"Don't stop," Nudin said greedily. "Show me more."

"Will you lend me your body?"

"Let me—"

Runes glimmered in the air while distant voices reverberated in unknown tongues. The sun dimmed over a breathtakingly beautiful meadow and the landscape dissolved away. Stacks of books swayed dangerously and learned volumes of spells and incantations moldered, leaves perishing and turning to dust.

"Will Nudin the All-Knowing save Girdlegard?" the mist whispered. "Will he help a mother protect her child?" The magus's defenses crumbled.

"I will help you," he whispered hoarsely, peering into the mist. By letting the spirit in, he would be able to control it, or so he told himself. *If I find out it's lying about the threat to Girdlegard, I'll force it to give back our lands and send its servants over the Northern Pass. Whatever happens, I'll get the promised knowledge and Girdlegard will win.* "What must I do?"

The mist glimmered excitedly. "Nothing. Lie still and don't stop me. Open your mouth, empty your mind, and think of nothing. You'll know when I'm in."

Nudin lay back and did as instructed.

Three tendrils of mist snaked toward him and slipped between his lips. It felt as if they were reconnoitering the territory in preparation for an invasion.

What happened next took Nudin by surprise. Suddenly, the mist contracted and forced itself inside his mouth. The pressure was so great that his jaws seemed to break apart and his ears were filled with the sound of cracking. His hands dug into his bedclothes, ripping the sheets.

Once inside him, the mist pushed onward with no regard for his body. It expanded along his gullet, cutting off his airway and expelling the breath from his lungs. His veins throbbed frantically, his blood racing at four times its usual speed.

Red fluid spurted from his nose and eyes and he realized with horror that he was losing blood from every pore. His lifeblood was seeping from his body, streaming over his skin and staining his sheets.

He sat up, gurgling unintelligibly, and tried to reach the door. The floor rushed toward him.

He had no control over his legs or any other part of his body; even his mind refused to obey him. Babbling, laughing, and choking, he screamed in pain and terror, crawling and writhing through his chamber and leaving a glistening crimson trail.

He could feel the mist pushing through every vessel in his body, pounding his flesh, foraging in his guts, torturing his manhood, and never pausing for a moment on its agonizing path.

Then at once the suffering was over.

Nudin lay on the cold marble floor, struggling to regain his breath. Slowly, his dazed senses cleared, and his thoughts and perceptions became extraordinarily acute.

He clambered to his feet. Blood was caked to his skin and the smell of excrement clung to his robes. Repelled by the filth, he hurried along the corridors and stood beneath a fountain to wash away the dirt. The cold water revived his spirits, leaving him refreshed and alert.

And now for a test...He tried to recall the spells he had heard. The words and gestures returned to him effortlessly, but more remarkably, he knew their purpose and the correct inflection of every syllable: It was all imprinted on his mind.

Strictly speaking, it wasn't his mind that was furnishing the information, but he brushed that thought aside.

With a rush of exhilaration he thought of all the wonders he had seen, and at once they returned to him, only this time he could hear, taste, and smell them. The beautiful meadow had its own distinctive aroma, which he recognized instantly. He remembered the melodies sung by the birds, and he knew that Pajula, for that was the name of the spot, was located beyond the mountains of his homeland in a place that no one in Girdlegard had heard of, let alone mapped.

Chuckling delightedly, he let the water splash over his skin.

Well, are you satisfied? asked a voice inside his head. *Have I kept my side of the bargain?*

"Yes," he said aloud, then corrected himself. *Yes, your knowledge is everything you promised it would be.* He decided on a further test. *I want you to leave.*

At once he felt an unpleasant burning sensation, then a sudden chill and a feeling of abject loneliness and abandonment. The mist was preparing to depart. Nudin shuddered at the thought of experiencing such agony a second time.

Stop! he commanded. *You can stay. I wanted to be sure I could trust you to go.*

I entrusted you with my knowledge and memory; you have to trust me. We two are one.

"We two are one," the magus murmured. He clambered out of the fountain to look for a mirror. There was nothing peculiar about his reflection: He looked the same as before, although the shirt he took from his wardrobe seemed tighter than usual and the sleeves were a little too short.

The soul of the Perished Land shared his satisfaction. *I chose well,* it whispered. *You needn't feel ashamed. You're not a traitor.*

So you can read my thoughts? Nudin felt embarrassed that his doubts had been detected.

We are one.

Then I should be able to read yours.

Patience! Such things take practice, and practice you shall have. For now our pact must remain a secret. Buy me some time and say nothing to the other magi until I am ready to be a mother to these lands. Begin your preparations, but work alone and be sure not to arouse their suspicions. They will accuse you of treachery, Nudin the All-Knowing, but you're not a traitor; you're my friend—my one and only loyal friend. The whisper faded and the magus was alone.

He strolled to the window and looked out. Sunrise was only a few hours away, but Porista was still slumbering. He turned his back to it and scanned the rows of books that lined his room.

All these folios, encyclopedias, and grimoires contained only a fraction of the knowledge that was stored in his head. It gave him a feeling of contentment, infinite wisdom, and completeness. No sooner had a thought occurred to him than he knew everything there was to know on the matter. He could sate his lust for knowledge without the help of study, travel, experiments, or books.

A moment later he felt bored: Everything he yearned for was already accomplished. *Saving Girdlegard is the last remaining challenge and nothing and no one can take it from me.*

* * *

Nudin drew up a plan of action and devoted himself to his task. It seemed wrong to leave the responsibility of saving Girdlegard to his knowledgeable friend. He could picture the terrible threat bearing down on his homeland, ready to sweep over the high mountains and take Girdlegard by storm, and he knew that it was up to him to stop it.

There was no doubt that his new knowledge was useful, but incantations and formulae weren't enough. In order to apply the magic, he needed power—more power.

He had already devised a way of acquiring it, channeling it, and making it his own. When the magi next gathered in Porista to renew the girdle, he would harness their magic energies and present his colleagues with a choice: Join him—or get out of his way.

Every waking moment was devoted to his plan. He ensconced himself in his laboratory and selected a few of his most loyal famuli to assist him; when the time was right, they would help him with whatever he had to do.

Älfar emissaries took to visiting him in secret, bringing intelligence gathered in the mountains of Urgon, the plains of Gauragar, and the highlands of Idoslane. His scouts informed him that the orcs in Tilogorn's kingdom were prepared to fight on his behalf.

Nudin's greatest fear was betrayal. Resistance was not to be tolerated: Anyone who challenged him was a threat to Girdlegard and a traitor to the cause. Dissenters were crushed.

Sometimes, in rare moments of doubt, he wondered whether he was in charge of his actions or whether the spirit inside him was governing his will.

His misgivings soon disappeared, vanishing as mysteriously and abruptly as they had come. Every now and then his friend would speak to him and offer his advice, rounding out his plan with helpful suggestions and ideas.

We are one, he thought gratefully. *Together we will save the race of men.*

And yet your cause has been betrayed.

How so?

One of your apprentices, Heltor, talked to a man by the name of Gorén, a former famulus of Lot-Ionan's. Our friends heard them talking at the doors of the palace when the council was in session. He thinks he knows our secret and how we can be sundered.

Nudin was aghast. *Sundered? That's impossible. I can't allow it!*

Listen to me, Nôd'onn. Gorén won't be working alone. Lot-Ionan gave him books that tell of our pact. They're jealous of your knowledge and power. Don't let them tear us apart. We are one!

Nudin decided to have Gorén killed. *The älfar will deal with him. They'll bring back the books and have the famulus punished.*

If you kill Gorén, the others will be suspicious. You'll have to kill them all.

No, I'll reason with them. They're bound to understand if I explain it to them, as you explained it to me. Just think what we could achieve with the power of six magi. We'll be able to advance on different fronts and our friends will be grateful for the speedy victory.

The spirit doubted the wisdom of the scheme but said nothing to oppose it, fearing that a disagreement might alienate the magus. *I'm afraid you'll be disappointed, my one and only friend.*

"I hope not," Nudin said softly. He turned his attention to

a book whose contents he knew by heart: There was nothing in his library that wasn't present inside his head.

A drop of blood fell onto the open page, obscuring four characters so that the word became unreadable. Blood seeped from his nose and his eyes, slowly at first, then faster and faster until it became a constant stream.

Nôd'onn knew what lay in store. He rose quickly and hurried to his bed. His bones creaked, his head throbbed, his brain hissed, and his skin stretched painfully as he suddenly gained another few inches in height.

He screamed, cried, bit his lips until they bled, and thrashed about so violently that he fell out of bed and blacked out.

When he woke, the suffering was a distant memory and all he felt was the habitual desire to eat. His regular feasts resulted in enormous weight gain, obliging his tailors to replace his wardrobe every week.

He scrubbed the blood from his face and his hands. *How much longer until it stops hurting?*

Not long, the voice whispered. *All this knowledge is too much for a human body. It needs more room. You won't come to any harm, I promise. We are one.*

Nudin made his way hungrily to the dining hall and had his servants set the long trestle table. He ate enough to feed a whole family, but his appetite wasn't sated and the cook had to bring out a pair of sizzling roast chickens before he declared himself full. As he rose from the table he noticed that his sleeves were too short.

A female älf entered the room, holding a letter in her hand...

PART TWO

PART TWO

I

Enchanted Realm of Oremaira,
Girdlegard,
Late Autumn, 6234th Solar Cycle

Tungdil was so wrapped up in the story that he couldn't be sure how much of the drama had been enacted by the players and how much he had imagined for himself.

The spell was finally broken when a hand reached out from the curtain at the rear of the box, took hold of his knapsack, and pulled it carefully by the straps.

Tungdil saw none of this and was alerted only when the villain lost patience and jerked the bag across the floor. He turned just in time to see the filcher's fingers disappearing behind the curtain, together with his pack.

"Hey! Stop thief!" he shouted furiously. "Come back with my bag!" Whipping out his ax, he stormed into the aisle, his hobnailed boots clattering on the floorboards. "I'll teach you to respect other people's property!"

The dramatic tension barely withstood his heavy footsteps and was demolished by his booming voice. There were angry shouts from the audience, most of them directed at the victim and not the thief.

Count yourselves lucky, Tungdil thought grimly, ignoring the outcry. He raced after the dark-robed figure, his short legs powering up and down and filling the auditorium with a thunderous rumble.

"Perhaps the gentleman could make a little less noise!" boomed the counterfeit Nôd'onn from the stage. His älf emissary put her hands on her slender hips and frowned. She was clad in black armor and looked remarkably convincing despite the ruined play. The fearsome magus was just an indignant actor. "If you don't mind, I'm trying to entertain our audience!"

"I've been robbed!" the dwarf bellowed without slowing. "Your precious theater is harboring a thief!"

"The only thief in this theater is you, my stunted friend," the actor said waspishly. "You're stealing my time, not to mention plundering my patience, neither of which you can afford. Kindly take your thieving presence out of my theater and allow those of more cultured sensibilities to see the rest of the play, which shall have the finale it deserves!"

On hearing the cheers and laughter, he took a deep bow.

Jackass, muttered Tungdil. Bursting out of the theater, he stopped on the street, looked both ways, and ran on. On rounding the next corner, he spotted his man. The scoundrel had slung the stolen pack over his shoulder in order to free his hands.

"Stop! That's my bag you've stolen!" Tungdil set off in hot pursuit.

At the end of the third street he still had the thief in his sights, but somewhere along the fourth street, after what must have been the tenth sudden change in direction, the fellow vanished into a marketplace. Tungdil was left stranded among a crowd of people with no hope of spotting his knapsack amid the seething mass.

The sigurdaisy wood! He felt hot and cold all over at the thought that the relic was lost. Of all the misfortunes that could have befallen him, this was surely the worst. *I didn't come all this way to be thwarted by a petty criminal!* he thought determinedly, forcing himself to continue the chase.

Still gripping his ax with one hand, he used the other to push his way through the crowd until he reached a table piled high with woven baskets. He clambered on top.

From this angle the situation looked no better than before. The only way of recovering the bag was to enlist the help of the guards, but his plight was unlikely to elicit much sympathy—and understandably so. What could he possibly say to convince them of the importance of retrieving his pack?

Er, excuse me, I know the town's surrounded by orcs, but I've lost a lump of wood. I was hoping to use it to save Girdlegard and its inhabitants from the Perished Land.

No one would ever believe him.

He jumped to the ground and set off toward the tavern where, Vraccas willing, Bavragor and Boïndil would be waiting. To his unspeakable dismay he realized that he was lost.

Tungdil had sent his companions to the tavern without checking its name. Now his only hope of finding them was to return to the gates.

Which gates? Did we enter from the north?

He started on his way, grumbling to himself and glancing up from time to time to check his position against the watchtowers that rose above the sloping roofs. Striding along determinedly, he passed a dingy side street without slowing and heard a muffled groan.

He stopped in his tracks, gripped his ax with both hands, and doubled back. Stepping warily into the darkness, he spotted a tall, slender figure whose garments were enveloped by a dark gray cape.

At his feet was the villain who had stolen Tungdil's pack.

The thief was lying on the cobbles, bleeding from a dozen stab wounds, while his killer rummaged eagerly through the bag.

Tungdil's instincts told him something was wrong. In height and build the stranger looked less like a man than an älf. *Vraccas be with me,* he murmured.

The knapsack's new owner buckled the lid, grabbed the straps with his left hand, and hid the bag beneath his cape. Groaning in agony, the thief rolled onto his back and clutched the ground. His assassin was unmoved by his suffering and strolled away without looking back.

"Excuse me! That's my bag," shouted Tungdil.

The stranger whipped round and his cape flew open, obscuring his face. Tungdil was still trying to get a proper look at him when two heavy objects collided with his chest. The throwing knives glanced off his chain mail, clattering to the cobbles.

Before Tungdil could recover, his crafty assailant had taken off down the alleyway and rounded the next bend. The dwarf was at a disadvantage because of his stumpy legs, and by the time he reached the corner, the stranger was nowhere in sight.

Tungdil stepped back into the shadows and leaned against a wall to catch his breath. *One blasted misfortune after the next! What have I done to displease you, Vraccas?*

He felt an arm wrap itself around his neck. A narrow blade flashed in front of his face and came to rest against his bare throat.

"It's your knapsack, is it?" whispered a voice in his ear. "In that case, you must be Tungdil. We weren't expecting you here. A friend of mine has been longing to make your acquaintance ever since you murdered his companion in Greenglade."

Tungdil tried to prize away the arm, but the pressure on his neck increased.

"Keep still," the voice commanded. "You've got some explaining to do."

"I'm not telling you anything," Tungdil said defiantly, now certain that the stranger was one of Nôd'onn's älfar.

"We'll see about that." His attacker stepped backward, dragging Tungdil beneath a covered archway at the front entrance to a house. Total darkness engulfed them. "Where are you taking the relic?"

The dwarf maintained a stubborn silence.

"Talk or I'll kill you."

"You'll kill me anyway. What difference does it make?"

The älf laughed. "The difference between a quick death and an agonizing end. Let's try again. Are you alone?"

Footsteps hurried along the alleyway, accompanied by clunking mail. Two figures rounded the corner. The älf fell silent.

By some vindictive twist of fortune, Boëndal and Goïmgar chose precisely that moment to make their appearance.

Boëndal was doing his best to reassure the wary artisan that neither Bavragor nor Boïndil had any intention of carrying out their threats. Tungdil heard him vow to protect Goïmgar from any rash acts of vengeance; then he and the fourthling disappeared from sight.

"Very well," the älf whispered, "so there are five of you. What is the purpose of your journey?"

"To foil you, your master, and all of your ilk!" Tungdil said loudly, choosing that moment to make his escape. He made a grab for the knife and threw his weight backward, hoping to ram his captor against the wall. The älf stepped aside, and Tungdil barreled into the brickwork, still struggling ferociously to fend off the blade.

The noise was enough to alert the other dwarves. They rushed to his aid.

"Is that you, scholar?" Boëndal skidded to a halt in front of the archway, leveled his crow's beak, and barred the way. Skulking behind him was Goïmgar, doing a convincing impression of a two-legged shield.

The älf thrust his knee into Tungdil's nose guard, forcing the metal into his face. Tungdil's eyes watered, blurring his vision; then the knife tore a gash in his unprotected left arm. The älf set about making his escape.

I don't think so! Tungdil darted after the knapsack and managed to catch hold of the flap. He clung to it, growling, and aimed his ax at his antagonist's wrist.

The älf whipped his hand away and the blade missed, slicing through the air, hitting the knapsack, and slitting the canvas. The flap came away in Tungdil's hands, and he lost his balance and fell.

The situation was too perilous for the älf and he turned to leave, trying to wrong-foot the experienced Boëndal, who saw through the feint and timed his attack to perfection. The deadly tip of the crow's beak passed through the leather armor, penetrating deep into the flesh.

The älf uttered an unintelligible curse and staggered sideways, stepping into a lone shaft of light. His deep blue eyes became two dark pits.

But that was only the beginning of his transformation. Thin lines appeared on his pale skin, and in no time his face and throat were patterned with what looked like tiny cracks. Clutching his wounded side, he stumbled down the alleyway, the knapsack bouncing on his back.

"He's not going anywhere!" Boëndal was about to sprint after him when Tungdil called him back.

"Let him go. For all we know, it might be a trap."

"But he's got the knapsack!"

Tungdil wiped the blood from his nose, then proudly produced the sigurdaisy relic. "This is what he was after, and it's right here with me!"

"How did he find you in the first place?"

"I'll explain on the way. We'd better get back to the others." He gave a quick nod to Goïmgar. "Don't worry, those hotheads won't hurt you."

"I told them to close the door *after* you," the artisan said softly. "Honestly, I did."

"It's all right, Goïmgar," Tungdil reassured him, although deep down he wasn't sure what to believe. The fourthling had forfeited his right to be trusted, and there was still no sign of him understanding what the mission was all about.

"We ought to warn the guards that at least one älf has found his way inside the gates," Boëndal reminded him. "Whichever way you look at it, it's bad news for Mifurdania. It's probably a trick to open the settlement to the orcs."

"They know we're here now," Goïmgar pointed out. "Do you think they'll come after us?"

"They've been after us all along," Tungdil told him bluntly. "It's a shame they had to find us. We need to get back to the tunnel as soon as we can. The älfar don't know about the underground network."

The trio hurried through the streets until they reached the southern gates, where Tungdil told the sentries of his brush with the älf. Then they set off toward the alehouse where Bavragor and Boïndil had been instructed to wait.

They were still some distance from the rundown tavern when the sound of Ireheart's ranting reached their ears. They heard cracking wood, then a chorus of screams.

"Bavragor and Boïndil! The älfar must have found them!" Boëndal charged ahead to save his twin.

Just then glass sprayed everywhere as a narrow window shattered and a man hit the cobbles with a thud. The next unfortunate was ejected from the tavern together with the door. Bruised and bleeding, he picked himself up and fled.

The three dwarves rushed inside to be met with a scene of devastation. It looked as if a tornado had hit the bar. Nothing was in its proper place, the chairs, tables, and benches broken or upturned and the floor strewn with groaning bodies. All had taken a beating, some more severely than others.

At the heart of the carnage was Boïndil, glowering like a dwarven god of vengeance. He was busy ridding a man, hair by hair, of his mustache. There was no sign of Bavragor.

"What's got into you?" his brother asked incredulously, staring at the mess. "Is this your doing?"

Ireheart turned to face them, and they saw his singed beard. "You'd better believe it!" he slurred. "The long-uns set fire to my whiskers, so I gave them a good walloping." He giggled and plucked out another hair. "This ruffian started it. I only meant to punish him for ruining my beard, but the others piled in. I suppose I should thank them, really; it made a better fight."

"Tell him I'm sorry," groaned his victim. "It was a misunderstanding. I was offering him a light for his pipe, that's all. I'm begging you, make him stop hurting me."

Ireheart seized him by the ears and looked at him blurrily. "Will you never, ever burn another hole in a dwarf's bearded glory?"

"Never," the man whimpered.

"Then swear it!" The man complied and was released.

"Get out of my sight," barked Boïndil. As a parting shot, he grabbed another clump of hair and aimed a kick at the man's behind. He sat down on the table, laughing, and reached for his tankard. He took a noisy slurp. "I haven't had this much fun in ages," he burped. Just then he spotted Goïmgar. "Ah, there's our little flower."

"He's drunk as a skunk," said his brother, pursing his lips.

"Where's Bavragor?" asked Tungdil. *Keeping tabs on this lot is worse than herding cats,* he thought crossly. "Don't tell me we'll have to look for him too."

"Oh, him...He'll be back in a moment. He went to buy a pony so we can fetch the ingots from the—"

"Boïndil!" His brother snatched away the tankard and pulled him down from the table. "What in the name of Vraccas are you thinking? We're in a strange town, the orcs are at the gates, and all you can do is drink yourself silly. You're as bad as Bavragor!"

"So that's the thanks I get for buying two ponies," came an offended voice from the door. "He's the one who's been beating up locals, not me!"

"I told you he'd be back!" Boïndil said happily. He seized the tankard from Boëndal and knocked it back. "There, try taking it from me now!" He grinned and burped again.

"Orcs!" They heard the shout even before the guard rushed in. "To arms! To arms! The southern gates have fallen and the enemy has invaded! To arms, good people of Mifurdania, to arms!" He stopped short, noticing the bodies strewn around the room. "What in the name of..."

"To arms!" shouted Boïndil excitedly. "Let's get the runts! Oink, oink!" He drew his axes and stumbled to the door. His brother pulled him back and gave him a good talking to.

"Boëndal didn't mean what he said," Tungdil told Bavragor, hoping that the comment wouldn't spark another feud.

"Old Hookhand can say what he likes; he's usually right," the mason said mildly. "You'll find a couple of ponies waiting for us outside. I got them cheap, but they're sturdy little beasts."

"We need to get out of here," muttered Tungdil, deciding to save the story of what had happened in the theater until they were safely out of town—not that he had the faintest idea as to how they would escape. "The älfar are after me."

"In that case, we need a plan," observed Bavragor.

"I've been thinking, scholar," said Boëndal. "Our enemy will be focusing on the main gates, so all we need is a side exit. Once we're out, we can hack our way through the fringes of the battle." He glanced at his brother, whose uncharacteristic silence was explained by the fact that he was snoring in the doorway. "Obviously, the circumstances aren't ideal," he finished with a sigh.

Goïmgar shuddered. "Through the battle?" In his mind's eye he was already fleeing from snarling orcs, grunting bögnilim, and nimble-footed älfar, while arrows rained down on him and swords, spears, and pikes slashed and jabbed all around. "Are you sure that's wise?"

"I don't suppose you can fly, can you?" asked Bavragor. The artisan shook his head wretchedly. "In that case, we don't have a choice."

There was a loud crash behind them. Ireheart had gone down like a felled oak and was lying inert on the floor. His loud snores were the only indication that he hadn't been smitten by Vraccas's hammer.

"A fat lot of use he is," Goïmgar said accusingly. "Just

when we could do with a bloodthirsty warrior, he knocks himself out on beer. Think of how many orcs he could have butchered for us."

"I know." Bavragor nodded, helping Boëndal to drape the unconscious Boïndil over one of the ponies. "It beats me how he got into this state. The long-uns' beer is no better than flavored water."

"He drank five whole tankards of it," Goïmgar told him. He looked at the mason in sudden amazement. "You're not saying..."

"I had seven, not counting the two at the market." He winked at the smaller dwarf and passed him both sets of reins. "Here, look after the ponies."

Hefting his mighty war hammer, he took up position at the rear of the procession. Boëndal and Tungdil took the lead.

From time to time they heard the clatter of swords, but they avoided trouble by taking frequent detours and keeping out of sight. The tactic was to Goïmgar's taste.

People were charging past them in every direction, some armed and rushing to defend the town, others clutching their children and possessions and hoping to find refuge in passageways and backstreets that hadn't yet fallen to the orcs.

Another doomed settlement, thought Tungdil, remembering the charred wreckage of Goodwater. He knew what the orcs would do to Mifurdania and he was tempted to forget about the mission and rush to the townspeople's aid. They were desperately in need of a few extra axes. He wondered whether to declare a change of plan.

What if one of us gets killed? If we don't forge Keenfire, Girdlegard will be lost. He agonized for a moment and decided that he had to put the mission first, regardless of how hard it was to leave the Mifurdanians to their fate. *May the gods preserve you,* he thought bleakly, lowering his head.

Boëndal laid a comforting hand on his shoulder. It was clear from his expression that he shared Tungdil's torment.

At length they reached the eastern battlements and discovered a small door watched over by a pair of sentries. Moments later, a bugle sounded and the sentries grabbed their spears and raced to the northern gates. The streets and marketplaces echoed with the sounds of fighting as the orcs advanced through Mifurdania, beating back the defenders.

The dwarves inspected the door. Heavy-duty chains and padlocks prevented anyone from tampering with the four steel bolts.

"Well, well, well," said a disapproving voice. "What do we have here? Five plump cannonballs on legs…I hope you weren't intending to slip out unnoticed."

The man who stepped out of the side street had an aristocratic face and a pointed beard. His flamboyant robes looked expensive. Behind him was a tall, slender woman in leather armor with a crimson head scarf over her long black hair. A plainly dressed man with gray-green eyes, dark hair, and a thin mustache brought up the rear. All three were carrying duffel bags.

"Dear me, little giants," said the man with the pointy beard, "didn't anyone tell you that this door is out of bounds?"

"Thieves, are you?" growled Bavragor, grasping his hammer in his brawny hands.

The man laughed theatrically. "Thieves! That's a good one! What funny little fellows…No, my bearded warrior, we're not even commoners, let alone common thieves! Surely you don't need two eyes to see that?"

The snarling and grunting was getting louder all the time.

"Let me through," the dark-haired woman commanded. She pushed past the bewildered dwarves and lifted her sword belt to reveal a leather pouch. Producing a number of finger-length implements, some sharpened to a point, others curved or bent at right angles, she set to work on the locks. Soon there was a click.

"I knew they were thieves," said Bavragor, pleased to be proven right.

"We're nothing of the sort, my good fellow." The man with the pointed beard gestured to his male companion. "Meet Furgas, the most accomplished prop master since"—he waved vaguely, unable to think of a suitable period of time—"since time began." He pointed to the woman. "It is my pleasure, nay, my *privilege,* to introduce you to the delightful Narmora, whose exquisite beauty caused the mayor of Mifurdania's roses to wither in shame. As for myself, I am—"

"The fabulous Rodario!" exclaimed Tungdil, who had suddenly placed the actor's voice.

At once the man seemed to warm to him. "An admirer of my art? Who would have thought it! And I took you for a—" He stopped short and his features hardened. "Drown me in a privy, if it isn't the racket maker, the despoiler of my scene, the saboteur of the illusion skillfully woven for the delectation of the public." His brown eyes stared accusingly at Tungdil's boots. "That's him, all right, the dwarf and his accursed footwear. His trampling and shouting ruined my act!"

There was another click as Narmora opened the final padlock and unthreaded the chain, letting it clatter to the ground. "Hurry!"

"Aren't you coming?" Furgas said anxiously.

She smiled and gave him a lingering kiss on the lips. "You

go through and I'll lock up behind you. I don't want to be blamed for handing Mifurdania to the orcs. I'll climb over the parapets."

The dwarves led the way, followed by Rodario and Furgas.

It was immediately obvious that the invaders were throwing all their energy into besieging the main gates and had forgotten about the flanks of the town. The runaways were spotted by a pair of Mifurdanian soldiers, who shouted at them from the parapets to identify themselves, but the order went unheeded. Only the actor turned to wave. "Take good care of my theater for me. We'll be back when you've fought off the orcs. The very best of luck!"

"This is real life, Rodario, not one of your plays," Furgas chided, dragging him on.

The impresario seemed not to grasp the full seriousness of their plight. "All the hallmarks of drama are there, though," he said thoughtfully. "What an excellent suggestion, my dear Furgas. I shall write a new work." He put his hands on his hips and struck a heroic pose. "A fearless guardsman—that's me, of course—spots an army of orcs advancing and, in a pitched battle with, say, half a dozen of them, saves the town from certain ruin."

Just then a rope unfurled from the top of the wall and Narmora descended nimbly, hand after hand, and joined them at the base. Shouting wildly, the guards stormed along the parapet and hauled up the rope before it could be spotted by the orcs.

Tungdil and company hurried toward the shelter of the forest, the other three following purposefully behind.

"A word, oh worthy hoarders of gold and gems. Would you consent to us accompanying you for a while on your overland excursion?" inquired the fabulous Rodario, doing his best to dazzle them with his smile. "I don't mean to be personal, but you look like the sort of fellows who could tackle the green-hided beasts. These are dangerous times, and my friends and I are feeble artists, aficionados of the stage." He turned his tanned face toward his thin arms, which protruded like broomsticks from his expensive cloak. "A fine group of soldiers we'd make: two men as slender as saplings and a beautiful, yet vulnerable woman who wears her armor merely for show. I shudder to think what would happen if the orcs were to..."

"Very well, you can join us," conceded Tungdil. With Boïndil still under the influence, they were two axes down, and in the event of a skirmish, the gasbag and his companions would serve as a distraction while he and the others attacked.

"*A word,*" Goïmgar echoed in disbelief. "I think I lost count of them."

"Men talk a lot when they're frightened," Bavragor said knowledgeably. "If you ask me, he must be scared silly. Have you seen their teeny beards? I had more hair when I was born!"

Tungdil headed in the direction of their ingots and gems, steering a course through the forest toward the plateau. He was only grateful that his new companions were oblivious to the comments being bandied about in dwarfish.

We'll have to carry the ingots up the stairs, past the waterfall, and out to the ponies, he thought. *It's bound to take a while.* The delay was infuriating, particularly since the wagon's mishap seemed to have been planned.

He decided not to wonder where Gandogar and his companions might be. *There I go again,* he cursed, banishing the thought of their rivals from his mind. He focused on picking a path through the forest and listening for noise.

"Little man," opened Rodario, blundering through the undergrowth in an effort to catch up with the dwarf. He didn't seem to notice the snapping twigs or his echoing voice. "Unless I'm much mistaken, you are the leader of this merry band, and so I address myself to you. Groundlings—"

"Dwarves," Tungdil corrected him automatically.

"As you prefer...As I was saying, dwarves are a rare sight in these lands, and so I wonder: Why did the five of you abandon your underground home? Were you driven out by your kin?"

"That's our business, Mr. Rodario."

"True, very true. It was impolite of me to ask. But perhaps you and your companions would consent to join my itinerant theater and collaborate on a play?" He beamed at Tungdil. "With your permission, I'd like to pen a script especially for five dwarves. People would come from far and wide to see our show. There wouldn't be anything like it in Girdlegard. They'd shower us with coins!"

"I'm sorry, Mr. Rodario, but we've business to attend to."

"Business? What kind of business?" He frowned. "Are you in search of treasure?"

"We're on a quest to forge Keenfire!" came a rambunctious shout from the back of the pony. In spite of the slurring, the words were clearly audible. "We'll go to the Gray Range and fashion a weapon more powerful than Nôd'onn himself. The fat wizard won't be bothering us much longer—"

"Shut up, you drunken fool!" Boëndal barked gruffly. "If you're going to give away all our secrets, at least have the decency to do it in dwarfish!"

"Sorry about him," said Tungdil, turning to Rodario with an apologetic shrug. The impresario's face had lit up with interest. "I'm afraid his imagination gets the better of him when he's had too much to drink." He did his best to sound nonchalant, not wishing to give the impression that Boïndil's ravings bore any relation to the truth.

"Don't apologize," Rodario said lightly. "I'm all in favor of imagination. A good writer welcomes inspiration, whatever its source. Besides, I like the sound of the idea. It's just the sort of story that audiences love to see on stage. The trouble is, who would I cast?" He threw up his arms despairingly. "I can't use children or gnomes or kobolds with false beards! I need stocky fellows, proper groundlings, like you. Nothing else would do! Are you sure I can't persuade you?"

"We're dwarves, not groundlings," Boëndal told him crossly. "And keep your voice down, unless you're looking for inspiration on the tip of an orcish sword."

With an offended toss of his long brown locks, the man fell into line with his friends and drew them into a whispered conversation.

"Actors," tutted Boëndal. "You wait: He'll perform our story in every marketplace in Girdlegard before we've finished forging Keenfire. If Nôd'onn finds out what we're up to because of that peacock..." He left the rest of the sentence unsaid.

"Nôd'onn will be long dead before he gets round to writing his play," said Tungdil, clapping him reassuringly on the back. He glanced round to see the fabulous Rodario scribbling frantically in a little notebook that dangled on a ribbon round his neck. Suddenly Tungdil's optimism seemed a little misplaced. "We'll have to take them with us," he said, having thought the matter through.

"You can't seriously suggest that we—"

"I mean it, Boëndal. We'll take them as far as the firstling kingdom. The impresario won't be able to resist an adventure like that. We'll get Borengar's dwarves to lock them in their stronghold for a while—or until the mission is over, if need be. I'm sure they'll find somewhere cozy where our friends will be obliged to enjoy their dwarven hospitality for as many orbits as it takes."

"Assuming they fall for it."

Tungdil gave him a confident wink. The full brilliance of his plan was dawning on him. "Don't worry, they will. When the impresario hears the incredible stories I'm going to tell him, he'll be desperate to see the firstling kingdom for himself."

Boëndal muttered unhappily into his beard.

"Fine," said Tungdil, "I'll warn the others. I don't want them looking too surprised."

He stopped to talk to Goïmgar, then Bavragor, on the somewhat flimsy pretext of checking their armor, and informed them in whispers of his plan.

They were almost on the other side of the forest when they came to the last resting place of the slaughtered unicorns. Rodario immediately stopped to sketch the corpses and make notes on the once-beautiful and peaceable creatures.

Was it wrong to abandon Mifurdania? The sight of the dead unicorns was a painful reminder that they had abandoned the settlement and left Girdlegard's last surviving unicorns to their fate. *The gods will understand that we had no other choice.*

The group approached the foot of the narrow path that wound its way up to the plateau. From ground level, the track was completely hidden.

"On guard!" Stopping abruptly, Boëndal drew his crow's beak. Bavragor responded by reaching for his war hammer, while Goïmgar interpreted the warning in his own fashion and hid behind his shield.

"On guard? My dear fellow, whatever for?" said the bewildered Rodario. His female companion drew her weapons. The first seemed to consist of a pair of scythes mounted on either side of a metal haft, while the second was a straight-bladed version of the same. Judging by the shimmering keenness of the blades, both the inner and outer edges were deadly sharp. She wore metal baskets on her wrists to protect her fingers from enemy swords.

The impresario turned to her. "What could you want with those, precious rose of Girdlegard?"

If Tungdil had learned anything since the start of his journey, it was to trust his friends' instincts. He steeled himself to face the threat.

A moment later he detected the stench of their hidden foes. They smelled sweeter and stronger than orcs, but there was definitely a whiff of rancid fat on the gentle breeze.

Suddenly the enemy disgorged from the bushes.

Shouting and shrieking, the bögnilim stormed toward the humans and dwarves. Bringing up the rear were two orcs wielding studded riding crops, which they used to whip the beasts into a frenzy and galvanize the attack.

The bögnilim, cowardly creatures by nature, were carrying short swords whose notched blades were encrusted with gore from their previous victims. Lolloping and leaping like apes, they screamed and screeched, partly in terror, partly in hatred. Their fighting technique relied on numbers, not skill: If one fell, two or three others would rush into the breach, biting, scratching, and slashing or hurling themselves at their opponents and knocking them off their feet. They descended on the company, stabbing and hacking with indiscriminate rage.

"Back-to-back!" came the terse order from Boëndal. Bavragor took up position, dragging Goïmgar with him, so the artisan had no choice but to join the fight. Rodario was nowhere to be seen, but Furgas and Narmora lined up with the others.

The dwarves' weapons swooped back and forth relentlessly, cleaving skulls and hewing bones, but they had to be careful that none of their slippery assailants sneaked past their guard. Goïmgar barricaded himself behind his shield, his short sword darting out like a flash of silvery lightning and slashing through the bögnilim's insubstantial leather armor. Pus-colored fluid spurted from the gashes and dripped down his shield.

Narmora fought at triple the speed of her companion, her light yet phenomenally sharp weapons giving her an immense advantage over their foes. Just as it seemed the bögnilim had lost the battle, the orcs gave their smaller relatives such a thrashing that they relaunched their attack with a ferocity fueled by mortal fear.

The surging bögnilim caused the defenders to draw closer together until there was barely enough room for the dwarves to swing their weapons. The long blade of the crow's beak caught on the haft of the war hammer, and Bavragor's weapon was torn from his grip. Two or three of the beasts darted forward and knocked the mason to the ground. Others poured through the breach and Tungdil found himself dangerously overextended.

Just then there was a loud hiss and a cloud of green smoke took shape between two trees, crackling and spluttering menacingly. As the air cleared, an enormous two-headed monster loomed out of the mist. With a terrible roar, it opened its vicious jaws and engulfed the bögnilim in a torrent of flames. Two died in the blaze; the others were rooted with shock.

The ensuing commotion sufficed for Bavragor to retrieve his hammer and overwhelm the bögnilim who had infiltrated their circle, pounding them to a pulp. Tungdil and Boëndal also went on the attack.

"I'll take care of the monster if it ventures our way," said Boëndal. "If it sticks to killing bögnilim, so much the better."

Narmora ducked out of the circle and vanished into the bushes, reappearing behind one of the orcs. Her curved blades sliced through his beefy neck, and his headless body toppled to the ground. The second orc lashed out at her, but she dove beneath the whistling whip and launched herself into the air, landing coiled at his feet. Her straight-bladed weapon drove into his belly. The sharp blades cut through his mail, spilling intestines and killing the beast.

Alarmed by the appearance of the fire-spewing monster and thrown into confusion by their flagellators' deaths, the bögnilim panicked and fled in all directions. None were left, save the thirty or so whose corpses were littered about the ground.

Boëndal turned to the two-headed dragon. "Now for you, foul beast of Tion," he growled, preparing to charge. The monster hastily retreated behind the fading smoke.

"Don't strike!" Furgas cried suddenly. "It's Rodario!"

"Rodario?" echoed Bavragor, bewildered. He was brandishing his weapon, ready to join the attack. Hurriedly, he stayed his hammer's momentum by swinging it round his head.

They heard a rustling in the bushes, then a peal of laughter. "Did you see them run?" the impresario said happily, stepping out of the smoke. He was dressed in a leather costume that was several paces too long for him. In his right hand he held two enormous heads; in his left was a pair of hinged stilts.

"I had a feeling I'd be more useful as a monster than a swordsman. I prefer to reserve my fighting prowess for the stage—outside the theater my enemies tend to laugh instead of tremble. Thankfully, I had time to grab a few props and teach the wee beasts some respect. With a little bit of alchemy, anything is possible."

"But we nearly killed you," Bavragor said, stunned.

"I looked the part, didn't I?" Rodario smirked, gratified. He gave a deep bow. "What's this, worthy spectators? Don't I deserve a round of applause?" The dwarves continued to look at him in mute disbelief.

"All humans are barmy," the mason observed. "He makes Boïndil look sane."

"He might be barmy, but he probably saved your life," Tungdil reminded him. "Vraccas knows what would have become of us if it hadn't been for him. To think we were fooled by a man in fancy dress!" He chuckled, and after a while the others saw the funny side too.

The impresario gave another low bow, straightened up, and smiled. "Thank you. You're most kind. I gather from your laughter that you enjoyed my performance. I'm deeply flattered."

This was the moment that Tungdil had been waiting for. He summoned the three players. "My friends and I have been discussing the matter," he said solemnly, as if he had something of vital importance to convey. "You're a trustworthy trio, and we've decided to tell you where we're going. We're on a mission to the firstling kingdom, home of Borengar's dwarves, who guard the western pass."

"Aha! So you're gathering an army to fight against Nôd'onn!" Rodario said excitedly. "Does that mean the story about Keenfire is true?" He scrabbled for his quill.

Tungdil ignored him and plowed on. "You came to our aid, and we'd like to show our gratitude. You may accompany us to the firstling kingdom, where you will enter a dwarven stronghold and behold its splendor. That, and a bag of gold coins, should cover our debt." It seemed to Tungdil that only the foppish actor had been won over by his words, so he tried again, this time waxing lyrical about the wonders of a kingdom he had never set eyes on. For the benefit of Furgas, he invented all kinds of extraordinary machinery and ascribed it to the genius of the firstling engineers, while Narmora was treated to descriptions of wondrous jewelry and armor. On finishing his protracted speech, he fell silent and awaited their decision with mounting impatience.

To his horror he realized that Bavragor had reached for his blood-encrusted hammer and intended to attack the players should they decline. Boëndal looked equally resolute.

"Just think," mused Rodario, stroking his pointed beard. "I could found a new theater. We'll see wonders in this kingdom never known to humankind! Furgas, imagine all the new contraptions you could build!"

Furgas nodded enthusiastically, leaving Narmora looking unimpressed. He stroked her hair fondly and kissed her. "You'll come too, won't you?" She pouted.

Tungdil looked at her intently. He still thought of her as the actress who had played the älf. *Her face isn't quite elven enough,* he told himself. *She's just an unusually beautiful human, that's all.*

"I hope you don't mind me asking," he said brightly. "But how did you learn to use these?" He pointed to the weapons hanging in narrow leather sheaths from her belt. "I've never seen the like of them. What are they?"

"Their names are Crescent and Sunbeam. I designed them myself."

"You designed them?"

Furgas planted another kiss on her cheek. "She's our lead älf, and we didn't want her to have the same weaponry as everyone else." He glowed with pride at his mistress's ingenuity. "We had to ask around a bit until we found a smith with the skill to forge the blades."

"I'm not surprised," said Tungdil, refraining from further comment. He pointed to the steep track. "We'd better get going before the bögnilim recover from the shock."

He knew there had to be more to it than that. *You don't just invent those sorts of weapons and you certainly don't wield them with such proficiency unless you've been properly trained.*

He glanced at Bavragor and Boëndal, who were obviously thinking the same. None of them had any doubt that Narmora was really a warrior, an accomplished fighter who had abandoned the battlefield in favor of the stage.

Tungdil watched as Furgas looked at Narmora tenderly and drew her to him. *Did she lay down her weapons for love?* He would ask her when he had the chance. *I bet she was a mercenary in Umilante's or Tilogorn's army, although she still looks very young...*

Furgas and Narmora helped the impresario out of his oversize breeches, while Goïmgar turned his attention to the startled ponies, who, contrary to all expectations, had stood their ground throughout the fight. The inebriated Boïndil was still draped over the back of one of them, snoring.

"Listen to that racket," said Bavragor. "He's making more noise than a lumberjack in a forest."

"I can't wait to see his expression when he hears he missed a battle," said Boëndal with a wicked grin. "I bet he'll never want to drink again."

The humans and dwarves strung out in a line as they made their way up to the plateau that overlooked Mifurdania and its surrounds. Thick banks of smoke hung over the settlement and a swarm of tiny black dots surged back and forth around the walls. Nothing they saw gave them any reason to believe that the Mifurdanians would prevail against Nôd'onn's troops. Even the otherwise ebullient Rodario was distressed by the sight. Narmora stood impassively at the edge of the platform, peering down at the forest, while Furgas and the dwarves crouched by the waterfall and washed the blood from their hands.

"Where to now?" he asked, noticing that the track went no farther.

"Back down to the bottom, just as soon as we've loaded the ponies," Tungdil told him. "We stopped here on our way to Mifurdania and left our gifts for the firstlings in a cave."

"Can I give you a hand?"

"There's no need," said Tungdil, not wanting to reveal the existence of the underground network. "You should probably get some sleep. We'll need someone to sit watch for us later." He took his leave with a quick nod and edged behind the waterfall with Goïmgar, Bavragor, and Boëndal.

Shifting the ingots was every bit as onerous as Tungdil had expected. At last, after hours of hard work, the bars of gold, silver, palandium, vraccasium, and tionium were stacked safely at the top of the stairs. The sun was setting by the time the dwarves collapsed wearily on the floor, worn out from all the fetching and carrying, not to mention their earlier run-in with the bögnilim.

They were almost asleep when an embarrassed Boïndil emerged from his drunken slumber, mortified at getting sloshed on five tankards—which in his estimation was not nearly enough. Bavragor took particular pleasure in informing him that he couldn't hold his drink.

Later, Boïndil was introduced to the players, whom he viewed with suspicion. He made a point of ignoring them, preferring to treat them coolly until they earned his respect. Not having witnessed the battle, he hadn't seen their fighting spirit and refused to be swayed by his companions' reports. Rodario could be as obliging as he liked: Boïndil was impervious to his charm.

Beroïn's Folk,
Secondling Kingdom,
Girdlegard,
Late Autumn, 6234th Solar Cycle

Soon your kingdom will be ours," a voice warned Gundrabur. The älf was almost invisible in the darkness of the chamber. He stepped closer to the bed. "You'll lose your kingdom, as the fifthlings lost theirs."

"Nothing you can do will stop us," said a second älf, emerging from the shadows and stooping over the bed. Black runes were tattooed across his face, making his pale skin appear translucent and lending him a menacing air. "You're dying, Gundrabur. Vraccas will gather you to his eternal smithy, where you can weep and wail all you like."

"No one will remember you," a third älf told him, stepping noiselessly out of the darkness and stopping at the foot of his bed. "You're old and weak, a high king who waited until his dying cycle to do something worthwhile and failed in all his endeavors." He broke off, raising his violet eyes to the ceiling and listening intently. "Do you hear that?" A chisel was tapping away at the rock. "The secondlings are expunging your name from their annals. You failed them, Gundrabur." Even as he spoke, the tapping and hammering intensified so that Gundrabur could hear a thousand chisels working in unison, chipping away at his skull. "Nothing will remain of your works. Yours will be the Nameless Era that brought humiliation and defeat on the dwarves. You are to blame for their destruction, Gundrabur. You are to—"

"*Gundrabur! Gundrabur!*"

The älfar whirled round and turned to face the door. Light flooded into the chamber.

"We'll be back," they told him, melting into a darkness so complete that not even Gundrabur's dwarven eyes could fathom it.

"*Gundrabur!*"

The high king woke with a start. His heart was pounding and it took a moment for him to find his bearings. He covered his face with his hands and groaned.

Balendilín was sitting on the edge of the royal bed, mopping the sweat from his sovereign's brow. He wrung the cloth into a bowl that was resting on Gundrabur's chest and wobbling slightly as it rose and fell. "Your Majesty was having a nightmare," he said, pressing his hand.

"They're waiting for me," whispered Gundrabur. He looked even older than usual, a time-wizened dwarf so frail and ancient that he was in danger of being swamped by the sheets. He gave Balendilín a short, breathless account of his dream. "They were right," he sighed. "I'm not going to leave this bed alive. I wanted to die fighting Nôd'onn, or at the very least to cleave one more orcish skull." He tried to laugh, but it came out as a choke. "If it weren't for this confounded weakness..."

Balendilín was in no doubt as to what had prompted Gundrabur's decline. He himself had been sick for three orbits following their interview with Bislipur. The beer that had been brought to them after the fourthling's departure had given Balendilín an upset stomach and a temperature, but his constitution was sturdy enough to withstand the shock. The elderly king was unlikely to recover.

It had come to light that the attendant who had served the refreshments had collided with Bislipur on his way to the hall. There was no doubt that Bislipur had a koboldlike talent for skulduggery, but Balendilín couldn't accuse him of anything without proof.

He won't get away with it this time. Poisoning Gundrabur's beer is murder—murder and high treason. As soon as evidence came to light of Bislipur's wrongdoings, Balendilín was determined to put him on trial and execute him for his crimes. And if the fourthling didn't trip up of his own accord, the counselor intended to help him fall.

"I have no other heir but you, Balendilín. Be a strong leader to our folk. Serve them better than I did."

Balendilín dabbed at the beads of sweat on his brow. "You served the secondlings well," he told him. "You were a good king and you still are."

Tears welled in Gundrabur's eyes. "I should like to go to the High Pass, where I fought my proudest battles."

"Your Majesty, that's not wise. An excursion like that could kill you."

"If I die, it is Vraccas's will and you shall take my place." He lifted the bowl from his chest and sat up. "Fetch me my ax and armor," he ordered, becoming the dwarves' stately ruler as he donned his battle dress: leather jerkin, leather breeches, a light knee-length tunic of mail, and a bejeweled aventail, then helmet, gloves, and armored boots. Gathering his ax, the haft of which was as long as his legs, he hobbled to the door.

His counselor pleaded with him to reconsider, but Gundrabur had made up his mind and was as obstinate as any dwarf.

Together they marched through the passageways of the stronghold, Balendilín guiding the high king and steadying him during the frequent pauses after every flight of steps. At length they reached the defenses built by their ancestors to keep out the waves of invading orcs and other beasts and made their way to the highest parapet.

Groaning with effort, Gundrabur sat down on a ledge between two merlons. His hands and arms were trembling and his face was covered in a sheen of perspiration, but he was content. A light southerly wind blew in, ruffling his almost transparent white hair, and he closed his eyes.

"I expect you think Bislipur put something in my beer," he said. "You're probably right. He'll go to any lengths to achieve his goals, but you'll never defeat him by responding in kind. Don't play him at his own game, Balendilín, or he'll drag you down to his level."

Balendilín drew closer and looked the monarch in the eye. "What would you have me do? Is it wrong to fight fire with fire?"

"Bislipur's mask will slip, and when it does, you must be there to expose his duplicity. When the truth is out, even his closest friends will turn against him, but until then you must bide your time. If you speak too soon, the fourthlings will accuse you of troublemaking and slander. Fires are best fought with water: It puts out the flames without adding to the blaze." Gundrabur's cloudy eyes settled on his heir. "Be like water, Balendilín, not for me, but for the sake of our folks." He gazed down at the trench, surveying the bleached bones of the countless creatures who had died there. "Not a single orc entered our stronghold during my reign," he murmured, not without a hint of pride. "We defended Girdlegard against Tion's minions, and now you must protect it from the threat within."

There was a short silence as he took in the splendor of the stronghold's defenses; then he sniffed the air quizzically.

"Is this your doing, my loyal friend?" he whispered gratefully. "Am I to die in battle after all?"

At that moment the guards on the battlements spotted the advancing beasts and sounded the alarm. The gates of the stronghold flew open as the echoing blare of the bugles called the dwarves to arms. Warriors left their stations at the foot of the ramparts and streamed up the stairways to the battlements.

Balendilín stared at the high king's countenance. He looked visibly younger. The foul stench of the approaching orcs was fanning the flames of his inner furnace, steadying his hands and sharpening his sight.

"Lower the bridge," came the order from Gundrabur. He sprang to his feet. Moments earlier, his legs had trembled under the weight of his mail, but now they bore him with ease, and he seemed to have gained a few finger lengths in height. "Let's see whether the orcs have learned anything about fighting over all these cycles. I'll warrant they can't scare this old dwarf."

The portcullis lifted, pillars rose from the base of the trench, and the first slabs of stone were lowered to form a bridge across the trench. Already five hundred dwarves had formed a guard around their king.

Balendilín tried one last time to dissuade him. "I'm begging you, Gundrabur, you'll be killed—"

The elderly monarch patted his shoulder reassuringly, then took his hand and gripped it firmly. "My loyal friend, I would rather die like this than have the spirit sucked out of me by poison. Bislipur shan't have the satisfaction of ending my life." He clasped Balendilín to him. "I will die a glorious death, a death befitting a secondling king. History will remember me kindly." He stepped back and looked solemnly at his counselor and friend. "The first ten orcs that fall by my ax will be vengeance for your arm. Farewell, Balendilín. We'll meet again in Vraccas's smithy." With a smile, he turned and faced his troops. "Warriors of Beroïn," he cried, his voice traveling through the stronghold and echoing against the rock, "let us fight together and defend our kingdom. For Ogre's Death and Girdlegard!"

A cheer went up among the secondling warriors who knew nothing of their monarch's illness and rejoiced to see him fighting at their side.

We'll meet again. Balendilín felt a lump in his throat as he watched his friend stride majestically through the gates and across the bridge, shielded by the secondlings' arrows and catapults until he and his warriors were close enough to engage their orcish foes.

Balendilín didn't have long to wait until a cry went up among the horrified warriors that Gundrabur had fallen. It was then that he decided to ignore the late king's advice and see to it that Bislipur died. *Dwarves are no friends of water,* he thought grimly. *Fire is our element.*

On the fifth orbit after the high king's passing, the taverns, quarries, and workshops of the secondling kingdom were still closed. Thousands of dwarves from the seventeen clans of Beroïn's folk had gathered in the funeral hall whose vast pillars towered so high and dwindled into the distance.

The focal point was a stone sarcophagus, hewn by the secondlings' finest masons and decorated with wondrous carvings commemorating Gundrabur's glorious deeds, not least his last battle at the High Pass where the orcs had been routed.

Carved into the lid of the coffin was a perfect likeness of the monarch in his younger years. The marble Gundrabur was dressed in his finest armor, his right hand clasping the haft of his ax.

Even those at the back of the hall could see the sculpted body resting on the dais, high above the heads of the crowd. Slender rays of sunshine slanted through chinks in the ceiling, converging on the coffin from all points of the compass and bathing the effigy in iridescent light.

The moment of parting has come. Balendilín ascended the steps and stopped at the high king's feet. Kneeling down, he lowered his head and paid his respects to the fallen monarch. Then he got up and surveyed the secondlings for a final time before he was appointed king.

"Gundrabur sensed the invaders before they were spotted from the watchtowers. He was always the first to detect our enemies and preserve us from harm." As he spoke, he found himself looking at Bislipur, who was standing with the fourthling delegates at the edge of the crowd. Not even Gandogar's scheming adviser could excuse himself from an occasion such as this. "Our king was called to Vraccas before he could realize his dream of a united dwarven assembly, but he took the first step toward creating a new and stronger union of the folks. From this moment on, his goals will be mine, and I swear in the name of Vraccas to complete his work before I die."

Banging the hafts of their axes against the floor, the second-lings signaled their approval. A low roll of thunder rumbled through the mountain.

Balendilín was too choked with emotion to say anything further, so he walked to the head of the coffin, kissed the brow of the marble king, bowed again, and left the dais.

With that, fifty dwarves hurried over and hooked long poles into the metal rings subtly incorporated into the coffin's design. As soon as the order was given, they lifted the coffin, carried it from the dais, and bore it silently past the rows of dwarves, who bowed a final time as their dead monarch was taken to his resting place in the crypt of kings.

Balendilín walked behind the coffin. He would watch over Gundrabur's body during the long hours of the night, ending his vigil in the morning, when he would leave the crypt with the secondling crown. In time, he too would be laid to rest with the rulers of his folk.

From the corner of his eye he spotted Bislipur pushing his way to the front of the crowd. The fourthling's gaze was fixed on him as if to read his thoughts and divine the nature of the vengeance that Balendilín had in mind. *You are right to fear me, Bislipur. Your crimes won't go unpunished.* Looking straight ahead, Balendilín didn't let on that he had seen the brawny dwarf.

At length the pallbearers entered the crypt of kings and placed the coffin on its basalt stand. High above, an opening had been cut out of the mountain, allowing the light of Girdlegard to shine on Gundrabur's marble face. The attendants filed out of the vast crypt that housed the mortal remains of the secondling kings, twenty-six in all.

Balendilín walked to the far end of the vault, placed the haft of his ax on the floor, and leaned on the ax head. His gaze fell on the sculpted countenance of his friend and sovereign. *Fare you well, Gundrabur.* As the moments passed, he too became stone, insensible to the passing of time. His eyes stared blankly at the coffin, while his mind relinquished all thought and drifted on a sea of sorrow.

At times it seemed to him that voices were speaking to him in ghostly whispers, but he understood nothing of what they said.

According to secondling legend, Vraccas would open the eternal smithy and release the spirits of the dead kings, who would visit the prospective monarch and pass judgment on his worth. In some cases, the heir to the throne entered the vault and was never seen again.

Balendilín was spared such a fate.

The next morning, tired, aching, and bleary-eyed, he left the crypt to find the waiting dwarves exactly where he had left them many hours before. The secondlings bowed and drummed their axes against the floor, hailing their new king and offering him beer, bread, and ham to restore his strength.

Balendilín took a few mouthfuls, washed them down, and ascended the dais where Gundrabur's coffin had lain.

"I did not seek this office," he said in a loud, clear voice. "It was my hope that Gundrabur would reign for another hundred cycles so I could serve him loyally, but Vraccas decided otherwise. Fourteen orcs died by Gundrabur's ax and four arrows pierced his flesh before our king was gathered to the eternal smithy." His gaze swept the hall. "He named me as his successor, and so I ask you: Will you have me as your king?"

The crowd chorused a resounding "aye," wooden hafts pounded the stone, and Balendilín realized with a rush of emotion that the secondlings were chanting his name.

"Beroïn's folk has chosen. Let us never forget Gundrabur or his dream of uniting our kin. It is our shared duty, irrespective of clan or folk, to defend Girdlegard against all harm." His eyes sought Bislipur and found him where he had been standing before. "Join me," he said, extending his hand.

The startled Bislipur limped up the steps to the dais and greeted the new monarch with a nod. His cold brown eyes stared at him uncertainly.

"The death of Gundrabur has robbed our folks of their high king. The succession will not be decided until the fifth and final challenge is complete. As I'm sure you know, Bislipur and I have not seen eye to eye, but I cannot allow a rift to open between our folks. Friendship must not be turned to enmity, which is why I solemnly swear to put aside our differences until one or the other of the candidates has returned." He drew himself up to his full height. "When dwarf fights dwarf, only our enemies stand to gain. The new high king will set our course and we will obey his orders and submit to his will." Balendilín held out his hand to Bislipur. "Let us shake on it."

His antagonist had no choice but to comply. To Balendilín's astonishment, he seemed neither angry nor resentful.

"I swear that neither of us will promote our separate causes until the new high king has returned," he promised, choosing his words with care. "We may disagree on certain matters, but we share a common enemy: evil in all its forms. As dwarves, we are committed to wiping out evil wherever it occurs and we shall not tire in our duty."

A loud cheer went up as the pair shook hands and looked each other in the eye. No one could tell that their gazes were locked in an oath of eternal enmity.

"As a sign of my good faith, I should like to suggest that we begin our crusade against evil this very moment," announced Bislipur. "Will we stand by while orcs murder and pillage before the gates of this stronghold?" He turned to the crowd and raised his voice to a rallying shout. "We must clear Ogre's Death of this plague!"

On hearing the cheers, he knew he had judged the mood right. "My messenger is heading through the tunnels to the fourthling kingdom, as I speak. He will return with five thousand of our finest warriors," he proclaimed to the astonished Balendilín and the crowd. "Together the dwarves of Beroïn and Goïmdil will chase the orcs from these gates. United our folks will prevail!" He threw up his arms and brandished his double-bladed ax, dazzling the dwarves with reflected light. "This is our chance to realize Gundrabur's dream of a common dwarven army!"

The cheering redoubled and the mountain shook with the drumming of axes.

Balendilín bore the treachery smilingly and gazed intently into Bislipur's hard face. *You don't fool me, you devious bastard. Are the warriors meant for your protection, or are you after the high king's throne? Would you stage a coup so you can have your elven war?*

Bislipur stared back, his cold eyes boring into him mercilessly. "May the hunt begin, King Balendilín," he said, descending from the dais. Balendilín was left to wonder who the quarry might be.

II

The following morning, after a cold night that heralded the coming of winter, they loaded the ingots onto the ponies and headed west. The smoke had cleared above the deserted streets of Mifurdania and tiny black dots lay unmoving at the foot of the settlement's walls. Every dot was a corpse and they covered the area in a sea of black.

Tungdil hated Nôd'onn and the orcs more violently than ever. *First Goodwater, then Greenglade, and now Mifurdania and all the other villages, hamlets, and farms: Half of Girdlegard has been razed to the ground.* He spotted a cloud of dust on the horizon: The army of orcs was heading northwest. *I'll do whatever it takes,* he promised himself.

Much to the dwarves' disgust, their provisions for the journey consisted almost entirely of bread and dried fruit, which they were forced to eat for want of anything else. In their haste to leave Mifurdania, they had forgotten to stock up on victuals and no one was inclined to venture back. They were all the more grateful when Goïmgar found a few wild mushrooms, even though they had to eat them raw.

"Do you really mean to take them with us?" asked Boïndil, casting a quick look over his shoulder at Rodario and his companions, who were bringing up the rear.

"We'll decide when we get to the tunnel," said Tungdil.

"It's eighty miles to the next entrance, and if we can't find it, we'll continue on foot."

"On foot? Can't you buy us each a pony?" demanded Goïmgar.

Boïndil harrumphed. "A bit of exercise might be just the thing for your puny little legs. It's time you pulled yourself together and started acting like a dwarf. Even the female long-un is tougher than you."

After two orbits of marching in the pouring rain, they reached a low-lying area bounded to the north by imposing mountains—the Sovereign Stones, as they were labeled on the map. Nestled in the foothills was the human settlement of Sovereignston, which Tungdil remembered was famous for its wealth. It was the fashionable place for Weyurn's gentry to build their palatial villas and stately homes. The attraction was not so much the mountain air, but the prestige to be gained by living there—and of course, the social whirl.

"We'll stay only long enough to buy some ponies," Tungdil told his companions on approaching the gates. "It'll be cheaper and safer to look for provisions and ponies in the poorer parts of town. We'll leave the rich folk and their villas well alone."

"What a terrible pity," said Rodario in an exaggeratedly aristocratic voice. "It seems churlish not to visit our wealthy neighbors after living on their doorstep all this time." He was relieved to see that the solid city walls were lined with armed guards: The orcs would never be able to get hold of them once they passed through the gates. He turned to his companions excitedly. "Why don't we put on a play? Nothing long or complicated—just a short, impromptu performance. We'd earn enough bronze coins to fill our bags with victuals and keep the proverbial wolf from the door."

"Can't you speak normally for a change?" growled Boïndil, scratching his stubbly cheeks, which were long overdue for a shave.

"I shall speak in whichever way I choose, master dwarf," the actor said huffily. "Some people are blessed with communicative talents beyond the level of primitive grunts, burps, and growls. I don't see why I should disguise the magnificence of my education when you do nothing to hide the paucity of yours."

"Fine," Boïndil muttered malevolently. "We'll see how far your fine words get you when we meet a pack of orcs."

His brother changed the subject by asking how the impresario had breathed fire at the bögnilim.

Rodario beamed. "You can thank Furgas for that. The trick is to fill a tube with lycopodium spores, put on the dragon mask, and blow through the tube. The spores pass over a burning wick at the mouth of the mask, and the monster spews fire." He rolled up his sleeves. "I use a smaller version when I'm playing the magus. The tube runs down my forearm, connecting a leather purse of spores at my elbow with a miniature tinderbox just inside my cuff." He held up his arm and gestured expansively to demonstrate the technique. "I squeeze the purse like so, and the seeds shoot down the tube. Meanwhile, the pressure on the pouch activates a cord that pulls the flint backward and produces a spark. Presto, the seeds are ignited as they exit my sleeve!" His hands mimicked the flight of a fireball. "So there you have it: a magic trick for magic flames."

Boëndal, who had been following the explanation carefully, shot Furgas an admiring look. "An ingenious invention!" The prop master accepted the compliment with a nod.

They joined the back of a queue of wagons and carriages

owned by Mifurdanians and merchants who had fled the unfortunate city.

Sentries were checking the vehicles, noting exactly what they were carrying, and demanding a toll. No distinction was made between farmers, traders, and other travelers, so the city of Sovereignston made a considerable profit from the dwarves. Not only that, but as visitors to the kingdom of Weyurn, Tungdil and the others were restricted to the poorest districts of the city and given the address of a boardinghouse in which they were required to stay.

Thus constrained, they trudged up a narrow street and turned into a passageway that was barely wide enough for single file. Both sides of the alley were crammed with timber houses whose upper stories jutted out dangerously, almost meeting overhead. The uneven cobblestones never saw daylight. All in all, it wasn't dissimilar to an underground gallery, except for the stench of sewage and detritus. Mounted on one of the bulging walls was a sign showing a prancing pony; they had found their address.

With a shudder of disgust, Rodario searched the pockets of his rain-drenched coat, pulled out a handkerchief, and pressed it to his mouth and nose.

"With all due respect," he said firmly, "nothing could induce me to sleep in such a hovel." It was evident from their expressions that Furgas and Narmora felt the same. "Fortunately, I have a solution to our dilemma. My companions and I will spend the night in more salubrious accommodations, and we'll meet you tomorrow morning at the gates. You'll have time to buy your ponies and so forth, and we'll find a venue and put on a play. How does that sound?"

The suggestion was greeted enthusiastically by Boïndil, who was tired of the actor's voice.

Rodario didn't wait for further permission, but strode away at once, his vibrant robes flapping around his legs. There was no denying that he looked like a nobleman, but the duffel bag rather ruined the effect. Furgas and Narmora followed him down the alleyway, boots squelching as they trudged through the foul-smelling mud.

"To be honest with you, I think they've got a point," ventured Goïmgar, peering after them regretfully. "I don't much like the look of it either."

"We were told to stay here," Boëndal reminded him, steering the ponies into the barn while the others made for the door. "I'll see to the ponies and keep an eye on the ingots. They'll be safer in the stables, I'll warrant. I'll sound my horn if I need you."

"Very well. I'll order you some food," Tungdil promised. He pushed open the door and stepped into an impenetrable fog of smoke. Quite apart from the cloud of tobacco, it was evident that the chimney needed a thorough sweep. They made their way through the crowd of drinkers, sat down at a table by the fire, and stretched their soggy boots toward the flames.

"At least we won't be sleeping outside again," said Goïmgar, softening. "I can't stand the rain." The others nodded in silent agreement: None of them were accustomed to coming into contact with water unless they chose to—which was seldom enough. "If only it were a bit more homely..."

Tungdil was happy to forgo all other comforts, provided that the roof didn't leak. The heat from the fire was beginning to dry his leather garments, and he closed his eyes with a contented sigh. Soon the conversation faded to an indistinct hum as he gave into his tiredness and dozed. He woke when the publican arrived with a tray of food and beer ordered by

Bavragor. "Do you have a room for us? We're not fussy, so long as it's warm and dry."

The man nodded. "Come this way." The dwarves grabbed their packs, picked up their plates and tankards, and filed out behind him. They weren't sorry to be leaving the other drinkers, whose demeanor failed to inspire much trust.

The chamber to which the publican led them was a garret room with a chimneybreast at one end. The warmth exuding from the brickwork was enough to heat the whole room. "Another beer for the gentleman?" Bavragor accepted with a nod.

They hung their clothes to dry on a rope around the chimney, then Boïndil, wearing nothing but chain mail and breeches, left the chamber to take his turn in the stables.

Tungdil waited until Boëndal had joined them, then took off his boots, stood them next to the chimneybreast, and climbed into a little bed. "Time for an afternoon nap," he told the others, pulling up the sheets. "I'll go into town and ask about the firstlings later. It would be good to know what to expect."

"It's been such a long time since anyone heard from them," said Bavragor, shaking his tankard and gazing at the swirling beer. "What if something's happened to them?"

"I expect they're just loners like you," Boëndal teased him. He stripped to his chain mail and underwear and climbed into bed.

The mason finished his beer, burped, and polished off the leftovers of Boëndal's meal. "I'd really like to meet them," he admitted. "I've been asking Vraccas to keep them safe." He fell silent and stuffed his pipe with tobacco.

Tungdil was staring at the beams overhead. The fine cracks in the paint reminded him of the way the älf's face had fractured. "He knew my name."

"What's that, scholar?" Boëndal asked drowsily.

"The älf knew my name." He reached for the head scarf that Frala had given to him. There was something soothing and reassuring about the cloth. "They know more about me than I thought," he said uneasily.

"The most powerful of Tion's creatures are frightened of a dwarf," observed Bavragor with a low chuckle. He lit his pipe, filling the chamber with the smell of tobacco spiced with a hint of brandy. It was surprisingly pleasant. "That's the way we like it."

Goïmgar glanced over at Tungdil. "I don't blame you for being concerned," he said with feeling. "I wouldn't want to be chased by a band of älfar who know exactly who I am."

"Yes, but that's because you're a coward." The insult left Bavragor's lips before he had time to consider.

"If you haven't got anything useful to say, you may as well go to bed," Tungdil told him sharply. *They won't give each other a chance.*

He saw Goïmgar look at him, then pick up his sword and shield and take up position on his bed, keeping a careful eye on the window and the door.

Tungdil couldn't be sure whether the artisan was sitting watch for himself or the others. He was still considering the matter when he fell asleep.

It was dark outside when Tungdil opened his eyes.

His boots and clothes were drier than they had been in ages. No one else was awake, not even Goïmgar, who was snoring with his head lolling back against the wall. From the nose down, there was nothing to be seen of him except for his shield.

It seemed a good time to get on with procuring the ponies

and provisions, so Tungdil pulled on his warm clothes and
dry boots, slipped into his mail tunic, and jammed his ax
into his belt. At the last moment he decided to leave the sigurdaisy wood behind for safekeeping; then he left the chamber
and went down to the bar, stopping to tell the publican that
he'd be back in a couple of hours. He stepped outside.

The rain was still falling in torrents. A cold, malodorous
wind gusted through the narrow streets. Nothing in his surroundings hinted at the opulence of the dwellings that graced
the city's upper slopes. *It's all very well for the rich folks in
their mansions, high above the slums,* he thought to himself.
*Everyone down here is forced to look up at them, not know-
ing whether to hate them or admire them for their wealth.*

He had several run-ins with particularly persistent beggars
and on one occasion he was chased by a pair of aging harlots
who demanded to know if certain parts of his anatomy were
as small and hairy as the rest.

Tungdil ignored them because they offended his romantic
sensibilities. His idea of love was gleaned from fiction and
from Frala and her husband. He stroked his lucky scarf and
tried to picture her in his mind. Knowing that he would never
see her or her children again was even harder to deal with
than the death of Lot-Ionan. He would have done everything
in his power to be a good guardian to Sunja and Ikana.

The incessant rain, gray skies, and general squalor of Sovereignston did nothing to improve his mood. He had to walk
for what seemed like hours before he found a dealer who sold
ponies, and even then he was instructed to call back the next
morning. His next stop was a grocery store, where he bought
provisions for the journey and succumbed to the temptation
of buying a cake. He hadn't felt hungry until he saw it, but the
mixture had risen perfectly to form a soft brown crust. The

cinnamon streusel topping had melted in places, and delectable golden clumps nestled alongside rum-soaked raisins and sunken slices of fruit. Tungdil took a deep breath and bought the whole cake to share with the others, trusting to the baker to brighten his mood.

In the dark he set off through the streets, carrying his well-wrapped cake and other purchases. Mud and detritus clung to his boots, making them squelch unpleasantly. Not all the streets were properly cobbled, and parts of the waterlogged city were no better than mud slicks. *Why would anyone want to live in this godforsaken place?*

It was inevitable that he would fall over, and fall over he did. He stepped on a soggy pile of horse dung, skidded on his right leg, and stumbled, reaching down with one hand to save his clothes from the worst of the muck. Somehow or other he managed not to drop the cake. *Underground vaults and strongholds are a thousand times better than this.*

His thoughts were cut short by a sudden gust of wind. Something whizzed to the left of his head, grazing his ear. Whatever it was, it was painful, and he yelped in surprise, reaching up to touch his neck. Warm blood trickled over his fingers.

Turning sharply, he whipped out his ax. "If you think you can part me from my money or my cake—" The threat was left unfinished. *They've found us.*

Waiting at the other end of the alleyway was the älf from Mifurdania who had tried to slit his throat. His cloak was fluttering in the stinking wind. He nocked a second arrow to his imposing bow and drew back his hand to release it.

At precisely that moment, Tungdil was bowled over by something that charged toward him from the side. All he saw was a flash of violet light and a mask of gleaming silver before he was hit with such force that he soared through the air and landed in the next passageway, skidding four paces and cutting a channel through the mud.

What on... Head spinning, he rolled onto his back and held his ax at the ready, bracing himself for the älf to find him and kill him. Nothing happened. Groaning, he stumbled to his feet. Every link in his mail shirt was oozing thick black mud. He looked dirtier than a pig that had been rolling in the muck.

He peered around the corner warily. His cake was lying where he had dropped it, but the alley was deserted and his footprints had been washed away by the driving rain. The only evidence of the disturbance was a black arrow and a strange yellow fluid that formed a garish trail through the puddles and the mud.

Tungdil's earlobe was throbbing. *Why didn't the älf kill me? Did someone stop him?* His body felt as if he'd collided with a wall. He tried to recall what had happened. *If I didn't know better, I'd think Djerûn had...*

He gave up on the idea and bade a mournful farewell to the cake, then hurried through the streets, keeping an eye out for any älfar who might be on his tail. On reaching the tavern, he raced upstairs and burst into their chamber to find Boëndal on the point of going out.

"Hello, scholar. Is everything all right?"

"Not exactly," said Tungdil, telling him quickly of the älf's ambush and his miraculous escape.

"The sooner we leave Sovereignston the better." Boëndal frowned in concern. "What possessed you to go wandering through the city on your own? An ax and a bit of learning aren't enough to protect you in a place like this." He thought for a moment. "If you ask me, it's not just the sigurdaisy wood they're after. Nôd'onn wants us dead because we know his secret." He woke Bavragor and Goïmgar to tell them what had happened, then went to join his brother in the stables. There would be no more sleep for any of them that night.

What if it was Djerûn after all? Tungdil dismissed the idea. The armored giant and the maga were miles away in the Outer Lands.

At first light, the three players were waiting at the gates as agreed. Narmora was wearing a leather cape and the red head scarf that she never seemed to be without; and Furgas had put on a long coat to keep himself as dry as possible while the downpour showed no sign of letting up. The impresario seemed to have dressed in a hurry and was scanning the crowds nervously.

The dwarves rolled up with their ponies and provisions.

"What's wrong?" Boïndil asked Rodario. "Are the älfar about?"

"It's not älfar he's worried about," replied Furgas. His tone implied that he had witnessed the scene before. "After last night's performance, he put on a private showing for the innkeeper's daughter and his wife."

"Shush! Do you want me hounded out of town?" hissed Rodario, glancing back and forth on the lookout for angry faces. "They told me they were separated!"

"There's always an excuse," Narmora said cynically. "It's a pity their cuckolded husbands won't believe you."

Boïndil whinnied with laughter. "The innkeeper's wife *and* his daughter?"

"Thirty-four cycles the one, and sixteen the other: spring and summer in one bed, with me, the king of seasons," he bragged.

Narmora was unimpressed. "I'd say you're more of a wanton farmer who can't help plowing foreign fields. For the most part, they accept your attentions because they're neglected by their own farmers—or because they pity a man with such a miniscule plowshare."

Rodario stopped searching the crowd and focused on sparring with Narmora. "My dear lady, I understand your fascination with my mighty apparatus, but I'm most discerning about my choice of fields. Stony meadows give you bruises; they may appeal to some laborers, but not to me." He flashed a smile at Furgas, then remembered what Boïndil had asked him. "Älfar, did you say?" he inquired with sudden seriousness. "Right here in Sovereignston? Why didn't you—"

"That's him!" the shout went up. "That's the scoundrel!" Rodario spotted the approaching pitchfork and fled. In no time he was through the gates and wending his way nimbly among the queuing carts. A moment later four men rushed past in hot pursuit.

Bavragor and Boïndil fell about laughing, Boëndal shook his head silently, and Goïmgar clung to his shield, ready to take shelter in case the long-uns gave up on the adulterer and took their anger out on him.

But the cuckolded husbands and their friends were intent on apprehending Rodario, who had successfully evaded them, leaving his pursuers searching furiously in the rain.

The rest of the company left Sovereignston in a more dignified fashion.

"Älfar?" said Narmora, returning to the initial question. "Where?"

"Yesterday in the city. I was attacked by one. You didn't see any, then?" Tungdil couldn't help feeling a mild aversion toward the actress, perhaps because of her elven looks. *She's an ordinary woman,* he told himself. *That's all.*

She shook her head. "They left us alone. At least we're forewarned." She laid her right hand on Crescent.

About a mile from Sovereignston they were reunited with the philandering impresario, who was waiting under a fir tree and trying to shelter from the rain.

Bavragor couldn't help laughing. "I hope they were worth it!"

"Indeed they were." A look of delectation came over Rodario's face. "I suspect I wasn't the first to enjoy their combined attentions, but they certainly knew how to please." Realizing that the ponies were getting away from him, he sped up to a jog. "That's all in the past now. Come, my loyal companions, let's make haste to the firstling kingdom where unparalleled wonders await us!" His stirring words were somewhat spoiled by the squelching beneath his feet, but he still cut a dash as an adventurer.

Tungdil's memories of Sovereignston weren't nearly as fond. He picked up the pace, unmoved by the city's fluttering pennants and colorful panorama of tiled roofs. Nothing could induce him to look back. Hurrying away from the pride of Weyurn, he tried not to think of the älf's murderous eyes.

I hope my mysterious rescuer killed him.

III

Kingdom of Weyurn,
Girdlegard,
Winter, 6234th Solar Cycle

As soon as the opportunity arose, the travelers purchased a small cart for their baggage and a pair of horses—one for Rodario and the other for Narmora and Furgas. From then on, the journey westward proceeded considerably faster, not to mention more comfortably.

Rodario, fearing the wrath of the cuckolded husbands, was especially keen to make progress—although it didn't deter him from using his charm and eloquence to make a string of conquests on the way.

A fierce northerly brought with it the season's first snowstorm, the white flakes settling on the frozen ground to form a thick icy layer. Winter seemed to descend on the land and its inhabitants faster and more vigorously than usual. Sleeping in the open was too dangerous, so the company camped out in places where they would be sheltered from the elements, under trees or rocky overhangs, or in derelict houses or ruined forts.

The vast lakes that made up three-quarters of Weyurn's surface were covered in ice. The sun and clouds played on the frozen water, creating glorious displays of shadow and light, but the glittering spectacle could do nothing to win over the twins, who were too afraid of the icy depths to go fishing with Rodario and Furgas.

"Ice is just as dangerous as water," Boïndil told them. He

set about making a fire in the ruined temple where they were camping for the night. "It looks so pretty that you forget to be careful, and then whoa, you find yourself sinking to the bottom, never to be seen again."

"It's like marriage," observed Rodario. "Women tempt you into their arms and before you know it, you're trapped for life. I'm more of the type for—"

"Bedding other people's wives. Not to mention being beaten by angry husbands and dying of the clap," Narmora finished for him.

"Still jealous, I see," he riposted, flashing her a dazzling smile as he hurried after Furgas, who was heading for a nearby stream.

Boïndil chuckled. "My old billy goat was a bit like Rodario. He mounted anything that stayed still for two seconds."

"What became of him?"

"The old lecher jumped on a nanny goat and didn't notice that she was grazing near a cliff. He plummeted to his death." He ran a razor over his cheeks to get rid of the stubble that was drawing attention away from his magnificent beard.

"In other words, Rodario will get his comeuppance by falling out of bed and breaking his neck," said Tungdil, grinning.

"Who said anything about a bed? It might be the window!" Boëndal pointed out.

His brother hooted with laughter. "What a sight!" He scrambled along a fallen column that was propped up amid the ruins and came to a halt at the top end where he could see for miles around. He took a seat and lit his pipe. Boëndal tossed him his share of the food. "It would serve the old prattler right," chuckled Boïndil, turning his attention hungrily to the cheese.

Goïmgar, wrapped in two blankets with his shield laid across him like a third, had said nothing for some time. Eyes closed, he seemed to be asleep.

The temple's moss-covered walls were alive with flickering shadows. Over the cycles, the frescoes had faded and there were holes in the crumbling plaster. Not that the dwarves would have recognized the painted deities anyway: To their minds, there was only one god and that was Vraccas. The rest weren't worth the time of day.

The warmth from the blazing fire spread rapidly, casting a soft light throughout the temple and making the timeworn sculptures seem strangely alive.

Tungdil found himself thinking of the performance in the Curiosum. He still couldn't decide how much of what he had seen had been acted by the players and how much had unfolded in his mind. *It all seemed so real.*

Muttering to himself, Bavragor returned from his tour of the ruins. "Not bad," was his verdict on the masonry, "but not worthy of us dwarves."

Tungdil offered him some bread and ham. "Do you mind if I ask you something?"

Bavragor accepted the food. "Sounds ominous."

"It's been playing on my mind. You know the business with your sister..."

"Smeralda." Bavragor placed the sandwich on a stone to warm the bread and bring out the flavor of the meat. He took a long slug of brandy before continuing and said bitterly, "I can't forgive him for what he did."

Tungdil didn't press him. He had a feeling that Bavragor was ready to open up to him, and after a while the mason cleared his throat.

"She was a slip of a thing, a lass of forty cycles, but as soon as he clapped eyes on her, he wanted her for himself. She was as much of a warrior as he was, and she trained like a demon because she wanted to be able to fight by his side." He clenched his fists as the memories flooded back. "The rest of us were worried about his fiery spirit, and we begged her to stay away. Smeralda wouldn't listen, and everything went on as before. The two of them were fighting a band of orcs when he..." He broke off, covering his good eye with one hand and raising his pouch to his mouth with the other. "He killed her, Tungdil. He was so far gone in bloodlust that he took her for an orc."

Tungdil pushed back the lump in his throat and blinked.

"An orc! Afterward they said it was a tragedy and a terrible accident and he swears he can't remember a thing, but I couldn't care less: My sister died because of him. I don't know if you could forgive him, but I don't intend to."

Tungdil knew there was nothing he could say. The story was unspeakably sad. He laid a hand on Bavragor's arm. "I'm sorry I put you through it again," he said simply.

Listening to the mason had brought back the pain of losing Lot-Ionan and Frala, who had been like a sister to him. *I can almost understand how he feels.*

"So now you know," sighed Bavragor, taking a deep breath and flushing away the memories with a long draft of brandy. His ham sandwich lay untouched and forgotten by the fire.

Tungdil looked up and glanced at Boïndil, who was guarding the camp from his lookout on the fallen pillar and puffing on his pipe. Blue smoke rings wafted into the darkness, rising through the falling flakes, and Tungdil thought for a moment that he could hear the hiss of hot tobacco on snow.

"The fieriness of his inner furnace is a curse," Boëndal said sadly. "He still can't remember what happened on the bridge. All he knows is that Smeralda was lying dead at his feet and he thought the orcs had killed her. When Bavragor and the others told him that she'd died by his axes..."

"Weren't you with him?"

"I wish I had been. I keep telling myself that if I hadn't been injured, I might have stopped him before it was too late." He scratched at a rusty patch on his chain mail and oiled the corroded links. "He calls out to her in his sleep sometimes. Trust me, scholar, he suffers just as much as Bavragor, but he'd never admit it."

Boëndal filled his pipe and they took turns smoking, each pursuing his thoughts. Tungdil looked out of the crumbling window and saw that the snow was falling faster than before.

A pair of snowmen appeared in the doorway: Furgas and Rodario were back from fishing. The prop master had caught two fully grown carp, but the impresario was clutching a single, insubstantial tench.

"A god among plowmen, but a terrible fisherman," commented Bavragor, hoping that a bit of banter would dispel his gloomy thoughts.

Rodario didn't rise to the taunt. "What's the use of being a god when the mortals forsake you?" He pointed to the crumbling, damp-ridden frescoes. "Deities need lesser beings to adore them, or they fade and die. They lose their purpose; there's no reason for them to exist."

"Vraccas doesn't need a purpose," Boëndal told him firmly. "He created himself because it suited him, not because of anyone else."

"I'm familiar with the creation myths, thank you, and I certainly don't need any sermons from you." The impresario turned his attention to filleting his fish. "We used to perform them on stage—very successfully, I might tell you. It's true what they say: Old stories are always the best, although in the present circumstances our play about Nôd'onn seems to strike a chord."

That was Tungdil's cue to ask him about the theatrical

effects he had witnessed in the Curiosum. Ever since the performance he had been longing to find out how they made the illusions seem so real.

"You're interested in how we did it?" Rodario pointed his scaly knife at Furgas. "Ask the expert."

While the impresario continued to hack away at the unfortunate tench, Furgas finished gutting the first carp and started on the second. "I know a fair bit about alchemy. That's how we make the smoke, for example. Thick smoke, wispy smoke, red smoke, black smoke, whatever we need. The science of the elements is fascinating."

Alchemy was one of the subjects taught by Lot-Ionan at the school and Tungdil was familiar with some of the chemicals, having fetched and carried them often enough. "But how did you extinguish all the lamps at once?"

"Magic," Rodario whispered, trying to look enigmatic. "You thought Nôd'onn was the only magus left in Girdlegard, didn't you?" He leaned over to Tungdil, fiddled with his ear, and pulled out a gold coin. "What do you say to that?"

"Thank you," said Tungdil, snatching up the coin. He tested it with his teeth and knew at once that he'd been had. "Gold-plated lead," he reported. "And not even good-quality gold." He tossed back the coin. "Your magic's not up to much."

"He's a conjurer, not a magus," laughed Boëndal, pointing at the impresario with the stem of his pipe.

Rodario wagged a finger at him. "But the audience falls for it, and that's what counts. Why, even the ugly little bögnilim were tricked by my art, and that, my friends, is what's known as success."

"So it's all a case of conjuring, illusion, and alchemy," said Tungdil, summing up.

Furgas nodded. "And makeup," he added, glancing at his slender mistress. "Makeup convinces the eye of what it otherwise only suspects. It turns Narmora into an älf and sends the youngsters screaming to their parents." He laughed. "That's when we know that we're doing something right."

"Just be thankful it was Tungdil and not our lunatic ax man who visited your theater," Bavragor said darkly. "He would have stormed the stage."

"Poor Narmora," Boëndal murmured unthinkingly. "Even without makeup she looks remarkably like an elf. Nature can be cruel sometimes."

The comment prompted smiles from Furgas and Rodario, but Narmora shot the startled secondling a murderous look. Tungdil and Bavragor fell about laughing, thereby waking Goïmgar, who peered nervously over his shield.

"Oh," said Boëndal, embarrassed. "That came out all wrong. I didn't mean it that way," he apologized.

"Are you sure I look like an elf, not an älf?" Narmora said threateningly. Her eyes, so dark they were almost black, glowered at him angrily. "I hope none of you get a nasty shock tonight..." She stood up, straightened her head scarf, and left the ruined temple. Her silhouette melted into the darkness.

"Ye gods, she's a natural," Rodario gushed. "Doesn't she play the role to perfection? Of course, I've no intention of telling her. She'd only demand a raise." He looked excitedly at the others for confirmation, and the dwarves concurred with mute nods. Boëndal was genuinely perturbed about what might befall him when he fell asleep that night.

The men finished filleting their catch and soon there was a smell of roasted fish. They all tucked in hungrily.

"There's one thing I don't understand," Tungdil said to Furgas. "How did you make the set? Everything—the woods, the palace...It looked so real."

"Can you keep a secret?"

"Of course!"

"Do I have your word?"

"Absolutely!"

"Swear by the blade of your ax."

Tungdil swore himself to absolute secrecy.

"Magic," announced Furgas with a mischievous grin. He smoothed his mustache.

"Uh-huh," sighed Tungdil, kicking himself for falling for the routine.

Boëndal sat up with a jolt and stifled a scream. For all the shock of being woken, he was glad to have escaped the visions that had plagued his sleep.

His relief was short-lived. On reaching for his crow's beak, he was alarmed to discover that the weapon was gone. Slender fingers encircled his wrist.

He rolled over to find himself staring into the cruel, lean face of an älf. Clad in full armor, she was crouched beside him, studying him with cold, dark eyes. *I'm still dreaming*, he told himself frantically. *It can't be...*

"Let that be a lesson to you," he heard her hiss menacingly, just as his eyelids grew impossibly heavy and he drifted off to sleep.

When he woke for the second time, he leaped up, spluttering and gasping, and whirled round to face the threat. This time his crow's beak was in its proper place and he snatched it up hastily.

The players were asleep: Narmora in Furgas's arms, and Rodario, head resting in a pile of discarded fish skin, nestled beside the dying fire.

Boëndal studied them carefully. It didn't *look* as though they were playing a joke on him. Heart still pounding, he recovered some of his composure and vowed never to offend the actress again.

It occurred to him that Goïmgar was supposed to be keeping watch for them, but the lookout post was empty and the sentry had vanished. The horses and ponies were all safely tethered, but a trail of footprints led away from the door.

Surely he's not daft enough to run away in a snowstorm? Boëndal took a few steps outside and was almost knocked over by a flurry of snowflakes that seemed intent on laying him out. Suddenly he spotted a figure crumpled in the snow.

"Goïmgar!" Boëndal rushed over but the artisan didn't respond. Blood was trickling from a narrow gash in his head. Boëndal carried him into the ruined temple, laid him next to the fire, and threw on a couple of extra logs.

"I…" Goïmgar's teeth were chattering furiously. "I slipped."

Boëndal covered him with two blankets. *He can't even pee without getting himself in a fix.* Tactfully, he refrained from comment: Goïmgar had humiliated himself sufficiently already. Why Tungdil had picked the troublesome artisan was beyond him, especially with four perfectly acceptable diamond cutters to choose from. *Vraccas is bound to have his reasons,* he thought philosophically, as the bundle of misery slowly began to thaw. His beard, hair, and eyebrows were streaming with icy water.

Boëndal leaned over to talk to him. "Were you trying to get yourself killed out there?"

"No," came the eventual reply.

"Be more careful in the future. We need you for our mission."

"You mean the *impostor* needs me to help him steal the throne," the shivering artisan muttered darkly.

Boëndal didn't bother to reply: The fourthling still hadn't grasped that more was at stake than the succession, despite

Tungdil's well-meaning attempts to set him straight. *How can anyone be so obtuse? Everything depends on the success of our mission, but he's too stubborn to see it.*

Goïmgar stopped shivering and stared straight past him toward the rear of the temple, where the marble gods were grouped. He gulped. "How many?" he whispered.

"I beg your pardon?"

"How many statues were here when we arrived?"

Boëndal thought for a moment. "Seven. Four big ones and three small ones."

Goïmgar closed his eyes. "There are eight of them," he hissed. "Five big ones. What are we going to do?"

"Which one wasn't there before?" Boëndal's fingers were already wrapped round the haft of his crow's beak. He tensed his muscles.

"The third from the right."

"Fine. I'll go in for the attack and shout to wake the others. Meanwhile, you grab your shield and back me up until Boïndil takes over."

"Me?"

"Who else am I supposed to ask?"

Before Goïmgar could protest, the crow's beak swung up in a half circle, its long tip speeding toward the area just above the hips where there were no bones to slow its path. The wound would be deep and deadly. Like a miniature pennant, Boëndal's plait traced the weapon's movement in the air.

"For Vraccas!" he bellowed.

The statue shattered under the force of the blow, the crow's beak smashing through the crumbling stone and dashing it to pieces. The damage to the deity, carved lovingly by humans, was absolute and irrevocable.

"Sorry," Goïmgar said contritely, "I meant third from *my* right." By then it was too late.

The hitherto inanimate statue suddenly came to life. Its eyes glowed lilac beneath its visor.

"Of all the dumb mistakes..." Boëndal swore under his breath and made to strike again.

His titanic adversary had other ideas. Moving with a speed that belied its size, the statue seized the dwarf's forearms in its enormous hands and lifted him clean into the air. Boëndal found himself dangling two paces above the ground. His weapon clattered to the cracked marble floor.

His brother was on his feet already. "Let go of him!" Whipping out his axes, he was about to launch himself on his colossal opponent when he was blinded by a flash of light. The glare was so bright that he had to look away.

"That's enough, Boïndil," commanded a distinctive female voice. The glare softened to a weak glow, allowing them all to see.

The speaker emerged from behind the remaining statues and joined the giant's side. Her crimson cloak was streaked with melting snow and she was holding a glowing sphere. "You can put Boëndal down now, Djerûn. I think they know who we are."

"Andôkai!" cried Tungdil in astonishment, lowering his ax. "You're back!"

She threw back her hood to show them her face.

"Andôkai? Andôkai the maga of Brandôkai? Andôkai the Tempestuous?" inquired Rodario. He didn't seem to notice that his cheeks were covered in fish scales and that he was scarcely looking his best. "Isn't she supposed to be dead?" He stared at her brazenly. "Confound it, you're right!" He turned to Furgas and Narmora. "Andôkai's alive. We'll have to rewrite the play."

"What play?" Slipping the globe inside her cloak, the maga strode to the fire and warmed her hands. Djerûn lowered

Boëndal to the floor. "What's he talking about? Who is he, anyway?"

"An impresario," Tungdil said apologetically. It took all his self-control not to bombard her with questions.

"I see. I've been immortalized in a play already, have I? I hope the actress is suitably—"

Rodario was about to launch into a flattering explanation when Boëndal rounded on the maga.

"What the blazes was your giant up to? How was I supposed to know he was spying on us? I could have killed him!"

"He wasn't spying; he was guarding your camp. And no, there was never any danger of you killing him," she informed him in a condescending tone. She took off her cloak to allow the warmth to penetrate her other clothes. Underneath she was wearing full armor, thick winter garments, and a sword. She was broad-shouldered by nature, and the layers only added to her bulk. "He was here at my request to protect you from the älfar. They've been following you since Mifurdania."

"I *knew* they were hunting us," wailed Goïmgar.

Boïndil laughed. "I'd rather die in a fight with the älfar than be saved by a beast. Leave the pointy-ears to me." He stroked the short hafts of his axes.

"I doubt you would have spotted them in time. They managed to follow you this far without you seeing them," the maga said gravely. "Djerûn killed a couple of them three miles from here, but two escaped. I sent Djerûn ahead in case they tired of tracking you and decided to attack."

"So it was him who rescued me in Sovereignston! I thought as much," said Tungdil.

Andôkai nodded. "I'm afraid your attacker got away."

"I wouldn't have let the pointy-eared murderer escape with his life," growled Boïndil. "My enemies never get the better of me, even if I have to chase them down."

"I'm assuming you've never been shot at by an älf archer." She gave the dwarf a pitying look. "And anyway, warriors who run after their enemies should be careful about being trapped."

"My enemies *never* trap me," Boïndil said mulishly. He took up his old position atop the fallen pillar.

The extra height brought him level with the giant. He peered through the visor, curious to see what lay among the shadows, but his eyes, despite being accustomed to darkness, failed to penetrate the gloom. It was as if Djerŭn's helmet contained nothing but bottomless space.

The others sat down in a circle around the fire.

By this time the players were wide-awake. While Narmora returned her fantastical weapons to her belt, Rodario whipped out his notepad and quill, only to discover that the ink was frozen solid. Djerŭn had already retreated to the rear of the temple, where he transformed himself into a statue and waited in the gloom.

Tungdil waited for everyone to settle. "What changed your mind, maga?" he asked at last. "How did you find us?"

"Your new companions can be trusted, I assume?"

"They helped us get here. You can trust them."

Boïndil grunted disapprovingly from his perch.

"You can trust us with your lives," Rodario declared expansively, seizing the opportunity to introduce the troupe in characteristically florid style. "We know all about Keenfire, of course. In fact," he said, waving his arms extravagantly, "we rescued these future heroes, these champions of legends as yet unwritten, from a fate most foul by plucking them from the claws and swords of a pack of vicious bögnilim. We're completely reliable, most Estimable Maga."

Under normal circumstances his smile had the power to melt the thickest ice and soften the hardest stone, but this time it failed: Andôkai was unmoved.

"You *made* me come back," she said accusingly, glaring at Tungdil. "It's your fault for hounding me about my duty. Everything you said kept running through my head until I couldn't take it any longer. My conscience wouldn't let me abandon Girdlegard and so I returned. Besides, there are a thousand reasons why Nôd'onn deserves to die."

Her face seemed less severe in the flickering light of the fire, her features somehow softer, more feminine. Rodario couldn't take his eyes off her and was hanging on her every word. He seemed to regard her forbidding charm and stern manner as a challenge to his seductive powers.

"So I went back to Ogre's Death and took another look at the passage that I hadn't been able to make sense of. You remember, don't you? The only remaining uncertainty in the plan..." Gazing into the flames, she motioned with her hand, marshaling the sparks into the script of the common tongue. One by one the words flared up and faded in an instant.

Rodario read them aloud: "Keenfire must be forged by the undergroundlings, then wielded by the undergroundlings' foe." He snatched up a piece of charred wood. "I need to write it down before I forget. What use is a quill without ink? I could kick myself for letting it freeze."

"You write, and I'll kick," Bavragor said magnanimously.

"The gods save me from your hulking boots," exclaimed Rodario, shooing him away. "Wait and see, we'll have the best play ever performed in Girdlegard!" His hand moved busily across the page. "They'll be fighting to get through the door!" He was about to launch into another effusive speech, but Furgas jabbed him in the ribs.

"The undergroundlings' foe," murmured Tungdil, unable to mask his disappointment. *What could it mean?*

Boëndal couldn't make sense of it either. "We've got no shortage of foes. Ogres, for example"—he cast a sideways glance at Djerûn—"not to mention orcs, bögnilim, and all the other beasts created by Tion to plague the kingdoms of men, elves, and dwarves. Come on, scholar, surely you can think of something. A bit of book-learning might be exactly what we need."

Bavragor took a swig of his brandy. "We could have a bit of fun with this. Why don't we catch an orc and torture him until he agrees to clobber Nôd'onn? Or maybe we could talk an ogre into taking a swipe at him with our ax."

"I guess that's the end of the expedition, then," said Goïmgar, readily accepting defeat. He suddenly paled. "Who's going to tell the others? King Gandogar doesn't know!"

Tungdil expelled his breath in a long sigh. "Are you absolutely sure of the meaning?" he asked slowly.

The maga nodded. "I'm afraid so. I read it over and over again."

"Do you have any suggestions?" He glanced at Djerûn.

She smiled. "Djerûn isn't your foe, if that's what you're thinking. He can't do it."

Tungdil scratched his beard, which had grown to something approaching its former length. "Then we're facing a considerable obstacle." He looked into the faces of his companions. "I don't know what to suggest." He lay down and pulled up his blanket. "Maybe Vraccas will send me some inspiration in the night. Get some rest; we're bound to need our strength for whatever lies ahead."

They settled down by the fire while Djerûn kept watch.

I have to think of something. I'm in charge, thought Tungdil, tossing and turning restlessly. *If I don't come up with a solution to the riddle, Girdlegard will be doomed*. It wasn't the sort of thought that would lull anyone to sleep.

*   *   *

Tungdil still hadn't received divine inspiration by the time they broke camp at first light. They decided to carry on regardless: With a bit of luck, one of them would think of something on the way, and if not, there was always a chance that the firstlings would be able to help.

We'll get there in the end, Tungdil told himself firmly, slipping his freshly oiled and rust-free mail shirt over his leather jerkin.

Andôkai rode with Rodario. The impresario had imagined himself sitting behind her on the saddle, with his arms wrapped chivalrously around her waist, but she insisted on riding bareback to give them both more space. Not only that, she forced him to take his place in front of her while she held the reins — much to Furgas's amusement.

More snow had fallen overnight, adding to the existing coating by the length of a forearm or so. The horses had to plow a path for the short-legged ponies to follow, and so they proceeded in single file with Djerûn trudging behind them. From a distance it looked as if one of the marble deities had left the tedium of the temple and joined the procession instead.

The going was tough for the unusual band of travelers. Winter slowed their progress considerably, and Tungdil realized the advantage of traveling underground. They needed to get to the Gray Range as fast as possible, and by foot, or even on horseback, the journey would take too long. In a week, they advanced two hundred miles, a distance that could be covered in one or two orbits on the underground rail.

That afternoon, while they rested their horses, he pestered Andôkai to tell him how she had tracked the company down.

"It was no great challenge," she said dryly. "I left the Outer

Lands, went back to Ogre's Death, and persuaded the second-lings to show me the tunnels. We came up near Mifurdania, Djerûn found your tracks, and the rest was easy. People tend to notice a group of traveling dwarves. It wouldn't have been hard for the älfar to find you either."

Tungdil glanced at Narmora, who was helping Furgas shovel snow into a pan and melt it over the fire.

The maga's gaze settled on Rodario. "These actors... How did you meet them?" Tungdil recounted the story. "Aha," laughed the maga on hearing how Narmora had got them out of Mifurdania by picking the locks, "so she's a woman of many talents. Have you seen their play?'

"I certainly have! The production was a sellout. It's called *The Truth About Nudin the Knowledge-Lusty and the Grisly Circumstances Leading to His Reincarnation as Nôd'onn the Doublefold and Resulting in Girdlegard's Demise.*"

"A snappy title," she observed.

For the first time Tungdil saw the corners of her mouth turn upward and it occurred to him that smiling suited her better than her usual stern expression. Rodario chose precisely that moment to look over his shoulder and naturally assumed that the friendly smile was meant for him. He beamed back delightedly.

"And that's the star of the show, the fabulous Rodario. According to the others, he keeps a mistress in every town."

"I don't doubt it. Who plays me?"

"I'm afraid I left early, Estimable Maga. I had to chase a thief." He beckoned to Rodario. "You'll have to ask him."

The impresario bounded over to be cross-examined by the maga. "My players are the most accomplished in all Girdle-gard. Your role was played by the talented Narmora, who alone could emulate your prowess with a sword." At her request he embarked on an explanation of the plot, but she cut him short when he was halfway through.

"The rise of the Perished Land, Nôd'onn's visitation, his compact with evil—what gave you the idea?"

"I listened to the rumors, combined them with some ancient legends, and added a dash of inspiration of my own." He looked at her brightly. "Does it meet with your approval?"

"It's incredibly accurate, at least as far as Nudin's transformation is concerned."

"Really?" Rodario seemed genuinely surprised. "But then, truth is at the heart of all great art, wouldn't you say?"

"Thank you, Rodario, you can go now," Andôkai told him briskly. "And don't forget to rewrite my part in your play. I'm not dead yet."

"My dear maga, you're positively blooming," he said, turning on the charm and gazing seductively into her clear blue eyes. "No man could—"

"I'm busy," she informed him, turning back to Tungdil.

Rodario's magnificent smile was wiped off his face. His pointed beard seemed to droop in dismay. "I respect your wishes," he said in a dignified tone.

"The maga has sent the peacock packing," chuckled Bavragor, who had followed the little scene. "Poor Rodario, his magnificent feathers are trailing on the ground. I'd advise him to back off now while he's still in possession of his plumage." He rummaged around for his drinking pouch and started humming a ballad under his breath.

"No chance," said Furgas. He lay back in the snow. "When Rodario's got his eye on a woman, he never gives up. Her sternness will only encourage him." He kissed Narmora and pulled her close. "One day he'll stop playing the field and settle down."

"If he doesn't get beaten to death by a pack of angry husbands," put in Boïndil, guffawing. "He must be pretty good at running because he certainly can't fight."

After a short rest, it was time for the company to continue. Tungdil and Andôkai broke off their conversation and Djerûn bent down on one knee, joining his hands to create a chair for the maga. The crestfallen Rodario was consigned to riding alone.

In the orbits that followed they battled through Weyurn's snowdrifts, sometimes struggling to find a safe path. Whenever the lead horse sank up to its belly, they knew for certain that the ponies would never get through. Djerûn, burdened with the weight of the maga, spent much of his time hip-deep in cold snow.

On several occasions they were forced to retrace their steps and seek another route, but at last the Red Range was firmly in their sights. The mountains towered before them, guiding them on their way, the red slopes blazing like fire whenever the winter sun scored a hard-fought victory against the somber clouds.

At last they reached the mouth of a narrow gully that meandered toward a blood-red peak. The entrance to the gully was sealed by a wall, as were each of its five sweeping curves. The firstlings had taken extensive precautions to secure their kingdom against unwanted guests.

"Well, we made it," Tungdil said happily. He rubbed his beard, dislodging a collection of tiny icicles that had formed beneath his nose. He was tired, his feet were numb, he felt cold to the core, and he couldn't risk touching his chain mail for fear that his hand would stick to the frozen steel. *It's nothing a tankard of dwarven beer won't fix.* "Look," he told them, "there's the entrance."

The twins followed his gaze, taking note of the six stone

barriers in their path. "It makes you wonder what all the fortifications are for," said Boëndal, giving voice to their concern. His plaited hair was wrapped around his neck like a
scarf to protect him from the cold. "Anyone would think
Tion's hordes were approaching from this side and not the
western pass."

"My dear fellows, couldn't we save the discussion for
another *warmer* time?" pleaded the shivering impresario.
"I'm in danger of losing my toes to frostbite." He too was
growing stalactites from his nose.

Bavragor looked at him scornfully. "You're as bad as a
girl—or as bad as Shimmerbeard, which comes to the same
thing."

"Take another slug of brandy," Goïmgar hissed angrily.
"With any luck, you'll trip over and freeze to death. I've got a
feeling you won't be much use to us anyway. With your shaky
hands, it'll be a miracle if the spurs ever fit."

"I'm surprised that someone as yellow-bellied as you can
feel anything except the warm sensation in your pants,"
Bavragor said scathingly, not bothering to look round.

Following Boëndal's advice, they fanned out in an arc
formation, weapons at the ready, and rode cautiously into
the gully toward the first of the defenses, forty paces away.
The wall of weathered stone rose high into the wintry sky, the
only way past it through a metal door inscribed with runes.
The bricks themselves were just roughly hewn blocks of stone;
the firstlings hadn't lavished much attention on the masonry.

Tungdil spelled out the runes, the metal glowed, and the
door swung open, allowing them to pass. "I wish everything
were that easy. If it were all down to metalwork and reading,
Nôd'onn would soon be dead." The company set off again.

"Reading doesn't come naturally to everyone," said
Boëndal from the back of the procession. "It's just as well

we've got a scholar with us. Without your—" The links of his mail shirt tinkled softly and he stopped, eyes widening in alarm. "W-what in the name of Vraccas..." he stammered, reaching behind him.

A black arrow was embedded in his back. Before he could alert the others, a second missile sang toward him, passing through his hand, piercing his armor, and tunneling into his back. By the time it came to a halt, the arrowhead had passed right through him and was protruding from his chest. Boëndal groaned and slid out of the saddle.

"Wait!" the impresario shouted frantically, calling to his companions to stop. He tugged on the reins and felt a rush of air near his throat. The arrow whizzed past him and hit his horse in the neck. With a loud whinny, the animal crashed to the ground, sending the impresario tumbling through the snow.

Djerůn whipped round, only to be hit. The long arrow missed Andôkai and pierced Djerůn's armor with a curious sound. Even now, the giant gave no audible sign of pain. Without hesitating, he turned away from the archer, putting himself between the maga and their foe.

Andôkai cursed volubly and invoked a spell.

"What is it?" cried Furgas, who was staring in confusion with the remainder of the group.

"Over there!" Narmora pointed to a tall, fair-haired figure at the mouth of the gully. Even as they looked, the älf nocked a fifth arrow to his bow. It hurtled toward them, this time heading straight for Tungdil.

Hurrying to escape the feathered missile, he caught his foot in the stirrups and was trapped. Suddenly he was out of time. The arrow was only a finger length away when it stopped in midflight, suspended in the air. Its tip was pointed directly at his heart. Tungdil shuddered.

"Quick, get Boëndal out of here," the maga panted. "We need to ride on. I can't maintain the charm for much longer."

Boïndil's eyes flashed dangerously. "Accursed älfar!" he shrieked dementedly. "Look, there's another one! Leave them to me!" He made to spur on his pony.

"Stop!" Tungdil peered at the mouth of the valley. Two älfar were standing side by side, waiting for the spell to break. "They'll shoot you dead as soon as you leave the maga's protection. Think of your brother, not revenge." He made a grab for Boïndil's reins.

"Out of my way!" raged Ireheart, staring at him without a glimmer of recognition. He raised his arm to strike.

"No, Boïndil!" shouted his brother, kneeling in the crimson snow. "You can't let it happen again!" He tried to lever himself up with his crow's beak, but one hand was still pinned to his back by the arrow. Eyes watering with pain, he mumbled something and keeled over.

Boïndil let out a terrible howl and leaped from the saddle. "Please, Vraccas, he can't be dead. He just can't." He crouched beside him. "His heart's still beating," he told them, breaking off the shafts of the arrows and gathering his brother into his arms. "We need to get him to the stronghold."

They tied the unconscious Boëndal to his startled pony and dragged the pair of them toward the next set of gates.

Tungdil felt a knot of fear in his stomach when he saw the trail of blood in the fresh white snow. *Even warriors aren't safe on a mission like this.*

He risked a glance over his shoulder. The fair-haired älf looked remarkably like Sinthoras. Tungdil thought back to their last encounter in the desert village. *Somehow, Sinthoras must have survived Djerûn's attack.* The tenacious älf had returned to avenge himself and his mistress, whom the twins had slain in Greenglade.

Sinthoras yanked something from his neck, wound it around an arrow, and took aim. There were 250 paces between the archer and his target, but Tungdil didn't doubt for a second that the deadly missile would cover the distance and more. The älf released the string and a moment later a second shot followed from his companion's bow.

"Look out!" Tungdil yelled to the others, promptly losing sight of the arrows, which were speeding toward them at an impossible rate.

The air crackled as the first arrow hit Andôkai's protective shield, ripping through the magic barrier and allowing the second arrow to embed itself in Djerûn's back.

This time a dull moan sounded from the visor as the arrow penetrated the giant's armor and a jet of yellow fluid spurted from the wound. It was as if the tip had lanced a festering blister.

Tungdil had seen the substance once before in Sovereignston when Djerûn had saved his life. *He came to my aid and got hurt in the process*. The giant swayed, shook his head sluggishly, and walked on, his pace considerably slowed. "We need to keep moving!" someone shouted.

They hurried on, running or riding accordingly, toward the second set of gates. Tungdil gave the command, they slipped through, and the door closed behind them; they no longer felt quite so exposed.

"Hurry!" shouted Boïndil, spurred on by the circle of blood spreading from his brother and soaking the pony's coat.

Meanwhile, the fluid seeping from Djerûn's wound was turning from yellow to dark gray and his movements were increasingly labored.

They scrambled down the gentle slope toward the third set of gates. Man, dwarf, or pony, it made no difference; they were floundering to their waists in snow.

The landscape reminded Tungdil of a hill near Lot-Ionan's vaults where he used to go sledding with Frala and Sunja. He had an idea. Snatching the shield away from Goïmgar, he turned it over and laid it flat. "Put Boëndal on top. You'll get there faster like this."

They placed the wounded dwarf on the shield, his brother squatted next to him, and the pair of them swooped down the white slope, speeding toward the third door, which opened mysteriously as they approached.

The smooth underside of the shield raced over the snow, gathering speed all the time, but Boïndil could neither steer nor brake. He looked up to find himself heading straight for a group of sentries who had gathered in the gateway, weapons at the ready.

Tungdil cupped his hands to his mouth. "We're from the secondling kingdom," he bellowed, his warm breath hanging in the air. "In the name of Vraccas, lower your axes!"

The firstlings recognized that the intruders were dwarves and stepped aside just in time. The strange craft hurtled past, spraying glistening snow in all directions. Incredibly, no one was hurt.

Panting and coughing, the rest of the company sprinted to the gates, only to be stopped by the guards. Dressed from head to toe in armor and wrapped up warmly against the cold, the firstlings looked at them suspiciously through a narrow chink in their cladding of metal and fur. They leveled their spears, axes, and war hammers at the ragged group.

"May Vraccas our creator bless you and may the flames of your furnace never die. My name is Tungdil Goldhand," he introduced himself, gasping for breath and glancing back to check for älfar. "These are my friends and companions. We were sent here by the dwarven assembly on a mission regarding the safety of Girdlegard. I need to speak with your king."

The thicket of metal parted to reveal a dwarf in chain mail, leather breeches, and a particularly striking cloak of white fur. "Many cycles have passed since we were visited by our cousins from the other ranges. Call me cynical, but isn't it strange that a collection of dwarves and long-uns should enter our kingdom just as Girdlegard is being threatened by the Perished Land?" The voice was unusually high-pitched for that of a man.

"A fine sort of welcome this is!" growled Bavragor. He took a step forward, towering over the speaker by at least a head. "Look here, dwarf-with-no-name, I'm Bavragor Hammerfist of the clan of the Hammer Fists, a child of the Smith, a descendant of Beroïn, and your equal in merit and birth. Is this what the firstlings' hospitality has come to?"

"Now, that's what I call a proper dwarven voice," said the other. The scarf was pulled away, unmasking the speaker's identity.

Tungdil gasped in surprise. The face looked distinctly feminine. There was no beard, the features were soft and delicate, and the cheeks were covered in soft down that grew thicker and darker toward the hairline.

"My name is Balyndis Steelfinger of the clan of the Steel Fingers," she told them, not in the least bit intimidated. "I'm in charge of these gates, and I make no apology for vetting our visitors before I let them in."

IV

Borengar's Folk,
Firstling Kingdom,
Girdlegard,
Winter, 6234th Solar Cycle

I t's a woman," said Bavragor, clearly nonplussed.

"Oh, well spotted, Master Hammerfist," she teased smilingly. "What sharp eyes, I mean, *eye*, you have!" Turning to her guards, she gave orders for the injured Boëndal to be taken care of. Four firstlings shouldered the shield and carried it like a stretcher to the next set of gates. After waiting for Tungdil to nod his assent, Boïndil hurried after them.

"The rest of you come with me. Her Majesty will be waiting in the great hall." The guardswoman looked Tungdil up and down curiously, then turned and led the way. No sooner had Tungdil warned her about the älfar than she instructed a group of warriors to take up position by the trebuchets and ballistae on the third rampart.

"What prompted you to build the defenses?" he asked.

"Many cycles ago we had a problem with trolls. Tion tried to sneak them in through the back entrance. Our forefathers built the walls to keep them at bay and eventually the beasts were defeated." She glanced up at the sentry, who gave the all clear. "Looks like the älfar have retreated. Why were they following you?"

"That's something I'll have to discuss with your queen," said Tungdil, lowering his eyes to avoid her probing stare.

"A dwarven queen!" exclaimed Rodario. "I wonder how

the women came to wear the breeches." He sighed. "If only my blasted ink hadn't frozen. I'm never going to remember it all. Was it a female revolution?"

Balyndis laughed. "A revolution? No, it's all very peaceable here. I thought men and women always shared the work."

Djerûn had stopped carrying Andôkai and was stumbling at the back of the group. On reaching the final set of gates, he came to a halt and leaned against the wall.

He's badly hurt, thought Tungdil in alarm. In a way, he felt responsible because the giant had sustained his original injury in Sovereignston while fighting on his behalf.

"It's not far now," the guardswoman reassured them. "I'll send for our healers as soon as we're inside." It didn't seem to occur to her that Djerûn was far taller than any ordinary man.

"That won't be necessary," Andôkai said quickly. "You go ahead, and I'll see to his injuries. He's too far gone for a physician; only my art can save him." The giant slid down the wall and slumped into the snow. Andôkai knelt beside him. She was exhausted from her confrontation with the älfar, but she summoned the last of her strength. "We'll catch up with you," she said sharply. "Just go!" Her companions complied.

So this is the firstling kingdom. Tungdil gazed up at the mountain's red flanks. Hewn into the lower slopes was a stronghold with nine giddy towers. The architectural style was different from that of Ogre's Death, the lines more flowing and not as angular and severe, although the building was similarly sturdy. Curiously, Borengar's masons had dispensed with ornamentation altogether.

Abandoning their ponies, they made their way onto a wooden platform at the base of a tower. "Try to keep still. It'll probably feel a bit funny at first." Balyndis threw back a lever and up they shot, racing toward the top of the tower, past a narrow spiral staircase that led up to the battlements.

On the way up, Tungdil heard the rattle of chains uncoiling and scraping over metal. *Some kind of pulley system, but for passengers, not supplies.* "You don't like stairs, then?"

The guardswoman smiled. and Tungdil thought she looked awfully pretty. "It's less effort like this," she said.

They drew level with the top of the tallest tower and walked out onto a parapet that led toward the main entrance via a single-span arch bridge

On either side of the walkway was a two-hundred-pace drop. Crows and jackdaws circled overhead and the chill wind blew stronger than ever. Narmora kept a hand on her head scarf to stop it from flying away.

The vast gates, ten paces wide and fifteen paces high, remained closed as they approached. Instead, Balyndis led them into the great hall via a separate door.

Bavragor glanced around and smiled smugly. "Just as I thought..." He didn't have to elaborate: His assessment of the masonry was sufficiently clear.

The stronghold made little impression on the master mason, but Furgas, Narmora, and Rodario were blown away.

"You hear stories about vast halls hewn into the mountain, but I never thought they were true," said Furgas, lowering his voice to a reverential whisper.

"We'll have to build a new theater," the impresario told him. "A bigger stage will give the audience a better sense of the splendor." He reached out to touch the stone. "It's real, all right. I almost suspected it was cardboard. Ye gods, it's incredible, nay, *miraculous!*"

The copper statues and bronze friezes proved popular, especially with the dwarves, who delighted in their intricacy.

The artwork commemorated battles against Tion's minions, immortalizing great firstling warriors such as Borengar, founding father of the kingdom, and other great heroes and heroines of his folk.

"This way," called their guide, hurrying ahead of the dawdling group toward the next of the kingdom's wonders, a series of breathtaking bridges.

This time Bavragor was forced to admit that in matters of engineering, the firstlings were unsurpassed. There was insufficient rock to span the plummeting chasms, so gleaming plates of metal had been added to straddle the gaps, the sides secured with wrought-iron balustrades tipped with silver.

When they came to the last of the bridges, their hobnailed boots rang out against the metal, each plate creating a different tone. The notes echoed through the cavernous passageway in a simple but pleasing tune.

"I give in," said Rodario, overwhelmed by the magnificence of it all. "We'll go back to performing idiotic farces and forget the whole idea. No illusion in the world could do justice to this."

"Nonsense," Furgas said briskly. "We can do it, but it'll cost a bit of coin."

They slowly began to thaw out, the snow and ice melting from their garments and running down their mail, leaving them feeling immensely tired but warm.

At length Balyndis came to a halt and knocked on a vast door. A shaft of gold shone through the crack, heralding the glories within.

The rectangular chamber was clad from top to bottom in beaten gold. Warm light emanated from countless candles and lamps, reflecting off the burnished walls. The statues were cast from gold, silver, vraccasium, and rare precious metals quarried from the heart of the mountain. Each gleaming figure was draped with trinkets that could be swapped around at will.

The queen was seated twenty paces away on a throne of pure steel. Guards of both sexes, all dressed in gold-plated mail, watched over her. The ceiling sparkled with ornate mosaics made of beaten silver, gold, and vraccasium tiles.

"Did I say a bit of coin?" Furgas whispered to Rodario. "I meant, *a lot*."

"Borengar's folk welcomes you," the queen said benevolently, signaling for them to approach.

They filed into the hall, with Tungdil at the head of the procession. He bowed courteously, then sank to one knee. The other dwarves followed, but the players contented themselves with a bow. Tungdil introduced them, not forgetting Andôkai, Djerûn, and the absent twins.

"As for me," he concluded, hoping that his speech conformed to protocol, "I'm Tungdil Goldhand of Goïmdil's folk. A matter of grave importance brings us to your court."

"Thank you, Tungdil Goldhand. My name is Xamtys Stubbornstreak the Second of the clan of the Stubborn Streaks, ruler of the Red Range for thirty-two cycles. Your visit intrigues me. I have been without news of my royal cousins and their kingdoms for a good long while." Her mail was made of golden rings and she carried a four-pronged mace as a scepter. Her brown eyes regarded them keenly but kindly.

They were offered refreshments: beakers of piping-hot drink. Rodario sipped contentedly, sighing as the warmth returned to his body for the first time in orbits.

"You say you were brought here by a matter of grave importance?"

"I'm afraid it's bad news," said Tungdil, launching into an

account of the danger threatening Girdlegard, the deaths of the magi, the high king's frailty, and the trouble surrounding the succession. At last he turned to the purpose of their mission.

"Which is why we're here, Your Majesty. We need you to lend us your most talented smith, a smith who can forge the blade by which Nôd'onn will fall. Help us, Queen Xamtys," he implored her. "Help us and save your folk."

The firstling queen turned her brown eyes upon him and stroked the fair down on her cheeks. Suddenly she stopped fiddling and sat up straight. "It seems from your report that Girdlegard is in danger," she said thoughtfully. "We haven't seen the other candidate, which makes me fear the worst. The älfar are accomplished marksmen, and perhaps Gandogar's expedition wasn't blessed with such protection…"

"Pardon me, Your Majesty," Goïmgar broke in indignantly. "King Gandogar has Vraccas's blessing. He's the high king's rightful heir!"

"It isn't my place to judge," the queen said kindly before returning her attention to Tungdil. "I shall be happy to help. What better time than now to renew the bonds between our folks." She lowered her mace and pointed to Balyndis. "This is your new companion. Not only is Balyndis the firstlings' best warrior, she's also our finest smith."

"I don't mean to speak out of turn," interrupted Rodario, "but I was wondering if Her Majesty could tell us how she came to be queen. I thought the line of succession was always male…"

"The long-un has an inquisitive mind, I see. Very well, he shall have his explanation. It all began with a quarrel. Boragil, my father, valued my mother's advice, but considered her incapable of ruling the kingdom on her own. That angered my mother, who demanded to be given the opportunity to try. After much argument, it was decided that my mother should govern the firstlings' destiny for a period of fourteen orbits. It was during this time that the trolls attacked, but my mother had no intention of relinquishing the crown. Instead she marched at the head of the army and defeated the enemy with a combination of cunning and military skill. In so doing, she proved to be a more proficient ruler than my father, and when the fourteen orbits were over she reneged on their agreement and refused to step down. The clans stuck by her and that was that." She rose. "My mother died thirty-two cycles ago, and I ascended the throne."

"I thank Her Majesty for indulging a humble dramatist's curiosity. I shall write her a magnificent part in my play."

An attendant entered the hall with news that Boëndal was seriously hurt. The maga had rushed to his bedside and was doing her best to treat his wounds.

The three dwarves were filled with dread.

"Someone will show you to your quarters so you can get some rest. Our tailors will provide you with warm clothes and fur coats to keep out the cold. I assume you mean to continue your journey tomorrow?" She didn't wait for a response. "In any event, I'll show you the way to the tunnels once you've recovered your strength."

"You know about the tunnels?" Tungdil said, surprised. He was so tired that he could barely suppress his yawns. "Why haven't you used them?"

"My mother wasn't sure what the other rulers would think about a dwarven queen. She kept quiet for fear of conflict and I did the same."

"In that case, Your Majesty, you must send a delegation to Ogre's Death," Tungdil said urgently. "In the name of the assembly, I invite you to join the other rulers and chieftains in deciding our future. You spoke of renewing the bonds between the folks; this is your chance."

"The situation is every bit as serious as he says," Rodario seconded him. "The Perished Land is a formidable foe. I've seen with my own eyes what the orcs have done to Girdlegard, and without your kinsfolk, Nôd'onn will prevail. Speak to the other folks and don't worry about what they might say. This isn't a time for caution."

Tungdil looked at him gratefully. *Who would have thought it?*

Xamtys tapped her scepter firmly against her throne. "As soon as you and your company have commenced your journey to the Gray Range, I shall lead a delegation of firstlings to Ogre's Death and the folks shall be reunited after many long cycles." She smiled at them munificently. "You are right: There is no time to lose."

I know you're only trying to help," said Boëndal, gritting his teeth with pain, "but I don't want your magic. The wounds will get better by themselves."

The firstlings had laid him in a warm chamber, removed his mail, and exposed the afflicted flesh. He had already bled through the first set of bandages and was waiting for the next.

Andôkai, her face as ashen as her patient's, was leaning over him, inspecting the damage. His body was struggling to cope with the puncture wounds: Some of his internal organs had been damaged and he was rapidly losing blood. "I know a great deal about injuries, and quite frankly, I can't share your optimism," she said candidly, her blue eyes clouded with concern. "Put aside your pride, Boëndal, and think of the mission."

"Pride? This isn't about pride!" protested his brother from across the bed. He was determined to keep an eye on things and had refused all offers of refreshment, barely stopping to take off his coat. "It's your sorcery that's the problem. It's not right! Your wretched Samusin might conjure some devilry into his soul."

"Don't be ridiculous," she snapped.

Boëndal closed his eyes, his breath coming in shallow gasps. "Leave...me...alone!"

"By rights you should be dead," she said coolly. "If it weren't for your dwarven constitution, you wouldn't have made it this far. Sheer bloody-mindedness is keeping you going, but your life is in the balance. I need to help while I still have the power. My magic is waning."

Boëndal was in no state to answer. His brother nodded to the door. "Save your hocus-pocus for your own patient, maga. We dwarves can take care of ourselves."

Andôkai got up, one hand resting lightly on the pommel of her sword, and walked silently to the door.

"He didn't mean to offend you," Boëndal whispered. "We appreciate your offer, really we do, but Vraccas will see me through this."

Andôkai flung her cloak over her shoulders. "I hope for your sake that he does." The door slammed and silence descended on the chamber.

"Perhaps she's right..." ventured Boëndal.

"That's enough," Boïndil shushed him. "Vraccas has seen your plight and he'll keep you alive for many more cycles. If either of us deserves to die, it won't be you, so stop fussing and get some rest." He gave his brother another sip of water and hurried to see why the physicians were taking so long with the dressings.

His armor seemed a thousand times heavier than usual and his legs were bowing beneath the overwhelming weight. All he could think about was his brother. "Vraccas be with him," he muttered, remembering Boëndal's deathly pale face. His twin was languishing on the threshold of the eternal smithy and what the maga had said about dwarven resilience and stubbornness was true: A human would never have survived such injuries, and whether or not a dwarf could withstand them, only time would tell.

On his way down the corridor, he bumped into Tungdil, who was hurrying to visit the wounded dwarf. "How is he?" Tungdil asked anxiously.

"Sleeping. He needs new bandages. The first lot are drenched already," said the warrior, visibly distressed. The crazed spark in his eyes had given way to profound concern.

"What about Andôkai? Can't she do anything for him?"

"We don't want her sort of help," Boïndil shut him off. "I always said magic was no good, but Samusin's magic is worse." He hurried away, calling out to the physicians, who came running with bandages.

Tungdil knew it was pointless to argue; the twins had made up their minds. Determination was a virtue, whereas intransigence... *Boëndal would rather die than be healed by the maga.*

He tiptoed into the chamber and saw Boëndal lying waxen-faced in the bed, seemingly dead but for the shallow rise and fall of his chest. The physicians washed away the dried blood and carefully sewed the gaping flesh together, then applied a compress of moss to ease the pain.

"We'll have to go on without him," Tungdil said softly. "He won't last more than a hundred paces in his present state."

"I'll be fine, scholar," came a faint but determined whisper from the bed. Boëndal looked at him pleadingly and reached for his hand. "Another few orbits, and I'll be back on my feet. It's just a couple of scratches, that's all."

Tungdil glanced at one of the physicians, who promptly shook his head. "It's out of the question. The wounds are deeper than they look and there's the internal damage to consider. Any movement will make things worse and he'll die in agony. He's not fit to go anywhere."

"I'm sorry, Boëndal," Tungdil told him, heavy-hearted, "but you have to stay here and rest. You've done your bit for now; just be sure you're back with us when it comes to the great battle against Nôd'onn."

"I'm coming, like it or not," Boëndal threatened. "Boïndil and I stick together! Forging Keenfire is the most important mission in dwarven history and I won't—" He tried to sit up but had barely succeeded in moving when he gave a low groan, his fresh dressings flushing crimson with blood. "I suppose that settles it," he said through gritted teeth. He looked up at his twin. "It's up to you now to protect Tungdil and the rest of the company."

Boïndil was standing stiffly by the bed, searching for the right thing to say. "All our lives we've been together," he said thickly, "and now I'm leaving you behind. It won't be the same fighting without you." He squeezed Boëndal's hand. "The first hundred runts will be for you."

"You've got great plans, then," said his brother, smiling weakly. "Don't overreach yourself, Boïndil; I won't be there to watch your back." They embraced, tears streaming down their bearded cheeks. Never before had they faced a parting such as this.

"You'll have to keep a better check on your temper when I'm not around. Promise you won't let it run away with you?"

Boïndil gave his solemn word. "Get some rest now, brother." He and Tungdil left the chamber. "When do we leave?"

"As soon as possible. Andôkai has done her best to patch up Djerûn with her magic and he's fit to travel. He might be too big for the wagon, though."

"We'll be cramped as it is. There's the three long-uns, Andôkai and her pet warrior, Hammerfist and Shimmerbeard, not to mention the materials for Keenfire—we'll need a couple of wagons at least."

"Don't forget Balyndis," Tungdil reminded him.

"Who?"

"Our new smith."

"A woman?"

"You sound as enthusiastic as Bavragor."

"I've got nothing against women, don't get me wrong. I like a nice well-built lass with plump cheeks and big bosoms, a real woman who you can hold on to and warm yourself against, but—"

"Come on, Boïndil, you know as well as I do that some of the secondling women are excellent smiths. They can be handy on the battlefield as well. Smeralda could fight like a —" He checked himself. *Blast*.

Boïndil stiffened at the mention of his dead lover's name. "Fine, we'll take the woman. If you'll excuse me, I'm tired." He disappeared along the passageway in the direction of his chamber.

Tungdil watched him go. *That was stupid*, he remonstrated with himself. *I need to watch what I say*.

"I'm no stranger to the smithy, believe me," said a high-pitched voice behind him. He whipped round in surprise. "Sorry, I didn't mean to startle you." Balyndis was still dressed in her mail, and her long dark hair framed her rounded face. "I wanted to tell you that it's an honor to be chosen for your mission."

His heart gave a little leap. He was so taken with the idea of traveling through Girdlegard in the company of the female smith that he almost forgot his worries about the twins. He gazed into her brown eyes, unable to say a single word.

"I can handle an ax as well as a hammer, you know."

Tungdil smiled weakly, still incapable of summoning his voice.

Balyndis didn't know what to make of his silence. "If you don't believe me, I can show you."

"Vraccas forbid!" he cried, raising his arms hurriedly. "I believe you, absolutely. I daresay that women are good at fighting too."

The new smith seemed to take offense at his words. "In that case, Tungdil, I insist," she said, reaching for her ax.

Tungdil's eyes were drawn to the formidable muscles in her arms and chest. "Honestly, Balyndis, I didn't mean it like that," he said, trying desperately to repair the damage. "I was worried you might get hurt."

"I see. So you think you can hurt me, do you?"

I wish she'd stop twisting everything I say! "Of course not," he explained hurriedly while Balyndis hefted her ax belligerently and took a few experimental swipes. "Not unless you weren't paying attention. Really, Balyndis, there's no need to prove anything. I believe you!"

"Well, I don't!" boomed a baritone voice. Bavragor stepped up to the smith, his war hammer at the ready. "It's bad enough that Goïmgar fights like a girl. The firstling must prove that she won't be a burden."

She squared her shoulders menacingly. "For that, mason,

your one eye will soon be seeing stars." Already the war hammer and the ax were hurtling toward each other, and Tungdil barely succeeded in leaping clear.

The weapons collided forcefully. It was clear from Bavragor's grunts that he was impressed, but he soon got into difficulties, having failed to allow for Balyndis's strength and speed. By lunging at him from his blind side, she kept forcing him to turn his head. He was so intent on parrying her blade that he didn't notice when she raised her ax suddenly and whacked him on the head. He took a few dazed steps backward and slumped against the wall.

For a moment he looked at the grinning Balyndis in astonishment, then slowly raised his hand and felt his head. His shoulders shook slightly, rising and falling with increasing rapidity until he was roaring with laughter, the passageways echoing with his mirth.

"No one could say I didn't deserve it," he said, still chuckling as he clambered to his feet and extended a rough, calloused hand, which she gladly shook. "You're a fine lass, all right. There's no messing with you."

"Thank goodness we've cleared that up," Tungdil broke in, thankful to have been spared the ordeal. He nodded to Balyndis. "I think everyone agrees that you're an excellent fighter, so maybe we could go to bed and get some sleep before our early start."

The firstling smiled and was about to retire when Bavragor hauled her back. "I've got a better idea. How about taking me to the Red Range's finest tavern so I can taste a draft of your firstling beer? There'll be a song in it for you," he promised. Balyndis didn't need further persuasion and the two of them started down the corridor.

"Aren't you coming, Tungdil?" she shouted as they rounded the corner.

"He's our leader, remember! He's got maps to read, tunnels to check...Of course he's not coming!" said Bavragor, only half joking.

"Don't overdo it," Tungdil warned them. "Those tunnels have got lots of sharp curves!" He saw them off with a wave and retired to his chamber to ponder the events of the orbit. No matter how tempting it was, he knew it wouldn't be wise to fall for Balyndis; the mission required his full attention.

Inside his chamber, the light from the lone oil lamp steeped the polished walls in a gentle glow. It was the perfect ambience for relaxing before the big journey.

"Tungdil?"

He swung round to confront the voice behind him. Ax at the ready, he peered warily into the shadows by the door. "Narmora? Is that you?"

The actress was wearing her black leather armor and exuded a vague air of menace. For some reason Tungdil found himself thinking of Sinthoras.

He kept hold of his ax, his secret antipathy toward the woman growing all the time. *Don't be ridiculous,* he told himself. *She's an ordinary woman.* "What can I do for you?" he asked, trying to smile convincingly.

"Remember what Andôkai said about wielding the ax," she said hesitantly.

"*Keenfire must be wielded by the undergroundlings' foe.* Do you have a suggestion?" he said, perking up.

"What about the älfar?" she said cautiously. "The älfar are your enemies, right?"

"Real älfar are our enemies," he corrected her. "Actresses won't do, but it's kind of you all the same."

She pulled off her head scarf, revealing two pointed ears.

Tungdil took a step backward and tightened his grip on the ax. Long moments of horrified silence passed. "But that's not... I mean, y-you can't be an älf..." he stuttered. Then he laughed out loud in relief. "You almost had me going there, but I know your eyes don't look black in the light!"

Narmora stretched a hand toward the lamp, turned her palm to the ceiling, and muttered unintelligible words. The flame dwindled until there was nothing but a smoldering wick.

She must know some trick. Alchemy or... He stared at the candle in amazement, then turned to Narmora and discovered she was gone. "Narmora?"

Suddenly she loomed behind him. "Half human, half älf," a voice whispered in his ear. "I inherited my mother's gifts and her weapons. My father left me little of value, but his eyes are a boon." The next moment her menacing air was gone. She went over to the lamp and restored the flame by blowing on it gently. "I'm sorry I scared you. Do you believe me now?"

Tungdil composed himself. *That explains why I've never really taken to her.* "I certainly do," he said with a vigorous nod. "I think you've solved the dilemma as to who should wield Keenfire." He looked at Narmora with new respect. "It can't have been easy for you to tell me—but it's nothing compared to the challenge ahead."

"I can't see any other solution," she said simply, her savagery and malevolence suddenly gone. "It's not as though we could ask an orc or a real älf." She stroked the hafts of her weapons. "I've never really fought with an ax. The magus won't have much to fear from Keenfire unless you drill me in axmanship first."

"We'll have to tell the others, you know."

Narmora considered. "Yes, I suppose so—although I don't know how they'll react." It was clear she was thinking primarily of Boïndil.

Tungdil smiled encouragingly. "It's nothing to worry about, I promise."

She smiled roguishly, and for a moment there was something älflike about her after all.

On receiving Tungdil's summons, the rest of the company hurried to his chamber, where he told them of the turn of events. "Which means we'll be able to defeat the magus after all," he finished, waiting anxiously for their reaction.

"Strictly speaking, I ought to kill her," Ireheart said slowly. He showed no sign of making good on the threat.

"Strictly speaking," Tungdil corrected him, "you ought to kill half of her, but which half would that be? Is the left side human and the right side älf, or the other way round? What if it's top and bottom?" He sighed. "Seeing as she's agreed to save Girdlegard, I think Vraccas will let us spare her. There's no other way."

Furgas was hugging the half älf and looked worried, which seemed natural to Tungdil, who realized what a risk Narmora was taking in pitting herself against such a formidable foe.

"Furgas and Rodario will stay here in the firstling stronghold until we—"

"She's not going without me," the prop master said flatly. "Besides, someone with my technical ability would be an asset."

"And you're bound to need a first-rate impresario," added Rodario. A moment later, it occurred to him that the company had no obvious use for his talents, so he settled for looking handsome and putting on a winning smile.

"He's right, you know," said Boïndil unexpectedly. "The enemy won't be able to concentrate with his incessant jawing."

The other dwarves smiled, save for Goïmgar, who seethed quietly in the corner until he finally erupted. "Gandogar is in the Gray Range already," he hissed. "He'll be the one to forge Keenfire, just wait and see! You'll never be made high king." He looked scornfully at Narmora. "I don't know what you're relying on *her* for. She's only half an älf." He flounced to the door and stormed out.

"Fine," said Bavragor, breaking the strained silence. "Narmora can half kill Nôd'onn, and we'll do the rest." Whipping out a tankard that he had smuggled from the tavern, he took a long sip.

The tension dissolved and they laughed in relief.

The following morning Queen Xamtys and her entourage of chieftains and elders accompanied Tungdil and the others over the shimmering bridges and deep into the stronghold's passageways and galleries that reminded the secondlings of home.

Bavragor kept stopping to inspect the masonry, tapping on the walls, running his fingers over the stone, and stamping critically on the floor. "It's certainly not *superior*," he said with unusual diplomacy, "but it's still very good."

At length they came to a vast steel door inlaid with runes of glittering gold. The queen recited the formula and they entered a chamber whose every detail Tungdil recognized from its counterpart in Ogre's Death. At the center of the room were eight rails, and around them a jumble of vats, pulleys, and gears. The engineers soon got the machinery going, and the air filled with hissing, steaming, and rattling, not to mention a smell of hot metal and grease.

"You've taken good care of the equipment," observed Furgas. "No rust, no dust. You could have been out of here in minutes, whenever you decided to go."

"I should have done this cycles ago," Xamtys said regretfully. She gave instructions for two convoys to be made ready for departure—the first for her own delegation, and the other for Tungdil and his friends.

Djerůn had made a full recovery and was allocated a carriage of his own. The firstlings had repaired his armor overnight and it looked almost as good as new. Owing to his great height, they decided to remove the seats from the wagon so he could lie down on the floor. That way he wouldn't run the risk of beheading himself if the height of the tunnel changed.

The rest of the company were spread over two wagons: the five dwarves and the ingots in one, and Andôkai, the players, and the gems in the other.

She looks tired, thought Tungdil. He went up to the maga. "How are you feeling? You said yesterday that you were nearing the end of your strength."

Andôkai tied her blond hair with a strip of leather to stop it from blowing in her eyes during the blustery ride. "Are you prepared for the truth?"

"You don't have to lie to me."

She sat down on the side of one of the wagons and watched the bustle. "My magic will soon be exhausted. Unless we pass through a force field, I won't be able to replenish my stores."

"Is that why wizards like to keep to their realms?"

Her eyes settled on Tungdil's bearded face. "Yes, it's our secret weakness. As you've seen, we can still use our magic outside the enchanted realms, but we can't store it effectively. Straying from the force fields turns us into leaky pouches that lose their contents even when they're not in use. It takes only a powerful charm or two, and our energy is spent." She glanced at Djerûn. "I don't like the idea of being defenseless when my magic runs out. That's why I learned to fight and why I always keep Djerûn with me."

Tungdil thought for a moment. "Maybe we could see to it that Nôd'onn runs out of magic too."

She shook her head. "The spirit inside him has lent him extraordinary powers. I'm sure it won't work."

The dwarf caught sight of Narmora and remembered her trick with the lamp. "Narmora can use magic, can't she?"

"Not exactly. I don't know much about the älfar, but they don't use real magic. It's more a case of innate abilities: the power to conjure up darkness, extinguish fire, influence dreams—small things that strike fear into human hearts and add to the älfar's aura of power."

"But things have changed, haven't they? Sinthoras broke through your magic shield."

"That was cunning, not magic. Remember how the älfar in the desert warded off my magic with amulets? The amulets were a present from Nôd'onn to protect them from the magi. Sinthoras tied his to an arrow and broke my spell." Andôkai rose. "We may as well get going." Their vehicles were ready, and the queen's wagon had been lowered onto its rail. "You mustn't rely on my intervention, Tungdil. I need to conserve my strength."

"I'll tell the others," he promised. *Don't you worry, Keenfire will be forged, with or without your magic,* he added silently to himself.

They joined Xamtys at the top of the ramps. The queen was studying a map. "I can't wait to find out what it's like in the tunnels," she said excitedly, stroking her downy cheeks. "Just think of the looks on their faces when I arrive; those menfolk won't know what's hit them." She jumped into the wagon and released the brakes. "Fashion Keenfire and make haste for the secondling kingdom. We'll be waiting for you." The wagon rolled away and vanished through the mouth of the tunnel. "May Vraccas be with you!"

"And with you!" Tungdil called after her. He climbed up the next ramp and took his seat in the wagon. The map of the tunnels, given to him by the queen, was tucked safely beneath his chain mail. Boïndil took his place next to him, while Bavragor and Balyndis sat together, laughing and joking, on the bench behind.

"Keep it down, can't you?" Boïndil said crossly. Leaving without his brother made him irritable and uneasy, and he felt thoroughly out of sorts.

Rodario made a few scribbled notes, then replaced the cork on his inkwell. He took particular care to seal the bottle tightly so as not to spill its recently thawed contents all over his clothes. "My, my," he said excitedly, "what an adventure! We should build a contraption like this for our theater. The audience could experience for themselves the thrill of traveling through a tunnel like the heroes of our piece."

"It's not an adventure and it won't be thrilling," Goïmgar contradicted him. "Just wait: Your stomach will turn somersaults, your beard will blow in your face, and you'll want to be sick."

"It can't be that bad," the player said blithely. He fastened the safety rope around his waist "I'm not as soft as you think."

The wagon reached the end of the ramp and plummeted almost vertically into the tunnel. At that moment Rodario emitted a terrified scream, closing his mouth only when he felt an uncontrollable urge to vomit. For the first time in ages, Goïmgar looked genuinely pleased.

Beroïn's Folk,
Secondling Kingdom,
Girdlegard,
Winter, 6234th Solar Cycle

Balendilín was in his chamber, ax in hand. He raised it tentatively and took a few practice swipes to check if he could swing it one-handed.

"There's more of them coming, Your Majesty," came an anxious shout from outside. "You ought to see for yourself."

Anyone would think Bislipur's warmongering had lured them to our gates, he thought darkly, leaving his chamber and striding past row upon row of grim-faced warriors until he reached the highest battlements of Ogre's Death and surveyed the land below.

The enemy was everywhere. Black figures, some larger than others, were milling about on the ground, and the air reeked of rancid fat. An unwholesome stench of orcs wafted over from their encampment a mile from the gates where they were preparing to attack. The muffled sound of their shouts reached the battlements.

In the distance, gigantic wooden siege engines, each forty or more paces in height, were rolling toward the stronghold. *They'll be over the first rampart in no time with the help of those things.*

To the dwarf's eyes, the contraptions looked crooked and ungainly, but the beasts cared nothing for the engines' durability or elegance, provided that they fulfilled their purpose, which was to breach the outer defenses so the real invasion could begin. The timber towers had been draped with human skin to protect against firebombs, and the orcs intended to keep them watered for the duration of the assault.

"I didn't expect them to attack so soon," said Bislipur, joining him on the battlements and looking down at the hordes. Dressed in full armor, he looked every bit the dwarven warrior. "There must be ten thousand of them at least. What a blessing I'd already sent word to my kingdom and summoned our troops." He waited for a word of praise, but none came.

"Orcs, bögnilim, a handful of ogres, some trolls, and a contingent of älfar," enumerated Balendilín, surveying the enemy ranks. "Nôd'onn is determined to annihilate us, just as Tungdil said." He watched the combined force of secondlings and fourthlings take up position behind the first rampart and prepare for the attack. *The magus would never send an army of such proportions without securing the human kingdoms first. There's something not right about this.* "If the ramparts fall, we'll retreat inside the mountain," he decided.

"Then what?"

"They'll be lost if they follow us. We know the territory and they don't."

"Are you saying we might not hold the ramparts?" Bislipur asked, surprised. "With two armies of five thousand warriors apiece, we should be able to defend the stronghold for as long as it takes."

"In these dark times nothing is certain. I'm saying we shouldn't count on it." He sent some of his finest warriors to buttress the troops at the entrance to the underground network. *Just in case,* he thought bleakly.

On ascending the parapet, he obtained his first full view of the invading hordes, a motley collection of beasts, vile products of Tion's creation, poised to massacre the dwarves and open the High Pass to their foul kinsfolk in the Outer Lands.

The orcs and bögnilim are wearing armor stolen from Umilante's men. Her soldiers could do nothing to halt their advance. Balendilín watched as the enemy troopers marshaled themselves into disorderly groups, ready to launch their assault and test the dwarves' defenses. "We need two thousand soldiers behind the main gates," he commanded firmly. "Be ready to fight!"

He waited until the snarling, grunting orcs had almost reached the rampart; then he signaled for the gates to be opened, and his warriors sallied forth.

To his satisfaction, the dwarven axes wrought havoc among the brutes who were caught off guard by the counterattack and tried to flee, only to be rounded up and driven back into battle by the trolls.

By then, the dwarves were safely behind the solid walls of Ogre's Death. Three dozen of their number had suffered minor injuries, while several hundred beasts lay dead or dying on the dry earth before the gates. There was great rejoicing among the united armies of Beroïn and Goïmdil.

"See what a formidable force we are when we fight side by side!" Balendilín shouted down to them proudly. He glanced around to see if Bislipur had anything to say.

The fourthling was nowhere in sight.

Underground Network,
Kingdom of Weyurn,
Girdlegard,
Winter, 6234th Solar Cycle

The wagons shot through the tunnels, tearing cobwebs from the walls and ceilings and stirring up clouds of centuries-old dust. Every now and then a shadow took flight from the rattling, rumbling carriages and scampered out of the torchlight into the darkness of a side shaft. What life there was beneath the surface of Girdlegard was of a harmless, nervous variety that left the travelers well alone.

Tungdil and company were approaching the fifthling kingdom from the west. He kept count of the markers on the walls, calculating that they had traveled 250 miles by the end of the first orbit.

He shared the good news when they stopped for a while and lit a fire. "At this rate, we'll be there in four orbits. We're making excellent progress."

They were in a large chamber that served as a junction between two rails. The ceiling of the cavern was supported by naturally formed pillars and carefully hewn arches engraved with runes that testified to their dwarven origins. The wood now spluttering merrily in the flames had come from a left-over stockpile of moldering timber.

"We'll never be able to outwit the dragon," Goïmgar said dismally. "She'll burn us to cinders with her fire."

"We could always shove a long-un down her throat; that should do the trick," retorted Boïndil through a mouthful. "This is delicious, Balyndis. You firstlings certainly know a thing or two about salting and smoking meat." He plucked dried herbs from the rind of the ham and tasted them experimentally.

Bavragor gave Tungdil a nudge. "Isn't she lovely? I've never seen a more handsome—I mean, beautiful—smith." His chestnut eye gleamed contentedly. "And look at her chain mail! She's a master with a hammer."

"Since when do you know anything about smiths?" teased Tungdil, although he too had been admiring the metalwork. He grinned. "You've changed your tune, haven't you?"

"That was before our duel," Bavragor chuckled. "I took a blow to the heart."

Apparently so. The pair had bonded from the moment Balyndis had conquered the mason with her ax and they seemed to be getting closer all the time. Tungdil couldn't begrudge the one-eyed dwarf his happiness. "I thought she whacked you on the head, not the chest."

"Don't talk so fast," Rodario scolded. "I can barely keep up." Sprawled next to the fire, the impresario had been eaves-dropping on their whispered exchange and was frantically transcribing every word. "I want the script to be as authentic as possible."

Meanwhile, Furgas had got up to examine the rail and Narmora was beside him, keeping watch. Djerůn was sitting a few paces away from the others, his weapons laid out around him. As usual, he kept completely still.

"I wish she'd thumped him a bit harder," muttered Goïmgar in a voice so low that only Tungdil could hear. "Oh, Gandogar, if you weren't my beloved sovereign, I'd hate you for lumbering me with such insufferable companions." Like most nights, he was the first to pull up his blankets and settle down to sleep.

The impresario had brought his bag of costumes with him. Bavragor was amused to see that he refused to be parted with them. "Couldn't you have left them with the firstlings?"

Rodario gave him a disapproving look. "Absolutely not! There's no telling when I might need them, and besides, do you know how much they're worth?"

He was interrupted by a sudden bang. It sounded like a single rap of a hammer on stone. The echo rumbled through the tunnels, then faded.

They turned to look at Furgas, who was bent over the rail. "It wasn't me," he said quickly. "It came from the next stretch of tunnel."

Goïmgar sat up. "I know that noise." He reached nervously for his shield. "The spirits of the dead masons are haunting us," he whispered, cowering behind his steel screen. "Vraccas protect us from their ghosts!"

The sound was familiar to Tungdil too. "We heard the exact same noise just before our wagon was derailed near Mifurdania," he said softly. *I wonder if it's a signal. But what would it be conveying? And to whom?*

"Quiet, everyone." Boïndil's warlike instincts had been stirred. He got up and jogged to the mouth of one of the tunnels, while Narmora stood guard by the other. Sticking his head into the darkness, he listened intently. They held their breath for what seemed like an eternity.

Only Andôkai looked untroubled, rummaging casually for her pipe. She filled it and lit it with a burning splint. Balyndis smiled broadly and followed suit, picking up a smoldering ember with her gloved hand and holding it to the tobacco. The two women, who couldn't have been more different in appearance, disappeared in clouds of smoke.

At length Boïndil returned to the fire. "Nothing," he reported. "No noises, no smell."

"We don't want any more accidents," Tungdil told them. "We'll have to be careful.' He settled down to get some sleep.

Furgas and the half älf took their places beside him. "I think we're not the only ones on the move down here," Furgas confided in a whisper. "There's not a speck of rust on the rail ahead."

"So the tunnel is being used on a regular basis," Tungdil conjectured.

"I thought you should know."

"Thank you, Furgas. I'd rather you didn't tell the others. We don't want Goïmgar dying of fright."

Beroïn's Folk,
Secondling Kingdom,
Girdlegard,
Winter, 6234th Solar Cycle

What can I do for you, Bislipur?" asked one of the two sentries politely as the fourthling approached the door to the underground network.

"Die," he said smilingly. "Die nice and quietly." His ax

whipped up and swooped diagonally toward the sentry's unprotected throat.

There was no time to escape the double-handed blow and the guardsman succumbed with nothing but a muffled groan.

His companion managed to reach the bugle with his left hand and the hilt of his club with the other, but already the bloodied ax was slicing through the flesh beneath his chin. The blade jerked upward, cleaving his skull.

Well, that wasn't too hard. Bislipur wiped the blood from his face and gave a short whistle, whereupon two hundred of his most loyal soldiers appeared in the corridor.

"You know what to do," he said tersely before reciting the runes that opened the door to the tunnels. "Show Gandogar's enemies no mercy: They will show none to you."

Underground Network,
Kingdom of Weyurn,
Girdlegard,
Winter, 6234th Solar Cycle

Just as they reached the three-hundred-mile marker, disaster struck. Moments earlier they had exited the tunnel and turned onto a narrow bridge. As far as they could tell, there was nothing but thin air and darkness beneath them.

The first carriage was traveling at full speed when the dwarves felt a sudden judder and the wheels were thrown from the track, tilting the wagon to the side. Sparks flew everywhere as they skidded along on two wheels, trying to right the wagon before it tipped too far. The next moment, they hit the ground and flipped over.

There was a screech of brakes as the second wagon stopped just paces from the scattered bodies.

Tungdil, Balyndis, and Boïndil were in luck: They landed on the bridge, tumbled over, rolled for a bit, and slowed to a halt. Their gloves and armor saved their skin from serious cuts and grazes.

Tungdil discovered to his embarrassment that he was lying on top of Balyndis. His cheeks reddened. She gazed up at him and seemed about to say something, but swallowed her words and just stared.

The spell was broken by the sound of Goïmgar's frantic screams. "Sorry," Tungdil said awkwardly, picking himself up to see what was wrong.

The little dwarf was dangling from the side of the bridge. His hands clung desperately to the stone coping, but his knapsack and his armor were exerting an inexorable downward pull. "Somebody do something!" he whimpered desperately. "I'm falling!" Tungdil broke into a sprint.

Bavragor was lying near the edge of the bridge, a few paces from the stricken artisan. He got up, muttering, groaning, and clutching his head. "I think an ogre just kicked me." Suddenly he noticed the plight of his companion and threw himself forward to grab his arm.

It was too late.

Goïmgar's panicked face vanished from view, his shrill scream fading rapidly.

"Vraccas forfend," stuttered the mason. Boïndil, Tungdil, and Balyndis reached the spot a moment later, only to watch helplessly as the shrinking figure was swallowed by the darkness.

"Move!" Andôkai sped past them, bounded onto the coping, and pushed off forcefully, arms outstretched like a diver.

Her scarlet cloak billowed behind her like a flag; then she too was gone.

The dwarves could hear the swoosh of her cloak but were powerless to intervene. Rodario lit his torch and dangled it into the gloom, but the light was too weak to cut through the blackness.

Long moments passed and at last they saw a faint blue glow in the murkiness below.

"Do you think she hit the bottom and died?" asked Boïndil. "It might be her soul."

Tungdil shot a quick glance at Djerûn, who was immobile as ever. He didn't seem overly concerned about his mistress's safety, which gave Tungdil grounds for hope. *I'm sure she knows what she's doing.*

"It's getting closer," Balyndis shouted excitedly. "It's flying up."

A fierce gust blew toward them, propelling two figures out of the chasm below. The current of air carried the maga and her passenger to the bridge, set them down gently, and died away.

Andôkai's long blond hair was tousled, and the artisan's shimmering beard seemed to have been ransacked by mice. His face was ashen but he wasn't in the least bit hurt.

"That was incredible, Estimable Maga!" exclaimed Rodario. "Absolutely incredible! How selfless and courageous of you. To think that you risked your own precious life to save the dwarf!" He turned to Goïmgar apologetically. "Not that your life is any less precious, of course."

Andôkai seemed determined not to dwell on the incident. "Have you checked the wagon?" she asked Furgas. She gave her cloak a tug and set about plaiting her hair. "Can you fix it?"

The prop master walked over to the vehicle and shook his

head. "The wheels have buckled. We won't get them back on the rail." He bent down. "Someone's been busy," he said. "We're lucky that the other wagons didn't meet the same fate."

"The gold and tionium," cried Boïndil, who had crawled round to the other side of the wagon to check the cargo. "They're gone."

Bavragor gazed gloomily into the chasm. "It's not hard to guess where they are: on a never-ending journey to the bottom of the world." He looked at the maga hopefully.

"No," she said, dismissing his unspoken request. "We'll have to think of something else."

They fell silent. Two key components of the magic weapon had been wrenched from their grasp.

"I knew we'd never make it," whined Goïmgar, unable to hide his glee.

"A fat lot of use you are," Boïndil growled. "I say we throw him back down again. We've lost half the ingots, so we may as well get rid of the pesky artisan as well."

"So what if we've lost a few ingots?" said Tungdil, determined to raise their spirits. "We're on our way to a dwarven kingdom, remember! We're bound to find enough gold and tionium to make a solitary ax."

"Problem solved." Andôkai nodded, giving her leather armor a final tug.

"Excellent. If we've all recovered sufficiently, we may as well get going. Divide yourselves up between the wagons," ordered Tungdil, who was beginning to warm to being in command. "We'll take turns pushing until we reach a downward pitch."

"Don't worry about that," said the maga. She motioned to Djerûn. "Leave it to him."

Beroïn's Folk,
Secondling Kingdom,
Girdlegard,
Winter, 6234th Solar Cycle

This time Nôd'onn's army attacked from the sides.

Dwarven missiles sped toward the approaching siege engines, passing through the moist cladding of human skin, punching holes in the timber and shattering the joists. The sheer scale of the invasion ensured that some of the engines approached unscathed.

At length three wooden towers drew alongside the parapets. As the ramps clapped down, hordes of screeching orcs spewed forth, but the ferocious dwarves stood firm.

Balendilín proved himself an able commander, defending the stronghold so successfully that not a single assailant made it through the dwarven lines.

"Pour oil on the wood," he shouted as soon as the first wave of invaders had been repelled. Already the next wave of beasts was streaming into the towers.

The plan worked. In no time the siege engines disappeared in a blaze of yellow flames. The wood burned like tinder, the flammable sap fueled the fire, the ropes ignited, and the towers collapsed, raining debris to the ground. The enemy retreated, yelping with fear.

Victory came at a price. Fourteen dwarves were slain by an älf who concealed himself on the ramp of the third tower and bombarded them with arrows, showing no regard for the hungry flames. At last his cloak caught alight, but the onslaught continued, ending only when his bowstring was consumed in the blaze.

In spite of the casualties, the mood was upbeat. There was no reason to believe that Ogre's Death would fall.

"You fought bravely and well," Balendilín praised his troops. "Our fallen brothers will live on in our memories and their names shall be etched in gold in the kingdom's great hall." His eyes roamed over the rows of defenders. Their bearded faces gazed back at him, sweaty but smiling; there was plenty of fight in them yet. "Vraccas gave us—"

"Orcs!" The shout came from a sentry who had turned his back to the gates and was listening to the king. "They've got into the stronghold!"

There were hundreds of them. The snarling, roiling brutes were demolishing anything and anyone in their path. In no time they had seized the inner rampart. They held up their swords, axes, lances, and shields triumphantly, taunting the assembled dwarven army.

The tunnels. They must have come up through the tunnels! "The High Pass must not be breached. Children of the Smith, I call on you to destroy the invaders!" cried Balendilín, rousing his soldiers from their shock. "Every beast must die!"

The dwarves jolted into action, storming up the mountainside to fight their ancient foe. Among them was their one-armed king whose courage and tenacity were an inspiration to them all.

At that moment an ogre emerged from the underground hall, lips pressed to an enormous bugle. His piercing call drew cheers and roars from the troops outside the stronghold. The second assault on the ramparts began.

V

Beroïn's Folk,
Secondling Kingdom,
Girdlegard,
Winter, 6234th Solar Cycle

T*hey shouldn't have got this far. Why weren't they stopped by the guards?* Balendilín had no time to consider what had happened to the warriors who were guarding the entrance to the tunnels: He and his army were battling a seemingly endless onslaught of ogres, orcs, and bögnilim. For every beast he felled, two more appeared before him, and he could always be sure of hewing flesh.

At last Balendilín's guards managed to turn the tide of the surprise attack and drive the invaders back to the tunnels. The battle was bloody and cost many dwarven lives, but the king's troops finally reached the threshold of the hall where the underground network began. They could advance no farther.

How many more? Balendilín's heart sank as he surveyed the waiting beasts. They were trapped in the hall, but by no means defeated, and their numbers were swelling as the tunnels disgorged more orcs.

A messenger pushed his way through the dwarven ranks, bringing more bad tidings for Balendilín. "The beasts have outmaneuvered us," he gasped. "They've attacked from the rear. The gates of Ogre's Death are open and the first two ramparts have been taken."

By now Balendilín was beginning to suspect that the

dwarves had been betrayed. "Flood the ramparts with boiling oil," he ordered. "That will—"

"We can't. They've destroyed the vats."

Destroyed? A moment ago, he had been confident that the enemy would be defeated; now his faith seemed misplaced. *To destroy the vats they'd have to know where to find them, in which case...* "Give the order to retreat. We'll defend the stronghold from within. Close the gates and abandon the ramparts." He clapped him on the shoulder. "Hurry!"

The messenger nodded and sped away.

Balendilín was certain that the secondlings' predicament had nothing to do with bad luck. Not only had they been attacked through tunnels whose existence had been secret for hundreds of cycles, but their defenses had been sabotaged by enemies who seemed to know the stronghold inside out, and now they were in danger of being outmaneuvered.

Someone with intimate knowledge of Ogre's Death had helped them to plan the invasion. *What kind of dwarf would do such a thing?* Balendilín could think of no one who would stoop so low as to ally themselves with orcs. *Nôd'onn must have used his sorcery to draw out our secrets.* There was no time to hesitate: He had to act fast.

"I need two hundred warriors. The rest of you stay here and hold back the orcs," he commanded, turning and marching away.

He was on course for the High Pass, where he intended to destroy the bridge before the orcs got hold of it and allowed fresh hordes to flood into the stronghold from the Outer Lands. His fury and hatred of Nôd'onn grew stronger with every step.

Underground Network,
Kingdom of Weyurn,
Girdlegard,
Winter, 6234th Solar Cycle

Surely he must be tired by now," said Rodario, puzzled. "I'd be exhausted if I had to push both wagons."

"Unlike some people, Djerûn is no stranger to hard work," the maga said sternly.

The impresario gave her an injured look and stuck out his chin. "Perhaps the Estimable Maga could tell me what I've done to be treated with such contempt?"

She turned her back on him. "Climb in, Djerûn; there's another downward pitch."

The armored giant squeezed into the rear wagon, trying to make himself as small as possible so as not to injure the others or crack his head on any low archways.

"Very well," said Rodario, refusing to give in. "You can ignore me if you like, but prepare for the consequences. I happen to be writing a drama in which you play a leading role. You'll have only yourself to blame if you make a bad impression."

The maga's eyes bored into his. "Perhaps Djerûn should attend the first performance. You'll know from his reaction whether I like your play. If he raises his ax, you should run." The impresario held her gaze, but she refused to back down. "It isn't because of anything you've done, Rodario. Quite frankly, I don't like your manner. It's foppish."

Rodario frowned, his mood completely spoiled. "Why don't you come straight out and tell me that I'm not a real man? In your opinion, a man must have muscles, know how to wield a sword, and command the mystic arts."

"You understand me better than I thought," she said scathingly. "Since you fail on all three counts, you should stop your tiresome flirting. It's getting on everyone's nerves."

The maga's put-down was delivered in her usual strident voice. Rodario went a deep shade of red and was about to retaliate when the wagon plunged and picked up speed. Ink spilled out of the open bottle, washing over the parchment and onto his clothes. He fell into a wounded silence.

With one hand resting on the brake, Tungdil peered ahead, hoping to spot any potential obstacles before it was too late. Of course, if the rail was broken, nothing would save them. Boïndil was sitting beside him, eyes straining into the darkness too.

There was a generous gap between the two wagons and soon they were traveling at top speed. Suddenly the temperature seemed to rise, and the warm wind buffeting their faces acquired the sulfurous odor of rotten eggs.

"There's light ahead," shouted Boïndil. "It looks orange."

Shooting out of the tunnel, they raced toward another bridge whose basalt pillars spanned a vast lake, the surface of which was incandescent with light. Lava twisted and snaked its way along the bottom, causing the crystal-clear water to bubble and boil. The rising vapors warmed the air and made the atmosphere so humid that sweat started streaming from their pores. Breathing was difficult, not least because of the stench.

The molten lava lit up the cavern, a vast irregular hollow of two or more miles across, with a ceiling some five hundred paces above the water.

Their wagons trundled over the long bridge. Tungdil glanced over the side. *A spectacular place, but I'll be glad to get out of here.*

At that moment they heard hammering again.

It began with a single rap, a piercing tone that rose above the gentle bubbling of the water.

Goïmgar's head whipped back and forth as he strove to locate its source. "It's the ghosts of our forefathers," he whispered. "My great-grandmother told me stories about bad dwarves who trespassed against the laws of Vraccas. They were barred from the eternal smithy and condemned to roam the underground passageways. They avenge themselves on any mortal who crosses their path."

"I suppose you believe the stories about man-eating orcs as well," said Bavragor with a scornful laugh.

"Oh, those stories are true," Boïndil growled from the front. "I can vouch for that. His great-grandmother was probably right." Goïmgar shrank down farther into the wagon until only his eyes were visible over the side.

"That's enough, Boïndil," Tungdil said sharply. Even as he spoke, a second rap echoed through the grotto, reverberating against the glowing stone walls.

This time it didn't stop.

The raps grew louder and the intervals briefer until the hammering swelled to a deafening staccato that shook the rock, dislodging loose stones from the ceiling. Small fragments rained down on them, missing the bridge by a matter of paces and splashing into the bubbling lake.

"Look!" shrieked Goïmgar, beside himself with fear. "Vraccas have mercy on us! The spirits are coming to drag us to our deaths."

They looked up to where he was pointing. Figures detached themselves from the rock and stared down at them. Tungdil counted at least three hundred before he gave up.

Still they kept coming. There was no denying that they

looked like dwarves: Some were wearing armor, some dressed in normal garb, others clad in little more than a leather apron. Male, female, warriors, smiths, and masons, their pale faces stared accusingly at them and the hammering increased. Suddenly their arms flew up in unison and pointed in the direction the travelers had come.

"They want us to leave," whispered Goïmgar. "Turn back, I beg you. Let's walk across Girdlegard; I'll fight the orcs, I promise."

Spirits. Tungdil's blood ran cold at the sight of their empty stares. The molten lava stained their ashen faces with its blood-red glow. He had read about ghosts in Lot-Ionan's books and now he'd seen the living proof. *I'm not going to let you ruin our mission.*

They swept into the next tunnel, away from the cavern, the lake, and the spirits. After a while the hammering faded too.

Beroïn's Folk,
Secondling Kingdom,
Girdlegard,
Winter, 6234th Solar Cycle

It was just as Balendilín had feared.

On reaching the High Pass, he and his warriors found dead dwarves strewn across the ramparts, blood trickling across the stone. They hadn't had time to draw their weapons and defend themselves, which seemed to suggest that the murderer had been a friend. *A friend bewitched by Nôd'onn and turned traitor. Confound the wizard and his magic!*

The air was foul with the stench of orc and they could

hear the rattle of cogs and the clatter of stone as the bridge unfolded, slab by slab. The traitor had beaten them to it.

"Run!" shouted Balendilín. There was no need to say more; everyone knew what had to be done if disaster was to be averted.

Tearing up the steps, they made for the chamber that housed the mechanism operating the bridge. On the other side of the chasm, the beasts were braying and cheering in excitement as the gangway unfurled. The dwarves tried not to listen to their shouts.

Suddenly they found themselves confronted by a guard of one hundred orcs, tall, powerful specimens, bristling with weaponry. Balendilín and his warriors would have to fight tooth and nail to get through.

Both sides threw themselves into the battle with ferocity, each more determined than ever to wipe their enemies from the face of the earth. Green blood mingled with red, limbs were severed, teeth sent flying, and the bloodcurdling noise of the fighting competed with shouts and jeers from the hordes across the chasm whose rapacious hunger could barely be contained.

Balendilín's arm grew heavier with every blow. His muscles were tiring from the strain of wielding his ax, but stubbornness kept him from flagging. "Show no mercy!" he cried. "The bridge must be destroyed before it's too late."

"It's too late already, Balendilín," said Bislipur. The words echoed through the stone stairway, but of the speaker there was no sign. He didn't sound particularly troubled by the secondlings' plight. "The dwarves of Beroïn and Goïmdil will meet their doom together. It was easy enough to arrange, once the orcs were acquainted with the tunnels."

"You told them?" The king's ax slashed the vile visage of

an orc. There was a sound of shattering bone and the beast toppled over, his skull a bloodied wreck. The path was clear and the dwarves surged into the chamber to attack the last dozen foes who were prepared to die rather than lose control of the bridge. Gasping for breath, Balendilín stopped for a moment. "Why?"

"This isn't what I wanted, but you thwarted my plans with your ridiculous challenge to the succession. Thanks to you and the high king, I had to improvise a little, but I'm not one to mourn what might have been. I wanted a war against the elves, but orcs will do the job just as well—if not better."

Balendilín tried to see where the voice was coming from, but the echo was deceptive. "I'll kill you for your treachery," he vowed, full of loathing.

His words were met with mocking laughter. "Others have threatened the same, but they've never made good on their promise. You won't either, King Balendilín, not now that I've deprived you of your subjects and your stronghold."

Balendilín lingered no longer, rushing instead to join the surviving warriors in the battle for the chamber. At last he risked a glance through an embrasure.

Two-thirds of the bridge had been lowered already and a few of the beasts, unable to restrain themselves, were jumping the gap. Some fell to their deaths, others caught hold of the edge and dangled for a moment before plummeting into the chasm below.

We have to stop them. Balendilín let out a ferocious battle cry and threw himself against the last remaining orc, driving his ax with all his might into the creature's side. The blade ate its way through the grease-smeared armor, releasing a jet of dark green blood. He pulled out his weapon, parried his antagonist's sword, and struck where he had hit before. After a third blow, the beast staggered and died.

It was only then that Balendilín caught sight of the twisted levers and broken handles that served to operate the bridge.

"The bridge is down," one of his soldiers reported. "The beasts are storming the kingdom, Your Majesty."

Frozen in horror, Balendilín stared at the mangled machinery. He grabbed the lever on which the future of his kinsfolk, the future of all Girdlegard, depended, but it was jammed.

"Don't forsake your children, Vraccas," he cried in desperation, leaning against it with all his force. Changing his tactics, he tore out the lever, rammed his blade into the slot, and pulled down on the shaft. He looked out.

It was working! The columns retracted and the walkway dropped a few paces, sagging dangerously in the middle. Balendilín heard the vast stone slabs snapping and cracking; then the noise was drowned out by screams of terror as the invading beasts realized that nothing could stop them from plunging to their deaths. At that moment the bridge gave way, pulling the creatures with it. The assembled hordes on the far side of the chasm howled in disappointment.

"Your Majesty, you're wounded," said one of his warriors in concern. Balendilín looked down to see blood seeping from the left side of his torso. There was a huge slit in his chain mail where an orcish sword had struck.

"It's nothing," he mumbled, wrenching his ax from the slot. "We'll finish off the creatures who made it over the bridge, then go back to help the others. We'll deal with the traitor later."

As they battled their way back to the tunnels, it became apparent that the Blue Range was riddled with enemy troops. Every corridor, every passageway, every chamber brought forth more orcs and bögnilim patrolling the territory in small groups or big gangs.

How much longer will we be able to hold them back? Balendilín prayed to Vraccas for help.

On approaching the entrance to the tunnels, they heard the bestial cries of dying orcs. From the sound of it, the enemy troops were being massacred.

"I gave the warriors strict instructions not to attack! A pitched battle would be fatal. We'll be outnumbered!" The king and his company hurried to the aid of their comrades, but were greeted by an entirely unexpected—and inexplicable—sight.

Advancing in the opposite direction was a battalion of dwarves who had popped up behind the orcs and taken them by surprise. While the battalon cut its way through the beasts from the rear, Balendilín's own troops had seized the initiative and launched an offensive, thereby squeezing the enemy between two fronts.

Balendilín ordered his company to attack, and they joined the fray. At length the two dwarven armies met in the middle, their gleaming axes making quick work of the last orcish troopers.

"I don't like to be late for a battle," declared a warrior in beautifully fashioned mail. The voice was a little high-pitched, the beard on the thin side, and the armor revealed two large bulges that seemed distinctly unmanly. The dwarf was clutching a golden mace, now stained with orcish blood.

"I am Xamtys II of the clan of the Stubborn Streaks, queen of Borengar's folk and commander of the firstlings." She turned one of the corpses over with her foot. "I came here for a meeting of the assembly, and what do I find? Orcs! I suppose it's one way of letting off steam between debates."

Balendilín quickly recovered from the surprise. "Queen Xamtys, you are most welcome here. Thank you for coming to the aid of your cousins in their hour of need. My name is Balendilín Onearm of the clan of the Firm Fingers, king of the secondlings. Was it Tungdil or Gandogar who asked you to come?" He prayed silently that it was Tungdil.

"It was Tungdil. He convinced me to put an end to the cycles of silence." She held out her hand and he shook it. "What's going on here?"

He described in as few words as possible the fate that had befallen Ogre's Death and the betrayal of the dwarves by their own. He was interrupted by a messenger bearing news that the main gates were about to fall to the besiegers.

"Leave the range," Xamtys advised him. "If you've been betrayed, they'll know every passageway and every cavern." She placed a hand on his shoulder. "Come to my kingdom and shelter with the firstlings until Nôd'onn has been defeated and the beasts thrown out of your lands."

"I can't," he said quickly.

"King Balendilín, this is no time for stubbornness," she said gently. "You and your folk will be overwhelmed by the enemy, and for what gain? My warriors will have their work cut out saving Girdlegard without you. I propose that we take the tunnel back to my kingdom and send messages to Tungdil and Gandogar to inform them of the change of plan." She studied Balendilín's face and saw with relief that he knew she was right.

"Get the womenfolk and children out of here," he instructed his guards. "Squeeze as many of them as possible into the wagons. Anyone left behind will have to wait for our return; lone dwarves will have no trouble concealing themselves in the mines and quarries. Destroy the key bridges. The orcs will be hard-pressed to track them down."

Withdrawing the troops and abandoning the kingdom amounted to a defeat, but Balendilín had no choice if his folk were to survive. *We wouldn't be in this position if it weren't for Bislipur,* he thought bitterly.

He put his mind to organizing the retreat and dispatched volunteers to convey the news to the far reaches of the kingdom and warn the clans that the army had withdrawn. "Tell them it won't be for long," he commanded. "I give my word that I'll be back in a few weeks to kill the orcs."

He hurried away to the great hall, anxious to save the ceremonial hammer from desecration by the beasts. There was no need to worry about the secondlings' hoard: The treasures were protected by a runic password known only to the king.

Balendilín picked up the hammer from its place beside the abandoned throne and listened to the battering rams thudding against the main gates. The pounding noise went straight through him, heralding the doom of Ogre's Death as clearly as if Tion himself were thumping on the door.

He took a last melancholy look at the throne, the stone pews, the tablets inscribed with Vraccas's laws, the lofty columns, and the beautifully sculpted bas-reliefs. Golden sunshine sloped through the chinks in the ceiling, bathing the hall in warm light. *How much of this will be left when I return?*

"Surely the king isn't abandoning his realm?"

"Bislipur!" Balendilín whipped round toward the marble tablets. The traitor stepped out from behind one of them, the stone trinkets in his beard tinkling softly as he walked.

"I was hoping to meet you alone without any of your slavish attendants. It was tiresome of you to destroy the bridge.

I was sorry to see it go." He raised his ax and drove it into one of the sacred tablets, cracking the stone and breaking it apart. "But patience is a virtue. The orcs will destroy your kingdom, just as I will put pay to your laws."

The king descended from the dais. "You can shatter the tablets, but the words will be carved again. You shan't destroy us, Bislipur. The children of the Smith stand united. Haven't you heard? The firstlings have come to our aid, and many of your allies have been slain by their axes."

"They're not allies; they work on my behalf. The orcs are only instruments of my revenge," Bislipur said calmly. He demolished the remains of the tablet. "Enjoy your little victory while you can. You'll never defeat Nôd'onn: He's dangerous in his insanity, and he's far too powerful for you." The second tablet shattered, splinters of polished stone striking the flagstones and scattering across the floor.

"Enough!" Balendilín was at the foot of the dais and nearly upon the traitor. Without stopping he dropped the hammer and drew his ax from his belt. The fourthling was stronger, he knew, but his lameness made him slow and clumsy. "Tell me why."

"A fine duel this will be," laughed Bislipur. "Two cripples locked in combat."

"This isn't a battle of words," the king said grimly.

Bislipur smiled. "I guess the dwarves of Beroïn will have to find a new leader." His ax hurtled out of nowhere, but Balendilín ducked, flinging out his arm and using his momentum to strike.

Cursing, Bislipur leaped back, but the metal spike on Balendilín's ax head caught his unarmored calf, ripping through leather and fabric. Blood oozed from the wound.

"Why are you doing this?" Balendilín demanded. "Is it

because your favorite wasn't elected high king? Are you so obsessed with waging war on the elves that you betrayed your own kin? Is that it?"

Bislipur rushed forward and launched a series of feint attacks, but Balendilín saw through them and drew back, steeling himself for the real assault. They had crossed the breadth of the vast hall and were battling along a passageway that led to a bridge. The ground was twenty or more paces beneath them.

"The succession never interested me," spat Bislipur. "My only desire was for war. The elves would have destroyed you."

He dealt the blow so forcefully that it was impossible to parry. At the last moment Balendilín managed to deflect it, but he almost lost his ax.

"It makes no sense, Bislipur. Has Nôd'onn bewitched you? Why would you betray your folk?"

"My folk? The fourthlings aren't my folk! You were closer to the truth than you realized." His ax whistled through the air. Balendilín blocked it, but the force of the blow numbed his hand.

"I'm too strong, too warlike to be a puny son of Goïmdil. Remember, you said so yourself." He struck again and this time the ax flew out of Balendilín's fingers and clattered to the bridge. "I'm a child of Lorimbur, and I will go down in history as the thirdling who brought misery on the other dwarven folks," he said darkly. "I have succeeded where all others failed."

Balendilín grabbed his arm and stopped the next blow, but the traitor head-butted him with his helmet. The king staggered backward, his vision starry and bloodied. Bislipur's cocky laughter rang in his ears.

"What a blow to you that Tungdil is a thirdling or he could

have succeeded you on the throne. Oh, he'll weep when he sees the ruins of Ogre's Death. I've a good mind to stick around and ambush him. Killing him and his miserable company would give me pleasure."

"A thirdling? Never." It was all Balendilín could do not to fall from the bridge.

"I know my kind when I see them. It's an instinct we've got. Trust me: Your protégé is a thirdling, a dwarf killer. You may as well get used to the idea—before I kill you and feed your entrails to the orcs."

"You lie!" The king leaned back against the parapet, his legs giving way.

Smiling malevolently, Bislipur raised his ax. "What if I do? You're going to die anyway."

The blade swooped down but Balendilín saw only a fleeting shadow.

Underground Network,
Kingdom of Tabaîn,
Girdlegard,
Winter, 6234th Solar Cycle

The sound of falling rock gave Tungdil just enough warning to pull on the brake. Even so, the force of the collision sufficed to throw the wagon from the rail and give its passengers a thorough shaking.

"The spirits need to work on their timing," said Bavragor, wiping the dust from his brow. He turned to Balyndis, who let him wipe her face. "I bet the ceiling was meant to collapse on us." He reached for his drinking pouch and took a sip of brandy.

"It's nothing to worry about." Rodario scowled, springing from the wagon. "Our industrious giant will clear away the debris and we'll soon be on our way." He glanced at Andôkai. "Unless, of course, the Estimable Maga would prefer to blast through the tunnel with one of her gusts." His tone was deliberately sniffy: He was still cross with the maga for spurning his advances in front of the group.

Goïmgar, pale with fear, kept his eyes suspiciously on the ceiling and refused to leave the safety of his seat. Meanwhile, Andôkai was already inspecting the blocked tunnel and giving instructions for the rubble to be cleared. It soon became apparent that the task was too much even for Djerûn.

"By the look of things, the ceiling has gone entirely," said Bavragor, who was clambering over the fallen rock and studying the walls. "I'd say someone went to a lot of trouble to organize this."

Furgas hurried to take a closer look. He ran his hands over the rock, then nodded. "You're right. The roof of the tunnel is riddled with holes. Whoever it was wanted to make certain that the ceiling would collapse once the struts were knocked away."

"Ghosts," whispered Goïmgar tremulously. "We should have listened to their warning. They're trying to get us killed."

Boïndil turned on him fiercely. "I never thought I'd say this, but Hammerfist's drunken singing is a thousand times more bearable than your complaining." His inner furnace had been burning high for some time, and he needed to let off steam.

"Keep a check on yourself, Boïndil," Tungdil pleaded. "I know it's hard and it's been a long while, but you mustn't let your temper get the better of you." He rummaged through his knapsack and brought out Xamtys's map. "We have to turn back. There's an exit about a mile from here." He turned to Goïmgar. "The spirits have answered your prayers: We're going back to the surface."

"Whereabouts are we?" asked Andôkai.

"According to my calculations, we're in the southeastern corner of the kingdom of Tabaîn. It shouldn't be too much of a problem to find the next entrance. Tabaîn is dead flat; it's just one vast plain."

"It's not fair," Bavragor grumbled moodily. "Why should cowardly little Shimmerbeard get his way? All that blasted riding was bad enough. I'm not built for traipsing around overland, and I can't say I'm fond of the sun."

"You'll get used to it soon enough," snapped Boïndil. "If you'd taken your turn at the High Pass with the rest of us, you'd know that sunshine can be pleasantly warming."

"It wasn't worth the risk," Bavragor snapped back. "I didn't want to end up like my sister."

Balyndis stiffened. Sensing the sudden tension, she stepped in front of Bavragor to stop things from getting out of hand. He grabbed her arm and pushed her away.

"Be careful," he warned her. "Don't turn your back on him when he's angry. His ax moves faster than his mind."

The warrior's muscles tensed, his hands gripping the hafts of his axes. "Is that right?" he growled, lowering his head belligerently.

"Stop it, both of you!" commanded Tungdil. "The two of you can carry the ingots until you've used up your excess energy. Djerûn will take over when you're tired." They reluctantly obeyed.

Tungdil fell into step with Balyndis and briefly recounted the history of the feud. "Neither will give an inch. One of them is overburdened by grief, the other by anger."

"It's sad," she said, her plump face full of compassion. "Sad for both of them."

He dropped his voice, stopped walking, and leaned toward her. "Maybe we'll run into a pack of orcs so Boïndil can work off his anger. I'd rather we didn't have to, but it might be for the best." Her scent filled his nostrils: She smelled as delectable as fresh oil or polished steel.

"What are you waiting for, Tungdil?" shouted Goïmgar, who had finally left the wagon and was hurrying after the others. "Maybe I'm mistaken, but I thought leaders were supposed to *lead*..."

"You're absolutely right." He hurried past him and joined Boïndil and Bavragor, who were carrying their burdens in silence. Neither wanted to appear weaker than the other by handing their ingots to Djerûn and admitting defeat.

Suddenly they heard a loud rattling ahead. The next instant, a wagon sped down the rail toward them. In the nick of time they leaped aside.

Djerûn whipped out his ax and brought it down in one fluid movement. The wagon flipped off the rail and flew into the wall. At once the giant was beside it. He turned it upside down to check for passengers. There were none.

"That's funny. I suppose someone must have left it in a side passage, and now it's worked its way free," said Rodario. "Luckily I've got the reflexes of a panther; otherwise I'd be dead." Furgas responded with an incredulous look.

"The ghosts," whimpered Goïmgar. "They're trying to kill us."

"Don't be ridiculous," Boïndil said witheringly. He set down the ingots, went up to the wagon, and sniffed at it. "Well, it certainly hasn't been near any orcs. I'd be able to smell the fat on their armor." He crawled into the wagon and emerged only when he had something to show for his efforts. "A shoe buckle," he announced, lifting it up for the others to see. "Silver alloy. It's not especially old, but it looks quite worn, judging by the dirt and scratches." He pocketed it.

I've seen that buckle somewhere before, thought Tungdil to himself. "We can't do anything about it now," he told the others. "Let's carry on."

Boïndil scooped up his ingots and the company marched off.

Beroïn's Folk,
Secondling Kingdom,
Girdlegard,
Winter, 6234th Solar Cycle

Balendilín flung himself to the ground. The blade whistled over his head and crashed into the side of the bridge. He kicked up at Bislipur, driving his foot into his groin, then drew his dagger and rammed it into his boot. In an instant, the traitor's groan became a bellow.

At last Balendilín's vision cleared and he could see his antagonist above him—just in time to avoid the furious blow rushing his way. He rolled to the side and the ax hit the bridge.

This time Bislipur was prepared and the weapon rose again, swinging up toward Balendilín. The blade sliced through his chain mail, penetrating his wounded chest. The spike on top of the ax head embedded itself in the metal rings.

"Fly away, you one-armed cripple," laughed Bislipur. He gripped the ax with both hands and pulled his enemy toward him, only to hurl him against the balustrade. Balendilín slid to the edge of the bridge and saw the chasm beneath him. "That's if you can fly with one hand."

"Let's see if you do any better," cried the king, reaching out to stab him with his dagger. The blade entered the traitor's forearm just as Balendilín rolled over the side.

Hanging on to the dagger with all his might, he pulled the screaming Bislipur with him. *I'm taking the traitor with me,* he vowed.

To his great surprise, his flight ended after only two paces as he slammed onto a ledge that was all that remained of an ancient archway erected beneath the bridge. The dagger tore through his enemy's arm.

Bislipur shot past him, letting go of the ax to make a grab for the protruding stone. He succeeded in stopping his fall, but dangled by one hand; the dagger had slit his other arm from the wrist to the elbow.

"It isn't over yet," he gasped, choking with pain and exertion as he dragged himself onto the ledge. His eyes blazed with hatred. "I only need one hand to strangle you, Balendilín." He crawled across the stone toward him.

With a terrible shriek, the king seized the ax embedded in his chain mail and tore it out of his chest. "Oh, it's over, all right," he shouted, smashing the blade against the traitor's helmet. There was a cracking and splintering noise as the metal crashed into his skull. Blood streamed down Bislipur's face. "I promised to kill you, and I've kept my word."

He let go of the haft, thrust his foot into the traitor's face, and pushed him over the edge. The bleeding body plunged down, hitting the ground twenty paces below with a muffled thud and splattering over the stone.

May your soul smolder forever in Vraccas's flames. Balendilín closed his eyes and lay down on the ledge. The next moment he blacked out with pain.

They found him barely conscious and dangerously close to

falling from the narrow shelf. He was carried to the tunnels, where his wagon was the last to leave.

Kingdom of Tabaîn,
Girdlegard,
Winter, 6234th Solar Cycle

The snow sparkled for the last time that afternoon as the sun dropped below the flat horizon. Thousands of glittering diamonds studded the immense white plain as daylight faded to dusk.

Suddenly, in the middle of the untouched snow, a boulder began to stir. Cracks opened in its white cladding; then it rolled to one side and a woman struggled out of the ground beneath it. She stood up and took a few paces, cutting a channel through the immaculate blanket of flakes.

"Samusin protect us," gasped Andôkai as she surveyed the perfectly flat land. In the far distance, dark splodges marked the site of settlements, and each was topped with a column of smoke. She knelt down to make herself less visible and pulled her cloak tighter to keep out the biting cold. "The orcs are here already. They must have invaded from the north." The winter air, fresh and frosty, filled her lungs and made her cough.

Looking around, she saw black flecks moving across the horizon on their way to a town, village, or hamlet, wherever was next on their mission of destruction.

Andôkai closed her eyes and focused her mind. Almost immediately she sensed the weak force field running through the earth beneath her, its energy harnessed by Nôd'onn for his black art.

"We're in what's left of Turguria," she said slowly. "The enchanted realm was rich in magic energy, but there's almost nothing left." All the same, she took the opportunity to replenish her powers, her face contorting with pain as she siphoned the magic from the land.

A helmet popped out of the hole in the snow, followed by a pair of keen brown eyes that flicked to and fro. "The sooner we get out of here, the better," Boïndil said surlily. He emerged into the open, while the others hurried up the last few steps. "Now I know why I've been feeling so peculiar. It's this magical malarkey; it never did anyone any good." He gave himself a shake and pushed the boulder back over the hole, thereby concealing the entrance to the underground network. "Let's go."

"Wait." Tungdil had followed Andôkai's gaze. He shivered. His breath left plump white clouds in the air and his beard was already frozen solid. "You're right, maga. The orcs must have crossed over from the Perished Land. The hordes from Toboribor could never have got here this quickly."

"That makes it worse," commented Goïmgar in his customary whine. "I—"

"If you don't shut up, I'll make you," Boïndil threatened. "Can't you see we're trying to think?"

"You're trying to think? You're not even capable of—"

Ireheart whirled around and threw himself on the artisan with a wild shriek. Goïmgar ducked behind his shield and cried for help.

"Stop that, Boïndil!" The warrior paid no attention. *He'll tear him limb from limb.* Tungdil launched himself on Boïndil, and Bavragor followed suit. The three dwarves disappeared in a cloud of snow from which loud curses, the sound of punches, and a great deal of coughing could be heard.

With Djerůn's help they succeeded in pulling Boïndil away. By some miracle, he had refrained from using his axes, thus sparing the others more serious injuries. Their bloody noses and bruised faces were proof enough of his formidable strength.

"I'm sorry," panted Boïndil. "It's my fiery spirit." He scrabbled in the snow for his helmet and tried to come up with an appropriate excuse. "He provoked me and then I..."

"Let's forget about it." The right half of Tungdil's face was throbbing painfully and he wasn't in the mood for delivering a lecture. "You're welcome to slaughter the next lot of orcs by yourself."

Balyndis took care of their wounds by clumping snow together and pressing it against their bruised and battered limbs. They set off in silence on a northeasterly bearing.

Andôkai drew alongside Tungdil. "There's no smoke ahead," she said. "Nôd'onn must have ordered the orcs to quell any resistance in Turguria and the other enchanted realms before taking on the human kingdoms." She pointed to the east. "There's a fortified city in Tabaîn, just across the border from here. I vote we find ourselves a room. We're not dressed for sleeping in the open, especially not when it's freezing outside. Besides, the citizens will be glad of a few extra swords."

Tungdil nodded his agreement. It was nighttime when the company reached the gates of a city marked on the map as Roodacre.

Beroïn's Folk,
Secondling Kingdom,
Girdlegard,
Winter, 6234th Solar Cycle

No sooner were the wagons rolling along the rail than Balendilín and Xamtys encountered the next setback. Nôd'onn's troops had already started to occupy the tunnels and barricade the tracks.

They managed to speed past the first band of waiting orcs, but a little farther along the tunnel they were pelted with stones by ogres and trolls while the second band of orcs charged onto the rail.

The ambush cost them four wagons, but the remaining carriages turned off at a junction, only now they were heading north and not west.

Before they reached the next corner, Xamtys signaled for them to halt. She made her way to the king's wagon to confer with Balendilín. "They've blocked the rail to my kingdom," she said, clenching her jaw in frustration. "It's too dangerous for us to use the tunnels. For all we know, the orcs have sabotaged the tracks and we'll plunge straight into a chasm."

"Bislipur must have told them about the tunnels some time ago," said Balendilín. His attendants saw their chance and redressed his wound. *It doesn't bear thinking about. The dwarves built these tunnels for the protection of Girdlegard and now Tion's creatures are using them to conquer our kingdoms.*

"We can't go overland, Balendilín." Xamtys inspected his wound and shook her head. "It's winter and we won't find anything to eat on the way. None of us are equipped to trudge through snow and ice. We'd be lucky if half of us survived without freezing or starving." She took off her helmet and two plaits unfurled, draping themselves over her shoulders. "We'll have to come up with another idea. The Red Range—"

"No, Xamtys." He stopped short, gasping with pain. His strong hand gripped the side of the wagon while the dressing was removed. "The Red Range is out of the question." He pulled out a map and placed his finger over a dot at the heart of Girdlegard. "This is where we'll go. It's a somber place, I know, and a curse hangs over its history, but it's our only safe bet."

She ran a hand over her face as if to wipe away the dark thoughts and tiredness. "What makes you so sure?"

"It's not connected to the tunnels and there's no other way in. We'll have to cover a few miles overland, but once we're there, the women and children will be out of danger. The surrounding area is flat and easy to survey. We'll be safe until Tungdil or Gandogar finds us." He cursed Bislipur silently; he could barely move because of the wound in his chest, and he felt dangerously weak.

"Girdlegard is a big place. We can't count on sending messengers." Xamtys studied the section of map beneath Balendilín's hovering finger. "I've never heard of the place."

"We won't need messengers. Provided we make sure everyone knows where we're going, our two friends will find us in the normal course of events. They're bound to realize that the orcs have seized the tunnels and they'll start making inquiries."

"Hmm." The queen didn't seem entirely convinced. "But then the beasts will be able to find us too. Is that what we want?"

"Absolutely." He nodded vigorously, his brown eyes gazing earnestly. "That's exactly my intention. I want Nôd'onn to lead his army to us."

Xamtys looked at him as if he were out of his mind. "He'll never show up in person, and if he does, we'll be dead. If you want a swift end, Balendilín, you should have stayed in the Blue Range. We needn't have bothered to escape."

"No, Nôd'onn must come to us. He's been scouring Girdlegard for the books and relics. If he thinks we've got them, he'll gather his hordes and attack us in person."

"But why would we *want* him to attack us?" She leaned over the side of the wagon and looked at him imploringly. "Balendilín, I need to know why I should lead my warriors to certain death."

He met her worried gaze. "We need to draw Nôd'onn close to us so Gandogar and Tungdil can find him. Otherwise he'll barricade himself somewhere in the depths of Girdlegard and we won't get a chance to use Keenfire against him."

At last the queen saw the logic of the plan. "So we'll act as bait. Of course, the only drawback is that no one knows when Gandogar or Tungdil will arrive."

"Or if they'll make it at all," he admitted frankly, closing his eyes. The loss of blood was sapping his strength, making him dizzy. "But it's our only hope."

"Very well." Xamtys let go of the wagon. "But I must warn my subjects first."

"It's too late for that. The orcs know all about the tunnels; they'll be there already. It's the obvious thing to do." He gripped her hand. "Your Majesty, we must resign ourselves to being the last dwarven army in these lands. The task of destroying Nôd'onn falls to us alone."

She took a deep breath and stared at his chapped hand. "To think that they're butchering my folk and I can't even stop them." A tear trickled down her soft cheek. "We must avenge ourselves a thousand times over, Balendilín. The fields of Girdlegard will be awash with orcish blood, and I shall pursue our enemies tirelessly, stopping only when my royal mace shatters on an ogre's skull." Balendilín could see from a glance that her weapon would never break. Suddenly Xamtys looked concerned. "But what if Nôd'onn defeats us before either expedition returns?"

He smiled at her, trying to look more confident than he felt. "We won't let him," he said firmly.

Xamtys held her head high, her brown eyes scanning the rows of anxious, determined faces in the wagons. Some of the children were crying, their wails rising above the clunking armor and weaponry as the other passengers fidgeted in their seats. The air smelled stuffy and old.

"As you wish, Balendilín. I will follow your lead." She shook his hand and returned to her wagon.

The news of their destination spread like wildfire through the carriages. The secondlings had left their kingdom with misgivings, but on hearing where Balendilín was taking them, they reacted with disbelief, horror, and, in a few cases, unmitigated fear.

Roodacre,
Kingdom of Tabaîn,
Girdlegard,
Winter, 6234th Solar Cycle

Once again the company passed the sentries' muster without anyone remarking on Djerûn's great size.

Roodacre was a vast place. The population was listed as seventy thousand in one of Lot-Ionan's books, but the study had been written some time ago and the city was still expanding.

"I don't blame the orcs for not touching it," commented Boïndil. "I'll wager that Roodacre could rally thirty thousand trained defenders, not to mention the rest."

"It won't take long for the orcs to gather an army to rival them," said Andôkai. "Either that, or the älfar will capture the city by stealth." Mifurdania had taught them that nowhere was safe from Tion's hordes. "If all else fails, Nôd'onn will send one of his famuli to tear down the walls and let the orcs in. Once they're inside the settlement, Roodacre will be lost. Humans are no match for orcs." She pointed to a tavern where a light was still burning in the bar. "Shall we go in?"

"I wouldn't want to live in a place as flat as this," Bavragor said to Balyndis. "How are you supposed to hide from the sun when there isn't any shade? It must be baking in the summer."

"I've nothing against warmth, provided it comes from my forge," said the smith, ushering him in front of her.

"Yes, there's nothing better than smiting red-hot iron on the anvil and letting the hammer sing." Tungdil sighed. "I miss my smithy."

"Your smithy?" echoed Balyndis, surprised. "I thought you were a fourthling. Aren't Goïmdil's dwarves supposed to be gem cutters?"

"Exactly," said Goïmgar in an I-told-you-so tone of voice. "Gem cutters and diamond polishers. But he's not one of—"

"I'm a fourthling, all right, but I've always felt more of an affinity for a craft beloved of all our folks," Tungdil cut in.

"He's not one of us," Goïmgar continued dismissively. "He's just a foundling. He lived with the long-uns until someone talked him into thinking he was a fourthling, and then he took it upon himself to steal the crown."

"Oh," she said in confusion, "but if you were raised by men, who taught you to love the smithy?"

"I've always loved metalwork," he confided. "Even with sweat pouring into my eyes, arms as heavy as lead, and sparks singeing my beard, there's nowhere I'd rather be than at the anvil."

Her eyes lit up as she laughed. "I know what you mean." She rolled up her mail shirt to show him the scar on her right arm. "Look, that's what Vraccas did to me when I tried to forge a sword. He doesn't approve of dwarves fashioning anything but axes and maces. He sent a message through the anvil, and I've never been tempted to make another one since."

Tungdil pulled off his glove enthusiastically and held out his left palm, which was marked by a deep red scar. "It was a horseshoe. I knocked it off the anvil and put my hand out to catch it before it landed in the dirt. It was my best-ever horseshoe, and I wasn't about to see it ruined."

Balyndis was swept away by Tungdil's hitherto unsuspected passion for the forge. Soon they were deep in conversation about the particulars of metalwork and had quite forgotten their companions.

Andôkai called them to order by clearing her throat. "There'll be plenty of time for talking later. First we need to find somewhere to stay."

Tungdil glanced around for the first time and saw that they were in a large room of staring humans. Djerûn towered above them like a statue. The enormous warrior would have looked more at home on a plinth outside the town hall than in the front room of a tavern.

The innkeeper lodged them in a dormitory usually used by traveling merchants. Because of the threat facing Girdlegard, trade between towns had practically ceased, and so Tungdil and his friends had the place to themselves at no extra cost. None of them felt like talking to the locals, so they ordered their meal to be brought to their room.

Feeling sidelined by Balyndis's and Tungdil's enthusiasm for the smithy, Bavragor tried to interest Balyndis in the art of masonry, with only moderate success.

He was a few notes into a traditional song of the Hammer Fists when Tungdil delved into his knapsack and brought out the sigurdaisy wood. Balyndis saw him inspecting it and leaned over to get a closer look. The melody stopped abruptly, ending in an unintelligible grunt.

"Is it metal?" The firstling frowned as she stared in fascination at the surface. "I've never seen anything like it. We don't have it in our kingdom."

Tungdil gave her a brief account of the wood and its purpose and handed her the relic. "The trees were all chopped down, so this is the last piece in Girdlegard—except Gandogar's, of course. Without it, we'd never be able to make Keenfire."

She ran her hands over it reverently, trying to feel the details with her fingers. Bavragor looked on jealously.

"Ha, look at him stare!" cackled Goïmgar, hiccuping with glee. "His one eye is falling out of its socket! Don't you get it?" he jeered. "She's not interested in you anymore. You're a stone splitter, not a fancy smith! It's too bad you've got the wrong gift." He stopped to fill his pipe, then jabbed the stem toward Tungdil. "Charlatans are in the habit of taking what doesn't belong to them."

Tungdil's cheeks reddened with anger and shame. "That's enough from you, Goïmgar," he said harshly. "Don't you see that spitefulness doesn't do you any favors?"

"Oh, I'm fine, thanks for asking," he hissed back. "How would you feel with everyone picking on you all the time?"

"Why can't you see that this isn't about Gandogar or the succession? We're here to stop Nôd'onn because—" Tungdil was about to launch into yet another explanation, but opted instead for the truth. "But you know that, don't you? You don't *want* to understand. You *like* being the one with a grievance!"

"What I think is *my* business, not yours! Anyhow, I was forced to join this expedition against my will and I don't see why I should suffer in silence. It wasn't my idea to come on this mission, and I'm going to keep reminding you of that."

"Actually, Goïmgar, you're not. No more insults, no more snide comments, no more cussed remarks, or I'll solder your lips together with red-hot metal. Do you understand? We need your hands and your craftsmanship, not your poisonous tongue." Eyes flashing, he turned to Bavragor and Boïndil. "As for you two, you're to leave him in peace. The teasing stops now."

Goïmgar puffed furiously on his pipe, sending clouds of blue smoke shooting toward the ceiling. He got up and walked to the door. "Don't worry, I'm not running away," he said scornfully when he saw the alarmed expression on Tungdil's face. "I'm going outside so I can walk up and down and be as insulting, snide, and cussed as I like—and you'd better not get in my way!"

He marched out, letting the door slam behind him.

Rodario was the first to break the silence. "Would anyone like the last of this delectable sausage?" he inquired. "I'm still a little hungry, but good manners dictate that..." He broke off when no one showed any sign of responding, and decided that the lack of interest entitled him to help himself. Having finished the sausage with gusto, he dipped his hands in the tub of warm water provided by the publican and lathered the soap in preparation for a wash.

He was watched by Boïndil, who sighed incredulously to communicate his opinion of washing and water in general.

The secondling stared up at Djerûn, who had taken his place on the floor while Andôkai stood at the window and drew the rudimentary curtains. She had taken off her cloak. "Well, long-un," he said to the giant, "you and I are both dying to slay a dozen runts, but don't forget: If we come across a pack of them, the first ten belong to me."

Djerûn maintained his customary silence.

Boïndil shrugged, went to the window, and climbed out onto the roof. He soon spotted Goïmgar. "You should see this," he called out to the others. "The artisan is marching up and down the street."

"Tell him to come back in," said Tungdil, who was poring over the map. The city walls did nothing to assure him of their safety. *We've had proof enough that the älfar can slip past sentries with ease.* If their enemies had spies anywhere near the city, they would know by now that the odd-looking group had found its way to Roodacre. *They'll come for us and they won't give in until they've seen their mission through.*

"He says he won't," Boïndil bellowed through the window.

"Pretend you've seen an älf," suggested Bavragor, offering a morsel of genuine dwarven cheese to Balyndis. "That should do the trick." Andôkai wrinkled her nose in disgust at the smell, but said nothing.

Sure enough, a few moments later they heard the rush of footsteps on the stairs; then the artisan burst into the dormitory, banging the door behind him and dropping the heavy oak panel into the latch.

Boïndil abandoned his post and climbed back inside, his chain mail clinking softly. "You were lucky," he said gravely. He curled his long plait into a pillow and lay down. "The älf was right behind you."

Goïmgar turned a deathly shade of pale.

VI

Roodacre,
Kingdom of Tabaîn,
Girdlegard,
Winter, 6234th Solar Cycle

Tungdil was woken by the sound of scraping metal. He opened his eyes.

Djerůn had got to his feet and drawn his mighty sword. He was holding the weapon outstretched in his right hand, blade angled toward the door. Andôkai, still in bed, was wide-awake too. She signaled to Tungdil, instructing him to keep quiet and lie still.

They watched as a thin strip of wood slipped through the doorframe and rose toward the latch, pushing the oak beam noiselessly out of the catch. Little by little the door came open. Faint light sloped into the dormitory from the corridor, illuminating the outline of a stocky figure.

The intruder was roughly the size of a dwarf. He was wearing a helmet and, judging from his silhouette, was blessed with an exceptionally bushy beard. In his left hand he was clutching a sack. The sight of Djerůn stopped him in his tracks. Andôkai gave the command.

The giant shot forward to seize the intruder, but his phenomenal speed was not enough. Ducking away, the little fellow surprised them all by darting in instead of out.

"Stop right there!" Tungdil sprang out of bed and barred his path. He made to grab him, but the dwarf proved astonishingly agile, leaving the startled Tungdil with a clump of whiskers in his hand.

The intruder leaped nimbly onto the windowsill, hurled his sack at his pursuers, and fled across the roof. The bag smacked Tungdil in the chest, spilling its contents across the roughly hewn tiles.

The clattering and jangling woke the others. Boïndil was up like a shot, running around the room, brandishing his axes and bellowing for the orcs to fight him if they dared. The rest of the company reached for their weapons.

Balyndis, dressed only in her undergarments, had taken up position on her bed and was gripping her ax with both hands. A shaft of moonlight slanted through the curtains, exposing her curves. It occurred to Tungdil that she probably didn't realize how much she was revealing, but he couldn't bring himself to look away.

"Where did they go?" demanded Boïndil, spoiling for a fight.

"We had an uninvited guest," said Andôkai, leaning out of the window to see where the fellow had got to. "A dwarf. There must have been something funny about him because he didn't respond to my spell. And now he's gone."

"Gold," exclaimed Tungdil in surprise, finally noticing the shiny coins on the floor. He bent down and scooped them up. Some of them were stuck together and left damp traces on his hands.

"And a dagger," observed Goïmgar, who was cowering in a corner.

Boïndil picked it up and eyed it carefully. "Forged on a dwarven anvil," he said slowly, handing it to Balyndis. "You're the expert. What do you reckon?"

Booted feet thundered up the stairs and across the landing to their room. The next moment, armored guards burst inside, halberds pointing menacingly toward them.

"Light, I need more light!" shouted someone, and in an

instant lamps were passed forward and more guards thronged inside.

The coins and the knife! Tungdil was about to throw the gold out of the window and tell Boïndil to put away the dagger, but already the room was bathed in light, revealing telltale red smudges on his fingers: The coins and the dagger were covered in blood.

"By Palandiell," exclaimed the captain of the guards, a strong man of some forty cycles with a small scar on the left side of his face. "I've never seen such brazen criminals. Just look at the ruffians! Sitting here calmly, dividing their loot." His eyes shifted to the dagger in Boïndil's hand. "He's even holding the murder weapon!" He waved his men forward. "Arrest the lot of them, the men as well as the little fellows. We'll soon find out which of them were embroiled in this dastardly business."

"What business would that be, oh worthy guardian of our municipal safety?" inquired Rodario in his most amiable and gracious tone. He could easily have been inquiring about the weather. He adjusted his undergarments with aristocratic elegance. "Perhaps you would care to enlighten us?"

"Sir Darolan was murdered at knifepoint not three streets from here." He glared at Boïndil. "The game's up. You were seen and followed." He turned to one of his men. "There's a whole band of them. Professionals, I'll warrant."

"I'm afraid there's been a terrible misunderstanding," chimed in Tungdil. He outlined what had happened before the arrival of the guards, holding up the lock of beard as evidence. On closer inspection, it turned out to be a snippet of fleece.

The captain laughed in his face. "A likely story, groundling. I've never heard such nonsense."

"I know it sounds strange, but—"

"Strange? It's preposterous! I'm arresting you and your accomplices in the name of King Nate. One of you will sign a confession soon enough. We've solved every murder in this city by putting the suspects on the rack."

"As I was saying," Rodario resumed smoothly, "the dwarves are nothing to do with us." He winked furtively at Tungdil. "In fact, my companions and I were accompanying the lady when—"

"Save your stories for the interrogator," the captain interrupted him harshly. Just then his dour face brightened and he looked at them with sudden kindness. "Although, I must say, the evidence in your favor is quite compelling…" He took the strand of fake beard from Tungdil and gestured to the door. "We've been wasting our time," he told his guards. "The real murderer led us here on false pretenses. We need to get after him before the trail goes cold."

"But, Captain!" one of his subordinates protested vigorously. "We saw the dwarf run into the tavern—"

"Get a move on," the captain ordered. "Outside on the double! We'll never find him at this rate." Realizing that he was not to be dissuaded, the baffled guardsmen followed his instructions and exited the room. Soon afterward their clunking armor could be heard through the open window.

"That was close. Thank goodness he changed his mind." Rodario breathed a deep sigh of relief. "Can we go to bed now?"

Andôkai was already packing her things. "He'll come to his senses before too long. The sooner we leave, the better. The spell won't last forever."

"What do you mean, *come to his senses?* He's always like that," objected Boïndil, scratching his beard in confusion.

"She means the captain, not Rodario," explained Tungdil with a grin. It dawned on him why no one ever challenged Djerûn; the maga could obviously control people's thoughts. "She put a spell on him. Why else would he let us go?" He stared pensively at a tuft of fleece that had stuck to his fingers. *The whole thing was a setup and it almost succeeded.* "Someone was trying to get us into trouble."

"And it nearly worked! The villain disguised himself as a dwarf," said Boïndil, scandalized. He started to pack. "Just wait until I get my hands on him. He'll wish he'd never been born."

"Children can't move that fast," mused Balyndis, gathering her things. "It must have been a gnome or a kobold or..."

Tungdil raised his hands to his head in sudden understanding. "Of course! Bislipur's gnome!" They hurried out of the room and down the stairs. "Sverd must have followed us and waited for the opportunity to land us in real trouble. Bislipur's behind it all!"

"You can't fault the gnome's persistence," said Bavragor admiringly, tugging on the straps of his pack. "To think he followed us all this way."

"It would have been easy enough to track us," argued Boïndil. He peered into the front room of the tavern before waving the others on.

"Not necessarily," countered Balyndis, impressed by Sverd's tenacity. "He must have snuck into the firstling kingdom and found his way into the tunnels. That takes some doing."

"Remember the buckle we found in the runaway wagon?" Tungdil tiptoed to the door and scanned the street. "I knew I recognized it from somewhere." He slipped out of the tavern with Boïndil at his side. "We're safe," he said. "They're searching another street."

"You mustn't run," Boïndil told Goïmgar. "Running in the

middle of the night only attracts attention. They'll assume you're a criminal."

The travelers proceeded at a leisurely pace, chatting and smiling as if they were out for a nighttime stroll. Nothing in their behavior suggested they were engaged in illicit activity or fleeing a murder scene. Djerůn stayed in the shadows, trying to keep a low profile.

Before they could reach the gates, a group of guards approached on a routine patrol.

"Remember, Goïmgar: Just stay calm," whispered Boïndil.

"Shush," hissed Balyndis with one eye on the trembling artisan. "You're only making things worse!"

The guards were getting closer and had almost drawn level when a thin voice piped up. "Arrest the villains! Those are the culprits! Arrest them, guards! They're getting away!"

"That blasted gnome. I'll wring his scrawny neck," growled Ireheart, whipping out his axes to defend himself. The bewildered guardsmen looked to their leader for direction.

Just then the captain of the first patrol burst onto the street, shouting orders for their arrest. Candles blazed in the windows, shutters were opened, and the city awoke from its slumber.

"We don't have time for explanations," said Andôkai, drawing her sword. "They won't believe us and we'll rot in their dungeons."

"So what do we do?" demanded Bavragor, gripping the haft of his hammer, ready to fight his way out of the gates.

"It's probably best if I slip away now," said Rodario, shouldering his precious bag of costumes and hastily taking his leave. "I'll see you outside the city. I don't want to get in your way." He hurried into a side street before the guards could surround them.

"Never trust an actor." Narmora grinned and pulled out her weapons.

Tungdil held up his ax, poll first. "Don't kill unless you have to," he instructed them. "We're leaving Roodacre—whether they like it or not."

Tungdil couldn't help noticing that their opponents were woefully underprepared. More accustomed to chasing purse snatchers and incarcerating drunks, the guards had little experience with combat and stood no chance of restraining four staunch dwarves, a maga, a half älf, and a giant.

Furgas wasn't much of a warrior, but he held his ground valiantly and cleared enough space for Narmora to swing her weapons unimpeded. Goïmgar was tasked with guarding the rest of the ingots.

After the shortest of skirmishes, they hurried to the gates, where Rodario was conversing with a guard. The whole company descended on the distracted sentry before he could sound the alarm. When he eventually noticed the maga, it was already too late.

"You will let us through," she intoned. "You will let us through and tell no one that we passed this way." Even as she spoke, the sentry's eyes glazed over and he raised the portcullis without a word.

"Didn't I do well?" the impresario said to Andôkai. "I bewitched his senses with my silvery speech, thus enabling the Estimable Maga to cast her spell. Magic certainly has its uses. I don't suppose you'd consider a spot of backstage conjuring? Together we could put on a spectacle of such—"

Furgas shook his head despairingly. "For pity's sake, Rodario!"

"There's no harm in asking. We need to earn a living some-how when our amazing adventure is at an end."

Bavragor laughed. "Assuming you survive that long."

Buffeted by the wind, the rising portcullis made enough of a racket to wake the other sentries, whom Boïndil attacked with enthusiasm. He stuck to using his poll as instructed, but Tungdil detected the sound of splintering bone.

He's desperate to finish them off. He looked in consterna-tion at the bloodied and oddly misshapen face of a sentry. The man keeled over as Ireheart landed a follow-up blow. With at least one dead, the company would be wanted for multiple murder as well as theft.

Meanwhile, the portcullis was still rising slowly, but Sverd had followed them and was hiding in an alleyway, prepar-ing to alert the guards a second time. "They're escaping! The murderers are escaping through the gates!"

Even the last determined sleepers in the city were torn from their slumber by his shouts. Everyone with two legs and a weapon found their way onto the street, including the first courageous members of the militia, who came running out of their houses, having barely stopped to dress.

"Do something, Andôkai," shouted Tungdil, terrified of what would happen to the citizens of Roodacre if the battle-crazed Boïndil was to rampage through the city. "We won't be able to hold them off."

This time she didn't turn to sorcery. "Djerûn," she barked, and issued an unintelligible order.

The giant stepped forward. The torches of the assembled crowd bathed his armor in flickering light, bringing the threatening visor to life. At that moment the helmet produced a noise unlike anything Tungdil had heard in his life. It was a cross between a reptilian hiss and the dull, ponderous rumble of an earthquake, a sound so full of aggression and menace that anyone in earshot knew instantly not to approach. Tungdil felt the hairs on his neck stand on end. He took a nervous step back.

Inside the helmet, the violet glow intensified, streaming out of the eyeholes and outshining the torches. The horrified faces of the transfixed crowd were steeped in a purple light that was painful to behold.

The second roar was even louder and more terrifying than the first. This time everyone, including the guardsmen, turned in panic and fled, running back through the streets and alleyways to safety.

The portcullis was almost fully raised. "Let's g-go," stuttered Tungdil, still shaken by the sound of Djerûn's voice. *Assuming it was his voice...*

They ran into the night, glancing over their shoulders as they hurried down the snowy road. No one followed. The giant's performance had made enough of an impression to dissuade the townspeople from hunting them down.

As for Tungdil, he was more curious than ever about the armored warrior, although he suspected the truth would be less than reassuring. *It's not a human, at any rate,* he decided.

The company jogged in silence through the snow. After a while, Bavragor, who had fallen in line behind Goïmgar, pointed to the artisan's back. "Where are the ingots?" he panted breathlessly, listening in vain for a response. "Hey, I asked you a question!"

Goïmgar sped up, intent on getting far enough ahead before he dared to answer. "I lost them," he said plaintively. "A guardsman knocked the bag from my hand and I couldn't reach it in the scrum. I'm sorry, I honestly didn't mean to—"

"Didn't mean to...? I'll give you *didn't-mean-to,* you worthless little—" Bavragor lunged at him but was restrained by Tungdil from behind.

"It's all right, Bavragor."

The mason was beside himself. His chestnut eye glinted angrily. "All right? We've lost every single one of the ingots! We can't exactly fetch them now!"

"We'll be in the fifthling kingdom before you know it; we're bound to find something there," said Tungdil in a firm, confident voice that reminded everyone that he was the leader. To his mind, the matter was closed.

"But you said we shouldn't rely on finding materials on the way," Bavragor objected stubbornly. "So why—"

"What's done is done," Tungdil said sharply. "We'll have to make the best of things." He loosened his hold on Bavragor and clapped him on the back. "No matter what happens, we're not going to let it stop us. We can't! No one else is going to forge the ax and save Girdlegard. It's up to us."

"It would be a darned sight easier without Goïmgar," grumbled Bavragor. "He only drags us down."

"Vraccas must have made him part of this mission for a reason." Tungdil noticed that the mason was wheezing. "Steady on, Bavragor, you'd better stop talking before you get a stitch. Goïmgar's fitter than you."

"Cowards always make good runners." Even as he spoke, there was a jangling noise and he stiffened. Before he could take another step, his legs buckled and he toppled over, raising a cloud of glistening snow. When the flakes settled, he was buried beneath a layer of white crystals. Sticking out of his neck was a bolt fired from a crossbow.

The others, with the exception of Djerûn, threw themselves to the ground so as not to fall victim to the archer.

Once again, Andôkai barked an unintelligible command, whereupon the giant scanned their surroundings and set off at a sprint.

It definitely wasn't an älf, thought Tungdil. Unlike Djerûn, he could see no sign of their hidden assailant. *Guardsmen? But guardsmen carry torches...*

The maga crawled through the snow to examine the mason's wound. Balyndis wriggled over to join her.

"The tip stopped just short of his spine," said Andôkai, after a cursory inspection. "If it weren't for his cloak and the metal-plated nape of his helmet, it would have penetrated farther." She gripped the shaft of the bolt resolutely and pulled it from his flesh. With her right hand she stemmed the blood from the wound. "I hope he'll forgive me for using my dastardly magic to save his life." She closed her eyes in concentration. "I can't say I've had much experience in healing dwarves. I hope I can do it."

So do I. Something whirred past Tungdil, just missing his head; then a third missile rebounded off Goïmgar's shield. They heard a high-pitched scream, which stopped abruptly as Djerûn seized his prey.

He cast their tormentor into the snow beside them. A yellowy-green circle sullied the pristine snow around the diminutive corpse. A head with two long pointed ears plumped beside it.

Goïmgar shrank back in horror. "Sverd!" The dead crossbowman was Bislipur's former slave. The artisan looked at the mangled gnome and shuddered, then stared at the dent in his shield where the third bolt had struck. "But why would he..." He broke off, not wishing to draw attention to the matter, but Tungdil finished the question for him.

"Why would Sverd be aiming at you?" He stared into the

gnome's unseeing eyes, but Djerûn's ruthless solution to the problem had ruled out all hope of an answer. "You were traveling with the wrong party, I suppose."

He bent down to pick up the now-redundant choker. Sverd was free at last, but not in the way he had hoped. Pensively, he pocketed the collar, intending to confront Bislipur with the evidence when they next met. As he looked down, he noticed a shiny lump of butter-yellow metal. *Gold!* There could be no further doubt that the gnome was responsible for the mishaps that had befallen them on their journey.

Boïndil got straight to the point. "Bislipur is the most contemptible dwarf that ever lived." He wiped the snow furiously from his thick cloak and beard. "Setting his lackey on us and trying to have us killed! Dwarves don't assassinate their kinsfolk; it's the most dastardly crime a child of Vraccas could commit!"

"The gnome did all his dirty work," commented Tungdil, his mind still whirring. "Bislipur wasn't going to kill us himself. He would have washed his hands of all responsibility."

"Just wait until I get hold of his wretched king," threatened Boïndil, praying to Vraccas to hasten their encounter. "I'm going to beat him black-and-blue."

Still struggling to digest what had happened, Goïmgar shook his head slowly. "No, Gandogar would never have agreed to it; he's not a murderer, whatever you think. Bislipur must have taken it upon himself to…" The artisan lapsed into a helpless silence, no longer sure what to believe.

"Hang on a minute; you want Gandogar to be high king, don't you?" Boïndil accused him suspiciously.

"Of course I do! I said so from the start. But to murder a dwarf because of it…" He shuddered. "Bislipur must be mad," he murmured, staring at Bavragor's motionless form.

"He must be so desperate for Gandogar to be crowned that he doesn't know what he's doing. He's insane."

Balyndis took Bavragor's hand to comfort him. Slowly the open wound in his neck shriveled until only a small scar was left. Exhausted, Andôkai sank down and cooled her face on the snow.

"I've healed the wound," she said faintly. "In a moment he'll..."

"Magic," Bavragor muttered sleepily. "I've been thinking; maybe it's not so useless after all." Groggily, but with a profoundly serious expression, he nodded to the exhausted maga. There was no need for him to thank her in any other way.

A question if I may, glorious captain of our troupe." The sun was just rising when Rodario, shivering with cold but gripping his duffel bag with grim determination, drew alongside Tungdil. The impresario pointed furtively at Djerûn. The events of the previous night had reminded him and the others that the giant was unlikely to be an unusually tall man. "What kind of creature is he?" The question was barely audible through the layers of scarf wrapped around his head.

"I have no idea," Tungdil said frankly without slowing his pace.

Rodario displayed his customary persistence. "No idea? But I thought the lot of you had been traveling together for a while..."

"She told us that he isn't a monster." Tungdil suddenly remembered the night in the desert when he had caught a glimpse of what lay behind the terrifying visor. A shiver ran down his spine.

The impresario blew on his frozen fingers. "Not a monster, eh? Then what in the name of Palandiell is he? I've never known a human to light up a darkened street with the power of his eyes. If it's a trick, I'd give anything to know the secret; the audience would love it."

Hoping that Rodario would give up and go away, Tungdil said nothing and trudged energetically through the snow, glancing at the map to get his bearings.

"Very well. I'll have to assume that he's a creature of Tion." Looking pretty pleased with himself, Rodario stuck his hands into the pockets of his fur coat. "It adds a bit of drama to the plot. Ye gods, the play will be brilliant. The whole of Girdlegard will flock to see it." He stopped and cursed. "I wish my blasted ink would stop freezing. At this rate, I'll have forgotten the best bits before I get a chance to write them down."

"You should carry the inkwell next to your skin," Tungdil advised him. "That way the ink will be nice and warm and you can scribble as much as you like."

Rodario gave him a friendly pat on the back. "There's a sharp mind hiding under all that hair, my little friend. I was thinking the same thing, but thank you nonetheless."

Not a single footprint marred the snowy road ahead. The wintry weather and marauding orcs had convinced the people of Tabaîn to stay by their hearths and barricade their doors.

The terrain was so flat that raiding parties could be spotted well in advance. In clear weather the watchtowers commanded views of over a hundred miles, but no amount of warning could save the settlements from the orcs. The northern hordes could be stopped only by good swordsmen, and Tabaîn had precious few of those.

Tungdil checked their position against the map. They were closer than ever to the southernmost reaches of the Perished

Land. *Who knows how far the pestilence has spread? There's no way of telling with the landscape blanketed in snow.*

"Orcs," came Boïndil's warning from the front of the procession. "Twenty miles to the west. They're...Hang on, they're turning east," he reported, surprised. "They're moving fast. You don't think they're looking for us, do you?"

Bavragor pointed to a hamlet situated in the direction that the beasts had been heading originally. The superior vision in his remaining eye enabled him to see what the others could not. "That would have been their next stop, but they've abandoned their quarry." He wiped the sweat from his forehead. A red glow had settled over his face.

"Are you sure you're all right?" Balyndis asked. "You look a bit feverish."

"What if it's gangrene?" said Boïndil. "Maybe the hocus-pocus hasn't worked as well as it should."

The allegation spurred Andôkai into action. She asked the mason to lean forward so she could inspect the wound on his neck. Boïndil was beside her in a flash. They came to the same conclusion.

"The wound has healed nicely," he admitted. "I can't argue with that."

"I've lost a bit of blood, that's all," said Bavragor, trying to allay the others' fears. He was obviously uncomfortable at being the center of attention, but Balyndis persevered. She pulled off her left glove and laid her hand on his forehead.

"For the love of Vraccas, I could forge a horseshoe on there," she said in alarm.

"With a skull as thick as his, I don't suppose it would do much harm," Tungdil joked. "He's a tough customer, our Hammerfist."

"I'm serious, Tungdil, he's feverish. Either that, or he's got a nasty cold. We need to get him inside before he loses consciousness or worse."

"Don't be ridiculous," objected Bavragor. "I'm perfectly—" He doubled up in a coughing fit that went on and on until he was shaking so violently that his legs caved in. Tungdil pulled him upright and steadied him.

"I'd say it's a cold." Balyndis scanned the horizon. "He needs a warm bed for the night."

Tungdil nodded. "We'll stop at the next hamlet. Sorry, old fellow, but a dead mason won't be any good to us."

"A cold!" Goïmgar chuckled maliciously. "So who's the weakling now? I might not be big, but at least I'm hardy." He was practically glowing with satisfaction at not being the underdog anymore. Head held high, he strode past the ailing mason with a smug smile that prompted Furgas to throw a snowball in his face.

Tungdil soon realized that their efforts to find a bed were destined to fail; there wasn't a single farmhouse, let alone a hamlet, between them and the Gray Range. Since Bavragor refused to make a detour, they walked without stopping in order to reach the entrance to the tunnels as soon as they could.

A nasty surprise awaited them when they finally reached the spot. The mouth of the shaft had transformed itself into a frozen pond.

"We'll have to walk, then," said Bavragor cheerily, doing his best to downplay his illness and seem sprightly despite his fragile state. His bright red face and the beads of perspiration forming beneath his frozen helmet told a different story. "I can see the range from here."

"The range has been in sight since the moment we entered Tabaîn," moaned Goïmgar, dreading the prospect of another long march in the cold. "Are you trying to get us all snow-blind or something?"

Grumpily, he set off through the snow, the others following in his wake. Toward evening they came to a deserted barn filled with bales of hay.

They lit a fire in spite of their qualms and made themselves comfortable, then cleared a spot for Bavragor to lie beside the flames, swaddling him in three blankets so he sweated out the cold. Rodario curled up in the warmth, while Djerûn stood guard by the door, leaving the others free to look after the invalid. They clustered around him.

"It's nothing, honestly." Just then he choked and spat out a large clot of blood. He was gasping for air, groaning rather than breathing, and he seemed to be losing strength. The warmth was making things worse. "If you give me a sip of brandy, I'll be fighting fit."

"It can't be a cold," Boïndil said firmly. He got up. "It's gangrene, I know it. Sometimes it spreads beneath the skin, even after the wound has healed."

"No, Boïndil," snapped Andôkai, "I cleaned the flesh thoroughly."

A terrible thought occurred to Tungdil. He got up, went over to Goïmgar, and picked up his shield to examine the dent. Where the bolt had hit, the metal was discolored and there were traces of a clear frozen liquid that neither he nor the artisan had noticed before. His spirits sank. The bolt had been dipped in something that had stuck to the shield.

Vraccas, give him strength. "Do you have a spell against poison?" he asked Andôkai hoarsely. "By the look of things, Sverd wasn't relying purely on his aim."

"Poison?" Bavragor swallowed his cough and grinned. As

his lips parted, his companions saw the blood leaking from his gums and coloring his teeth. His mouth was full of blood. "I knew it! Did you hear that, Goïmgar? What's the betting you'd be dead already? I've drunk enough brandy and beer in my lifetime to toughen me up. Ha, a cold!"

The maga closed her eyes. "I can't do anything against poison. My art is...I'm afraid, it's not my kind of magic," she said in a soft, apologetic tone. "Healing the wound drained a lot of my energy. My strength is all but exhausted."

A terrible silence settled over the group. There was no mistaking what Andôkai's words meant for the mason. Balyndis reached for his calloused hand and squeezed it encouragingly. She was too choked to speak.

"I know what you're thinking," croaked Bavragor at length. "Things don't look good for the merry minstrel. It's all right; I wasn't intending to return from the mission anyway." He looked up at Tungdil. "Still, I'd give anything to see the fifthling kingdom and fashion Keenfire's spurs. I wanted to go out with a bang, not in a dingy barn miles away from my beloved mountains."

Blood was seeping through his pores, the droplets merging into rivulets and soaking his straw mattress. In no time his garments were drenched with red.

"You're not going to die," Tungdil told him shakily. His smile, which he hoped would be encouraging, looked more like a grimace. "We can't fashion Keenfire without you! You're Beroïn's best mason."

Bavragor had to swallow a mouthful of blood before he could reply. "In that case, you'll have to take me with you. We'll make the ax to kill Nôd'onn, you'll see." He nodded to the door. "Carry me to the Perished Land. I'll fulfill my mission after my death."

"But...but you'll be a *revenant*," stuttered Boïndil, horrified. "Your soul—"

"I'll do my bit for Keenfire and confound the rest!" The outburst ended in another coughing fit.

"What if you turn against us? The other dead souls tried to kill us and eat us!" Boïndil glanced at the others for support. Some were struggling with their emotions, the remainder looked embarrassed.

"Chain my hands together, if you're worried," the mason told them. "My will is stronger than the drive to do evil. Dwarves are too stubborn to be conquered by darkness." He closed his eyes. "You'll have to hurry," he gasped. He coughed again and blood spewed from his mouth, trickling into his well-kempt beard.

"Djerûn!" At Andôkai's bidding, the giant stooped to lift the dwarf. Cradling Bavragor gently in his arms like a mother would carry her child, he left the barn and stomped through the snow.

His long tireless limbs bore the mason toward the north, where the Perished Land had established its dominion, awakening anything that died to hideous life.

The rest of the company packed their things and followed the giant as fast as the sparkling snow and the dwarves' stumpy legs would allow.

Tungdil looked up at the stars and wept silent tears for the mason who was sacrificing his soul for the sake of the ax on which Girdlegard's future depended. For all Bavragor's eccentricities and occasional crotchetiness, he was a good dwarf whom Tungdil regarded as a friend.

He heard a sniff beside him and turned to the tearful Balyndis. Her eyes were red with crying, but she smiled and squeezed his hand. Suddenly his courage, which had all but deserted him in the barn, came flooding back.

So much had happened since they had left the secondling kingdom—too much, in fact. Their adventure had turned into something far bigger and more perilous than they'd ever imagined. Even Rodario, renowned for his pompous comments, had fallen silent and was brooding over the mason's death.

"I hope Girdlegard is worth it, Vraccas," murmured Tungdil, gazing up at the sparkling firmament. "When all this is over, I shall see to it that our folks don't barricade themselves back in their mountains. From now on, we'll work together."

Balyndis gave his hand another squeeze, but he pulled away and hurried to join Boïndil at the head of the procession. It was the wrong time to be thinking of anything except Keenfire.

"You like her, don't you?" the secondling said immediately, without glancing round.

"Don't start," Tungdil told him. "It's the last thing I want to talk about."

"I can't say I blame you. She's an attractive lass, and to someone like you, with no experience of the fairer sex, she must look as pretty as Vraccas's own daughter."

"I've decided not to think about it until Nôd'onn has been defeated. My duty is to Girdlegard."

"Trust a scholar to want to *think* about it." Boïndil took care not to meet his eye: For all intents and purposes, he was addressing Djerûn's snowy footprints. "Think about it if you must, but remember: If something is worth pursuing, you shouldn't waste time. Situations change faster than you can split an orcish skull, and a moment's hesitation could cost you your chance."

"What makes you say that?"

"No reason." He peered into the distance. "They're up ahead." He whipped out his axes. "Let's hope the drunkard can defy the bidding of the Perished Land." It was evident from his hefted weapons that he was prepared to take decisive action.

The maga called out to Djerůn, who raised his armored hand and beckoned them over. At his side was Bavragor, arms dangling limply and gaze fixed blankly on the Gray Range.

"Bavragor?" Tungdil said gently, searching the pale face for a trace of recognition. His features had aged terribly; he looked waxen and corpselike.

"I feel...nothing," came the ponderous response. It seemed to cost him a great deal of effort to open his mouth and form the words. "I can't feel my body. My mind is...empty." The soulless eyes roved over the group and settled on Tungdil. "It feels bad; everything feels bad. Things I loved, I hate. Things I hated..." He stared past Tungdil and fixed his gaze on Boïndil. "I want to slaughter the things I hated—tear them apart and devour them. Tie my hands together; I don't know how much longer I can resist. The evil is inside me."

"Very well," said Tungdil, unthreading the leather strap from Goïmgar's shield. He bound Bavragor's hands behind his back.

"Tighter," growled the mason. "You don't have to worry about my blood flow: My heart stopped beating when I died." He seemed tense and agitated, but once the bonds had been tightened to his satisfaction, he relaxed a little and turned to Tungdil. "I want you to behead me as soon as my work is done. I don't want to serve the Perished Land for eternity and patrol the abandoned fifthling galleries, massacring innocents and spreading the pestilence."

"No dwarf will ever serve the Perished Land," Tungdil promised. "You have my word."

"As for you," the mason snapped at Boïndil, "take my advice and stay away. I want nothing better than to sink my teeth into your gullet and tear you to shreds." He squared his shoulders and his chestnut eye glimmered cruelly before he looked down and stared at the snow. He took a first step, then another. "Hurry, I don't want to be a soulless corpse for a moment longer than necessary."

On a signal from the maga, Djerûn assumed the role of Bavragor's keeper, walking close behind him so the others were shielded from his jaws by a solid metal frame.

Time wore on, orbit after orbit, as they trudged across the never-ending flats of Tabaîn. The Breadbasket, as the fertile fields were nicknamed in summer, was so inhospitably cold that it was essential to keep moving in order not to freeze.

Tungdil had read somewhere that light reflected by the snow could harm the eyes and cause permanent damage. To protect his companions from blindness, he ordered them to bind cloth around their faces and look out through tiny slits.

Their journey was slow and laborious. The only members of the company who didn't seem to mind the march were Djerûn and the undead mason, who plowed their way impassively through the snow. Since their provisions were frozen solid, they had the onerous task of thawing their food by the fire every evening before they could eat. Without the warm garments given to them by Xamtys, they would surely have perished in the cold.

At length Boïndil became more restless, his fighting instincts ever harder to repress, while Bavragor had been stripped of the very things that made him who he was; he didn't drink, didn't sing, didn't laugh, just stared into the distance. On one occasion he took the edge off his hunger with a mountain hare. Ripping it from a metal trap, he ate it alive, leaving nothing but bones and fur. The sound of his frenzied eating and the cracking of bones made Goïmgar, whose hand rested permanently on his sword, more nervous than ever.

The Gray Range edged closer and closer. Its peaks seemed almost in touching distance, yet still they struggled through the snowdrifts of Tabaîn, finally crossing the border into Gauragar and, after an exhausting march of many orbits, reaching the slate-gray foothills of the range.

On their way they encountered neither orcs nor any other beasts, although they occasionally saw their tracks. Great armies were advancing southward, but fortunately for the company, their paths never crossed.

At last they neared the stronghold's outermost defenses. Even from a distance they could see that no one had been posted to defend the ramparts against intruders from Girdle-gard's interior.

The beasts from the north had torn stone from stone, destroying walls and toppling towers until nothing remained of the stronghold's former splendor. Their work had been done so thoroughly that Tungdil and the others were hard-pressed to imagine how the kingdom had looked during Giselbert Ironeye's era. Fragments of stonework testified to the fifthling masons' skill, but the glorious ramparts were nothing but ruins. It was a harrowing sight for the dwarves.

Although the defenses seemed deserted, the company approached the gates with caution.

"Stay here and don't make a sound," Boïndil told them as

they struggled to the top of a steep pathway. "Narmora and I will check for sentries."

The pair slipped away, darting between the gray rocks and hiding behind sections of masonry that loomed out of the snow. Their goal was an open gateway, as tall as a house, leading straight inside the mountain.

Tungdil scanned their surroundings and listened intently. A chill wind whistled through the cracked ramparts, producing high-pitched notes that rolled together in a tune. Icicles hung like glassy stalactites from the mountain ledges, and fifty paces to their left, a waterfall had stopped midstream in a frozen sculpture of ice.

No orcs, no ogres, no älfar, nothing.

"Did you hear what he said?" Goïmgar smiled bitterly. "He told us to be quiet! If only he could hear himself."

"He's not exactly graceful," agreed the impresario, "although the comparison with the delightful Narmora certainly doesn't help."

Tungdil watched as they stole forward, Boïndil relying on his diminutive size, while the half älf sprang between the rocks with the elegance of a dancer. There were no telltale noises from the snow beneath her feet; she seemed barely to land at all, skimming across the ground as light as a feather. Boïndil's chain mail, by contrast, made a terrible racket, even through his thick fur coat.

Narmora was the first to reach the gates. She pressed herself against the wall, listening intently to the darkness before slipping inside. Her silhouette melted into the gloom and she disappeared from sight.

Furgas fiddled determinedly with his gloves. "Sometimes I wish she wasn't so daring," he whispered.

"Don't worry, old chap," Rodario soothed him. "Narmora

is a woman who knows her talents and isn't afraid to use them. You know the sort of thing she got up to before the three of us were a troupe. This is child's play by comparison."

"I'd rather not talk about Narmora," Goïmgar chipped in hurriedly. "She's scary enough as it is."

Boïndil had also reached the gates to the fifthling kingdom, conquered over a thousand cycles earlier by the Perished Land. He stopped, apparently undecided, and looked about, but the coast was clear.

At that moment, Narmora emerged from the enormous tunnel. The black shadows stuck to her like cobwebs, wrapping themselves around her lovingly, reluctant to set her free. She waved to them, her relaxed manner signaling that there was nothing to fear.

"How did she do that?" Goïmgar whispered nervously. "It was like she was covered in ink."

"Half magic," came the maga's answer. "It's something she was born with. Älfar are children of darkness."

"She'll swap sides as soon as we meet any of her kind," Goïmgar predicted darkly. "Blood is thicker than water."

"And love is stronger than both," Furgas countered firmly. "Narmora would rather die than betray me, and I'd give my life to protect her from harm."

The puny dwarf grumbled unintelligibly and followed the others to the gateway. He held his shield in front of him, ready to ward off an attack.

"All clear," said Narmora, not bothering to lower her voice. "They seem to have contented themselves with knocking down the defenses and vandalizing the gates to the point where they can't be closed."

"So where are all the runts?" demanded Boïndil, whirling his axes over his head.

"At the Stone Gateway, I expect—and for our sake, I hope they stay there," said Tungdil, who remembered the stronghold's layout from a book he'd once read. He turned to the archway. "Time to relight the great furnace of Dragon Fire!"

It was with reverence, apprehension, and a good deal of emotion that he took his first careful step into the tunnel, knowing that no dwarf had set foot in the stronghold since the fifthlings' defeat.

Life flooded back to the kingdom as Rodario and Furgas lit their lamps. The walls reflected the light so radiantly that they hastily damped the flames.

At last they could see that they were standing in a passageway whose walls were clad with polished palandium. A thousand cycles of neglect had done nothing to subdue the metal's white sheen. The likeness of dwarven kings had been etched into the polished panels and a row of bearded rulers gazed benevolently at the visitors, their shiny red axes of cast vraccasium raised in greeting.

"Such majesty," murmured Rodario.

Filled with wonderment, the dwarves sank to their knees and prayed to Vraccas. Even the soulless Bavragor was awed by his surroundings, but every word of his prayer was uttered with immense concentration as the evil within him strove to break his will and seize control of his thoughts and beliefs. It hadn't reckoned with his resolve and the legendary stubbornness of the dwarven mind.

Andôkai, Djerûn, and the players waited patiently.

At length Tungdil rose and breathed deeply. The passageway smelled old, dusty, and venerable; it had retained its character in spite of the invasion of orcs and other beasts. "We'll have to do some exploring if we're going to find Flamemere." He set off with Boïndil at his side.

Their boots raised clouds of dust, and from time to time a small creature scurried to safety. The ground was littered with fragments of bone, shields, and mail.

They proceeded in silence until they reached a second archway. The door had been ripped from its hinges, allowing them to enter the many-columned hall. Leading out from the vast pentagonal chamber were fifteen passageways. The stone signposts had been smashed to smithereens.

"There's such a thing as *too* much choice," Rodario said glumly. "Especially when we haven't got all day to scamper around like mice until we find the right tunnel."

"We could pick the one with the least footprints," proposed Tungdil. "I can't imagine orcs are frequent visitors to Flamemere. There's no reason for them to go there."

"Good idea," agreed Boïndil, making a beeline for one of the passageways. Narmora, Djerûn, and Andôkai set about inspecting the others, while the rest of the company found a less exposed corner of the hall to sit and rest.

Rodario scribbled a few thoughts, then shared a meal with Furgas, while Bavragor stayed standing and stared emptily ahead. Goïmgar took shelter behind his shield, chewing nervously on a strip of cured meat and scanning the room for threats. The thought of fifteen passageways converging on his resting place did nothing to help him relax.

"He must be wondering what's happened to Gandogar," Balyndis said softly to Tungdil.

"He's not the only one. We've come all this way and no one's said anything about another group of dwarves. Your folk hadn't seen him either. I hope nothing dreadful's happened," he said, concerned. He closed his eyes, only to open them suddenly and unbutton his fur coat. It was much warmer in the hall than outside and the heat was making him tired.

"Get some sleep," Balyndis told him. "I'll keep watch and wake you as soon as there's anything to report."

"I'm your leader; I'm not supposed to sleep."

"Tired leaders make mistakes," she said firmly, pushing on his shoulders until he capitulated and lay down. "There, that's much better. Now you can dream of rescuing our kingdoms." Smiling, she pushed a wayward lock of hair behind her ear and turned to get a better view of the hall.

Sitting next to him like that, her gaze watchful and one hand resting confidently on her ax, she looked every inch the warrior.

It's definitely this way." To nobody's great surprise, Boïndil, his mind made up, had no intention of listening to anyone else.

"Fine," said Tungdil, signaling for them to start moving, "we'll start with this one and if it doesn't work out, we'll try Andôkai's next."

They had snatched a few moments' sleep to recover their strength in preparation for facing the dragon, but now it was time to move on.

"Argamas is the mate of Branbausíl," Tungdil explained to Balyndis. "Branbausíl lived in the Gray Range until Giselbert's folk stole his fire, killed him, and plundered his lair. Argamas fled to Flamemere…"

"…never to be seen again," Goïmgar finished gladly. "Let's hope the fire-breather stays there. I can't say I'm particularly convinced by our strategy. Dragon scales are as hard as steel."

"We don't need to kill her, only to steal her fire," said Andôkai, unconcerned. "I thought you'd be happy about that."

"Happy?" chimed in Boïndil. "It's a waste! Why do we have to let her live? Argamas is the biggest beast in Girdlegard, or thereabouts, and I'm not allowed to kill her!" From the injured look on his face, it was obvious that the warrior felt cruelly misunderstood. He tried again. "Name me one other place where I can find a real dragon! It would be scandalous to pass up an opportunity like this!"

"I'm afraid the Estimable Maga is right," said Rodario.

"That's exactly the kind of reaction I'd expect from a coward like you," Boïndil told him dismissively. "Balyndis, what do you say the two of us—"

"Quiet," cautioned Tungdil. There was a smell of sulfur in the air and the temperature was rising. Their route had taken them down countless flights of stairs and through endless shafts, and now at last they were closing in. "Not another word until we know what's out there. We don't want Argamas leaving her lava bath until we're absolutely ready."

Goïmgar shrank behind his shield. "Maybe we should ask her to help. Dragons aren't stupid, you know, and she might be quite reasonable."

"You can't *ask* the dragon to give us her fire," Boïndil blazed up angrily. "Are you determined to ruin everything? You've got to *take* it! *Take* it, do you hear?"

"Goïmgar, Argamas's mate was killed by dwarves. I hardly think she'll be willing to help us," said Tungdil, shaking his head. "Our priority is to stay alive, so we'll settle for stealing her fire." He patted the stash of torches on his belt. "We need to bait her, nothing more."

"Unbelievable," grumbled Boïndil. "Why does everyone have to spoil my fun?"

They stepped out of the passageway and were bathed in an intense yellow glare. There was a pervading smell of rotten eggs and it was difficult to breathe, but the view made up for the other unpleasantness.

A wave of heat rose toward them as they approached the seething lake. The molten lava was alive with bubbles, some swelling and showering incandescent droplets as they burst, others collapsing meekly, while new pockets formed on the surface in a boiling, churning mass.

Tungdil couldn't be sure of the lake's exact proportions, but the expanse of simmering lava measured at least four thousand paces across. Islands of solid rock rose above the surface and strange basalt columns hung from the cavern's ceiling, where cycle after cycle of spitting magma had cooled. Everything was suffused with the lake's yellow glow.

"Is that where the dragon lives?" asked Goïmgar, who was staring with the others in amazement. "Thank goodness we're not going to fight her. Any creature tough enough to survive in that inferno won't be slain by our blades."

Djerûn raised his sword to direct his mistress's attention to something a thousand paces farther along the shore. "You can stop worrying about Argamas," said Andôkai. "Take a look over there."

To their horror they saw a gigantic skeleton, which, judging by its size and shape, was all that was left of Branbausíl's mate.

VII

Boïndil prodded the enormous skeleton with his boot. Broken arrow shafts, lances, spears, and smaller bones lay in and around the dragon's remains. "Orcs. From the look of the bones, they killed her a good few cycles ago." He appraised the fossil critically and a look of distant longing passed over his face. "What a fight it must have been."

Goïmgar snorted and shrugged. "We're wasting our time here. We may as well go home. I don't know about you, but I'd like to be in my own kingdom with my own clansfolk when Nôd'onn comes banging on the gates."

"A fat lot of use you'd be," Boïndil said scornfully. "You can't even fight!" He gave one of the ribs an experimental kick. The bone stood firm.

"I didn't say anything about fighting," Goïmgar corrected him. "If we're all going to die, I'd rather be back in my kingdom, that's all. I don't want to meet my end in the company of an ax-happy lunatic, an impostor, and an undead drunk." He glanced at the smith. "No offense, Balyndis, I've got nothing against you."

"Couldn't we light the furnace with ordinary fire?" asked Furgas.

Tungdil looked out across the lava. "We may as well give it a shot. It's better than giving up and doing nothing while

Nôd'onn lays waste to Girdlegard. We don't stand a chance of stopping him otherwise." He wiped the sweat from his eyes and peered at the tongues of fire licking across the lake. He had seen flames of all kinds and colors in his smithy, but these looked somehow different. "Is it my imagination," he said to Balyndis, who was similarly knowledgeable when it came to fire, "or are those flames unusually bright?"

"They're unusually bright." she said, guessing his thoughts. She pulled out a torch and held the end above the twisting flames. The wood flared up with incredible intensity.

"Perhaps you could put it out for us, Narmora," said the maga.

The half älf nodded and focused her mind. Her eyes closed and opened again a moment later, but the torch was still alight. "I can't do it," she said, surprised. "Normally it's no—"

"Precisely." The maga laughed in relief. "There's your proof, Tungdil. Argamas left her fiery legacy in the lake."

The excitement was too much for Balyndis, who planted an exuberant kiss on Tungdil's cheek. He smiled shyly. "In that case we've got what we came for," he declared. "We'll light the torches and get going. The fifthlings' furnace is waiting to be kindled back to life." With that he set off toward the mouth of the tunnel.

"Bravo, bravo," gushed Rodario. "Thank goodness it's so warm down here. My ink has never flown so freely. Such emotion! Such excitement! The scene is positively begging to be recorded in my notes!" He was still scribbling furiously as he walked. "Furgas, my dear friend and worthy associate, the sheer scale of this adventure will soon exceed the limits of any conventional play. We could open our doors in the morning," he suggested. "Hire some extras, double the ticket price. What do you think?"

Furgas took one last look at Flamemere before commencing the ascent through the passageway. "We should probably leave out the lava," he ruled. "We won't be able to afford enough coal to simulate the heat."

"Good thinking. We need to be careful with the costs. Besides, we can't have our valued spectators vomiting because of the smell."

"They'll vomit anyway if they have to put up with your acting," said Boïndil, handing him a torch. "Take this. Since you won't be fighting, you may as well make yourself useful. And woe betide you if you let it go out!"

"I swear by all four winds and every conceivable divinity, even the evil ones, that if, in spite of my best efforts and the intervention of all the relevant weather systems and supernatural powers, I was to suffer such a mishap, then I would, no matter what the circumstances or the extent of my guilt, lay the blame, fair and square, at your door."

Boïndil, who had been nodding in satisfaction, stopped short. "Very funny," he growled as Rodario and Goïmgar fell about laughing. "I'll wipe the smiles from your faces."

Bavragor's behavior had become increasingly erratic.

Since entering the fifthling kingdom, he hadn't said a word, his one eye rolling wildly as he walked. Every now and then he growled or groaned for no apparent reason and the leather strap around his wrists tightened with a menacing snap. Djerůn maintained a safe distance between him and the others.

Meanwhile, Boïndil was unhappy about the light from the torches, which he said drew attention to their presence and played into the enemies' hands—but no one could think of a workable alternative.

He was right, though. The fierce flames lit up the passageways, the panels of vraccasium, palandium, gold, and silver
gleaming with light, rendering even the smallest details visible from a distance of twenty paces and making the company
equally easy to spot.

Tungdil ran a hand over the panels. *They must have known
we'd be in need of precious metals.* At the risk of angering
the dead fifthlings, he decided to break off sections of the
portraits for use in making the ax. Djerûn snapped the metal
with ease and soon they had enough of each material for the
inlay. All that was missing was the iron for the blade. He
glanced at the ax that Lot-Ionan had given to him. *I could
smelt it, I suppose.*

The company had been marching through the lost king-
dom for some time when Boïndil signaled for them to stop.
"There's something ahead," he said, tensing in anticipation.
"Beasts of some kind, but not orcs."

Tungdil sniffed the air and detected the odor too. "They're
in front of us." He turned to Narmora, who nodded briefly
and set off to investigate.

"Come here, you cowards," thundered a deep voice from
somewhere along the passageway. "It takes more than that
to scare a dwarf!" A moment later, blades crashed against
shields and high-pitched squeals rent the air. "I may be the
last one standing, but I'll slay at least four dozen of you before
you cut me down. Vraccas is with me!"

I know that voice, thought Tungdil. He was still trying to
place it when someone got there first.

"King Gandogar!" shouted a jubilant Goïmgar. "Stand
firm, Your Majesty, I'm on my way!" Discarding his heavy
cloak, he grabbed his shield, whipped his sword from its
sheath, and stormed forth.

"Such courage!" exclaimed Rodario. "What's got into old Shimmerbeard? I never thought he had it in him."

"Me neither," said Boïndil. "All the same, we shouldn't let him fight alone." The prospect of clashing blades with Tion's beasts filled him with visible euphoria. "As for you," he threatened, nodding at Djerûn, "you know the rules. Keep an eye on our undead mason. I don't want him stabbing me in the back." He threw off his cumbersome cloak and looked expectantly at Tungdil.

The company's leader hefted his ax, having already decided that the fourthling monarch deserved their aid. "Stand by our rivals like true children of the Smith," he told them, preparing to charge. "Death to our enemies!"

They barreled along the corridor and found themselves in a small, dimly lit hall filled with hairy, hunchbacked bögnilim. Clad in armor several sizes too big for them and wielding maces and notched swords, the squawking creatures were shoving their way up a stone staircase at the top of which towered a statue of Vraccas cast in gold.

Blocking their path was Gandogar, as godlike in his heavy armor as the sculpture he was protecting. Gripping his double-bladed ax with both hands, he mowed down the first wave of aggressors with a single swipe. His diamond-studded helmet showered the walls and pillars with dappled light, adding to his heavenly aura.

At the bottom of the steps lay dead or dying beasts that had fallen from a height of ten paces. The stairs dripped with slimy olive and bottle-green blood, which further hindered the bögnilim's attack.

Yet the enemy showed no sign of retreating. Pushing and shoving, the beasts fought their way to the front, only to be cut down by Gandogar's swooping blade.

Boïndil raced ahead of his companions, sounding his bugle to herald their advance.

"Here's another dwarf who's not afraid of Tion's beasts!" Laughing maniacally he threw himself into the battle, becoming Ireheart the Furious from whom there was no escape. His axes seemed to seek out his enemies instinctively, zeroing in on unprotected flesh and damaged mail. At the end of his first sally, six bögnilim lay twitching on the floor.

Ireheart powered on, channeling a path through the hordes, with Tungdil and the others following in his wake. Even the usually timorous Goïmgar launched himself into the battle. For the first time he was prepared to fight and even die.

During the commotion Bavragor succeeded in tearing off his leather manacles. Not possessing any weapons, he tore the creatures apart with his hands, thrusting his blood-smeared muscular fingers deep into their flesh to inflict the fatal wound. The bögnilim fought back with their swords, but the revenant continued undeterred, stopping only to seize two maces and swing them with terrible strength.

Stooping low, Djerûn swiped at the knee-high creatures with his club. They crashed down amid their comrades, squashing some of them with their weight.

"To the stairs!" bellowed Tungdil on seeing that Gandogar was overextended. The king seemed to be the only survivor among his group; none of the others were visible amid the mass of heaving bodies.

The company closed ranks to thrash their way forward. Djerûn stayed at the foot of the steps and repelled the advancing bögnilim with murderous force, while the others worked their way up, engaging their enemy from behind until the last beast on the stairs had fallen. The ruler of the fourthling kingdom stood before them on the steps.

Gandogar looked dreadful, his face pale, haggard, and drawn. A mighty weapon had left two deep gashes in his bloodied chain mail.

"My king!" Goïmgar said joyfully. Not even the present danger could prevent him from sinking to one knee.

Tungdil gave him a brief nod. "Where are the others?"

"Dead," he said, struggling to regain his composure. "We need to get out of here before—"

Five figures, broader, uglier, and nastier than orcs, appeared at the far end of the hall. They were four paces tall and looked incredibly strong.

"Ogres!" Boïndil clapped excitedly. "This is where it gets really fun! Hey, Armor-Face, I'm leaving the tiddlers to you." He knocked the butts of his axes together and licked his lips. "This is more like it."

The smaller beasts drew back without a murmur, allowing the ogres to pass.

"The rest of you run," commanded Andôkai. "Djerûn and I will keep them busy. We'll see how far my remaining magic gets us. Go!"

Even as she lowered her sword and began the incantation, a thunderous rumble filled the hall and a giant tore itself out of the flesh of the mountain, taking shape beside the statue. Cavernous eyes stared at the maga from a long stony face, and a fist sped down toward her.

Andôkai spotted the danger just in time and diverted her magic toward the unexpected foe. She managed to stop the blow, but was brought to her knees by the effort. "A golem," she coughed. "There must be a wizard controlling it. Find him and kill him before my strength deserts me. I can't hold off the creature for long."

A great cry went up among the surviving bögnilim when they saw their apparently invincible enemies struggling to repel the new threat. The squawking and shouting grew louder until the creatures resolved to try their luck again, advancing in a wave of arms, legs, teeth, and whirling weapons.

The onslaught of bögnilim drove Djerûn slowly up the stairway until he stopped and opened his visor, steeping his assailants in a beam of purple light. The hall echoed with his terrible, menacing roar and the whimpering bögnilim fled from the armored giant. Djerûn followed them, lashing out with his sword and mace to regain the lost ground.

"He's over there!" Narmora pointed to a man-sized figure in the malachite robes of Nôd'onn's school. He was standing a hundred paces away, flanked by a mob of muscular orcs who served as his bodyguards. It was clear from his gestures that he was responsible for steering the golem's attack.

"They're determined not to let us near the furnace," said Tungdil. *Nôd'onn doesn't want us to forge Keenfire. We're on the right track.*

Gandogar looked at the swelling ranks of beasts that were piling into the hall. "It's hopeless. The door to the furnace is on the far side of the adjoining hall. It's sealed with dwarven runes so the beasts can't get in. We were almost inside when they ambushed us. They must have known we were coming."

Tungdil's mind whirred feverishly. "Everyone with a role to play in forging Keenfire needs to make it through that door. You or I will go with them. Since I never intended to be crowned high king, I cede my place to you, King Gandogar. My only concern is the safety of Girdlegard and our kinsfolk." He looked his rival in the eye. "Narmora will explain her role in this later, but I need you to promise you'll do everything you can to help her slay the magus."

Gandogar bowed his head. "I swear in the name of Vraccas our Creator and by the memory of Giselbert Ironeye, founding father of this kingdom, that I shall fight the magus to the end." They shook hands. "Which doesn't mean to say you won't be there too," he added.

They turned to face the enemy and raised their weapons. Tungdil placed the bugle to his lips and sounded the attack.

Giselbert's Folk,
Fifthling Kingdom,
Girdlegard,
Winter, 6234th Solar Cycle

Djerûn led the advance, flanked by the dwarves, with Rodario, torches in both hands, following close behind, shielded by Furgas, who was doing his best to fend off the bögnilim and protect the precious flames.

Back on the steps, Andôkai was still under siege from the golem. All her efforts were focused on defending herself, leaving her no time to deal with the famulus and stop the attack at its source. "Hurry!" she shouted hoarsely. "Another couple of charms and my magic will be spent."

"Leave it to me," volunteered Narmora. Launching herself into the air, she alighted on Djerûn's shoulders and pushed off again, soaring another five paces to land on a bögnil's head. In no time she was away again, using the heads and shoulders of the bewildered beasts as stepping stones. She had almost reached the famulus when a dagger nicked her calf. She missed her step and fell among the howling brutes.

"Narmora!" cried Furgas, so overcome with horror that he neglected his duty as Rodario's guard. In a flash the beasts surged forward and closed in on the impresario.

"Shoo!" he shouted, thrusting the torches in their direction. Squealing, the bögnilim backed away from the tongues of fire, only to be struck by flying sparks. In an instant they were reeling backward, consumed by flames. The dragon fire burned them to ashes before they had time to retreat.

Rodario's strategy guaranteed his own safety, but at the cost of the torches, whose light was ebbing after numerous brushes with the bögnilim's swords. At length he was left with a single torch. "Furgas," he shouted, trying to alert his companion to his plight. "Furgas, I need your help!"

But Furgas was still staring anxiously at the spot where Narmora had fallen.

"For the love of Vraccas, wake up!" Balyndis scolded him. She fought her way through the fray and thrust herself between the bögnilim and the impresario.

All of a sudden Narmora appeared out of nowhere, looming up behind the famulus's bodyguards and hewing the first orc's head with a mighty blow. She dispatched the other beasts before they had time to respond.

"Very impressive," the famulus said furiously, pointing his staff in her direction, "but not as effective as this."

A thick bolt of light shot toward Narmora, who darted nimbly aside. The bolt latched on to her movement.

Just as it seemed certain that Narmora would be hit, the bolt struck an invisible obstacle and dissipated harmlessly. It was instantly followed by a powerful flash of lightning that arced toward the famulus from the direction of the statue. There was a terrible crackle as it seared through his flesh, the flames subsiding only when nothing remained but a pile of reeking cinders. The next moment, the golem collapsed. Huge chunks of rock rained down on the enemy troops, squashing dozens of bögnilim and flattening three of the ogres who were too ponderous to escape.

The two remaining ogres stopped in their tracks and stared fearfully at the triumphant maga before retreating into the adjoining hall and vanishing from sight.

Narmora gave Andôkai a wave and the maga returned the greeting, then drew her sword in a single fluid movement. It was the only defense she had left.

"Excellent, excellent, so Narmora's still alive. Unless there's another lead actor you'd rather work with, you might want to lend me a hand," the impresario said to Furgas. "At this rate, the fabulous Rodario will die a heroic death."

Andôkai abandoned the statue and stormed down the staircase, her blade wreaking havoc among the enemy troops.

"She always ruins everything," Boïndil said testily. "I was looking forward to those ogres." He threw himself with added fury on the fleeing bögnilim. "At least I can have some fun with you."

Disregarding Tungdil's warnings, Boïndil chased after his victims, slicing into their necks from behind and shooing them along as if he were herding pigs. On reaching the doorway to the adjacent hall, he came to a sudden halt.

"What's wrong? Don't tell me your brain's caught up with you," Goïmgar said spitefully, hurrying with the others to join him. They stopped and froze as well.

"I say we leave this scene out of the play," Rodario whispered hoarsely. "I have a feeling we won't enjoy it."

The hall was at least three thousand paces long and two thousand paces wide. It was obvious what purpose the chamber had once served, for among the disused blast furnaces, ramps, and rope pulleys lay abandoned slag heaps and scattered mounds of pig iron and coal.

Now a thousand orcs, bögnilim, and trolls occupied the fifthlings' smelting works, sealing the entry to the Dragon Fire furnace.

The defeated ogres and bögnilim had already reached the foremost line of beasts and were hastily relaying what had happened in the adjoining hall. An angry murmur swept through the chamber as the beasts drew their weapons, growling in readiness for the fight.

"It's..." Boïndil was lost for words. He lowered his axes in an admission of defeat. The vast army was more than just another of the big challenges that he was so fond of. Even he could see that the odds were stacked overwhelmingly against the plucky band.

"Do you think you could fly to the other side and take us with you like you did for Goïmgar?" Tungdil whispered to the maga.

"The battle with the golem and his master drained my last reserves of magic. There's nothing left." Andôkai's eyes scanned the crowds bitterly. "Had I known what awaited us, I would have held back, but even then..."

"Let's go home," Goïmgar implored them. He turned to Gandogar. "Your Majesty—"

He stopped short, silenced by a look from Tungdil. "We can't go home now," he said. "We'll get to the furnace or die trying." He squared his shoulders stubbornly. "We're Girdlegard's last line of resistance. No one else is going to make it past this hall."

"Then it's decided." To Goïmgar's horror, Gandogar gave his assent. "We'll stay and fight together." He raised his double-bladed ax.

"We're dwarves!" thundered Ireheart, who had finally found his voice. Tucking in his head, he squared his shoulders and took a deep breath. "We never give in," he bellowed at the beasts, beating his axes together until the smelting works echoed with the noise. "Do you hear that, you worthless scoundrels? It's the sound of your deaths!"

Tungdil offered a silent prayer to Vraccas. "There's nothing for it but to fight our way through." He looked into the faces of his companions. "There's a good chance that not all of us will make it. What matters is that the right ones survive." He glanced at Balyndis. "I'm expendable. I'll gladly give my life if it means Girdlegard and its peoples have a future."

Furgas's eyes filled with tears as he kissed Narmora passionately: She was among those who had to survive at all costs. She stroked his cheek tenderly.

"One to a hundred," was Boïndil's assessment of their respective numbers. "It could be worse." This time he blew the bugle, sounding the ancient dwarven call to war. It was answered by hostile shouts. Boïndil glanced at his companions. "Race you to the other side."

After five hundred paces, they had fought themselves into an impasse, unable to advance or retreat.

Surrounded on all sides by the foulest of creatures, the company stood shoulder to shoulder and faced the prospect of fighting until their arms were too heavy to deflect the deadly blows.

Worse still, they had lost Rodario in the first ten paces. He had been swallowed among the mass of orcish bodies and by the time Tungdil noticed his absence, the impresario was nowhere to be seen.

With Rodario, they lost the dragon fire with which the furnace was to be lit.

We're so close now, Vraccas. "We need to go back," he shouted over his shoulder. "We've lost Rodario and the only torch."

Andôkai was about to reply when roaring flames shot toward the ceiling.

"Get back," a voice rasped imperiously from the door. "Let me deal with them."

The noise stopped instantly. In a flash, a path opened through the rabble, the beasts drawing away to let their master pass. A corpulent figure in malachite robes strode toward them, extinguishing the last spark of hope that Tungdil had been kindling with dwarven obstinacy.

"Nôd'onn." An awed whisper swept through the ranks of beasts, who were staring at the magus in fascination, some bowing or falling to their knees.

"I thought I would find the villains here," he rasped, his voice giving way to a cough. A bright red globule of saliva spattered onto the face of a bögnil whose tongue shot out hungrily and licked it away. "I sent my servants here to ambush you. I wanted to have the pleasure of destroying you myself."

An orc leaped forward, whipping out his sword. "Let me do it for you, Master," he said slavishly.

"Silence, ingrate!" The magus stretched a hand. There was a flash of light and flames shot out of his fingers, setting the orc ablaze. The beast staggered backward, stumbling in agony until at last he lay still. "Out of my way," commanded Nôd'onn. "If you crowd me, I can't destroy them without destroying you." His pale face was almost entirely obscured by a cowl, with only a chink of white skin visible through the folds of cloth.

"I'll do what I can," Andôkai whispered to Tungdil. "The rest of you run." She pushed her fair hair back from her severe visage, seized her sword, and prepared to strike. All of a sudden she stopped.

Tungdil sensed her hesitation. "What's wrong?"

She seemed puzzled. "I can't see his staff. Nôd'onn would never be parted with it, no more than I would go anywhere without my sword. It must be an illusion."

"Ye gods! It's Rodario!" hissed Furgas, trying not to blow his friend's cover by looking too relieved.

Tungdil stared in disbelief. The impresario's transformation was as complete as it had been on the stage, but now he was playing to an audience who would kill him and eat him if his performance was anything less than faultless. *How does he do it?*

"As for you," the sham magus rasped at the company, "you shall suffer. But first I shall be merciful: You may advance to the forge and touch the hallowed door. Only then will my servants rip you to pieces. Is that not exquisitely cruel?" The beasts cheered excitedly.

This time the crowd parted on the other side of the company, allowing them to proceed through a narrow corridor toward the locked door. The sham magus followed behind them, swaying, coughing, and whipping his followers into a frenzy as he threatened the company with increasingly diabolical fates.

They were ten paces from the door when the impresario swayed more vigorously than usual and stumbled.

"Stop!" Tungdil grabbed Narmora and Furgas before they could rush to his aid. "You'll give the game away for all of us."

The costumed Rodario struggled upright. A helmet rolled

out from beneath his robes and his left leg seemed suddenly a good deal shorter. Without the makeshift stilt that had allowed him to tower majestically at the real magus's height, the fakery was obvious. It took the beasts a few moments to fathom the situation.

"That's not Nôd'onn!" An orc rushed toward him, brandishing his sword, as the company closed ranks around the hobbling Rodario and the battle recommenced.

"What have you done with the torch?" demanded Tungdil.

Clutching his side, the impresario coughed up another mouthful of blood; this time he was wounded and not just relying on his props. Even so, he managed a smile as he held up a small lantern. The wick was burning brightly. "No self-respecting magus would dream of carrying a torch."

Their courage restored, they fought their way more determinedly than ever toward the door, while the orcs pushed aside their smaller colleagues and attacked with full force. They were determined to put an end to the indefatigable men and dwarves.

Every member of the company was struck by an ax, sword, or mace. Some of the wounds were more serious than others, but the dwarves stood their ground. Tungdil focused on deciphering the runic password that would gain them entry to the forge. For once his knowledge failed him.

"I can't read the runes," he cried despairingly to Andôkai. "It must be a riddle."

"How awfully inconvenient," gasped Rodario. He clutched the door, trying to hold himself up as his legs gave way. "I don't expect my death to trouble you greatly, but remember this: Girdlegard has lost a luminary of the stage." He closed his eyes and slumped to the ground, suffocating the lantern as he fell. The flame flickered dangerously.

"No!" murmured Gandogar, who had been watching the dying actor out of the corner of his eye. "We can't let the flame go out!" As he turned to save the lantern, an enormous orc seized his chance and waded in. With a terrible shout he thrust his notched sword toward the king's back.

"Your Majesty!" Goïmgar realized midshout that the warning would come too late. Without thinking, he threw himself—shield first and head ducked—into the path of the blade.

With a high-pitched ring the sword struck the edge of the shield, forcing it down. The dwarf's head and neck appeared above the rim.

The orc bared its teeth, expelling a foul rush of breath, which swept through Goïmgar's beard. The beast's long blade settled on the shield, using its contours to draw a perfect line from right to left.

Goïmgar thrust his blade forward, but it was no match for the orcish sword. His stumpy weapon shattered, shards of metal jangling to the floor, and the sword continued, cleaving through skin, flesh, sinew, and bone.

As the artisan's head fell to the right, his twitching body toppled left, brushing against Balyndis, who let out a furious howl and swung her ax with fresh savagery.

Gandogar turned in time to see Goïmgar die in his stead. Even as the head hit the floor, the flame died, a thin wisp of smoke snaking its way to the ceiling. "May Tion take you!" Gandogar raised his ax and split the murderer from skull to chest.

With two of their number dead and the dragon fire extinguished, the company struggled against the heaviness in their arms. Their resistance was weakening.

"Did you get us this far in order to destroy us, Vraccas?"

Tungdil shouted accusingly as he drove his ax between the jaws of an orc.

At that moment there was a welcome grinding noise and the right-hand panel of the door swung open.

The deep tones of a bugle rang out, echoing the melody that Boïndil had sounded at the beginning of their attack. Stocky figures streamed through the doors and threw themselves on the beasts. Their axes and hammers raged mercilessly among the hordes.

It took Tungdil a good few moments to realize that their rescuers were dwarves.

One of their number, a warrior whose polished armor outshone everything save the diamonds on his belt, nodded toward the open door.

"Hurry, we can't hold them back for long," he bellowed, his deep voice sending shivers down Tungdil's spine.

He was more used to seeing the warrior's features cast in vraccasium and gold, but he had encountered the visage often enough during their long march through the fifthling kingdom to know exactly who he was: Giselbert Ironeye, father of Giselbert's folk.

"I thought you were..."

"We'll talk later," the ancient dwarf told him. "Just get your company inside."

Tungdil gave the order. Furgas hoisted Rodario to his shoulders, and Gandogar carried Goïmgar's corpse. As soon as the group was safely in the forge, Giselbert's dwarves abandoned their attack and slammed the door behind them. A moment later there was a furious hammering and pounding, but blind rage alone was not enough to breach the door.

"Welcome," Giselbert said solemnly. "Whoever you may be, I hope your coming is a good omen."

There were ten of them in all: ashen-faced dwarves with absent eyes that made them seem vaguely trancelike. Each was clad in lavishly splendid mail and their beards reached to their belts. Determination, a Vraccas-given trait of their race, was stamped on every face.

"My warriors and I have been fighting Tion's minions since the fall of my kingdom eleven hundred cycles ago," said Giselbert, who seemed the most venerable, the most majestic of them all. "We are the last of the fifthlings, killed by the älfar and resurrected by the Perished Land. As you can see, we chose not to serve it."

Tungdil shot a quick glance at Bavragor, who was covered from head to toe in every imaginable shade of green. Orc and bögnil blood was dripping from his hands and splashing to the floor.

"It takes a lot to kill an undead dwarf, but most of our companions were eventually slain. The rest of us retreated to the furnace, our folk's most treasured relic." He held Tungdil's gaze.

"And you're sure you don't hate other dwarves and want to murder every living creature?"

Giselbert shook his head. "We taught ourselves not to. In eleven hundred cycles you can learn to stifle the pestilent hatred." His eyes shifted to the door. "The creatures used to content themselves with guarding the entrance, but during the last few orbits they've laid siege to the doors. I daresay the change has something to do with you."

"Very likely." Tungdil ran through the introductions and gave a hasty account of the threat facing Girdlegard and the reason for their coming. "But it's all been in vain. We were supposed to light the furnace with dragon fire, but the flame went out while we were fighting by the door."

Giselbert clapped a hand on his shoulder and a kindly smile spread across the creases and wrinkles of his ancient face. "You are wrong to give up hope. The fire is burning as fiercely as ever." He stopped and listened. "The furnace has always been under our protection. Vraccas must have known we would need it one day." He and his companions stepped aside to reveal the rest of the chamber.

The hall, fifty paces long by thirty wide, boasted twenty abandoned hearths, lined up in two rows, and four times as many anvils, arranged around an enormous furnace ablaze with fierce white flames.

Countless pillars supported the ceiling eighty paces above and the walls were filled with neat rows of tools: hammers, tongs, chisels, files, and all manner of implements needed for the blacksmith's craft. Fine sand covered the floor and the upper reaches of the chamber were coated in a thick layer of soot. A stone stairway led to the flue.

The bellows and grindstones were attached to metal chains that ran through a system of rollers and pulleys to the ceiling, where they looped through the rock. Tungdil was instantly reminded of the lifting apparatus in the underground network.

He found himself imagining the smithy in its heyday when Girdlegard's finest weapons and most splendid armor had been forged by Giselbert's dwarves. He breathed out in relief and prayed to Vraccas to excuse his lack of faith. "That's the best news we've had since Ogre's Death," he said cheerfully. *We're nearly there. And to think I'd resigned myself to failure...*

"He's alive!" exclaimed Furgas. "His heart is beating! Rodario's alive!"

"Let me take a look at him." Andôkai swept back her hair, knelt beside the wounded impresario, and inspected his wound. "He's had a blow to the head and a slight gouge to the side. It's nothing too serious," she announced, cleaning the afflicted area with Bavragor's brandy to stave off infection.

The impresario's eyes fluttered open. "Thank you, Estimable Maga," he gasped, gritting his teeth as the alcohol stung his raw flesh. "Had I known, I would have begged the orc to strike me on the mouth so you could kiss me back to life."

"If you were a warrior, things might have been different between us," she said, responding remarkably favorably to the flirtation.

"A good actor can be many things, even a warrior."

"But it's only an act."

"I'm a warrior in spirit. Isn't that enough?"

"Maybe," she said, "but your weapon has fought for so many causes in every kingdom that I couldn't rely on you not to swap sides." Her blue eyes looked at him smilingly as she patted his cheek. "Save your charm for the women who adore you."

Giselbert pointed to a quiet corner of the smithy. "Lie down and get some rest. The doors won't fall; we'll see to it that they don't. It's important that you recover your strength before we get going with Keenfire. There are some matters we need to attend to before we can forge the blade."

"Such as...?"

The ancient monarch chuckled when he saw the look of alarm on Tungdil's face. "It can wait until you're rested. I'm sorry we can't offer you any sustenance, but you'll be safe here, at least."

The travelers were too tired to do anything but follow his advice; even Boïndil was so spent that he forgot to be suspicious of their undead hosts. In any case, no one could claim that the revenants weren't putting their lives to good use.

Tungdil went to join Gandogar, who was sitting in silence beside Goïmgar's corpse. The fourthling king had removed his battered helmet, his brown hair resting on his mighty shoulders. "He died trying to save me," he said somberly. "He threw himself in front of that orc, even though he must have known the brute would kill him." He glanced at Tungdil. "I didn't think he had it in him. I was pleased when you picked Goïmgar because he seemed too much the artisan and too little the dwarf. I misjudged him. He was a dwarf, all right."

Tungdil placed the pouch of diamonds in Gandogar's hands. "You're our diamond cutter now. You must finish his task for him."

"Gladly, although I can't promise to emulate his skill. Goïmgar was a far better artisan than I am."

Tungdil paused before broaching a rather delicate subject. "There's something I need to tell you, Gandogar." He quickly told him of Gundrabur's plan and Bislipur's trickery, and finished by producing Sverd's collar as proof.

The king recognized the choker at once. "By the beard of Goïmdil, I wish these accusations were unfounded, but the loathsome collar speaks for itself. Sverd was in thrall to his master; he could never have acted alone." He shook his head incredulously. "How could Bislipur be so blind? How could I be so blind?"

"So you don't want to wage war on the elves?"

"Absolutely not! Isn't Girdlegard in enough trouble already?" He took a deep breath. "Honestly, Tungdil, nothing could be farther from my thoughts. Gundrabur was right after all. We've been through so much since the start of this mission that the thought of another war...No, an alliance is what we need." He stopped and frowned. "I'm not saying we have to be best friends with the elves or anything. The way they betrayed the fifthlings was—"

"We weren't betrayed by elves," interrupted a fifthling who had approached in time to hear the end of their exchange. His thick black beard hung in decorative cords that reached to his chest.

"Your folk was betrayed by the pointy-ears," the king insisted. "I saw the evidence myself."

"Evidence provided by Bislipur," Tungdil reminded him.

The stranger gave them a wan smile. "My name is Glandallin Hammerstrike of the clan of the Striking Hammers." He turned to Gandogar. "I witnessed the terrible demise of our kingdom, and I saw the traitor who opened our gates."

"Yes," Gandogar said stubbornly. "A backstabbing elf."

"It was a dwarf." He paused as the others, including Balyndis, who had joined them, stared in disbelief. "Glamdolin Strongarm was the traitor who spoke the incantation and opened our gates."

"But why?"

"It was the opportunity he had been waiting for. That dreadful morning he pretended to succumb to the fever that the älfar had spread among our folk. The battle was fierce and no one gave him a second thought. He skulked down to the gates and cleared the way for Tion's hordes. It was his doing that the älfar found their way into our underground halls and took us by surprise."

"But I don't see..."

"He was a thirdling," Glandallin said flatly. "A child of Lorimbur, a dwarf killer, who inveigled himself into our folk and masked his true intentions so cunningly that we suspected nothing. He waited until we were fatally weakened, then struck the final blow. He died by my ax but was raised by the Perished Land to incant the secret runes. After our deaths we captured him and questioned him. Glamdolin was beheaded, never to rise again."

"I hope you're writing this down for me," Rodario whispered to Furgas. "We'll make our fortunes with this play!"

"So the elves had nothing to do with it!" said Tungdil, delighted that the path was clear for an alliance. *Bislipur's treacherous scheme has come to naught.*

They buried Goïmgar's body in a corner of the forge, erected a pile of stones to mark the grave, and dedicated his soul to Vraccas. As soon as they felt sufficiently rested, they began their preparations for forging the mighty ax. " 'The blade must be made of the purest, hardest steel, with diamonds encrusting the bit and an alloy of every known precious metal filling the inlay and the runes. The spurs should be hewn from stone and the grip sculpted from wood of the sigurdaisy tree,' " recited Tungdil, reading from the manuscript that would serve as their guide.

They stacked the gold, silver, palandium, and vraccasium neatly on the table along with the pouch of diamonds and the sigurdaisy wood for the haft. The fifthlings furnished them with iron ore for the blade and stone for the spurs.

Tungdil realized with alarm what it was they were missing. "We didn't bring any tionium," he said, scolding himself for his laxness. "You don't have any, I suppose?"

There was a short silence. "Not in the forge," said Glandallin. "We were never especially fond of Tion's metal, so there wasn't much call for it."

Narmora unhooked an amulet from her neck and laid it on the table. "It's pure tionium. My mother gave it to me to ward off the forces of good. Since I've allied myself with them, there's not much point in wearing it. I just hope there's enough for you to use."

Tungdil gave her a grateful look. His doubts and reservations about the half älf had been canceled out by her deeds. "Girdlegard is in your debt twice over. No matter how expertly we fashion the weapon, Keenfire would be powerless without tionium—or without the undergroundlings' foe."

"It's the least I can do, given the amount of suffering my mother's race has caused," she demurred.

He glanced at the glowing furnace. "Shall we begin?"

"I'm afraid it's not that simple," said Giselbert. "The furnace is alight, but the temperature isn't high enough. Usually, we'd use the bellows to breathe life into Dragon Fire, but the equipment has rusted and we haven't been able to get it to work."

"Thank goodness for that!" Furgas leaped to his feet. "What with Narmora being the savior of Girdlegard, I was beginning to think I was just a hanger-on." He chuckled good-humoredly and the others joined in. "I hope you're ready for a demonstration of my expertise."

He was rewarded with a kiss from Narmora, who picked up her ax to practice wards, attacks, and strikes with Boïndil. Andôkai sat watching them, while Djerûn, motionless as usual, crouched beside her. For some reason Tungdil was half expecting the helmet to give off a purple glow.

"You're wondering what's behind the visor, aren't you?" said Narmora, recovering her breath. She pressed the canteen of water thirstily to her lips.

He turned to her. "Is there something I should know?"

Narmora leaned against the wall of polished rock, still panting with exertion. Boïndil was a hard taskmaster and the combat sessions left her exhausted. "When I was little, my mother told me stories about a terrifying being, the king among Tion's and Samusin's creatures, the predator of predators, the hunter who hunted his own kind, destroying the weak and fighting the strong to make them stronger—or to kill them if their ascendancy was undeserved." Narmora dabbed the sweat from her brow. "She said that his eyes shone with violet light and that weaker beings fled for their lives at the sight of him. All the beasts are terrified of Samusin's son. She used to scare the living daylights out of me with those stories." She grinned, then averted her gaze, careful not to glance in the giant's direction. "And back then I didn't know that they were true."

The explanation didn't take Tungdil entirely by surprise. Samusin was Andôkai's chosen deity, and she would doubtless feel honored to be traveling with a creature who was said to be his son. Whether or not Djerûn was more than just a servant to the maga was a question that Tungdil was reluctant to ponder. "No wonder the bögnilim bolted."

"Most creatures would run away from him, beasts of Tion or not." Narmora got up to resume sparring with Boïndil.

Tungdil watched as Balyndis kindled one of the hearths with ordinary flames. After stripping off her mail and leather jerkin, she donned a leather apron that covered her chest and her midriff, although her undergarments left a good deal of flesh on show. He made his way over to see what she was doing. "What are you up to?"

"Making steel," she said, signaling for him to tie her apron at the back. Standing behind her, he caught his first proper glimpse of female skin. It was pink and covered in wispy down. There hadn't been much opportunity for washing of late, so she had a strong smell about her, but it wasn't unpleasant—not clean, exactly, but still quite arousing. "The blast furnaces are on the other side of the door, so I'm having to smelt the metal by other means. It's a trick of the trade."

Balyndis's apron strings were safely knotted, but Tungdil found himself clasping her sturdy hips. Her skin felt smooth and warm. He stroked the fine hairs.

"Come here so you can see what I'm doing." He did as he was told. "First we have to get rid of the impurities, which is why I'm placing the ore in a shallow crucible. The heat will burn them off. Unfortunately, it means we can produce only small quantities of steel at a time, but it should be enough for a blade." She stood there, waiting patiently for the temperature to rise and the iron to melt. "Surely you've done this before?"

"No," he said regretfully. "I was only a blacksmith."

"How many strikes for a horseshoe nail?"

"Seven, if I concentrate. Nine, if I don't."

"Not bad," she said with a smile that made his cheeks flush redder than the molten ore. "It takes me seven strikes too."

"How many for an ax?"

"Seven, if I concentrate; nine, if I don't. Orbits, that is, not strikes. Since time is of the essence right now, I'll work straight through and it should be done in five orbits, without the quality suffering at all." She drew his attention to Giselbert, who was waving at them from the doors. "I think he wants to show you something."

Tungdil raised his hand to indicate that he was coming. "It's hard to believe that he and the others are older than anything we've ever encountered, save the mountains themselves."

"And to think that they're revenants as well. It's so sad that their souls were stolen by the Perished Land. I wish there was something we could do to get them back."

"Only Vraccas can restore their souls, but you're right,

it must be awful for them." He hurried over to the anxious Giselbert.

"The beasts are preparing to attack."

Tungdil studied the heavy metal doors. They were reinforced with steel bindings and protected with Vraccas's runes. "I thought you said the forge was safe?"

"It was—until you gave them a reason to breach the doors. They know you're here and they know you're forging a weapon that will bring about their doom. Their priorities have changed." He pointed to a peephole and Tungdil peered through.

In the course of a single orbit the ragged hordes had become an orderly army under the älfar's command.

A short distance from the doors was a growing pile of pillars and stalactites, torn down and stacked by a unit of ogres. Beyond that, further divisions of beasts were putting the finishing touches on what looked like hoists.

"You're right; it looks serious. I'll have to warn the others. What do we have in the way of defenses?"

Giselbert raised his ax.

"Is that all?"

The fifthling raised another ax and gave a wry smile. "It's not enough, I know. We—"

He was interrupted by muffled shrieks and jangling armor; ogres bellowed, orcs snarled anxiously, bögnilim yelped in terror.

What's going on out there? Tungdil pressed his face to the peephole just as the fires went out in the encampment. Dwarf-sized warriors with pale faces poured out of the darkness, swarming among the beasts and cleaving through their ranks. They seemed to be deliberately beheading their opponents so that none could be raised from the dead.

The attack was over in moments. The flames were rekindled and the invaders disappeared without a trace.

The spirits of the dead dwarves! He thought back to the pale figures and their mysterious warning. Tion's hordes had colonized their realm against their wishes, and the vengeful ghosts had made them pay. "What do you know about dwarven ghosts?"

"Ghosts? Nothing...but I'm glad they've decided to help."

Tungdil hurried to tell the others of the imminent attack. Everyone not involved in forging Keenfire was put to work hewing boulders to barricade the doors.

All that mattered for the moment was keeping the beasts at bay. Later they would have to figure out a way of getting themselves and the weapon out of the forge.

The company's faith in Furgas proved well founded. It took him less than an orbit to get to grips with the bellows. According to him, the pulley system worked in much the same way as a stage curtain, a parallel that he found especially apt.

Having located the damage, he repaired it, improvising a solution with the presence of mind and ingenuity befitting a prop master who had rescued plenty of performances from mechanical disaster. He even got the grindstone turning again.

Meanwhile, the others continued their efforts to barricade the doors. The beasts had already launched an initial offensive, which failed because the stalactites shattered against the doors.

When the second orbit dawned, Gandogar began work on the diamonds. The environment could scarcely have been less conducive to his task, but he was fortunate to have use of Goïmgar's tools. Bavragor sat at a table and fashioned the spurs, his hands moving with the mechanical jerkiness of a puppet on strings.

Giselbert prepared the casts for the precious metals, while Balyndis threw herself into forging the blade and its shaft, which itself was the length of a forearm.

She set up her workshop in the middle of the chamber near Dragon Fire. With every sigh of the machine-driven bellows, the coals hissed and crackled, sometimes spitting white flames.

Her work was spread between three anvils of different sizes and shapes. Time after time she reached confidently for the appropriate tool among the rows of rivet tongs, wolf jaw tongs, duck bill tongs, and six dozen or so similar implements, extracted the red hot steel from the fire, hammered it approximately into shape, and replaced it in its fiery bed of coals as soon as the metal cooled.

Tungdil had never seen such a magnificent forge. Whereas he was accustomed to four types of hammer, there was a choice of fifty and all with different heads, not to mention the chisels, files, saws, and other tools that Balyndis employed with obvious skill.

"I could use your help," she said suddenly, handing him some tongs. "Draw out the steel to the thickness of a knife blade, halve the metal with your ax, and lay the sections on top of each other."

Tungdil did as instructed, reaching into the furnace with his long-handled tongs. White flames licked the coals, emitting a phenomenal warmth.

The steel was white-hot when he placed it on the anvil. He drew it out quickly and returned it to the flames, waiting for it to glow before transferring it to the anvil, dividing it in half, and hammering the two sections vigorously into a single strip.

It had been so long since he had last stood at the anvil that he felt a rush of elation as he brought down the hammer and tapped out a rhythm. This was the wizardry of the dwarves, their ability to induce metal to perform wondrous miracles that a magus or famulus would never understand.

He glanced at Balyndis happily; without realizing, they were hammering in unison.

At length he laid down his tools. "I ought to go back to shifting boulders before the others start accusing me of ruining the blade. How many layers will it have when it's finished?"

"About three hundred," she replied, still hammering. "It's good steel so it can take it. Thanks for the help."

Tungdil gave her a wave and joined the working party at the doors. The fifthlings hurried back and forth tirelessly, their undead bodies able to function without rest, but Tungdil and Boïndil were only too aware of the importance of conserving their strength. Most of their provisions had been eaten already and the rest would have to be rationed until they left the forge.

"Vraccas must be really farsighted," said Boïndil after a time. "To think that he brought us all together like this!'

"What do you mean?" asked Tungdil, surprised to hear the warrior pondering such matters.

Boïndil, his skin bronzed from orbits in the sun, turned his bearded face toward him. "Each one of us has a vital role to play. We needed you to come up with the plan in the first place, Balyndis and the others to make the blade, the impresario to save us from the runts, Furgas to repair the bellows, and the pointy-eared actress to strike the magus down." He sat down on a rock. "There couldn't be a better team..."

"What about Goïmgar?"

"Er...Well, we needed Goïmgar to save Gandogar."

"Aren't you forgetting the warrior twins? You and your brother wiped out anyone who stood in our way and kept fighting when others would have lost their nerve. We wouldn't have got this far if it weren't for you." He gave him a hearty thump on the back.

Boïndil grinned. "More incredibly, we turned our scholar into a proper, respectable dwarf. Living with the long-uns sent your instincts to sleep, but we've woken them up for you, Tungdil." He made to strike him with his ax. "Truth be told, you're pretty handy with a weapon. You must have been born a warrior."

Born a warrior. Tungdil was painfully reminded that he still knew nothing of his birth.

For once Boïndil picked up on his mood. "Cheer up, Tungdil! If the fourthlings won't have you, you can always live with us," he promised breezily. "I'll swear by the beard of Beroïn that you're the illegitimate cousin of my estranged aunt thirty-four times removed." They both laughed.

Giselbert, who had been peering through the peephole at regular intervals, headed over from the door. His expression was grave. "They've fashioned new battering rams. This time they might actually work."

"Is there any other way out?" asked Tungdil. "Rodario's act won't fool them again." He looked up at the chimney towering above the furnace. "Would that do the trick?"

"Our scholar is full of inspiration," Boïndil said admiringly.

"It might, but the stairs are pretty steep."

"We'll manage," Tungdil assured him. "Nothing can stop us from saving Girdlegard, especially not now that the ax is almost finished."

Just then, an almighty crash shook the walls as if the mountain were collapsing around them.

The doors shuddered, fragments of rock rained all around them, and the metal panels strained and groaned. The attack had begun in earnest.

VIII

For three whole orbits the forge echoed with continual pounding and thudding against the doors and the beasts' persistence began to pay off. The solid iron panels were already bulging in the middle, and the metal showed signs of cracking under the force of the brutal assault.

Tungdil had requisitioned one of the anvils and was frantically forging bars to add to the barricade, but it was obvious that the beasts would eventually force their way in.

Balyndis had almost finished the blade and was about to begin the fine-tuning. The task of engraving the metal was entrusted to Giselbert, who marked the warm steel with runes and patterns for the inlay. Gandogar had cut the diamonds to size and left them on his makeshift workbench. Each gem had been sharpened to a deadly point that would slit the magus open. The spurs, carved by Bavragor from black granite, were as long as a human index finger and were waiting to be attached.

Tungdil, under directions from Narmora, sculpted the grip using a hacksaw, a file, and a grindstone to shape the metal-like sigurdaisy wood to fit her hand. He left the sanding to her and went back to reinforcing the doors. On the fourth orbit the heated blade was edged with diamonds and the spurs were put in place.

Balyndis worked with utmost concentration. The metal was unforgiving, and every strike of the hammer was vital: The slightest mistake could cost her the blade, and there wasn't enough time to reforge it. The constant gonglike pounding on the doors was a distraction that they could all have done without.

Giselbert was almost ready to combine the precious metals and create a single alloy, a process made possible by the incredible heat of the dragon fire. The others looked on in fascination as he heated the metals in individual pans: rich gold, shimmering silver, orange vraccasium, white palandium, and a coin-sized lump of black tionium.

One by one he emptied the molten contents into a bell-shaped vessel lined with glass. When it came to pouring the tionium, the black liquid hissed with Tion-like malice, angry at being united with an element as pure as palandium.

Another loud boom shook the hall, followed immediately by a cracking and snapping of metal. A battering ram smashed into the reinforced door, opening a gap half a pace across. In no time a bögnil had squeezed through and was staring wide-eyed at his surroundings. He squealed in excitement.

"Come here, you ugly piglet!" bellowed Ireheart, whooping exuberantly as he charged. At last he could allow his fury to run riot. "So you think you're brave, do you? Let's see if my axes change your mind!"

"Narmora, you stay here," ordered Tungdil. "Everyone else, after him!" Balyndis, Giselbert, Andôkai, and Djerûn rushed to help Boïndil, who shouted at them to go away.

The pounding on the doors became faster and more violent. With victory in sight, the beasts redoubled their efforts. At last the opening was wide enough for an orc to storm through. Arrows ripped through the gap, but inflicted no damage, save the occasional scratch.

Tungdil knew that the breach could not be allowed to open further if he and the others were to stem the attack. *We'll drive them back with dragon fire.* He ran to the furnace, heaped on some coals, and pumped the bellows until the fire roared with bright white flames.

Hurriedly he shoveled a few loads onto a wheeled anvil and rolled it to the doors. Without wasting a second he filled his spade and hurled its contents over the heads and shoulders of the invaders.

Red-hot coals showered over the beasts, covering them in sparks and coal dust that singed their faces, danced down their collars, and penetrated their chain mail. Loud screams rent the air, increasing in volume when the second fiery hail descended. There was an overwhelming stench of charred flesh, smoldering hair, and scorched leather. The orcs raised their shields above their heads in panic, allowing Tungdil and his companions to plunge their axes and hammers into their unprotected chests.

Furgas kept them supplied with hot coals until the enemy retreated. The orcs went back to bombarding the forge with arrows.

"Sooner or later they're going to force their way in," predicted Andôkai. "They'll form a shield wall and we won't be able to stop them. It's time we left."

They made a concerted effort to close the doors, but the beasts had been cunning enough to jam them open with wedges.

She's right; we need to get out of here as soon as we can. Tungdil returned to the furnace. "How much longer until the inlay is ready?" he asked Giselbert.

"The tionium and the palandium need to simmer for half an orbit. Once they've melded, the others will follow. After that I'll be able to pour the alloy into the grooves, but then there's the cooling time. Will the doors hold?"

"They'll have to," growled Tungdil, nodding resolutely. "We'll see to it that they do."

From then on, Nôd'onn's servants gave them no respite. The assault on the doors was unrelenting and the beasts proceeded as the maga had predicted: Shields raised above their heads, they advanced in formation, protected from the glowing coals.

Two of the fifthlings were beheaded, never to rise again. Their loss was a serious blow to the defenders, and already the next battering ram was pounding against the doors. The destructive will of the Perished Land was bent on assailing the forge.

It is time." The long and wearying wait ended as Giselbert lifted the vessel containing the mountain's precious metals and poured them into the indented runes and symbols. The alloy's color was strangely indeterminate: somewhere between orange and yellow with a peculiar shimmer and swirling black pinpoints. It streamed through the grooves with the assurance of a river that was familiar with its course, filling the channels without a drop to spare.

"Done," announced Giselbert, heaving a sigh of relief. "In another half an orbit, when the inlay has cooled, we can set the blade on the haft and—"

A battering ram exploded through the ravaged metal doors. The protruding end of the pillar withdrew quickly, only to reappear just above the existing hole. The beasts had decided to fashion their own entrance.

Tungdil took a deep breath. His arms were about to drop off, he had never felt hungrier in his life, and he was tired enough to sleep for an orbit. Instead he raised his ax. "We need to keep them at bay until the inlay has cooled."

He paid no attention to the pain in his back and shoulders, determined not to flag. He was leader of the company, after all, and Gandogar deferred to him without a murmur, never questioning his authority. His selfless cooperation made Tungdil respect him all the more.

Already the invaders were squeezing through the breach. In a flash, Ireheart had thrown himself on the beasts, his enthusiasm for combat apparently undiminished. He hacked at the orcs so savagely that his axes were barely visible amid the scraps of flying armor and bloodied flesh.

But even Ireheart's fury could do nothing to stem the attack. As time wore on, the battle swung steadily in favor of the beasts. With a third of the doorway smashed open, it was only thanks to Djerûn and the indomitable fifthlings that the company hadn't been defeated already. Time was against them.

Giselbert fought his way to Tungdil's side. "You should go. The alloy has cooled enough for you to take Keenfire." He raised his ax. "We'll hold the beasts back until you're safely inside the flue; then we'll shut the vents and destroy the mechanism. Without it, they won't be able to get into the chimney. You'll be miles away by the time they force their way inside."

Tungdil nodded gratefully and signaled for his company to retreat.

The finished blade was lying on the central anvil, shimmering enigmatically in the bright light of Dragon Fire. The diamonds twinkled, the inlay glistened, and the runes shone with the fierce glow of the furnace, brought to life by the roaring flames.

"To think that Vraccas gave us the means to accomplish this." Tungdil gazed in awe at the result of their joint labor. "Balyndis," he said solemnly, "attach the blade." She picked up the grip and inserted it into the long metal shaft of the blade. Her face paled.

"Vraccas forfend, it doesn't fit," she said hoarsely. "See how loose it is? The blade will fly off as soon as Narmora swings the ax. But how could we have made the grip too narrow? I'm sure it—"

One by one the runes lit up. The shaft glowed, then the wood seemed to swell. Crackling and straining, it expanded to fill the gap, until the grip and the shaft were one.

Tungdil took it as a sign that Vraccas was happy with their work. He ran his fingers over the blade, cherishing the feel of the metal. Deep down, he wished he could wield the ax himself, and he held on to it for a moment before handing it to Narmora.

Giselbert stepped forward. "May I?" he asked tremulously.

"Of course. If it weren't for you and the others, it would never have been forged."

The ancient king grasped the ax, gazing at it reverently before trying a few swings. He entrusted it ceremoniously to the half älf.

"So this is it," he said, his voice choked with emotion. "The agony of the undead, all those cycles of waiting, of fighting...There was a reason for it all." He shook hands with each of the company in turn, lingering when he came to Tungdil. "Don't abandon my kingdom to the creatures of Tion. Free Girdlegard and drive out the pestilence, then come back and rebuild my kingdom for the dwarves. Will you promise me that, Tungdil Goldhand?" He fixed him with a piercing stare.

Tungdil could do nothing but nod, rendered speechless by the zeal in the fifthling's eyes.

Giselbert unfastened his diamond-studded weapons belt and laid it around Tungdil's waist. "Wear this in memory of my folk and let it be known that we defended our kingdom to the last, in death as well as life."

Tungdil swallowed. "Your gift is too generous."

"From what I have come to know of you, it is no less than you deserve." They embraced as friends; then it was time for the company to leave.

"Let's get going," said Tungdil, looking up at the narrow staircase leading into the gloomy chimney. He glanced back at the doors, where the last of the fifthlings were locked in bitter combat with the orcs.

"But what will become of you?" Boïndil asked the fifthling king.

Giselbert stood tall, eyes fixed on the doors. "My warriors will hold them back while you get yourselves out of here. We'll fight until they chop off our heads and put an end to our undead existence," he said proudly. "Now go! The steps are shallower in the upper reaches of the chimney. Djerůn will have to take care."

It was decided that Narmora, as the nimblest among them, should lead the way and test the stairs. The humans and dwarves lined up behind her, with the giant at the rear. Bavragor stayed by the furnace, a new war hammer in his hand.

"Aren't you coming with us?" Tungdil asked cautiously.

He shook his head. "I said from the beginning that I'd never go home. I set out to die a glorious death and so I shall. This is what I wanted." A profound calm had descended on him, allowing his mind, which had been battling against his undead state, to find peace. He turned his one eye toward Tungdil. "Thank you for bringing me here and for letting me be part of this."

"I gave you my word."

"You could have gone back on it. No one would have blamed you. They warned you about the merry minstrel, but you honored your promise." He took a step forward and looked him in the eye. "I shall die in the knowledge that my hands carved the most important bit of masonry in the history of the dwarves. No mason will trump it—not unless Girdlegard needs another Keenfire, which I sincerely hope it never will."

"Is there anything I can say to persuade you?"

The mason chuckled, and something about his laughter reminded Tungdil of the cheerful ballad singer and joker of old. "Persuade me? Tungdil, I'm a dwarf! I made my decision orbits ago." He nodded toward the door. "They need my help and I shall fight alongside them. There could be no greater honor than to die side by side with the founding dwarves of the fifthling kingdom, the most ancient and venerable of our kin." His calloused fingers gripped Tungdil's hand. "You're a good dwarf and that's what matters, not your lineage. Be sure to remember me—and old Shimmer-beard as well."

They embraced, and Tungdil let the tears course down his cheeks. Another friend was being taken from him, and he wasn't afraid to show his grief.

"As if I could ever forget you, Bavragor Hammerfist! I shall remember you always." He turned to look at Goïmgar's grave. "I'll never forget either of you."

Smiling, Bavragor hurried to join the fifthlings in the battle against the hordes. After a couple of paces he stopped and looked across at Boïndil. "Tell him that I forgive him for what he did," he said softly.

Tungdil stared at him in amazement. "I can't tell him that," he protested. "He'd think I was making it up to make him feel better about himself."

"Then tell him I knew he loved my sister as much as I did, but I couldn't stand losing her. I was filled with hatred, and I couldn't hate death for taking her, so I hated the one who swung the blade. Hatred helped to silence the pain and the sorrow, and it was easier to live that way. Deep down I knew he loved her and he never meant to kill her." He chuckled gently. "Death has made me wiser, Tungdil. May Vraccas protect Boïndil and the others, but especially you."

He turned and, belting out a rousing melody, hurled himself into the unequal battle. His hammer smashed into an orcish knee, then crushed a beast's skull, and still he kept singing.

Tungdil swallowed and hurried after his companions, who were rushing up the steps. Narmora had already reached the entrance to the flue.

As they ascended, Bavragor's voice accompanied them through the darkness until Giselbert set the machinery in motion to close the vents. There was a whirr, then a rattling of metal as chains unfurled and tumbled to the floor. The mechanism had been destroyed.

When the noise settled, Bavragor's singing could still be heard, softer and more muffled, but still audible.

There was no talking among them as they listened to his songs of dwarven heroism and glorious victories over the

orcs. He was mocking the vast army, provoking his antagonists, luring them to their deaths.

Then everything was quiet.

There's no one here," Narmora called down to the others.
"Just me and the mountains." Tungdil looked up at her slim
black form silhouetted against the pale sky. She disappeared
from view.

One by one they clambered to the surface. The flue terminated in a crater large enough to swallow a fair-sized house.

Tungdil ascended the final paces with weary, leaden legs.
At three thousand steps he had stopped counting the soot-
stained stairs that wound their way up the chimney's walls.
There had been no moments of panic, no tripping, stumbling,
or teetering on the edge, and the ascent had passed without
incident, even for Djerûn in his cumbersome mail.

We made it. Tungdil emerged from the shelter of the rock
to find himself on a snow-capped mountain at the heart of
the Gray Range. An icy wind whipped about them, whistling
through his beard and making him shiver with cold.

Looking down, he was filled with wonderment at the
mighty valleys and gorges below. All around them were
mountains: the towering summit of the Great Blade, the great
pinnacle of the legendary Dragon's Tongue, and the sheer
sides of Goldscarp. Clad in snow and buffeted by wind, the
peaks rose majestically toward the clouds, enduring and eternal. Few had seen the range from such a privileged vantage
point, and Tungdil was loath to tear himself away.

He sent the half älf ahead as their scout. The decision
caused him considerable heartache: On the one hand, he
wanted to protect Narmora because of her role in the mission; on the other, he knew that she stood the best chance of

leading the company to safety. Furgas was sick with worry on her behalf, but she struck out confidently through the snow, allowing the others to tread in her footsteps.

Their path took them over shimmering bridges of ice, through sheer-sided chasms, and past deep gulleys. From time to time they clambered over snow-covered scree and through stone archways that seemed liable to collapse.

They walked in silence, their tongues stayed by tiredness and all that had gone before. It was enough to focus on putting one foot in front of the other without tripping.

Tungdil's thoughts drifted back to Giselbert and Bavragor. He could imagine them defending the gates against the enemy hordes, and if he closed his eyes for a second, he could almost hear the mason singing. *The merry minstrel,* he thought sadly.

Later, as daylight faded and the wind picked up, they sheltered inside a cave, huddling around the torchlight. Boïndil didn't seem to mind the cold, but Andôkai brushed the snow from her cloak, pulled it close, and leaned back wearily against the bare rock. She lowered her blue eyes and cursed.

"I need to find a force field," she said, putting an end to the silence. "The sooner we're back on charmed land, the better. My powers are exhausted. I never thought this would happen and it's not an experience I'd choose to repeat."

"Quite apart from that, we're bound to need your magic before too long." The shivering Tungdil produced his map of the underground network. "I get the feeling that Nôd'onn knows about the underground network. He'll guess we're heading for Ogre's Death, and he'll probably be lying in wait." He scanned the map attentively, his eyes coming to rest at a point two hundred miles from their present location. *He'll never think of looking there!* "We'll go to Âlandur."

"To Âlandur?" blustered Boïndil, who was carefully plucking ice from his beard. "Whatever for?"

"There's a shaft leading down to the network," he told him, pointing to the map. "There's a good chance that this part of the kingdom won't have fallen to the älfar. We'll ask the elves to join us and take up the fight against Nôd'onn, just as the high king proposed. Unless you've got a better suggestion, of course."

"Er, no'..." the secondling conceded. "But I can't help...I mean, it takes a while to get used to the idea. Elves are our enemies, our sworn rivals."

"I can't imagine it either," admitted Balyndis, nodding in agreement. She stretched her hands to the burning torch.

"How extraordinarily easy it is for one to dislike something," said Rodario philosophically. He clutched his stomach just as it growled in protest. Like the others, he was ravenously hungry. Desperation drove him to break off an icicle and pop it in his mouth.

"The gods made us too dissimilar. Sitalia created the elves to love the skies and forests. Vraccas gave us our caverns and underground halls." Balyndis hugged her knees to her chest. "They look down on us for not being beautiful like them. They despise us."

"Consequently, you despise them," the impresario divined. "Well, if one of you could see fit to stop despising the other, neither side would have reason to continue the feud. A whole history of hostility, resolved just like that." He laughed, then gripped his injured side. "Blasted orcs! Do you happen to have any other enmities that I can put to rights?"

"There's always Lorimbur's folk," Boïndil said slowly. "You heard what Glandallin said about the thirdlings. But it's no good trying to reconcile me with them." He clenched his fists. "To think that they betrayed the fifthlings!"

Rodario propped himself upright against the wall. "What was the origin of the quarrel? We humans know shamefully little about dwarves." He took up his quill. "Keep it short, if you will. My ink is running low."

Balyndis grinned. "We hate each other."

His pen froze. "That was a little *too* short, worthy metal-worker of Borengar." He flashed her a winning smile.

"I was afraid you'd say that." Without further ado, she launched into the tale.

The five founders of the dwarven folks were created by Vraccas, who gave each of them a name. The father of the thirdlings cast off his Vraccas-given name and called himself Lorimbur, which is how he has always been known.

The other dwarves each received a particular talent for their folks, and so the smiths, the masons, the gem cutters, and the goldsmiths were born. But when it was Lorimbur's turn, Vraccas told him: "You chose your own name, so you must choose your own talent. Teach yourself a trade, for you can expect nothing from me."

Lorimbur tried to teach himself a trade and apprenticed himself to each of his brothers in turn, but his efforts went unrewarded. The iron cracked, the stone split, the gems shattered, and the gold burned.

And so it was that Lorimbur came to envy his brothers and his spiteful heart was filled with eternal hatred for all dwarves.

Determined to excel at something, he applied himself secretly to the art of combat. His aim was not merely to defeat his enemies, but to kill every dwarf in Girdlegard so that none of his kin could overshadow him again.

Rodario was hurriedly taking notes. "This is wonderful," he murmured. "Enough to keep me going for a hundred cycles or more."

Balyndis cleared her throat. "Do you see why we're afraid of Lorimbur's folk? They're not to be trusted."

Andôkai changed position, trying to get comfortable on the rocky floor. "The thirdlings aren't the ones we should be worrying about. How are we going to convince the elves of our intentions? Lord Liútasil is known for his reluctance to forge new friendships. I hardly think he'll rush to the aid of a company of dwarves."

Tungdil watched the shadows cast by the torch and smiled. "I've learned from this journey that nearly everything is possible, even against the odds. I'm sure the elves will come round."

At Balyndis's request, Narmora handed over Keenfire, and the smith took to removing the excess inlay with a file. Tungdil looked on in fascination while she polished the metal. All of a sudden she put down her tools.

"It's the cold," she said apologetically. "My fingers are really numb."

He glanced at Furgas and Narmora, who were snuggled under a blanket. His mouth went dry. "You can sit a bit closer, if you like," he offered nervously.

She sidled over and nestled against him. "Like sitting by a furnace," she said with a sigh of contentment.

Tentatively he laid an arm across her shoulders. There was something indescribably wonderful about having Balyndis by his side.

Kingdom of Gauragar,
Girdlegard,
Winter, 6234th Solar Cycle

They walked quickly, speeding up to a march as soon as the terrain permitted and descending the southern slopes as fast as they could. Soon the mighty peaks of the Gray Range were behind them and they found themselves among Gauragar's hills.

They were all so exhausted that they didn't have much time to talk. After a while, Tungdil took Boïndil aside and told him of Bavragor's last words. The secondling pressed his lips together tightly and said nothing, but his eyes welled with tears.

Where possible, they avoided settlements, although on one occasion Furgas and Rodario were sent to buy provisions from a farm. Had the decision been left to the impresario, the pair would have posed as impoverished noblemen, but Tungdil, conscious of the need to keep a low profile, insisted that they pass themselves off as cobblers instead.

The food tasted dreadful. The coming of the Perished Land had spoiled the winter crops and shriveled the apples, and even the bread was so heavy that it sat in their stomachs like lead. Still, it contained enough energy to restore a little of their strength. Since the groundwater was unpalatable, they melted snow to quench their thirst.

At length Djerûn hunted down a scrawny doe, which they roasted briefly over the flames and wolfed down hungrily, trying not to notice the slightly moldy taste.

They hadn't been troubled by orcs since their escape from the fifthling kingdom, but after seven orbits the company's relief turned to puzzlement: The Perished Land had seized Gauragar, but there was no sign of runts or bögnilim.

By rights the roads should be crawling with beasts. Unable to make sense of it, Tungdil sent Furgas and Rodario to find out what was happening from the inhabitants of a nearby town.

They returned with alarming news.

"The orcs were called away," said the impresario, waving

his arms to convey the drama of his report. "They've abandoned their encampments. A while ago, thousands of the beasts descended on the human kingdoms to rout the race of men, but now they're marching south on Nôd'onn's orders. The townsfolk said something about besieging a stronghold in a mountain." He frowned in concentration. "I'll remember the name in a moment."

"Ogre's Death," Boïndil shrieked excitedly. "It's got to be Ogre's Death. Ha, they need thousands of orcs to attack the dwarves of Beroïn, do they? I always said the runts were worse than useless. Oh, what I'd give to fight beside my clansmen!"

To the others' astonishment, Rodario shook his head. "That's not it," he said. "Dark…no, brown…no! I've always learned my lines perfectly and now I can't remember a simple thing like this. It was something to do with leather." His hands gesticulated frantically in the air. "With leather and riding…"

"Reins," suggested Balyndis.

Tungdil made the leap. "The Blacksaddle! They're besieging the Blacksaddle!"

Andôkai searched her memory. "The name means nothing to me. What is it?"

"A flat-topped mountain. The thirdlings built a stronghold inside it and tried to wage war on the other folks. It's right in the middle of Girdlegard." Tungdil pictured the Blacksaddle's abandoned chambers and galleries. *So why all the orcs?*

"Do you think someone important might be sheltering there?" asked Narmora. "You know, someone Nôd'onn is intent on getting his hands on, like one of the human kings."

Tungdil remembered telling Gundrabur and Balendilín about the stronghold, but he couldn't see why either of them would ensconce themselves in such a dark, benighted place.

"We should probably go there. The Blacksaddle is practically en route."

They resumed their journey.

Twelve orbits after leaving the fifthling kingdom they sighted Âlandur. There was no need for Tungdil to consult his map; nature was their guide.

They were trudging through a snow-filled valley when they first spotted a lush forest of beeches, oaks, and maples in the distance, surrounded by a protective fence of pines. The vibrant colors and thriving trees were proof enough that, contrary to rumor, the last elven kingdom hadn't fallen to Nôd'onn's hordes. This part of Girdlegard was free from the pestilence.

"I never thought I'd live to see the day when I'd welcome the sight of greenery," muttered Boïndil, whose spirits were suffering from the long march through the Perished Land. His eyes swept the thick line of trees that formed a natural palisade against intruders. He reached for his axes. "Looks like we'll have to chop our way through."

"And give the elves every reason to wage war on your kingdom?" said Andôkai sharply. "No, we'll have no need of weapons in the woods. Besides, they'll spot us soon enough." She stared at the forest. "What did I tell you? They've seen us already." Four tall figures detached themselves from the trees. Their longbows were raised, ready to shoot. "Who's going to talk to them?"

"I will," Tungdil said quickly. He took a step forward, laid his ax on the ground for the elves to see, and walked toward them with measured steps.

"The woods of Âlandur have seen a great deal," called the voice of one of the archers, "but never a groundling. Stay where you are and state your purpose."

Tungdil looked at the four forest-dwellers. They were clad in white leather armor, with swords hanging from their belts. Each wore a white fur cloak, and their fair hair hung loose about their shoulders. As far as Tungdil could tell, their perfectly formed faces were identical. He didn't like them.

"My name is Tungdil Goldhand of the fourthling kingdom. My companions and I left our homes to forge Keenfire and destroy Nôd'onn the Doublefold," he declared firmly. "Good friends of ours have died that we might accomplish our goal. If you will permit it, we should like to enter your kingdom."

"There's no need. You won't find Nôd'onn here."

"No, but we'd like to access a tunnel built by our ancestors. The entrance is within your borders. We intend to journey underground to the Blacksaddle," he explained briefly. "We heard the magus is there."

"You're going to kill him with this Keenfire, are you? You and a handful of warriors?" The elf stared at him incredulously. "I bet Nôd'onn sent you here!"

"More than likely," Tungdil said crossly. He felt like boxing the elf's pointy ears. "What a fabulous plan that would be! Sending a bunch of dwarves to talk their way into an elven kingdom. He must have known how pleased you'd be to see us. You'd welcome us into your forests, we'd deliver you up to the magus—and you'd never suspect a thing!"

"Nôd'onn's a traitor, not an idiot," muttered Balyndis not quite softly enough.

Tungdil couldn't help grinning, and a fleeting smile crossed the elf's slender face. It wasn't enough to change the dwarf's opinion of him. "How can we convince you that we mean no harm?"

The elves conferred in their own tongue. "You can't. Wait here," came the unfriendly reply. "Set foot on our land and we'll kill you." With that they disappeared among the mighty trees.

"Ha, we've got them worried." Boïndil grinned and crossed his arms in front of his powerful chest. "That's something."

They made a virtue of necessity and tried to get some rest. There were enough fallen branches to make a roaring fire and so the time passed. The sun was already sinking behind the forest when the sentries reappeared, this time accompanied by twenty archers and a warrior clad in shimmering palandium, which marked him out as an elf of rank.

"So these are the travelers." He was handsome, so handsome that he could never look anything but arrogant. Long red hair framed his face, setting off his dark blue eyes. "A strange group claiming an even stranger purpose. Let me find out the truth."

He raised his arms, his hands tracing symbols in the air. Andôkai responded immediately with a countercharm.

On seeing the maga, the elf broke off in surprise. "It seems you can use magic. Few among the race of men are capable of that. We heard Nôd'onn had killed them all." He studied her intently. "In appearance you resemble the woman once known as Andôkai."

"I am Andôkai the Tempestuous." She gave the most cursory of curtsies. "I am weak from our journey, Liútasil, and my magic is no match for yours." She tapped the hilt of her sword. "But I have a certain reputation as a swordswoman and if you care to cross blades with me, I shall prove I am no impostor."

Tungdil's eyebrows rose in surprise. Liútasil wasn't any old warrior; he was lord of Âlandur.

The elf laughed—a kind, gentle laugh, but still somehow superior. "Ah, the tempestuous maga. Very well, Andôkai,

I believe you, but I need to reassure myself. The älfar have played too many tricks on us of late."

His fingers moved gracefully through the air, conjuring a golden haze that settled over the group. In an instant the tiredness that had been eating into every fiber of Tungdil's body lifted and even his hunger disappeared. Beside him Narmora was gasping with pain and the air was rent by the same terrible noise that Djerûn had made at the gates of Roodacre. The elves nocked their arrows, spanning their bows, and took aim at the pair. Liútasil lowered his arms. "Andôkai, it can't have escaped your attention that two of your traveling companions will never be granted entry to our glades," he said carefully.

"They're with us," Tungdil said quickly. "They may be descended from Tion and Samusin, but we can't defeat Nôd'onn without them." He pointed to the half älf. "Narmora must wield Keenfire, and Djerûn is almost as accomplished a warrior as Boïndil here." He hoped the dwarf would appreciate the flattery. "Orcs and bögnilim flee at the sight of him."

Liútasil pondered the matter while one of the elves advised him in an urgent whisper.

"An unusual company indeed," the elven lord began. Tungdil could tell from his tone that he had conquered his doubts and decided in their favor. "Too unusual to be anything but genuine. You may enter Âlandur and proceed through your tunnel." He turned to leave.

Tungdil felt sufficiently encouraged to make his next request. "I beg your pardon, Lord Liútasil, but there is something else we should like to ask. We know the älfar are laying siege to Âlandur and that your kingdom is under threat. You won't be able to defend your lands alone. Join us in our fight against Nôd'onn and we will destroy the Perished

Land. Afterward you can reclaim your kingdom with our assistance."

The elf gazed at him earnestly. "Your generosity does you credit, but it will take more than a few axes to reclaim our lands."

"He speaks on behalf of the dwarven assembly," explained Gandogar. "The assistance he promises would come from my folk, the dwarves of the fourthling kingdom, of which I am king. And I know the secondlings would gladly rid your forests of the älfar."

"We've done it before, you know," Boïndil hastened to assure him. "We kicked them out of Greenglade."

Liútasil could no longer disguise his astonishment. "A dwarven king? It gets more and more intriguing." He beckoned for them to approach. "Come, you shall explain to me why the dwarves are willing to help their oldest enemies and save Âlandur from destruction."

He led the way, and the company followed, escorted on all sides by elven archers.

"Well spoken," Tungdil said to Gandogar.

The fourthling king smiled. "It was our only hope. Personally, I set no store by my status, but perhaps it will convince the pointy-ears to give us the loan of their army."

They walked on, squeezing their way through the palisade of trees. Djerûn struggled at first, encumbered by his armor, but Liútasil gave an order and the boughs swung back, allowing him to pass.

Once they had crossed the buffer of pine trees, they entered the forest proper. Even in winter, the oaks, beeches, and maples kept their foliage, and the branches showed no signs of bowing or snapping beneath the heavy snow. The towering trees reminded Tungdil and Boïndil of the splendor of Greenglade before it had succumbed to the northern pestilence and vented its hatred on every living thing.

The sheer size of the trunks took the travelers by surprise; even ten grown men with outstretched arms could not have spanned their girth.

Such was the peacefulness and serenity of the forest that the pain of what they had seen on their journey melted away from them, and they found an inner calm that deepened with every step.

Dusk was falling by the time they reached a building that was roughly equivalent to a dwarven hall. There were no stone columns, of course, only trees whose crowns formed a canopy two hundred paces above the forest floor, keeping out the rain and snow. A profusion of glowworms bathed the interior in welcoming light.

The elves' elegant architecture was the perfect complement to the beauty of the woods. Tungdil had experienced the same feeling in Greenglade, where the carved arches, elven inscriptions, and smooth wooden beams had seemed so at one with the trees.

This corner of Âlandur, as yet unconquered by the Perished Land, was the very essence of harmony. Tiny squares of gold and palandium, each no thicker than gossamer, dangled from the boughs, forming shimmering mosaics that sparkled in the starlight. As the company progressed through the living hall of trees, they passed a hanging mosaic of elven runes so dazzlingly beautiful that they gasped in admiration.

"I'm not saying that I *like* the pointy-ears," whispered Balyndis, sneaking a sideways glance at the tiles, "but their artwork's pretty good."

"Houses made of trees." Boïndil shook his head doubtfully. "I wouldn't feel comfortable. I'd rather have good solid rock above me. It protects you from the elements and it doesn't burn."

"What about volcanoes?" Rodario asked

"Volcanoes don't burn; lava does," Tungdil corrected him.

"What do you think lava is..." The impresario dried up under Narmora's fierce glare. "There's no point arguing with a dwarf," he finished.

The appearance of the company drew stares from the elves in the hall. It was the first time that a child of the Smith had visited their kingdom, and most of them had never seen a dwarf before.

"They all look the same to me," said Boïndil, voicing his thoughts as freely as ever. Luckily he chose to speak in dwarfish. "Long faces, cheeks as smooth as babies', and so conceited you wouldn't believe. I bet they think Girdlegard should be thankful that they live here at all." He gave his head a little shake and his black plait bounced on his shoulders. "I know it's not their fault that the fifthlings were conquered, but I'm not ready to trust them yet." The smith nodded in agreement.

Tungdil sighed and stuck his thumbs in Giselbert's belt. He was glad that Lot-Ionan had raised him: Unlike his companions, he was able to surmount his antipathy to the elves.

Liútasil sat down on a wooden throne, the back and arms of which were decorated with rich intarsia of palandium and gold. Amber and semiprecious gems added to the opulence. Stools were brought for the guests, but Djerûn had to stand.

Rodario's quill moved tirelessly across the page as he took notes, made sketches, and complimented the elves effusively. Furgas stared reverently at his surroundings, while Narmora's älf ancestry made it hard for her to relax. Her lips were pressed together in a thin line and she clung to her stool, appearing agitated and unwell.

Liútasil gave an order, and his attendants brought out bread, water, and other offerings, which they served with visible reluctance to Tungdil and friends. The dwarves, whose presence in Âlandur had obviously caused an upset, weren't familiar with most of the victuals, but felt obliged to eat. Boïndil was the first to take a wary bite.

"I don't care what it tastes like; you'd better not complain or spit it out," Tungdil warned him sharply.

The look of disgust that was beginning to take shape on the warrior's face mutated into a wonky smile. Boïndil forced down his mouthful, swallowed noisily, and reached for some water to wash away the taste. "Don't touch the yellow stuff," was his whispered advice to Balyndis, after which he restricted himself to bread.

More elves arrived in the course of the meal and took their places on carved chairs to either side of their monarch. They eyed the dwarves with interest.

Rodario added a little water to his last remaining drops of ink. "That should do the trick," he said, smiling.

"Perhaps we could speak of the purpose of your visit," began the elven lord. "I shan't be able to reach a decision until you've told me all that has gone before. Speak only the truth; we will know if you try to deceive us."

It's my job to convince them. Tungdil glanced at the others and rose to his feet. He looked into the waiting faces of the elves. Until recently, Liútasil and his kind had been under suspicion of the most heinous betrayal, but the fifthlings' story had cleared the way for a new beginning. It was up to Tungdil to forge the alliance that the high king had dreamed of. *Speak with a scholar's wisdom and authority,* he told himself. More nervous than ever, he took a sip of water, stuck his hands in Giselbert's belt, and commenced his account of their journey.

As he talked and talked he saw the stars wander above the glittering mosaics and watched as the dark sky turned a deep shade of blue, the moon paling as the horizon glowed red. Finally, as the sun rose above Girdlegard, sending its rays through the banks of snow-laden cloud, he concluded his report.

Liútasil's blue eyes had not left him for an instant: He had listened to every word. "I see," he said slowly. "So it started as a contest for the succession and became a mission of far greater consequence. I can see from your faces that the journey has been testing."

"Indeed it has, Lord Liútasil. The dangers were many, but we survived, and now we're here." Andôkai rose, eyes flashing impatiently, her stormy temperament unwilling to tolerate further delay. "We're running out of time. You've heard what we have to say; make your decision while we still have the choice. Girdlegard will be lost if we don't act soon." She took a step forward, knowing full well how imposing she looked. "What have you decided, Liútasil?" Her eyes searched his handsome face. "What have the elves decided?"

IX

Unbelievable!" Boïndil had no intention of letting the matter go. He sat down heavily in a wagon. "How can they need more time? Time to think about what? I've never heard anything so ridiculous! They'll be sorry when Nôd'onn rules Girdlegard and the älfar chop down their forest to make a bonfire! They won't need time for thinking then!" He thumped the handrail angrily. "I'd like to slice four of those elv—er, orcs—in two!"

What a blow for Gundrabur, thought Tungdil disappointedly. He took a seat beside the warrior. "I know how you feel," he confessed. "I thought Liútasil would overrule the doubters, but obviously I was wrong."

Furgas, who had been examining the track, took a few steps into the tunnel to assess the condition of the rail. "It looks pretty solid. There's a bit of rust, but nothing serious. It's almost as good as new." Satisfied, he returned to the wagon and sat down beside Narmora. "Let the journey begin."

The company had stayed the night in the forest while the elves were conferring. Âlandur's beds were the softest in Girdlegard, which suited the humans very well. The dwarves, unaccustomed to such luxury, had slept badly and woken up with sore backs. After a simple breakfast, they had packed their things and set out in search of the tunnel. The trapdoor, built into a boulder and camouflaged by a thicket of ferns, had opened without a hitch. Once inside, they had discovered four empty wagons and a ramp.

"Finished," said Rodario, putting away his quill. "You'll be pleased to know that the elves play a none-too-courageous role in this epic." He beamed at them. "Girdlegard will hear how the warriors of Âlandur declined to come to its rescue."

"At least we found the entrance to the tunnel," Balyndis said brightly, trying to lift the mood.

Boïndil ran his finger experimentally along his blades. "I suppose that's something. The question is, will we reach our destination, or end up being ambushed and eaten by a war band of orcs?" A menacing smile crept over his face. "Don't worry, my axes will take care of them. I'm longing to slit their runty throats." As always on such occasions, he glanced sharply at Djerûn to remind him not to interfere.

Tungdil turned to Narmora, who seemed calmer now that they were leaving. "How are you feeling?"

She smiled. "Better. It was hard for me in the forest, surrounded by so much elvishness. I've got my mother to blame for that."

He cleared his throat. "Are you nervous?"

"About the showdown with Nôd'onn?" She squeezed Furgas's hand. "No, not really—although once the magus is standing in front of me it will be a different story. Still, I've rehearsed what to do, so it should be all right."

"Of course it will be all right!" roared Boïndil. "We'll pop up behind the army and plow through the ranks. Before the runts know what's hit them, you'll whip out Keenfire and strike the magus in the back. He'll die, and Girdlegard will be saved!"

Narmora smiled. "A fine plan, but I'd like to try something a little more daring. How about I pretend to be an älf? I can play the part to perfection. I'll be able to get past Nôd'onn's guards and apprentices without arousing suspicion."

"I don't mean to be rude," Andôkai said doubtfully, "but why would Nôd'onn be interested in an ordinary älf? You'll never get close enough."

Narmora rearranged her head scarf. "I'll think of something."

Of course! Tungdil broke into a grin. He had just remembered a story from one of Lot-Ionan's books. The heroes had used a simple but effective trick that could work for them as well. "He'll be interested, all right, when you deliver the hostages that he's been waiting for."

"What kind of hostages?" asked Boïndil. Then it dawned on him. "What? You want us to give ourselves up?" he protested. "No, we'll fight our way through like I said!"

"My dear fellow," Rodario interrupted sweetly, "I don't wish to reawaken painful memories, but remember what happened in the fifthling kingdom? Your axes made little impression on the hordes of baying beasts."

"Precisely my point." Tungdil nodded. "We'll be outnumbered. That's why Rodario, Furgas, and Andôkai will pretend to be mercenaries who helped Narmora to capture us. Djerûn will have to stay here; his presence would give us away."

"It's a risky strategy, but it might just work," Andôkai said earnestly. "I'm in favor."

Rodario tapped his lip pensively. "Haven't I read something like that before?"

"Do you mean *The Death of Herengard*? In the story the heroes need to kill the evil monarch. They use the same tactic and it works," explained Tungdil, owning up to his source.

"You mean you borrowed it from a book?" Boïndil pro-tested, aghast. "But you can't—"

"Remember what I told you when we met? Reading is important!" Tungdil clapped the warrior on the back. "Maybe you'll believe me now. Let's have a show of hands."

The motion was passed with only one objection. Offended at not being listened to, Boïndil sulked in silence, not even cheering and whooping when the wagon plunged downhill.

Tungdil chose not to mention the end of the story: King Herengard's valiant killers had been slain by his guards. It was a good strategy nonetheless.

Once again their journey took them deep below the surface of Girdlegard. They were headed for the Blacksaddle, where Nôd'onn was mustering his army of orcs and other vile beasts.

Little did they know that the tunnel was preparing to surprise them again.

On rounding a corner, they saw upturned wagons and mounds of orcish corpses piled on both sides of the rail. There must have been at least two hundred bodies in all. They couldn't stop because of the momentum, so they leaned out of the wagon to get a better look.

"By my beard, this is the work of axes if ever I saw it," growled Boïndil. "You can bet they were slaughtered by dwarves. Our kinsfolk must be doing better than we thought."

"It seems funny to be fighting in the tunnels when there's a perfectly good stronghold in the Blacksaddle. Why haven't they ensconced themselves there?" Tungdil dangled over the side to inspect the corpses, which were stacked neatly away from the rail. *Someone wanted to make sure that nothing and no one got in our way.* He was instantly reminded of the spirits whom they had encountered twice before. "The ghosts! They helped us in the fifthling kingdom, remember?"

Balyndis pointed to a niche in the tunnel, where a small figure lay contorted on the floor. An orcish spear protruded from its side. "That's not a ghost!" she said. "Ghosts don't have corpses."

"I wonder if there's such a thing as tunnel-dwelling dwarves," speculated Furgas. "It struck me a while ago that the rail looked nice and shiny. Someone's been using it regularly, I'd say."

Tunnel-dwelling dwarves? The network had been abandoned for such a long time that a band of dwarves could easily have settled in the tunnels. Tungdil could only guess at an explanation. *They must have been banished by the ancient folks.*

He was gripped by excitement. It was entirely plausible that outcasts from the various clans and folks had learned of the tunnels and founded their own community many cycles ago. *Perhaps they didn't want to go back to their kingdoms?*

"Quick, lend me your quill, Rodario!" he said, grabbing the ink and parchment and scribbling a hurried thank-you letter. His handwriting was almost illegible because of the juddering wagon. They sped past a stalagmite, and he pinned the note on top.

"Can spirits read?" inquired Andôkai.

"They're not spirits," he answered. "If my suspicions are correct, they're dwarves — outcasts from the five kingdoms who claimed the tunnels for themselves. We've been trespassing on their territory." He gave a quick explanation. "Remember how they kept warning us? The hammering, the collapse of the tunnel, the faces in the cavern. They were trying to make us leave."

"Fascinating, fascinating," said Rodario. "And when the orcs turned up, they decided to help their kinsfolk instead of scaring them away. Blood is thicker than water, I suppose." Rodario snatched back his quill. "I'll add it to my notes."

"We've seen so many new things—good as well as bad," murmured Balyndis. "I hope the good outweighs the bad when it's over."

"It will," Tungdil said confidently. As they rattled around the next corner, he took a last look at the stalagmite. Unless he was much mistaken, a small figure was clutching his note.

Their arrival in the former realm of Lios Nudin gave Andôkai an opportunity to replenish her powers. She closed her eyes and waited. Almost immediately the walls of the tunnel began to glow, revealing the veins and pockmarks in the rock. Andôkai's breathing quickened; the light became brighter and intensified to a dazzling glare, then faded abruptly.

Slowly the maga opened her eyes, turned to the right, and vomited over the side of the wagon.

"What's the matter?" Tungdil was about to pull on the brake, but she stopped him with a wave.

"It's nothing; just keep going. Nôd'onn corrupted the force fields." She leaned back, and Balyndis handed her a pouch of water. "I channeled some of the energy, but it would probably kill me if I took any more." Her mouth snapped shut as she struggled to contain the next wave of nausea.

After traveling for two orbits they reached a set of points and continued alongside another rail. Suddenly a second wagon rolled up and drew level with theirs. Its passengers, a dozen or so orcs, seemed just as surprised as they were.

Ireheart was the first to recover from the shock. He reacted true to type.

"Oink, oink! Come here, you runts," he screeched excitedly, whipping out his axes. He glared at the others. "Leave them to me."

Before anyone could stop him, he had launched himself out of the wagon and landed ax-first among the startled beasts. In his battle-crazed fury, he accidentally killed the driver, leaving no one in charge of the brakes. The wagon hurtled through the tunnel while the scuffle continued inside.

Ireheart spotted a row of stalactites ahead and used them to his advantage. Maneuvering skillfully, he tricked a careless orc into dodging his ax and colliding face-first with the hanging calcite. There was an explosion of gore and a peal of maniacal laughter; then the dwarf pushed the headless creature over the side.

The runts struggled to defend themselves as Ireheart slashed through their ranks; the suddenness of the attack and the cramped circumstances worked in his favor, and his frenzied cackles, along with the shrieks and howls of his victims, vied with the noise of the wagons. Soon he reached the last of the orcs, a muscular beast whose armor was superior to his companions'.

"Stop! Don't kill their leader!" shouted Tungdil. "I want to interrogate him."

But the warrior was in the grip of his fiery spirit. Brandishing his axes, he charged toward the orc, who didn't stand a chance of deflecting both blades at once.

Andôkai barked an order, and Djerûn seized the doomed beast by the scruff of his neck. Like the boom of a crane, the giant's metal-plated arm swung toward the company's wagon and deposited the creature at the rear. The orc stopped struggling as soon as he felt the giant's sword against his throat.

"Hey! That's cheating!" Undaunted, Boïndil leaped back

into their wagon, still intent on hacking the orc to pieces, but Andôkai barred the way.

"Don't be foolish, Boïndil," she warned him coldly. "I've replenished my powers, remember. Stop of your own accord, or I'll make you. Tungdil's right; we need to find out what we're up against."

Reason and fury struggled for mastery of the warrior's mind. Panting for breath, he returned to his seat: Good sense had triumphed. "Question him if you must. I'll kill the other runts when we get to the mountain."

Tungdil turned to the orc and looked at him keenly. "What's Nôd'onn doing at the Blacksaddle?" he asked in orcish.

"I'm not telling you anything, groundling."

"Maybe you'd prefer to tell my friend." He reached toward the seated giant and flipped back his visor. Violet light bathed the hideous features of the prisoner, who looked away in horror and fear. Tungdil took care not to look at Djerûn; what he had glimpsed in the desert village would haunt him forever. "Or do you want him to bite off your arms?"

The orc squealed something that Tungdil couldn't understand, then said more clearly, "No, don't let him touch me!"

"What are you doing at the Blacksaddle?"

"We're besieging the groundlings," the orc answered, his voice cracking with fear. "They tried to hide from us, but Nôd'onn wants them dead."

"Why?"

"How should I know?"

"Is he there?"

The orc fell silent but kept a wary eye on Djerûn.

Tungdil could practically smell his fear. "Is the magus at the Blacksaddle?" he repeated. When nothing happened, the giant seized the initiative. His head sped forward, and they heard a loud crunch.

Screaming, the orc stared at the mangled stump where his arm had once been. "You're right, you're right," he cried, howling with pain. "The magus is at the Blacksaddle!"

"When is he going to attack?" Tungdil asked pitilessly.

"I don't know. I was ordered to be there in four orbits." The beast groaned, trying to stop the gushing blood with his other hand. Green gore spurted through his fingers. "That's all I—"

Djerûn hadn't eaten for ages, and the sight of a fresh meal was too tempting to resist. Without consulting Andôkai or Tungdil, he seized the orc, killed it, and devoured its twitching corpse. His back was turned, so none of the dwarves could see his face.

At the sound of the maga's voice, he dropped the body like a shot, closed his visor, and sat back down. Drops of green blood trickled from his helmet and there was a sickening smell of orc guts.

"Throw the rest away," Andôkai ordered. Djerûn dropped the remains of the beast over the side of the carriage.

"By the hammer of Vraccas, if we didn't need the giant for our mission..." Ireheart broke off his threat. "He's a monster—a tame one, but a monster all the same." He glanced at the maga. "I hope your god doesn't get tired of you and turn the brute against us." His axes disappeared back into his belt. "I'm here if you need me; just say the word."

Andôkai declined to comment.

So Samusin's son devours his father's creatures. Tungdil stared in fascination at the demonic visor. Djerûn's helmet was still glowing violet as if an eternal fire were blazing inside his head. Tungdil caught Narmora's eye. "The orcs were sup-

posed to be there in four orbits. We've got a new deadline."
He turned to face the front and felt a rush of air that cleared
his nostrils of the smell of dead orc. *Girdlegard will soon be
free of evil—or forever in its thrall.*

*Underground Network,
Kingdom of Gauragar,
Girdlegard,
Winter, 6234th Solar Cycle*

Later on they came across another fifty orcs whose bodies
had been stacked to the side of the track. Their mysterious
protectors had been at work again, although they continued
to hide themselves from view.

The rest of their journey was uneventful, and they sur-
faced in the former kingdom of Gauragar, not far from the
Blacksaddle.

Tungdil recognized the area straightaway. "It's this way,"
he told them, leading them to the hill from which he had first
seen the Blacksaddle. Crouching low, they scrambled to the
top, hoping not to be spotted by sentries. They weren't ready
to don their disguises yet.

"Vraccas almighty, we're not a moment too soon," he
whispered.

The murky forest of conifers was gone, replaced by a
ring of wooden structures whose platforms were crawling with miniature figures that looked like orcs. The towers were already dizzyingly high, but the beasts were adding
extra stories in the hope of storming the stronghold from the
summit or the upper slopes. They must have tired of banging their heads against the solid base of the Blacksaddle or

perhaps the growling mountain had shaken them from its
flanks.

It looks more sinister than ever without the trees.

Every now and then black torrents cascaded from the hidden stronghold, forcing the besiegers to flee the steaming liquid or perish in its flow. Elsewhere, fiery projectiles rained down on the army from chinks in the rock, landing among the beasts and dousing them in oil. Countless troopers were incinerated in the blaze.

They've resurrected the old defenses.

But despite their losses, Nôd'onn's soldiers continued undeterred. The beasts were swarming like ants around the base of the Blacksaddle, scouring the flat ground for anything that could be used in their assault on the flanks.

A detachment of ogres had been put to work splitting tree trunks and building siege engines. The defenders focused on toppling the towers or setting light to them before the orcs could climb high enough to pose a threat; but it did nothing to discourage the ogres, who collected the debris and started again. Their smaller comrades milled about impatiently, desperate for the attack to begin.

"It's strange, isn't it?" said Tungdil to his dwarven companions. He kept his eyes fixed on the mountain ahead. "The thirdlings built the stronghold to wipe out the other dwarves, but now it's the only thing protecting us from Nôd'onn." He suddenly remembered the runes that he had found on his first visit to the mountain. *Roused by the thirdlings / Against the will of the thirdlings. / Drenched again / In blood, / The blood / Of all their / Line.* He wondered what it could mean.

"I've never seen so many of them," said Balyndis, staring wide-eyed at the beasts below.

The enemy had pitched their tents in a circle around the

mountain about a mile from its base. Their shelters barely looked sturdy enough to withstand the snow and winter winds. Here and there black puffs of smoke rose skyward.

"Eighty thousand at a guess," Boïndil said evenly. He thumped Tungdil on the back. "I'm not saying you were right about books, but I'd need more than my axes to deal with a rabble like that. Your plan will work better after all."

Rodario pointed west. "Do you think those are Nôd'onn's quarters?" He indicated a stately tent, far larger than the others and draped in malachite-colored cloth. "I'd certainly want a tent like that if I were the magus. Canvas is all very well for the riffraff, but a man of authority deserves something better."

Furgas sighed. "Thank goodness you weren't born a nobleman. Your subjects would have strung you up cycles ago."

"Not if you were around to invent a slower way of killing me." They smiled at each other companionably.

"Speaking of inventions." Furgas gestured away from the main battleground and pointed to a band of ogres who were constructing a rolling siege engine. It towered two hundred paces above the ground and looked far more robust than its foregoers. "That should do the trick for them. They've used tiles on the outside to make it less flammable."

Hundreds of orcs descended on the contraption, swarming over its many platforms, arming it with crossbows and catapults, and stocking the slings with missiles and spears. The ogres finished the building work and bent down to push the tower toward the mountain. Bugles were sounded, heralding an all-out attack.

"It's time we did something," ruled Tungdil. "Narmora, bring the prisoners to Nôd'onn."

She nodded resolutely and donned her disguise.

A few moments later they were faced with one of the deadliest creatures in Tion's creation. The transformation went deeper than the change of clothes; with each piece of älf armor, Narmora looked crueler and more menacing, her face hardening and paling. As she straightened up, her voice sounded oddly sinister. "And now for the most important part..." The whites of her eyes darkened, leaving nothing but fathomless blackness, the distinguishing feature of the älfar by day.

If I didn't know better... To Tungdil, she looked exactly like a real älf, which was precisely what they needed for their plan to succeed. "Perfect," he praised her.

Andôkai got out the dark blue amulet that belonged to the dead älf in the desert and hung it around Narmora's neck. "The crystal will ward off Nôd'onn's magic," she said. "I want you to wear it in case we get separated and you find yourself fighting on your own."

Narmora smiled at her. "Wait here. I'll fetch the armor for my mercenaries." She slipped away noiselessly and disappeared.

Tungdil noticed that Balyndis had reached for her ax. "She's...she's changed," the dwarf said defensively. "She's all sinister and threatening, just like a real älf."

"What if her dark side takes over?" asked Boïndil, who didn't mind voicing his doubts. "She'll have Keenfire and we can't kill Nôd'onn without it. The maga won't be able to hurt her because of the amulet. How are we supposed to stop her if she turns against us?"

Furgas rushed to his mistress's defense. "She's still Narmora, you know," he said fiercely. "Don't forget that she's an actress. No matter what she says or does, you mustn't doubt her. She's had plenty of opportunity to—"

Narmora returned with an armful of bloodied armor belonging to some careless sentries. She threw the garments into the snow. "You'll have to wipe them clean," was all she said.

Once Rodario had taken some "special precautions," as he mysteriously referred to them, the company began the most perilous phase of their journey yet.

Tungdil, Gandogar, Balyndis, and Boïndil took their places at the heart of the group, surrounded by their captors, whose faces were hidden by their foul-smelling helmets. Narmora had swaddled Keenfire in rags and was carrying the weapon on her back. Djerûn stayed behind, poised to charge down the hillside and cut down the enemy if his mistress should signal for help.

Boïndil found it especially difficult to be separated from his beloved axes. Worse still, his hands were bound, a circumstance he tolerated only because they couldn't get to Nôd'onn by any other means. A worrying thought occurred to him. "Tell me again how the story ended."

Rodario opened his mouth to enlighten him, but Tungdil cut him off. "Happily," he said firmly. He locked gazes with the impresario, pleading with him to let the falsehood stand. Rodario rolled his eyes, but refrained from comment.

"Just as well," growled Boïndil, who luckily wasn't interested in specifics.

Furgas had stowed the dwarves' axes in a sack and was ready to return them to their owners at the first sign of trouble. The captives were bound with leather manacles that would rip at the jerk of a wrist. All that mattered was that they *looked* like prisoners.

The afternoon shadows were growing long when they finally entered the enemy encampment.

Narmora glared menacingly at the sentries, three orcs and four bögnilim, and demanded to be allowed to deliver her prisoners to Nôd'onn in person. The company was allowed to pass.

One of the bögnilim rushed ahead to announce the arrival of the heroic älf. The company strode purposefully between the tents, heading in the direction that the bögnil had taken.

"So I was right," came a muffled voice from Rodario's helmet. "I knew it had to be Nôd'onn's tent."

"Silence," commanded Narmora in her sinister älf's voice, and the impresario refrained from further comment.

By now they had a clear view of the dark green cloth that was housing the source of Girdlegard's ills. They were only twenty paces away when the tent opened and an old acquaintance emerged: pointy ears, handsome features, and long fair hair. "Sinthoras," gasped Tungdil in horror.

Boïndil leaned over. "Was he in the story too?"

The älf was smiling maliciously. He was wearing a tionium breastplate and a long tionium mail shirt that reached as far as his knees. He was prepared for battle. "It's always a pleasure to see you," he said to Tungdil with a bow. Then he turned to Narmora. "Congratulations on capturing the prisoners, Miss...?"

"Morana," she said, furnishing herself with an älf name.

"Morana," he repeated. "Tion must prize you highly. Caphalor and I hunted the groundlings across the length and breadth of Girdlegard with no success." His cruel eyes roved coldly over the little band. It was impossible to tell exactly who he was looking at. "We inflicted some casualties, it seems."

"And yet they evaded you," she said scornfully. She decided

not to be intimidated and to play the part of the arrogant stranger.

"Yes, they evaded us." Sinthoras sighed with feigned regret. "But we have them now. I'll take them to Nôd'onn. You may go."

Narmora stood her ground. "I captured them. Why should I let you steal my reward?"

Sinthoras circled her menacingly. "You've got courage, young älf. It's strange that I've never heard your name."

"Dsôn Balsur is a big place. I don't believe we've met."

"You're from Dsôn Balsur? I know every inch of our kingdom; I founded it." He stopped in front of her. "What of your mother and father? Where do you live, Morana?"

"That needn't concern you," she retorted, unmoved. "Hurry up and tell Nôd'onn I'm here to see him—or get out of my way."

"The magus is asleep."

"Then wake him."

Tungdil was still reeling from the shock of meeting Sinthoras. *What are we to do? Should we walk past him? If it comes to a fight, some of us will die.* He glanced at Nôd'onn's tent, which was tantalizingly close. *If we wait too long, we'll only attract an audience, which is the last thing Narmora needs.* He couldn't see that they had a choice.

"Come and listen to this, Caphalor." Sinthoras threw back his head and laughed. "I've got a young älf here who isn't afraid of her elders. It could be the death of her one day."

"She ought to be taught some respect," someone said behind them.

Rodario was caught off guard by the voice and whipped round, almost taking Balyndis's head off with his lance. His armor, which was slightly too big for him, clunked noisily.

Behind them was an älf with long dark hair. Tungdil recognized him immediately as the sinister bowman who had shot at him in Goodwater and tracked the company through the Red Range. He knew they had to do something, but he couldn't for the life of him think what.

"I knew a Morana once, but she didn't look like you. Besides, the Morana I'm thinking of is dead." Caphalor's fathomless eyes settled on Narmora. He was wearing tioniumplated leather armor that seemed to swallow the sunlight. "You're not from Dsôn Balsur, are you?" He laid his slender fingers on the hilt of his sword. "Why did you lie to us? Tell us where you're from."

By now Boïndil was becoming restless. His eyes darted back and forth and he glanced at Tungdil, waiting for his command.

Should we attack? If we do, they're bound to overpower us. Tungdil didn't know what to do. The älfar's ambush was entirely unexpected and it looked as though neither Sinthoras nor Caphalor had any intention of allowing Narmora to deliver her prisoners to Nôd'onn.

"I've had enough of your games," she said, her voice trembling slightly. For all her acting experience, she couldn't control her fear. "If you won't take me to him, I'll call him myself." She shouted out to Nôd'onn.

The älfar laughed.

"That's too bad," Sinthoras said spitefully. "You're not the only one who's been lying. The magus is mustering his troops by the tower. We're just about to join him. My spear is looking forward to whetting itself on dwarfish blood."

"The tower?" She glanced at the mercenaries and the dwarves. "Then that's where I'll take them." She was about to push past Sinthoras when he whipped out his sword. Before the blade reached her neck, she parried the blow. "Another trick like that and I'll kill you," she said menacingly.

A knife whistled over the dwarves' heads, its sharp point embedding itself in the half älf's armpit. She cried out in pain.

"*My* Morana sounded different as well," Caphalor said grimly.

Furgas couldn't contain himself any longer and lunged at the aggressor. The älf stepped nimbly out of the way of his spear, drew his sword, and feigned a swipe at his head. Furgas fell for the ruse and readied himself to parry the blow. The dark-haired älf rammed his sword into Furgas's belly. The prop master sank to his knees, groaning.

"Quick," Tungdil shouted to Rodario, who was rooted with shock. The impresario grabbed the sack and tossed the weapons to the dwarves. Throwing off their leather manacles, they seized their axes and hurled themselves on their hated foes.

As Rodario backed away from the smiling Sinthoras, Ireheart leaped into the breach, his axes twirling ferociously.

"So you want to dunk your toothpick in some dwarf blood, do you, hollow eyes?" He slashed at the älf's hips, forcing him away from Rodario. The impresario seized his chance and fled. Ireheart took another step toward his opponent. "You'd better be quick because my axes are hungry for älf flesh." They fell on each other, and Balyndis and Gandogar threw themselves into the mix, ignoring Boïndil's indignant shouts.

Andôkai and Tungdil were left to deal with Caphalor, while the injured Narmora went to Furgas's aid.

The half älf's wound was relatively minor. The knife had missed the vein, nicking the flesh and drawing blood, but

Furgas was in a critical state. By the time Narmora got to him, he was breathing shallowly, fumbling with his visor, and struggling for air.

"Furgas, my love," she said soothingly, pressing on his abdomen to stem the bleeding. The color returned to her eyes as she tended to him anxiously. Blood continued to gush from the wound. With a wild curse, she jumped to her feet, pushed Andôkai away from Caphalor, and harried the älf with a series of blows. "I'll take care of him. You see to Furgas," she ordered. "He'll die if you don't." Her eyes darkened to hollows.

Andôkai retreated with a nod.

"How moving," Caphalor said scornfully. "I shouldn't worry, though. You'll be united in death." He dodged her weapon and kicked Tungdil elegantly in the chest. The dwarf fell backward and sat down with a thud. Caphalor smiled at Narmora. "Let's have some fun before I kill you."

He parried her next blow and punched her in the face. Struggling to keep her balance, she managed to duck beneath his sword, but his knee powered into her nose and she straightened up, placing herself unknowingly within reach of his blade.

Without stopping to think, Tungdil hurled his only ax at the älf. Boïndil would have disapproved of the tactic, but he didn't know what else to do.

The blade whistled as it arced through the air, alerting Caphalor to the danger.

In a movement so swift that Tungdil scarcely saw it happen, Caphalor caught the weapon by the haft and tossed it back. The älf used the momentum to whirl like a spinning top toward Narmora and knock her sideways. He raised his sword to kill her as she fell.

Tungdil had no time to dodge the flying ax, which hit him poll-first in the chest. His ribs cracked audibly and the pain was terrible, but it could have been far worse.

"Leave her to me, Caphalor," a hoarse voice commanded. The älf froze and turned to see Nôd'onn, who had appeared out of nowhere.

"But, Master, you..."

His confusion lasted long enough for Narmora to sit up and thrust her blade into the crouching älf's neck. The blow almost parted his head from his shoulders, but Caphalor took one last lunge at her, slashing at her throat, then toppling over and burying her beneath him.

Sinthoras let out a terrible howl. He realized that his friend was dead and that the distraction was the work of an impostor. Glancing at his opponents, he decided that the odds were against him. He had sacrificed his amulet already and was no match for the maga on his own. "We'll meet again," he promised. "Sinthoras will be your death." With that he disappeared into the tent.

Tungdil and his companions chased after him but found the magus's quarters deserted. *Damn that älf! He's tricked us again.*

Rodario, still posing as the magus, had stayed outside to disperse the crowd of startled beasts. He instructed them to return to the battle and kill any of their comrades who weren't fighting savagely enough. "I'll take care of the treacherous sorceress myself." He stabbed a finger at Andôkai and muttered a few unintelligible words. "Take that!" The maga sank obligingly to the ground. Impressed by the magus's power, the orcs and bögnilim backed away, bowing respectfully.

"An unsophisticated audience is a gift from above," he murmured gratefully into his malachite cowl. His heart had been in his throat throughout the scene. He checked that the coast was clear and beckoned to Andôkai. "No one's looking. Come quickly, Estimable Maga! Narmora needs your help!"

The maga crouched over the half älf and began a healing incantation to close the wound, while Rodario stood in front of them, spreading out his voluminous robes to hide them from view. "Incidentally, you'd make a wonderful actress. I've never seen anyone die with such conviction."

"This is no time for flattery," she rebuked him, concentrating on her charm.

As quickly and discreetly as possible they carried the dead älf and their two wounded companions into the tent and held a whispered conference. Boïndil peered out of the flap and kept watch.

"Sinthoras is bound to tell the magus about us," said Tungdil. He glanced down at Furgas's motionless form. Andôkai had induced a deep healing sleep in the hope that he would recover. Narmora was stroking his hand comfortingly, but she herself was shaking all over and her throat was smeared with blood.

"Nôd'onn will be expecting us," said Andôkai, glancing around the tent. "It won't make things any easier, but at least we've got another älf outfit." She stripped the dead Caphalor unceremoniously of his mail and strapped it to her body. It was tight in some places and loose in others, but with her visor down and in the company of Narmora she looked reasonably convincing. "With any luck, Nôd'onn won't notice the difference until it's too late."

"How do you feel about posing as the magus again, Rodario? Do you think you'd be able to get us as far as Nôd'onn?" Tungdil was already working on a new plan.

"With pleasure." He tugged on the straps that looped

beneath his improvised stilts. He was standing on a pair of helmets. "I get quite a kick out of being a notorious wizard." Grinning, he made a final check of his flamethrower and rearranged the air-filled leather pouches that inflated his girth. "Let the show begin! Our beastly spectators are waiting."

"Don't lay it on too thick or they'll tear you to pieces before we can stop them," warned Tungdil. "All right, here's the story." He pointed to Balyndis, Boïndil, Gandogar, and himself. "The four of us are defectors. We're under your spell, and we're showing you how to infiltrate the stronghold."

Andôkai picked up Furgas's helmet and placed it on her head. It didn't look right with the elaborate älf armor, but at least it hid her face.

"Blasted ogres," gasped Boïndil, peering through the tent flap. "They've pushed the tower right up against the mountain. They're going to do it this time." He screwed his eyes up in concentration. "I think I can see the magus. He's on the middle platform and he's—" He stopped short, too anxious to continue.

The others rushed to the door to see for themselves what was happening.

The Blacksaddle was quaking under the force of Nôd'onn's attack. Black bolts sped from his staff and zigzagged over the slopes. The noise of crackling, spluttering lightning carried as far as the tent.

The stubborn mountain stood firm, resisting the assault. Just then a mighty bolt slammed into its flank, forcing it apart.

A mass of fractured rock thundered down the slopes, raising vast clouds of dust. Ledges and overhangs collapsed, laying open the passageways that led into the stronghold.

The troops on the tower prepared to disembark. Each

platform was equipped with hastily constructed gangplanks, which the beasts angled toward the pitted surface of the once-sheer slope. The first orcs were halfway across before the planks had touched down. They stormed into the stronghold, to be met by dwarven axes.

Nôd'onn made certain that enough troopers were inside, then stepped onto a gangplank and followed them unhurriedly into the stronghold.

At least we know where he is. Tungdil took a deep breath. "We'll have to leave Furgas here," he decided. "It's safer than taking him with us. Are you ready?"

Narmora and Rodario nodded.

As they strode past rows of kneeling beasts who were too dim-witted to see through their disguise, Boïndil had a sudden feeling that they had forgotten something important, and he couldn't think what.

They remained on guard, knowing that Sinthoras was still at large and could ambush them at any moment. Mercifully, the crowds were too thick for him to take aim at them with his bow, so he would be forced to attack at close range. He hadn't shown himself yet.

No one challenged them as they headed for the tower. Farther away, four smaller siege engines had started attacking the stronghold. They ascended the broad steps that led up to the platforms and strode over the gangplank that Nôd'onn had used.

To their intense relief, they survived the defenders' hail of stones and arrows and made it safely into the Blacksaddle. Orcish shrieks echoed through the passageway, accompanied by the peal of colliding swords, axes, and maces. A battle was raging deep within the stronghold.

"I'll see to it that we don't have to worry about enemy reinforcements," said Andôkai. She turned and focused on the besiegers' main tower. Ogres were scaling its sides, hoping to use the uppermost platform as a stepping-stone. Unable to squeeze through the tunnels, they were intent on assailing the defenders from the mountain's flat summit.

"You mustn't exhaust yourself," warned Tungdil, scanning the area for orcs. "We're bound to need your magic when it comes to tackling Nôd'onn."

"Don't worry; I know how to deal with them." The fair-haired maga conjured luminous blue runes that coalesced into a sphere. Hissing furiously, the ball of energy swooped toward the base of the tower and exploded on Andôkai's command.

The air crackled with the sound of an oncoming storm, and a gale blew up, blasting through the tower's solid timber and blowing away the tethers. The lower platforms folded like cardboard, causing the tower to wobble and tilt dangerously to the side.

The walls blew out, and the ogres were thrown backward, arms and legs thrashing frantically like upturned beetles. They fell to earth amid the milling mass of orcs, bögnilim, and beasts. A moment later, the tower collapsed entirely, burying several hundred more creatures under its weight. The shrill screams of terror sounded sweeter than the sweetest music to Tungdil's ears. The wreckage of the tower lay directly below the entrance to the stronghold, so the debris would have to be cleared before any of the smaller siege engines could be wheeled into place.

"That should keep them busy for a while," said Andôkai, eyeing her work with satisfaction.

"Now for the traitor. We'll have to fight our way through

to him, I'm afraid." Tungdil gave up all pretense of being enslaved to the counterfeit magus. "Enough of the act, Rodario. If our kinsfolk mistake you for the real Nôd'onn, they'll rip you limb from limb."

Rodario stepped down from his makeshift stilts and took off his robe to reveal his armor. He stowed the props hastily in his bag.

Balyndis was still scanning the besieging troops. A cloud of dust had appeared on the horizon. "We need to hurry," she said in alarm. "There are more of them. Where the deuce are they coming from?"

Tungdil didn't care where they were coming from, provided that he and the others could beat them back. *How are we ever going to defeat them? Even if we kill the magus, we'll never get rid of them on our own.* It would take a combined army of dwarves, elves, and men to see off the threat. He drew closer to Balyndis and took her hand, drawing strength and courage from her touch. "We'll deal with Nôd'onn; then we'll worry about his troops."

They raised their weapons and prepared to charge into the tunnels and overwhelm their enemies from behind. Boïndil was in his element.

"This is the way it should be," he whispered, eyes glinting as his fiery inner furnace took control. "A narrow tunnel, more enemies than we can count... The first ten are for my brother, but Vraccas can have the rest."

"Narmora is our priority," Tungdil reminded them. "She's the only one who can kill Nôd'onn, but the rest of us must protect her as best we can."

Gandogar patted his double-headed ax. "No one will touch her while I'm alive to stop them. Destroying Nôd'onn is all that counts."

Rodario was happy to settle for a less heroic role and stood back politely to let the others pass. While they stormed down the tunnel, he took a last look outside.

"Come back, everyone, it's..." He stared at the fluttering banners of an army approaching from the east. "Aren't those the colors of Ido? Surely Prince Mallen wouldn't ally himself with Nôd'onn?" His eyes roved over the other banners flying above the rows of troops. *The crests of all the human kingdoms!*

The first wave of warriors flowed into the back of a unit hurrying to lend Nôd'onn their support. Rodario watched in astonishment as the new arrivals mowed down the startled beasts.

Not having reckoned with enemy troops, Nôd'onn's soldiers took a while to realize that they were under attack. A moment later, the sky darkened and a hailstorm of arrows ripped through the air. The iron-tipped missiles glittered in the light as they sped toward the beasts. The magus's warriors forgot about the humans and tried to locate their other mysterious foes. Firebombs were already whining toward them, crashing down and engulfing them in flames. Panic broke out.

"Bravo for the elves!" cheered Rodario, relaying the news to his friends.

Gandogar grinned. "So the pointy-ears have found their courage, have they?"

"What are we waiting for?" demanded Ireheart, fired up by the prospect of orc blood. "Do you want to kill Nôd'onn or not?"

They charged into the tunnel, their confidence buoyed.

As it turned out, they had nothing to fear from the orcs. Not expecting to be attacked from the rear, the runts put up almost no resistance, and the first forty died without knowing what had hit them. The company found themselves at a junction with no sign of beasts or dwarves.

"That was brilliant fun! Where to now?" Ireheart panted eagerly. "You know your way around here. Which direction will Nôd'onn have taken?"

"He's probably helping his troops at a spot where he can't get any farther by brute force alone," Tungdil said, wishing fervently that the walls of the stronghold would speak to him as they had once before. Nothing happened. "The trouble is, I can't think where." There was a hint of desperation in his voice. "It's..."

A dull rumble shook the ground beneath their feet, and a fierce red light radiated from the passageway to their left. Flames licked the walls in the distance; then the glow faded and was gone.

Tungdil didn't need to give the order: He and the others were already sprinting toward the blaze. The smell of charred flesh hung thick in the air, the black fatty smoke stinging their eyes and burning their lungs.

They stormed out of the passageway and entered the first of three halls. The chambers were divided by roughly fashioned walls, but vast archways, each nine paces or more in height, allowed them to see through to the final hall.

A fierce battle was raging between the dwarves and the beasts. They seemed to be fighting for control of a wide door at the far end of the third hall, where the clatter of blades was at its most deafening. Bright pennants fluttered above the warriors of Borengar, Beroïn, and Goïmdil.

Poorly fashioned pillars supported the ceiling, fifty paces above. Crumbling staircases without kerb or rail wound up the columns, which were connected by bridges that ran the length of the halls. The fighting had spread to the walkways too.

"Come on, we're bound to find him here," Tungdil said firmly.

At first the company passed undetected through the turmoil, but their fortunes changed in the final hall when they spotted Nôd'onn pacing along a bridge. He was watching the dwarven warriors struggling to defend the door against his troops.

"Look! I bet he's going to help them with his wizardry." Boïndil ran ahead, speeding toward the staircase that would take them to the magus's walkway. The rest of the company made to follow, but fate had ordained that they should fight a different battle.

A dark arrow sang toward them from the right. Tungdil felt a searing pain in his leg and looked down to see an arrow embedded in his thigh.

"Sinthoras will be your death," hissed the älf. He was leading a band of fifty orcs and a second arrow was notched on his bow. "I will take your life and the land will take your soul."

Not mine, you won't, Tungdil thought stubbornly. He saw Sinthoras release the bowstring and managed to raise his shield to ward off the feathered shaft of death.

Cursing, the älf bounded toward them and ordered the orcs to attack.

"Quick, Narmora and Boïndil, you take the steps," instructed Tungdil. "Kill Nôd'onn before he sees us. We'll watch your backs." With a muffled groan he reached down and snapped the arrow shaft in two. *Stand by us, Vraccas.* Bracing himself, he raised his ax to strike an orcish knee.

The stone staircase crumbled as they ran. The thirdlings had chosen their material badly and over the course of time it had chipped and fractured. Narmora and Boïndil were risking their lives with every step.

They swept up the spiral stairs, winding their way to the top and never once glancing at the fighting below. All their thoughts were focused on the bloated man in malachite robes who was standing on the walkway. With every turn of the staircase he flashed in and out of sight. The air was getting warmer, and there was an overpowering stench of blood and orc guts.

Only a few steps remained. Narmora rounded the final corner, only to be confronted by a famulus who was standing guard behind the pillar.

"Who said you could come up here?" he asked rudely, mistaking her for one of Nôd'onn's älfar. "You're supposed to be commanding the orcs, not—"

Boïndil charged past Narmora and rammed his left ax into the famulus's crotch. The next ax sliced into the man's right shoulder, and he staggered against the pillar and collapsed.

"Ha, I guess wizards aren't always in favor of surprises." The dwarf grinned. He peered round the corner. "There's no one else in sight. I'll wait here, or Nôd'onn will get suspicious. Just call if you need me." He looked at her keenly. In the darkness of the underground hall, Narmora's eyes looked like hollows once more. "Are you sure you can do this?"

Narmora tossed the rags to the floor and practiced reaching for Keenfire. "You're worried that my dark side will make a traitor of me."

He nodded. "Yes."

"Well, Boïndil Doubleblade, at least you're honest." She bent down and laid a hand on his shoulder. "Don't you think it's a little too late to doubt my loyalty?" Her expression was as hard and cruel as an älf's and she looked more terrifying than ever.

He tapped his axes together nervously. Her words and gestures were making him jumpy. "Just do something so I know what's what," he said grumpily.

She smiled and left the shelter of the pillar. "Very well. I'll do something." Her face remained an inscrutable mask.

Nôd'onn was standing halfway along the walkway. He raised his right arm and traced a symbol in the air, conjuring the first runes of a devastating spell that would put pay to the defenders' determined resistance. In his bloated left hand he held his onyx-tipped staff of white maple. The black jewel was glimmering malevolently.

Narmora could tell that it was no use sneaking up on him and that an all-out assault would be equally doomed. She would have to rely on cunning and dissimulation to get within striking distance of Girdlegard's most dangerous and powerful wizard.

She held her hand to her bloodied neck, pressing on her wound. All her efforts were focused on appearing injured, and she made her performance as authentic as possible, swaying and stumbling along the bridge.

"Master," she groaned, "they've destroyed the tower...It was Andôkai..."

He froze and turned sharply. His waxy skin wobbled as if it were filled with rippling water. "Andôkai?" he rasped. "Where is she?"

"Outside, Master. She's using her magic against our troops." She took a few faltering steps toward him. Only ten paces remained, an impossibly long distance. "How can we stop her?"

Nôd'onn shuffled round to face her. She saw his huge girth, the puffed-up face that bore no resemblance to Nudin's, the blood seeping from his pores and running in red trickles across his skin and soaking his robes. Dark patches, some still glistening moistly, stained the green cloth that was caked with blood and grime. The smell was enough to make anyone retch.

"She's too powerful for you," he said, his voice cracking as if two people were speaking at once. "You won't be able to stop her. Show me where you last saw her and I'll take care of her myself. Lead the way."

Five paces.

I need to get closer to him. Narmora stumbled and sank to her knees. "Master, I'm hurt. Have pity on me and heal my wounds so I can serve you better."

"Later," he told her sharply. "Get up and..." His gaze had fallen on a particularly ferocious skirmish at the center of which was Tungdil, still locked in combat with Sinthoras and his orcs. "Lot-Ionan's groundling? But that's not... I mean, I thought the artifacts were..." He fell silent and collected his thoughts. "Well, things have got a good deal easier."

The magus closed his eyes. Narmora saw her opportunity and decided to act.

Slowly and silently so as not to attract attention, she rose from her knees and took a nervous step toward him, then another.

Four paces, three paces, two paces. She reached for Keenfire. *One more pace.*

"Master, look out!" someone shouted across the hall.

Narmora drew the ax and brought it down with all her might. Nôd'onn turned away from Tungdil and directed the curse at her.

Narmora felt as if she were staring into the sun. The dazzling light seared into her eyes, and before she knew it, she was flying backward through the air. She thudded down, landing heavily on the walkway, still blinded, but with Keenfire gripped tightly in her hand.

She couldn't see Nôd'onn, but it was obvious that he'd evaded her blow. *Why am I still alive, then?* She ran her hands over her body and felt the smooth surface of the amulet given to her by Andôkai. *That must be it.*

"Finish her off, and bring the ax to me," she heard the magus order. The clicking of his wooden staff against the flagstones receded into the distance.

Little by little her eyes cleared and she caught a hazy glimpse of the malachite robe disappearing down the staircase. Gasping with pain, she struggled up, intent on running after the traitor and cutting him down. The amulet would protect her.

She was almost on her feet when a shadow hurtled out of nowhere. Whooshing over her head, the dark figure landed lightly on the walkway in front of her. Two short swords pointed menacingly at her chest.

"You should have known that the Perished Land would allow me to avenge myself," said Caphalor.

Narmora stared at the deep wound where her blade had gashed his throat. "If I thought you were a danger, I would have beheaded you," she said coldly. "You're no threat to us." She held the ax on high, knowing that Caphalor would kill her if he sensed she was afraid.

The älf lunged at her, snarling, and Narmora realized that she would never keep pace with his attack. She retaliated with an offensive of her own and laid open the undead warrior's shoulder. The ax cut into his flesh, but Caphalor was undaunted.

"I'll cut you to ribbons, eat your flesh, and paint a portrait of your ravaged body with your blood," he spat, raising his weapons again. Harrying her with his swords, he maneuvered her closer and closer to the edge of the walkway. Belatedly she noticed that she was only a hand span away from plummeting to her death.

Caphalor dropped down suddenly and swiped at her calves. She leaped over him, whirled around, and swung her ax to finish his undead existence.

But the älf had thrown himself to the floor and rolled over, ready to thrust his swords toward her as she delivered the final blow.

The ax head scraped along the stone floor, sparks flying everywhere, then sliced sideways into the älf's neck, settling the matter forever. Caphalor's eyes widened.

But his final maneuver had not been in vain.

His swords had pierced Narmora's armor and embedded themselves beneath her collarbone. The half älf found herself skewered above his corpse, unable to think or move. Through the haze of her consciousness she saw the amulet fall from her neck, hit Caphalor, and bounce off the walkway. The leather band, sliced in two by the älf, unraveled onto his chest.

I still haven't... She tried to call to the others, but her gored chest and her ebbing strength turned her shout to a whisper. She could feel herself slipping out of consciousness and there was nothing she could do.

Her legs gave way and she slumped over Caphalor, her chest still propped up by his swords. Suddenly she felt unbearably cold. Incapable of even the smallest movement, she dangled above her foe.

Furgas... She had nothing left to give. Her fingers opened against her will, and Keenfire fell from her grip. Clattering to the walkway, the ax bounced against the flagstones and flew over the edge.

X

Tungdil glanced up and saw Narmora on the walkway. The sight of her impaled on Caphalor's swords filled him with helpless rage.

Meanwhile, Nôd'onn was descending the final steps of the staircase only paces away from Tungdil and the others. They were running out of time. *We'll be lost without Keenfire.*

"I'll get the ax," he shouted to Balyndis. "Keep the orcs busy and watch out for Nôd'onn. Andôkai will have to take care of him until I get back."

The firstling nodded grimly and felled a beast that was about to lunge at Tungdil. "Hurry!"

Tungdil detached himself from the scrum and blew his horn to summon the warriors of the three dwarven folks who were fighting in the other halls. His call was answered by blaring bugles and the sound of dwarven axes on orcish mail. He hoped that the upsurge in fighting would preoccupy the enemy and allow him to slip past unnoticed.

"Vraccas, your name will be worshipped forever if you help me now." He finished his quick prayer, took a deep breath, and charged into the jumble of stinking armor and legs.

No matter how tempting it was to clear a path with his ax, he knew that his safety depended on stealth. Crouching low, he tried to scurry past the beasts without brushing against them. It would have been easy for a scrawny gnome like Sverd, but Tungdil was considerably broader.

Every now and then he was spotted by an orc, but he kept moving to avoid being caught. Twice he was seized by a clawed hand and had to use his ax to slice his way free.

At last he reached the place where Keenfire had fallen to the ground. He scanned the flagstones, but the ax had vanished.

"Tungdil, I've got something for you. Over here!" He turned in time to see the back of a dwarven warrior disappear from view. Keenfire's ax head glittered in his hands. "Come and get it."

This is no time for silly games. Tungdil set off in pursuit, dragging his wounded leg across the floor. He left the muddle of orcish shins and made for the shelter of a pillar. The beasts rushed on, too focused on defeating the dwarven army to notice what was unfolding behind them.

To his surprise, the dwarf turned and held out Keenfire toward him. Tungdil stared at him in bewilderment. "You?"

"Looking for this?" asked Bislipur. His body was twisted out of shape, his face a mass of shattered bone. Judging by his fractured skull, he had fallen from a great height. Tungdil could barely stand to look at him.

"I see you've been punished for your plotting, then," he said grimly, gripping his ax in readiness. *He must be a revenant.* "I told King Gandogar—"

"I don't give a damn about Gandogar."

"You lowered yourself to all kinds of trickery to have him crowned and now he means nothing to you?"

"All I ever cared about was having a high king who would do my bidding, a high king whom I could control." He swung the ax playfully. "A war against the elves—that's what I wanted. I even murdered Gandogar's father and brother so I could blame the elves and stoke his fury. How was I to know that I wouldn't need the pointy-ears? It's turned out better than I expected." He pointed to the dwarves locked in combat around them and laughed. "Don't you get it, Tungdil?" he said, noticing the other's uncomprehending stare. "I'm a thirdling—and so are you."

"No," whispered Tungdil. The shouts, screams, and ringing metal seemed to fade into nothingness as he stared into Bislipur's knowing eyes. He tried not to remember how he had initially felt drawn to him. "A thirdling? But I can't be. I'm a fourthling, a dwarf of Goïmdil."

"Like me, you mean?" Bislipur laughed in his face. "Tungdil, our destiny is revenge. Lorimbur was scorned by his brothers. They wouldn't share their talents and they mocked the thirdlings because they thought they were better. The gifts they received from Vraccas made them arrogant like the elves. Don't you see how they treated you?" He took a step forward. "Noble Gundrabur and his loyal counselor, Balendilín, used you to suit their purpose. Why else do you think they were interested in you? If Lot-Ionan's letter had arrived at any other time, they would never have bothered fetching you from the long-uns. That's how much they care! They're worthless, every last one of them. They all deserve to die."

Tungdil felt the words cut into his heart and found himself succumbing to Bislipur's hypnotic stare. "No," he said hesitantly. "Balyndis..."

Bislipur laughed spitefully. "So you've fallen for someone, have you? And how do you think she'll react when she finds out you're a dwarf killer and a traitor? Your future is with the thirdlings, not here. You'll die with the others if you stay."

"A traitor?" Tungdil stared at the battle in sudden understanding. At last he grasped the full meaning of Bislipur's words. "It was you! You betrayed us to Nôd'onn!"

"Nôd'onn is a great ally, the greatest. I promised him that the thirdlings would do nothing to stop him, provided that the other kingdoms were destroyed. It was the perfect opportunity."

Tungdil swallowed and tightened his grip on his ax. "You're crazy. You delivered up Girdlegard just because—"

"No!" the thirdling screeched suddenly. "Not *just* because of anything! This is our destiny! For thousands of cycles we've been waiting for a moment like this. No deed could be more glorious, Tungdil. Our folk, the dwarves of Lorimbur, will rule all five ranges of Girdlegard once the others are dead!"

"I don't want anything to do with you or your folk! I came here to stop Nôd'onn and save the dwarves. I don't belong to Lorimbur!"

"You're one of us," Bislipur told him fiercely. "I knew it from the moment I saw you. Look inside your heart and embrace your hatred. You're a thirdling, believe me."

"Believe *you*? Why should I believe a traitor?" Tungdil glared at him scornfully and took a deep breath. "Now give me Keenfire."

Bislipur stared at him suspiciously. "Why?"

"So Nôd'onn can be killed. As for your punishment, I'll leave that to Gandogar and the others to decide."

"It's like that, is it?" He thumped the ax regretfully. "I'm afraid I'll have to kill you, Tungdil. You risked everything for Keenfire, and now the weapon will be your death. It seems a shame to—"

Tungdil raised his ax without warning, but Bislipur countered his blow. From then on, both dwarves fought mercilessly, but neither could win the upper hand.

"So you still think you're not a thirdling, do you?" the traitor asked mockingly. "How else would you have learned to fight so well in such a short space of time? You were born a warrior."

"No!" thundered Tungdil, slashing at him furiously. "I'll *never* be a thirdling."

The two axes collided, and Keenfire shattered Tungdil's weapon. The ax head spun into the air and struck Tungdil's nose guard with enough force to make him see stars.

Bislipur didn't wait for him to recover, but moved in fast. Tungdil tried to step out of the way and stumbled. At the last moment he pulled Bislipur with him, and they wrestled each other to the ground.

The battle continued on the floor, the two dwarves hacking at each other until Keenfire fell from Bislipur's grasp. He whipped out a dagger and rammed it into Tungdil's arm. Gasping, Tungdil grabbed his knife and plunged it into Bislipur's throat.

"You're wasting your time," Bislipur said derisively. "See what Balendilín did to me? He couldn't kill me; the Perished Land wouldn't let him." He landed a punch that knocked off Tungdil's helmet, then seized his chance to scramble to safety. A well-aimed kick sent Tungdil's knife flying out of his hand. "It's not a fair fight, Tungdil, and you're about to lose."

His fingers wound their way into Tungdil's hair and hauled him up. "I'll give you one last chance because you're a thirdling," he snarled. "Do you want to die with the other scum, or come back with me and celebrate our victory?"

Tungdil had run out of weapons and had only one option. Fumbling in his pouch, he pulled out Sverd's collar and looped it around the startled Bislipur's neck.

"The gnome's choker? What good will that do? I'm dead already! I don't need air!"

"Sure, but you can't do without your head." Tungdil shoved him backward. The maneuver cost him a clump of hair, but allowed him to reach for the magic wire on Bislipur's belt. "And it's your head that I'm after."

A sudden jerk, and the noose closed around Bislipur's neck. The collar tightened, cutting into Bislipur's throat. At last the thirdling realized what Tungdil was intending to do.

Grunting inarticulately because of the pressure on his throat, he jabbed his dagger toward Tungdil, who tugged on the wire. The choker passed through Bislipur's neck, slicing through his spinal cord. The wire ran through its clasp, the noose sprang open, and the traitor's head rolled across the floor. The hateful collar fell apart, its evil charm broken.

There was no time for Tungdil to savor his victory. Gathering up Keenfire, he ran as fast as his injuries would permit him, determined to stand by his friends in the fight against the magus.

The ax was back in their possession. Now all they needed was an enemy of the dwarves who could wield it against Nôd'onn.

The orcs drew back to let the magus through. Suddenly everyone stopped fighting.

"Hello, Andôkai," rasped Nôd'onn, inclining his head toward her. "You should have allied yourself with me from the beginning, instead of squandering your strength in futile resistance. I'll need your power to fight the peril from the west."

"The peril is here already. It lives within you, confusing your thoughts and steering your deeds." She focused her energy on maintaining her protective shield. "The demon is using you, Nudin."

"He's my friend, a loyal friend of Girdlegard." He shook his head despairingly. "You don't understand. No one understands."

"You're right, Nudin; we don't understand. How many men, elves, and dwarves must die so you can protect our kingdoms? It seems a high price to pay, especially when the supposed peril is a figment of your poisoned mind."

"My name is *Nôd'onn!*" His voice became a shrill, nasal shout. "When you see what's coming from the west, you'll be grateful that my friend and I protected you. Lay down your weapons, and I'll spare you." There was an urgency to his doublefold voice; he seemed fully convinced of everything he said. "I did what I did because you gave me no choice. If you'd relinquished your power, it would never have come to this."

Andôkai's sword flashed as she raised her arm defiantly. "How I am supposed to believe you after all the suffering you've caused?"

He looked at her sadly. "In that case, we'll have to finish things properly. You've had your chance." With a wave of his hand, he shattered her protective spell.

Sinthoras heard the shield collapse and lunged at the maga. She batted away his spear, only to find herself under attack from three orcs who crowded round her, cutting her off from her companions.

Suddenly the älf was beside her and this time his spear was headed straight for her chest. It collided with a shimmering shield.

Sinthoras was sheathed in violet light. A terrible roar shook the hall, then Djerûn's sword swooped down. The älf barely had time to raise his weapon.

No wood in the world, not even sigurdaisy wood, could have withstood such a blow. The giant's sword sliced through the spear and sped on. A wide sweeping blow parted the disbelieving älf's head from his shoulders, and Sinthoras's headless body slumped to the ground, never to rise again.

Grunting in terror, the orcs shrank back from the king of

the beasts as he straightened up, howling, and opened his visor. His face was invisible in the blinding light, but the orcs were rooted with fear, allowing the company to regroup.

Tungdil, still clutching Keenfire, limped toward the maga. "I've got the weapon." He pointed to Djerûn. "Is he an enemy of the dwarves?" he asked, panting for breath.

"I don't know. Are you prepared to give him Keenfire?"

"We don't have a choice." He tossed the weapon to the giant.

Without hesitating, Djerûn discarded his sword by ramming it through two orcs and reached out to catch the ax.

Let's get this over with. Tungdil raised his horn and sounded a long, powerful call. The dwarves of Beroïn, Borengar, and Goïmdil answered with cheers and blaring bugles. "For Vraccas and Girdlegard!" he shouted, leading the charge against the magus. Balyndis and Gandogar were already at his side; the others stormed after them.

They hewed down the orcs and bögnilim in their way, cutting a path of gory destruction that brought Djerûn within striking distance of their foe. Andôkai conjured a bolt of lightning, whose purpose was to dazzle the magus, then gave the command for Djerûn to strike.

Before Nôd'onn had time to compose himself, the mailed giant brought down the ax. It hit the magus's unprotected back, sliced through his body, and sped out of his chest. Stinking black fluid spurted everywhere, showering the transfixed onlookers.

Nôd'onn let out a terrible howl. The hall was still echoing with his screams when the wound began to heal.

"No," whispered Tungdil in horror. "It's not possible. Keenfire was supposed to..."

Nôd'onn hurled bolts of black lightning at the giant, who fell backward and lay still among the orcs. "I told you that nothing can hurt me," thundered the magus. He bore no sign of injury, save for the gash in his robes.

We can't let it end this way! Filled with desperate fury, Tungdil went on the offensive. While his friends tried to preoccupy the magus by engaging him in an increasingly hopeless battle, he set off a second time in search of the ax.

He found Keenfire in Djerûn's stiff metal grasp. Prizing away the giant's fingers, he picked up the ax and felt a strange sensation in his hand. *What...?*

Light pulsed through the intarsia, and the diamonds came to life, shining and sparkling like a thousand miniature suns. At first he thought Nôd'onn had worked a spell on it, but then he saw that the ax itself had wrought the change. Keenfire was readying itself to fight the demon.

By Vraccas, Bislipur was right: I'm a thirdling. No sooner had he grasped the significance of what was happening than he decided to turn his heritage to the good.

He tightened his grip on Keenfire, squared his shoulders, and charged. Orcs tried to block his path but perished in a blaze of white fire as he swung the shimmering ax. A trail of smoke followed the swinging Keenfire, and Tungdil could feel the heat from its blade. It burned with the fierce ardor of the fifthlings' furnace.

Nôd'onn recognized the danger before it was upon him. His self-assurance vanished, replaced by pure terror. His magic could do nothing against the charging dwarf; Tungdil was protected from harm by Keenfire's runes.

"Kill me, and Girdlegard will be doomed," the magus prophesied. "Terrible forces are gathering in the west and you won't be able to stop them." He thrust his staff at Tungdil, who deflected the blow and lunged closer. "*You'll* be to blame for Girdlegard's destruction. You must let me live!"

Tungdil slashed at the magus's onyx-tipped staff. The black jewel shattered in a shower of dark crystals.

"No, Nôd'onn, evil will never triumph over Girdlegard.

We'll protect our kingdoms, just as we protected them from you." Tungdil swung his ax again. *For Lot-Ionan, Frala, and her daughters.*

The corpulent magus tried in vain to sidestep the blow. Even his final incantation failed to halt the blade, his hastily conjured runes flickering briefly as Keenfire smashed through them. The diamond-studded ax head buried itself in Nôd'onn's waist.

Like an overripe fruit, the magus burst, spilling a foul mess of flesh, blood, and entrails. A finger-length splinter of malachite shot out and was swept away in the reeking cascade.

Slowly, a shimmering wisp of mist detached itself from the wreckage. It expanded rapidly, coursing with black, silver, and crimson flashes and looming five paces in the air. Fist-sized orbs burned red within its cavernous eyes as it stared with hatred and malice at Tungdil. Then it shifted its gaze to the maga.

It needs a new victim.

The swirling mist reached out toward Andôkai, who took a step backward. She raised her sword, but the blade slid straight through it. The mist shrank, sprouting thin transparent arms and imprisoning the maga in its grasp.

Groaning, Andôkai staggered and fell to her knees as fingers of mist prized themselves experimentally between her jaws. The being was determined to find a new home, with or without her permission.

Tungdil leaped toward her, bringing down his ax just as the flickering column of mist readied itself to glide down her throat.

Keenfire's runes sparkled as it hewed the mist in two. There was a loud hiss as the mist drew back like a wounded beast. Tungdil closed in, swinging his ax and slashing at the mist. Thin wisps floated through the hall and dispersed into nothingness, but the demon was still alive and seemed intent on escaping to the ceiling.

In that case I'll have to try another tactic. Tungdil climbed onto an upturned pillar. Pain shot through his wounded arm and leg as he sprinted forward, casting himself into the air and brandishing Keenfire. "For Vraccas!"

He had timed the leap well. Soaring into the middle of the mist, his blade found its target. Runes blazing, the ax head left a cometlike trail of light. The diamonds sparkled fiercely.

For the span of a heartbeat Tungdil hovered at the heart of the demon. At first it seemed as if the mist had stopped his fall; then there was a tearing noise and a terrible groan.

Tungdil plunged through the mist, skidded across the floor, and was saved by his chain mail from serious cuts and grazes. Looking round, he saw he had punched a hole through the flickering demon. Slowly the being sank to the ground, turning first gray, then black, then disappearing altogether. In the end there was nothing left.

No one moved. Dwarves and beasts alike had witnessed the death of the magus and the destruction of the demon. It was deathly still.

One of the älf, who moments earlier had been spurring the hordes against the dwarves, reached to his neck, screaming with pain. Suddenly his amulet burst apart, tearing him to pieces. Soon the other älfar and a number of orcish chieftains were dead or dying, slain by the magus's gifts.

A bugle sounded the attack, and the dwarves of the three kingdoms fell upon their foes.

The bögnilim were the first to flee, followed by the orcs, but the children of the Smith showed no pity or mercy, funneling them into the narrow passageways where the battle continued. In the vast halls, the ceilings echoed with the clatter and ringing of furious axes.

Slowly Tungdil picked himself up from the floor. Balyndis

was beside him, helping him to his feet. "You did it!" She leaned forward and gave him a lingering kiss on the lips.

It was a moment he had dreamed of, but the truth about his lineage spoiled it. "Only because I'm a thirdling," he said bitterly. *A dwarf killer,* he added silently.

She nodded. "Praise be to Vraccas! Nôd'onn would still be alive if you weren't!" She smiled. "You're a true dwarf, Tungdil. I don't care which folk you belong to. I know in my heart that I can trust you, and that's what counts."

He gave her hand a grateful squeeze. *Let's hope the others are as understanding.*

Meanwhile, Andôkai and a unit of dwarves had stormed the walkway and were attending to the wounded Narmora. Boïndil had been cut down by Caphalor and needed the maga's attentions as well. Djerûn was back on his feet again, his visor firmly closed and his face still a mystery.

Dwarven healers hurried over with water, balms, and dressings. Now that the duel with the demon was over, Tungdil was acutely aware of his injuries and allowed himself to be salved and bandaged. He found a worthy place for Keenfire in Giselbert Ironeye's belt.

He didn't have much opportunity to relax. Already Rodario was hurrying toward him.

"My apologies for bothering Girdlegard's valiant hero, but I think we should check on Furgas," he said anxiously. "Who knows what…"

"Valiant hero?" Tungdil grinned. *Not bad for a scholar. I hope Frala and Lot-Ionan can see me now.* He straightened up and checked his bandages. "In that case, I'll have to rejoin the battle. In books the hero always keeps fighting to the end."

"Blasted älfar, they always creep up on you. I didn't hear him coming. He loomed up like a shadow and attacked me from behind." Boïndil, his chest swathed in bandages, hobbled down the stairs. "That's right, scholar, just like in a book. My brother would be proud of you."

"Boïndil!" Smiling with relief, Tungdil thumped him gently on the back: The thought of losing another friend had been too much to bear. "Let's check on Furgas."

Tungdil, Rodario, Balyndis, Boïndil, and Djerůn hurried away. Andôkai caught up with them after a few paces: They had started the journey as strangers and wanted to end it as friends.

Blacksaddle,
Kingdom of Gauragar,
Girdlegard,
Winter, 6234th Solar Cycle

A chill wind was buffeting the flat summit of the Blacksaddle, but shafts of sunlight shone through the clouds and warmed the earth, heralding the coming of spring.

"For many cycles this mountain was known as a place of foreboding, a dreaded stronghold where a plot was hatched to destroy the dwarven race. Today's events have changed all that. From this day forth, the Blacksaddle will be seen as a symbol of hope, a symbol of a better future in which elves, men, and dwarves will work together for the good of Girdlegard." Gandogar paused for a moment and surveyed the assortment of leaders and warriors gathered on top of the Blacksaddle.

Half a cycle ago he would have ridiculed the idea of elven, human, and dwarven rulers uniting on the accursed peak to celebrate a battle fought as allies, not foes.

His eyes traveled over the faces before him. Prince Mallen of Ido was sitting beside Lord Liútasil of Âlandur. Next came

King Balendilín Onearm of the clan of the Firm Fingers and Queen Xamtys II of the clan of the Stubborn Streaks, and behind them were Nate, Bruron, and the other human sovereigns, not forgetting Andôkai, of course.

After that, there was a short gap to the first row of commoners, made up of Girdlegard's most distinguished warriors—dwarves, elves, and men. They were straining to hear what their leaders were discussing. Gandogar could see Tungdil and Balyndis among them, with Djerûn towering like a pinnacle at their side.

"Together we defeated the monstrous issue of Nudin the Knowledge-Lusty's alliance with a demon from the north. Nôd'onn is dead, the Perished Land has been banished from Girdlegard, and nature is returning to her ancient ways. Together we achieved all this, and our kingdoms were *saved,* saved because we buried old grudges, overcame our mutual distrust, and joined forces in Girdlegard's hour of need." He raised his arms. "We prevailed! Is this not reason enough to forget our past quarrels?"

He waited for a moment, allowing his words to take effect.

"You, Prince Mallen of Ido, rallied the human warriors after their defeat at Porista and led the united army to the Blacksaddle in a courageous stand against Nôd'onn." He smiled solemnly at Idoslane's ruler, then turned to face the elven leader. "And you, Lord Liútasil of Âlandur, welcomed us into your kingdom when we asked for your help. Your heart must have counseled you against it, but you came to our aid." He looked at Balendilín and Xamtys. "And you, worthy children of the Smith, you reforged the bonds between our kingdoms and honored the duty entrusted to us by Vraccas." He raised his voice triumphantly. "Friends, *together* we rescued Girdlegard!"

The warriors of the assembled races thumped their shields and banged their weapons together.

"We must rid our hearts of hatred. Our past battles are just that: They belong in the past and are best forgotten. This orbit marks the start of a new age: one of peace, cooperation, and friendship." He held his ax aloft, and the other monarchs rose to their feet to pledge a new era of friendship.

This time his speech was met with deafening cheers. Swept away by the excitement, Balyndis planted another kiss on Tungdil's lips. Even in the last moments of the battle she hadn't known whether or not they would succeed, and now she was overcome with gladness and relief. "You must be really proud," she said.

"Proud of what? Being a thirdling?" he retorted, only half joking. His voice was edged with resentment.

"Proud of being the only thirdling to save the dwarven folks instead of trying to destroy them." She smiled. "Come on, Tungdil, we're lucky to have made it alive."

He thought of Narmora and Furgas lying side by side in the stronghold. They would have shared a different fate if Andôkai hadn't summoned the last of her strength to invoke a healing charm. Dwarven physicians were still tending to their wounds. Then there were those who had been gathered to Vraccas's smithy: *I haven't forgotten you, Bavragor and Goïmgar.*

He looked up to see Gandogar pointing straight at him.

"But above all we owe our thanks to Tungdil Goldhand," announced the dwarven king. "Step forward, Tungdil."

Nervously, he obeyed.

"Take a good look at him, for without Tungdil, without his stubbornness, his ingenuity, and most important, his unshakable faith in our mission, none of us would be standing here today. Without Tungdil Goldhand, Nôd'onn would have killed or enslaved us all."

Suddenly it seemed to Tungdil that every dwarf, elf, and man on the Blacksaddle was staring at him. He blushed and felt terribly embarrassed. He reached down and rested a hand on Keenfire, which made him feel slightly less shy.

"We will never be in a position to repay our debt," said Gandogar gravely. "But know this: For as long as you live, Tungdil Goldhand, I will do everything in my power to satisfy your every wish."

Liútasil turned his slender, graceful face toward him. "We have never numbered among the dwarves' closest friends, but we are beholden to you, Tungdil Goldhand. We too will grant you whatever you desire."

The human sovereigns swore similar oaths of gratitude while Tungdil squirmed in embarrassment.

"Prithee, stop, Your Majesties," he interrupted.

Boïndil rolled his eyes. "Here he goes again. Wake me up when he's finished."

Tungdil took a deep breath. "You don't owe me anything. My only wish has been granted already: All I want is for dwarves, elves, and men to come together in friendship, not war. You pledged an end to our quarreling, and what more could I desire? Gold and riches count for nothing without peace. I can't accept your gifts, but I shall gladly accept your thanks, especially on behalf of my companions, Bavragor Hammerfist of the clan of the Hammer Fists and Goïmgar Shimmerbeard of the clan of the Shimmer Beards. Bavragor and Goïmgar risked everything for Girdlegard, and they paid the highest price. Keenfire would never have been forged without them."

The elven lord inclined his head toward him. "You speak with the wisdom of a true leader, Tungdil Goldhand. If ever we are in danger of resuming our old rivalries, you must remind us of the oaths of friendship sworn today. You will always be welcome in Âlandur."

There was thunderous applause from the warriors, who

hammered on their shields, sounded their bugles, and cheered tirelessly. Tungdil scurried back to Balyndis's side.

Boïndil pretended to scowl at him. "Show us your tongue," he demanded. "I bet you've talked it into knots."

Tungdil just grinned. He was happy that his lessons in rhetoric had been put to proper use.

After a while the assembly dissolved and the allied armies retired to the stronghold to celebrate their victory and negotiate their newfound friendship.

Balendilín and Gandogar joined the others. "What an orbit this has been!" the secondling king said happily. "Who would have thought it would turn out so well?" He thumped Tungdil on the shoulder. "Vraccas sent us the dwarf of all dwarves, and if anyone cares to dispute it, I'll set up another contest with five new tasks." He laughed and the others joined in.

Gandogar noticed that Tungdil's jollity seemed a little forced. "Is something the matter?"

"It's nothing."

"No, something's wrong. Is it because you think you're a thirdling?"

"I *am* a thirdling! How else could I have awoken Keenfire's power?"

"Then be proud to be a thirdling, Tungdil," Balendilín exhorted him solemnly. "Show your kinsfolk, show every dwarf in Girdlegard, that Lorimbur's descendants aren't all as dastardly and conniving as Bislipur and Glamdolin. Incidentally," he added with a mischievous smile, "were you planning to return to Ogre's Death or is there somewhere else you'd rather be?"

"Balyndis and I won't be going to the firstling kingdom, if that's what you mean," he said, grinning bashfully. "We're both smiths at heart, and our interests and experiences have soldered us together. We've decided to go to the Gray Range. Boïndil's coming with us and we'll pick up Boëndal on the way. I promised Giselbert Ironeye that I wouldn't abandon his kingdom and I intend to keep my word."

The rising winds carried a foul smell to their nostrils. It came from the plains around the Blacksaddle, where the corpses of ogres, orcs, bögnilim, and älfar were strewn. The combined army of elves, dwarves, and men had laid waste to the enemy battalions. A few undead troopers had survived the massacre, only to lose their lives forever with the defeat of the Perished Land. Their corpses were rotting in the winter sunshine, but the carnage would soon be frozen overnight.

"It will take time to bury all the bodies," Gandogar said grimly. "I hope the earth can suffer so much death."

Rodario joined them, quill and notebook in hand. "A magnificent finale for a play, don't you think? Too many corpses for practical purposes—we'd never fit them on stage." He stopped making notes and extended his hand toward Tungdil. "It was a privilege to accompany you. If you find yourself in Mifurdania, be sure to visit the Curiosum. We'll be celebrating our grand reopening." He winked at Tungdil. "As the star of the show, you'll qualify for free admission—and Balyndis as well."

"When are you off?"

"As soon as my prop master and my leading lady are fit to ride. A fortnight or so, I expect. In the meantime, they've found room for us here."

Andôkai strode toward them. "Djerûn and I are leaving. I need to get back to my realm and find some new famuli."

"Why the hurry, dear heart?" Rodario said lightly.

The maga refused to be drawn. "I don't want to spoil the mood."

"Impossible!" he declared with overblown enthusiasm. "Nothing could spoil a victory like this!"

"I wouldn't be so sure." Her lips were unsmiling. "What if Nôd'onn wasn't lying after all?"

"About the western peril?" The impresario laughed incredulously. "My dear lady, you shouldn't be fooled by a cheap trick like that. You disappoint me!"

"Say what you like, but I intend to be vigilant." She laid her hand on Tungdil's arm. "At least I'll know where to find Keenfire and its valiant bearer, should Nudin prove right." At last her stern face relaxed. "You're stubborn enough to take on any kind of peril single-handed," she told him.

She took her leave of the company, giving everyone except Rodario a long embrace. He pouted and stalked away, only to turn after a few paces and wave. "Farewell, enchanting maga. I shall take your advice and devote my attentions to women who know how to appreciate me—and believe me, *they do!*"

Andôkai hurried away, followed, as always, by Djerûn. The others watched in silence as the strange pair passed from sight. Balendilín called the group to attention by clearing his throat.

"I must take my leave as well, dear friends. The assembly will soon be meeting to decide the succession, and I need to make sure that everything's in place." He inclined his head toward Gandogar. "I don't doubt that the delegates will vote in your favor. You have proven yourself a worthy heir since stepping out of Bislipur's shadow; I know you will make an excellent high king."

"I'd even vote for him myself," said Tungdil with a grin. He held out his hand to Gandogar, who shook it firmly and seemed moved. "Don't forget to send a hundred of your best warriors and artisans to the fifthling kingdom. That goes for all the folks—Balyndis and I will appreciate the company, and we won't be able to defend the Stone Gateway on our own. I want to rebuild Giselbert's kingdom." He paused for a moment, remembering the promise he had made. "The Gray Range will belong to the children of Vraccas. Who knows, perhaps our mysterious rescuers will join us? They might be glad to leave the drafty tunnels for a more comfortable home."

"You should certainly ask them," Gandogar concurred.

"Vraccas will be proud to see us forging a folk of our own. But what should we do about the thirdlings?" Balendilín asked.

Tungdil turned to the east and gazed in the direction of the Black Range, where Lorimbur's descendants had made their home.

"I can't be the only thirdling who wasn't born to hate his fellow dwarves," he said softly. "Once things are settled in the fifthling kingdom, I'll pay them a visit and see what they have to say." He looked into the eyes of the three dwarven rulers. "I meant what I said when I asked for peace. The thirdlings are no exception."

Balyndis smiled and took his hand. He gave it a little squeeze.

Gradually the others made their way down from the mountain. Balyndis and Tungdil lingered on the summit until the sun dropped below the horizon and stars filled the sky. There was a crisp chill in the air, reminding them that Girdlegard was still in the grip of winter.

Tungdil had wrapped his fingers around Balyndis's hand and had no intention of letting go.

Just then a shooting star left a glittering trail from east to west, the white light turning red as it shot across the sky. There was a brief red flare; then the light dispersed into myriad crimson dots that reminded Tungdil of scattered blood. At last they were swallowed by the darkness of the sky.

"Was that a good or a bad omen, do you think?" Balyndis asked uncertainly.

He gave a shrug, then stepped back and hugged her from behind. "A good omen," he said after a short silence, running his hand over her downy cheeks.

"How do you know?"

He studied the night sky and spotted the distant lights of settlements. He was glad of the stillness that peace had brought with it. The prospect of spring, when trees and plants would blossom throughout Girdlegard, was exciting. *All Girdlegard will be covered in greenery for the first time in a thousand cycles.*

"After everything we've been through, it has to be a good omen," he whispered in her ear. "It was red, the color of love, so it must mean something good. Come on, let's find the others. We've got something to celebrate."

Hand in hand they made their way down from the Blacksaddle, whose looming presence had lost its terror for the dwarven folks.

They were halfway down the steps that led into the stronghold when a second streak of light flashed above them.

Unseen and unnoticed, the comet sped toward the west. Still shining brightly, it dipped toward the earth, sailing through the clouds and leaving a deep red trail in the sky. At last it disappeared on the horizon beyond the firstling kingdom. It hit the ground with a muffled thud, sending a shudder through Girdlegard. Even the Blacksaddle trembled.

Then everything was quiet...

Dramatis Personae

DWARVES

Firstling Kingdom

Xamtys Stubbornstreak II of the clan of the Stubborn Streaks, queen of Borengar's folk.

Balyndis Steelfinger of the clan of the Steel Fingers, blacksmith and custodian of the gates.

Secondling Kingdom

Gundrabur Whitecrown of the clan of the Hard Rocks, high king and leader of Beroïn's folk.

Balendilín Onearm of the clan of the Firm Fingers, counselor to the high king.

Bavragor Hammerfist of the clan of the Hammer Fists, mason.

Boëndal Hookhand and **Boïndil Doubleblade**, known also as **Ireheart**, of the clan of the Swinging Axes, warriors and twins.

Thirdling Kingdom

—

Fourthling Kingdom

Gandogar Silverbeard of the clan of the Silver Beards, king of Goïmdil's folk.

Bislipur Surestroke of the clan of the Brawny Fists, adviser to the fourthling king.

Tungdil Bolofar, later **Goldhand**, foundling and Lot-Ionan's ward.

Goïmgar Shimmerbeard of the clan of the Shimmer Beards, gem cutter.

Fifthling Kingdom

Giselbert Ironeye, father of the fifthlings, king of Giselbert's folk.

Glandallin Hammerstrike of the clan of the Striking Hammers, warrior.

HUMANS

Andôkai the Tempestuous, maga and ruler of the enchanted realm of Brandôkai.

Djerûn, bodyguard in the service of Andôkai.

Lot-Ionan the Forbearing, magus and ruler of the enchanted realm of Ionandar.

Maira the Life-Preserver, maga and ruler of the enchanted realm of Oremaira.

Nudin the Knowledge-Lusty, magus and ruler of the enchanted realm of Lios Nudin.

Sabora the Softly-Spoken, maga and ruler of the enchanted realm of Saborien.

Turgur the Fair-Faced, magus and ruler of the enchanted realm of Turguria.

Gorén, wizard formerly apprenticed to Lot-Ionan.

Frala, maid in the service of Lot-Ionan, mother of Sunja and Ikana.

Jolosin, famulus apprenticed to Lot-Ionan.

Eiden, groom in the service of Lot-Ionan.

Rantja, famula apprenticed to Nudin.

The fabulous **Rodario**, actor and impresario.
Furgas, theater technician and prop master.
Narmora, actress and companion to Furgas.

Hîl and **Kerolus**, peddlers.
Vrabor and **Friedegard**, envoys to the council of the magi.

Prince Mallen of Ido, exiled heir to the throne of Idoslane.
King Lothaire, sovereign of Urgon.
King Tilogorn, sovereign of Idoslane.
King Nate, sovereign of Tabaîn.
King Bruron, sovereign of Gauragar.
Queen Umilante, sovereign of Sangpûr.
Queen Wey IV, sovereign of Weyurn.
Queen Isika, sovereign of Rân Ribastur.

OTHERS

Sinthoras and **Caphalor**, älfar from the kingdom of Dsôn Balsur.
Liútasil, lord of Âlandur, kingdom of the elves.
Bashkugg, **Kragnarr**, and **Ushnotz**, orcish princes of Toboribor.
Sverd, gnome enslaved by Bislipur.

Acknowledgments

When I finished the final volume of my Ulldart series, I decided to tackle a new project: dwarves. It was a nerve-racking prospect. Most readers have fixed ideas about how they like their dwarves to look and act; I didn't want to disappoint their expectations, but at the same time I needed to do something new.

And so I went ahead and created my dwarves. I invented clans and folks for them to belong to, and I gave them particular talents and traits. I was careful not to stray too far from the traditional dwarf, but I added bits here and there, and I gave my dwarves a chance to prove their mettle. I didn't want them to be extras or sidekicks, so I made them into proper protagonists who outshine the humans and elves. My dwarves are the valiant defenders of Girdlegard, true heroes who fight—and sometimes die—in the line of duty.

I sent Tungdil and his companions on a perilous mission, and it had me on the edge of my seat. These pages are chock-full of dwarven dedication, passion, determination, exuberance, war, and death. Writing them was great fun, and with any luck, reading them will be entertaining as well.

My particular thanks go to those who made this a better and more interesting book. Among the first to see the manuscript were Nicole Schuhmacher, Sonja Rüther, Meike

Sewering, and Dr. Patrick Müller. Their thoughtful comments and suggestions were immensely helpful, as always.

Many thanks to translator Sally-Ann Spencer, who taught the dwarves a new language.

I would also like to thank those who allowed me to send the dwarves on their very own adventure. It was time the little fellows had their big chance.

extras

orbit

www.orbitbooks.net

about the author

Markus Heitz was born in 1971 in Germany. He studied history, German language, and literature and won the German Fantasy Award in 2003 for his debut novel, *Shadows Over Ulldart*. His Dwarves series is a bestseller in Europe. Markus Heitz lives in Zweibrücken.

Find out more about Markus Heitz and other Orbit authors by registering for the free monthly newsletter at www.orbitbooks.net

if you enjoyed
THE DWARVES

look out for

THE EDGE
OF THE WORLD

Terra Incognita: Book One

by

Kevin J. Anderson

These foreign seas looked much the same as the waters of home, but Criston Vora knew the lands were different, the people were different, and their religion was contrary to everything he had been taught in the Aidenist kirk. For a twenty-year-old sailor eager to see the world, those differences could be either wondrous or frightening—he wouldn't know which until he met the people of Uraba, which he was about to do.

The *Fishhook* had made this voyage several times, and Criston's captain, Andon Shay, was confident in his abilities to negotiate another trade deal with the Uraban merchants. The young man kept his eyes open and studied the unfolding coastline as the ship sailed far, far south of everything he had known.

From his fishing village of Windcatch, he had always felt the call of the sea, wanting to see what lay beyond the horizon, yearning to explore. Though he had signed on for only a short trading voyage, at least he was seeing the other continent: *Uraba*. A place of legends and mystery.

Though connected by a narrow isthmus, the world's two main continents, Uraba and Tierra, were separated by a wide gulf of history and culture. Ages ago, at the beginning of time, when Ondun—God—had sent two of his sons in separate sailing ships to explore the world, the descendants of Aiden's crew had settled Tierra, while those from Urec's vessel colonized Uraba. Over the centuries, the followers of Aiden and the followers of Urec developed separate civilizations, religions, and traditions; despite their differences, they were bound together by ties of trade and necessity.

On a bright sunny day with a brisk breeze, Captain Shay called for the sails to be trimmed for a gentle approach to the city of Ouroussa, where they hoped to find eager customers. The hold of the *Fishhook* contained barrels of whale oil from Soeland Reach, large spools of hemp rope from Erietta, grain from Alamont, and in a special locked chest in the captain's cabin, beautiful metal-worked jewelry made by the skilled smiths of Corag Reach. Though the bangles and ornaments would be sold to the followers of Urec, the Corag metalworkers had subtly hidden a tiny Aidenist fishhook on each piece of jewelry.

Captain Shay would sell his cargo at prices greatly reduced from what the other Uraban merchants and middlemen could offer. With fast vessels, intrepid Tierran sailors braved the uncharted currents and sailed directly to Uraba's coastal cities, bypassing the much slower overland merchants (much to their consternation).

Near the ship's wheel, Criston paused to look at the two compasses mounted on a sheltered pedestal, a traditional magnetic compass that always pointed toward magnetic north and a magical Captain's Compass that always pointed *home*. The silver needle of the Captain's Compass came from the same piece of precious metal as an identical needle in the

Tierran capital city of Calay. These twinned needles remained linked to each other by sympathetic magic, as all things in Ondun's creation were said to be linked.

Now, as the *Fishhook* closed in on Ouroussa, the crew saw a flurry of activity in the distant harbor; a ship with a bright red sail set out to meet them, sailing toward the open water. Captain Shay gestured to Criston. "Go aloft and have a look, Seaman Vora." Shay's dark hair ran to his shoulders, and instead of wearing a full bushy beard like most ship captains, he kept his neatly trimmed.

Nimble and unafraid of heights, the young man scrambled up the shroud lines to reach the lookout nest. During the voyage, Criston had enjoyed spending time high atop the main mast overlooking the waters; he had even seen several fearsome-looking sea serpents. but only at a distance.

As the Uraban ship approached, Criston noted its central painted icon on its square mainsail, the Eye of Urec. He spied additional movement in the harbor, where two fast Uraban galleys launched, their oars extended, beating across the water at a good clip. They spread apart, approaching the *Fishhook* from opposite directions.

Captain Shay called for a report, and Criston scrambled back down the lines to relate what he had seen to Captain Shay. "I couldn't see many crewmen aboard the main ship, Captain. Maybe they just want to escort us into port."

"Never needed an escort before. These aren't waters that require a pilot." Shay snapped orders to his crew, and all twenty-eight men came out on deck to stand ready. "Once they know what we're offering, they'll welcome us with open arms, but don't let your guard down." He turned back to the young sailor. "This could be a very interesting first voyage for you, Seaman."

"It's not my first voyage, sir. I've spent most of my life on boats."

"It's your first voyage with *me*, and that's what counts."

Criston's father, a fisherman, had been lost at sea, and Criston himself had served aboard many boats, working the local catch but dreaming of more ambitious voyages. Though young, Criston owned his own small boat for carrying cargo up to the Tierran capital of Calay, but the prospect of paying off the moneylenders seemed daunting. So when the *Fishhook* had passed through Windcatch on her way south and Captain Shay asked for short-term sailors to accompany him on a two-month trip to Ouroussa, offering wages higher than he could make on his own boat, Criston had jumped at the chance.

Not only would it help him pay off the debt, but it would give Criston a chance to see far-off lands. And when he returned to Windcatch with his purse full of coins, he would finally be able to marry Adrea, whom he had loved for years. Once the *Fishhook* unloaded her cargo in Ouroussa, Criston could be on his way home....

As the scarlet-sailed Uraban ship closed to within hailing distance, he spotted a man standing near the bow dressed in loose cream-colored robes, his head wrapped in a pale olba. Only five crewmen stood with the man on the foreign vessel's deck. The robed man shouted across to them in heavily accented Tierran. "I am Fillok, Ouroussa's city leader. What goods have you brought us?"

Shay lowered his voice to Criston. "Fillok...I know that name. I think he's the brother of the soldan of Outer Wahilir, an important man. Why would *he* come to meet us?" He frowned in consternation. "Men who consider themselves important sometimes do brash things, and it's rarely a good sign." The captain raised his voice and called back across the water, "We are on our way to port. I can give your harbormaster a full list."

"It is my right to inspect your cargo here and now! How do we know your boat is not filled with soldiers to attack Ouroussa?"

"Why would we do that?" Shay asked, genuinely perplexed. If Fillok did not change course, his ship would collide with the *Fishhook* within minutes. Captain Shay eyed the two swift war galleys coming toward them from both port and starboard. "This doesn't feel right, Vora. Go up there and have another look." The young sailor slipped away and scrambled back up the ropes to the lookout nest.

Tierran traders often made great profit from selling to Uraban cities, but many vessels vanished, more than could reasonably be accounted for by storms and reefs. If Fillok were an ambitious and unprincipled man, he could have attacked those traders and seized their cargoes. No one in Tierra would know.

When Criston reached the lookout nest and peered down at the foreign ship, he was astonished to see far more than just the five Uraban sailors standing at the ropes. At least a dozen armed men crouched out of sight behind crates and sailcloth on the deck; the hatches were open, and even more Uraban men crowded below, holding bright scimitars. Criston cupped his hands around his mouth and yelled at the top of his lungs, "Captain, it's a trap! The ship is full of armed men!"

Shay shouted to his crew, "Set sails! All canvas, take the wind *now*!" Already on edge, the men jumped to untie knots, pull ropes, and drop sails abruptly into place.

Criston's warning forced Fillok into abrupt action. The Ouroussan city leader screamed something in his own language, and hidden men burst into view, lifting their swords. Shrill trumpets sounded a call to battle. Ropes with grappling hooks flew across the narrow gap between the two ships; several fell into the water, but three caught the *Fishhook*'s deck rail. Answering horns and drumbeats came from the two closing war galleys, and the rowers picked up their pace.

Shay reached down to grab a long harpoon stowed just below the starboard bow of the *Fishhook*. The Tierran men armed themselves with boat-hooks, oars, and stunning clubs. Criston clambered back down to the deck, ready to join the fight. He held a long boat-knife to defend himself, though its reach was much shorter than that of a Uraban scimitar.